READER'S DIGEST CONDENSED BOOKS

READER'S DIGEST
CONDENSED BOOKS

Volume 1 • 1976

THE READER'S DIGEST ASSOCIATION

Pleasantville, New York

READER'S DIGEST CONDENSED BOOKS

Editor: John T. Beaudouin

Executive Editor: Joseph W. Hotchkiss

Managing Editor: Anthony Wethered

Senior Editors: Ann Berryman, Doris E. Dewey (Copy Desk), Marcia Drennen, Noel Rae, Robert L. Reynolds, Jane Siepmann, Jean N. Willcox, John S. Zinsser, Jr.

Associate Editors: Barbara Bradshaw, Istar H. Dole, Barbara J. Morgan, Marjorie Palmer, Frances Travis, Patricia Nell Warren, Angela Weldon, Angela C. Woods

Art Editor: William Gregory

Associate Art Editors: Marion Davis, Soren Noring, Angelo Perrone, Thomas Von Der Linn

Art Research: George Calas, Jr., Katherine Kelleher

Senior Copy Editor: Olive Farmer

Associate Copy Editors: Jean E. Aptakin, Catherine T. Brown, Estelle T. Dashman, Alice Murtha

Assistant Copy Editors: Dorothy G. Flynn, Jean S. Friedman, Enid P. Leahy, Marian I. Murphy

Research Editor: Linn Carl

SPECIAL PROJECTS

Executive Editor: Stanley E. Chambers

Senior Editors: Marion C. Conger, Sherwood Harris, Herbert H. Lieberman

Associate Editors: Elizabeth Stille, John Walsh

Rights and Permissions: Elizabeth Thole

Reader's Digest Condensed Books are published every two to three months at Pleasantville, N.Y.

CONTENTS

THE
GREAT
TRAIN
ROBBERY

A CONDENSATION OF THE NOVEL BY

MICHAEL CRICHTON

ILLUSTRATED BY GINO D'ACHILLE

"The crime of the century"
and the "most sensational exploit
of the modern era"...

. . . that's what the Victorians labeled The Great Train Robbery of 1855. The amount stolen—£12,000 in gold bullion—was large but not unprecedented; the meticulous planning, involving many people and extending over a year, was similarly not unusual. Yet the adjectives applied to this crime were strong: it was "unspeakable" and "appalling."

To understand why the Victorians were so shocked, one must understand that England was the first industrialized society on earth, and the most visible proof of its progress was the railroads, which symbolized moral as well as material advancement. So it was absolutely astonishing to discover that "the criminal class" had found a way to carry out a theft aboard the very hallmark of progress, the railroad.

Many of the features of the criminal subculture were brought to light in the trial of Burgess, Agar, and Pierce, the chief participants in The Great Train Robbery. It is from their voluminous courtroom testimony that the following narrative is assembled.

—M.C.

CHAPTER ONE

ORTY minutes out of London, in the rolling green fields and cherry orchards of Kent, the morning train of the South Eastern Railway attained its maximum speed of fifty-four miles an hour. Riding the bright blue-painted engine, the engineer in his red uniform stood upright in the open air, unshielded by any cab or windscreen, while at his feet the fireman crouched, shoveling coal into the glowing furnaces. Behind the chugging engine and tender were three yellow first-class coaches, six green second-class carriages, and, at the very end, a gray, windowless luggage van.

As the train clattered down the track on its way to the coast, the sliding door of the luggage van opened suddenly, revealing a desperate struggle inside. The contest was most unevenly matched: a slender youth in tattered clothing against a burly, blue-uniformed railway guard. The youth made a good showing, landing one or two telling blows against his hulking opponent. But then the guard, having been knocked to his knees, sprang forward, catching the youth unprepared. Flung through the open door, he landed tumbling and bouncing like a rag doll upon the ground.

The guard, gasping for breath, looked back at the fast-receding figure of the fallen youth. Then he closed the door, and the train sped on, its whistle shrieking. Soon it was gone around a gentle curve, and all that remained was the lingering gray smoke that settled over the tracks and the body of the motionless youth. After a minute or two the youth raised himself up on one elbow and seemed about to rise to his feet. Then he collapsed back to the ground, gave a final convulsive shudder, and lay still.

Half an hour later an elegant black brougham came down a dirt road that paralleled the tracks, and the driver drew up his horse on a hill. A red-bearded gentleman emerged, dressed in a dark green velvet frock coat and high beaver hat. He pressed binoculars to his eyes and swept the length of the tracks until he saw the youth's body. But he made no attempt to approach him. When he was certain the lad was dead he climbed into his brougham and drove back the way he had come, northward toward London.

THIS red-bearded gentleman was Edward Pierce, a man in his early thirties. For one so notorious later, he remains an oddly mysterious figure. Tall and handsome, in his speech, manner, and dress he seemed to be a gentleman and well-to-do. He was apparently very charming. He claimed to be an orphan of Midlands gentry and to have attended Winchester College and Cambridge University. He was a familiar figure in London social circles and counted among his acquaintances members of Parliament, ambassadors, and bankers. Although a bachelor, he maintained a house in fashionable Mayfair. But he spent much time traveling abroad. To contemporary observers the idea of a gentleman adopting a life of crime was so titillating that nobody wanted to disprove it.

Yet there is no evidence that Pierce came from the upper classes; indeed, almost nothing of his background is known. In an era when birth certificates were rare and fingerprinting unknown, it was difficult to identify any man with certainty. Even Pierce's name is doubtful; during his trial, witnesses claimed to have known him as John Simms, Andrew Miller, or Robert Jeffers.

The source of Pierce's obviously ample income was also a mystery. Some said he owned several public houses and a fleet of cabs, headed by a sinister-appearing cabby named Barlow, who had a white scar across his forehead. This could have been true, for the ownership of pubs and cabs was an occupation where underworld connections were useful. But there was nothing brought out at the trial to substantiate it.

Of course, it is not impossible that Pierce was a wellborn man with a background of aristocratic education. But one thing is certain: he was a master cracksman, or burglar, who over the years had accumulated sufficient capital to put up a lay, or finance a criminal operation, from time to time. And toward the middle of 1854 he was well into an elaborate plan to pull the greatest theft of his career: The Great Train Robbery.

ROBERT Agar, a screwsman, or specialist in keys and safecracking, testified in court that when he met Edward Pierce in late May, 1854, he had not seen him for two years. Agar was twenty-six and in fair health. But he had a bad cough, the legacy of his years as a child working for a match manufacturer in Bethnal Green, where phosphorus vapor filled the air. Phosphorus was known to be poisonous, but there were plenty of people eager to work. Agar had nimble fingers, and eventually he took up the trade of screwsman. He had worked at it for six years without being apprehended.

Agar had never had any direct dealings with Pierce, but he knew him by reputation. Their first 1854 meeting occurred at the infamous Bull and Bear public house, at the periphery of the notorious slum of Seven Dials. The Bull and Bear was frequented by gentlemen of quality with a taste for low life, and two fashionably dressed young bloods lounging at the bar while they surveyed the females in the room attracted no particular attention.

The meeting was unplanned, Agar said. He recalled that when Pierce arrived the conversation began without preliminaries.

Agar said, "I heard Spring Heel Jack's left Westminster."

"I heard that," Pierce agreed, rapping with his silver-headed cane to draw the attention of the barman. Pierce then ordered two glasses of the best whiskey.

"I heard," Agar said, "that Jack is on a south swing to dip the holiday crowd." London pickpockets often traveled to other cities. One could not dip a particular locale for long without being spotted by the crusher, or policeman, on the beat.

"I didn't hear his plans," Pierce said.

"I also heard that he took a South Eastern train. I heard"—
Agar's eyes were on Pierce's face—"that on this train he was doing
some crow's peeping for a gent who is putting up."

"He might have done," Pierce said.

Agar grinned. "I also heard that you are putting up."

"I may." Pierce sipped, then stared at the glass. "It used to be
better here. Neddy must be watering his stock. What have you
heard I am putting up for?" he asked.

"A robbery. A ream flash pull, if truth be told."

"If truth be told," Pierce repeated. He seemed to find the phrase
amusing. "Everybody hears the pull bigger than life."

"Aye, that's so." Agar sighed. (In his testimony Agar recalled,
"Now I goes and gives a big sigh, you see, like to say my patience
is wearing thin, because he's a cautious one, Pierce is, and I want
to get down to it, so I gives a big sigh.")

There was a brief silence. Finally, Agar said, "It's two years gone
since I saw you. Been busy?"

"Traveling," Pierce said. He looked at the whiskey in Agar's
hand and the half-finished gin and water Agar had been drinking
when Pierce arrived. "How's the touch?"

"Ever so nice," Agar said. To demonstrate, he held out his hands,
palms flat, fingers wide; there was no tremor.

"I may have one or two little things," Pierce said.

"Spring Heel Jack held his cards close," Agar said. "He was all
swelled mighty and important, but he kept it to his chest."

"Jack's put in lavender," Pierce said curtly. This might mean
that Spring Heel Jack had gone into hiding; more often it meant
that he was dead.

"These little things," Agar asked, "could they be tricky?"

"Very tricky," Pierce said. "And you will want a tight lip. If the
first lay goes right enough, there will be more."

"Is it keys?" Agar asked.

"It is. And on the fly."

"Right, then," Agar said. "I'm your man. What's the lay to be?"

"You'll know when the time comes," Pierce said.

"You're a tight one," Agar said.

"That is why I have never been in," Pierce said, meaning that he had no prison record. At the trial, witnesses testified that Pierce had served three and a half years for cracking, under the name of Arthur Wills.

Pierce gave Agar a final word of caution, and then moved away, crossing the smoky, noisy Bull and Bear to bend briefly and whisper into a pretty woman's ear. The woman laughed. Agar turned away, and recalled nothing further from the evening.

MR. HENRY Fowler, forty-seven, knew Edward Pierce in rather different circumstances. At the trial Fowler admitted freely that he had little knowledge of Pierce's background; but the man was clearly educated and well-to-do, keeping a most excellent house—and Henry Fowler found him amusing for an occasional dinner.

He recalled, with difficulty, a dinner of eight gentlemen at Pierce's home in late May, 1854. The conversation had chiefly concerned a proposed underground railway in London, and Fowler found it tedious. Then, over brandy in the smoking room, the talk turned to cholera, of late an epidemic in certain parts of the city. The dispute over the proposals of Mr. Edwin Chadwick, one of the sanitary commissioners, for a cleaning up of the polluted Thames was also profoundly boring to Mr. Fowler.

He was thinking of taking his leave when Pierce asked him about a recent attempt to rob a gold shipment from a train. It was only natural that Pierce should ask him, for Fowler was the brother-in-law of Sir Edgar Huddleston, of the banking firm of Huddleston & Bradford, Westminster. Fowler was general manager of that prosperous enterprise, which specialized in foreign transactions.

This was a time of extraordinary English domination of world commerce. England mined more than half the world's coal and produced three-quarters of the world's cotton cloth; her foreign trade was valued at twice that of her leading competitors, the United States and Germany. Foreign business concerns of all sorts therefore made London their financial center, and the London banks thrived. When England and France declared war on Russia in March 1854, the firm of Huddleston & Bradford was designated to arrange for the payment of British troops fighting in the Crimea. It was precisely such a consignment of gold for troop payments that had been the object of a recent attempted theft in a railway luggage van.

"A trivial endeavor," Fowler declared. He felt obliged to put down any suspicion of the bank's inadequacy. "There was not the slightest chance of success."

"The villain expired?" asked Pierce, puffing his cigar.

"Quite. The railroad guard threw him from the train at a goodly speed, poor devil."

"Has he been identified?"

"His features were considerably—disarrayed," Fowler said. "It was said he was named Jack Perkins, but one doesn't know. The whole robbery speaks of the rankest amateurism."

"I suppose," a Mr. Bendix said, "that the bank must take considerable precautions."

"Considerable precautions indeed!" Fowler said. "One doesn't transport twelve thousand pounds in bullion to France each month without the most extensive safeguards."

"We should all be curious to know the nature of your precautions," Pierce said. "Or is that a secret of the firm?"

"No secret at all." Fowler withdrew his watch from his waistcoat pocket and flicked open the cover. Past eleven, but the necessity·to uphold the bank's reputation kept him there. "In fact, the precautions are of my own devising. And I invite you to point out any weakness in my plan." He glanced from one face to the next as he talked. "Each gold bullion shipment is loaded within the confines of the bank itself into ironbound wood strongboxes, which are then sealed and taken by armed guard to the railway station. The convoy follows no established route and keeps to populous thoroughfares; thus there is no chance that it may be waylaid. The guards are all long-standing servants of the firm. At the station the strongboxes are loaded into the luggage van of the Folkestone train, where we place them in two of the latest Chubb safes."

"Indeed, Chubb safes?" Pierce said, raising an eyebrow. The firm was universally recognized for its skill and workmanship.

"Nor are these ordinary Chubb safes," Fowler continued, "but specially built to our specifications, of one-quarter-inch tempered steel, with interior door hinges which offer no chance for tampering. Their very weight is an impediment to theft: each safe weighs in excess of two hundred and fifty pounds."

"Most impressive," Pierce said.

"We have added further refinements. Each safe is fitted with two locks. Not only that, but each of the four keys—two to each safe—is individually protected. Two are stored in the railway office. A third is in the custody of the bank's senior partner, Mr. Trent. I myself am entrusted with the fourth key." Here Fowler lapsed into a dramatic pause.

A Mr. Wyndham, a bit stiff with drink, finally spoke up. "Damn it all, Henry, tell us where you have hidden your bloody key!"

Mr. Fowler smiled benignly. "I keep it," he said, "about my neck." And he patted his starched shirtfront. "I wear it even while bathing and asleep." He smiled broadly. "So, gentlemen, you see that the young ruffian had no more chance of stealing that bullion than I have of—well, of flying to the moon."

"I must congratulate you, Henry," Pierce said. "It is really quite the most ingenious strategy I have ever heard for protecting a consignment of valuables."

"I rather think so myself," Fowler said. Soon thereafter he took his leave, with the comment that if he were not soon home, his wife would think him dallying with a judy—"and I should hate to suffer the chastisement without the antecedent reward." His comment drew laughter; it was, he thought, just the right note on which to depart. Gentlemen wanted their bankers prudent but not prudish.

"I shall see you out," Pierce said.

AT THE time of Napoleon's defeat at Waterloo, England was a predominantly rural nation of eleven million. By 1855 the population had nearly doubled, to twenty million, and England had become a nation of cities. The new cities glittered with wealth, yet they stank of abject poverty. There were many calls for reform, but also there was widespread complacency. For prices had fallen; consumption had increased; taxation, per capita, had been reduced by half. Living conditions for all classes had improved. Factory working hours had been reduced from seventy-four to sixty hours a week for adults, and from seventy-two to forty for children. Average life span had increased five years. The outstanding symbol of progress, however, was the railroads. By 1850 five thousand miles of track crisscrossed the nation, providing cheap, swift transportation for people of all classes.

England's railroads grew at such a phenomenal rate that the city of London had never managed to build a central station. Instead, each of the lines had run its tracks as far into London as it could and then erected a terminal, until by 1899 there were fifteen—and the bewildering array of lines and schedules was apparently never to be mastered by any Londoner except Sherlock Holmes, who would know them all by heart.

In the 1850s the South Eastern Railway, which ran from London to Folkestone on the southeast coast some eighty miles away, leased tracks, platforms, and office space in the London Bridge Station from the London & Greenwich line. On the south shore of the Thames, near its namesake, the London Bridge terminal was the oldest station in the city, originally constructed in 1836 and rebuilt in 1851. Victorians regarded stations as the "cathedrals of the age"; they were expected to blend aesthetics and technological achievement, and many of them fulfilled that expectation with elegant, arching glass vaults. But the London Bridge terminal was depressing. It had a row of dreary shops under an arcade, and an unadorned main station.

The South Eastern traffic supervisor's offices were located in glass-doored rooms on the second floor of the terminal, accessible by an ironwork staircase leading up from the train platform. Anyone using the stairs was in plain view of the offices as well as of all passengers, porters, and guards on the platforms below.

The traffic supervisor or dispatcher, Mr. McPherson, was a

white-haired, elderly Scotsman who saw to it that his clerks did no daydreaming out the window. Thus no one in the office noticed when, in early July, 1854, two travelers took up a position on a bench on the platform and remained there the entire day, consulting their watches frequently, as if impatient for their journey to begin. Nor did anyone notice when the same two gentlemen returned the following week and again watched the activity in the station while frequently checking their pocket watches.

In fact, Pierce and Agar were not employing pocket watches, but stopwatches. After the second day of observing the office routines Agar announced, "It's bloody murder. She's too wide open. What's up there, anyway?"

"Two keys I happen to want," Pierce said.

Agar squinted up at the offices. "Well, I reckon they're in that storage space just past the clerks. See the cupboard?"

Pierce nodded. Through the glass he could see a shallow, wall-mounted cabinet. It looked like a storage place for keys.

"There's my money, on that cupboard," said Agar. "She has a cheap lock on her; that will give us no great trouble."

"What about the front door?" The frosted door to the offices—with SER: TRAFFIC SUPERVISOR DIVISION stenciled on it—had a large brass lock above the knob.

"Appearances," Agar snorted. "I could open her with a ragged fingernail. Our problem is the bloody crowds." Pierce nodded, but said nothing. This was essentially Agar's operation. "Two keys is four waxes," Agar went on. "Four waxes is nigh on a minute, to do it proper. But cracking the door and the cabinet, that's more time again." Agar looked around at the crowded platform and the clerks in the office. "Bloody flummut to try and crack her by day," he said. "At night, when she's empty, that's best."

"At night the crushers make rounds," Pierce reminded him. They had learned that during the evening policemen patrolled at four- or five-minute intervals. "Will you have time?"

Agar frowned. "No," he said finally. "Unless—unless the offices were already open. Then I make my entrance neat as you please, do the waxes quick-like, and I'm gone in less than two minutes flat.

I'm thinking of a snakesman." He nodded to the supervisor's office.

Pierce looked up. Through the broad window he could see McPherson, in his shirt sleeves, with a green shade over his forehead. And behind McPherson was a foot-square window for ventilation. "I see it," Pierce said. "But damn small."

"A proper snakesman can make it through," Agar said. (A snakesman was a youth adept at wriggling through small spaces, usually a former chimney sweep's apprentice.) "And once he's in the office he unlocks the cupboard, and he unlocks the door from the inside. That will make this job a bone lay, and no mistake."

"Who's the best snakesman?" Pierce said.

"The best?" Agar said, looking surprised. "The best is Clean Willy, but he's in Newgate Prison. There's no escaping Newgate."

"Perhaps Clean Willy can find a way."

"Nobody can," Agar said. "It's been tried before."

"I'll get a word to Willy," Pierce said, "and we shall see."

Agar nodded. "I'll hope," he said. "But not too excessive."

The two men resumed watching the offices. Pierce stared at the little cabinet. What if there were dozens of keys inside? How would Agar know which ones to copy?

"Here comes the esclop," Agar said.

The police constable was making his rounds. Pierce flicked his stopwatch: seven minutes forty-seven seconds since the last circuit. But the routine would be more rapid at night.

"You see a lurk to use?" Pierce inquired.

Agar nodded to a luggage stand where there was ample place to hide. "There'd do."

"Well enough."

At 7:00 p.m. the clerks left the office. At 7:20 the supervisor departed, locking the door after him.

The two men remained another hour, until the last train had departed and they were too conspicuous. They clocked the constable on night duty as he made his rounds. He passed the traffic supervisor's office once every five minutes and three seconds.

"Five and three," Pierce said. "Can you do it?"

"I can," Agar said, "if I have a snakesman like Clean Willy."

As they left the station in the fading twilight Pierce signaled his cab. The driver, who had a scar across his forehead, whipped up his horse and clattered toward the entrance.

"When do we knock it over?" Agar said.

Pierce gave him a gold guinea. "When I inform you," he said.

CHAPTER TWO

ALFRED Nobel would not discover dynamite until 1866, so a decently constructed metal safe represented a genuine barrier to theft in 1854. A thief had three options. He could steal the safe outright, carrying it off to break open at his leisure. But this was impossible if the safe was of any size or weight. Alternatively, a thief could employ a petter-cutter, a drill that clamped to the keyhole of the safe and permitted a hole to be bored above the lock. Through the hole the lock mechanism could be manipulated. But the petter-cutter was noisy, slow, and uncertain.

The third choice was to get hold of the key. Combination locks had not yet been invented; all locks were operated by key, so Victorian crime literature often seems obsessed with keys. As the master safecracker Neddy Sykes said in his trial in 1848, "The key is everything in the lay."

It was Edward Pierce's unquestioned assumption in planning the train robbery that he must first obtain copies of the necessary keys. And he must do this by gaining access to the keys themselves. Wax impressions of a key could be made in a few moments, and any premises containing a key could be cracked with relative ease.

But a key could be hidden almost anywhere, particularly in a cluttered Victorian room, where even a wastebasket was likely to be covered with layers of fringes and tassels. Furthermore, the Victorians adored concealed spaces; a mid-century writing desk was advertised as containing a hundred and ten compartments, including many "most artfully concealed from detection."

So information about the location of a key was almost as useful as an actual copy of the key itself. A thief might break into a house if he knew in which room a key was hidden, but if he did not know where in the house it was, the difficulty of making a thorough search was not worth the attempt.

By mid-July, 1854, Pierce knew the location of three of the four keys he needed to rob the safes. Two were in the traffic supervisor's office; a third hung around the neck of Henry Fowler. To Pierce these three keys presented no major problem. The real difficulty centered around the fourth key. It was in the possession of the bank's senior partner, Mr. Edgar Trent, but Pierce did not know *where*—and this lack of knowledge represented a formidable challenge indeed.

The first question was whether the key was kept in the bank. Junior clerks of Huddleston & Bradford dined at one o'clock at the Horse and Rider, across the street from the firm. This was a smallish pub, crowded at the dinner hour. There Pierce struck up an acquaintance with a clerk named Rivers. Normally the junior clerks in a bank were wary of casual acquaintances; but Rivers was relaxed, in the knowledge that the bank was impregnable to burglary—and perhaps because he had a deal of resentment toward his employer.

The RULES FOR OFFICE STAFF posted by Mr. Trent in early 1854 were as follows:

1. Godliness, cleanliness and punctuality are the necessities of a good business.
2. The firm has reduced the working day to the hours from 8:30 a.m. to 7:00 p.m.
3. Prayers will be held each morning. The clerical staff will be present.
4. Clothing will be of a sober nature.
5. A stove is provided for the clerical staff. Each member should bring 4 lb. of coal each day during the cold weather.
6. No member of the clerical staff may leave the room without permission from Mr. Roberts. For calls of nature, staff may use the garden beyond the second gate.
7. No talking is allowed during business hours.
8. Tobacco, wines and spirits are forbidden to the staff.

9. Members of the staff will provide their own pens.
10. The managers expect a great rise in the output of work to compensate for these near-Utopian conditions.

However Utopian, the working conditions of Huddleston & Bradford led Rivers to speak freely about Mr. Trent, and with less enthusiasm than one might expect for a Utopian employer.

"Snaps his watch at eight thirty sharp," Rivers said, "and checks to see that we are at our places. God help the man whose omnibus is late in the traffic of the rush. No excuses. He's a stiff one. Getting on in years, but he's vain; grew whiskers longer than yours, on account of the fact he's losing the hair up top. He has this brush, Dr. Scott's electric hairbrush, from Paris. You know how dear it is? Twelve shillings sixpence." Rivers would find this expensive; he was paid twelve shillings a week.

"What's it do?" Pierce inquired.

"Cures headaches, dandruff, and baldness," Rivers went on, "or so it's claimed. He locks himself into his office and brushes once an hour, punctual." Rivers laughed.

"He must have a large office."

"Aye, and comfortable, too. The sweeper's in every night, dusting and arranging just so, and every night as he leaves at seven o'clock Mr. Trent says to the sweeper, 'A place for everything, and everything in its place.'"

The rest of the conversation was of no interest to Pierce. He already knew what he wanted—that Trent did not keep the key in his office, or he would never leave the place to be cleaned in his absence; sweepers were notoriously easy to bribe.

But the key might still be kept in the bank, perhaps in a vault. To determine this, Pierce could have struck up a conversation with a different clerk, but he chose another method.

A POPULAR theory of the Victorian era was that the progress in technology would lead inevitably to the eradication of social evils and criminal behavior. A few daring commentators, however, had the temerity to suggest that crime was not linked to social conditions at all, and such opinions remain today. Western man still clings to the belief that crime results from poverty, injustice, and poor education, although experts now agree on the following points: First, crime is not a consequence of poverty. Second, criminals are not limited in intelligence. Third, the vast majority of criminal activity goes unpunished. Similarly, criminologists dispute the traditional view that "crime does not pay." In reality, according to them it does; and a century ago in mid-Victorian England there were, without question, professional criminals.

Teddy Burke, one of the swellest of the swell mob, or elite street thieves, was working the Strand at two in the afternoon, a fashionable hour. Like the gentlemen around him, he was decked out in a high hat, frock coat, and narrow trousers.

In the throng of gentlemen and ladies who browsed among the elegant shops, Teddy was working his usual operation, with himself as dipper, a stickman at his side, and two stalls front and back— altogether four well-dressed men attracting no attention.

There was plenty of diversion. On this fine early summer day the air was warm and redolent of horse dung, despite a dozen street-urchin sweepers. Carts, drays, omnibuses, four-wheel and hansom cabs, and carriages rode past. Ragged children turned cartwheels for the crowd, some of whom threw them a few coppers.

Teddy Burke's attention was fixed upon a fine lady wearing a flounced crinoline skirt. In a few moments he would dip her.

One of Teddy's stalls had taken up a position three paces ahead; another was five paces back. They would create disorder and confusion should anything go wrong with the dip.

"Right, here we go," Teddy said. The stickman moved alongside him. It was the stickman's job to take the pogue once Teddy had snaffled it. With the stickman, Teddy moved so close to the woman he could smell her perfume.

He carried an overcoat draped across his left arm, though it was a warm day. The coat looked new, so he could conceivably have picked it up from a fitting at a shop. It concealed the movement of his right arm across his body to the woman's handbag. He took a deep breath, praying that the coins in her purse would not clink,

22

and lifted it from her bag. Immediately he eased away, shifted his overcoat to his other arm, and in the course of that movement passed the purse to the stickman, who drifted off. Ahead and behind, the stalls moved out in different directions. Only Teddy Burke, now clean, continued to walk along the Strand, pausing before a shop that displayed crystal from France.

A red-bearded man was also admiring the wares. He did not look at Teddy. "Nice pull," he said.

The speaker was too well dressed to be a plainclothes crusher. Teddy said carefully, "Are you addressing me, sir?"

"Yes. I said, a nice pull. You tool her off?"

Teddy Burke was insulted. A tool was a wire hook that inferior dippers employed to snare a purse if their fingers were shaky. "Beg pardon, sir. I don't know your meaning."

"I think you do," the man said. "Shall we walk awhile?"

Teddy shrugged and fell into step alongside the stranger. He was clean; he had nothing to fear. "Lovely day," he said.

The stranger did not answer. They walked on in silence. "Do you think you can be less effective?" the man asked after a time. "I mean, can you buzz a customer and come out dry?"

Teddy laughed. "It happens often enough without trying!"

"There's five quid for you, if you can be a prize bungler."

Teddy Burke's eyes narrowed. Plenty of con men set up an unwitting accomplice to take a fall. "Five quid's no great matter," he said.

"Ten," the man said in a weary voice.

"What's the lay, then?" Teddy Burke said.

"Just a ruck touch, to make the quarry pat his pockets."

"Who's the quarry, then?" Teddy Burke said.

"Gent named Trent. You'll touch him in front of his offices, Huddleston & Bradford Bank. He's near sixty; gray beard and a paunch. He'll arrive in a brougham at eight thirty."

Teddy Burke whistled. "Westminster. Sticky, that is. There's enough crushers about to make a bloody army." He walked on a few moments, thinking things over. "When will it be, then?"

"Tomorrow morning. Be there eight o'clock sharp." The red-bearded gentleman gave him a five-pound bill, and said he would get the rest when the job was done.

"What's it all about, then?" Teddy Burke asked.

"Personal matter." And the man slipped away into the crowd.

BETWEEN 1801 and 1851, London had tripled in size, to two and a half million; it was by far the largest city in the world. And it continued to grow, literally exploding outward, with the flight of the newly affluent middle classes to suburban areas where the air was better and the atmosphere in general more pleasant. Some older sections of London retained a character of great elegance, but they were often cheek to jowl with the most dismal rookeries, or slums, which were refuges for "the criminal class."

Then, as now, these slums existed in part because they were profitable for landlords. A nethersken, or lodging house, of eight rooms might take a hundred boarders, each paying a shilling or two a week to sleep with as many as twenty members of the same or opposite sex in the same room. (Perhaps the most bizarre example was the famous waterfront sailors' penny hang. Here a drunken seaman slept the night for a penny, draping himself across chest-high ropes, like clothes on a line.)

No rookery was more famous than St. Giles, the six acres in central London that were called the Holy Land. Not far from the prostitute center of the Haymarket and the fashionable shops of Regent Street, it was strategically located for any criminal who wanted to "go to ground."

On a foggy summer evening in late July, 1854, Pierce walked fearlessly through the Holy Land's malodorous and dangerous lanes. The loiterers watching him no doubt observed that his silver-headed cane looked ominously heavy and might conceal a blade; and a bulge about the trousers that implied a hidden gun probably also intimidated many who might be tempted to waylay him.

He went from street to stinking street, inquiring after a woman called Maggie. Finally he found a lounging soak who knew her.

"Little Maggie?" the man asked, leaning against a yellow gas lamppost, his face deep shadows in the fog.

"She's Clean Willy's judy."

"I know of her. Pinches laundry, she does." Here the man paused significantly.

Pierce gave him a coin. "Where shall I find her?"

"First passing up, first door to yer right."

As Pierce continued on, the man called after him, "But it's no use your bothering. Willy's in Newgate now."

Pierce did not look back. Dogs barked; whispers, groans, and laughter came to him through the fog. Finally he arrived at the nethersken. A rectangle of yellow light at the entrance shone on a crudely painted sign: LOGINS.

He entered the building and asked one of the throng of dirty, ragged children clustered about the stairs for the woman named Maggie. He was told she was in the kitchen, so he descended to the basement.

The kitchen of every nethersken was a warm and friendly place, a focus of heat and rich smells. Half a dozen men stood by the fire talking and drinking; at a table men and women played cards while others sipped bowls of steaming soup. He found Maggie, a dirty child of twelve, drew her aside, and gave her a gold guinea, which she bit. She flashed a half-smile.

"What is it, then, guv?" She looked appraisingly at his fine clothes, a calculating glance far beyond her years.

"You dab it up with Clean Willy?" Pierce said.

She shrugged. "I did. Willy's in Newgate."

"You see him?"

"I do, once and again. I goes as his sister, see."

Pierce pointed to the coin. "There's another one of those if you can slip him a message."

The girl's eyes glowed, then they went blank. "What's the lay?"

"Tell Willy to break at the next topping. It's to be Emma Barnes, the murderess. They'll hang her in public for sure."

She laughed, a harsh laugh. "There's no breaks from Newgate."

"Willy can. Tell him to go to the house where he first met John Simms, and all will be well."

"Are you John Simms?"

"I am a friend. Tell him the next topping and he's over the side, or he's not Clean Willy." Pierce turned to leave.

At the kitchen door he looked back at her, a skinny, stoop-shouldered child in a ragged dress spattered with mud.

"I'll tell him." She slipped the coin into her shoe.

UNLIKE the rookeries, respectable London was quiet at night. The business and financial districts were deserted except for the Metropolitan Police constables making their twenty-minute rounds. As dawn came the silence was broken by the crowing of roosters and the mooing of cows, for animal husbandry was still common in London. At 7:00 the first of the armies of women and girls employed as seamstresses in the West End dress factories appeared. At 8:00 the shops took down their shutters. Between 8:00 and 9:00 the streets became crowded with clerks, bank cashiers, stockbrokers, bakers, soap-boilers, making their way to work by the marrowbone stage—that is, on foot—or in omnibuses and dogcarts.

In the midst of this, street sweepers began to collect the first droppings of horse dung. Each horse was said to deposit six tons of dung on the streets each year, and there were at least a million horses in the city. Gliding through the confused and jammed traffic, a few elegant broughams of gleaming dark polished wood, with delicately sprung, lacy-spoked wheels, conveyed substantial citizens in utter comfort to the day's employment.

Pierce and Agar, crouched on a rooftop overlooking the imposing façade of the Huddleston & Bradford Bank across the way, watched as one such brougham came down the street toward them. "There he is now," Agar said.

Pierce checked his watch. "Eight twenty-nine."

The brougham pulled up, the driver jumped down to open the door, and Edgar Trent stepped out. The moment the heavy, gray-bearded Trent reached the pavement, a well-dressed young man jostled him, muttered an apology, and moved on in the crowd. Mr. Trent walked toward the impressive oak doors of the bank. Then he stopped in mid-stride.

"He's realized," Pierce said.

Trent looked after the young man and then patted his side coat pocket. Apparently what he sought was still in place; his shoulders dropped in relief, and he continued on into the bank.

Pierce grinned and turned to Agar. "That's what we needed to know, that Mr. Trent brings his key with him, for—" He broke off. He had not yet informed Agar of his plan.

"You're a tight one," Agar said. "Wasn't that Teddy Burke, trying a pull? The swell that works the Strand?"

"I wouldn't know," Pierce said, and they left the rooftop.

IN THE coming weeks Pierce learned a great deal about Edgar Trent. He was rather devout, rarely drank, never smoked or played at cards. He was the father of five children; his first wife had died. His second wife, Emily, was thirty years his junior and an acknowledged beauty, but as severe as her husband. The family resided at number 17, Highwater Street, Mayfair, in a large Georgian mansion. Twelve servants were employed. The children, even a twenty-nine-year-old daughter, all lived in the house. The youngest child, a four-year-old son, had a tendency to somnambulation, so that the household was often roused at night. Pierce also learned that Mr. Trent kept two bulldogs, which were walked at 7:00 a.m. and at 8:15 p.m.; they were penned in a run behind the house.

Mr. Trent arose at 7:00 a.m., breakfasted at 7:30, and departed for work at 8:10. He invariably lunched at Simpson's. He left the bank promptly at 7:00 p.m., returning home no later than 7:20. Although he was a member of several clubs, he rarely frequented them. The Trents dined out occasionally and gave a dinner for a dozen once a week or so. An extra maid and manservant were laid on then, but they were obtained from adjacent households and could not be bribed. The family sometimes weekended in the country, but then most of the servants remained in the mansion. At no time, it seemed, were there fewer than eight people in the house.

The tradesmen who worked the street were careful never to associate with a potential thief—a "polite" street was not easily come by. A chimney sweep named Marks also worked the area and was known to inform the police of any approach by a lurker seeking information. The daytime constable, Lewis, made his rounds once every seventeen minutes, and the night man, Howell, made his every sixteen minutes. Neither was susceptible to bribes.

Pierce accumulated this information at some risk, adopting various disguises when he talked with servants in public houses or loitered in the neighborhood. But Trent seemed to have no vices, no eccentricities. As Pierce continued his surveillance it became evident that the information he needed could be obtained only through striking up a personal acquaintance with Mr. Trent.

Henry Fowler, who now shared with Pierce an occasional gentleman's evening on the town, had been approached, but Fowler said Trent would bore Pierce, and added that his wife, though pretty, was equally tedious. Pierce could hardly press for an introduction to such a dull couple. Nor could he approach Trent directly, pretending business with the bank; Fowler would rightly expect that Pierce bring any business to him.

By the first of August, Pierce was desperately considering staging an accident in which he would be run down by a cab in front of the Trent household or the bank. But these tricks would require some degree of genuine injury to Pierce. Then, on the evening of August 3, Mr. Trent suddenly changed his routine. He returned home at 7:20, went immediately to the dog run and put one of his bulldogs on a leash. Petting the animal elaborately, he climbed back into his waiting carriage and drove off.

When Pierce saw that, he knew he had his man.

CHAPTER THREE

THE livery stable of Jeremy Johnson & Son was a smallish establishment, in which a visitor might hear, besides the whinny of horses, the sounds of barking dogs. Many such reputable establishments operated a side business of training fighting dogs.

Jeremy Johnson, a jovial old man, led his red-bearded customer back through the stables, slapping the hindquarters of a horse to push it out of the way. "Now what is it you'll be wanting?"

"Your best," Pierce said.

"You're seeking a learner to polish yourself?"

"No, I want a fully made dog."

"That's dear, very dear."

"I know."

Johnson pushed open a creaking door, and they came out into a small courtyard with three circular pits, each perhaps six feet in diameter, and caged, yelping dogs on all sides.

"Takes a proper long training to have a good made dog," Johnson said. "First we jogs the dog day and day again, to toughen him. Then we puts the learner in with a gummer—all his teeth yanked." He pointed. "Very good gummer, this one. Knows how to worry a learner."

Pierce looked at the gummer. It was a healthy dog, barking vigorously. All its teeth were gone, yet it continued to snarl and pull back its lips menacingly. "I want your very best made dog," Pierce repeated.

"And you shall have it, I warrant. Here is the devil's own." Johnson paused before a cage with a bulldog who growled but did not move. "See that? He's a confident one, vicious as ever I saw. Some dogs just have the instinct, you know, to get a good mouthful straightaway."

"How much?" Pierce said.

"Twenty quid. He'll do you proud, I warrant."

"I want your best veteran. This dog has no scars."

Johnson moved two cages down. "This one took the neck off old Whitington's charger a week past, at the pub tourney—perhaps you was there. Twenty-five quid."

Pierce tapped his foot and stared at Johnson. "I want the *best dog* you have."

Johnson looked away as if embarrassed. "Well, there *is* one more, but he's very special. He has the killer instinct, the taste of blood, the quick move, and a tough hide." He led Pierce to another area, where there were three dogs, heavier than the others, in larger pens. Johnson tapped the middle cage.

"This 'un," he said. "Thought I'd have to top him off." Johnson rolled up his sleeve to reveal a set of jagged scars. "But he has the spirit, see, and the spirit's everything."

"How much?" Pierce said.

"Couldn't let him go for less'n fifty quid."

"I will give you forty."

"Sold," Johnson said quickly. "You'll take 'im now?"

"No," Pierce said. "I'll call for him soon." He gave the man ten pounds down, had him pry open the dog's jaws, and checked the teeth. Then he departed.

CAPTAIN Jimmy Shaw, a retired pugilist, ran the most famous of the sporting pubs, the Queen's Head, off Windmill Street. On the evening of August 10, 1854, the dingy place was filled with all manner of well-dressed gentlemen rubbing shoulders with hawkers, costermongers, and navvies in a state of excited, noisy anticipation. Nearly everyone had brought a dog. There were bulldogs, Skye terriers, English terriers, and mongrels nestled in the arms of their owners or tied to tables or the bar. They were hefted to gauge their weight, their limbs were felt for strength, their teeth were inspected. Dog collars hung from the rafters; there were stuffed dogs mounted over the bar, and prints of dogs by the hearth.

Jimmy Shaw, a burly figure with a broken nose, moved about the room calling, "Give your orders, gentlemen." Then at nine o'clock he gave the order to light up the pit, and the entire company began to file upstairs, each man carrying his dog and dropping a shilling into the hand of a waiting assistant.

The bare second floor was dominated by the pit—an arena six feet in diameter enclosed by slats four feet high. As the spectators reached it the dogs barked and strained on the leashes. They barked and snarled more fiercely when Captain Jimmy waved a cage over his head. It contained fifty scampering rats. "Every one country born," he announced. "Not a sewer rat among 'em. Who wants to try a rat?"

By now fifty or sixty people had crammed into the narrow room, money in hand. Over the din of lively bargaining a voice spoke up. "I'll have a try at twenty of your best for my fancy."

"Weigh the fancy of Mr. T.," Captain Jimmy said.

The assistants took a bulldog from the arms of a gray-bearded, balding gentleman and weighed him. "Twenty-seven pounds!" came the cry, and the dog was returned to its owner.

"That's it, gents," Captain Jimmy said. "Twenty-seven pounds is Mr. T.'s dog, and he will have a try at twenty rats. Four minutes?" And as Mr. T. nodded in agreement, "Four minutes it is, gentlemen. Wager as you see fit. Make room for Mr. T."

The gray-bearded gentleman moved up to the edge of the pit, cradling the snarling animal. "Let's see them," Mr. T. said.

The assistant opened the cage and took out twenty rats with his bare hands, to prove they were indeed country animals, not diseased. He tossed them into the pit and they huddled together.

"Ready?" called Captain Jimmy, a stopwatch in hand.

"Ready." Mr. T. made growling sounds to his dog.

"Blow on 'em! Blow on 'em!" came the cry, and otherwise dignified gentlemen puffed on the rats, sending them into a frenzy.

"Aaannnddd . . . *go!*" shouted Captain Jimmy, and Mr. T. flung his dog into the pit. Then he leaned over the wooden rim, urging the animal on with shouts and growls.

The dog leaped into the mass of rats, snapping at the necks like the well-blooded sport he was. In an instant he killed three or four, while the spectators screamed and yelled. "That's it!" shouted Mr. T. "Now *go*, Lover. *Grrrrrr! Good! Go! Grrr-rugh!*"

Lover moved quickly from one furry body to the next. One rat caught hold of his nose, but the dog writhed free and raced after the others. Now six bodies were lying on the pit floor.

"Two minutes," called Captain Jimmy.

"Hi, Lover," screamed Mr. T. "Go, boy. *Grrrrh!*"

The dog raced around the pit; the crowd screamed and pounded the wooden slats. At one point Lover had four rats clinging to him, but he kept going, crunching a fifth in his jaws. In the midst of the excitement a dignified red-bearded gentleman came to stand by Mr. T., whose attention remained focused on the dog.

"Three minutes," Captain Jimmy called. There was a groan from those who had bet on Mr T.'s fancy. Only twelve rats dead!

But Mr. T. still barked and screamed orders.

"Time!" shouted Captain Jimmy. The crowd sighed and relaxed. Lover was pulled from the arena; the three remaining rats were deftly scooped up. Mr. T. had lost.

"Good try," said the red-bearded man, in consolation.

EDGAR Trent's presence at the Queen's Head pub requires some explanation. In Victorian days there were a few places where all classes mingled freely; and chief among these were the prize ring, the turf, and the baiting sports. Most of these activities were disreputable or illegal, and their supporters shared a common interest that permitted them to overlook the breakdown of convention.

One common interest—animal baiting—had been a cherished amusement throughout Western Europe since medieval times. But in Victorian England animal sports were dying out, the victim of legislation and changing public tastes. The baiting of bulls or bears was rare; cockfighting was found only in rural centers.

In London in 1854 ratting was the most common dog sport, although technically illegal. Signs read: RATS WANTED and RATS BOUGHT AND SOLD, for the owner of a sporting pub might buy two thousand rats a week. Country rats were most prized, for their fighting vigor and their absence of infection. The more common sewer rats were timid and their bites more likely to infect a valuable fighting dog.

There is no good explanation why Victorians looked away from the sport of ratting, but they were conveniently blind, and the gentlemen who participated considered themselves "staunch supporters of the destruction of vermin."

One such staunch supporter, Mr. T., retired to the downstairs rooms of the Queen's Head, now virtually deserted, and called for gin for himself and peppermint for his fancy. He was washing his dog's mouth out with peppermint, to prevent canker, when the red-bearded gentleman came down the stairs and said, "May I join you for a glass?"

"By all means." Mr. T. continued to minister to his dog.

Upstairs, shouting indicated another episode of the destruction of vermin. The red-bearded stranger shouted over the din, "I perceive you are a gentleman of sporting instinct."

"And unlucky," Mr. T. said, equally loudly. He stroked his dog. "Lover was not at her best this evening. At times she lacks bustle." Mr. T. sighed. He ran his hands over the dog's body, probing for deep bites, and wiped the blood of several cuts from his fingers with his handkerchief. "But my Lover will fight again."

"And I shall wager upon her again when she does."

Mr. T. showed a trace of concern. "Did you lose?"

"Ten guineas. It was nothing," said the red-bearded man.

Mr. T. noticed the fine cut of the stranger's coat and the excellent silk of his neckcloth. "I am pleased you take it so lightly. Permit me to buy you a glass for your ill fortune."

"Never, for I count it no ill fortune. Indeed, I admire a man who may keep a fancy. I should do so myself, were I not so often abroad on business."

"Oh, yes?" Mr. T. signaled for another round.

"Why, only the other day," said the stranger, "I was offered an excellently made dog, a true fighter. I could not make the purchase, for I have no time to look after the animal."

"What was the price asked?" said Mr. T.

"Fifty guineas."

"Excellent price," Mr. T. said, as the waiter brought drinks. "I am myself in search of such a dog. But I don't suppose . . ."

"I could inquire whether the animal is still available."

"That would be very good of you. Very good indeed. But were I you, I should buy it myself. While you are abroad, your wife can instruct the servants in its care."

"I fear," Pierce replied, "that I have devoted too much of my energies to the pursuit of business concerns to marry. But of course I should like to."

"Of course," Mr. T. said, with a most peculiar look.

IN VICTORIAN England there was a worrying number of single women of marriageable age. Women of lower stations could take jobs as seamstresses or any of a dozen other occupations. But the daughters of middle- and upper-class households had been raised for no other purpose than to be "perfect wives," and one who remained a spinster became a social misfit and a burden to her father. An unmarried upper-class woman could use her education to become a governess. Her other choices were less appealing: she might be a clerk or a nurse, but these occupations were more suitable for an ambitious lower-class woman than a gentlewoman.

The Victorians tended to marry late, but Edgar Trent's daughter Elizabeth was now twenty-nine and somewhat past her prime. This evidently well-to-do young man might be drawn to her, and with this in mind Mr. Trent invited Mr. Pierce for Sunday tea, on the pretext of discussing the purchase of a fighting dog. Mr. Pierce, with apparent reluctance, accepted the invitation.

ELIZABETH Trent was of medium height, darker in complexion than was the fashion, and had features that were regular without being pretty. She apparently had few suitors, save for openly ambitious ones eager to marry a banker's daughter, and these she staunchly rejected. But she must have been impressed with the dashing Pierce. A servant testified as to their initial meeting.

Mr. Pierce and the Trents were taking tea on the lawn when Elizabeth arrived, wearing white crinoline. "Ah, my darling daughter," Mr. Trent said, rising, Pierce with him. "May I present Mr. Edward Pierce, my daughter Elizabeth."

"I confess I did not know you had a daughter," Pierce said. He bowed deeply at the waist, took her hand, and seemed about to kiss it, but hesitated, appearing flustered. "Miss Trent," he said, releasing her hand awkwardly. "You take me quite by surprise."

"I cannot tell if that is to my advantage or no," Elizabeth Trent replied, quickly taking a seat at the tea table.

"I assure you, it is wholly to your advantage," Mr. Pierce replied. And he was reported to have colored deeply.

Miss Trent fanned herself; Mrs. Trent picked up a tray of biscuits and offered them to the guest.

Mr. Trent said, "Mr. Pierce was telling us of his travels. He has recently returned from New York."

Elizabeth picked the cue up neatly. "Really?" she said. "How fascinating!"

"I fear it is more so in the prospect than the telling," Mr. Pierce replied, avoiding the glance of the young woman to such a degree that all observed his abashed reticence. He was clearly taken with her. "It is a city like any other, and chiefly distinguished by the lack of niceties which we residents of London take for granted."

"Are there native predators in the region?" Elizabeth asked.

"I should be delighted if I could regale you with adventures with the Indians in New York, but the wilderness of America does not begin until the Mississippi is crossed."

"Have you done so?" asked Mrs. Trent.

"I have," Mr. Pierce replied. "It is a river many times broader than the Thames. They are constructing a railway across the vast colony"—Mr. Trent guffawed at the condescending reference—"and I expect the savagery will soon vanish. But if the delicate ears of the ladies will not be offended, I shall give an example of the savagery which persists there. Do you know of buffaloes?"

"I have read of them," said Mrs. Trent. "They are large beasts, like wild cows, and shaggy?"

"Precisely so," Mr. Pierce said. "The western portion of America is populated with these creatures, and buffalo hunters sometimes seek the flesh of the animals, which is like venison."

"They lack tusks," Mr. Trent said. The bank had at this very moment a warehouse filled with five thousand ivory tusks.

"Yes, although the male possesses horns."

"Horns. But not of ivory."

"No, not ivory. Well, buffalo hunters utilize rifles for their purposes, and—here I must beg excuses for the crudity of what I must report—once the beast has terminated existence, its innards are removed. And this is the peculiar part. The hunters prize as the greatest of delicacies the small intestines of the beast. These are consumed on the spot, in a state wholly uncooked."

"Do you mean *raw?*" Mrs. Trent wrinkled her nose.

"Indeed, madam, while they are still warm."

Mrs. Trent turned pale. She rose. "You must excuse me."

"My dear," Mr. Trent said.

"Madam, I hope I have not distressed you." Mr. Pierce also rose.

"Your tale is remarkable," said Mrs. Trent, turning to leave.

"My dear," Mr. Trent said again, and hastened after her.

Thus Edward Pierce and Elizabeth Trent were briefly alone and were able to exchange a few words. Miss Trent later admitted that she found Mr. Pierce "quite fascinating in a rough-and-ready way," and it was generally agreed that Elizabeth now possessed that most valuable of all acquisitions, a "prospect."

●

CHAPTER FOUR

THE execution of the notorious axe murderess, Emma Barnes, on August 28, 1854, was a well-publicized affair. On the evening before, crowds began to gather outside the granite walls of Newgate Prison in order to be assured of a good view of the spectacle the following morning. The owners of lodging houses that overlooked Newgate square were pleased to rent rooms for the night to the better class of those eager to get a room for a "hanging party." When a well-spoken gentleman named Pierce asked Mrs. Edna Molloy if he could hire the best of her rooms for the night, she struck a hard bargain: twenty-five guineas.

Mrs. Molloy could live comfortably for a year on that amount, but she knew that to a gentleman like Mr. Pierce it was only the cost of a butler for six months. The proof of his indifference lay in the ready way he paid her, on the spot, in gold guineas.

She took little note when Mr. Pierce and his party filed upstairs later. There were two other men and two women, all smartly turned out, but she knew by their accents that the men were not gentlemen, and the women were no better than they looked, despite the wicker baskets and bottles of wine they carried. When they were in their room she did not bother to listen at the keyhole. She'd have no trouble from them, she was sure of it.

Inside, Pierce stepped to the window and looked down at the crowd, which gathered size each minute. The square was dark, lit only by the baleful glare of torches around the scaffolding. He could see the gallows taking shape.

"Clean Willy will never make it," Agar said behind him.

Pierce turned. "He has to make it, laddie."

"He's the best snakesman in the business, but he can't get out."

The second man, Barlow, was stocky and rugged, the white knife scar across his forehead usually concealed beneath his hatbrim. Barlow was a pickpocket who had degenerated to plain mugging, and whom Pierce had hired five years back. He was precisely what Pierce wanted for a buck cabby—a man holding the reins, ready to make the getaway, or ready for a bit of a shindy. "If it can be done, Clean Willy can do it," Barlow said.

The women were the judies of Agar and Barlow. Pierce did not know their names and did not want to know. He regretted that they must be present, but there was no way to avoid it. Barlow's woman was an obvious soak; you could smell her gin breath across the room. Agar's woman was little better, but at least sober.

"Did you bring the trimmings?" Pierce asked.

Agar's woman opened a picnic basket. In it he saw a sponge, medicinal powders, bandages, and a small, carefully folded dress.

"Well enough." Pierce then stared out at the prison.

"Here's the supper, sir," said Barlow's woman.

Pierce looked at the cold fowl, jars of pickled onion, lobster claws. "Very good, very good," he said. "I'll have a leg of that chicken. We shall disport ourselves while we wait."

PIERCE slept part of the night; he was awakened at daybreak by the noisy, rough crowd that jammed the square below, now swollen to more than fifteen thousand. He knew the streets would be filled with ten or fifteen thousand more, coming to see the hanging on their way to work. Employers were not strict on a morning when there was a hanging. Pierce glanced at his watch. It was 7:45, just a short time now.

The crowd began to chant, "Oh, my, think I'm going to die! Oh, my, think I'm going to die!" There was laughter and shouting, and fights broke out.

They all went to the window to watch.

Agar said, "When do you think he'll make his move?"

"He'll make his move whenever he thinks best," Pierce said.

At 8:00 the chimes of St. Sepulchre signaled the hour, and the crowd roared in anticipation. A door in Newgate opened and the prisoner was led out, her wrists strapped behind her. In front was a chaplain, behind the executioner, in black. The crowd saw the prisoner and shouted, "Hats off! Down in front!" Every man's hat was removed as she stepped up the scaffolding.

Emma Barnes was in her thirties and looked vigorous enough, but her eyes were glazed. The executioner turned to her, making slight adjustments, as if he were a seamstress positioning a dress, and then fitted the rope to a chain around her neck.

The clergyman read loudly from a Bible, keeping his eyes fixed on the book. Then the executioner slipped a black hood over the woman's head, and at a signal the trap opened with a wooden *crack!* The body fell, and caught, and hung instantly motionless.

"He's getting better at it," Agar said.

There was a moment of silence, and then an excited roar.

"Will you take some punch?" asked Agar's judy.

"No," Pierce said. And then he said, "Where is Willy?"

CLEAN Willy Williams was a tiny man. Once famous for his agility as a chimney sweep's apprentice, he had later been employed by the most eminent safecrackers, and his feats were legendary. It was said that he could climb a surface of glass.

Newgate guards had kept a close watch on him, though they knew that escape from Newgate was flatly impossible. It was the most secure prison in all England. In more than seventy years no convict had ever escaped. And this was hardly surprising: Newgate was surrounded on all sides with fifty-foot granite walls, the stones so finely cut that they were said to be impossible to scale. Encircling the top of the walls was a spiked iron bar fitted with revolving, razor-sharp spiked drums.

As the guards grew familiar with Willy they ceased to watch him closely. He never broke the rule of silence, never spoke to a fellow inmate; he suffered the cockchafer, or treadmill, without complaint, worked at oakum picking with no surcease. Indeed, there was some grudging respect for the cheerful little man. He was a likely candidate for a ticket of leave—a shortened sentence.

Yet at eight on that morning Clean Willy Williams had slipped to a corner of the prison walls, and with his back to the angle skinnied up the sheer rock surface, bracing with his hands and feet. He reached the top of the wall and grabbed the bar with its iron spikes. His hands were immediately lacerated, but from childhood Clean Willy had had no sensation in his palms, which were covered with calluses and scar tissue. It was the custom of homeowners to keep a hearth fire burning right up to the moment when the chimney sweep and his assistant arrived. Clean Willy's hands had been burned again and again when he hastened up still-hot chimneys, so he felt nothing now as blood trickled down from his slashed palms and ran along his forearms.

He moved slowly along the length of one wall, then turned the corner to the second wall, and then to the third. It was exhausting work, but he made his way around the perimeter of the prison yard until he reached the south wall. There he waited while a patrolling guard passed beneath him. The guard never looked up, although Willy later remembered that drops of blood landed on the man's cap and shoulders.

When the guard was gone Willy clambered over the spikes—cutting his chest, his knees, and his legs, so that the blood now ran very freely—and jumped down to the roof of the nearest building. From there he jumped to another, and another, leaping six- and eight-foot gaps without hesitation. Once or twice he lost his grip, but he always recovered. He had spent much of his life on rooftops.

Finally, less than half an hour from the time he began to inch his way up the prison wall, he slipped through a gabled window at the back of Mrs. Molloy's lodging house, padded down the hallway, and entered the room of Mr. Pierce and his party.

There Pierce directed his swift treatment, for Willy was barely conscious. His clothes were stripped off by the women; his many wounds were stanched with styptic powder, then bandaged. Agar gave him a sip of coca wine for energy, and beef-and-iron wine for sustenance, with two Carter's Little Nerve Pills and some tincture of opium for his pain. The women cleaned his face and bundled him into the waiting dress. He was given a sip of Bromo Caffein and told to act faint. A bonnet was placed on his head, and his prison garb was stuffed in the picnic basket.

No one among the crowd of more than twenty thousand paid the slightest attention when a well-dressed party departed Mrs. Molloy's lodging house—with one woman so faint that she had to be carried by the men into a waiting cab—and rattled off. A faint woman was a common enough sight and in any case nothing to compare to a woman turning slowly at the end of the rope.

AFTER his escape Clean Willy was taken to Pierce's house, where he spent several weeks in seclusion while his wounds healed. It is from his later statement to police that we first learn of the mysterious Miss Miriam, who was Pierce's mistress.

The servants were told that Willy was a relative of Miss Miriam's who had been run down by a cab. Willy said of Miss Miriam that she was "well carried, a good figure, and well-spoke." Her eyes were said to be captivating, and her grace "dreamlike."

Willy recalled only one conversation with Miss Miriam. He asked, "Are you his canary, then?" Meaning Pierce's accomplice.

"Oh, no," she said, smiling. "I have no ear for music."

From this he assumed she was not involved in Pierce's plans, but this was later shown to be wrong.

At the trial there was considerable speculation about Miss Miriam. Evidence points to the conclusion that she was an actress, for she could mimic the accents and manners of different social classes, wore makeup, and lived openly as Pierce's mistress. The dividing line between an actress and a prostitute was then exceedingly fine, and actors were likely to have connections with criminals. She seems to have been Pierce's mistress for several years.

Pierce himself was rarely in the house by day, and on occasion he was gone overnight. Clean Willy recalled seeing him once or twice in the late afternoon, wearing riding clothes.

"I didn't know you were a horse fancier," Willy once said.

"I'm not," Pierce replied shortly. "Hate the bloody beasts."

Pierce kept Willy indoors after his wounds were healed, waiting for his convict's short hair to grow out. By late September his hair was longer, but still Pierce did not allow him to leave. When Willy asked why, Pierce said, "I am waiting for you to be recaptured or found dead."

A few days later Pierce came in with a newspaper under his arm and told Willy he could leave. The body of a young man had been found floating in the Thames, and police had identified him as the escaped convict from Newgate. Willy went back to the Holy Land, where he found Maggie. He lived under cover off her earnings, cheerful and at ease, and waited for Pierce to call.

On the muddy pathway in Hyde Park called the Ladies' Mile of Rotten Row, hundreds of splendidly dressed men and women rode in the golden sunshine at four in the afternoon: the women with uniformed foot pages trotting along behind, and sometimes accompanied by stern, mounted duennas or by their beaus. Many of the women were of dubious character. "There is no difficulty," one observer would write, "in guessing the occupation of the dashing *equestrienne* who salutes half-a-dozen men at once with whip or with a wink, and who sometimes varies the monotony of a safe seat by holding her hands behind her back while gracefully swerving over to listen to the compliments of a walking admirer."

These were members of the highest class of prostitute, the demimondaines. At the opera and the theater more than one young lady found her escort's gaze fixed not on the performance but on some box where an elegant woman openly returned his glances. It is usual to dismiss Victorian prostitution as a manifestation of profound hypocrisy. But the issue is more complex; it has to do with the way that women were viewed in Victorian England.

It was believed then that the power of reasoning was small in women, who were governed by their emotions and hence required strict controls on their behavior by the more rational, levelheaded males. Because of their presumed intellectual inferiority, reinforced

by their education, many well-bred women probably were the sim-
pering, tittering fools depicted in many Victorian novels. Ladies in
general were "very unsatisfactory mental food," as one late-
Victorian critic wrote, adding, "I doubt greatly whether there were
ever many men who had thoughts worth recounting, who told
these thoughts to their wives at first, or who expected them to
appreciate them."

There is good evidence that both sexes were bored silly by this
arrangement. Women, stranded in servant-filled households, dealt
with their frustrations in fainting spells, loss of appetite, even loss
of memory. Frustrated men had recourse to prostitutes, who were
often lively, gay, and witty. In their company, men could discard
the formalities of Victorian society and relax. This freedom from
restraints was at least as important as the availability of a sexual
outlet, and allowed such women to intrude boldly into arenas of
Victorian society like Rotten Row.

By late September, 1854, Edward Pierce had begun to meet
Elizabeth Trent on riding excursions there. The first encounter
seemed accidental, but later, by unstated agreement, they occurred
with regularity. Elizabeth spent all morning preparing for these
afternoon meetings, and all evening discussing them with her
friends. The twenty-nine-year-old woman apparently never thought
it strange that Mr. Pierce should single her out from among the
stunning beauties on Rotten Row.

At the trial their conversations were summarized as "light and
trivial," except for one in the month of October, 1854. This was a
time of political upheaval and military scandal; the nation had
suffered a severe blow to its self-esteem, for the Crimean War was
turning into a disaster. In *Victoria's Heyday*, J. B. Priestley notes
that "the upper classes welcomed the war as a glorified large-scale
picnic in some remote and romantic place. . . . Wealthy officers
like Lord Cardigan decided to take their yachts. Some command-
ers' wives insisted upon going along, accompanied by their personal maids."

The picnic quickly became a debacle. The British troops were
badly trained and ineptly led. The military commander, Lord Rag-

43

lan, was sixty-five and often seemed to think he was still fighting Waterloo. He referred to the enemy as "the French," although the French were now his allies. On one occasion he was so confused that he took up an observation post behind the Russian enemy lines. By October the atmosphere of "aged chaos" culminated in Lord Cardigan's charge of the Light Brigade, a spectacular feat which destroyed a large part of his forces in an effort to capture the wrong battery of enemy guns at Balaklava.

Nearly all upper-class Englishmen were profoundly concerned, but on that warm October afternoon in Hyde Park, Pierce gently guided Elizabeth into a conversation about her father.

"He was most fearfully nervous this morning," she said. "He is nervous every morning when he must send the gold shipments to the Crimea. He is distant and preoccupied in the extreme."

"He bears a heavy responsibility," Pierce said.

"So heavy, I fear he may take to excessive drink."

"I pray you exaggerate!"

"Well, he does act strangely. You know he is entirely opposed to the consumption of alcohol before nightfall, but each morning of a shipment he goes to the wine cellar. He spends some time there, and then emerges to make his journey to the bank."

"I think," Pierce said, "that he merely checks the cellar for some ordinary purpose. Is that not logical?"

"No, indeed," Elizabeth said. "At all other times he relies upon my stepmother to deal in the stocking and care of the cellar and the decanting of wines before dinners."

"Then I trust," Pierce said gravely, "that his responsibilities are not placing an overgreat burden upon his nervous system."

"I trust." The daughter sighed. "Is it not a lovely day?"

"Lovely," Pierce agreed. "But no more lovely than you."

Elizabeth replied that he was a bold rogue to flatter her so. "One might even suspect an ulterior motive," she added, laughing.

"Heavens, no." Pierce placed his hand lightly over hers.

"I am so happy," she said.

"And I am happy with you," Pierce said, and this was true, for he now knew the location of all four keys.

CHAPTER FIVE

HENRY Fowler, seated in a dark recess of the taproom at the lunch hour, showed some agitation. He twisted his glass in his hands and could hardly bring himself to look into the eyes of his friend Edward Pierce. "The matter is somewhat embarrassing," he said.

"Then speak of it forthrightly, as one man to another."

Fowler gulped his drink and set the glass back on the table with a sharp clink. "Very well. The fact is that I have a strong craving for a fresh country girl."

"How may I help you?" Pierce asked, knowing the answer.

"I hoped that as a bachelor you might have knowledge—ah, that you might make an introduction on my behalf."

Pierce frowned. "It is no longer so easy as it once was. But I know a woman who sometimes has a fresh or two. I can make inquiries, and you may expect to hear from me in a day or so."

"Oh, thank you, thank you," Fowler said.

"I warn you, it may be expensive. They are much in demand."

"Well, then, it shall be," Fowler said.

And so, two days later, he received by penny post a letter addressed to him by Pierce. It told him to present himself in four days' time, at eight o'clock, at a house in Lichfield Street near St. Martin's Lane. Mr. Fowler sent off a quick note of thanks.

When he found himself at the address given to him, he eyed the establishment with some trepidation, for the exterior was not prepossessing. Thus it was a pleasant surprise when a knock at the door was answered by an elegantly dressed woman, who asked him to address her as Miss Miriam. Her face was in shadow in the rather dark hall. Fowler saw that this was not one of those crude five-shillings-an-hour establishments. The furnishings were plush velvet, with rich drapings and fine Persian carpets. Miss Miriam comported herself with extraordinary dignity as she requested a large sum; her manner was so wellborn that Fowler paid without a quibble and was directed to an upstairs room.

Once in the room, Henry Fowler could scarcely believe his eyes. Here was a delicate, young, rosy-cheeked creature. Her name was Susan Lang, she said, and she had come from Derbyshire; her parents were dead, and she had a brother in the Crimea. She talked of these events lightly, though she seemed nervous.

The room was superbly furnished, and the air softly scented with jasmine. Fowler looked about briefly, for a man could never be too careful. Then he bolted the door and faced the girl.

"Well, now," he said. "Shall, we, ah . . ."

"Oh, yes, of course, sir," she said, and began to unbutton his shirt. "What is this?" she asked suddenly, touching a key which hung around his neck on a silver chain.

"Just a—ah—key," he replied.

"You'd best take it off," she said. "It may harm me."

He took it off, and the next hour was so magical that Henry Fowler did not notice when a hand slipped around one of the red velvet curtains and plucked the key from atop his clothing; nor did he notice when, a short time later, the key was returned.

ON THE same day that Fowler was writing a letter of thanks to Pierce, Pierce was preparing to crack the Trent mansion. Involved in the plan besides Pierce, who now knew the layout of the house, were Agar, who would make wax impressions of the key; his judy, who would act as crow, or lookout; Barlow, who would be a stall, providing diversion; and Miss Miriam. She would carry out "the carriage fakement." This was a method of breaking into a house which relied upon the tipping of servants. In Victorian England roughly ten percent of the population was "in service," and nearly all were poorly paid. Some of the poorest paid were those brought in contact with visitors. Footmen, some of whom served as hall porters, for instance, relied on tips for most of their income. Thus the notorious disdain of the footman for insubstantial callers—and thus, too, the carriage fakement.

By nine o'clock on the evening of November 12, 1854, Pierce had his confederates in their places. The crow lounged across the street from the Trent mansion. Barlow had slipped down the alley toward the dog pens. Pierce and Agar were concealed in shrubbery by the front door. When all was ready an elegant carriage drew up in front of the house, and the bell was rung.

The Trents' porter heard the ring and opened the door. He saw the carriage, and when after a moment no one emerged, being conscious of a possible tip, he went down to the curb to see if he could be of service. Inside the carriage was a handsome, refined woman, who asked if this was the residence of Mr. Robert Jenkins. The porter said it was not, but that the Jenkins' house was around the corner. He gave directions.

Meanwhile, Pierce and Agar slipped into the house through the open front door and proceeded directly to the basement door. It was locked, but Agar employed a twirl, or skeleton key, and had it open in a moment. The two men had closed the basement door by the time the porter received his shilling from the lady, walked back into the house, and locked the front door.

That was the carriage fakement.

IN THE light of a narrow-beam lantern Pierce checked his watch. It was 9:04. That gave them an hour to find the key before Barlow was to provide his diversion to cover their escape.

Pierce and Agar moved stealthily down the creaking stairs. The wine cellar was locked by iron gratings, but the locks yielded easily to Agar's twirl, and at 9:11 the grating swung open. Pierce could make only one assumption about the hiding place: since Mrs. Trent often went into the wine cellar, and since Trent did not want her coming across the key, he probably hid it at some inconveniently high location. They felt the tops of the wine racks with their fingers. There was soon a good deal of dust in the air, and Agar, with his bad lungs, had difficulty. Several times his stifled coughs alarmed Pierce, but the Trent household never heard them.

By 9:30 time was beginning to work against them. Pierce searched frantically, hissing complaints to Agar, who wielded the shaded lantern. Ten more minutes passed, and Pierce began to sweat. And then, with startling suddenness, his fingers felt something cold on the top of a rack. The object fell to the ground with a metallic clink. A moment of scrambling around on the earthen floor and he had the key. It was 9:45.

Pierce held the key up to the lantern. Agar groaned.

"That's the wrong key."

Pierce turned it over in his hands. "Are you sure?" he whispered, but even as he spoke he knew Agar was right. The key was no safe key; it was small and delicate; there was grime in the crevices.

"Nobody's touched her in ten years," Agar said.

Pierce swore, and continued his search. He felt his heart thump in his chest, not daring to look at his watch. Then his fingers again felt metal. He brought it to the light. It was a shiny key.

"That's for a safe," Agar said.

"Right," Pierce said, taking the lantern. Agar fished two wax blanks from his pockets. He warmed them in his hands, then pressed the key into them, first one side, then the other.

"Time?" he whispered.

"Nine fifty-one," Pierce said.

"I'll do another." Agar repeated the process with a second set of blanks. Then Pierce returned the key to its hiding place.

"Nine fifty-seven."

"Crikey, it's close." They left the wine cellar, locking it behind them, and slipped up the basement stairs.

Meantime, Barlow, lurking in the shadows near the servants' quarters, checked his watch and saw it was 10:00. He hesitated. His accomplices might not have finished their work on schedule, and he had no wish to be greeted by angry faces when they made their escape. Finally he muttered to himself, "Ten is ten," and, carrying a bag, moved to the dog pen. Three dogs were there, including the new gift from Pierce—the made dog. Barlow bent over the run and pushed four squeaking rats out of the bag and into the enclosure. Immediately the dogs began to yelp, raising a terrible din.

Barlow slipped into the shadows as lights came on in the servants' quarters. Pierce and Agar, hearing the commotion, opened the basement door and moved into the hallway, locking the door behind them. Hearing running footsteps at the back of the house, they unbolted the front door and disappeared into the night.

49

They left behind them only one sign of their visit: the unlocked front door. They knew that in the morning the footman would be reminded of the incident of the carriage the night before, and would probably assume that he had forgotten to lock up.

No burglary at the Trent residence was reported to authorities. The commotion of the dogs was explained by the bodies of dead rats in the kennel. There was some discussion of how the rats had got into the dog run, but the Trent household was large and busy, and there was no time for speculation on trivial matters.

Thus, by dawn of November 13, 1854, Edward Pierce had waxes of two of the four keys. He directed his attention to the others.

BUT the ease with which Pierce and his fellow conspirators had obtained the first two keys gave them a sense of confidence that was soon to prove false; for the South Eastern Railway unexpectedly changed its routine at the dispatcher's offices in London Bridge Station.

Miss Miriam had been checking that routine in late December, and she returned to tell Pierce and Agar that the company had hired a jack, or detective, to guard the premises at night. "He comes on duty at lockup, at seven sharp. He's forty or so—a ream esclop." Miss Miriam meant he was a real policeman. "Square-rigged, fat. But he's armed."

"Where's he lurk, then?" Agar said.

"Sits at the top of the steps, by the door, with a paper bag at his side, which I think is his supper."

"I wonder why they put on a night guard," Pierce said.

"Maybe they knew we were giving it the yack," Agar said. They had kept the office under surveillance now, off and on, for months. Someone might have noticed.

Pierce sighed. "Just a little more difficult is all. We don't yet know the full night routine. We never had an all-night watch." At night the station was deserted, and loiterers were briskly ordered off by the policemen making their rounds, but a concealed man could remain there all night.

"Clean Willy?"

"No," Pierce said. "Clean Willy is glocky."

Clean Willy, dead at the time of the trial, was noted in courtroom testimony to be of "diminished faculties of reasoning."

"Who shall we have instead?" Agar asked.

"I was thinking of a skipper," Pierce said. "Do you happen to know of a skipper?"

"I can find one. But what's the lurk, then?"

"We'll pack him in a crate," Pierce said.

The term "skipper" implied a way of life—more specifically a way of spending the night. Even with massive building programs and densely crowded slums, a sizable fraction of the London population lacked the means to pay for shelter. Skippers spent their nights wherever the police would leave them alone: in the arches of railway bridges, in ruined buildings, shop doorways, boiler rooms, empty market stalls, even outhouses. Skippers were at the bottom of the social order, and were often soaks, which no doubt helped them tolerate their uncomfortable resting places.

So Pierce ordered a packing crate to be built and delivered to his residence. Agar obtained a very reliable skipper, and arrangements were made to send the crate to the railway station. The skipper, Henson, was never tracked down; he was a very minor figure in the entire scheme.

The crate with Henson in it was placed strategically within London Bridge Station. Through the slats Henson was able to watch the behavior of the night guard. After the first night the crate was hauled away, painted another color, and returned to the station again. This routine was followed three nights in succession. Then Henson reported his discouraging findings.

"The jack's solid," he told Pierce. "Regular as this clock." He held up the stopwatch Pierce had given him. "Comes on at seven prompt, with his little paper bag of supper. Sits on the steps, always alert, greeting the crusher on his rounds. First crusher works to midnight, goes every eleven minutes regular round the station. Second crusher works midnight to dawn. He keeps to no beat but pops up here and there like a jack-in-a-box. And he's got two barkers at his belt."

51

"What about the jack by the office door?" Pierce said. "Does he ever leave his place?"

"No," the skipper said. "He sits right there. Each time the church bells ring the hour he cocks his head and listens. At eleven he opens his bag and eats his tightener, for maybe ten, fifteen minutes, and has a bottle of beer. Now the jack waits until half past eleven or thereabouts, and then he goes to the loo. The crusher passes him by."

"Then he *does* leave," Pierce said. "How long is he gone?"

"I clocked it proper," Henson said. "He's gone sixty-four seconds one night, and sixty-eight the next night, and sixty-four the third night. Always near about eleven thirty. And he's back to his post when the first crusher makes the last round, quarter to midnight, and then the second crusher comes on to the beat."

"He did this every night?"

"Every night. Beer makes a man have a powerful urge."

"Yes," Pierce said, "it does have that effect. Now you're sure he doesn't leave his post at any other time. You never slept?"

"When I'm sleeping here all the day through on your nice bed? I swear, Mr. Pierce, I never slept a bit. The jack's as regular as this jerry"—he held up the stopwatch—"that jack is."

Pierce paid the skipper and sent him on his way. As the door closed on him, Pierce told Barlow to worry, or strangle, the skipper; Barlow nodded and left the house by another exit.

When Pierce returned to Agar he recounted the night guard's movements and said, "Well?"

"Sixty-four seconds," Agar said, shaking his head.

"You keep telling me you're the best screwsman in the country; here's a fitting challenge for your talents."

"Maybe," Agar said. "But I got to practice the lay. Can we pay a visit?"

"Certainly," Pierce said.

"OF RECENT weeks," wrote the *Illustrated London News* on December 21, 1854, "the incidence of bold and brutal street banditry has reached alarming proportions. Only yesterday a constable, Peter Farrell, was lured into an alley, where a band of thugs fell upon him, taking all of his possessions, even his uniform."

The article went on to describe Constable Farrell as "faring no better than could be expected." Farrell said that he had been called by a well-dressed woman who was arguing with her cab-driver, "a surly fellow with a white scar across the forehead." When the policeman interceded the cabby fell on him, beating him with a blackjack; and when the unfortunate policeman came to his senses he discovered he had been stripped of his clothing.

In 1854 many urban-dwelling Victorians were concerned over street crime by rampsmen, or footpads. The usual method of foot-padding called for a victim, preferably drunk, to be lured into a corner by an accomplice, preferably a woman, whereupon the foot-pad would beat and rob the victim.

The attack on Constable Farrell made little sense. Then, as now, criminals tried to avoid confrontations with the police, for the police took a special interest in attacks on their own kind. To prop, or hit, a crusher was asking for an all-out manhunt through the rookeries. Besides, a policeman was more capable than most victims of defending himself and never carried much money. And, finally, there was no point in stripping a policeman, for his uniform had no resale value. Secondhand shops were always under surveillance and always accused of taking stolen goods; they would never accept a police uniform. Thus any thoughtful observers must have pondered why the attack on Constable Farrell had occurred at all.

In late December, 1854, Pierce met a man named Andrew Taggert in the King's Arms public house, off Regent Street. Taggert had survived a varied career. Born around 1790 outside Liverpool, he had come to London with his prostitute mother. By the age of ten he was employed in the resurrection trade—digging up corpses from graveyards to sell to medical schools. He soon acquired a reputation for uncommon daring; it was said that he once transported a body through London streets in daylight, with the man propped up in his cart like a passenger.

When the Anatomy Act of 1832 ended the business in corpses,

Taggert shifted to passing counterfeit coins. This was petty work, and he soon tired of it. He moved on to a variety of con games, took a respectable flat, and also a wife, one Mary Maxwell, a widow. Mary was a coiner, who had served time in prison on several occasions.

A woman's legal position was already the subject of active attempts at reform; but women still did not have the right to own property or to make wills, and the earnings of a woman who was separated from her husband were still the property of her husband. Although the law appeared overwhelmingly to favor men, there were some odd legal quirks, as Taggert soon discovered.

In 1847 the police raided Mary Taggert's coining operation, catching her red-handed in the midst of stamping out sixpence pieces. She greeted them with equanimity, announced pleasantly that she was married, and told them the whereabouts of her husband; for by law a husband was responsible for any criminal activities of his wife. So Taggert was arrested and sentenced to eight years in prison for counterfeiting; Mary was released without so much as a reprimand, and is said to have displayed "a roistering, bantering demeanour" when her husband was sentenced.

Taggert served only three years, but afterward it was said the steel had gone out of him; he turned to hoof-snaffling, or horse stealing. By 1854 he was a familiar face in sporting pubs.

Pierce met him in the King's Arms with a most peculiar suggestion. Taggert gulped his gin and said, "You want a *what?*"

"A leopard," Pierce said.

"Now, where's an honest man like me to find a leopard?"

"I wouldn't know," Pierce said.

"Never in my life," Taggert said, "would I know of any leopard, excepting the bestiaries here and there, which have all manner of beasts. Is it to be christened?"

Taggert was an expert christener—a man who could remove marks of identification from stolen goods. He could disguise a horse so that even its owner would not recognize it. But christening a leopard might be hard.

"No," Pierce said. "I can take it as you have it."

"What's it for, then?"

Pierce gave Taggert a severe look. "It is a present," he said, "for a lady. On the Continent. In Paris."

"You could buy one. Cost you no more than buying from me."

"I made you a business proposition."

"So you did. But you didn't mention what's in it for me. If you want a leopard, you'll pay me forty guineas and count yourself lucky."

"I'll pay you twenty-five and *you'll* count yourself lucky."

Taggert looked unhappy. He twisted his gin glass in his hands. "All right, then," he said. "When's it to be?"

"Never you mind," Pierce said. "You find the animal. You'll hear from me." He dropped a gold guinea on the counter.

Taggert picked it up, bit it, nodded, and touched his cap. "Good day to you, sir," he said.

"Good day," Pierce said.

T HE current attitude of fear or indifference to a crime in progress would have astounded the Victorians. In those days any person being robbed or mugged raised a hue and cry, and the victim got an immediate response from citizens around him, who joined with alacrity in an attempt to catch the villain.

There were several reasons for this. In the first place, the organized police force was only twenty-five years old, and people did not yet believe that crime was "something for the police to take care of." Second, as firearms were rare, there was little likelihood of a bystander stopping a charge by pursuing a thief. Finally, many of the criminals were children, even young children, and adults did not hesitate to go after them.

If an alarm was raised, the chances were that the criminal would be caught. For this reason thieves often staged a fracas to cover their activities. This maneuver was known as a jolly gaff.

On the morning of January 9, 1855, Pierce looked around the

cavernous interior of the London Bridge Station and saw that all his players were in position. Pierce was dressed as a traveler, as was Miss Miriam. She would be the plant, or victim.

A few yards distant was the "culprit," a child nine years old, scruffy and noticeably out of place among the crowd of first-class passengers. Pierce had selected him from a dozen children in the Holy Land for his speed. Farther away still was Barlow, wearing a constable's uniform, with the hat pulled down to conceal his scar. Finally, not far from the steps to the dispatcher's office was Agar, disguised in fine gentleman's clothing.

As it came time for the eleven-o'clock train to depart for Greenwich, Pierce scratched his neck. Immediately the child brushed against Miss Miriam's side, rustling her velvet dress. Miss Miriam cried, "I've been robbed!" patting her pocket.

Pierce shouted, "Stop, thief!" and raced after the boy.

Startled bystanders grabbed at the youngster, but he tore free and ran toward the back of the station. There Barlow in uniform came forward menacingly. Agar, as a civic-spirited gentleman, also joined in the pursuit. The child's only escape was up the stairs to the railway office. He ran hard, with Barlow, Agar, and Pierce on his heels. The boy's instructions were to get into the office, past the clerks' desks, and back to a high rear window looking out on the station roof. He was to break this window in an attempt to escape. Then Barlow would apprehend him, and he was to struggle until Barlow cuffed him as a signal that the jolly gaff had ended.

The child burst into the office, startling the clerks, and Pierce dashed in immediately afterward, shouting, "Stop him, he's a thief!" In his pursuit Pierce knocked over one of the clerks. The child was scrambling for the window when Barlow came in.

"I'll handle this," Barlow said, in an authoritative voice. But he clumsily knocked a desk over and sent papers flying.

"Catch him! Catch him!" Agar called, entering the offices.

The child scrambled onto the dispatcher's desk, going toward a narrow high window; he cracked the glass with his fist, cutting himself. The dispatcher kept saying, "Oh, dear, oh, dear!"

"I am an officer of the law, make way!" Barlow shouted.

Glass fragments fell on the floor, and Barlow and the child rolled in a struggle that took longer to resolve itself than one might expect. The clerks watched in confusion.

No one noticed that Agar had turned his back on the commotion and was trying several of his ring of skeleton keys until he found one that fitted the lock on the office door. Nor did anyone see him move to the wall cabinet and try one key after another until he found one that worked.

The young ruffian, who kept slipping from the hands of the red-faced "constable," was finally caught by Pierce. The lad handed up the stolen purse and was carted away by the constable. Pierce dusted himself off, looked around the wreckage of the office, and apologized to the clerks and the dispatcher.

Then the other gentleman who had joined in the pursuit said, "I fear, sir, that you have missed your train."

"By Gad, I have," Pierce said. "Damn the little rascal!" And the two gentlemen departed, leaving the clerks with the mess.

WHEN Clean Willy Williams arrived at Pierce's house the afternoon of January 9, 1855, he was confronted by a strange spectacle in the drawing room. Pierce, wearing a red velvet smoking jacket, lounged in an easy chair, smoking a cigar, utterly relaxed, a stopwatch in his hand. Agar, in shirt sleeves, stood in the center of the room, in a kind of half crouch.

"Ready?" Pierce said. Agar nodded. "Go!" Pierce said, and flicked the stopwatch.

To Clean Willy's amazement, Agar dashed across the room to the fireplace, where he began to jog in place, counting to himself, ". . . seven . . . eight . . . nine . . . ."

"That's it," Pierce said. "Door!"

"Door!" Agar said and, in pantomime, turned the handle on an unseen door. He then took three steps to the right, and reached up to shoulder height, touching something in the air.

"Cabinet," Pierce said.

Agar fished two wax flats out of his pocket, and pretended to make an impression of a key. "Time?" he asked.

"Thirty-one," Pierce said.

Agar made an impression on a second set of flats, counting to himself. "Thirty-four . . . thirty-five . . ."

He reached into the air with both hands, as if closing something. "Cabinet shut," he said, and took three paces back across the room. "Door! Steps!" He ran in place once more, then sprinted across the room to Pierce. "Done!" he cried.

Pierce looked at the watch and shook his head. "Sixty-nine."

"It's better than it was," Agar said in a wounded tone.

"But not good enough. Maybe if you don't close the cabinet and don't hang up the keys. Clean Willy can do that."

"Do what?" Willy said, watching.

"Open and close the cabinet," Pierce said.

Agar went back to his starting position. "Ready," he said.

Once again this odd charade was repeated.

"Time?" Agar called.

Pierce smiled. "Sixty-three." And as Agar grinned, gasping, Pierce said, "Once more, just to be certain."

Later, Clean Willy was given the lay. Pierce said, "Once it's dark, you'll go up to London Bridge, and get onto the roof of the station. Cross the roof to a little window that is broken. Inside you will see a green cabinet on the wall." Pierce looked at the snakes-man. "You'll have to stand on a chair to reach it. Be very quiet; there's a jack posted outside the office."

Clean Willy frowned.

"Unlock the cabinet," Pierce said. He nodded to Agar, who gave Willy a skeleton key. "Open it and then wait. Around ten thirty there'll be a bit of a shindy; a soak will come into the station to chat up the jack. Then you unlock the office door"—Agar gave him another key—"and wait till eleven thirty, when the jack goes to the loo. Then Agar comes up the steps, through the door, and makes his waxes. He leaves, and you lock the door right away. Then lock the cabinet, put the chair back, and go out the window quietlike."

"That's the lay?" Clean Willy said doubtfully. "You popped me out of Newgate for *this?*"

"Just you look sharp and be ready," Pierce said. "Then do the lay. And quiet."

Clean Willy nodded. "What's for dinner?" he said.

THAT evening, in a London pea-soup fog, Clean Willy Williams eased down Tooley Street. He could not see the second story of London Bridge Station, but after maneuvering around the terminal he found his spot. By climbing onto a luggage cart he was able to jump to a drainpipe and from there to the sill of a second-story window. From there he inched along a stone ledge until he reached a corner. Then he climbed up the corner, his back to the wall. By eight o'clock he was standing on the terminal's broad roof. Cautiously he edged around the building until he found the broken window and looked in. The dispatcher's office was still somewhat in disarray.

Clean Willy reached through the jagged glass, turned the lock, and raised the window. He wriggled through easily, stepped down onto a desk top, and paused to look through the glass in the office doors. He could see down to the deserted station. He could also see the jack on the stairs, a paper bag at his side.

Clean Willy climbed down off the desk. His foot crunched on a shard of glass; he froze. But the guard gave no sign. After a moment Willy crossed the office and moved a chair to the high cabinet. He stepped onto the chair, plucked the twirl Agar had given him from his pocket, and opened the cabinet. Then he sat down to wait, hearing church bells toll the hour of nine.

AGAR, wedged into a cramped corner of the station, also heard the bells. He sighed. Another two and a half hours. He knew how stiff and painful his legs would be when he finally made his sprint for the stairs. He could see Clean Willy make an entrance into the office, and he could see Willy's head when he stood on the chair and worked the cabinet lock. Then Willy disappeared.

Agar wondered, for the thousandth time, what Pierce intended to do with these keys. It must be a devilish flash pull. A few years earlier Agar had been in on a Brighton warehouse pull, involving nine keys. That pull had meant ten thousand pounds, and the putter-up had spent four months arranging the lay. Now here was Pierce, flush if ever a cracksman was, spending eight months just to get four keys. What *was* he after? The question preoccupied him more than the mechanics of timing a sixty-four-second smash and grab. He was cool and confident as he stared across the station at the jack on the stairs. But what *was* the pull?

THE drunken Irishman with the red beard and slouch hat stumbled through the deserted station singing "Molly Malone." Shuffling along, he suddenly noticed the guard on the stairs and eyed the guard's paper bag suspiciously before making an elaborate and wobbly bow. "And a good evenin' to you, sir," the soak said.

"Evening," the guard said.

"And what, may I inquire, is your business up there, eh?"

"I'm guarding these premises here," the guard said.

The drunk hiccuped, and tried to point an accusatory finger. "So you say, my good fellow, but I think—I think, sir, we shall have the police to look you over!"

"Now, look here," the guard said.

"You look here, and lively, too," the drunk said, and abruptly began to shout, "Police! *Po-lice!*"

"Here, now," the guard said, leaving the office door and coming down the stairs. "Get a grip on yourself, you soak."

The constable came running around the corner, drawn by the shouts, and the drunk said, "Officer, arrest that scoundrel!" He pointed to the guard. "He is up to no good." The drunk hiccuped again. The constable and the guard exchanged open smiles.

"You find this a laughing matter?" said the drunk.

"Come along, now," the constable said, "or I'll have you in for creatin' a nuisance."

"A nuisance?" the drunk said, twisting free. "I think you and this blackguard are a pair of—"

"That's enough," the constable said. "Come along smartly."

The drunk allowed himself to be led away, saying, "You wouldn't be havin' a beer, would you, now?"

The guard sighed and climbed back on the stairs to eat his supper. The chimes rang eleven o'clock.

While Agar was amused by Pierce's performance, he worried whether Clean Willy had taken the opportunity to open the office door. There was no way to know until he made his own mad dash. He looked at his watch. Less than half an hour now.

PIERCE was led by the constable out onto Tooley Street. He did not want to disrupt the policeman's regular rhythm in the terminal, so he had to disengage himself rapidly. "Ah," he said, "and it's a lovely evening. Brisk and invigorating."

The copper looked around at the fog. "Chill enough."

"Well, my dear fellow!" Pierce made a show of straightening up, as if the air had sobered him. "I am most grateful for your ministrations. I can carry on from here."

"You're not going to be creating another nuisance?"

"My dear sir, what do you take me for?"

It was the copper's business to stick to the terminal beat. "Stay clear of trouble, then," he said, and let Pierce go.

Pierce wandered into the fog, singing. But he went less then a block. There, hidden in the shadows, was a cab. He looked up at the driver. "How'd it carry off?" Barlow asked.

"Smart and tidy. I gave Willy two or three minutes. It should have been enough." He glanced at his watch. "We'll know soon."

He slipped back toward the station, and at 11:30 took up a position in a shadowy recess where he could see the stairs. The copper made his round; he waved to the jack, who waved back. The copper went on; the jack yawned and stretched. Pierce poised his finger on the stopwatch button. The guard came down the stairs, and moved off toward the WC around a corner.

Pierce hit the button, counting softly, "One . . . two . . . three . . ."

He saw Agar appear, running hard, barefoot to make no sound, and dashing up the stairs to the door.

"Four . . . five . . . six . . ."

Agar reached the door, twisted the knob; the door opened and Agar was inside. The door closed.

61

"Seven . . . eight . . . nine . . ."

"Ten," Agar said to himself, panting, looking around the office.

Clean Willy, grinning in the shadows in the corner, took up the count. "Eleven . . . twelve . . . thirteen . . ."

Agar crossed to the opened cabinet and removed the first of the wax blanks from his pocket. "Crikey!" he whispered.

"Fourteen . . . fifteen . . . sixteen . . ."

Dozens of keys hung in the cabinet, large and small, labeled and unlabeled. He broke into a sweat.

"Seventeen . . . eighteen . . . nineteen . . ."

Agar was going to fall behind. He knew it with sickening suddenness. He could not wax them all; which were the ones to do?

"Twenty . . . twenty-one . . . twenty-two . . ."

Agar stared at the cabinet in rising panic. He remembered what the other two keys looked like; perhaps these were similar. He peered close, straining; the light was bad.

"Twenty-three . . . twenty-four . . . twenty-five . . ."

"It's no bloody use," he whispered to himself. And then he realized something odd: each hook had only one key, except for a single hook which had two. He quickly lifted the two off. They looked like the others he had done.

"Twenty-six . . . twenty-seven . . . twenty-eight . . ."

He set out a blank and pressed one side of the first key into it, plucking it out with his fingernail; the nail on the little finger was long, one of the hallmarks of a screwsman.

"Twenty-nine . . . thirty . . . thirty-one . . ."

He took a second blank, flipped the key over, and pressed it into the wax to get the other side, then scooped it out.

"Thirty-two . . . thirty-three . . . thirty-four . . ."

Now Agar's professionalism came into play. He was five seconds off count but he knew that at all costs he must avoid confusing the keys. Quickly but carefully, he hung up the first finished key.

"Thirty-five . . . thirty-six . . . thirty-seven, Lordy," Clean Willy said. Clean Willy was looking out the glass windows, down to where the guard would be returning in less than thirty seconds.

"Thirty-eight . . . thirty-nine . . . forty . . ."

Swiftly, Agar pressed the second key into his third blank, then lifted it out.

"Forty-one . . . forty-two . . . forty-three . . ."

Agar plucked up his fourth wax and pressed the other side of the key into it.

"Forty-four . . . forty-five . . . forty-six . . . forty-seven . . ."

Abruptly, while Agar was peeling the key free of the wax, the blank cracked in two. "Damn!"

"Forty-eight . . . forty-nine . . . fifty . . ."

He fished in his pocket for another blank. His fingers were steady, but there was sweat dripping from his forehead.

"Fifty-one . . . fifty-two . . . fifty-three . . ."

He drew out a fresh blank and did the second side again.

"Fifty-four . . . fifty-five . . ."

He plucked the key out, hung it up, and dashed for the door.

"Fifty-six," Willy said, and moved to the door to lock up.

Below, Pierce saw Agar exit, behind schedule by five full seconds. His face was flushed with exertion. He sprinted down the stairs three at a time.

"Fifty-nine . . . sixty . . . sixty-one . . ."

Agar streaked across the station to his hiding place.

"Sixty-two . . . sixty-three . . ."

Agar was hidden.

The guard, yawning, came around the corner and took up his post at the stairs. He began humming to himself, and it was a while before Pierce realized it was "Molly Malone."

THE Casino de Venise on Windmill Street was a large and lively gaslit dance hall, where young men spun and wheeled colorfully dressed girls. The impression of fashionable splendor belied its reputation as a notorious place for whores and their clientele.

Pierce went to the bar, where a burly man in blue uniform hunched over a drink. "Have you been here before?" Pierce asked.

The man turned. "You Mr. Simms?"

"That's right."

The burly man looked around at the women, the bright lights.

"No, never before. Bit above me," he said, and stared at his glass.

"And expensive," Pierce said. "Let me buy you another drink." He raised a gray-gloved hand and indicated two drinks. "Where do you live, Mr. Burgess?"

"I got a room on Moresby Road," the man said.

"I hear the air is bad there."

Burgess shrugged. "It'll do."

"I hear you're married. What's your wife do?"

"She sews," Burgess said impatiently. "What's this all about?"

"Just conversation, to see if you want to make more money."

Pierce already knew a good deal about Richard Burgess, a Mary Blaine, or railway train, guard. He knew that he had two children and that his four-year-old son needed the frequent attentions of a doctor, which the Burgesses could not afford. He knew that their room on Moresby Road was squalid, and ventilated by the sulfurous fumes of a gasworks. And he knew that the train guard was paid fifteen shillings a week and his wife made ten.

"Only a fool doesn't want more money," Burgess said shortly.

"You work the Mary Blaine," Pierce said.

Burgess, with still more impatience, nodded and flicked the silver SER letters on his collar: the insignia of the South Eastern Railway. "What's it to be?" he said, not looking at Pierce.

"I was wondering about your vision. I wonder what it would take for your eyes to go bad."

Burgess sighed. Finally he said in a weary voice, "I done a stretch in Newgate. I'm not wanting to see the inside again." He gulped his drink. "What's the sweetener?"

"Two hundred quid," Pierce said.

Burgess coughed and pounded his chest with a thick fist. "Two hundred quid?" he repeated.

"That's right," Pierce said. "Here's ten now, on faith." He took out two five-pound notes, holding his wallet in such a way that Burgess could see it was bulging. He put the money on the bar.

Burgess did not touch it. "What's the lay?"

"You'll never see the inside of a lockup again, I promise you."

"Speak plain," Burgess said.

Pierce sighed. He reached for the money. "I'm sorry," he said, "I fear I must take my business elsewhere."

Burgess caught his hand. "I'm just asking," he said.

"I can't tell you."

There was a moment of silence. Finally, Burgess picked up the two five-pound notes. "Tell me what I do."

"It's very simple," Pierce said. "Soon you will be approached by a man who will ask you whether your wife sews your uniforms. When you meet that man you simply . . . look away."

"That's all? For two hundred quid?"

"For two hundred quid."

Burgess frowned for a moment, and then began to laugh.

"What's funny?" Pierce said.

"You'll never pull it," Burgess said. "Few months past, a kid works into the baggage car to do those safes. Have a go, I says to him, and he has a go for half an hour, and gets nowhere. Then I threw him off smartly, bounced him on his noggin."

"I know that," Pierce said. "I was watching."

IN JANUARY 1855 the first modern war correspondent, William Howard Russell, was in the Crimea with the British troops. His dispatches to the London *Times* had aroused furious indignation at home. The disastrous charge of the Light Brigade at Balaklava, the devastating winter when British troops, lacking food and medical supplies, suffered a fifty-percent mortality—these were all reported to an increasingly angry public.

By January the British commander, Lord Raglan, was ill, and Lord Cardigan—"haughty, rich, selfish and stupid," the man who led the Light Brigade to utter disaster and then returned to his yacht to drink champagne—had come home. The press hailed Lord Cardigan as a national hero. He was mobbed. Hairs from his horse's tail were plucked for souvenirs. London shops copied the jacket he had worn in the Crimea—called a cardigan—and thousands were sold. The man known to his troops as "the dangerous ass" went about the country delivering speeches recounting his prowess, and only later did historians chastise him.

But despite all the news from the Crimea, the dispatches which most intrigued Londoners that January concerned a man-eating leopard which menaced Nainital in northern India. The man-eater was said to have killed more than four hundred natives, and accounts were remarkable for their lurid detail. One correspondent wrote: "The majority of its victims have been children under the age of ten, but it has been seen to carry off a fully grown female in its jaws, while the victim cried out piteously." Such stories became the talk of London, and a working model of a tiger devouring an Englishman was visited by fascinated crowds; it can still be seen in the Victoria and Albert Museum.

So when, on February 17, 1855, a caged leopard arrived at London Bridge Station, it created a considerable stir—much more than the arrival, a short time previously, of armed guards carrying strongboxes, which were loaded into the South Eastern Railway luggage van. The snarling beast charged the bars of its cage as it was loaded onto the same van of the London–Folkestone train. The animal's keeper, who accompanied it, explained to curious onlookers that the leopard was four years old and that it was destined for the Continent, where it would be a present to a wellborn lady.

The train pulled out of the station just after eight that morning, and the guard closed the van's sliding door. There was a short silence while the leopard stalked its cage and growled; finally the guard said, "What do you feed her?"

The attendant turned to the guard. "Does your wife sew your uniforms?" he asked.

Burgess laughed. "You mean it's to be you?"

Agar did not answer. He opened a satchel and removed a jar of grease, several keys, and files. He went to the two Chubb safes, coated the four locks with grease, and began fitting his keys. Burgess was impressed; he had never thought the lay would be carried off with such boldness.

"Where'd you make the impressions?" he said.

"Here and there," Agar replied, fitting and filing.

"They keep those keys separate. How'd you pull them?"

"That's no matter to you," Agar said, still working.

Burgess watched him for a time and then he watched the leopard. "How much does he weigh?"

"Ask him," Agar said irritably.

"Are you taking the gold today, then?" Burgess asked, as Agar got one safe open. Agar did not answer; he was staring transfixed at the strongboxes inside. "I say, are you taking the gold today?"

Agar shut the door. "No," he said. "Now stop your voker."

Burgess fell silent, and for the next hour Agar worked on his keys. He had opened and closed both safes. He wiped the grease from the locks, and cleaned them with alcohol. Finally he placed his four keys in his pocket, and sat down to wait for Folkestone.

Pierce met him there and helped to unload the leopard.

"The finishing touches are done," Agar said. Then he grinned. "It's the Crimean gold, isn't it? That's the flash pull!"

"Yes," Pierce said.

"When?"

"Next month," Pierce said.

The leopard snarled.

CHAPTER SEVEN

PIERCE had originally intended to take the gold during the next Crimean shipment. Under the plan, he and Agar were to board the train in London, each checking several heavy satchels loaded with packets of lead shot onto the luggage van.

Agar would ride in the van. While Burgess looked away he would open the safes, put the gold in the satchels, and replace it with the shot. The satchels would be thrown from the train at a predetermined point and collected by Barlow, who would drive on to Folkestone to meet Pierce and Agar. Meanwhile the strongboxes—still convincingly heavy—would be transferred to the steamer going to Ostend, where the theft would be discovered by the French authorities hours later. By then so many people would have been involved in the process that no particular suspicion would fall on Burgess. In any case British-French relations were at a low level because of the Crimean War, and it would be natural for the French to blame the English for the theft, and vice versa.

The plan seemed foolproof when the robbers prepared to carry it out on the shipment scheduled for March 14. But on March 2 "that fiend in human shape," Czar Nicholas I of Russia, died suddenly. News of his death caused confusion in business and financial circles, and the gold shipment was delayed until March 27. By then Agar was desperately ill with an exacerbation of his chest condition, and the opportunity was missed. Thus the robbers had to wait until April. Pierce was now getting his information on shipment schedules from Susan Lang, the country girl who had become a favorite of Henry Fowler's. Fowler liked to impress the simple girl with his importance in the banking world, and she seemed fascinated by everything he told her.

Susan was hardly simple, but somehow she got her facts wrong. The gold went out on April 18, and when Pierce and Agar boarded the April 19 train, Burgess informed them of their error. To maintain appearances they made the trip anyway, but Agar testified later that Pierce was in "very ugly humor indeed."

The next shipment was scheduled for May 22. Pierce took the risky step of opening a line of communication between Agar and Burgess through Smashing Billy Banks, a betting-shop proprietor. Burgess would get in touch with Banks if there was any change of routine. Agar would check with Banks daily.

On May 10, Agar brought a piece of ghastly news—the two safes had been returned to the manufacturer, Chubb, for overhaul. Pierce frowned. "Overhaul? Those are the finest safes in the world. What's wrong?" And as Agar shrugged, Pierce said, "Did you scratch the locks? I swear, if someone's cooled your scratches—"

"I greased 'em lovely," Agar said calmly. "They had nary a tickle on 'em."

Pierce sighed. "Then *why?*"

"I don't know," Agar said. "You know a man who will blow on the doings at Chubb?"

"No," Pierce said. "No informers there." He stared into the distance thoughtfully. "But I have another idea."

WHAT ROLLS-ROYCE WOULD BECOME to automobiles, Chubb's had long been to safes. The head of that venerable firm, Laurence Chubb, Jr., later said he did not remember a visit by a handsome young woman in May 1855. But an employee of the company was sufficiently impressed by her beauty to remember that she arrived in a handsome coach, with liveried footmen, swept in imperiously, and demanded to see Mr. Chubb himself.

When Mr. Chubb appeared the woman announced that she was Lady Charlotte Simms; that she and her invalid husband maintained an estate in the Midlands, and that recent thievery in the neighborhood had convinced her that they needed a safe.

"Then you have come to the best shop in Christendom," said Mr. Chubb. "Indeed, our safes excel even the best of the Hamburg German safes. What, specifically, does your Ladyship require?"

Lady Charlotte seemed to falter, gesturing with her hands. "Why, just a, ah, large safe, you know."

"But," said Mr. Chubb severely, "we manufacture steel safes and iron; lock safes and throw-bolt; safes with a capacity of six cubic inches and those of twelve cubic yards; safes mounted with single locks and double locks—even triple locks."

At this recitation Lady Charlotte appeared nearly helpless— quite the ordinary way of a female when asked to deal with technical matters. "I—I don't know. . . . Mr. Chubb, I must beg your assistance, since my husband is ill. In truth, I know nothing of these matters. Can you perhaps show me your safes?"

"Of course, my lady. We maintain no showroom, but if you will follow me into the workrooms—and I apologize for any dust and noise—I can show you the various safes we make."

He led Lady Charlotte into a workroom, where a dozen men were hammering, welding, soldering. The noise was so loud that Mr. Chubb had to shout and Lady Charlotte fairly winced from the din. "Now, this version," he said, "has a one-cubic-foot capacity and is double-layered, sixteenth-inch tempered steel, with an insulating layer of dried brick dust. An excellent safe."

"It is too small."

"Very good, my lady, too small. Now this one"—he moved down

the line and then turned to the workman. "What is the capacity?"

"This 'un here's two and a half," the workman said.

"Two and a half cubic feet," Mr. Chubb said.

"Still too small."

"Very good, my lady. If you will come this way." Lady Charlotte coughed delicately in a cloud of brick dust. Then she pointed across the room. "There! That's the size I want."

They crossed the room. "These safes," said Mr. Chubb, "represent our finest workmanship. They are owned by the Huddleston & Bradford Bank. They are generally sold to institutions, not to private individuals."

"But this is the safe I want," she said, and then looked at them suspiciously. "They don't appear very new."

"Oh, no, my lady, they are nearly two years old now."

This seemed to alarm Lady Charlotte. "Two years old! Why are they back? Have they some defect?"

"No, indeed. A Chubb safe has no defects. They have merely been returned for replacement of the undercarriage mounting pins. You see, they travel on the railway, and the vibration from the roadbed works on the bolts which anchor the safes to the luggage-van floor." He shrugged. "But these details need not concern you. There is nothing wrong with the safes; we are merely replacing the anchor bolts."

"I see they have double locks."

"The banking firm requested double-lock mechanisms."

Lady Charlotte peered at the locks. "They are burglarproof?"

"Oh, absolutely. There is no breaking them."

Lady Charlotte looked thoughtfully at the safes for some moments, and finally nodded. "Very well," she said, "I shall take one. Please have it loaded into my carriage outside."

"My lady," Mr. Chubb said patiently, "we must first construct the safe. Each is built to the customer's specifications."

Lady Charlotte appeared quite irritated. "Well, can I have one tomorrow morning?"

Mr. Chubb gulped. "Tomorrow morning! My lady, we require four weeks to construct a safe."

"Mr. Chubb, I have come here for the purpose of buying a safe today, and now I discover you have none to sell—"

"My lady, please—"

"—but on the contrary will construct one for me only in weeks. By that time the neighborhood brigands will very probably have come and gone. Good day to you, sir, and thank you for your time." With that she swept out.

And Mr. Laurence Chubb, Jr., was heard to mutter, "Women."

Thus Pierce and Agar learned that the overhaul did not include changing the locks on the safes. So they made their final preparations to carry out the robbery on May 22.

Then their plans were thrown into further disarray by the arrival of a letter, written to Pierce in a graceful and educated hand.

> My dear sir:
> I should be greatly obliged if you could contrive to meet with me at the Crystal Palace this afternoon at four, for the purpose of discussing matters of mutual interest.
>
> Most respectfully, I am,
> William Williams, Esq.

Pierce looked at the letter in consternation. Agar could not read, so Pierce read the contents aloud to him.

Agar stared at the penmanship. "Clean Willy's got himself a screever for this one," he said. "You going to meet him?"

"Absolutely. Will you crow for me?"

Agar nodded. "But 'twon't be easy in the palace."

"I'm sure Clean Willy knows that," Pierce said gloomily.

THE Crystal Palace, a magical, three-story glass building covering nineteen acres, was erected in Hyde Park to house the Great Exhibition of 1851. Even in drawings it is stunning to the modern eye, and to see about a million square feet of glass shimmering in the afternoon light must have been a remarkable sight for anyone. After a fire in 1936, the palace was demolished.

The building committee had originally planned a brick monstrosity, four times as long as Westminster Abbey, with a dome even larger than St. Peter's in Rome. The public balked at the destruction of trees in Hyde Park; meantime the building committee discovered that their plans required nineteen million bricks. It was then already too late in 1850 to make all those bricks in time for the exhibition's opening, and at this point the Duke of Devonshire's head gardener, Joseph Paxton, came forward with the idea of erecting a large greenhouse as the Exhibition Hall.

Paxton's plan, drawn up on a piece of blotting paper, saved the trees by enclosing them in the vast conservatory; also, the glass could be manufactured quickly, and the building could be taken down after the exhibition and installed elsewhere. The giant structure was completed in seven months, to almost universal acclaim. Thus the reputation of an empire was saved by a gardener; and thus a gardener was eventually knighted.

There was only one unforeseen problem with Paxton's idea. The building contained trees, and the trees contained sparrows, and the sparrows were not housebroken. The birds couldn't be shot in a glass building, and they ignored traps. Finally, Queen Victoria was consulted, and she said, "Send for the Duke of Wellington."

"Try sparrow hawks, ma'am," the famous soldier suggested, and he was once more victorious.

After the exhibition the Crystal Palace was taken down and rebuilt in Sydenham, a pleasant suburban area. There, shortly before four o'clock, Edward Pierce entered the vast structure to meet Clean Willy Williams.

The giant hall held several permanent exhibits, the most impressive being full-scale reproductions of the huge Egyptian statues of Ramses II at Abu Simbel. But Pierce paid no attention to them or to the lily ponds and pools of water everywhere about. A brass-band concert was in progress, and Pierce saw Clean Willy sitting in one of the rows to the left. He also saw Agar, disguised as a retired army officer, apparently snoozing in another corner. Pierce slipped into the seat alongside Willy.

"What is it?" Pierce said in a low voice.

"I'm needing a turn," Willy said.

"You've been paid."

"I'm needing more," Willy said.

Pierce shot him a glance. Willy was sweating, and he was edgy, but he did not look around him as a nervous man would.

"Willy," Pierce said, "if you've turned nose on me, I'll put you in lavender!" A nose was a police informer.

"I swear it, no," Willy said. "Ten pounds or so is what I need, and that's the end of it."

The band played loudly. Pierce said, "You're sweating, Willy."

"Please, sir, ten pounds and that'll be the end of it."

Pierce drew out two five-pound notes. "Don't blow on me," he said, "or I'll do what must be done."

"Thank you, sir, thank you," Willy said, and quickly pocketed the money. "Thank you, sir."

Pierce left. He came out of the park, entered Harleigh Road and paused to adjust his top hat. The gesture was seen by Barlow, whose cab was drawn up at the end of the street.

Pierce walked on slowly, to all appearances a relaxed gent taking the air. Near St. Martin's Church he hailed a cab and rode it into town to Regent Street, where he got out. He strolled casually, never glancing over his shoulder, but pausing frequently to look in the shopwindows and to watch the reflections in the glass.

He did not like what he saw, but he was wholly unprepared for the familiar voice that cried, "Edward!" Groaning inwardly, Pierce turned to see Elizabeth Trent. She was shopping, accompanied by a livery boy, who carried packages. Elizabeth colored deeply. "I must say, this is an extraordinary surprise."

Pierce bowed and kissed her hand. "I am so pleased to see you."

"I—I—" She snatched her hand away and rubbed it with her other. "Edward," she said, taking a deep breath. "I did not know what had become of you."

"I must apologize," Pierce said smoothly. "I was very suddenly called abroad on business, and I am sure my letter from Paris was inadequate to your injured sensibilities."

"Paris?" she said, frowning.

"Yes. Did you not receive my letter from Paris?"

"Why, no."

"Damn!" Pierce said, and then apologized for his language. "The French are so inefficient. If only I had known—but I never suspected—and when you did not reply, I assumed you were angry. . . ."

"I? Angry? Edward, I assure you—" she began, and then said, "When did you return?"

"Just three days past," Pierce said.

"How strange," Elizabeth said, with a sudden shrewd look. "Mr. Fowler was to dinner a fortnight past, and spoke of seeing you."

"I do not wish to contradict a business associate of your father's, but Henry has the deplorable habit of mixing his dates." Pierce added quickly: "And how is your father?"

"My father is well, thank you. Edward, I—my father, in truth, spoke some rather unflattering words concerning your character. He called you a cad. And worse."

"I wholly understand, given the circumstances, but—"

"But since you are returned to England," Elizabeth said, "I trust we shall be seeing you at the house once more."

Here it was Pierce's turn to be greatly discomfited. "My dear Elizabeth, I do not know how to say this," and he broke off. It seemed that tears were welling up in his eyes. "When I did not hear from you in Paris, I naturally assumed that you were displeased with me and . . . well, as time passed . . ." Pierce suddenly straightened. "I regret to inform you that I am betrothed."

Elizabeth Trent stared. Her mouth fell open.

"Yes," Pierce said. "I have given my word. To a French lady."

"A *French* lady?"

"Yes. I was most desperately unhappy, you see."

"I do see, sir," she snapped, and turned abruptly and walked away. Pierce remained there, trying to appear as abject as possible, until she had climbed into her carriage and driven off. Then he continued down Regent Street, with nothing in his manner to indicate remorse. Again he took a cab, to Windmill Street, where he entered one of the better accommodation houses.

In the plush velvet hallway Miss Miriam said, "He's upstairs. Third door on the right."

Pierce went upstairs and entered a room to find Agar seated, chewing a mint. "What did you see?" Pierce said.

"I cooled two," Agar said. "Both riding your tail. One's a crusher in disguise; the other's dressed as a square-rigged sport. Followed you all the way down Harleigh, and took a cab when you did."

Pierce nodded. "I saw the same two in Regent Street."

"Probably lurking outside now. How's Willy?"

"Willy looks to be turning nose," Pierce said.

"I'd bump him," Agar said.

"I don't know about bumping, but he won't have another chance to blow on us," Pierce said. "I've got to think a bit." He sat back, lit a cigar, and puffed in silence.

The robbery was only five days away, and the police were on to him. If Willy had sung, the police would even know that Pierce's gang had broken into the railway terminal offices.

"I need a new lay," he said, "a proper flash lay for the Peelers to discover." He watched the cigar smoke curl upward, and frowned.

CHAPTER EIGHT

I n LONDON the Metropolitan Police, founded by Sir Robert Peel in 1829, was headquartered in a district known as Scotland Yard, a term then denoting an area of Whitehall containing many government buildings. The police station's address was number 4, Whitehall Place, but it had an entrance in Scotland Yard proper, and the press always referred to the police as Scotland Yard, until the term became synonymous with the force itself.

From the beginning the Yard adopted a posture of modesty in solving crimes; official explanations always mentioned lucky breaks—an anonymous informant, a jealous mistress, a surprise encounter. In fact, the Yard employed informers and plainclothesmen, and this was the subject of heated debate, for many feared that an agent might provoke a crime and then arrest the participants. Entrapment was a hot political issue of the day.

A Mr. Edward Harranby oversaw the ticklish business of working with undercover agents and informers. From his office strange figures could be seen coming and going, often at night. In the late afternoon of May 17, Harranby's assistant, Mr. Jonathan Sharp, said to him, "The snakesman blew, and we have had a look at our man. He appears a gentleman; lives in a fine house in Mayfair. The snakesman doesn't know where, but he's been there."

"Perhaps we can assist his powers of memory. Do we know the intended crime?"

Sharp shook his head. "The snakesman says he doesn't know. He's afraid to blow all he knows. He says this fellow's planning a flash pull."

Harranby turned irritable. "That is of remarkably little value to me. Who is on this gentleman now?"

"Cramer and Benton, sir."

"They're good men. Keep them on his trail, and let's have the nose in my office, and quickly."

"I'll see to it myself, sir," Sharp said.

CLEAN Willy had been drinking. Very nervous, he left the Hound's Tooth pub about six and headed for the Holy Land. He ducked into an alley, jumped a fence, slipped into a basement, crawled through a passage to an adjoining building, climbed the stairs, came out onto a narrow street, and disappeared into another house. Here he ascended to the second floor, climbed onto the roof, jumped to an adjacent roof, scrambled up a drainpipe to the third floor of a lodging house, crawled in through a window, went downstairs to the basement, crawled through a tunnel, and came up into a narrow mews. By a side door he entered another pub, the Golden Arms. He looked around and exited from the front door.

He walked to the end of the street and went into his lodging house. Immediately he knew that something was wrong; normally there were children yelling and scrambling all over the stairs, but now the entrance and stairs were deserted and silent. He was about to turn and flee when a rope snaked out and twisted around his neck, yanking him into a dark corner.

Clean Willy had a look at the white scar as Barlow strained on the garrotting rope. Willy coughed and struggled, but Barlow's strength was such that the little snakesman was literally lifted off the floor, his feet kicking in the air. The struggle continued for almost a minute, and then Clean Willy's body sagged.

Barlow let him drop to the floor. He unwound the rope, removed the two five-pound notes from the snakesman's pocket, and slipped away. Many minutes passed before the children reemerged and approached cautiously. Then they stole Clean Willy's shoes and all his clothing and scampered away.

SITTING in the third-floor room of the accommodation house with Agar, Pierce finished his cigar and sat up in his chair. "We are very lucky," he said finally.

"Lucky? To have jacks on us five days before the pull?"

"Yes, lucky," Pierce said. "If Willy blew, he probably told them we knocked over the London Bridge Station."

"I doubt he'd blow so much, right off." An informant let out information bit by bit, with a police bribe at each step.

"Yes, but we must take the chance that he did. Now, that's why we are lucky, for London Bridge is the only station in the city with more than one line operating from it."

"Aye, that's so," Agar said, with a puzzled look.

"We need something to keep the crushers busy while we're on that train, and it would be pleasant if they were in Greenwich."

"So you need a nose to pass them the word. Then Chokee Bill will do you proper."

"Chokee Bill? The uncle?" An uncle was a pawnbroker.

Agar nodded. "He did a stretch in Newgate. But not for long."

"Oh, yes?" Pierce was suddenly interested. A shortened sentence could imply that the man had agreed to become an informer.

"Got his ticket of leave uncommon early," Agar said. "And the crushers gave him his broker's license quick-like, too. His shop is in Battersea, on Ridgeby Way."

"I'll see him now," Pierce said, getting to his feet.

"Here, now," Agar said. "It just came to me mind: what's there for a flash pull in Greenwich, of all places?"

"That," Pierce said, "is the very question the crushers will be asking themselves."

"But *is* there a pull?"

"Of course," Pierce said. He grinned at Agar's perplexed look and left the room.

When he reached the street it was twilight. He immediately saw the two crushers on opposite corners, made a show of looking nervously about, then walked to the end of the block and hailed a cab. He jumped out of the cab in Regent Street, crossed over, and took a hansom going in the opposite direction. To all appearances he was operating with the utmost cunning. In fact, Pierce would never bother with a simple crossover fakement; it rarely worked. When he glanced out the cab's back window he saw his pursuers.

He rode to the Regency Arms, a notorious pub, entered it, exited from a side door in plain view of the street, and crossed over to New Oxford Street, where he caught another cab. In the process he had lost one of the crushers, but the other was still with him. Now he proceeded directly across the Thames to Battersea.

AT THAT time it was not uncommon for a pawnbroker to serve the middle as well as the lower classes as a sort of impromptu bank, operating more cheaply than established banking concerns. A person could buy an expensive coat, hock it to pay the rent, reclaim it to wear on Sunday, hock it again on Monday, and so on. The number of licensed pawnshops doubled during the mid-Victorian period. The middle class was drawn to the broker more for the anonymity of the loan than the cheapness of it; people often equated economic prosperity with moral behavior. Actually, the pawnshops themselves were not very shady, although they had that reputation. Criminals usually turned to unlicensed fences, who were not regulated by the police as pawnbrokers were.

Pierce found Chokee Bill, a red-faced Irishman whose complexion gave the appearance of perpetual near strangulation, sitting in the back of his shop. Bill jumped to his feet quickly, recognizing a gentleman, and said, "Evening, sir."

"Good evening." Pierce looked around. "Are we alone?"

"We are, sir, as my name is Bill, sir." But Chokee Bill got a guarded look in his eyes.

"I am looking to make a certain purchase." Pierce adopted a broad Liverpool accent. "Some items you may have at hand."

"You see my shop, sir. All is before you."

"This is all?" Pierce shrugged. "I must have been told wrongly. Good evening to you." And he headed for the door.

Chokee Bill coughed. "What is it you were told, sir?"

Pierce looked back at him. "I need certain rare items."

"Rare items? What manner of rare items, sir?"

"Objects of metal," Pierce said, turning back. He made a deprecating gesture. "It is a question of defense. I have valuables."

"I may have such a thing as you require," Bill said.

"Actually," Pierce said, looking around as if to reassure himself that he was truly alone with Bill, "I need five."

"*Five barkers?*" Chokee Bill's eyes widened.

"That's right." Pierce seemed nervous, glancing about.

"Five's a goodly number." Bill frowned.

Pierce immediately edged back toward the door.

"Wait, now," Bill said, "I'm not saying I can't snaffle them. But a man doesn't keep barkers about in an uncle shop, no, sir."

"How quickly can you get them?" Pierce seemed more nervous.

As Pierce became more agitated Chokee Bill became more calm, more appraising. Pierce could almost see his mind working. A request for five pistols implied a major crime, and as a blower he might make a penny or two, if he knew the details.

"It would be some days, sir, and that's the truth." Bill seemed to tick off the days on his fingers. "A fortnight would be safe."

"A fortnight!"

"Eight days, then."

"Impossible. In eight days I must be in Greenw— No."

"Seven?" Bill asked. "Thursday next?"

"At what hour on Thursday next?"

"A question of timing, is it?" Bill asked, with a casualness that was wholly unconvincing.

Pierce just stared at him.

"I don't mean to pry, sir," Bill said quickly.

"Then see you do not. What hour on Thursday?"

"Noon," Bill said.

Pierce shook his head. "Impossible. It must be not a minute later than ten in the morning on Thursday."

Chokee Bill reflected. "Ten o'clock here? Will you be coming yourself to collect them?"

Once again Pierce gave him a stern look. "That hardly need concern you. Can you supply the pieces or not?"

"I can. But there's an added expense for the quick service."

"That will not matter." Pierce gave him ten gold guineas. "You may have this on account."

Chokee Bill turned the coins over in his palm. "I reckon this is the half of it."

"So be it."

"And the rest will be paid in gold?" At Pierce's nod he went on, "Will you be needing shot as well?" Pierce nodded again. "Another three guineas for shot," Chokee Bill said blandly.

"Done." Pierce paused at the door. "A final consideration. If, when I arrive Thursday next, the pieces are not waiting, it shall go hard with you."

"I'm reliable, sir."

"It will go very hard. Think on it." And Pierce left.

In the street, dimly lit by gas lamps, Pierce did not see the lurking crusher, but he knew he was there. He took a cab and drove to Leicester Square, where the theater crowds were gathering. He bought a ticket for *She Stoops to Conquer*, then lost himself in the lobby. He was home an hour later, after three cab changes and four duckings in and out of pubs. He was quite certain he had not been followed.

THE next morning, May 18, was uncommonly warm and sunny, but Mr. Harranby took no pleasure in the weather. Things were going very badly, and he had treated Jonathan Sharp with notable ill temper when he was informed of the death of Clean Willy. When he was later informed that his tails had lost the man they knew only as Mr. Simms in a theater crowd, Mr. Harranby had flown into a rage and complained about the ineptitude of his subordinates, including Mr. Sharp.

Now the Yard's only remaining clue, Chokee Bill, was sitting before Harranby, perspiring profusely, wringing his hands.

"Now, Bill," Harranby said, "five barkers tells me there is something afoot, and I mean to know the truth behind it." He dropped a gold guinea on his desk. "Try to recall," he said.

"It was late in the day, sir, with all respects, and I was not at my best," Bill said, staring pointedly at the gold piece.

"Many a memory improves on the cockchafer," Harranby said.

"I'm honest as the day is long, sir," Bill protested. "And I'd keep nothing from you."

"Then try to remember, and be quick about it."

Bill twisted his hands in his lap. "He comes into the shop near six, he does. Dressed proper, with good manner, but he speaks a wave lag from Liverpool, and he can voker romeny."

Harranby glanced at Sharp, in the corner. "He had a Liverpool sailor's accent and he spoke criminal jargon," Sharp translated.

Bill nodded. "Wants me to snaffle five barkers, and he wants them quick-like, and he's nervous."

"What did you tell him?" Harranby kept his eyes fixed on Bill, who was not above playing each side against the other.

"I says to him, five's a goodly number, but I can do it in a fortnight. He says he needs it quicker than a fortnight. I says eight days. He says that is too long, and he starts to say he's off to Greenwich in eight days, then he catches himself, like."

"Greenwich," Harranby said, frowning.

"Aye, sir, Greenwich was on the tip of his tongue, but he stops down. So I says how long? And he says Thursday, no later than ten o'clock. So I says, after a hem and a haw, I says I can have his pieces then. And he says that's fly enough, but he's no flat, this one, and he says any gammy cokum and it will go hard on me."

Harranby looked at Sharp again. Sharp said, "The gentleman is no fool and warned that if there were delay or false dealings, it would be hard on Bill."

"So he gives me ten gold pushes," Bill went on, "and he takes his leave and says he'll be back. And that's the lot."

"What do you make of this, Bill?" Harranby said.

"It's a flash pull and no mistake. This gent's a bloke who knows his business."

Harranby tugged at an earlobe, a nervous habit. "What in Greenwich has the makings of a proper flash pull?"

"Damn me if I know," Chokee Bill said.

"There's another guinea in it for you if you can say."

A look of agony passed across Chokee Bill's face. "I wish I could help you, but I heard nothing. It's God's own truth, sir."

"I'm sure it is," Harranby said. He finally dismissed the pawnbroker, who snatched up the guinea and departed.

Harranby, alone with Sharp, said again, "What's in Greenwich?"

"Damn me if I know," Sharp said.

"You want a gold guinea, too?"

Sharp said nothing. He was accustomed to Harranby's sour moods. He watched his superior light a cigarette. Sharp regarded cigarettes as silly. They had been introduced the year before by a London shopkeeper, and were favored by troops returning from the Crimea. Sharp liked a good cigar, and nothing less.

"Now, then," Harranby said. "We know this fellow Simms has been working for months on something. The snakesman was killed yesterday. Does that mean they know we're on the stalk?"

"Perhaps."

"*Perhaps* is not enough," Harranby said irritably. "What else do we *know*? We know that this fellow Simms suddenly finds himself, on the eve of his big pull, in desperate need of five barkers, though he has had months to obtain them quietly, one at a time. Now, is it well known that Bill's a nose?"

"There are suspicions about."

"And yet our clever Mr. Simms chooses this very person to arrange for his five barkers." He stared moodily at his cigarette. "Mr. Simms is deliberately leading us astray."

"I am sure you are right," Sharp said, hoping his boss's disposition would improve.

83

There was a long pause. Harranby drummed his fingers on the desk. "We're giving this Simms fellow too much credit. We must assume he is really planning on Greenwich. But what in the name of God is there in Greenwich to steal?"

Sharp shook his head. Greenwich was a small seaport town. It was chiefly known for the Royal Greenwich Observatory, which maintained the standard of time—Greenwich Mean Time—for the nautical world.

Harranby began rummaging in his desk. "Where is the damned schedule? Ah, here it is." He brought out a small folder. "London & Greenwich Railway . . . Thursdays . . . ah. Thursdays there is a train leaving London Bridge for Greenwich at eleven fifteen in the morning. Now, what does that suggest?"

Sharp looked suddenly bright-eyed. "Our man wants his guns by ten so he can make that train."

"Precisely," Harranby said. "All logic points to the fact that he is, indeed, going to Greenwich on Thursday. By a process of deduction we can conclude that his need for the guns is genuine. His plans for obtaining them may have been thwarted. Or perhaps he regards the purchase as so dangerous—everyone knows we pay well for information about anyone buying them—that he postpones it to the last moment. What matters is that he needs those guns for some criminal activity in Greenwich."

"Bravo," Sharp said, with a show of enthusiasm.

Harranby shot him a nasty look. "Don't be a fool; the question is still, *What is there to steal in Greenwich?*"

Sharp stared at his feet. Harranby lit another cigarette. "The principles of deductive logic can still aid us," Harranby said. "The crime must figure around a predictable situation."

Sharp continued to stare at his feet.

"Furthermore, we may deduce that this is a major crime, with high stakes. In addition, we know our man is a seafaring person, so his crime may have something to do with the ocean, or—"

Sharp coughed and said, "I was thinking, sir, that if it is Greenwich, it's out of our jurisdiction. Perhaps we should telegraph the local police."

"If we were to telegraph Greenwich, what would we tell them? Eh?" Harranby stood up. "Of course! The telegraph cable!" Harranby rubbed his hands together. "It fits perfectly!"

Sharp was puzzled. He knew that the proposed transatlantic telegraph cable was being manufactured in Greenwich. There were already cables under the Channel, linking England to the Continent, but these were nothing compared to the twenty-five hundred miles of cable being constructed to join England to New York.

"But surely," he said, "to steal some cable—"

"Not *cable*," Harranby said. "The *payroll* for the firm. It's an enormous project. And if our man is in a hurry to leave on Thursday, he wishes to be there on Friday—"

"Payday!" Sharp cried.

"Exactly. It's the logical conclusion."

"Congratulations," Sharp said cautiously.

"A trifle." But Harranby was still excited. "Oh, he is a bold one! To steal the cable payroll—what an audacious crime! And we shall have him red-handed. Come along, Mr. Sharp. We must journey to Greenwich and apprise ourselves of the situation."

"Four of them boarded the train to Greenwich," Miss Miriam said. "The leader was a squarish man with whiskers."

"Harranby," Pierce said. "He must be very proud of himself. He's such a *clever* man." He turned to Agar. "And you?"

"Fat Eye Lewis, the swindler, was in the Regency Arms asking about a lay in Greenwich—wants to join in."

"So the word is out!" Pierce said. "Feed it."

"Who shall I say is in?"

"Spring Heel Jack, for one. Jack's under, so you can mention him. And make Fat Eye pay. This is valuable information."

Agar grinned. "It'll come to him dear, I promise you."

Agar departed, and Pierce was alone with Miriam.

She smiled. "Congratulations. Nothing can go wrong now."

"Something can always go wrong," Pierce said.

"In four days?" she asked.

"Even in the space of an hour."

CHAPTER NINE

O N THE evening of May 21, just hours before the robbery, Pierce was dining with Miriam in his house in Mayfair when their meal was interrupted by the sudden arrival of Agar, who stormed into the dining room, making no apologies for his abrupt entrance.

"Burgess," Agar said breathlessly. "He's downstairs."

Pierce frowned. "You brought him *here?*"

"I had to," Agar said. "Wait until you hear."

Pierce went down to the smoking room. Burgess was standing there, twitching his guard's cap in his hands.

"What's the trouble?" Pierce said.

"It's the line," Burgess said. "They changed it all today."

Pierce frowned impatiently. "Tell me *what* is changed."

Burgess squeezed his cap in his hands until his knuckles were pale. "For one, they have a new jack, started today—a new bloke, young one. He works the platform at the station."

"What of it?" Pierce said.

"Well, it's the new rule. Nobody rides in the baggage car now, save me as guard. There's this new jack to keep the rule proper."

"I see," Pierce said. That was indeed a change.

Burgess went on. "They've gone and fitted an outside lock to the luggage-van door. They lock up in London Bridge, just before the train pulls out, and don't unlock till Folkestone."

"*Damn,*" Pierce said. "Why have they changed the routine?"

"On account of the afternoon train," Burgess explained. "It was robbed. Gentleman lost a valuable parcel. The other guard's been fired, and there's all bloody hell to pay. Dispatcher his very self called me in and warned me proper. And the new jack on the platform is his nephew. He locks up in London Bridge."

"Can we get Agar aboard in a trunk?"

Burgess shook his head. "Not if they do like today. Today this nephew—his name's McPherson—he makes the passengers open every trunk large enough to hold a man."

"Can we slip Agar in while he's not looking?"

"Not looking? He looks here and there and everywhere, like a starved rat after a flake of cheese. And when the baggage's loaded he climbs in, pokes about all the corners for lurkers."

Pierce plucked out his watch: 10:00 p.m. They had ten hours before the Folkestone train left next morning. Pierce could think of a dozen ways to get Agar past the Scotsman, but nothing that could be quickly arranged.

Agar, the picture of gloom, was thinking the same thing. "Shall we put off until next month, then?"

"No," Pierce said. "Now, this new lock on the door. Can it be worked from inside?"

Burgess shook his head. "It's a padlock—hooks through a bolt and iron latch, outside."

Pierce was still pacing. "Could it be unlocked at a stop and then locked again farther down the line?"

"She's a fat lock, big as your fist, and it might be noticed."

Pierce continued to pace, while Agar and Burgess watched him. Finally, Pierce said, "If the van door is locked, is there any apparatus for ventilating the van?"

"Well, there's the slappers in the roof—"

"What is a slapper?" Pierce said.

"A slapper? A slapper's a hinged door up in the roof. Inside, you've a rod to open or shut the slapper."

"And you have two of them in the luggage van?"

"Aye," Burgess said, "but they're not true slappers, with hinging. They're fixed open, so when it rains, there I be, soaked through—"

"So the slappers give access to the luggage van?"

"They do. But if you're thinking of slipping a bloke through, it can't be done. They're only a handbreadth square, and—"

"I'm not," Pierce said. "Now, where are the slappers located?"

"They're near center, and no more than three paces separate."

"All right," Pierce said, "that's what I need to know." He turned to Agar. "Would this padlock on the door be hard to pick?"

"A padlock's no trick," Agar said. "They have fat tumblers on account of their size. A man can tickle one open in a flash."

87

"Could I?" Pierce said.

Agar stared. "You might take a minute or two. But you heard what he said, you don't dare break her at the station stops."

Pierce turned back to Burgess. "How many second-class coaches are there on the morning train?"

"Six. Seven near the weekend. Now, first class—"

"I don't care about first class," Pierce said.

Burgess looked hopelessly confused. Pierce stared at Agar. Agar shook his head. "Holy Mother, you've lost your mind. Do you think you're Mr. Coolidge?" Coolidge was a well-known mountaineer.

"I know who I am," Pierce said tersely. He turned back to Burgess, who was now nearly immobilized, his face blank.

"Is your name Coolidge?" the guard asked. "You said Simms."

"It's Simms," Pierce said. "Our friend is making a joke. I want you to get up tomorrow and go to work as usual. Don't worry."

Burgess glanced at Agar, then back to Pierce. "Will you pull tomorrow, then?"

"Yes," Pierce said. "Now go home and sleep."

When Burgess left, Agar threw up his hands. "Damn me, make an end to it, I say. Next month, I say."

"I've waited a year," Pierce said, "and it can be done tomorrow." He went to a sideboard and poured two brandies.

"You'll not put enough of that in me to cloud my eyes," Agar said. He held up his hand and ticked the points off on his fingers. "I am to ride in the van, you say. But I cannot get past that eager jack of a Scotsman. Well, fair enough; I trust you to get me in. Now." He ticked off another finger. "The Scotsman locks up from the outside. I can't open the door and toss out the pogue. I'm locked in proper, all the way to Folkestone."

"Unless I open the door for you." Pierce gave Agar a brandy.

Agar gulped it. "And *there's* a likely turn. You come back over the tops of all those coaches, tripping light, and swing down over the side of the van like Mr. Coolidge to pick the lock."

Pierce said, "I know A. E. Coolidge. I climbed with him in Switzerland last year. I learned what he knows."

Agar stared at Pierce for any sign of deception. Mountaineering had recently captured popular attention, and the most notable climber was A. E. Coolidge. "No gull?" Agar said. "You did?"

"No gull. I have the ropes and tackle up in the closet."

"I'll have another," Agar said, holding out his empty glass. Pierce filled it and Agar drank it down. "Well, then," he said. "Let's say you *can* pick the lock, hanging on a rope, and lock up again. How do I get past the Scots jack, first?"

"There is a way," Pierce said. "Not pleasant, but a way."

Agar appeared unconvinced. "Say you put me on in a trunk. He'll open it, and there I am. What then?"

"I *intend* for him to open it and see you," Pierce said. "It will go smoothly enough, but you must take a bit of odor—the smell of dead dog or cat," Pierce said. "Dead some days. Now go to your lodgings, and come back with your best dunnage, and quickly."

When Agar had departed, Pierce sent for Barlow. "Hitch the horse to the flat carriage and get ready for a night's work," he said. "We have a few items to obtain."

When Barlow had left, Pierce returned to the dining room, where Miriam was still sitting. "There's trouble?" she said.

"Nothing beyond repair. Do you have a cheap black dress?"

"I think so, yes."

"Good," he said. "You will wear it tomorrow morning."

"Whatever for?" she asked.

"To show your respect for the dead."

WHEN the Scottish guard McPherson arrived at the platform of the London Bridge Station next morning, he was greeted by an unexpected sight. There by the luggage van of the Folkestone train stood a woman in black—a servant, by the look of her, but handsome enough—sobbing piteously. Nearby, on a baggage cart, was a plain wooden casket with several ventholes drilled in the sides. Mounted on the lid was a miniature belfry containing a small bell, with a cord running from the clapper down through a hole into the coffin. The sight was not mysterious to McPherson, or to any Victorian of the day. Nor was he surprised as he approached the coffin to detect the odor emanating from the ventholes.

During the nineteenth century there arose a preoccupation with the idea of premature burial; in the literature of Edgar Allan Poe and others, premature burial is a frequent motif. For the Victorians it was a genuine, palpable fear, shared by people of all social levels. There was evidence that premature burials did occur. In 1853, in Wales, the case of an apparently drowned ten-year-old boy received wide publicity: "While the coffin lay in the open grave . . . a most frightful noise and kicking ensued from within. The sextons ceased their labors, and caused the coffin to be opened, whereupon the lad stepped out. Yet the same lad had been pronounced dead, and the doctor said that he had no respiration nor any detectable pulse, and the skin was cold and gray."

There was reason to be skeptical about the reliability of any indicator of death. So Victorians dealt with their uncertainty by delaying interment—a week was not uncommon. They also contrived devices to enable a dead person to make known his resuscitation. One such alarm system, known as Bateson's belfry, after its inventor, was an iron bell mounted on the lid of the casket and connected by a cord or wire to the dead person's hand, "such that the least tremor shall directly sound the alarum."

On this morning of May 22, McPherson had more important things to worry about than the weeping servant girl and the coffin with its belfry, for he knew that the gold shipment from Huddleston & Bradford would be loaded upon the van at any moment. Through the open door of the van he saw the guard, Burgess, and waved. Burgess responded with a rather reserved greeting.

McPherson's attention was drawn back to the sobbing woman, and he proffered his handkerchief. "There, now, missy," he said. "There, now . . ." The girl was attractive, even in her grief. "There, now," he said again.

"Oh, please, sir," the girl cried, taking his handkerchief. "Can you help me? The guard upon the line is a heartless beast! He will not let me set my dear brother here upon the train, for he says I must await another guard. It's the rules. Oh, I am most wretched," she finished.

"Why, the unfeeling rogue!" McPherson noticed her heaving

bosom and her pretty, narrow waist. "Missy," he said, "I am the other guard, and I'll see your dear brother on the train."

"Oh, sir, I am in your debt!" She smiled through her tears.

McPherson was young, and it was springtime, and the girl was pretty; he also felt the greatest compassion for her. He turned to chastise Burgess for his overzealous adherence to the rules, but at that moment he saw the gray-uniformed Huddleston & Bradford guards bringing the bullion consignment down the platform.

The loading was carried out with sharp precision. First, two guards entered the van and searched the interior. Then eight more guards arrived, in formation around two carts, pushed by sweating porters and piled with sealed strongboxes.

At the van a ramp was swung down, and the porters joined together to push first one, and then the other laden flatcart inside.

Next, a bank official appeared with two keys. Soon after, McPherson's uncle, the dispatcher, arrived with a second pair of keys. The dispatcher and the banker opened the safes, the strongboxes were loaded into them, the doors were shut with a massive clang, and the keys were turned in the locks. The banker departed. McPherson's uncle pocketed his keys and came over to his nephew.

"Mind," he said, "open every parcel large enough to hold a knave." He sniffed the air. "What's that ungodly stink?"

McPherson nodded toward the girl and the coffin. His uncle frowned with no trace of compassion. "Scheduled for the morning train, is it? See that you open it." The dispatcher turned away.

"But, Uncle—" McPherson began.

"No stomach for it?" The dispatcher scanned the youth's agonized face. "All right, then. I'll see to it myself." And he strode off toward the girl, his nephew trailing behind.

It was at that moment that they heard an electrifying, ghastly sound: the ringing of Mr. Bateson's patented bell.

At the sound of the bell, which rang only once, and briefly, the girl let out a shriek, and the dispatcher and his nephew broke into a run to the coffin. The girl was already in a state of hysteria, clawing at the coffin lid. "Oh, Richard, dear Richard—oh, God, he lives. . . ." Her fingers scrabbled at the wooden surface, and the dispatcher and his nephew caught the girl's frantic anxiety. The lid was closed with a series of metal latches, which they opened one after another. They were soon at a fever pitch of intensity, and all the while the girl cried, "Oh, Richard—make haste, he's alive! Please, dear God, he lives!"

The commotion drew a crowd, which stood taking in the bizarre spectacle. "Oh, hurry, hurry!" the girl cried. It was only when the men were at the final latches that she cried, "Oh, I knew it was not cholera, he was a quack to say it!"

The dispatcher's hand froze on the latch. "Cholera?" he said.

"Oh, hurry, hurry," the girl cried. "It is five days now."

"You say cholera?" the dispatcher repeated. "Five days?"

But the nephew flung the coffin lid wide.

"Thank God!" cried the girl, and threw herself down, as if to hug her brother. But she halted in mid-gesture, for the body, dressed in Sunday clothes, hands folded across the chest, was already in a state of obvious decomposition, face and hands gray green. With a scream of heart-wrenching agony, the girl swooned on the spot. The nephew leaped to attend her, and the dispatcher closed the lid and began shutting the latches with even more haste than he had displayed in opening them. The watching crowd, when it heard that the man had died of cholera, dissipated swiftly.

The girl recovered from her swoon but remained in a state of profound distress. She kept asking softly, "How can it be? The bell rang. . . ." while young McPherson did his best to comfort her, saying that some gust of wind must have caused it.

The dispatcher, seeing his nephew occupied, himself supervised the loading of luggage into the van. There was only one further incident, when a portly gentleman placed a parrot on the van and then demanded that his manservant be permitted to ride with the bird and look after it. When the dispatcher explained the new rules the gentleman offered him ten shillings, but the dispatcher was aware that he was being watched by Burgess, whom he had admonished the day before. He was forced to turn down the bribe, to his own displeasure and also that of the gentleman, who stomped off muttering profanely. Feeling vaguely dissatisfied, the dispatcher

93

barked a final order to his nephew to lock up the van, and returned to his office.

The dispatcher later testified that he had no recollection of any red-bearded gentleman in the station that day. But Pierce had, in fact, been among the crowd that witnessed the dreadful episode of the opened coffin. When the crowd dissipated he moved forward to the van, with Barlow at his side carrying some luggage on a porter's trolley. Pierce had a moment of disquiet when he saw the dispatcher himself supervising the loading, for this luggage was unusual, to say the least: five identical satchels. The leather was coarse, the stitching crude and obvious; and none was large, so Pierce could have stowed them in his carriage compartment—the luggage van meant delays at both ends. Finally, Pierce's man-servant loaded each bag onto the luggage van separately, clearly straining under the weight. But the elder McPherson, somewhat pale, did not emerge from his distracted state until another gentle-man arrived with a parrot, and an argument ensued.

Pierce drifted away, but remained farther down the platform, apparently curious about the woman who had fainted. When she made her way toward the coaches he fell into step beside her.

"Are you fully recovered, miss?" he asked.

"I trust so," she said.

They merged with the boarding crowd, and Pierce said, "Per-haps you will join me in my compartment for the journey?"

"You are kind," the girl said, with a slight nod.

"Get rid of him," Pierce whispered to her. "I don't care how, just do it."

Miriam looked puzzled. Then a hearty voice boomed out, "Ed-ward, my dear fellow!" A man was pushing toward them.

Pierce waved a delighted greeting. "Henry," he called. "Henry Fowler, what an extraordinary surprise."

Fowler came over and shook Pierce's hand. "Fancy meeting you here," he said. Then he noticed the girl at Pierce's side and dis-played some discomfiture. Here was Pierce, dressed handsomely as usual, standing with a girl who was pretty enough, but by her dress and manner a very common sort.

Pierce was a bachelor and a blood, and might travel openly with a mistress for a holiday by the sea. But such a girl would be dressed with gentility. Contrariwise, if this was a servant in Pierce's household, he would hardly have her about in a public place, unless there was some reason Fowler could not imagine. Too, the girl had been weeping; her eyes were red. It was perplexing—

"Forgive me," Pierce said to the girl. "I should introduce you, but I do not know your name. This is Mr. Henry Fowler."

The girl, giving him a demure smile, said, "I am Brigid Lawson. How'd you do, sir."

Fowler nodded a vaguely polite greeting, as Pierce made the situation clear. "Miss, ah, Lawson, has just had a most trying encounter. She is traveling with her deceased brother, now in the van. A few moments past, the coffin bell rang. The casket was opened, but it was a false alarm."

"And thus doubly painful," Fowler said.

"So I offered to accompany her on the journey," Pierce said.

"And indeed I should do the same," Fowler said, "were I in your place. Would it seem an imposition if I joined you?"

Pierce did not hesitate. "By all means," he said.

"You are ever so kind, you two are," the girl said, with a brave but grateful smile.

"It's settled, then," Fowler said, also smiling. Pierce saw him looking at the girl with interest. "My compartment is just a short way forward." He pointed to the first-class coaches.

Pierce intended to sit in the last compartment of the final first-class coach. From there he would have the shortest distance to the luggage van at the rear. "Actually," he said, "my compartment is down there." He pointed to the back of the train.

"My dear Edward," Fowler said, "the choice compartments are all toward the front, where the noise is minified. You'll find a forward compartment more to your liking, particularly if Miss Lawson feels poorly."

Pierce said, "In truth, I selected my compartment on the advice of my physician, after experiencing some distress on railway journeys. This he attributed to the vibrations originating in the engine.

He warned me to sit as far back from the source as possible."
Pierce gave a short laugh. "He said, in fact, that I should sit second
class, but I cannot bring myself to it."

"There is a limit to healthy living," Fowler said. "My own physician advised me to quit wine—can you imagine the temerity? Very
well, we shall all ride in your compartment."

Pierce said, "Perhaps Miss Lawson feels, as you do, that a forward carriage would be preferable."

Before the girl could speak, Fowler said, "What? And steal her
away from you? Come, where is your compartment?"

They walked along the train to Pierce's compartment, Fowler in
unshakable good spirits. Inside the compartment Pierce glanced at
his watch: six minutes to eight. Time was short, and he had to get
rid of Fowler or he could not climb out onto the roof. But Fowler's
suspicions must not be aroused, for in the aftermath of the robbery
the banker would probably be questioned by the authorities, and
would be searching his memory.

Fowler's focus was directed toward the girl, who gave every
appearance of rapt attention. "It's extraordinary luck, running
across Mr. Pierce," he said. "Do you travel this route often, Edward? I myself do once a month. And you, Miss Lawson?"

"I never gone first class before," the girl said. "Only my mistress,
this time she buys me a first ticket, seeing as how . . ."

"Oh, quite," Fowler said, in a hearty, chin-up manner. "One
must do all one can for anyone in a time of stress. I am under no
little stress myself this morning. Now, Mr. Pierce may have guessed
the reason for it. Eh, Edward?"

Pierce had not been listening. He was considering how to get rid
of Fowler. "Do you think your bags are safe?" he said.

"My bags? I have no bags, Edward. I shall remain in Folkestone
only two hours, hardly time to take a meal and smoke a cigar
before I am back on the train, homeward bound."

Smoke a cigar, Pierce thought. He reached into his pocket and
withdrew a long cigar, which he lit. The girl stared, her mouth
slightly open.

Fowler said to the girl, "The truth is that this is no ordinary train. I am the general manager of Huddleston & Bradford, and today, aboard this train, my firm has stored a quantity of gold bullion for shipment overseas to our brave troops. A quantity in excess of twelve thousand pounds, my dear child!"

"Cor!" the girl exclaimed. "And you're in charge of all that?"

"I am indeed." Henry Fowler was looking self-satisfied, and with reason. He had obviously overwhelmed the simple girl. She now regarded him with dizzy admiration, and appeared to have forgotten Pierce. That is, until Pierce's cigar smoke billowed around her. Then she coughed suggestively. Pierce, staring out the window, did not seem to notice, so the girl coughed again, more insistently. Fowler said, "Are you feeling well?"

"I'm faint. . . ." The girl made a gesture toward the smoke.

"Edward," Fowler said. "I believe your tobacco causes Miss Lawson some distress, Edward."

Pierce looked at him and said, "What?"

The girl said, "I feel *quite* faint, I fear. Please?" She extended a hand toward the door, as if to open it.

Fowler opened the door and helped the girl, leaning heavily upon his arm, into the fresh air.

"I had no idea," Pierce protested. "Had I but known—"

"You might have inquired before lighting your diabolical contraption," Fowler said. The girl was leaning against him, weak-kneed, her bosom pressed to his chest.

"I'm most dreadfully sorry," Pierce said. He started to get out himself, to lend assistance.

The last thing Fowler wanted was assistance. "You shouldn't smoke anyway, if your doctor has warned you that even trains are hazardous to your health," he snapped. "Come, my dear," he said to the girl. "We can continue our conversation in my compartment with no danger of noxious fumes." The girl went willingly, and neither of them looked back.

A moment later the whistle blew, and the engine began to chug. Pierce stepped back into his compartment, shut the door, and watched London Bridge Station slide away past his window, and the train to Folkestone began to gather speed.

CHAPTER TEN

BURGESS, locked in the luggage van, could tell its location by the sound of the track. First the smooth clacking of the wheels on the well-laid rails of the yard; then the hollow tones as the train crossed Bermondsey on the long overpass; then a deader sound, signaling the rough southward run into the countryside.

Burgess had no inkling of Pierce's plan. He was astonished when the coffin bell began to ring, and attributed it to the vibration of the train, but a few moments later there was a pounding and then a muffled voice. He approached the coffin.

"Open up, damn you," the voice said. "It's Agar!"

Burgess hastily opened the coffin, and Agar—covered with green paste, smelling horrible—got out of the coffin. "Quick! Get me those satchels." He pointed to the five valises stacked in a corner.

Burgess hurried to do so. "But the van is locked," he said. "How will it be opened?"

"Our friend," Agar said, "is a mountaineer."

Agar opened the safes and removed the first strongbox, breaking the seal and taking out the dull gold bars—each stamped with a royal crown and the letters H & B. He replaced them with the bags of shot from the valises, while Burgess watched. The train was rumbling almost due south to Redhill.

"A mountaineer?" Burgess said finally.

"Yes," Agar said. "He's coming over the top of the train to unlock us after Redhill. He'll return to his coach before Ashford. It's all open country there. Almost no chance of being seen."

"But that is the fastest part of the run. Your friend is mad!"

AT ONE point in Pierce's trial the prosecutor lapsed into a moment of frank admiration. "Then it is not true," said the prosecutor, "that you had any knowledge of mountaineering?"

"None," Pierce said. "I merely said that to reassure Agar."

"Had you, perhaps, some past athletic experiences?"

"None," Pierce said.

"Well, then," said the prosecutor, "what on earth led you to believe you might succeed in such a nearly suicidal undertaking?"

Pierce smiled. "I knew there would be no difficulty," he said, "despite the appearance of danger, for I had read about railway sway, and the explanation, offered by scientists, that its forces are caused by swiftly moving air, and I felt sure that these forces would hold my person to the surface of the coach."

Actually, Pierce's confidence was completely unfounded. As railway trains began to attain speeds of fifty, even seventy, miles an hour, a bizarre phenomenon was noted: when a fast-moving train passed one standing in a station, the trains had a tendency to be drawn together in railway sway. In some cases this was so pronounced that passengers were alarmed, and there was sometimes minor damage to coaches. No one had the slightest idea why railway sway occurred; the confusion was precisely that of airplane engineers a century later, when the "buffeting" phenomenon of aircraft approaching the speed of sound was first observed.

However, by 1851 most engineers had decided correctly that railway sway was an example of Bernoulli's Law, which states, in effect, that the pressure within a moving stream of air is less than the pressure of the air surrounding it. This meant that two moving trains, if they were close enough, would be sucked together by the partial vacuum between them. So parallel tracks were set farther apart, and railway sway disappeared.

Apparently, Pierce believed that the airstream around the moving carriage would suck him down to the roof and help him to maintain his footing. But he would simply be exposed to a fifty-mile-an-hour blast of air that could blow him off the train.

Nor had Pierce, along with his contemporaries, much sense of the consequences of being thrown from a fast-moving vehicle, though he had seen Spring Heel Jack lying dead. Indeed, during the early 1830s, when most trains averaged twenty-five miles an hour, there had been a daredevil's sport called carriage-hopping—leaping from a moving railway carriage to the ground. Most hoppers suffered only a few bruises or a broken bone, and the fad bolstered the public belief that a fall from a train was much like a fall from a horse. By mid-century the speed of trains had doubled, and the consequences of a fall were quite different.

The prosecutor asked, "Did you take any manner of precaution against the danger of a fall?"

"I wore two pairs of heavy cotton undergarments," Pierce said.

Thus, wholly unprepared, Edward Pierce slung a coil of rope over his shoulder, opened the compartment door, and clambered up onto the roof of the moving carriage.

THE wind struck him like an enormous fist, screaming about his ears, stinging his eyes, filling his mouth and tugging at his cheeks, burning his skin. His frock coat flapped about him, whipping his legs. For a few moments he crouched, clutching the wooden surface of the rocking coach, disoriented by the unexpected fury of the shrieking air. The streaking particles of soot blown back from the engine rapidly covered him with a fine black film.

He very nearly abandoned his plan in those first moments, but after the initial shock had passed he determined to go on. Crawling on hands and knees, he moved to the end of the coach, and paused at the gap that separated his carriage from the next. Moments passed before he gathered the nerve to jump some five feet to the next car, but he did so successfully.

He crawled painfully along the length of that car. His coat was blown forward, covering his face and shoulders. After some moments of struggle he shucked it off and saw it sail away, twisting in the air. It looked like a human form, a kind of warning of the fate that might await him.

Freed of the coat, he made more rapid progress down the second-class coaches, jumping from one to the next with increasing assurance. He reached the luggage van after what seemed an eternity. Later, he concluded it had not been more than ten minutes.

Atop the van he gripped an open slapper and uncoiled his length of hemp. One end dropped down the slapper, and after a moment he felt a tug as Agar, inside the van, picked it up. Pierce turned to the second slapper. He waited there, his body curled tight against the wind, until a ghastly green hand—Agar's—reached out, holding the end of the rope. Pierce took it.

He now had a rope slung from one slapper to the next. He tied the loose ends about his belt, and then, hanging on the rope, eased himself over the side of the van until he was level with the padlock. There he hung suspended while he twirled the padlock with a ring of skeleton keys. He had tried more than a dozen when he heard the scream of the whistle.

An instant later he was plunged into blackness and churning sound. The tunnel was half a mile long; there was nothing to do but wait. When the train burst into sunlight again, he continued working the keys. Almost immediately one of them clicked in the mechanism. The padlock snapped open. It was a simple matter to remove the lock, swing the crossbar free, and kick the door with his feet until Burgess slid it open. The train passed a sleepy town, but no one noticed the man dangling on the rope, who now swung into the luggage van and collapsed on the floor.

Agar testified that at first neither he nor Burgess recognized Pierce with his clothing shredded, and black from head to toe. But Pierce recovered quickly, and they all worked with efficiency. The safes were locked up, with their new treasure of lead shot, and the five satchels with the bullion stood by the door in a row.

Pierce took out his watch; it was 8:37. "Five minutes," he said.

Agar nodded. In five minutes they would pass a deserted stretch of track, where Pierce had arranged for Barlow to pick up the satchels. Pierce sat down and stared through the open door at the countryside rushing past.

"Are you well, then?" Agar asked Pierce.

"Well enough. But I don't cherish going back."

"Aye, it frazzled you proper," Agar said. "And you're a sight, no mistake. Will you change in the compartment?"

"Change?" said Pierce, still breathing heavily.

"Aye, your dunnage." Agar grinned. "You step off at Folkestone as you stand now and you'll cause no end of stir."

Here was a problem Pierce had never considered. He couldn't step out at Folkestone looking like a chimney sweep, especially as

Fowler was almost certain to seek him out. "I brought no other clothing," he said. "I never expected . . ." He frowned.

Agar laughed heartily. "Then you'll play the proper ragamuffin, as you've made me play the stiff."

"It's nothing funny," Pierce snapped. "I have acquaintances on the train who will surely see me and mark the change."

Agar's merriment was quashed instantly. He scratched his head with a green hand. "They'll miss you if you're not there at the station?" Pierce nodded. "It's the devil's own trap, then," Agar said, and looked around the van at the luggage. "Give me that ring of tickles, and I'll find some square-rigged duns to fit you."

He held out his hand to Pierce for the skeleton keys, but Pierce was again looking at his watch. It was only two minutes to the drop-off point. Thirteen minutes after that the train would stop in Ashford; and Pierce had to be back in his own compartment. "There's no time," he said.

"It's the only chance—" Agar began, but broke off. Pierce was looking him up and down in a thoughtful way. "No," Agar said. "Damn you, no!"

"We're about the same size," Pierce said. "Now be quick."

The screwsman undressed, muttering oaths. Pierce, watching the countryside, bent to position the satchels at the open door. He saw a tree by the roadside, one of the landmarks he'd set. Soon there would be the fence. . . . There it was . . . and the abandoned, rusty cart. He saw the cart. . . . A moment later he saw the crest of a hill and Barlow beside a coach.

"Now!" he said, and with a grunt shoved out the satchels. He watched them bounce on the ground. He saw Barlow hastening down the hill. Then the train went around a curve.

He looked back at Agar, who had stripped to his underclothes and held his fine duds out. "Here you are, and damn your eyes."

Pierce took the clothes, rolled them into a tight ball, wrapped the parcel with Agar's belt, and without another word swung out the open door on the rope. Burgess closed the door, and a moment later Agar and he heard a clink as the bolt was thrown, and another as the padlock was locked. They heard the scratching of

Pierce's feet as he scrambled up to the roof; and then they saw the rope, which had been taut across the roof from slapper to slapper, suddenly go slack as it was pulled out. They heard Pierce's footsteps on the roof a moment longer, and then nothing.

"Damn me, I'm cold," Agar said. "You'd best lock me back up," and he crawled into his coffin.

PIERCE had not progressed far before he realized he had made another error in his planning: he had assumed it would take the same amount of time to return to his compartment as to go from his compartment to the van. But the return trip, against the wind, was much slower, and the parcel of clothing left him only one hand free to grip the roofing as he crawled forward along the train with agonizing slowness. He realized that he would still be crawling along the rooftops when the train reached Ashford. He would be spotted, and the jig would be up.

Pierce had a moment of profound rage that this final step in the plan should go irretrievably wrong; the fact that the error was his own doing merely increased his fury. He gripped the swaying carriage roof and swore into the wind, but the blast of air was so loud he could not hear his own voice.

He knew what he must do. He continued forward as best he could. He was midway along the fourth of the six second-class carriages when he felt the train slowing. The whistle screamed. Squinting, he saw Ashford Station, a tiny red rectangle in the distance. In less than a minute the train would be near enough for people on the platform to see him. For a brief moment he wondered what they would think, and then he sprinted forward, leaping from car to car without hesitation, half blinded by the smoke that poured back from the engine.

Somehow he made it to the first-class coach, swung down, opened the door, dropped into his compartment, and pulled the blinds. The train was now chugging very slowly, and as Pierce collapsed into his seat he heard the hiss of the brakes and the porter's cry: "Ashford Station . . . Ashford . . ."

Pierce sighed. They had done it.

TWENTY-SEVEN MINUTES LATER the train arrived at Folkestone and all the passengers disembarked. Although Pierce had hastily employed his handkerchief, the soot was recalcitrant. He could only guess at the condition of his face, but his hands were pale gray. Furthermore, his trousers were too short, and the cut of the coat, although elegant enough, was of the showy fashion that true gentlemen avoided as *nouveau riche*. And he reeked of dead cat.

Thus Pierce stepped out onto the crowded Folkestone platform with an inner dread. He knew that Henry Fowler would spot the peculiarity of his appearance and would almost certainly realize that he had changed clothing for some reason during the ride. So his only hope lay in making off, with a distant wave of good-by to Fowler and an air of pressing business. From a distance Pierce's bizarre dress might escape Fowler's eye.

But Fowler came charging through the crowd. The woman was beside him, and he did not look happy. "Now, Edward," Fowler began crisply, "if you would—" His mouth fell open.

Dear God, Pierce thought. It's finished.

"*Edward,*" Fowler said. "My dear fellow, you look *terrible.*"

"I know," Pierce began, "you see—"

"Why, you are gray as a corpse. When you told me you suffered from trains, I hardly imagined . . . Are you all right?"

"I believe so," Pierce said, with a heartfelt sigh. "I expect I shall be much improved after I dine."

"Dine? Yes, of course, and take a draft of brandy, too. I should join you myself, but they are now unloading the gold which is my responsibility. Edward, can you excuse me?"

"Perhaps I can help him," the girl said.

"Capital idea," Fowler said. "She's a charmer, Edward. I leave her to you." Fowler gave him a queer look at this last comment, then hurried toward the luggage van, turning back once to call, "Remember, a good draft of brandy's the thing."

Pierce gave an enormous sigh and turned to the girl. "How could he miss my clothes?"

"You should see your countenance," she said. "And I see you've a dead man's dunnage."

"Mine were torn by the wind."

"Then you have done the pull?"

Pierce only grinned.

PIERCE left the station, but Brigid Lawson remained to supervise the loading of her brother's coffin onto a cab. Much to the irritation of the porters, she turned down several waiting cabs at the station, claiming she had made arrangements in advance. The cab did not arrive until after one o'clock. The driver, who had a scar across his forehead, helped with the loading, then whipped up the horses and galloped away. No one noticed when, at the end of the street, the cab halted to pick up an ashen gentleman in ill-fitting clothes. Then it rattled off.

By noon the strongboxes of the Huddleston & Bradford Bank had been transferred, under armed guard, from the Folkestone railway station to the Channel steamer, which made the crossing to Ostend in four hours. At 5:00 p.m. Continental time French customs officials took possession of the boxes. They were then transported to the Ostend railway terminal for shipment to Paris.

The following morning French representatives of the bank of Bonnard et Fils arrived at the Ostend terminal to open the strongboxes and verify their contents, prior to placing them aboard the Paris train. Thus at about 8:15 a.m. it was discovered that the strongboxes contained a large quantity of lead shot and no gold.

This astounding news was immediately telegraphed to London. The message reached Huddleston & Bradford's Westminster offices shortly after 10:00 a.m. and provoked profound consternation.

The initial reaction was sheer disbelief. The French cable had been composed in English and read: GOLD MISSED NOW WHERE IS. It was signed VERNIER, OSTEND. Sir Edgar Huddleston announced that there had been, no doubt, some silly delay with the French customs authorities; the whole business would be unraveled before teatime. Mr. Bradford assumed that the stupid French had misplaced the bullion and were now trying to blame the English. Mr. Henry Fowler, who had seen the shipment safely onto the Channel steamship, speculated that the cable might be a practical joke.

Cables flashed back and forth across the Channel. As the day wore on, their tone became more acrimonious. By teatime there was a growing suspicion at Huddleston & Bradford that something had actually happened to the gold. The French were as worried as the English—Louis Bonnard himself had gone to Ostend to investigate the situation.

By 7:00 p.m. Sir Edgar was snappish, Mr. Bradford had the smell of gin on his breath, Mr. Fowler was pale as a ghost, and Mr. Trent's hands trembled. There was a brief moment of elation around 7:30, when the customs papers from Ostend arrived at the bank. They indicated that Raymond Vernier of Bonnard et Fils had signed for nineteen sealed strongboxes containing twelve thousand pounds sterling in bullion.

"Here is their bloody death warrant!" Huddleston said, waving the paper in the air. But this was not the legal situation, and he knew it.

And then Huddleston received a long cable from Ostend claiming that the lead shot seemed of British manufacture and that the seals had been broken and resealed in England. It ended:

NOTIFYING POLICE OFFICIALS ALSO GOVERNMENT IN PARIS REMINDING ALL OF BRITISH ORIGIN BRITISH RAILWAY BRITISH STEAMERSHIP BRITISH SUBJECTS GUARDING THROUGHOUT STOP REQUEST YOU INFORM BRITISH AUTHORITIES

LOUIS BONNARD

Sir Edgar's first reaction to the cable was reported to be "a forceful expletive." He was also said to have commented extensively on the culture and personal habits of the French. It was nearly 10:00 p.m. when he was calm enough to say to Mr. Bradford, "I shall notify the Minister. You notify Scotland Yard."

Private detectives were hired by the banks, the railroads, and the shipping line. The most widespread belief, on both sides of the Channel, was that it was an inside job. Though everyone who had the slightest relationship to the Crimean gold shipment was interrogated by the authorities, no significant progress was made until

June 17, nearly a month after the robbery. Then, at the insistence of the French, all the safes in Ostend, aboard the steamship, and on the South Eastern Railway were returned to their respective manufacturers for examination. The Chubb safes were discovered to contain telltale scratches inside the locks, as well as traces of metal filings, grease, and wax. The other safes showed no such signs.

This discovery focused new attention on Burgess, who had been previously questioned and released. On June 19, Scotland Yard announced a warrant for his arrest, but the same day the man, his wife, and his two children vanished. It was then recalled that South Eastern had suffered a robbery from its luggage van, only a week prior to the bullion theft. This fed the suspicion that the robbery must have occurred on the London–Folkestone train, and the press began to refer to The Great Train Robbery.

All during July and August, 1855, the crime remained a sensation. But no new developments occurred, and by October The Great Train Robbery was no longer of interest to anyone.

CHAPTER ELEVEN

NOVEMBER 5 had been celebrated in England as Powder Plot or Guy Fawkes Day since 1605. In 1856 a grand display of fireworks took place on the grounds of the Merchant Seamen's Orphan Asylum to raise funds for the institution. The large crowd included, of course, pickpockets and cutpurses, and dollymops, or part-time prostitutes, who were often servants or seamstresses. The police that night were busy indeed. One Constable Johnson, a man of twenty-three, was walking the grounds when, by the flaring light of the fireworks, he observed a female crouched over the prostrate form of a man. Constable Johnson went to offer help, but at his approach the girl took to her heels. He apprehended her a short distance away when she tripped on her skirts.

Observing her to be "a female of lewd aspect," he at once surmised that she was robbing the gentleman in his intoxicated stupor, and that she was therefore a very low criminal, a bug-hunter. Johnson arrested her, whereupon the minx put her hands on her hips and declared, "There's not a pogue upon me."

Constable Johnson faced a dilemma. Proper male conduct, and police regulations, demanded that even women of the lowest sort be treated with consideration for the delicacy of their feminine nature. This created obvious difficulties in handling female law-breakers. Indeed, criminals often employed a female accomplice precisely because the police were so reluctant to arrest.

Constable Johnson was fully aware of his situation. The woman claimed to have no stolen goods on her person; and without a pocket watch or some other indisputably masculine article, she would go free. Nor could he search her. His only recourse was to escort her to the police station, where a matron could be called. Furthermore, if it was then discovered the girl was clean, Johnson would look a fool and receive a stiff rebuke. But he had recently been advised by his superiors that his arrest record left something to be desired and had been told to be more vigilant. So in the sputtering glow of the fireworks he decided to take this bug-hunter in for a search—to the girl's astonishment, and despite his own considerable reluctance.

At the station the woman gave her name as Alice Nelson and her age as "eighteen or thereabouts." Dalby, the station sergeant, sleepily filled in the forms. He sent Johnson off to collect the matron and ordered the girl to sit in a corner.

Dalby had a flask in his pocket, and at late hours he often took a daffy or two when there was no one about. But now this little bit of no-good business kept him from his nip. He frowned into space, feeling frustrated.

After a time the judy spoke up. "If you think I've a pogue beneath me duds, see for yourself." She began languorously to scratch her limbs through the skirt.

"And earn the pox for my troubles," Dalby said wearily.

The judy sat up straight. "Let's us strike a bargain, then."

"Dearie, there's no bargain to be made." Dalby saw this tedious routine played out every night he worked at the station. Some little bit of goods would be tugged in on an officer's arm, all protestations of innocence. Then she'd make an advance of favors, and if that was not taken up, she'd talk a bribe.

"Let me go, and you'll have a gold guinea."

Dalby shook his head.

"Well, then," the girl said, "you shall have ten." Her voice now had a frightened edge.

"Ten guineas?" They must be counterfeit, Dalby thought.

"Ten is what I promise you, right enough."

Dalby hesitated. In his own eyes he was a man of principle, but his weekly wage was only fifteen shillings. . . .

"Well, then," the girl said, "it shall be a hundred!"

Dalby laughed. A hundred guineas! Absurd.

She chewed her lip. Finally she said, "I know a thing or two."

Dalby stared at the ceiling. Always after the bribe failed, there came the offer of information about some crime or other. Out of boredom he said, "And what is this thing or two?"

"I know who did the train-robbery lay."

"Holy Mother," Dalby said, "but you're a clever judy. That's the very thing we hear from every muck-snipe and bug-hunter who comes our way." He gave her a pitying smile.

"I know the screwsman did the pull, and I can put you to him. I swear." The girl was looking desperate. "I *swear*."

Dalby hesitated. "Well, then, where's he to be found?"

"Newgate Prison," the girl said.

"Newgate Prison?" Dalby said. "What's his name, then?"

The girl only grinned.

Here was a story so strange it likely had some truth to it. Dalby called for a runner to notify Mr. Harranby at the Yard.

By dawn the basic situation was clear to the authorities. The judy, Alice Nelson, was the mistress of one Robert Agar, recently arrested on a charge of forging five-pound notes. Agar had protested his innocence; he was now in Newgate Prison awaiting trial. Deprived of his income, the woman had turned to crime to support herself, and she was nabbed. She then turned nose on her lover and told all that she knew. It was little enough—but enough for Mr. Harranby to send for Agar to come to Scotland Yard.

"A THOROUGH COMPREHENSION OF the criminal mind," wrote Edward Harranby in his memoirs, "is vital to police interrogation." Harranby certainly had that comprehension, but he had to admit that the man seated before him presented a particularly difficult case. They were in their second hour of questioning, but Robert Agar stuck to his story. Harranby favored the introduction of abrupt new lines of inquiry to keep villains off-balance, but Agar seemed to handle this technique easily.

"Mr. Agar," Harranby said. "Who is John Simms?"

"Never heard of 'im."

"Who is Edward Pierce?"

"Never heard of 'im. I told you that." He coughed.

Harranby sighed. Agar's posture, his flicking downcast eyes, his gestures—everything suggested deceit. "Now, Mr. Agar. How long have you been forging?"

"I didn't," Agar said. "I swear it wasn't me."

Harranby paused. "You're lying," he said. "Make no mistake about it, we'll see you in the stir for many years."

"I swear," Agar said, getting excited. "There's no sense to it—" Abruptly, he broke off.

There was a brief silence, punctuated only by the ticking of a clock on the wall. Harranby had purchased the clock especially for its loud tick, which was irritating to prisoners.

"Why is there no sense to it?" he asked softly.

"I'm honest is why," Agar said, staring at the floor.

"What honest work do you do?"

"Local work. Here and there."

"Where have you worked?"

"Well, let's see, now," Agar said, squinting. "I did a day for the gasworks at Millbank, loading. I did two days at Chenworth, hauling bricks. I go where I can, you know."

"These employers would remember you?"

Agar smiled. "Maybe."

Here was a dead end. Employers often did not recall their casual workers. Harranby found himself staring at Agar's hands, clenched in his lap. One little finger's nail was long. It had been bitten at, to conceal this fact. A long fingernail might mean all sorts of things, for sailors or certain clerks. But for Agar . . .

"How long have you been a screwsman?" Harranby said.

"Eh?" Agar replied innocently. "Screwsman?"

"Come, now. Did you make the keys for the safes?"

"Keys? What keys?"

Harranby sighed. "You've no future as an actor, Agar. The keys to the train robbery."

Agar laughed. "You think if I was in on that flash pull I'd be in for forging? That's glocky."

Harranby's face was expressionless, but he knew that Agar was right. It made no sense for a man who had participated in a twelve-thousand-pound theft to be counterfeiting a year later.

"Simms has abandoned you. Why are you protecting him?"

"Never heard of 'im," Agar said.

"Lead us to him, and you'll have a fine reward."

"Never heard of 'im. Can't you see that plain?"

Harranby stared at Agar. The man was quite calm, except for his coughing attacks. He glanced at Sharp, in the corner. It was time for a different approach.

Harranby picked up a paper and put on his spectacles. "Now, then, Mr. Agar. This is a report on your past record."

"Past record?" His puzzlement was genuine. "I've no record."

"Indeed you do," Harranby said, running his finger along the print on the paper. "Robert Agar . . . twenty-six years old . . . born in Bethnal Green . . . hmm . . . Yes, here we are. Bridewell Prison, six months, charge of vagrancy, in 1849, and Coldbath, one year, charge of robbery, in 1852."

"That's not true!" Agar exploded. "I swear it, not true!"

Harranby glared at the prisoner over his glasses. "It's all here. I think the judge will be interested." He turned to his assistant. "What do you suppose he will get, Mr. Sharp?"

"Fourteen years transportation, at least," Sharp said.

"Umm. Fourteen years in Australia—that sounds about right."

"Australia," Agar said, in a hushed voice.

"Yes," Harranby said calmly. He knew that although transportation was popularly portrayed as a much-feared punishment, the criminals themselves sometimes viewed banishment to Australia with pleasant expectation. It was unquestionably preferable to a long stretch in an English prison. Indeed, at this time Sydney, in New South Wales, was a thriving seaport of thirty thousand. It was a place where "personal history is at a discount, and good memories are particularly disliked." And if it had its brutal side, it was also pleasant, with gaslit streets and elegant mansions. But Agar was greatly agitated. Plainly he did not want to leave England.

"That will be all for now," Harranby said. "If you have something you wish to tell me, just inform the guards."

After Agar was ushered out of the room Sharp came over. "What were you reading?" he asked.

Harranby picked up the sheet of paper from his desk. "A notification from the buildings committee," he said, "to the effect that carriages are no longer to be parked in the courtyard."

AFTER three days Agar informed the Newgate guards that he would like another audience with Mr. Harranby. On November 13, Agar told Harranby everything he knew about the robbery, in exchange for the promise of lenient treatment and the vague possibility that the bank, the railway, or even the government itself might present him with a reward for information.

Agar did not know where the money was kept; Pierce had been paying him a monthly stipend in paper currency. They had agreed to divide the profits two years after the crime, in May 1857. Agar did, however, know the location of Pierce's house. On the night of November 13 forces from the Yard surrounded the mansion and entered with guns at the ready. But the owner was not at home; the frightened servants explained that he had left town to attend a boxing spectacle in Manchester.

BOXING matches were illegal in England, but they were held throughout the nineteenth century, and drew an enormous following. To elude authorities a big match might be shifted from town to town at the last minute. The match on November 19 between

Smashing Tim Revels, "the Fighting Quaker," and the challenger, Neddy Singleton, had been moved from Liverpool to a small town called Warrington, outside Manchester. The fight was attended by more than twenty thousand supporters.

Under the PR, or prize ring, rules of the times, combatants fought barefisted. Fights had no prearranged length. They often went fifty or even eighty rounds. The object was for each man methodically to injure his opponent with a succession of small cuts and welts. Knockouts were not sought; the proper fighter literally battered his opponent into submission.

Neddy Singleton was hopelessly outclassed by Smashing Tim. He started dropping to one knee whenever he was struck, in order to halt the fight and catch his breath. The spectators hissed and booed, but the referee called out the count of ten with a slowness that demonstrated he'd been paid off by Neddy's backers.

With thousands of spectators about, including every manner of ruffian, the men from the Yard were at some pains to operate unobtrusively. Agar, with a revolver at his spine, pointed out Pierce and Burgess from afar; a gun was pressed to each man's side, with a whispered suggestion that he come along quietly.

Pierce greeted Agar amiably. "Turned nose, did you?"

"I had no choice," Agar blurted out.

"You'll lose your share," Pierce said calmly.

At the periphery of the crowd Pierce was brought before Mr. Harranby. "Are you Edward Pierce, also known as John Simms?"

"I am," the man replied.

"You are under arrest on a charge of robbery."

"You'll never hold me," Pierce replied.

By nightfall on November 19, Pierce and Burgess had joined Agar in Newgate Prison. Harranby made no announcement to the press, for he wanted to apprehend Miriam and Barlow and to recover the money. On November 22 he interrogated Pierce.

At 9:00 a.m. Pierce was ushered into the office and asked to sit in a chair, isolated in the middle of the room. Harranby directed his first question with customary abruptness.

"Where is the man called Barlow?"

"I don't know."

"Where is the woman called Miriam?"

"I don't know."

"Where," said Mr. Harranby, "is the money?"

"I don't know."

There was silence. "Perhaps," Harranby said, "a time in the Steel will strengthen your powers of memory." The Steel, or the Bastille, was the House of Correction at Coldbath Fields. Police frequently sent a man there if information had to be "winkled out" of him. It was the most dreaded of all English prisons. It featured the cockchafers, in stuffy narrow stalls, where prisoners remained for fifteen minutes treading down a wheel which sank away under their feet. Even less pleasant was shot drill, so rigorous that men over forty-five were usually exempted. In this the prisoners formed a circle three paces apart. At a signal each man picked up a twenty-four-pound cannonball, carried it to his neighbor's place, dropped it, and returned to his original position, where another shot awaited him. The drill went on for an hour at a time. Most feared of all was the crank, a sand-filled drum turned with a crank handle—a special punishment for unruly prisoners.

After six months in Coldbath Fields many a man emerged with his body damaged, nerves shot, and resolution enfeebled. As a prisoner awaiting trial Pierce could not be made to undergo the treadmill, the shot drill, or the crank; but if he broke the rule of silence, for example, he might be punished by a time at the crank. One may presume that the guards frequently accused him of speaking, and he was thus treated to "softening up."

On December 19, after four weeks in the Steel, Pierce was again brought to Harranby's office, but the second interrogation was as brief as the first.

"Where is the man Barlow?"

"I don't know."

"Where is the woman Miriam?"

"I don't know."

"Where is the money?"

"I don't know."

Mr. Harranby, the veins standing out on his forehead, dismissed Pierce in a voice filled with rage. As Pierce was taken away he calmly wished Mr. Harranby a pleasant Christmas.

MR. HARRANBY was under considerable pressure. Huddleston & Bradford wanted its money back and made this known to Harranby through the Prime Minister, Lord Palmerston himself. The inquiry was embarrassing, for Harranby had to admit that he had put Pierce in Coldbath Fields. The Prime Minister expressed the opinion that this was "a bit irregular." But Pierce remained in Coldbath, and on February 6 he was again brought before Harranby.

"Where is the man Barlow?"

"I don't know."

"Where is the woman Miriam?"

"I don't know."

"Where is the money?"

"In a crypt in St. John's Wood," Pierce said.

Harranby sat forward. "What was that?"

"It is stored," Pierce said blandly, "in a crypt in the name of John Simms, in the cemetery of Martin Lane, St. John's Wood."

Harranby drummed his fingers on the desk. "Why have you not come forth with this information earlier?"

"I did not want to," Pierce said.

ON FEBRUARY 7 the appropriate dispensations were obtained to open the crypt. Mr. Harranby, accompanied by Henry Fowler from the bank, opened the vault at noon that day. There was no coffin in the crypt—and neither was there any gold. It appeared that the lock on the crypt door had been recently forced.

Mr. Fowler was extremely angry at the discovery, and Mr. Harranby extremely embarrassed. The following day Pierce was returned to Harranby's office and told the news.

"Why," Pierce said, "the villain must have robbed me. Barlow! I always knew he was not to be trusted."

"So you believe it was Barlow who took the money?"

"Who else could it be?" Pierce did not seem greatly distressed.

There was silence. Harranby listened to the ticking of his clock with irritation; his subject appeared at ease.

"Do you not care," Harranby said, "that a confederate turned on you in this fashion?"

"It's just my ill luck," Pierce said calmly. "And yours," he added.

"By his collected manner," Harranby wrote later, "I presumed that he had fabricated still another tale to put us off the mark. But in further attempts to learn the truth I was frustrated. On the first of March, 1857, a *Times* reporter learned of Pierce's capture, and he could no longer conveniently be held in custody."

According to Jonathan Sharp, his chief read the London *Times* report on Pierce's capture "with heated imprecations," and demanded to know how the papers had been put on to the story. The *Times* refused to divulge its source. A guard at Coldbath was discharged under suspicion, but it was also rumored that the lead had come from the Prime Minister's office.

CHAPTER TWELVE

THE trial of Burgess, Agar, and Pierce began on July 12, 1857. It was a sensation. The prosecuting officials took care to heighten the drama of the proceedings. Burgess, the most minor of the players, was brought to the docket of the Old Bailey first, and the fact that he knew only parts of the story whetted the public appetite for further details.

Agar was interrogated next; but his testimony served only to focus attention on Pierce himself, whom the press referred to as "the brilliant malignant force behind the deed." Eager reporters conjured up wild and untrue accounts of the man: that he lived with three mistresses in the same house, that he was the illegitimate son of Napoleon; that he had been married to a German countess and had murdered her. Pierce's house in Mayfair was broken into repeatedly by avid souvenir hunters, and a "wellborn woman" was apprehended while leaving it with a man's handkerchief. With no embarrassment she said that she wished to have a token of the man. The *Times* complained that this fascination with a criminal was "unseemly, even decadent," and reflected "some fatal flaw in the character of the English mind."

Pierce was brought before the bar of the Old Bailey for the first time on July 29: "handsome, charming, composed, elegant and roguish." He gave his testimony in an even, calm tone of voice, but his statements were inflammatory. He referred to Mr. Trent as "an elderly nincompoop" and to Mr. Harranby as "a puffed-up dandy with the brains of a schoolboy." Mr. Harranby, in the gallery as an observer, was seen to color deeply, while the veins stood out on his forehead. Pierce's words not only gave no hint of remorse for his deeds but seemed to demonstrate an enthusiasm for his own cleverness as he recounted the various steps in the plan.

The witnesses were themselves most reluctant to testify. Mr. Trent was fumbling, nervous, and greatly embarrassed ("with ample reason," snapped one observer) at what he had to report, while Fowler recounted his experiences in so low a voice that the prosecutor continually asked him to speak up.

There were a few shocks in Pierce's testimony. One was the following exchange:

"Are you acquainted with the cabby known as Barlow?"

"I am."

"Can you tell us his whereabouts?"

"I cannot."

"Can you tell us when you last saw him?"

"Yes, six days ago, when he visited me at Coldbath Fields."

There was a buzz and the judge rapped for order.

"Mr. Pierce, why have you not brought forth this information earlier?"

"I was not asked."

"What was the substance of your conversation with Barlow?"

"We discussed my escape."

"You intend with the aid of this man to make your escape?"

"I should prefer that it be a surprise," Pierce said calmly.

The consternation of the court was great, and the outraged newspapers demanded that Pierce receive the most severe possible sentence. But Pierce's calm manner never changed. On August 1 he called Henry Fowler in passing "as big a fool as Mr. Brudenell."

Quickly the prosecutor said, "Do you mean Lord Cardigan?"

"You may refer to him however you wish, but he is no more than Mr. Brudenell, as he was born, to me."

"You defame the inspector general of the cavalry."

"One cannot," Pierce said, "defame a fool. I myself have killed no one, but had I killed five hundred Englishmen in the Crimea through my stupidity, I should be hanged immediately."

Pierce concluded his testimony on August 2, at which time the prosecutor turned to a final line of inquiry.

"Mr. Pierce," he said, rising to his full height, "did you never feel, at any time, some comprehension of unlawful behavings, some moral misgivings, in the performance of these criminal acts?"

"I do not comprehend the question," Pierce said.

The prosecutor was reported to have laughed softly. "Yes, I suspect you do not; it is written all over you."

At this point his Lordship cleared his throat and delivered the following speech from the bench: "Sir, it is a recognized truth that it is only by the rule of law that any civilization holds itself above barbarism. This we know from all the history of the human race, and this we pass on in our educational processes to all our citizens. Now, on the matter of motivation, I ask you: why did you conceive, plan, and execute this dastardly and shocking crime?"

Pierce shrugged. "I wanted the money," he said.

After Pierce's testimony he was handcuffed and escorted from the courtroom by two guards. He passed Mr. Harranby.

"Good day, Mr. Pierce," Mr. Harranby said.

"Good-by," Pierce replied.

Pierce was taken out of the back of the Old Bailey to the police van waiting to drive him back to Coldbath Fields. A sizable crowd had gathered on the steps and shouted expressions of luck to Pierce. One scabrous old whore, slipping forward, managed to kiss the culprit full on the mouth before the police pushed her aside.

It is presumed that she was actually the actress Miss Miriam, and that in kissing Pierce she passed him the key to the handcuffs.

When the two van guards, coshed into insensibility, were later discovered in a gutter near Bow Street, they could not reconstruct the precise details of Pierce's escape. The only thing they agreed upon was the sudden appearance of a tough brute of a man, with an ugly white scar across his forehead, who took over the van. It was later recovered in a field in Hampstead. Neither Pierce nor Barlow was ever apprehended.

In August 1857, Burgess, the railway guard, pleaded that the stresses of his son's illness had so warped his moral inclinations that he fell in with criminals. He was sentenced to only two years in Marshalsea Prison, where he died of cholera that winter.

The screwsman Robert Agar was sentenced to transportation to Australia. Agar died a wealthy man in Sydney in 1902. His grandson, Henry L. Agar, was lord mayor of Sydney from 1938 to 1941.

Mr. Harranby died in 1879. He had been flogging a horse, which kicked him in the skull. His assistant, Sharp, became head of the Yard and died a great-grandfather in 1919. He was reported to have said he was proud that none of his children were policemen.

Mr. Trent died of a chest ailment in 1857. His daughter Elizabeth married Sir Percival Harlow in 1858, and had four children by him. Mrs. Trent behaved scandalously following her husband's demise; she died of pneumonia in 1884, having enjoyed, she said, "more lovers than Sarah Bernhardt."

Henry Fowler died of "unknown causes" in 1858.

Pierce, Barlow, and the mysterious Miss Miriam were never heard from again. In 1862 they were reported to be living in Paris. In 1868 they were said to be residing in "splendid circumstances" in New York. Neither report has ever been confirmed.

The money from The Great Train Robbery was never recovered.

Very few writers have achieved as much—or as quickly—as Michael Crichton. He sold his first article to *The New York Times* when he was fourteen years old. Later, after graduating from Harvard University with high honors, he helped pay his way through medical school by writing thrillers under a nom de plume. When he graduated he chose writing instead of medicine for his life's work. His seventh novel, *The Andromeda Strain*, published in 1969 under his own name, became a best seller. In 1972 he was introduced to readers of Condensed Books as the author of *The Terminal Man*.

*Michael
Crichton*

Long fascinated by the cinematic possibilities offered by his books, Dr. Crichton moved to Hollywood to try his hand at directing films and writing screenplays. But his tolerance for making movies, he learned, was limited. "There's nothing that makes you want to get back to the typewriter more than being involved in a movie," he says. "In a book, nobody has to approve it, no conferences, no interference; it's all yours."

He had read about the train robbery of 1855 and been fascinated with the crime and with the era, because, as he puts it, "the Victorians were both very progressive and very repressed—and that leads to interesting crimes. . . . Going to England for research would have been too easy." Instead he went to the Los Angeles public library, where he pored over maps, rummaged through books on Victorian cities, on the language of the underworld and the like. "And when I couldn't find a fact, I had the option of making it up," he points out. "That's the nice thing about fiction."

Now that he has written *The Great Train Robbery*, of course he is anxious to see it made into a film. "There's nothing like writing," he says, "to make you want to get back of the camera again."

What Peter and Rennie learned that summer
would stay with them all their lives

I Take Thee, Serenity

A CONDENSATION OF THE NOVEL BY
DAISY NEWMAN

ILLUSTRATED BY TOM HALL

There were two named Serenity: the tranquil, joyful Quaker, whose kindness and trust warmed the memories of all who had known her; and Rennie, her modern great-granddaughter, who believed that her life was her own to live as she chose— as long as no one got hurt. She and Peter were happy in their special private world.

Then everything changed. The freedom that Rennie had claimed brought sorrow to those she cared for. And most of all to herself.

Bewildered, she sought the answer— at Firbank, the first Serenity's home, and in the old meetinghouse, where nobody preached and silence spoke louder than words. It was here, with her elderly cousin Oliver and his radiant, crippled wife, that Rennie discovered it is truly most blessed to give—an insight that was at last to grant her the right to her name, Serenity.

CHAPTER ONE

THEY were already late, but he stopped at the newsstand in the air terminal to buy two Chocomarshes, dropping one into her book bag. That was nice of him, except that all Rennie really wanted to take with her was Peter himself. She kept begging him to come, telling him again how she hated going to a strange place to see a strange old man.

"Please, Peter, won't you?"

Instead of answering, he gravely unwrapped the second candy bar. Then, grinning wickedly, he stuffed the candy in Rennie's mouth. That shut her up. She didn't dare laugh; she'd choke.

"Come on." Peter grabbed her hand. "Run!"

Rennie gasped. The Chocomarsh didn't go down till they reached the security check.

"This wasn't my idea," Peter murmured.

Rennie was hunting in her purse for the ticket. "What wasn't? Me going to see Oliver?"

"No. Getting married."

That made Rennie mad. "As a matter of fact," she retorted, "it wasn't my idea, either."

But Peter was cocking his bright yellow head to one side, grinning again, and Rennie saw he was only teasing. She should have known. He kissed her, licking the chocolate off her lips. When he handed over the book bag, the mischief had left his eyes. They were full of anxiety. "I hope this guy'll be nice to you."

The possibility that Oliver might not be nice alarmed Rennie. Nervously crumpling the ticket, she would have begged Peter again, only it was too late. A loudspeaker urged the passengers for Providence and Boston to board their plane. In that last minute Peter's eyes told Rennie how he loved her. He had such a nice face—more finished, she always thought, than most of the men's at college.

She wanted to tell him something, too. No, not tell; give—a keepsake, something for him to hold while she was gone. But she had nothing and there wasn't time to explain. She had to go.

"See you Sunday night," he called after her. "Come up to my room, soon as you get back."

A couple of women took the book bag and Rennie's purse. They went through everything, even peeking into her sneakers. Before they'd admit that she wasn't concealing any weapons, a guard made her walk through the metal detector.

I'm not a hijacker, she wanted to assure him. I'm only going to Rhode Island to ask my first cousin once removed— But Rennie was already out from under, retrieving her belongings, looking back at Peter.

"It's your wedding, too," she reminded him across the security table.

"I know," he called back. "Just get the address of the church. I'll be there."

The passengers around them burst out laughing. *Very* funny!

Rennie made a rush for the door, tagging after a stream of people into the blinding sun. It was hot for the beginning of May. The last thing she saw before her feet left earth was Peter waving from a window in the terminal.

Strapped in her seat beside the window, Rennie smoothed the pleats she'd worked so hard to press into her skirt. Peter hadn't noticed what she was wearing—at least he hadn't said anything about it. He never did. So Rennie still wondered whether he liked how she looked on those rare occasions when she dressed up.

Even more, she wondered whether he liked her face. Not many redheads have really blue eyes and clear skin. Once a guy in her art history class told her that the short hair, curling softly around her head, was cadmium red with a touch of burnt sienna, like autumn leaves. But Peter didn't talk like that. Was it her looks he went for? Her personality? Or was it simply that she had fallen into his arms?

The plane taxied down the runway, then rose sharply. Rennie's stomach preferred to stay on earth. Thankful that no one was sitting beside her, in case she got sick, she leaned back, feeling more and more uncertain. Then she thought, Maybe this is why Mother hates to fly.

Her mother wouldn't fly unless it was unavoidable. Rennie wasn't supposed to fly, either. The plane might crash, be hijacked. If her mother knew where she was right now, airborne, feeling queasy . . . But she didn't know.

Rennie's stomach was calming down. Opening her eyes, she turned to the window. Tiny houses were faintly visible below. Clouds floated over the wing, piled on one another like those dollops of whipped cream Rennie's mother used to shake off the beater before her father went on his diet and they stopped having desserts.

Now, cushioned on a cloud, Rennie sailed gently into the unknown. On the ground it had been threatening, but across the sky the unknown beckoned to her with a promise of something she must have felt homesick for all along, though she hadn't been aware of it—a reality she'd never experienced. Could one be homesick for something one never knew?

No walls. For the first time since Rennie came into the world, she was seeing it without walls. Neither in the foreground nor in the farthest distance did anything block her vision. Her eyes could travel across the horizon, taking in a universe more vast, more splendid than anything she'd ever encountered, even with Peter.

He was thousands of feet below and miles behind. I'm sorry, she told him, hoping he'd somehow hear. I'm sorry I was mad. I know teasing's just your way of saying you love me.

Rennie still wished that she'd had something to give him, a keepsake to hold while she was gone. What? Sadly she saw that it wasn't a *thing*, just serenity. That's what Peter wanted most from her. But, as her father'd said, she didn't have it. No one in her family did.

I'm sorry, she kept repeating. I should have been glad you were lighthearted for once—your old happy-go-lucky self.

Since this marriage business came up, he's been so serious. Before that, for almost three months, the two of them lived in a carefree world. It had always made Rennie think of primitive paintings of the Garden of Eden, where food hangs from trees for the picking, one doesn't need clothes and never has to work. Rennie hadn't dreamed such a world existed in real life till she happened on it in Peter's room.

Well, it wasn't quite like those primitives. For meals they had to go to the cafeteria. There they picked food from counters instead of trees. They had to work—study and attend classes. The rest of the time, though, they were blissful in their secret world, which was really a drab dormitory room. Their love made it sunny, safe, a place of completeness. The outside world never touched their secret one. They had the best of both.

Suddenly everything became complicated. The outside world butted in, demanding decisions, commitment, celebration. It threatened to saddle them with household linens, place settings.

"Rite of passage," Priscilla called a wedding, now that she was majoring in anthropology. "One of those vestigial tribal customs."

Rennie's parents had always maintained that a girl ought not marry till she finished college. Yet it was her parents' idea that she and Peter get married at the end of her junior year. They had sprung it on her in January, when she was home for intersession.

The day before she was going back to college, just casually at breakfast, Rennie'd mentioned that she and Peter were thinking of spending the summer camping in the Rockies.

"Who with?" her mother asked in a deceptively placid tone. Her right hand was working nervously, the thumb rubbing the tips of the fingers, back and forth, back and forth.

Hadn't Rennie just said? "Peter—Peter Holland."

"Just you and Peter?" her father expostulated. "That won't do. Unless you're going with a group—no."

"But I thought you liked Peter."

Neither parent responded. And Rennie dropped the subject.

Then, after supper that night, in the den, her father switched off the news abruptly and turned to Rennie. "Why don't you marry him?" he asked, almost fiercely.

Rennie jumped. "Peter?" No one had spoken about him since breakfast.

"You love him, don't you?"

"Oh, I do!"

"And you're certain he loves you?"

"Y-yes."

"Mother and I've been thinking about you a great deal lately and we've come to the conclusion that it would be best for you to get married in June. Then you two can go camping or anything else you decide to do together."

"Married?" Rennie repeated, appalled. "Me? Don't you think I'm too young?"

"Much too young! At nineteen few people know their own minds. But if you're going to run around with this man, it would be preferable. I'll support you, single or married, as long as you're getting your education."

Rennie's parents had been very nice to Peter when she brought him home. Yet, now, even while they were suggesting that she marry him, they disclosed a certain reserve, a coldness. Could it be that they suspected? Was that why they wanted her to get married, before something happened? But nowadays, who need worry? Marriage, she said to herself. Is *that* what we want? Why can't we go on as we are?

Rennie's father came across the room and tipped her chin up so that she had to look straight into his eyes. "You're still our little girl," he said. "Mother and I love you very much. We think marriage will give you the security you need. It troubles us that we don't seem able to give you that security ourselves."

"We just want you to be happy," Rennie's mother said, sounding anything but happy herself.

"But I am!" Didn't she and Peter have the best of both worlds?

WHEN Rennie got back to college, she rushed to Peter's room and described the whole scene. "For a second," she confided, recalling her father's face as he lifted her chin and looked into her eyes, "I thought I would break down and tell them everything."

Rennie was glad she hadn't. Her parents wouldn't understand. They were so naïve. They trusted Rennie completely and they were right. She wouldn't do anything she felt was wrong. It was simply that none of her friends, with one or two exceptions, believed that what she was doing was wrong. How could it be, as long as nobody got hurt?

"Would you want to get married?" she asked Peter. She was really asking herself. "So many couples break up after a while. If we broke up, there'd be no fuss. Just good-by, nice knowing you. But if we got married— Would you want to?"

Peter didn't answer and Rennie fought the fear that gripped her throat. Then he said something that stunned her. "I guess if I were your father, I'd feel the same way. We couldn't go on like this forever, Rennie. One of us would be bound to get hurt, sooner or later. I just never dreamed your parents would let you marry for ages."

"Would you want to?" she repeated.

"I don't know. But let's quit what we're doing."

"*Quit?* Why?" After playing it so cool with her parents, Rennie surprised herself by starting to cry.

Peter wiped the tears away, spreading them over her cheeks with the palm of his hand. "I need time, Rennie," he said softly, "to think things over."

"Daddy'll support me as long as I'm getting my education," she assured him, "even if I'm married."

"If you're married to me, *I'll* support you. But money isn't all we have to worry about. Marriage—it's a big step."

How big she only just realized, seeing the look on Peter's face.

He was frowning, the way he did on study dates when he was trying to do a math problem. "Give me a week," he said finally. "I'll tell you definitely next Thursday."

"Thursday!" How could she wait till Thursday?

He had to be by himself, he explained, go off on long walks. Rennie couldn't figure out why he didn't want her along, but she stayed away, returning to the company of the girls in her dorm.

The week was endless. Rennie's term papers on child development and classroom management were due, but she couldn't concentrate, what with the best of both worlds about to collapse. She could see now that her parents were right. She did need the security of belonging to Peter, and he wasn't willing to straddle both worlds any longer. But suppose he decided they'd had it? If she nearly died without him in just one week, how was she going to get through the rest of her life? It wasn't only that she missed him. Her being depended on his loving her.

Wednesday afternoon, when Rennie came back to the dorm from her French class, she found a florist's box lying on the mail desk. SERENITY MILLBURN ROSS, the label read. Nobody at Tilbury except Peter knew her middle name. Why would *he* be so official? With frozen fingers she picked at the knot on the box. Dewy red roses! He'd never sent Rennie flowers before. Was this his way of saying it was all over?

He didn't even wait till Thursday, she wailed to herself, opening the little envelope. Inside was a card: "I'm willing, if you are. Peter."

He was going to marry her! He really was.

Rennie's eyes filled up. It wasn't a romantic proposal, but she knew how much the words conveyed. Happily swinging the long, narrow box, Rennie rushed upstairs to put the roses in water. Then she flew to Peter's room in the men's dorm.

He looked years older. Only a week—how could he have changed so in a week?

"The reason I want to marry you," he whispered, holding her close, "is that I want to spend my whole life telling you how I love you—not just how much, but *how*. I know it'll be hard making you believe I mean it for keeps. That's because I started wrong. But I mean it." He leaned back so that he could look into Rennie's eyes. "I wish we could be married some morning at dawn in blue jeans on a hilltop, just you and me, no minister." He squeezed the breath out of Rennie. Then he let her go.

Just the two of them, no minister. Was that possible? Suddenly she remembered something. "Quakers don't have ministers, at least I don't think so."

"Oh?"

"My great-grandmother Serenity, the one I'm named for, was a Quaker. I don't know much about it, only that we have this old-fashioned picture on the third-floor landing at home. It's called *A Quaker Marriage*. The girl is wearing a beautiful, plain dress and a bonnet. The man has on knee breeches and a courtly sort of coat. They're standing, holding hands—and there isn't any minister, just people sitting around the couple on benches. I always loved that picture. When I was small," Rennie confided, hoping Peter wouldn't laugh, "I used to stop and talk to the girl every time I went to the third floor."

Peter didn't laugh at Rennie's childhood fantasy, but he failed to see that the picture still meant something to her. "Probably an illustration for one of those Victorian romances," he murmured.

"Oh, no," Rennie cried. She'd always believed in the reality of that picture. To have Peter reduce it to just a story . . . "It can't be," she said firmly. "I'll ask Daddy."

She hadn't called her parents yet with the wonderful news. That pay phone in the basement— She fished in the pockets of her jeans, hoping to find a couple of nickels for calling collect. There was nothing in them but lint.

"Peter, have you got a dime? I want to call home."

He paid no attention to her. Looking up, Rennie saw that he was throwing clothes into a suitcase. "What are you doing?" she cried.

"Going home. Phoning's no way to break news like this to one's family." There was a night bus he could catch if he left right now, he told her. That way he'd miss only one day of classes. Then he was gone.

Left alone, Rennie wondered if she ought to go home, too. But her parents were expecting the news, and it would take forever to get to Neville. She had to tell them right away. This was going to make them so happy! She put in the call and counted the rings. One, two, three, four. At last her father answered. Then he called to her mother to listen in on the kitchen extension.

"Daddy, guess what! Are you on the phone, Mother? I've got the most wonderful news. We're getting married, Peter and I!"

Instead of the joyful exclamations Rennie expected, there was a freezing pause. Her father, who was always the leader, said nothing. Her mother managed, after a bit, to murmur, "That's nice."

"*Nice?* It's terrific. It's what you wanted, isn't it?"

"Yes," Rennie's father finally answered. "It's just—well, you're our baby, you know, and it's hard having you leave us already. We hope the advice we gave you will turn out to be right."

"Oh, it is! How could it be anything but?"

There was another pause.

"You haven't changed your minds, have you?"

"No," Rennie's father declared without conviction.

Hadn't they meant it the other day? Were they simply playing with the idea of her marrying because they suspected that she and Peter were living together? Had they hoped, by bringing up the subject, that she'd see how they felt about what she was doing, and quit? Probably they had never believed Peter would marry her. Now they were drawing back.

I should have gone home, Rennie reproached herself. Peter's right. Phoning's no way.

But her father was fast rising to the occasion. "Well," he said, sounding as if he were determined to put a good face on the matter, "we'll make it a bang-up wedding. Our only daughter—"

"Yes," her mother broke in. "We'll make it the most beautiful wedding that ever was, a wedding to remember."

AFTER that conversation Rennie felt depressed. She'd done just what her parents wanted her to do, and they weren't pleased.

All through her childhood they'd been so proud of her. She'd

133

been the most satisfactory little girl any parents ever had. It was when she suddenly refused to put on those smocked dresses her mother was always making—other girls were wearing jeans—that this tug of wills developed. Now Rennie either pleased her parents or herself. Impossible to do both. Well, she told herself, when Peter returned, everything would be all right.

But the moment Rennie spied him on the breakfast line in the cafeteria, sleepy from spending two nights on buses, she knew everything was all wrong. To his surprise his parents had put up tremendous resistance. It wasn't, he explained, that they had anything against Rennie. Just that they couldn't see how he was going to support the two of them so soon. And didn't he want to go to graduate school?

"We should have thought about all this before the whole thing started," he told Rennie sadly.

The following week Peter flunked his math exam.

Rennie couldn't keep her mind on her work, either. Sitting in her room, trying to absorb *Teaching Creative Writing in the Primary Grades*, she stared mournfully at Peter's roses. Most of the petals had fallen. Those that still clung were droopy. But Rennie couldn't bring herself to throw them out.

In the end Peter's parents backed down. It would have been better, Mr. Holland wrote, if Peter were established. Nevertheless they didn't wish to stand in their son's way. Peter and Rennie's love for each other should be the determining factor.

That was in February.

The middle of March, Peter went home with Rennie and spoke to her father, who suddenly began calling him Pete. This annoyed Rennie. She supposed the nickname was her father's way of saying that Peter was going to be let into the family, although her parents still seemed cold toward him.

Two weeks later they put on a tea to announce the engagement. A photographer came to the house, and the next day Rennie's picture was in the paper, looking, she couldn't help feeling, surprised by the whole thing. Rennie's three brothers came, too—with all their wives and children—and each of them took her aside during the afternoon to tell her he thought Peter was a very nice guy.

Peter himself, all gussied up in his suit, with his hair cut, surrounded by a flock of new relations and everyone in Neville who was anyone, looked just plain mad. "What does all this have to do with us?" he asked Rennie. "So we're in love. Why does that mean people have to pile into your house and yak, yak, yak?"

By Easter vacation Rennie's mother was snipping pictures of wedding gowns out of magazines. After being the mother of three bridegrooms, she declared, she was coming into her own at last.

The Rosses didn't belong to a church, but they knew some of the ministers in town socially. Which one did Rennie prefer? Reverend Roberts? He was okay, she conceded, only she wouldn't be caught dead in his church—that pseudo-Gothic monstrosity. What about Dr. Johnson? *That creep?* Well, then, Pastor Noyes?

Rennie suddenly remembered what Peter had said about being married on a hilltop in blue jeans, without a minister. "Why can't we have a Quaker marriage? Then we wouldn't need any minister. Would we?"

"*No minister?* There has to be a minister to pronounce the couple man and wife. How else would the marriage be legal?" Rennie's mother exclaimed, smiling indulgently.

Now that she'd settled this matter, Rennie's mother switched to other details—the gown, the veil, the bridesmaids. It was all a familiar routine to Rennie. She'd been a bridesmaid in all of her brothers' weddings. Each time, the ceremony had moved her deeply. Yet each wedding had made her feel the way she did about medieval art, after she'd taken a course in it sophomore year. It was very beautiful, but it had no connection with her life.

Then one evening her father came home and inquired whether it wouldn't be nice to invite some of his business associates and their wives to the wedding. The more he thought about the idea, the longer the list became.

"Peter and I don't even know them," Rennie muttered.

"You'll meet everyone at the reception. When Joe Pitkin's daughter got married, the whole plastics industry was there. It was like a convention."

"But, Daddy, a wedding isn't a convention."

Rennie's mother backed her up. "I think that's disgusting. A wedding should just be a pretty, joyful occasion. Ours was, Ed."

"Yes, I guess it was. But your father had four daughters to marry off on a newspaperman's salary. I have only the one girl. I can afford to give her the best—always have given it to her, haven't I? Not that I'd agree to anything on the scale of the Pitkin wedding. Just happened to think of it." Rennie's father shrugged, dismissing the matter for the moment. "Well, Mother and I will work on this list, but until we find out the size of the church, we can't tell how many invitations to order. I wish you'd make up your mind where you want to be married, Rennie. How about Trinity? It's very spacious."

"Why can't we have a Quaker marriage? Like the picture on the third-floor landing. It *is* a real wedding, isn't it, Daddy?"

Her father looked at Rennie intently, as if trying to discover what lay behind the odd notion. "That old lithograph? I guess it does show the way Friends got married a century or two ago."

So it *was* real, not just an illustration for a story!

"I found that picture among my mother's things," Rennie's father recalled. "Don't know where she got it, but it must have meant something to her or she wouldn't have saved it. I couldn't bear to throw it away. I was taking it up to the attic when I got the idea of hanging it on the landing."

"A Quaker marriage would be appropriate with my name," Rennie said.

"Isn't that a little farfetched?" her father exclaimed. "Your name is the only Quaker thing about you."

"Besides," Rennie's mother objected, "I wouldn't know how to behave at a wedding like that. Would you, Ed? You scarcely remember anything about your Quaker ancestors."

"How can you say such a thing, Joan? I remember my grandmother very well. It's just that I lost touch with the rest of the family." He paused. "It's true, though, that I haven't the slightest idea what a Quaker wedding's like."

Rennie pressed him. "Isn't there anyone you could ask?"

"Not here. I never heard of any Friends in Neville."

"Have you, Mother?" Rennie asked.

"There were no Quakers on my side of the family. Just Daddy's."

"Friends," Rennie's father corrected. "I believe they prefer to be called Friends."

"Well, then, Friends," Rennie's mother repeated, giving him an impatient glance. "I never knew any. But I always loved your grandmother's name." She turned to Rennie. "Before each of the boys was born, I planned— And finally"—she smiled, reaching out to give Rennie a hug—"you came."

Something about the curve of her mother's arm, the almost wistful way she reached out, made Rennie feel a kind of pity, as if, in a curious reversal, her mother were a little child and she, Rennie, the parent.

"I remember my grandmother very well," her father repeated, and now his voice was nostalgic. He went to the coat closet to put his jacket away. Lost in recollection, he stood there holding the wire hanger. "That woman," he murmured, shaking his head. "*She* really *had* serenity. I wish some of it had come down to us."

Returning to the present, Rennie's father hung up his jacket. Then he stretched out in his chair to read the newspaper.

Rennie kept at him. "Where did she live, Daddy?"

He was scanning the headlines. "Who?"

"Your grandmother."

"On the old family farm—down in Rhode Island," he murmured absently.

"Firbank?"

The name seemed to trigger something. Rennie's father dropped the paper and looked at her. "Yes, Firbank."

"Where is it, anyhow? The way you talked when I was little, I used to think it was some pretend place—magical."

"It's eastward from Little Narragansett Bay, deep in the country. Nearest town's Kendal and that's minute."

"Did you know that your voice always gets moony when you speak about Firbank?"

Rennie's father laughed. "No. Does it?" He folded his hands over his stomach. "I guess the place is a bit magical for me, even now. We used to spend summers there when I was a little boy. Coming from New York, visiting Grandmother Serenity Otis was the event I waited for all year."

"Was she so nice?"

"I loved her! When I was naughty, she just took me on her lap and told me about the farm animals and the creatures living in the Salt Pond. That was more effective than my parents' punishments."

"Isn't Salt Pond where you sailed the catboat? I remember your telling me—"

"Yes. Grandmother let me hold the tiller. 'Thee steer, Edmund,' she said one day, when we were crossing to the dunes. I was five. Nothing that's happened since ever made me feel so important. She died a few years later, and we never went back to Firbank."

"Why not?"

"My parents had become real New Yorkers. The farm was pretty tame for them. Father wasn't a Friend, anyhow, and all that thee and thy, going to Meeting—well, we just didn't fit there."

"Isn't there anyone in Firbank you could ask about a Quaker marriage?"

Her father shook his head. "The only one left is my cousin Oliver Otis—if he's still alive. Haven't heard from him in years. He was always odd. Refused to fight in the First World War. Friends have this thing about going to war. He finally went to France, as I recall—stretcher-bearer or some such assignment."

"Daddy, couldn't you ask Oliver? Write, or even phone?"

"*Ask Oliver?*" Rennie's father shook his head. "We're out of touch. I can't even tell you much about him, except that he went to Harvard. And after the war he married this English girl he'd met in France, another Friend. Can't remember her name. A very beautiful girl. I remember that. He brought her back to Firbank. He never had a real occupation, as far as I know, only farming. Not that farming's anything to look down on. But Oliver and I didn't have much in common, and I rarely saw him and his wife, except at family funerals. Last one was Aunt Temperance's. Must be going on twenty years ago, wouldn't you say, Joan?"

Rennie's mother nodded absently.

"So you see, Rennie, I don't know what Oliver's like now. Old, that's for sure, up in the seventies. He's fifteen years older than I am." This seemed sufficient reason for not asking his cousin how to go about getting Rennie married in the way she wanted to be.

"Rennie," her mother put in, looking worried. "You simply must settle on your silver pattern. Here it is almost May, not two months till the wedding. People will be asking what you want."

"I don't want silver. You always complain about polishing it."

"Honey, if you just put it in an aluminum pan with a spoonful of baking soda—be sure it's aluminum—"

"I don't *want* any!"

It's true, Rennie thought, but why must I be so bitchy?

Rennie's father was still thinking of Firbank. "Now that you mention a Quaker marriage," he told her, "I remember, while I was down there, I saw the wedding certificate belonging to my grandparents, Edmund and Serenity Otis. He's the one I was named for, but I never knew him. Died before I was born. I always thought that was why Grandmother made so much of me—because I was his namesake."

"You were talking about the wedding certificate," Rennie reminded him.

"Yes. It had more signatures than the Declaration of Independence. Luckily it was hanging on the wall near where I was sitting during Aunt Temperance's funeral, because there was nothing else to occupy my mind. Most of the time people just sat there in silence. Some woman read a psalm. Someone else said a prayer—he wasn't a minister; they didn't have any. No music, either. I never was one for sitting around and meditating. So I studied the certificate. It described the procedure of the wedding."

"What was it, Daddy—the procedure?"

"Can't remember, just that the wedding took place in 1874."

"That's a strange thing to do," Rennie's mother remarked, "hang a marriage certificate on the wall. Rennie, Daddy and I are fitting you out with household linens. But if you leave everything till the last minute—"

What with all the arguments and plans, day after day, Rennie didn't open her bulging green book bag once all vacation. That was serious. She had a fine arts quiz on Monday.

Sunday afternoon, an hour before she left home, she got out her notes. Curled up in the den, she started to read through them. This was her favorite course, the only one she really cared about. The Impressionists had a way of looking at the world that touched something Rennie felt deeply—a drive to reach the truth about what they saw, even though this didn't correspond to the outward image. Studying the works of those artists—Monet, Pissarro, Renoir—Rennie lost herself in pure delight. It wasn't the moment for her mother to come barging in.

"We haven't settled anything, Rennie," she said. "How can I plan? Here you are, going back to college, and you haven't told me what arrangements to make. You ought to take some responsibility. It's *your* wedding."

Rennie had to clutch the book against her breast to keep from firing it across the room. "Then why can't I have it the way I want it? Why does everything always have to be what you and Daddy decide? Last year he was making a big thing about my major. I hate those ed courses. I don't want to be a teacher. Art history is all I care about, but Daddy put his foot down. Now I'm getting married and I can't even have the wedding the way I want it."

This was too much for Rennie's mother. She looked both furious and hurt. "That's what Daddy and I have been trying to find out your whole vacation—how you want it—and you won't tell us."

Rennie was furious, too, but she couldn't answer back. What was this elusive thing she and Peter thought they wanted? She really didn't know.

Defeated, Rennie slammed the notebook closed and went up to her room to pack. Priscilla was picking her up at four o'clock. When she came back downstairs, her parents started in again about the wedding, and it was a relief when Priscilla honked.

Rennie kissed her parents quickly and rushed out, promising to talk to Peter and let them know definitely about the arrangements in a week. "Maybe two," she called back as she ran down the walk.

WHEN RENNIE GOT back to school, she told Peter about her parents. "They never even listened," she cried. "I tried to explain that what you want is a Quaker marriage."

"I do? Who says?"

"Peter, you told me you wished we could get married in blue jeans, without a minister, just you and me. Don't you remember?"

"What's that got to do with a Quaker wedding? I bet even they don't wear blue jeans when they get married. Wouldn't want to myself. That was just—I don't know—an idea. I'd have to have a lot more information about the ceremony before I'd agree to something that far-out. From what you say, your folks aren't for it and I don't see mine liking it, either."

"All I was trying to do was find out."

"It was in that second that the idea came to Rennie. Within the next minute she had a plan.

"Peter! What if you and I went to see Oliver this weekend? We could borrow someone's car and drive down there, ask him what the wedding's like."

"Who's Oliver?"

"This old cousin of Daddy's. He's a Quaker."

"Where does he live?"

"Rhode Island. Near Kendal. We could call him up—ask Information whether he's listed. For all I know, he may be dead."

"Rhode Island!" Peter exclaimed. "That's a long trip. I can't go to Rhode Island. Costs too much. Besides, I have studying to do, and if we're getting married in June, Rennie, I have to find a summer job."

"If we're getting married in June, Peter Holland, we have to find a church. All vacation Daddy kept lecturing me about how some churches were already dated up for June weddings last Christmas. I promised Mother and Daddy—"

"Okay. You'd better fly. Otherwise you won't have enough time there. I'll borrow Jack's car and take you to the airport."

"You mean you won't come with me?"

But Peter didn't seem to hear her. "I hope you can stay at Oliver's house," was all he said. "Where else could you go?"

Rennie shrugged. She didn't know a soul in Rhode Island. She was thinking, If I wait now, if I wait five minutes, I'll never go.

"Be right back," she called over her shoulder, running out of Peter's room. She rushed downstairs to the pay phone and dialed Information. "Otis," she repeated, shouting above the racket of her heart. "Oliver Otis, Firbank, Rhode Island. There *is?*"

She gave the operator the number of her father's credit card.

As if in echo, the name was spoken back to her—not "Hello," quavered by an ancient voice, as she'd expected, but "Oliver Otis," deep and crisp.

Taken by surprise, Rennie could only murmur, "Mr. Otis?"

"Speaking."

"This is Serenity Ross. You don't know me. I'm your cousin Edmund's—"

"Serenity!" he exclaimed with such resounding delight that the receiver vibrated. "Serenity Ross—of course I know. I heard there was a child named for my grandmother."

"Right! The reason I'm calling—I wondered—would it be okay if I came over to see you Friday afternoon?"

"It would be first-rate. *First-rate!* Daphne and I'll be delighted."

He sounds as if he means it, she thought. "You're sure it's convenient? Could I spend the night? Do you have room?"

"Oceans of room in this old house. Where is thee now?"

"What—what did you say?" Rennie couldn't have heard right.

"Where is thee calling from?"

"Oh! Tilbury College. I don't suppose you've heard of it?"

"No."

"It's a hundred and seventy-five miles north of New York City."

"Thee's coming a long way."

"Yes. I have a ride to Albany County Airport, only I don't know where to fly to."

"Hillsgrove. That's our nearest airport. From there, thee'll have to get a bus. Stops right out in front of the terminal. Ask the driver to let thee off in Kendal. I'll meet thee there. The bus leaves Hillsgrove at seven. Does thee think thee could make it?"

"Easily. I get out of class at noon on Fridays."

"That ought to give thee plenty of time. Serenity?"

"Yes?"

"Does thee have enough money?"

"Loads. Thanks a lot just the same, Mr. Otis."

"Oliver, to thee," he said.

CHAPTER TWO

So HERE was Rennie, in the air, whizzing toward the unknown— Firbank, Oliver, Daphne. At the moment, cushioned on a cloud, securely fastened, she was weightless of worry. The serenity she'd longed to leave with Peter seemed almost within her grasp. What made it so nearly attainable here? Did she have to go up in a plane to get it?

Almost at once the peace was shattered as a stewardess announced that they were about to descend. A moment later they were beneath the clouds, sailing slowly over woods and cultivated fields. The sun sparkled on a wide bay with countless coves. Miniature houses, more woods, a white church whose steeple was like an inverted ice-cream cone. Then the plane landed with a bump.

Unfastening the seat belt, Rennie picked up her book bag. It was heavy. Not that her clothes weighed much. She'd brought only the tan shorts, the aqua turtleneck and sneakers. It was all those books that dragged her down, and so far she hadn't looked at one of them.

Surging forward, the noisy passengers filled the aisle. Rennie followed the crowd to a glassed-in lobby, where people stood waiting for their friends. Making her way through, she bumped against a tall man. He wore a white canvas sun hat, and his shirt collar was turned out over his tweed jacket. As she passed him, he stepped out of the crowd and caught up with her.

"Serenity Ross?"

She stood still, startled. It couldn't be Oliver. He was meeting her in Kendal, and from what her father'd said, he was feeble and old. This man was taller than her father, in much better shape, almost skinny.

143

"Oh, are you— You're not Mr. Otis?"

He lifted the sun hat, showing a bald scalp with a wisp of orange fuzz, and his weathered face crinkled into a delighted smile. "So thee *is* Serenity! I knew thee must be. I'm Oliver."

Taking the book bag from her, he began to guide Rennie into the terminal. "Welcome!" he exclaimed. "It was so fortunate—Mary Young came in to visit with Daphne, so I checked and found this was the only afternoon plane from Albany. Thought I'd run down and get thee. We'll go and claim thy baggage."

"This is all I have," Rennie said, pointing to the book bag. "Just for the weekend—"

He looked surprised. "We thought thee was coming for the summer. Thee didn't say. So we supposed thy father was sending thee to Firbank to become acquainted with the home of thy forebears."

"Daddy doesn't know I'm here," Rennie admitted.

For the first time Oliver looked grave. "Serenity," he asked, peering at her intently, "thee's—thee's not running away?"

Rennie laughed. "Oh, no!" Running away! From Peter?

"Not that we wouldn't be glad to have thee stay with us, anyhow," Oliver assured her, still grave. "But we wouldn't like to think of anyone's running away from home."

"I've got a reservation on the three-o'clock plane back to school on Sunday afternoon," Rennie explained.

This seemed to set Oliver's mind at rest. He beamed on Rennie again, and they stepped out into the sunshine. It was a lot cooler here, and the air was tangy. In the small parking lot, he stopped at an old pickup truck and opened the door on the passenger side. "Can thee hop up?" he asked. When she was settled, he hoisted himself into the driver's seat. Then he turned toward Rennie, as if this were his first chance to get a good look at her.

"How did you recognize me?" she asked, feeling shy.

"Thy hair," he answered, smiling. "It's the Otis hair. Mine was just like thine when I was young."

It was hard to imagine. He really was old, only his face was so lively that one forgot his age. Oliver must have a very carefree life. Peter needn't have worried about his being nice to her. Something already made Rennie glad she'd come. It was the way he looked at her—as though she mattered. She was used to people noticing her unusual coloring. But this man seemed to be looking past her face, searching beyond it.

His hand rested on the brake, ready to take off. Yet, for another few seconds, he went on looking at her. "So thee's coming home to Firbank," he said at last. "Wonderful! It's a good fifty years since we had a Serenity there."

OLIVER drove onto a highway bordered by woodland. Although every car on the road overtook the pickup, he never accelerated. He seemed to enjoy moseying along.

But Rennie felt urgency. With only two days for making all those arrangements, should she explain now why she had come? It seemed a littly pushy, plunging in right away.

"Everybody calls me Rennie," she said, temporizing.

Without turning his head, Oliver nodded, signifying that he had heard. But he never used her nickname.

"Reason I came," she finally told him, after such a long pause that she began to feel uncomfortable, "is, there's this boy, Peter Holland, in my class at college. We're getting married the end of June and I thought we might have a Quaker marriage, only we don't know what it's like." Put this way, their intention sounded so childish that Rennie fished around desperately for something to convey how mature she and Peter really were.

"Married?" Oliver exclaimed, before Rennie could think of anything to say. "How old is thee?" He wasn't hiding his surprise.

"Nineteen. I'll be twenty in September."

"And Peter?"

"He'll be twenty this summer."

"Do thy parents approve?"

"It was their idea. Now they're trying to decide on a church for the wedding—we don't belong to any—and I wondered if—" Rennie glanced sideways to see whether Oliver understood.

He seemed to be thinking. Then he asked, "Have you been in touch with Friends in your area—thee and Peter?"

"Daddy says there aren't any."

Oliver laughed. "There are Friends practically everywhere."

"You're the only one Daddy knows. That's why I came."

"I see," Oliver murmured, sounding a bit disappointed. But he quickly regained his good humor. "Well, thee'll meet a whole batch of Quakes here," he assured her, grinning.

"Did you say Quakes?"

Oliver burst out laughing. "Yes. Religion ought to be a purely joyous experience, but it's also terribly serious and if one doesn't look out, one ends up taking *oneself* too seriously. So we tend to poke fun at ourselves."

"Daddy's always correcting Mother because she says Quakers, and he thinks they want to be called Friends. Wait till he hears that you said Quakes!"

"Friends or Quakers—it's all the same. There was a time when people called us Quakers as an insult, but that's long past. A name makes no difference—just what one is."

"Do Friends all speak the way you do?"

"Plain language? No, it has practically died out. Old-fashioned Friends, like me, still use it in the family or the Meeting."

"I like it," Rennie said. She was considered "in the family"!

"We don't foist our language on outsiders," Oliver said, "the way our forebears did. They were protesting the custom of making social distinctions. People used to address their betters as you—it made their betters feel grander—and their equals or inferiors in the singular thee. So Friends dramatized their belief that all people are equal by speaking the same way to everyone, saying thee and thou even when they spoke to kings. Equality was a revolutionary idea three centuries ago."

"But now," Rennie argued, "everyone says you to everyone."

"Current speech is democratic," Oliver conceded, "but it isn't truth, addressing a single person in the plural."

Rennie'd never thought of this before. She could see why her father had called Oliver odd. But she liked his absolute honesty. It made her feel that she could trust him. And he held the key to the Ross happiness. If he wanted to, he could fix everything up this weekend. She'd go back to college with the wedding all arranged, and her mother and father could relax.

Oliver turned off into a country road. "We're almost home," he cried happily. "Daphne will be so pleased to see thee!" He looked at Rennie gravely. "Did thy father tell thee about her?"

"Yes."

"Wonder how he heard. It's years since we've had any contact."

Oliver stopped the truck before a long white farmhouse with huge maples at each corner and wisteria hanging in fringes from the roof of a stately semicircular porch. Behind the house, partly hidden by it, stood a white silo and a red barn.

Firbank, her father's dream place! As Rennie jumped out of the cab, she saw at once that it really had the quality he always conveyed when he spoke of it. The house needed paint, but, touched by the setting sun, it had a misty pink radiance, so that it was one with the earth, the trees and the sky that framed it.

That's what I've been missing all along, Rennie said to herself with surprise—beauty! That's the emptiness I feel sometimes, even though Peter and I have the best of both worlds.

A retriever and a little fox terrier came bounding over the lawn to jump up on their master. "This is Lion," Oliver told Rennie, as if he were introducing an exuberant child, "and this little scamp's our Duffy."

Only interested in the house, Rennie saw an old woman standing at the door, smiling in welcome. She was terribly homely. Rennie could barely conceal her disappointment. "Is that Daphne?"

"No. It's Mary Young, a neighbor of ours." Oliver looked at Rennie. His expression was troubled. "Thee said thy father told thee about Daphne?"

"Yes. He couldn't remember her name, but he said how beautiful she is."

"Thy father knew Daphne when we were all a great many years younger. She's still beautiful in spirit, only her appearance has changed," Oliver said, with such pain in his eyes that Rennie glanced away. "I didn't think thy father could have heard about her stroke. It paralyzed her. Not quite three years ago. She's better

147

now, but her speech is affected. Don't think, though, that because she can't talk, her mind is failing. If anything, her perception is keener than before."

The dogs, rushing into the house, almost knocked Rennie over.

Oliver took her arm and started up the porch steps. He only spent a moment introducing Mary Young, so eager was he to find Daphne. "Just try to speak naturally," he urged Rennie as they walked through the high-ceilinged entrance hall. "Before long thee'll guess what Daphne wishes to say." He drew her into the loveliest room she'd ever seen.

It was lined with bookshelves, painted a soft gray green. Above the shelves hung a whole gallery of pictures. At the far end of the room, in a bay window through which the last rays of the sunset streamed, Daphne sat in an armchair, with the dogs at her feet. Her hair, coiled on top of her head, was touched with the rose of the sun. As Oliver crossed the room with Rennie, Daphne leaned forward. In that instant her hair, no longer in the path of the sun's rays, turned pure white.

Devastating disappointment overtook Rennie; the face her father had remembered for its beauty was actually lopsided. Then she noticed Daphne's right arm, bent at the elbow, motionless, thin fingers dangling limply from the wrist. Pity, embarrassment in the presence of deformity, some disturbing uneasiness made Rennie start to draw back. But Oliver still had hold of her.

"This is Serenity," he told Daphne in the same affectionate tone with which he had just introduced the dogs. "Everyone calls her Rennie. Suits her all right, doesn't it? Just the same, I like Serenity better. She isn't staying as long as we thought, only till Sunday. Getting married next month. Can thee believe it?" He shook his head incredulously.

Daphne, smiling with one side of her face, reached out. When the cold hand touched her own, Rennie felt that disturbing uneasiness grip her again. Then, without quite letting go of Rennie, Oliver bent and kissed Daphne.

A strange sensation, almost like an electric current, passed through Rennie. Linked to them both, she seemed to be joined in the circle of their love. A comfortable sigh escaped her, as though she'd been holding her breath all her life and suddenly found she could release it.

Daphne and Oliver let go of Rennie in the same moment.

"I'll take Serenity up to Heather's room," Oliver said. "When she comes down again, supper will be ready. Mary brought a casserole." Seeing Daphne's look, he added, "She's gone home."

The room to which he took Rennie, leading the way up the curving staircase, was in an ell at the back of the house. It was a girl's room. A pale blue spread, sprinkled with irises and daffodils, covered the high brass bedstead. "This is the oldest part of Firbank," he explained, dropping Rennie's book bag onto a rocking chair. "Seventeen ninety-two. My great-great-grandfather Daniel Otis—let's see, what is he to thee?" Oliver interposed, grinning. "He's thy great-great-*great*-grandfather! He built the original house—three rooms down, two up. It was another hundred years before what we call the main wing was added."

"I've never slept in any place this old," Rennie murmured, noticing how the wide floorboards sloped dizzily downhill from the fireplace to the dormer windows.

"We put thee in here because this was our daughter's room," he said. "Also, we thought thee'd like the back of the house best on account of the view. These windows face the pond."

"Oh, Salt Pond! That's one of the things Daddy talks about."

"Still recalls it, does he?" This seemed to give Oliver pleasure. "He enjoyed coming here when he was a boy. Pity," Oliver said gently, "that he never comes back, except to pop in when someone has died and rush right off again."

"That's because of his business," Rennie explained, feeling she had to come to her father's defense. "Daddy works awfully hard." Then, to her surprise, she blurted out, "Oliver, please help Peter and me." She hadn't meant to say that. Wasn't it information she'd come for? Why was she suddenly asking for help?

Oliver placed a hand on Rennie's shoulder. "We'll do anything we can," he assured her. "After supper we'll sit by the fire and

149

talk. Now get ready and come down. Bathroom's next door. The towels on the rack are thine." He started to leave. "There's no one else in the house, just we three, so wander wherever thee wishes."

Left alone, upset because she'd blurted out more than she'd meant to, Rennie glanced around the room. There were pastels in gilt frames on the walls—not the work of an amateur, Rennie figured, as she looked more closely. The drawings were a series of portraits of a child. *Heather at six months* was written under one picture. There was *Heather at Cannes,* playing in the sand, and *Heather at Firbank, 1935,* a little girl of three or four.

Judging by the bookshelves, Heather had been less a reader than a collector. There were tiny, carved wooden animals and some

terra-cotta figurines of a woman playing with a child. In every one of the delicate pieces of sculpture the mother wore her hair on top of her head, like Daphne's.

Daphne. It was Daphne who'd upset her—the lopsided face. Beauty was what Rennie'd been hoping to find here—how eagerly, she only now realized. She'd come expecting to enter her father's dream place, to appropriate some of that magic herself. Instead . . .

Even the shame Rennie felt at being turned off by someone's trouble couldn't overcome her reluctance to go downstairs. Still, she couldn't stay up here all evening. And she *was* starving. She'd have to talk to Daphne, guess what Daphne meant to convey.

She found her way back to the curved staircase and down into the empty living room. Oliver's voice was coming from a distant part of the house. Following the sound, Rennie passed through a brightly lighted dining room with a table intended for a large family—not set for anyone just now. In the big warm kitchen beyond, Oliver, in his shirt sleeves, was standing at the stove stirring something. Daphne sat at a round table, with Lion and Duffy on the floor beside her.

"Come in, come in," Oliver called. "That's thy place, Serenity, on Daphne's left. Sit down. I'll dish up in a minute."

Rennie did as she was told, concentrating on the straw place mats, a blue-and-white pitcher filled with flowers, the nicks in the old pewter teapot—anything to avoid looking at Daphne. Even when Oliver began serving her food, Rennie just stared at the indigo design rimming her white plate. Without raising her eyes, she picked up her fork.

Oliver reached out and gently restrained the hand that held the fork. At the same time he took hold of Daphne's paralyzed fingers, and Daphne covered Rennie's other hand with her icy one. Glancing up in astonishment, Rennie saw that they were both bowing their heads. Oliver must be about to say grace. Rennie wasn't used to this sort of thing. She waited anxiously.

But Oliver said nothing. Rennie, sitting there in the eerie silence, waited for words that didn't come. Then, her hands still held in theirs, she was once more overwhelmed by that feeling she'd had when she first arrived, of being joined to Daphne and Oliver. A second later her hands were released.

Awkwardly, with visible determination, Daphne took up her fork. Oliver began eating, talking between mouthfuls about Mary Young's delicious casserole, the lady's slippers he'd found in the woods, his delight in having immediately recognized Rennie. "She looks exactly the way I imagined she would!" he told Daphne.

Listening to Oliver give an account of his day as if it had been a festival, observing the affection his eyes telegraphed to Daphne, Rennie felt reassured. This was a kind, caring man. He wouldn't let her go back to college without some solution to her problem.

AFTER the kitchen was tidied, with Rennie feeling clumsy in her efforts to help, Oliver ushered her into the living room. Would she sit here and enjoy the fire while he got Daphne ready for bed? He'd be down again soon, Oliver promised as he left the room.

So Rennie was going to have a chance to speak to Oliver without Daphne's disturbing presence. Greatly relieved, she sat down in a chair by the fireplace.

Judging by the sound of things, getting Daphne upstairs was a major operation. Oliver could be heard, encouraging her step by step. "Try again, dear one. We're almost at the top. There! Thee made it!"

Rennie looked around the room. The armchairs needed reupholstering and the rug was worn in spots. Still, this is exactly the kind of room I want when we're married, she thought—with a fireplace, and full of books and pictures. Peter would love it. She'd never visualized their home before. Next year they'd have one of those married students' apartments. And beyond next year, where would they be? Peter was worrying so much about this summer, he couldn't plan. Summer jobs, he'd been told, were scarce.

For Peter to be worrying was unusual. One of the things that had first attracted Rennie to him was his easygoing, lighthearted approach. He still joked now, still teased her, but underneath was a new seriousness that Rennie didn't know how to take and it frightened her. Was getting married going to change Peter?

Getting Daphne ready for bed was taking an awfully long time. Unable to sit still any longer, Rennie got up and looked at the pictures that crowded the walls. Light from the standing lamps didn't reveal details, but Rennie noticed oil paintings of flowers—bunches arranged in a blue-and-white pitcher, very much like the one on the table at supper. There were botanical plates, too, and a series of tiny watercolor drawings of children, dressed in what Rennie presumed were Quaker clothes of long ago.

After these attractive little figures, it was a shock to come to a series of charcoal sketches showing brutalized people, with crazed eyes and gaping mouths. Like Goya's *Disasters of War*. With relief Rennie noticed something less disagreeable on the adjacent wall—a framed document written in an antique hand on a long, narrow scroll. Every *f* turned out to be an *s*.

Whereas, the document read, *Edmund Otis and Serenity Millburn, having declared their intentions of taking each other in marriage, to Kendal Monthly Meeting of the Society of Friends . . .*

This was Rennie's great-grandparents' wedding certificate, which her father had studied during that funeral!

Now, these are to certify to all whom it may concern, that, for the full accomplishing of their said intentions, this Ninth Day of the Fifth Month, in the year of our Lord Eighteen Hundred and Seventy Four, they appeared at a religious meeting of the aforesaid Society in Kendal; and he, the said Edmund Otis, taking the said Serenity Millburn by the hand, did openly declare: in the presence of the Lord, and before this assembly, I take thee, Serenity Millburn, to be my wife, promising, with Divine assistance, to be unto thee a loving and faithful husband, until death shall separate us.

A Quaker marriage! Here were the words that went with the picture on the landing at home!

Then, in the same assembly, Rennie read on, *Serenity Millburn did in like manner declare: in the presence of the Lord, and before this assembly, I take thee, Edmund Otis, to be my husband, promising, with Divine assistance, to be unto thee a loving and faithful wife, until death shall separate us.*

And in further confirmation thereof, they, the said Edmund Otis and Serenity Millburn (she, according to the custom of marriage, adopting the surname of her husband) did then and there to these presents set their hands.

Edmund Otis
Serenity Millburn Otis

Intent on studying the signatures, Rennie didn't notice Oliver's return until he came up behind her and touched her shoulder.

"Did you know," she asked, turning to him in excitement, "that my middle name is Millburn?"

"Yes." He was evidently pleased by Rennie's interest in the scroll. "It used to be the custom for Friends to frame their marriage certificates and hang them in the best parlor—perhaps," he remarked with a chuckle, "to remind themselves when they were angry at each other of their promise to be loving! Also," Oliver added, "it gave them pleasure over the years to see the names of their old friends on the certificate."

Oliver ran his finger down the columns of names, under the couple's signatures, that reached to the bottom of the scroll. "At a Quaker marriage all the guests—even the children—constitute the legal witnesses and sign the certificate."

"Is getting married in a Friends meetinghouse the same today?"

"The procedure is unchanged."

"Tell me more," Rennie pleaded. "What else happens?"

"Come and sit down," Oliver urged as he dropped onto the couch. "I suppose thee knows that, in a sense, a Quaker marriage begins long before the wedding day?"

Rennie tried not to show her surprise. "Before the wedding day?" she repeated.

"Months before, the couple writes a joint letter to the Meeting, expressing the wish to be married under its care. This is the first and perhaps the most significant step. At that moment," Oliver said gravely, "the commitment begins."

"The legal stuff?"

Oliver looked at Rennie curiously. "No," he answered, without elaborating. After that he was silent.

Rennie felt uncomfortable, not knowing what to say next. "It's

155

true, isn't it," she finally ventured, "that Friends don't have a minister?"

"Kendal Friends don't," Oliver replied. "But some others do. Silent Friends, as we call ourselves—and we do an awful lot of talking—feel that every man is in direct contact with God. So we don't need anyone to do our praying for us—or to pronounce a couple man and wife. We believe only God can create such a union. What reason do thee and Peter have for wanting a Friends wedding?"

Rennie told him how Peter had spoken about being married without a minister, and how the idea had taken hold of her—she couldn't say why. "It's not really a reason," she admitted honestly. "It's more a feeling. Partly my name, I guess."

Oliver's reaction took her by surprise. "A feeling may be a better reason than a well-thought-out argument. It may be what Friends call a leading. But," he added, "thee should realize, Serenity, that it takes several months to arrange a wedding after the manner of Friends, even in the case of members whom we know and have worshipped with over a period of time. Thee spoke of June."

"Do you mean one has to join the church?"

"Nominal membership is immaterial. What counts with us is the experience of seeking together. Centuries ago a Friend Daphne and I greatly admire put this concept beautifully: 'There is a principle which is pure, placed in the human mind, which in different places and ages hath had different names.' " Oliver's audible delight in the words gave resonance to his voice. " 'It is deep and inward, confined to no forms of religion nor excluded from any, where the heart stands in perfect sincerity. In whomsoever this takes root and grows, of what nation soever, they become brethren. . . .' "

"Where the heart stands in perfect sincerity," Rennie repeated to herself. She wanted to remember those words.

But Oliver was asking, "Where were you thinking of holding the wedding?"

"Is there a Friends meetinghouse near Neville? If I had an idea where to find it, maybe I could persuade Daddy—"

"No!" Oliver exclaimed. "Thee and Peter must make the application yourselves. Your parents' approval is important, but if you are married in Meeting, thy father will not give thee away. Thee gives thyself to Peter and he gives himself to thee. You will enter the meetinghouse hand in hand."

How is Daddy going to feel about this? Rennie wondered. He's always wanted to walk down the aisle with me on his arm.

"I can tell thee where to inquire about the Meeting nearest thy home, Serenity," Oliver was saying, "but I'm afraid thee will find that Friends with whom thee and Peter have never had fellowship will be reluctant to undertake responsibility for your marriage. It's more than a ceremony with us; it's a deep and continuing concern for the permanence and rightness of the relationship. That's why a Friends Meeting first appoints a committee on clearness—two men Friends and two women Friends. When the committee is satisfied that the couple has clearness for marriage—"

"Clearness?" Rennie broke in.

"It's the Quaker term for establishing that nothing exists which might prove a hindrance; that both parties understand the responsibilities they are assuming and that they have every prospect of being happy together. If the committee feels comfortable about proceeding, the Meeting appoints another committee to have oversight of the wedding."

Rennie was floored. Strange people, poking their noses into her affairs. "I guess we'd better forget it," she muttered.

"Thee sees, Serenity," Oliver said in a gentle voice, "until thee and Peter have known Friends, you can hardly expect to understand what all this means to us. We have no forms or creed. We place our whole reliance on a common experience of the presence of God in the human heart. This makes us one with our fellow human beings. Thy heart is the only lasting gift thee has to give Peter, the only manifestation of love that can endure as long, the marriage promise puts it, as you both shall live."

"But marriage is something private," Rennie protested, "between the guy and the girl. What right do others have to intrude?"

"That is where we differ," Oliver answered. "Marriage is a great deal more than an understanding between two people. It affects

157

everyone around them, our whole civilization. It affects the unborn children, for whom we wish to prepare a harmonious home." Oliver paused a moment. Then he asked quietly, "If it's only yourselves you're concerned with, why bother with a religious ceremony? You could disregard these responsibilities completely and simply live together."

Rennie stared. She hadn't expected this from Oliver.

ALL she could think of when she went to bed in Heather's room was leaving Firbank. In the morning she'd ask Oliver to take her to the airport, or at least to Kendal. Rennie wished she could have brought herself to tell him when they were saying good night.

But it was too hard. After she'd left him and started upstairs, she'd felt a touch on her arm. Turning, she saw Oliver's blue eyes, which were almost level with hers now. "Way will open," he assured her. "Love is not a little bird that suddenly appears in springtime, alights awhile, then flits away when the season changes. We have to strive very hard sometimes. But way will open."

Rushing up the remaining stairs as soon as he withdrew his hand, Rennie thought bitterly that she was going back to college without the solution she'd counted on and more mixed up than when she came. What did he mean: Way will open?

She realized that the game she'd played so successfully with her parents all these years—avoiding every confrontation—hadn't worked in Firbank. Oliver was fifteen years older than her father. She'd expected that he'd be fifteen years more naïve. Instead he'd seen right through her. No need for any committee on clearness.

Sliding between sheets that smelled of outdoors, she wished she could get Oliver out of her mind, forget what he'd asked in that quiet tone. It didn't condemn Rennie, yet it told her firmly that, for himself, nothing less than premarital chastity would have been acceptable.

Stop thinking about it, she scolded herself. Oliver had raised questions she didn't have time to face. But they dodged around in her mind, pestering and prying until she felt blasted clean out of her world. She was like one of those tumbling bodies in Michelangelo's *Last Judgment*, careening wildly in space. Holding on to her blanket for dear life, she shut her eyes so she wouldn't see the terrifying void below.

The next thing Rennie knew, sunshine was streaming into the room. She jumped out of bed, still half asleep, and went to the window. There, at the bottom of a field speckled with boulders, not a house in sight, was Salt Pond. A sand dune enclosed it at the back, cutting off the view of the ocean, just the way Rennie's father had described it. Nothing was visible beyond but the horizon, making the little body of water a hidden, secret place on the edge of the world, sparkling in the morning sun.

Leaning her elbows on the windowsill, Rennie thought the pond didn't look nearly so big as her father had led her to believe when he told her about his exploits in his grandmother's catboat.

Serenity. Rennie tried to picture the woman with that tranquil sweetness, remembering how her father had wished sadly that some of her serenity had come down to his family. I want it! Rennie told Salt Pond. She felt like shouting, for suddenly she realized that she wanted serenity more than anything.

Turning from the window, she pulled on her shorts and turtleneck. To be serene about life; not to have another night like this last one, a tangle of nightmares! That bed of Heather's—tonight, anyway, she'd be back in Peter's.

Would she? Peter would never put her out of his room, but she knew he didn't want her there as much as she wanted to stay. The night she'd phoned Oliver, he'd tried again to explain how he felt. "If we go on making love, what will getting married prove? I don't think it should just be the legalization of an existing relationship. You feel this way, too, or you wouldn't be trying so hard to get a wedding we can believe in."

"But the relationship does exist," Rennie argued. "It has for months."

"I know. But now you're going to be my wife. That's something special. I'd like to have more chance to explore your thoughts and feelings; my own, too. Let's face it—when we have sex, we don't

159

do that. Will you try, Rennie? I may break down before the week is out, but let's try."

He put his arms around her and held her in a tender and protective embrace. Rennie knew then how strongly Peter meant this. But what would he feel tonight after she'd been gone all this time?

It was nine o'clock. Rennie went out into the upstairs hall. There was no sign of Oliver or Daphne. In daylight the house seemed different. Looking through open doors, she noticed tall headboards on old-fashioned bedsteads, a red-and-yellow patchwork quilt, bare wood floors bleached by sunlight. As she went down the stairs, running her hand along the smooth curve of the banister, she felt an almost seductive pull. Everything about this house was inviting and beautiful, with a character of its own.

Oliver must be in the living room. Rennie heard the vacuum cleaner. But when she looked in from the doorway, she found it wasn't Oliver. A boy in blue jeans with stringy hair was running the machine. He grinned at her. Who was he?

Still looking for Oliver, Rennie walked through the dining room and bumped into a woman coming out of the kitchen. "I just put a roast chicken in the refrigerator. They might like it tonight. Sorry, I have to run." The woman hurried away before Rennie had a chance to ask about Oliver.

Early though it was, the kitchen had been straightened. That pernickety Oliver—didn't he ever leave things around? On the counter, baking dishes and platters contained a variety of tempting foods. Had he been cooking all night?

He'd left a note for Rennie, a large, stiff sheet of paper, propped against the sugar bowl. Instead of writing her name he'd made a sketch of Rennie's head—not a line drawing, but a real portrait in delicate color, produced by just a few expert strokes. Beneath it he'd written:

We hope thee slept well. Help thyself. Coffee on the stove, eggs in the pan, bread in the toaster. When thee's broken fast, Daphne would be pleased if thee dropped in to see her. She's in the wood-shed beyond the back hall. Then will thee come and find me in the

Vietnamese Forest? Follow the little path behind the barn. We hope we can make this a happy day for thee. "The sun is but a morning star."

O.O.

"The sun is but a morning star." What did that mean? A Vietnamese forest in Rhode Island? And who were these people milling around the house? But Rennie was too fascinated by the sketch to wonder very long. In the picture her hair made a cloud around her head, just the right shade of red. The eyes, however, had an expression Rennie didn't associate with herself. Her father had said deprecatingly that Oliver was just a farmer. Little did he know! Only a real artist could have drawn this. Rennie felt impressed and terribly pleased.

She didn't want any breakfast, merely coffee, but she sat at the table, studying the sketch and sipping slowly. While she was there another woman came in, carrying a pie plate in one hand and a cookie tin in the other. With a friendly hello she placed both on the counter. "I brought a cherry pie and some meringues," she told Rennie.

"Are they having a party?"

The woman looked surprised. "Why, no. Since Daphne's stroke, we women of Kendal Meeting have looked out for their main meals. Most of us do our baking on Saturday, and we each stick in an extra pie or sheet of cookies for the Otises. Somebody fixes a casserole or roast. With their food mostly taken care of and the First-day school keeping the house clean, Daphne and Oliver manage beautifully now."

Rennie hadn't wondered about the mechanics of the household. Food had been provided for her, fresh towels hung in the bathroom. Who filled the woodbox so she could sit by a cheerful fire hadn't interested her. But she did wonder about the kid in the living room.

"Is that Heather's boy vacuuming in there?" she asked.

"No," the woman said. "Heather lives in England. We're all the family Daphne and Oliver have here—I mean, the Meeting is."

161

They have us, Rennie was going to say. But then she thought, Daddy doesn't even know about Daphne.

"We're a lot like a family," the woman was saying, "and with everyone in the Meeting doing a little, it's no trouble for any one person. It's been an absolute blessing for our children. We were beginning to have some problems with these youngsters—you know—like everybody else. Then this happened to Daphne. We'd been paying them for doing chores at home, and still we had to keep after them. Now we've asked them to work here purely out of love. I wish I could tell you how they rose to it. They must have been secretly yearning for grown-up responsibility—something to give them pride. We've learned more from this than the kids," the woman added, laughing.

She'd barely left when a couple of little girls—junior high, Rennie figured—burst into the kitchen. They made a comical picture— the one slim, dark and curly-headed, the other pretty, with straight blond hair.

"Hi," Rennie said as they stood in the doorway sizing her up. "I'm Rennie."

"We know," the short one said. "Oliver Otis told us. I'm Nancy. That's Sandy." They took a pail and mop out of the broom closet.

"Do you do this every Saturday?" Rennie asked as the girls started sloshing soapsuds around. Would any kid give up part of her weekend to wash someone's floor?

"No," they answered together.

"Just once a month," Sandy explained. "All the bigger kids in First-day school take turns doing something."

The other girl looked at Rennie gravely, as if she wondered whether this glamorous college student appreciated how indispensable she and her friend really were.

"What is First-day school?" Rennie asked.

"Sunday school. Quakers call it that because it's the first day of the week."

"Plain language?" Rennie asked, amused. She was getting to know her way around this place. "Do you say thee and thy?"

The girls giggled. "Nobody does," Nancy explained, "except

162

Oliver and Daphne Otis—well, she *used* to. Mary Lancashire and three or four others."

As the water level in the kitchen began rising, Rennie pushed her coffee cup aside and stood up. It was definitely time to leave.

"Is this the way to the woodshed?" she asked.

"Yes, but don't go in now," Nancy implored. "Daphne Otis is there. We're *never* to go in the woodshed when she's in there."

"It's okay," Rennie assured her. "Oliver told me to."

She didn't want to go at all. There was something spooky about the whole thing. What, she wondered, as she walked timidly down the back hall, could Daphne be doing in the woodshed that was so mysterious?

The back hall opened directly into the woodshed. Rennie saw an easel standing in the middle of the floor and dozens of canvases stacked against the unplastered walls. She stopped short. There sat Daphne, wearing a faded violet smock. In front of her was a little table with an open sketchbook, brushes, tubes and pans of paint, a jar of water. So *Daphne* was the artist!

She sat very close to the shed window, with her useless right arm toward Rennie. Something on the other side of the small panes attracted her attention. After a few moments she dipped a brush into the water, ran it lightly over a pan of paint and started dabbing the sketchbook with short, decisive strokes.

Rennie, almost holding her breath as she followed the progress of the brush, wondered why Daphne didn't notice her. Then the truth struck her: with that side paralyzed, Daphne's eye probably didn't move and she couldn't see out of the corner. Unless she turned her head, she'd never know someone was there.

Rennie was still overcome with surprise at discovering that Daphne was an artist, obviously the one who'd made the little sketch on Oliver's note. No doubt she'd also painted all those pictures around the house. The way Daphne worked showed she was a professional, or had been, before . . . Rennie was filled with enormous respect for this woman. She'd never known a real artist. To have a chance to see one at work!

The dabs on the paper were beginning to take shape. Rennie saw that what Daphne was trying to capture was the light of the sky filtering through the leaves of the tree. Some of the leaves appeared to let light shine through brilliantly. Where the light had to penetrate more than one layer of leaves, it was still bright, but a deeper green—leaf on leaf creating a pattern of subtly shaded color. Fascinated, Rennie stood watching, amazed by magic that evoked such beauty from blank paper.

Suddenly, Daphne's hand stopped moving. Looking up, Rennie found that she had turned her head and was smiling at her.

"Hi," Rennie said.

Daphne pointed to a chair. When Rennie sat down, Daphne looked eagerly at her, clearly waiting for her to speak.

Say something, Rennie commanded herself. "Oliver left me a note," she managed finally. "He told me to drop in for a minute and see you. Is it all right?"

Daphne nodded happily.

"You're the one who made that little sketch of me, aren't you? I thought it was Oliver. You painted it on that same paper."

Daphne nodded again. Then she looked down critically at the picture in the sketchbook.

"It's nice," Rennie said.

Holding the book at arm's length and squinting, Daphne began to smile to herself. She placed the book on the table again and turned toward Rennie, looking at her earnestly. Suddenly she pointed to Rennie, to the sketchbook, then to Rennie again, pleading with her eyes for some sign of understanding.

Was Daphne offering to *give* Rennie that picture? But the picture wasn't finished, and Rennie had to leave Firbank. She wondered whether she ought to tell Daphne. No. Oliver'd better take care of that.

Looking disappointed and frustrated, Daphne reached for a pencil and writing pad. Then, seeing that Rennie was getting up to go, she dropped the pencil and simply held out her hand. Rennie gave it a quick pat and hurried to the door. "I'm going down to the Vietnamese Forest, whatever that is," she told Daphne, relieved to have an out. "Oliver said I should come."

Rennie ran out the back door. She found herself between tulip beds, great masses of pink and yellow flowers. The air had a fragrance wholly unfamiliar to her. It smelled of pine, bayberry and other shrubs she couldn't name. She felt light and momentarily carefree as she found the path behind the red barn and followed it, wondering where it led. This evening she'd be back with Peter! But before she left, she wanted to ask Oliver what he meant about the sun being a morning star. And she must be sure to see Salt Pond, so she could tell her father about it.

Suddenly, Lion and Duffy came running at her, jumping up in a tumult of recognition. Oliver must be nearby. A few steps farther on, Rennie saw him in a group of men, digging around a tree.

"Serenity!" he called. "Come and meet these friends." When she reached them, he introduced her, and the men grinned and held out their earth-stained hands for her to shake. She was too confused to catch their names.

"This is a great day," Oliver exulted. "We think we've discovered the technique we've been searching for to make trees bloom again in Vietnam! Thee knows, the damage caused by American defoliation chemicals during the war is incredible. More than a third of the mangrove forests along the coast were destroyed and the inland forests were scarred extensively. If we've really succeeded in revitalizing soil, what a great day this is!"

The other men reflected Oliver's satisfaction.

"Come," he said, handing the shovel he was holding to one of them and taking Rennie's arm. "I want to show thee more of Firbank." Waving to his friends, he drew Rennie away.

"Is this what you call the Vietnamese Forest?" It was just woods.

Oliver laughed. "That's my private name for these acres," he explained. "When bombers began defoliating the trees of Vietnam, I was so distressed that I had to find a way to counteract the damage. A tree, Serenity, is as sacred, in its way, as a person. So I went over to the university to consult the forestry men. Thee knows, this is hardly the same climate as Vietnam's," Oliver admitted wryly, "but it's the only land I own. I learned from the foresters that here at home, where lethal doses of herbicides had been used as weed killers, the soil could be restored with activated charcoal. So I destroyed life in some old vegetable gardens we had here, then experimented with the charcoal and finally planted seedlings. I covered them in winter, even made smudge fires in the worst weather. Nursing these trees was pretty hard work. But now," he exclaimed jubilantly, "I *think* we may be on the track! It will have to be proved, of course. But I'm hopeful."

To Rennie his whole plan sounded impossible.

They were out of the woods now, and had come to a field dotted with boulders. This was the field she'd looked out on when she woke up. And there, at the bottom of the slope, lay Salt Pond. A dory was tied up at a small stone dock beside a boathouse.

"Oliver," she asked, "what was your grandmother like? You must remember even better than Daddy. He was wild about her."

"We all were. People sensed a special quality in her. When Daphne came here as a bride to a strange country, still haunted by the suffering she'd seen during the war, Grandmother did the most to make her feel at home."

"She had security, didn't she?"

"Does thee mean financial independence?"

"No. Was she sure—you know—of herself?"

"Yes, but I think she would have called it faith. It was a deep trust that there is something divine in every human being. Thee'll understand this better when thee sees her portrait. Daphne painted it shortly after we were married. I'll show it to thee when we go back." Oliver stopped and glanced at his watch. "Gracious! It's later than I thought. Daphne must be hungry, after working all morning. No doubt thee is, too."

This was it—the moment to tell Oliver she was leaving. But his next words took her breath away.

"Daphne would like to do thy portrait. Will thee sit for her?"

"My portrait? You must be kidding!"

"She's very anxious to do it. If thee would pose for her this afternoon, she thinks she can finish it in one sitting."

To have her portrait done by a real artist! But she had to leave. She couldn't go through another night in Heather's bed.

Oliver saw her hesitation and pleaded. "Do, Serenity. It would mean a lot to Daphne. She felt it the moment thee arrived. It was thy coloring at first, like Heather's; then at supper she found she was seeing beyond thy surface beauty to the woman unfolding in thee—its boundless promise. That's the beauty she wants to portray. She thought about it half the night. Thee reminds her of a leaf on the maple outside the woodshed. Was thee in there?"

"Yes."

"Then thee saw she's doing a sketch of those leaves, all new and tender, luminous against the sky. This is how she sees thee."

So that's what Daphne had been trying to show her!

"Thee's given Daphne an eagerness to draw she hasn't had in years," Oliver went on. "Not since she fell ill. Thee will sit for her, won't thee?"

How could she say no?

Oliver reached for her hand. "Thank thee," he said.

CHAPTER THREE

WHEN Rennie first saw her great-grandmother's portrait in Oliver's study, she was taken aback. She'd expected it to be like those massive pictures on the walls of the administration building at college—the dead deans and presidents, staring somberly down on the students. But Serenity's portrait was airily framed and smaller than those of the deans and presidents. The whole picture shimmered with light. Although her dress was an austere pale gray, it was made of some glowing material—silk or taffeta—and the fichu around her neck was so white one could almost feel the sun touching it. Sunshine lighted the whole background—the leafy, budding world of Firbank in spring. So it wasn't really surprising that, over her shoulder, Serenity should be carrying a jaunty pink parasol.

Serenity's face was different from what Rennie had expected, too. Yes, she had what Rennie called security, but it was a daring kind. It would risk trusting the unknown, and do what seemed right, without counting the cost. Despite, or perhaps because of, this cool courage, Serenity looked incredibly lighthearted. Daphne had caught her in the act of smiling at something close to the ground, not visible in the picture—a child, maybe, or a dog.

"Daphne's acceptance by leading American critics of the 1920s began with this portrait," Oliver was saying. "It was exhibited in New York, and commissions began pouring in. Her future was assured. Thee sees, up to that time the popular idea of an old person's portrait was something dark and solemn."

So Daphne had had a successful career. And this successful artist wanted to paint Rennie's picture—how fantastic!

When Oliver went off to prepare lunch, Rennie lingered, turning back to Serenity, seeking some rapport, like the conversations she used to have with the bride on the landing at home. But she was grown up now, and trained to look at pictures critically, not to walk through the canvas into the world of the subject.

Look at me, won't you? Rennie pleaded. I'm your namesake.

But Serenity showed no interest.

After lunch, while Daphne rested, Oliver brought the drawing board and a box of pastel crayons into the living room. The afternoon light was better here than in the woodshed, he explained.

"Heather sent those from England," he said, noticing Rennie's interest in Daphne's rainbow crayons. "Thee sees, they're square— easier to grip than her old round ones."

Rennie nodded. What changes in routine this illness demanded. "Shall I put on my skirt?" she asked Oliver.

"No need to," he assured her. "Daphne wants thee to feel comfortable—be thyself." He adjusted the position of Rennie's chair until it satisfied him. "She'd like thee to talk to her while she's drawing."

"Talk? What about?"

"Peter. Daphne wants to hear about him. She says ever since thee came I've monopolized the conversation. She insists thee hasn't had a chance to tell us anything about thyself or Peter." Oliver grinned.

"But how will I— How do *you* know what Daphne's saying?"

Oliver turned to the window and gazed out. "How can I tell?" He was silent a moment. Then he said, "We've loved each other, rejoiced together, endured pain, for well over fifty years. How can I help knowing what Daphne wants to say? And it's very important to listen to her, to make her truly believe that she's still the person she was before the stroke. For a time, the wonderful companion I'd known since she was nineteen seemed to have died. Another, less lovely, had taken her place."

Tears suddenly stung Rennie's eyes. To have the person you were married to change overnight, to go on loving that person, contending not only for her body but for her whole personality . . .

"Illness is devastating," Oliver was saying, "because it erects a barrier between the patient and the rest of the world, even those who care most. It requires that one concentrate on one's own needs instead of those of other people. For someone like Daphne, who'd been concerned with others all her life, this had a diminishing effect. She felt unworthy and depressed because the functioning of her limbs and speech became the focal point of her attention. Fortunately I was always able to reach her innermost self and hold on to it tightly till she emerged from those shadows."

"It's so cruel!" Rennie cried. "I mean—losing her speech and the use of her right hand, too. It isn't fair!"

"It does seem overmuch," Oliver agreed. "But that's the way the nervous system is hooked up. When the right side's paralyzed, it means the left part of the brain is affected. And that's where the speech center is located. At the time, I realized that the most important thing was to get Daphne painting again. As soon as her strength came back, we started training her left hand. Just holding the brush was agony. Sometimes it seemed all we had to work with was faith. Well," he said, turning to Rennie with an expression that was suddenly radiant, "all that's past now. Only the love that sustained us remains." He started toward the door. "Wait here, Serenity. I'm going to get Daphne."

Struck by another thought, Oliver came back and placed both hands on Rennie's shoulders. "Thy coming has meant a great deal to us," he said, smiling affectionately. "Thee knows, Heather's our only child and she lives in England. Married a Yorkshireman, Stephen Thirsk, who came here to study engineering in Cambridge and took her back with him. We find it hard, living so far apart. But her family always spends the summer with us. They'll be here July first. We can't wait."

Rennie suddenly remembered something she had wanted to ask. "Oliver, what did you mean in your note about the sun's being a star or something?"

Oliver's face lighted. "Those are the last words of Thoreau's *Walden*. Today is the anniversary of his death. That's what made Daphne and me think of it when we looked at the calendar this morning. More than a century later his glorious words are still vital. 'Only that day dawns to which we are awake. There is more day to dawn. The sun is but a morning star.'

"There's another reason we thought about those words," Oliver said a little reluctantly. "They express the way we see thee—more poised for flowering than thee thyself has any idea of."

DAPHNE was wearing the violet smock when she came into the living room on Oliver's arm, proceeding slowly, with a kind of majesty.

"Thee sees, Serenity," Oliver said, "this is how we walked into the meetinghouse at York the day we were married—arm in arm. Nowadays everything's less formal and couples are apt to come in hand in hand. It makes no difference."

Daphne turned and smiled at him. Her large gray eyes shone.

Rennie thought, That's how she looked at him that day. Why can't Peter and I . . .

She could see the moment Daphne was settled in her chair how excited she was about doing the portrait. Her cheeks were pink, and there was elation in the way she twisted the paper till she had it placed on the drawing board at an angle that pleased her.

Rennie, sitting down on her chair, was glad to discover that she had a view of the side lawn through the bay window. She'd have something to focus on during the long hours. "Be sure to remember everything Serenity tells thee, dear one," Oliver said as he was leaving, "so thee can tell me later. I want to hear about Peter, too." Then he was gone.

Forcing herself to do her part, fixing her attention on the lawn outside, Rennie took a deep breath. "His whole name," she began, "is Peter Hallburt Holland. He comes from a town in eastern Ohio called Charlesbury. It's about as opposite as you can get to Neville, where I live—suburban New York and sophisticated. Charlesbury is a small town, very conservative. So when Peter first got to college, he had sort of an identity crisis—he had to decide where he stood on a lot of issues—with the folks back home, whom he'd respected all his life, or with the kids at college, who were rebelling."

Rennie glanced at Daphne, wondering whether, back here in Firbank, she had any idea what Rennie was talking about.

"He almost quit college," she said, studying her own curled-up fingers while she spoke, as though she'd never seen them before. "Both his parents are schoolteachers and they'd been so proud of Peter. There isn't much money and they have two other kids to educate. They kept reminding Peter how he'd always wanted to be an astronomer. How could he just drop out? I guess it was pretty traumatic. But by the time we met, beginning of junior year, Peter had things under control. He even made dean's list last term. Then, when his parents objected to our getting married, he flunked his math exam."

Rennie looked at Daphne to see whether she understood. But Daphne was concentrating on the picture. Rennie had the feeling that she was talking to herself. It didn't matter what she said.

"It was funny, how we met," she went on, staring out the window, but visualizing the scene so vividly that she giggled. "We were in the school cafeteria. I was carrying my dinner tray to a table where these girls from my dorm were sitting. Well, somebody had spilled soup on the floor, and I didn't see it. I slid right across the room, tray and all. But instead of falling flat on my face, I landed in this strange guy's arms. He just happened to be there and he caught me. The whole cafeteria clapped. Peter was embarrassed. I guess he thought the way to cover it up was to do something smart, so he kissed me in front of the whole student body. He was full of the devil in those days," Rennie added wistfully. "Now he's turned awfully serious."

On the edge of her vision she could see Daphne looking at her. Was she interested in the story or was she concentrating on Rennie's features? Daphne had captured the character of Serenity Otis. How much of Rennie's secret self would this portrait show? She wasn't so sure that she liked having her portrait done, after all.

"I never did get to eat with those girls," Rennie concluded, trying to keep her mind from wandering. It was hard, sitting still in the same pose so long.

This time Rennie was sure Daphne was following the story. What happened next? the steady regard asked plainly.

Why had Rennie started to tell this? She couldn't go on.

What happened next? Daphne's gaze repeated.

We went to his room, Rennie answered, not out loud, just to herself, eyes fixed on the lawn. . . . Daphne was staring at her intently. Rennie's heart started to pound. She couldn't sit here another minute. She had to get up, run outdoors. Too bad about the portrait—she was already running as fast as she could from Daphne's eyes, even though her muscles wouldn't move. She had gripped the arms of the chair and she couldn't let go. She leaned forward tensely, but her fingers only clutched the arms more and more tightly. Burning tears spilled down her cheeks.

Daphne turned her eyes from Rennie and dropped the crayon she was holding into its box. She slammed down the lid and began rubbing her fingers on a rag. Her face was white.

"No!" Rennie suddenly cried out at the top of her voice. "I'm not going to tell you! As long as nobody got hurt—" This was one of those nightmares, when she kept calling for help.

Daphne's head fell back against the chair. Her eyes were shut.

Trembling, Rennie jumped up. Was Daphne having another stroke? She stood looking down at the motionless figure, the white face. What should she do?

She didn't notice Oliver rush into the room until, pushing her aside, he took hold of Daphne's good hand. "Dear one," he said, his voice confirming Rennie's anxiety.

Daphne opened her eyes and smiled. She was still white.

"Thee's done too much for one day," Oliver told her, sounding

relieved. "It's tired thee. Come." He drew her slowly to her feet, glancing over his shoulder to reassure Rennie. "Supper's nearly ready," he said. "I was just putting the kettle on." He helped Daphne across the room. "Thee'll have a tray, all cozy in bed."

Terribly shaken, Rennie watched them leave. As they reached the entrance hall, Daphne stood still and looked back. She detached her arm from Oliver's and held it out toward Rennie.

"Please come, Serenity," Oliver said. "Daphne would like to tell thee something."

Hesitantly, Rennie went toward her. The elation Daphne had expressed when she started the portrait glowed in her again. She reached out and, drawing Rennie to her, gave her a kiss.

THE next morning Rennie woke to a day of bright sunshine. Pulling Heather's quilt around her, she went to the window and knelt by it, trying to imprint the view on her memory.

It didn't register. She was thinking of the portrait—how, when Daphne and Oliver started upstairs yesterday afternoon, she'd run back to the drawing board, impatient to see her picture. But she'd stopped in her tracks, not daring to look. Those troubled feelings that had broken out—mightn't they show, give her away? She'd forced herself to face the portrait.

At first she couldn't take it in. There she was, exactly the way she thought she looked, in the aqua turtleneck and tan shorts, sitting on the chair, staring out the window. There was a simplicity about the whole thing, an ambience, as if she belonged to the room. But the eyes—minutes went by before Rennie grasped what they conveyed. Then she was shattered. She'd been braced to find them clouded by conflict. It was much worse! They were neutral, devoid of emotion, empty. Am I like that? Really?

Hearing Oliver come downstairs, Rennie had run out to the hall and asked anxiously, "Is Daphne sick?"

"Just tired. A night's rest will restore her."

"What happened?"

"She says thee ran away."

"I didn't! I wanted to, but I stayed right there."

"Thy body did. That was no use to Daphne, who was trying to portray thy spirit. It had fled. She said it wearied her, looking at an empty body, so she just closed her eyes." As Rennie followed him into the kitchen, Oliver exclaimed, "I'm so relieved! It's good thee called and that I was here."

Rennie couldn't get herself to admit that she'd lost her cool, but she did try to tell Oliver she hadn't called him. He had merely murmured offhandedly, "Oh? I thought thee did."

He knew very well, Rennie told Salt Pond now. He was only trying to make me comfortable, like Daphne when she kissed me.

Later, while they were eating supper, Rennie'd asked how Oliver and Daphne had met.

During an air raid in Paris, he'd told her, toward the end of the First World War. "We were both in the Anglo-American Friends Mission," he explained, "and Daphne happened to be in Paris, on leave from her volunteer job at a hospital in the Marne valley." He himself, after being court-martialed at home for refusing to bear arms, had been allowed to sail for France, where he'd helped to rebuild houses and replant trees in the Verdun area.

After supper Oliver had taken Rennie into the woodshed and shown her some portfolios of Daphne's drawings and paintings, beginning with the botanical plates she'd made as an art student, then examples of what he called her unfolding period, and finally the mature work, done in her free, unique style.

"When she recovered enough from her stroke to start painting again, she was helped by the example of Auguste Renoir," Oliver explained. "In his last years he was so crippled by arthritis that he couldn't use his right hand. Yet, in this period, he painted some of his finest canvases."

"I know! *The Bathers.*"

Oliver had glanced at Rennie approvingly, pleased that she was up on Renoir. "After the armistice Daphne was transferred to Savoy, near the Swiss border, where another Quaker team was helping to repatriate prisoners—undernourished Frenchmen going home to die, many of them on stretchers, or insane. It was a satisfaction to Daphne to give them a little comfort as their convoy passed through—a bowl of soup extended with that smile of hers. But it was such heartbreaking work that every night she had to draw to preserve her equilibrium. Those charcoal sketches in the living room—has thee noticed them?"

Rennie nodded.

"Horrible, aren't they? Those were the types Daphne saw in the convoys. It still hurts me to look at them."

"Me, too."

Rennie shivered, kneeling by the window, remembering last night. Gathering the quilt around her more closely, she wondered whether she'd been too fresh when she asked Oliver why he'd chosen farming instead of a more prestigious career. He hadn't answered immediately.

Returning some drawings to their portfolio and tying the tapes that held the cover, Oliver had said finally, "Daphne and I made a pilgrimage. It was a couple of months after we were married."

"A pilgrimage?"

"Yes. All we thought we were doing was traveling south in Grandmother's Model T. It turned out to be a great deal more." The recollection drained expression from Oliver's face; then he smiled at Rennie. "Because of the war, I'd been obliged to leave college in my junior year. After I got back from France, I returned to Harvard and graduated with the class of 1920, hoping to go into publishing. Conscientious objectors weren't getting the best jobs, and all I could land was some publicity work for a jewelry firm. Thee can imagine that with my bringing-up, this job—to encourage ostentation—was the least appropriate. But it paid well enough. It wasn't to start till the first of the year, so, in high spirits, I left for England and married Daphne. A few weeks later we came to Firbank. Grandmother had invited us to stay till we got a home of our own."

Oliver had turned to the window, though nothing was visible out there in the dark. "Daphne and I were deeply happy," he murmured, "and yet we were troubled, too. We'd seen such suffering during the war that we wondered whether we had a right to be so happy. And we were anxious about our future," he added, facing her again. "We believed in ourselves and each other, but we still had to prove our worth."

"You were lucky! You had a job. Peter—"

Oliver didn't seem to hear Rennie. "Daphne had a cough she couldn't shake. At the end of October, Grandmother urged us to go south for a few weeks. She offered to lend us her car, and suggested we stop at the Woolman House in Mount Holly when we got to New Jersey."

"What's the Woolman House?"

"John Woolman was a Quaker minister and writer from New Jersey who went about the American colonies in the eighteenth century, appealing to slaveholders to realize their humanity," Oliver explained. "He built the Mount Holly house for his daughter when she married, shortly before the Revolution. Daphne and I did go there, merely because it was a charming and inexpensive place to spend the night. But the next morning, when we woke up in our snug room under the eaves, I noticed a bookcase next to our bed. Inside were early editions of Woolman's works. I reached out for a volume, only to glance through it. Opening his *Journal*, I read the first sentence aloud: 'I have often felt a motion of love to leave some hints in writing of my experience of the goodness of God, and now, in the thirty-sixth year of my age, I begin this work.'"

Oliver paused, studying Rennie's face. "Thee sees," he said, "Woolman was talking about the goodness of God to Daphne and me, who'd seen so much evil during the war that we couldn't quite believe in that goodness."

He got up from the table. "Wait," he told her. "I want to show thee something." He went to his study and came back with a book that was bound in worn leather, splitting along the spine. Opening it carefully, he held it out to Rennie. *The Works of John Woolman,* she read, taking the book. At the bottom of the title page was a date: 1775.

"That's the house in Mount Holly," Oliver told her as she glanced at a picture in the front. "Daphne painted it that morning. When we got back, she gave the little watercolor to Grandmother, who pasted it into her own copy of Woolman."

177

Closing the book reverently, Rennie handed it back.

Oliver ran his fingers lovingly over the worn leather. "As I read on, I came to Woolman's account of his conflict between a business career and his beliefs. He had been apprenticed as a young man in a shop. One day he was asked to draw up a bill of sale for a black woman slave. He was disturbed at having to write an instrument of slavery for a human being and soon left the job to travel through the South speaking against slavery."

As Oliver caressed the book, he continued, "Downstairs at the Woolman House, I'd found some modern reprints of his *Journal* and *Essays* for sale. I put down the money and slipped our first copy of Woolman into the knapsack. After breakfast Daphne and I sat in the flower garden. While she painted this little picture of the house, I read her Woolman's account of his first southern journey. He appealed to the planters to consider what slavery was doing to their children—that it might lead to war. Daphne and I were deeply concerned about racial justice, too. We turned to each other and said at the same moment, 'Let's follow him.' We consulted the *Journal* for his route. We weren't aware of it, but that was the beginning of our pilgrimage."

Recalling last night, Rennie had forgotten the time. The grandfather clock in the hall informed her softly that it was eight. Oliver had asked her to be down by then. She flung the quilt on the bed and began to dress. While she combed her hair, she studied the face in the mirror, wondering what reflection Heather had seen when she stood here. What was she like inside, then? A mess, too? No, not with parents like that. Rennie envied her.

Daphne and Oliver were waiting for her at the kitchen table. Daphne looked better. Color was back in her cheeks, and she was wearing a soft blue shift which brought out the beauty of her hair. Oliver had on a white shirt, complete with tie. They took Rennie's hands again and bowed their heads. Once again this unfamiliar interlude eased her.

When they'd finished eating, Oliver helped Daphne to her feet. Taking his arm, she walked with him into the woodshed. In a few minutes he returned, only to disappear down into the cellar.

He came up with a bushel basket of apples. "The last of the crop," he announced, puffing. "We'll take them to Kendal for the fellowship meal after Meeting. Everyone brings something."

Meeting! It hadn't occurred to Rennie when she decided impulsively to come to Firbank that Friends Meeting would be part of the visit. "What time does thy plane leave?" Oliver was asking.

"Three ten."

He nodded. "Take thy belongings to the meetinghouse. Thee'll be going directly from there. But before we leave, Daphne would like to work on thy portrait again."

"I thought it was finished!"

Oliver looked at Rennie gravely. "Has thee seen it? Daphne doesn't want thee to till it's finished."

"I didn't know I wasn't supposed to. You never said."

Oliver nodded. "We *were* a bit upset last evening. It doesn't matter, unless thee's disappointed."

"Is that really how I look?"

"With expressionless eyes?" He laughed. "That's why Daphne needs thee to pose again—so she can put thy spirit into the eyes. It eluded her yesterday." Taking Rennie's hand, he said softly, "Thee needn't be afraid of Daphne. She's seeing way beyond thy present confusion to the person she believes will emerge. Thee may not like the finished portrait; either. To become the person Daphne sees will make demands thee may not care to accept. But, if not for thy sake, Serenity, do this for Daphne and me. Last night I studied the portrait a long time and I think thee is inspiring her to do something lasting."

"Do I—have to talk about Peter?"

"No. Speak or not, as thee feels moved. Do come," he pleaded. He drew her gently toward the back hall.

DAPHNE didn't look up when Rennie came into the woodshed. Oliver placed Rennie's chair so that she looked straight out, over Daphne's head, into the maple tree beyond the glass.

Light filtered through layers of leaves, just the way it had yesterday, only then the air was still. This morning a breeze tugged at the leaves, and as the patterns of light shifted and tumbled, Rennie had a flash of understanding. If this was how she appeared to Daphne, it must be that when Daphne looked right through her she didn't see the ugly fears and frustrations inside. Or, if she did, she disregarded them. With the heightened perception Oliver spoke of, Daphne had simply watched light from some outside source—what source?—shine through Rennie.

Daphne was studying a pastel crayon, rejecting it, choosing another. Because Rennie was facing the light, Daphne's features seemed blurred. That made it possible to imagine how she had looked in her twenties when she and Oliver began their pilgrimage.

As they'd traveled south, Oliver had told Rennie last night, they'd seen people working in the fields. "It seemed to us that, for the poor, conditions weren't much better than in Woolman's time," he said sadly. "All the way home we talked about the poverty we'd seen. Just before we crossed the Connecticut River, we stopped to picnic. While we ate, I read to Daphne from Woolman's *A Plea for the Poor:* 'To turn all the treasures we possess into the channel of universal love becomes the business of our lives.' All the treasures —*all*. Was this the business of our lives, Daphne's and mine? What had it to do with the jewelry business?"

It was Daphne who'd come up with the answer. "Why can't we stay at Firbank?" she had demanded. "Thee can run the farm. It's too much for Grandmother now, and she's worried about what will become of it after she's gone."

"Me? Farm?" Oliver had cried. "Farming's the last thing I've ever thought of doing." He had reminded Daphne that farmers lead a hard life; that he wanted her to have every comfort.

"I want thee to be happy," she'd retorted. "And thee's not going to be, competing in the business world. I'm a countrywoman. Farming doesn't frighten me. I'll paint, too."

As Oliver described this scene, the lightheartedness that had impressed Rennie when she first saw him returned. "Ever since that morning in Mount Holly," he confided, "Woolman had struggled with me. For weeks I managed to resist him. But I couldn't resist Daphne. I felt so eager to break the news to Grandmother that I threw everything into the car and raced home—at twenty-nine miles an hour! When we got to Firbank and told Grandmother, she smiled, as if she'd known all along this would happen. She'd never said a word about that job, but it didn't please her."

Rennie was so absorbed in her thoughts that she forgot she was posing for a portrait. Suddenly she felt rather than saw Daphne staring into her eyes.

"You know," Rennie told her, "to love the way you and Oliver do, one first has to have security in oneself, and one can't have security unless one loves that way. How does one break into that circle?" The moment the words were out of her mouth, Rennie regretted them. She'd asked a question, forgetting that Daphne couldn't speak. Rennie would have to give the answer herself.

"I guess—well—to begin with, I always thought love just happened. But, like Oliver said, one has to work at it. But you and Oliver can't understand how hard it is. You don't need to work at loving. With so much love, you can afford to share it, let it spill over onto other people. I—"

Turning her head, Rennie saw that Oliver was standing in the back hall, looking in. "Time to leave," he announced, as if he were sorry to interrupt. "We don't like getting to Meeting late," he told her. "It disturbs the Friends who've already begun to center down. Are thy belongings packed?"

"No. I'll run upstairs." Standing up, Rennie didn't dare look in the direction of the portrait. As she walked to the door, Oliver came in to help Daphne out of her chair. But Daphne waved him aside, reaching toward Rennie. Oliver understood.

"Serenity, Daphne would like thee to see the portrait. She may alter a little something later, but it's essentially finished."

Rennie, standing in the doorway, felt rooted to the spot. She couldn't face those eyes in the portrait. Yet she had to. Daphne was still holding out her hand.

Oliver gave Rennie an understanding glance. "It's humbling," he acknowledged, "to see oneself as someone else does. Thee knows, dear one," he exclaimed, turning to Daphne, "there's a marked resemblance to Grandmother! I hadn't seen it till this instant."

Rennie leaped forward and looked. The eyes were alive! This was a real person, a happy one, who really did have her great-grandmother's expression—lighthearted, trusting, courageous. But, except for the turtleneck and shorts, the shape and coloring of the features, it was another person—not Rennie Ross.

Oliver had helped Daphne to stand. "Come," he said, drawing them both toward the back hall. Feeling Rennie's reluctance to part from the portrait, he added, "On thy next visit, thee can study it longer. And someday, when thee comes to Firbank, thee'll suddenly find it's a true likeness."

Rennie didn't really know what happened after that. She must have gone upstairs and gotten her stuff. She remembered coming out of the house and finding the pickup in the driveway. Daphne was already sitting in the cab.

Oliver had let down the tailgate of the truck. "Does thee mind sitting on the floor?" he asked Rennie.

Rennie didn't mind. She climbed up and sat with her back against the cab. All she wanted was a last look at the house.

Fastening the tailgate, Oliver leaned toward Rennie for a moment. "Grandmother left Firbank to all her descendants," he told her. "I happened to be the only one who was willing to farm. But wherever thee settles with Peter, remember that Firbank's thine, too, waiting for thee to come home to, anytime."

BOUNCING along toward Kendal in the back of the truck, Rennie finally saw the ocean. It was breaking in slow ripples on the beach at the foot of a seawall. Those graceful birds, circling and diving over the water, that she'd taken for gulls, were terns, Oliver explained, shouting back to her from the cab.

The road left the shore and turned inland. From the town line on, it paralleled the Kendal River, running between a steep, grassy bank and houses that looked old and dignified, set wide apart on lawns shaded by huge trees. Finally the truck turned into a crescent-shaped street. "Here we are!" Oliver called to Rennie.

It can't be, Rennie thought—that little building without a steeple, those ordinary windows—is *that* the meetinghouse?

Plain clapboard, joined to the earth by a thick green hedge, Kendal Meetinghouse was the color of Great-grandmother Serenity's dress in the portrait—pale gray, austere, yet, like the dress, it glowed with sunshine. Children were running about the yard. The older people talked and laughed. Rennie recognized Mary Young and the two women who'd come in with food.

Beside the drive, two men stood with a wicker armchair. Oliver stopped the truck. "Sam! Jorim!" he exclaimed in greeting. "That's Serenity Ross in back. You met her yesterday at Firbank."

The men grinned at Rennie. Then they helped Daphne out of the cab. Lifting her into the chair, like experts, they carried her between them down the walk, up three stone steps and through a wide-open door. Oliver drove on to park behind the meetinghouse.

As Rennie walked up the drive with him, she stopped, panicked. "What do you— What am I supposed to do in Meeting?"

"Listen."

"But you said there was just silence."

Oliver smiled. "Yes, mostly we simply listen for God's presence, wait for guidance. Then a Friend who has a fresh insight may feel moved to share his or her thoughts. Thee'll find the strangeness wears off. Thee may even find the silence comforting."

To Rennie it seemed only terrifying. How could she listen for some presence when she didn't even know what it was?

Two little girls were running toward her—Nancy and Sandy, who'd swabbed the kitchen floor yesterday. They came alongside and tugged at Rennie's hands. "Sit with us," they begged.

Oliver glanced at Rennie. Sensing that she preferred to stay with him, he told the girls, "If Serenity sits with you, she'll be left alone on the facing bench when you go out for First-day school. Why don't you invite her to sit between you at lunch, instead?"

"Will you?" Nancy pleaded. Not waiting for an answer, she let go of Rennie and ran off. "See you then," she called back.

At the door of the meetinghouse, Oliver stood aside to let Rennie walk in ahead of him. They entered a vestibule lined with books. Beside the coatrack, Daphne's wicker armchair waited for her. Oliver dropped Rennie's book bag on the chair and took her into the quietest room she'd ever been in. It was bare. Nothing but benches—not an altar, a lectern, not even a bunch of flowers. The sun, streaming through the tall, clear windows, illuminated the features of the still worshippers. There was a kind of vacancy about their gaze, as if their souls had left their bodies. How different from the animated scene outside, moments ago.

Oliver led Rennie to the bench where Daphne was sitting. She gave them a welcoming glance, then returned to her meditation.

The bench was hard, not just the seat. The back stabbed Rennie between the shoulder blades. Stop wriggling, she told herself. This was supposed to be a solemn occasion. She tried to focus on that. Wasn't this what Oliver meant by centering down?

So this was what a Friends meetinghouse looked like on the inside. Her father would never agree to holding the wedding in such an undistinguished little place. She herself—would she want to walk down this short, gray-carpeted aisle with Peter, stand before the Meeting and promise, with divine assistance—what did that mean?—to be loving and faithful as long as nobody got hurt? No! Those weren't the right words. They were what kids at school said about sex outside of marriage—it was okay as long as nobody got hurt. The Quaker marriage promise was: as long as we both shall live.

How could anyone make that promise in absolute sincerity? Even if one meant it at the time, how could one know what would happen later? Right now she and Peter were loving and faithful without having promised anything, and nobody was hurt.

Is nobody hurt? she wondered suddenly, startled by the possibility. What a crazy idea! She and Peter were both okay.

Against the silence the question kept echoing, Is nobody hurt? It was roaring now so that Rennie wanted to stick her fingers in her ears to keep out the sound, *Is nobody hurt?*

But the sound was inside her head. She tried to confront it, argue it away, only she seemed to have lost the power to reason. A part of herself had taken off, drifted away on the silence, calling plainly to her as it receded, Is nobody hurt?

All that remained, she saw with a jolt, were the roles she played:

the teacher-to-be, who professed an interest in kids she didn't possess; the bride-to-be, about to walk down the aisle of a church—any church—a bride dressed in white, signifying a virginity she didn't possess. Is nobody hurt?

There was a small rustle, and looking up, Rennie found that the children were stepping down from the facing benches—a low gallery at the front of the room—and filing out. Nancy and Sandy winked at her as they went by. Rennie considered slipping out, too. But something held her back—she mustn't run away, leaving part of herself out there in the silence.

Suddenly a man's voice broke into her thoughts. He was just behind her, evidently standing, because she could feel a slight tremor as his hands gripped the back of her bench.

"In our family reading this morning," he said, without raising his voice, as though he were speaking only to Rennie, "we came across two quotations that are strikingly similar. They've stuck in my mind during Meeting. The first was written by a Friend in 1760; the other by a Jew who died in the 1960s."

Rennie heard the pages of a book being turned. Then the man said, "This is what John Woolman wrote: 'There is a principle which is pure, placed in the human mind, which in different places and ages hath had different names. It is, however, pure and proceeds from God. It is deep and inward, confined to no forms of religion nor excluded from any, where the heart stands in perfect sincerity.'" The speaker paused. At last he said, "And here are the words of Martin Buber: 'Everyone has in him something precious that is in no one else. This precious something in a man is revealed to him if he truly perceives his strongest feeling, his central wish, that in him which stirs his inmost being.'"

The speaker began to discuss these quotations. Rennie stopped listening. She was trying to hold on to the words. "Where the heart stands in perfect sincerity." She'd heard that before. Yes, Oliver had quoted it when he explained why she and Peter couldn't just walk into a Friends meetinghouse and be married. And what was the other? Something precious that's in no one else?

That's what Peter wants—the precious thing that's only in me.

Wistfully she thought, If we were starting now, if we were meeting tonight for the first time, things would be different.

How?

I'd listen, for one thing. I'd listen to Peter—not just to what he says, but to what he feels.

"It's the bride's family that decides about the wedding," he had said when she told him of her parents' plans for the reception. She'd heard the note of bitter resignation in his voice. As long as he hadn't protested, she'd disregarded it. Peter's parents care about him, too. Why shouldn't they have some say?

If we were starting now— But we're not.

Make a wish, she thought then, a *central* wish. She squeezed her eyes shut the way she used to do as a child when she saw the first star in the evening sky. What should she wish for? She wanted so much—serenity, mostly. But didn't serenity spring from something deeper? What was that precious something?

Suddenly, Rennie jumped. Someone had touched her hand.

Opening her eyes swiftly, she saw that Oliver was sending her a message with his handshake, his look telling her how happy he was to have her there.

And Rennie *was* there. Her fragments had come back together. For better or worse, the self that drifted off on the silence was once more joined to the rest of her.

All around the room people were shaking hands.

As Oliver let go, Rennie turned to Daphne. Reaching out, she took the paralyzed hand in her own and gently pressed it.

CHAPTER FOUR

HE HAD said he couldn't come to the airport to meet her, but there he was, waiting. Although eagerness shone in his face, Peter didn't kiss Rennie. He simply grabbed her hand and drew her toward the exit. "Have you got the address of a church?"

"No. A Quaker marriage is out. Their procedure is complicated. Takes months—committees on clearness and stuff. We wouldn't want it."

"That's okay with me," Peter said. "I only went along with the idea because you seemed to have your heart set on it. What's Oliver like? Was he nice to you?"

"Was he ever! Peter, wait till you see Firbank. It's the greatest. And you know something? It belongs to *me*, too! I can go back there anytime. I bet even Daddy doesn't know that."

"You have to phone him. He was trying to reach you all weekend. Called me, finally. Was he uptight!"

"What about?"

"Thought you'd gone off for the weekend with me."

Rennie giggled. "Did you tell him it was just Oliver?"

"Yes. That's when he really exploded. 'Pete,' he shouted, 'you don't mean Rennie would go to *Firbank* without *telling* me?'"

Rennie could just hear her father. "I should have phoned home Friday," she admitted. "I'll do it before supper. Peter, could we spend a little while in Firbank this summer? It wouldn't cost anything, and you'd hit it off with Oliver."

Peter's face clouded. "Depends on the job situation."

"Any nibbles?" At once Rennie was sorry she'd asked. She knew without being told that nothing had changed.

"You were sweet to come for me," she said when they were in the car Peter had borrowed. "It's just like Oliver meeting me at Hillsgrove. He told me to take the bus. Remember? Instead he came himself. Mary Young had happened to drop in. Well, I think she planned it so Oliver could leave Daphne."

But Peter knew nothing about Daphne or Mary Young, or that Austin and Judy, Mary's son and daughter-in-law, had driven Rennie to the airport after the fellowship meal—at long tables with checked cloths, heaped with food.

"Start at the beginning," he urged. "Oliver met you and—"

Rennie suddenly felt terribly tired. She rested her head on Peter's shoulder. Impatient as she'd been to tell him everything, she didn't know how to begin. It was going to take more effort to convey the deep meaning of Firbank, the love she'd seen in Oliver and Daphne, than she could put forth at this moment.

"Daphne made this little watercolor of the leaves outside the woodshed window," she began. "Daphne's a marvelous painter, though she's had a stroke. The picture shows how I look to her, full of promise." Rennie glanced at Peter, hoping he wouldn't laugh. The words that had seemed wonderful and exciting when Oliver spoke them sounded corny now. Peter didn't laugh.

"It's like the portrait. Oh, I haven't told you the most important part—I had my *portrait* done, Peter. By a real artist!"

This wasn't starting at the beginning. But Rennie felt certain that if she could just describe Daphne's pictures, Peter'd grasp something of what she'd experienced. Or if, when they reached college, they'd . . . That way, there'd be no need for words.

This morning, in the woodshed, while Daphne studied the expression of her eyes—her spirit, Oliver called it—Rennie had realized that there was more to love than making it with someone. She still thought so, but even as she repeated silently what she'd said about having to work at loving, all Rennie could *feel* was her need to love in the same old way.

Imagining the relief of being with Peter again, Rennie felt a rude jolt when the car stopped and she found that they'd already arrived at her dorm. The happiness that had filled her when she landed turned to such furious pain that she started to cry.

Peter reached for Rennie. "What's wrong?" he asked as sobs began to shake her. "I thought you had a good time."

"I did. It's just—I don't know. I hurt. I loved it there," she managed to say. "They loved me. Everything's different here. I liked myself better at Firbank."

Struggling to pull herself together, Rennie looked at the girls sitting on the steps of the dorm. How can I walk past them? she wondered. My face must be all streaked and swollen.

Peter rubbed his check against her curls. "You're being romantic. You were only in Firbank as a visitor. If you had to stay there and work, you'd feel about it the way you do about Tilbury."

Rennie shook her head. Peter couldn't understand.

But he did! Stroking her arm, he said, "Let me take you over to my place first. Wash your face before you have to talk to all those girls. You can phone your father from the men's dorm."

When they got to Peter's room, he wet his washcloth and dabbed her face. "There," he said. "Now go call home."

"Not now." Looking around, Rennie observed, "The room's just the same. Nothing's changed."

Peter laughed. "You were only gone two days."

"A lot might have happened," Rennie said, remembering that girl in his math class who always tried to get him to notice her.

She sat down on the bed. She was in her world again. Peter sat down beside her and took her in his arms, almost crushing her, though she could feel restraint in him, too. Her heart raced. She closed her eyes, abandoning everything, all her selves, to Peter. If he wants to, I'll forget the whole thing. Firbank. All that.

Letting go, Peter stood up.

Rennie's eyes flew open. A sigh escaped her. She didn't know whether she was relieved or disappointed.

HER father must have been sitting by the phone, waiting for her call, because he answered on the first ring. "Honey," he cried, "I've been trying all weekend to get through to you. Did you *really* go to *Firbank?* Why didn't you say something? I'd have driven you over. You know how nervous Mother is about flying."

"That's why I didn't tell you—so she wouldn't worry."

"To think of your going to see Oliver behind my back!"

"Daddy!" Rennie cried, appalled. "I didn't dream you'd feel that way. I just wanted to find out how Quakers get married, and you said Oliver was the only one you knew. So I went to ask him about the procedure. I guess it isn't really the kind of marriage we want."

"Of course not. I told you that."

"But it was nice there, Daddy. And wait till you hear—Daphne drew my portrait!"

"That's her name—Daphne! A beautiful woman."

"Except," Rennie said, dreading the effect on her father, "she's had a stroke."

"She has? Too bad."

"It's so awful. You should see her—"

"Tell me about it when you come home. This is a toll call and I have important news—your wedding. It's settled! June twenty-first. West Neville United Church. Isn't that wonderful? No need for any more shopping around. We've got it all arranged."

"*You've* got it—I thought Peter and I—"

"Yes, honey, I know. But the time kept getting shorter and shorter and you couldn't make up your minds, so your mother and I simply had to take matters into our own hands."

"We don't know a soul who belongs to that church, do we, Daddy? And how can Peter and I be married by a total stranger?"

"That's what I'm getting at. If you'd only *listen* to me! Dr. Mifflin—that's the minister at United—makes a practice of interviewing couples three or four times before the wedding. He wants you and Pete to go and see him this Saturday at three p.m. sharp. Please don't be late. He's a busy man."

"*He's* busy! Peter and I have *exams!* Peter wasn't planning to be in Neville till the wedding. His folks want him home. This'll be the last time."

"I told Mifflin it's a tough moment for you children, but he seemed adamant. Oh, I haven't told you about our piece of luck. The steward of the country club's agreed to squeeze in your reception, although he has two other weddings that afternoon."

Rennie tried to imagine Peter on the receiving line, shaking hundreds of hands, smiling politely at all those strange faces.

"You don't appreciate how lucky we are," her father was saying.

"I'll see how Peter feels about it," she promised.

At that, Rennie's father blew up. "Too late now for a lot of discussion. Everything's settled and I don't want any further arguments. We've had enough shilly-shallying. Your mother's worried to death about getting everything done on such short notice—the invitations, the gown, the bridesmaids' dresses."

It's Peter's wedding, too, Rennie started to say, but her father sounded as if he couldn't take much more. She suddenly felt sorry for him. He'd been so elated about fixing up his only daughter's wedding in the style he'd always dreamed of.

"Thanks, Daddy," she made herself say.

By the time Rennie got back to Peter's room the cafeteria had closed, so they went for hamburgers at a place they called The Grease Spot. It wasn't a festive meal. Brine from the pickle oozed across the paper plate in front of her. Before starting on the hamburger, Rennie wanted to reach out and take Peter's hands, the way Oliver and Daphne took hers when they bowed their heads. But, of course, she couldn't. How was Peter to understand? Rennie didn't herself. She only knew that as she sat at the polished kitchen table with Oliver and Daphne, joined in the circle of their love, she felt happy.

Now she felt depressed. So, obviously, did Peter. He said very little when she reported her conversation with her father. It was the way he looked that made Rennie desperate. Surprisingly, the only thing that didn't upset him was the minister's insistence on interviews.

"Getting there's going to be a problem," he said. "But speaking to that minister's our only chance to find out what his church stands for. I'm not going to be married in a church I know nothing about. Suppose we're expected to say things we don't believe."

"I don't even know what I believe. Do you?"

"Maybe not altogether. But I sure know what I don't."

"You think the minister is just going to talk to us about religion?" Rennie cried. "Maybe that's all the committee on clearness was going to do. I was afraid they were going to ask personal questions. That's why I gave up on a Quaker marriage. Peter, you really would have gone for some of the things Oliver said."

"Like what?"

"He talked a lot about truth. Something more than honesty, sort of like God. And he was always quoting, but not showing off. Bits from books are simply part of his conversation. The first night he said something about a principle that belongs to all religions. No one church has a monopoly on it. Men of all nations who cultivate it become brothers."

"Rennie, how great! Tell me more."

So Rennie told Peter about the Vietnamese Forest and the Salt Pond and the dunes. It was harder when she tried to communicate the outpouring of Daphne and Oliver's love. Even if she had found the words, it wasn't the moment. The mood Peter was in, speaking of love would only make matters worse.

"Hasn't he any faults?" Peter asked suddenly.

"Oliver? Oh, I guess so. He's terribly pernickety. The beds are always made. And he polishes the kitchen table so hard you can see yourself in it."

"That Vietnamese Forest idea doesn't sound too good."

"No. Judy Young called it quixotic. Austin, her husband, is a potato farmer, so I guess she knows what she's talking about. Still, faults wouldn't take away from Oliver's wonderful simplicity, would they? I mean, little faults?"

"You're sure hooked," Peter said, laughing at her.

"I wish you had come. Then you'd understand." But it wouldn't have been the same, Rennie had to acknowledge to herself.

Why? Until now she'd always clung to Peter, afraid of losing him. Was going to Firbank for her what those long walks were to him? Did he and she have to be whole persons separately as well as joined? Wasn't that a contradiction? It couldn't be, could it, that Oliver's views on life would come between them now? The thought that she might have to give up all that Firbank had become to her, or lose Peter, made her hurt again.

Peter was standing up, pulling her to her feet. "Come on," he said, "better get to bed early. You look bushed."

"I—am," Rennie answered shakily.

Back in her room, she shook the contents of her book bag out on her desk. On top of the pile of books was something that didn't belong to her—a package done up in corrugated paper.

Rennie fumbled with the wrappings. Her great-grandmother's copy of Woolman! That's what she was holding! The book opened at the flyleaf. In the upper corner was Serenity Millburn's name. Under it Oliver had added: "For our cousin, Serenity the Second, whose coming has brought great joy to Daphne and Oliver."

Rennie gasped. They were giving her their treasure! Oliver must have slipped the surprise into her book bag secretly. Daphne had signed her name. Rennie knew what effort went into shaping those six letters.

She flopped across the bed to look at the book. Turning the pages, she came to the words Oliver had read to Daphne as they lay in the little room under the eaves. "I have often felt a motion of love . . ."

ALL three of Rennie's sisters-in-law telephoned Monday morning, one after the other—Jane, then Matty, then Victoria—to talk end-lessly about the bridesmaids' dresses. Rennie decided to get out of the room fast, before her mother called, too. She dressed hurriedly, dropped off some books at the library, then sat through a confer-ence with her adviser. It was not until after lunch that she and Peter could spend an hour in the college garden, lying on their stomachs under a tree, looking at Serenity's book.

"It must be worth a fortune," Peter observed when he saw the date on the title page.

Rennie drew his attention to the watercolor, explaining why the house in Mount Holly had so much significance. "We could go there ourselves sometime," she said timidly.

Peter began the first chapter. Rennie hoped he wouldn't be put off by that bit about the goodness of God. But he was way past that now.

Suddenly he stopped reading. Some folded sheets of paper had fallen out of the book. They looked very old. Rennie noticed how carefully Peter spread them open.

"Great-grandmother must have written that," she told him. "See? It's the same handwriting as in her name on the flyleaf."

But Peter didn't turn to the front of the book. He was reading the top sheet aloud: Woolman's *A Plea for the Poor,* which had jolted Oliver. " 'To turn all the treasures we possess into the chan-nel of universal love becomes the business of our lives. . . . The business of our lives,' " Peter repeated. "I want to remember that. This guy's real."

On Thursday, Rennie's father telephoned to say that Dr. Mifflin was obliged to cancel the appointment for Saturday because of a funeral.

"Peter finally managed to borrow a car," Rennie wailed.

"That's all right. You have to come home anyhow to choose your gown. Bring Pete with you. He can study here. Oh, by the way, a letter came for you. It's from Kendal."

"Kendal! From Oliver?"

"No. Somebody named A. Young. Who's that?"

"Austin. Mary Young's son." Rennie was disappointed. "He and his wife drove me to the airport. I don't know what he'd write about."

"Would you like me to read it to you?" her father asked eagerly.

"Never mind," Rennie said. "I can wait."

On Saturday, less than an hour from Neville, Peter suddenly turned off the highway and parked at the side of an ice-cream shop. "Let's get some cones," he said. "It's hot."

He's putting it off as long as he can, Rennie thought sadly. How he hates going home with me.

They sat at the counter, swiveling on high stools. "What'll you have?" he asked. "French vanilla? Dutch chocolate? Burnt almond?" He read off the flavors painted in a long list on the wall behind the counter, turning to Rennie questioningly after each one. He came to the end and sat there, looking at Rennie, waiting.

"What'll you have?" he asked again.

"You," she said suddenly. "I want you, feeling good about things, the way you used to. Let's get out of here." She was losing control of her voice. She jumped down from the stool and escaped through the swinging door.

Outside, Peter grabbed her arm. "What's the matter? You sick?"

"I've got to go somewhere quiet and think." There was a picnic table at the edge of the parking lot. They sat down side by side on the bench.

Rennie tried to find words for her feelings. "When I saw all those flavors," she explained, "it hit me. There's more than one choice. We can have anything we want. Why do we have to take that wedding? It isn't real. We're simply being pushed around."

Peter's face lighted up. "Rennie, are you saying you'd be willing to wait? Oh, Rennie!" He had looked at her lovingly, longingly, for months, but never like this. Then he turned anxious. "What about your folks?"

"I know. It's going to be rough."

"Mine'll be in heaven," Peter admitted. "They couldn't see me marrying without a job and another year of school. And I've been feeling for a long time that they're right, only I promised you, and I wasn't going back on my word."

"Peter! It's not fair, keeping things from me."

A guilty look crossed his face. He said, "It was the only way I could be with you this summer. If they'd just leave us alone, let us wait till fall. By then I'll have a little money, I hope."

"Where could we go for the summer?" Rennie asked. "Someplace that wouldn't cost." She didn't need his reply. "Firbank!"

"No," Peter said emphatically. "I'm not going to Firbank. This summer I'm working, even if all I can get is mowing lawns in Charlesbury." He put his arm around Rennie's shoulders and brought his head down to the level of hers. "We can both stay there. My folks would love to have you."

Charlesbury! Amusing Peter's little sisters all day while he was out mowing lawns. To spend the whole summer in Charlesbury . . .

Leaving the parking lot, Peter stepped on the gas. Now he seemed eager to get to Neville. Rennie was the one who wanted to dawdle. How was she going to break the news to her parents?

Suddenly another thought struck her. "Peter, if we aren't getting married, do you mean we're never going to have sex, the *whole summer?*"

Peter didn't answer.

"Do you?"

All Peter said was, "My folks are trusting. If we sneak off while we're with them, they'll feel I've let them down. They'd worry about the girls, too. Try to hide something from my little sisters!"

"But, Peter, as long as nobody gets hurt—"

"Somebody would get hurt and I don't want it to be my parents. Matter of fact, you and I are hurt, Rennie, with your parents insisting on this rotten wedding, just because they suspect we've been up to something. They're hurt, too."

"They're hurt? Do you really think so?"

"Of course! You know they're not happy about you and me. And if you think there's nothing wrong, why are you feeling guilty?"

"I'm not!"

"You said yourself, when you told me about Daphne doing your portrait, that you panicked because you didn't want her to know. You must have felt guilty."

Rennie looked down into her lap. Guilty? Is that how she felt when she cried out and Oliver came running? No. It was that she just thought Daphne wouldn't understand.

Rennie looked at Peter. She had the feeling she'd thumbed a ride with a stranger. He was so different. By the time they reached the house and started up the walk, they were both grim.

When Rennie saw how happy her parents were to see her, how warmly they welcomed Peter, her heart sank further. Her mother had made some lemonade. She brought the pitcher into the living room. Rennie's father followed, pressing Peter for his opinion as to which team was likely to win the pennant.

"I'm just going up to my room for a second," Rennie announced, playing for time. "Be right back." As soon as she came down again, she'd tell her parents.

"Don't take long," her mother begged. "The manager of the Bridal Boutique is waiting for us at the shop."

The words hit Rennie like a slap. She barely made it up the stairs. On her bureau there was a letter, addressed in what looked like a schoolboy's writing. The Kendal letter! Rennie tore it open:

Dear Rennie,

Hope you got back to college okay. Judy and I stayed and watched your plane go up.

The man who drives my tractor broke his leg yesterday. He was on his motorbike, going to the beach. Oliver says the man you are marrying is looking for a job. Would he want to work on a potato farm? If he's interested, tell him to phone me right away collect.

Judy says hello.

Your friend,
Austin Young

196

Rennie rushed to the stairs. "Peter! Come here. Right away!"

He bounded up, looking alarmed. She handed him the letter.

Rennie's parents came rushing to her room. "What is it, Rennie?" her mother cried.

"Austin Young's offering Peter a job!" Rennie exulted.

"Running his tractor," Peter explained. "Gee, I'd love to work outdoors all summer. Mr. Ross, could I use your phone?"

In what seemed no more than a minute Peter came bounding up the stairs again, calling to Rennie, "It's okay! I'm going next week, right after my last exam. There's a room in the loft I can use."

"When will you be back?" Rennie's mother asked. "There's the rehearsal dinner and our boys will want to get together with some of your bachelor friends before the wedding."

For a minute Peter stood there, looking at Rennie. At length he said, "If you want to, you can still change your mind."

"Change her mind about what?" Rennie's mother cried.

"Getting married," Rennie told her. "I mean, not getting married." She turned to Peter. "Do you want to?" She remembered how Oliver had said, in describing the moment he and Daphne began their pilgrimage, that they were of one mind.

"It's up to you," Peter answered, looking at her in a way that left no doubt about his preference.

"We're of one mind," she told Peter, taking him by the hand.

He faced her parents. "Mr. and Mrs. Ross," he announced, "Rennie and I have decided to put off our marriage. This just isn't the time." Rennie was looking intently at the wall-to-wall carpet.

"But we've ordered the invitations!" her mother cried.

Rennie's father took a step toward Peter. "You can't do that!" Then he broke into a laugh. "Many couples get these last-minute jitters," he said. "Seems to me something like this happened to us, too. Didn't it, Joan? But I never would have given in to it. You're making a big mistake, children, acting up like this."

Rennie raised her head. "We're not acting up, Daddy. We mean it. We'll get married, only not June twenty-first."

"Of course you're getting married June twenty-first," her father shouted.

Rennie went over to her mother. "I know you're disappointed," she said as calmly as she could. "I'm sorry. But Peter and I can't face it right now."

She turned to her father, reached up and put her arms around his neck. She could feel the tension in his body. "In that case," he said sternly, "you'll stay with us this summer. We'll take you to Europe."

"No," Rennie cried, drawing back. "I want to be in Firbank. I can help Oliver and I have a right to be there. It belongs to me."

"It does nothing of the kind!"

"Your grandmother left Firbank to all her descendants. Didn't you know? It's yours, too, Daddy."

"It's Oliver's, no matter what Grandmother wrote in her will. But never mind about that. I don't want you running around with a man you're not married to." He gave Peter a warning glance. "If you're both going to Kendal—"

"We won't do anything you don't want us to, Daddy."

Rennie's mother didn't hear this. She had run out of the room.

Putting her arms around her father's neck again, Rennie looked at him, pleading for him to understand that she didn't mean to hurt him, that she simply wanted her heart to stand in perfect sincerity. She'd never looked at him so lovingly, so eager to have him back her up in a decision she knew was right. Then she had a shock. There were tears in her father's eyes.

CHAPTER FIVE

EVERY afternoon when Peter finished work, he biked over to Firbank. Then he and Rennie rowed across the pond and climbed over the dunes to the ocean. Hand in hand they stood there, leaning against the breeze, watching the surf pound and break along the shore. Below them the beach stretched as far as they could see.

"The beach belongs to us," Rennie exulted. "To you and me!"

Lying side by side on the sand, gently toasting, they were close enough to touch, but it was only with their eyes that they communicated love. They were content to wait. Like the beach, their lives

stretched endlessly before them, all theirs now, free of interference. They were free, too, of the physical fever they'd been consumed by at college, their mutual attraction slowed to the rhythm of the ocean—deliberate, constant, measured against eternity. In the fall, they told each other, they'd get married their own way.

They'd never taken time before to put their feelings into words. But this summer they talked endlessly—about themselves, about things that had happened, as if they'd only recently met.

"Just when I thought I had my career as an astronomer finally fixed," Peter said one afternoon, letting a fistful of sand run slowly through his fingers, "I go and find I'm happy farming. Austin's made me see how much more there is to it than just weeding and spraying. Don't worry"—he laughed—"this isn't another identity crisis, like that time, end of freshman year."

No, Rennie thought, that's past. He's happy now.

The one thing neither of them mentioned was Rennie's portrait. She avoided Oliver's study so she wouldn't have to confront it. Peter was obviously fascinated. Hardly a day went by that he didn't go in and stand before it. But when he came out, he said nothing, and Rennie felt shy about asking what he thought. She knew it would be years before she looked that way—if ever. So the portrait became a subject she was afraid to discuss.

Those afternoons were so perfect, why was it that Rennie would invariably have to remember suddenly how her father cried when she and Peter announced they weren't getting married yet, and how her mother had barely spoken to her since? She tried not to think about her parents, but they had a frightening way of disrupting her contentment. And in the back of her mind there was always something Oliver had intimated when she'd phoned to ask whether she might spend the summer at Firbank. He'd been delighted about that and about the postponement of the wedding.

"Thee and Peter have won the freedom to make thy own decisions," he'd exulted.

"Yes!" Rennie had sung out joyfully. "And they lived happily ever after!"

At that the telephone had gone dead. Were they disconnected?

No, this was one of Oliver's silences. "It will depend," he'd said then, "on what you do with that freedom." So Oliver thought this was just the beginning of their problems, not the end.

Strangely enough, when she thought of these worries in Meeting, they troubled her less. The silence really was comforting. As was Peter's presence beside her.

Rennie wasn't even terribly disturbed when she got her marks in the mail, along with a notice that, because she'd failed two education courses, she was on probation. Actually she was pleased. She had demonstrated her lack of talent for teaching. Maybe now her father would let her change her major to art history. Not easy to do in senior year. But if she was willing to work her head off, why should he object? "And I am willing," she assured Peter.

Daphne was giving her a whole new conception of art. Instead of assessing a work objectively, as scholars were trained to do, Daphne entered the creative core of a fellow artist's feeling and thinking. To her, every painting was an autobiographical note on canvas. She spent hours showing Rennie prints of a painter's work, then a page in his biography or in a contemporaneous history. These, she believed, revealed the sources of his inspiration. With her own brush she reproduced the artist's palette to show Rennie how he mixed his colors and why he juxtaposed them.

Occasionally, Rennie remembered that this woman, who conveyed more than any lecturer, actually couldn't talk. But Rennie seldom noticed this anymore, except on those rare occasions when Daphne's enthusiasm outran her patience and she opened her mouth to speak. Then the silence struck at Rennie's heart.

As soon as she'd arrived at Firbank, Rennie had seen that she wasn't only welcome; she was desperately needed. Heather's family had had to call off the annual visit. Stephen, her husband, was changing jobs and couldn't get away. In August, Oliver told Rennie, Heather would come by herself for a couple of weeks. He made no comment, yet his disappointment was obvious.

"There's a lot of work here in summer," he warned Rennie. "Thee mustn't do more than thee wishes to. When Heather comes, she'll put us to rights."

When Heather comes. Rennie found she was looking forward to this almost as much as Oliver and Daphne. At last she was going to have a friend, someone as wonderful as they were, but younger. She longed for such a friend. The girls at college were more mixed up than she was.

She'd be glad to have someone else take over the housekeeping, too. Rennie was working harder than she ever had in her life. In addition to the usual chores, this was preserving time. All of Oliver's garden and orchard seemed to be ripening at once.

"Wait till you taste the cherry pie we're having tonight!" she told Peter one day. "I'm getting to be a neat cook, you know it?"

At the outset Oliver had informed Peter that Daphne expected him to have supper with them every evening. They ate on the back porch, shaded by grapevine so thick with leaves that they could hardly see the barn. To Rennie the evening meal in this green bower seemed like a continual celebration. As she held Peter's and Oliver's hands during the moment of quiet before eating, she thought, Joy, that's what we have at last!

Oliver kept bringing in fruits and vegetables—far more than Rennie could cope with, even after he'd shown her what to do. Tomatoes to can, beans to freeze, berries—Rennie didn't know where to begin. Not that Oliver expected her to do anything. "When Heather comes," he'd murmur, surveying the mound of produce, "she'll take care of everything."

"But she isn't coming for weeks," Rennie complained to Peter. "This stuff can't wait. It'll spoil." And although Peter pitched in and helped, they couldn't get ahead of the garden.

"Austin says Oliver ought to retire. Sell out."

"*Sell Firbank?* Peter!"

"I know. But Austin thinks he's too old. And the Vietnamese thing is hopeless, according to him."

"Oliver doesn't think anything's hopeless," Rennie cried. "He may be old, but he's no fool. In fact, the head of the forestry department at the university phoned yesterday. He's bringing over some scientists to see Oliver's plants. Sell Firbank! Peter, don't ever say anything like that again."

While it sometimes seemed to Rennie that all she did was cook and freeze food, actually housekeeping was only incidental. A large part of her day was spent helping Daphne prepare for her fiftieth anniversary show of her work, scheduled for next April.

The invitation had come as a complete surprise. When it arrived, Oliver was jubilant. "Recognition is welcome to an artist anytime," he told Rennie. "But to think, to think that this should come to Daphne now, after all she's been through! The Museum of Contemporary Art. The leading one in the country! Isn't it wonderful?"

The museum had asked for an inventory of Daphne's works. She was to star the pictures she especially wished to exhibit. They would need the inventory by the end of August, at the latest.

"We'd always intended to make one," Oliver told Rennie, looking worried. "But we were too busy. It will take weeks just to go through the canvases in the woodshed and the attic. Then there are her sketchbooks, catalogues of shows she's exhibited in over the years. If only Heather had come!"

To Rennie this seemed the chance of a lifetime. "Could I—would you let me do that? I mean, if you showed me how?"

"Serenity! To have thee do it would make Daphne particularly happy. Did I tell thee she wants the exhibition to begin with Grandmother's portrait and end with thine? In fact, that's going to be the title of the whole exhibition: *The Two Serenitys*."

"*My* portrait. In a museum? Well, it doesn't really look like me."

"Peter thinks it does."

"Do you mean it? Has he told you so?"

Instead of answering, Oliver patted Rennie's shoulder and went on about the inventory. The first thing, he said, was to build a file, entering each work by title and date on three-by-five cards. He brought out a shoe box from a cupboard. To give Rennie a large working surface, he put leaves in the dining-room table.

Daphne sat beside Rennie, watching the number of index cards grow, signifying approval with her large gray eyes. Since the day she'd drawn the portrait, she'd made it clear that she wasn't put off by anything in Rennie. But now Daphne didn't simply accept Rennie; she *depended* on her. She was turning over the sum of her creative production to a girl who hadn't finished college. Awed by Daphne's trust, Rennie thought at the same time, I can do it!

Help—abundant help—suddenly arrived.

Rennie's little friends, Nancy and Sandy, dropped in one afternoon, hoping to take her for a swim. But, seeing the huge pile of string beans in the kitchen, they helped Rennie instead. When they went home, they must have reported that extra hands were needed at Firbank, because the Kendal women began arriving. In threes and fours they worked together until they'd disposed of all the fruits and vegetables. They brought Daphne the Kendal news.

Billy Green, who was only sixteen years old, had stolen a car. This got to Rennie. So a Quaker home was no guarantee that a kid wouldn't get in trouble. The whole Meeting seemed to feel responsible. "Where does thee think we made mistakes?" Edith Ellis asked Rennie. She explained that Billy and her son had gone through school together. "What ought we to have done?"

How should I know? Rennie felt like blurting out. Why ask me? But then she felt flattered. A grown-up was turning to her for advice!

Little Simeon, the Ashaway baby, was very sick. John Ludlow, the best pediatrician ever, said it was meningitis. Rennie didn't know the Ashaways, but she did know the doctor. The first Sunday she and Peter were in Kendal, John and Clara Ludlow had invited them to a cookout. And a few days ago they'd asked them to come for dinner Tuesday night, when Heather was due to arrive.

"Will it be okay if we go?" Rennie had asked Oliver. "I mean, wouldn't you like me to get supper for all of you?"

"We'll manage," Oliver had assured her. "John probably figured it would be less strain for Daphne not to have so many people at once when she's excited to see Heather. Go, by all means. I'm glad thee and Peter will have a chance to get to know them."

Firbank had come to seem like home to Rennie now. Heather's little room in the ell, with Rennie's record player on the desk and her books on the shelves, was a place where she fitted, where she belonged. She'd feared that when Heather arrived, she would want the room. But Oliver assured Rennie that Heather had used the big one in the main wing since her marriage.

When Peter came into the ell, he would survey the room as if he, too, felt it was home. The little terra-cotta figurines intrigued him. One day he took one up, carefully studying the details. Rennie knew now that Daphne had modeled them for Heather when she was small.

"Daphne thinks toys should be works of art," Rennie told Peter. "Even if they're soon broken, they should give tactile pleasure and delight the eye."

"Beautiful," Peter murmured, putting down the figurine and taking up another.

Watching him, Rennie thought, Now I understand why he didn't want to make love at his house. I wouldn't want to here, myself, not in Heather's room. Here, Rennie only wanted to do things she'd be willing to have Daphne and Oliver know about.

But, high above the beach, the night before Heather arrived, Rennie was released from this constraint. So, apparently, was Peter. They had climbed to the top of the dunes to watch the moon come up. Sitting in the soft fold of sand with Peter's arm around her shoulders, Rennie looked up at the stars, completely happy. Then it just seemed to happen, taking them both by surprise.

The next day Daphne and Rennie worked in the dining room, going through a stack of canvases without really putting their minds on them, simply marking time till Heather arrived. Rennie wondered whether having her here was really going to be that nice, after all. Would Oliver and Daphne withdraw their attention, transfer it to Heather? I mustn't be jealous, she warned herself. She's their daughter.

Going over to Daphne's chair, Rennie held up a canvas. "Is this one you'd like them to put on exhibition? Does it get a star?"

She studied Daphne's expression, trying to read the answer to her question. But Daphne glanced at the picture only briefly, then at the door in expectation. After that her eyes came to rest on Rennie's face. They revealed such tenderness that Rennie looked away and fixed her attention on the canvas she was holding. It was a seascape. . . . Blood suddenly rushed to her cheeks. That sand dune in the foreground—it was in this very hollow that she and Peter lay on their backs last night, looking up at the stars! The lapping of the waves at low tide had dissolved their wills and their intentions, drawing them together.

Rennie tried to push this memory away and kept her face averted, so Daphne wouldn't see it was red. But her head was being drawn down to Daphne's. Cool lips touched her burning cheek. Could Daphne really see through people? Somehow she'd guessed what Rennie was thinking, and she wanted Rennie to know that she loved her.

Turning to put the canvas on the table, Rennie stopped, frozen. A tall woman in a scarlet pantsuit stood at the door, taking in the scene. Instinctively, Rennie turned to Daphne again. And she saw how redundant the power of speech would have been at that moment. Daphne's eyes expressed a joy that needed no confirmation in words.

As Heather walked across the room and bent over her mother's chair to embrace her, Rennie felt acutely disappointed. This wasn't the friend she'd dreamed of. How could this cosmopolitan woman, with the Otis curly hair sprayed into a silver nimbus, be a product of Firbank?

Heather straightened up and smiled at Rennie like a guarded stranger, asking, "Where's Father?"

"Picking corn," Rennie said. "I'll go get him." But at the back door she bumped into Oliver, who had just seen Heather arrive in her rented car. Bursting with excitement, he brushed past, barely noticing Rennie.

She didn't return to the dining room. Nobody needed her now. Instead she walked slowly down the lane to wait for Peter. When he pedaled up to the Otis letter box and saw her, his face broke into a happy grin. Dear Peter! She could count on him. Sitting astride his bike with his feet on the ground, he put his arm around her waist. All the way to the house he kept his hand on her shoulder while he pedaled slowly, wobbling on the sandy road.

"Who's here?" he asked, seeing the strange car.

"Heather. She's arrived."

"What's she like?"

"Different. Not at all as I pictured her."

When they reached the house and entered the dining room, they found Heather sitting in Rennie's chair. She had pushed the shoe box and canvases aside to make room on the table for the gifts she'd brought her parents: a blue cashmere cardigan for Daphne, a camel's hair sweater for Oliver, a tin of custard powder.

"After all these years in the States, Daphne still loves her custard sauce," Oliver told Rennie, laughing.

When Peter was introduced, Heather was cordial. Yet, even with her parents, she conveyed reserve. This far and no farther, her smile seemed to say. From her handbag she drew a pack of photographs, passing them around, identifying her children for Rennie and Peter, talking rapidly, as if she didn't feel quite at home.

Later, driving to the Ludlows' in Oliver's truck, Rennie said to Peter, "I don't understand her. That reserve—when she was showing them the snapshots, it was almost as if she was placing her husband and children between herself and her parents, like a shield. If she had parents like mine— But Oliver and Daphne!"

"I'm sorry. I know you were counting on her being a sort of older sister. She still may. First impressions—"

Rennie shook her head. "I don't think so."

Clara Ludlow welcomed them at the door. A dainty and pretty woman, she had the fresh complexion of someone who lives near the ocean. John, she said, would be down directly. "I urged him to take a little rest before dinner. He was at the hospital all night."

The house was unusual—an old New England saltbox decorated with Chinese pictures and artifacts. "John's whaling forebears brought the Canton ware back from China," Clara told Rennie, observing her interest. "The other things he got himself."

"You mean," Peter asked, "he's been to China?"

"Yes, back in the 1940s, during the civil war. He was with a Quaker medical unit, caring for civilians. Sometimes they were behind Nationalist lines, sometimes in Communist territory. Whatever side they happened to be caught on, people needed help."

John came in, looking tired, but very pleased to see Rennie and Peter.

During dinner the Ludlows asked about life at Tilbury. Although their children had finished college, they were interested in education. In the middle of this conversation Peter suddenly asked them how one went about getting married by Friends. The question took Rennie by surprise. She didn't know he was considering this.

Clara Ludlow began to describe the procedure—the letter of application, the committee on clearness.

"But one has to belong," Rennie put in. "Not be a member, necessarily, but part of the religious community. Oliver said so."

"You belong," Clara assured her, laughing.

"All summer you've been part of our community. Haven't you felt it?" John asked.

"Yes, but—"

"That's all Oliver Otis meant. Ask him whether it isn't."

"How should the letter be worded?" Peter wanted to know.

"There's no fixed form," Clara replied. "Just state your wishes to be married under the care of Kendal Meeting. Both of you must sign it."

"How soon can it be arranged?"

"Ordinarily it takes at least two months for a couple to pass Meeting, as we call it," John told Peter. "Are you in a hurry?"

"We had planned to get married before we go back to school," Peter explained. "But I guess we could wait a couple of months."

"That will be more acceptable to the Meeting," John declared. "The reason our procedure takes so long is simply that Friends wish the couple to avoid acting impulsively."

Peter turned to Rennie. "How about it?"

Rennie didn't know what to answer, and Clara, sensing her uncertainty, quickly changed the subject, saying something about the dessert. All through the evening Rennie kept wondering what had made Peter suddenly decide on a Quaker marriage.

When they were on the doorstep saying good-by, John murmured, "Tell Oliver Otis—" He hesitated. Under the outdoor light Rennie saw that this competent doctor, whom parents trusted with their children's lives, looked defeated. "Tell him Simeon Ashaway died this afternoon. There's going to be a Meeting of thanksgiving Friday at two in the Kendal Meetinghouse."

"Thanksgiving?" Peter blurted out. "What's there to give thanks for when a little kid dies?"

"His life—what there was of it. A Meeting of thanksgiving's our term for a memorial service."

Looking at John, Rennie saw that the term seemed as inappropriate to him, in this instance, as it did to Peter.

HEATHER took everything over—not only the housekeeping, but the inventory as well. Thanking Rennie for beginning the job, she promised to get it finished before she went home, evidently convinced that Rennie wished to be relieved of it. "I tried to tell her that I like it," Rennie complained to Oliver, "but she doesn't seem to understand."

"Her ideas are a bit different," he admitted, looking embarrassed. "She's reorganizing the file."

"Reorganizing?" After all the work Rennie'd put in! She couldn't speak to Daphne about it because Heather was always there.

Overnight, Rennie became a fifth wheel at Firbank. For the past weeks she'd been run off her feet. Suddenly she had nothing to do. Oliver sensed that Rennie was suffering from the change in her status. He tried to make her feel welcome, as before, but he was seldom indoors. The forest claimed his attention. The scientists from the university had given him a lift. After their visit he merely reported that they thought his experiments were promising. But Rennie was on to Oliver now. This was an understatement. They had been impressed.

The days only began for Rennie now in the late afternoon, when Peter arrived. Then they rowed across the pond and swam. But their time was no longer measured against eternity. Summer was almost over; Kendal Friends were meeting for business the week after next. If Rennie and Peter wanted their application for marriage considered, they'd have to submit the letter soon. Why was it so hard to write?

"It really isn't that complicated," Peter argued. "We just state our wish to be married under the care of the Meeting."

Rennie looked at the ocean. Peter expected her to say something, but she couldn't.

"Isn't that what you wanted all along—a Quaker marriage?"

"That's right."

"What's the trouble? We don't have to do a thing but make the promise and sign the certificate."

"We'd have to promise in the presence of God. I don't know what that means. When I get up and promise, I want my heart to stand in perfect sincerity. And if I don't know what God is, how can I say—"

"You're taking me on faith. Why can't you take God?"

"That's different. How can I *promise* to be loving and faithful till one of us dies? How can I tell what's going to happen?"

"One promises on faith, too," Peter cried. Suddenly he blew his stack. "I can't be around you anymore and not make love! But when I sleep with you, Rennie, I want to be your husband. If we hadn't met so early, it would have been better."

"You mean you're sorry?"

"Of course I'm not sorry. Don't be an idiot. Well, maybe I am a little. If I'd finished school, I'd feel better about the whole thing."

They were quarreling. What about? They both wanted to get married, didn't they? Or were they, without knowing it, about to break up? Rennie shivered.

The next day was Friday. Sitting around the house all morning, Rennie thought how right Oliver was about Peter and her not living happily ever after. Now she wondered whether they would even make it to the wedding. *Tomorrow afternoon,* Peter had declared when he left last night—*this afternoon*—they were going to write that letter, definitely. Rennie told herself she'd have to stop shilly-shallying, as her father would say.

After lunch, when Oliver was starting off for the Ashaway memorial service, leaving Daphne with Heather, Rennie impulsively climbed into the truck with him. When they reached the meeting-house, there were more people gathered than on a First Day. A vase of lovely homegrown flowers stood in each tall window. Eventually all the benches were occupied, and latecomers were standing at the back. Rennie recognized a lot of people. Surprising, how many friends she'd made this summer.

Neil and Alice Hill, who moored their schooner in Little Narragansett Bay and had taken Rennie and Peter for moonlight sails, were sitting across the aisle with Mary Lancashire, Alice's mother. Whenever Mary saw Rennie, she beamed on her with extraordinary pleasure. "Thee looks so much like thy great-grandmother!" she would exclaim happily, forgetting, no doubt, that she'd said exactly the same thing last time.

Down front, Rennie saw the Ashaways, mother and father and three young children. They looked stunned, as if they were at a loss to understand how God could be so cruel as to let a little boy die. And yet they must be taking His love on faith, as Peter phrased it, or they wouldn't be here.

Oliver seldom spoke in Meeting. Rennie was startled when he stood up and in a conversational tone announced, "We're gathered in the presence of God to give thanks for the life of our little friend Simeon Ashaway."

In the presence of God! So already, without even a wedding, Rennie was there. Was all of life in that presence?

"Even as we give thanks for the joy it was to have him among us," Oliver continued, "we cannot deny the question that is in all our minds—why a child should not have been allowed to grow to maturity. Everything in us argues that Simeon should have lived."

How like Oliver! With his usual simplicity he'd put into words the bewilderment everyone must be feeling. He wasn't trying to tranquilize the parents with pious words. He acknowledged their outrage, which must be far greater than John Ludlow's or Peter's.

"So we have to accept without understanding," Oliver was saying. "And for beings like us, that's close to impossible. Nevertheless, we trust, we *know*, that the ordering of life is right, however wrong it may sometimes look. If we had more understanding, we'd not measure a life by its length, but only by the fullness of its love, which radiated so abundantly from little Simeon."

Oliver let himself down onto the bench and rested his hands on his knees. Rennie wished she could communicate to him the emotion swirling in her at his assurance that all of life was lived in a presence one couldn't understand, but which one trusted.

She sank into the silence that followed and felt a strange contentment, an ease of heart. Oliver had once remarked that love isn't a little bird which suddenly appears in springtime, alights awhile, then flits away when the season changes. If that were true, maybe Rennie *could* promise. If she really loved Peter—oh, I do!—then her love wouldn't ever fly away, would it?

CHAPTER SIX

AT THEIR Monthly Meeting in Eighth Month, Kendal Friends appointed a committee to determine the clearness for marriage of Serenity Millburn Ross and Peter Hallburt Holland.

The committee, Oliver told Rennie when he came home from Monthly Meeting, was to report at the next session, which would be held on September 29. It was hoped that Rennie and Peter would be present.

"School opens the fifteenth," Rennie answered. "But I guess we could come back for a couple of days."

"If the report of the committee on clearness is satisfactory, you'll pass Meeting. Kendal Friends will then undertake responsibility for the marriage." Oliver went on to describe the next step. Yet another committee would be appointed—overseers, who were to ensure that the ceremony was conducted in reverence and simplicity. "As soon as the Meeting has appointed overseers," he concluded, "thy parents will be at liberty to issue the invitations."

"Not before?" Now that Rennie'd decided it was possible to make that promise, she couldn't wait. But Oliver shook his head.

When Rennie had first broken the news to him that she and Peter planned to be married in Kendal Meeting as soon as possible, she'd expected him to exclaim, "First-rate!" He hadn't and she was disappointed. Now, as he described the arrangements in a cautious, almost tentative tone, she was furious.

Furious with Oliver? "Aren't you pleased?" she blurted out. "You said way would open."

"It will. I'm confident. As for the timing—the committee on clearness will help you decide that."

"We *have* decided! We wrote that letter, remember? You said yourself it's the most significant step. That's if we pass Meeting," Rennie added, suddenly uncertain. It was by no means a foregone conclusion. She'd better not tell her parents yet.

But she felt easier when Oliver announced that the committee consisted of the Ludlows and the Hills. "Thee'll hear from Clara Ludlow about arrangements for the interview," he told her.

Until recently, Oliver explained, the two men on the committee had talked with the prospective groom, and the two women with the bride. That was because it wasn't considered proper to discuss sexual matters in mixed company. But times had changed, and now the entire committee interviewed the couple together.

Rennie felt relieved to hear that Peter would be with her. And the Ludlows and the Hills—why would anyone be afraid of them? But she was. If only she could have talked to Daphne! But Daphne was never by herself now. Heather monopolized her completely.

All week Rennie hung around, waiting to hear about the interview. It seemed that John and Neil were having difficulty settling on a time when they would both be free.

Friday morning Rennie was sprawled on the bed in the ell, studying a set of Fra Angelico prints she'd found downstairs, when Heather appeared in the doorway. This was the first time she'd been in the room this summer.

"Would you mind," Heather asked hesitantly, "keeping Mother company this afternoon? Father wants to take me to call on some old friends."

Would she mind? To have Daphne to herself again!

Even after Rennie agreed, Heather lingered in the doorway.

The wistful way she looked around the room touched Rennie. "Come on in."

Heather didn't need to be coaxed. "My son always uses this room when he's here," she told Rennie, sitting down in the rocking chair.

"I wish I could have brought him and the girls, but Stephen didn't think we should spend the money this year. They love it here. When I was their age," Heather added, "I wanted to get away."

Get away? Rennie said to herself. How could anyone want to get away from Firbank?

"The inventory's almost finished," Heather announced.

So that's what she really came for—to crow.

But it was quite the contrary. "I couldn't have done it without the start you made, Rennie. It turned out that your system was really better. In the end I went back to it."

This was the first nice thing she had ever said to Rennie. And it wasn't all. "You've done a great deal for Mother, apart from the inventory," Heather went on. "The portrait—I think it's even better than Great-grandmother's. Don't you?"

"I—don't know. I try not to look at it."

"Why?"

Rennie shrugged. "I'm not sure."

"You've stirred something in her. The letters Father wrote about you! I was a bit jealous," Heather said shyly.

So it's not that she doesn't like me, Rennie thought. She just doesn't want her parents caring for someone else. Who can blame her for that? She must have felt awful the day she arrived, when she walked in and her mother was kissing me.

Reaching for one of the terra-cotta figurines of a mother playing with her child. Heather ran her fingers over the surface and shook her head incredulously. "Imagine making a work of art like this for a child to play with! Who but my mother . . . ?"

"You're so lucky! Mine never would let me touch her things for fear they'd break. Ever since I first came here, *I've* been jealous of *you*. I kept wishing for parents like yours."

"They've mellowed," Heather conceded. "They're better than they used to be."

"Better? They must have been wonderful to start with."

"Oh, they were. Only I didn't always think so." Heather smiled faintly. "Maybe I'm the one who's mellowed. But it wasn't much fun here for an only child. All Mother ever did was paint. She had to, I suppose. It was as necessary to her as breathing. Besides, portraits were our cash crop, like potatoes or the Christmas trees Father raised. He didn't have time for me, either."

Heather put the figurine back on the bookshelf. "I should have been a boy," she murmured. "With all the work on the farm, a son was what Father needed."

Rennie thought of Austin's telling Peter that Oliver ought to sell out. That was ridiculous now. But someday wasn't it bound to happen? If there'd been a son, Firbank could have stayed in the family. This must be on Heather's mind.

"I used to keep a jackknife in my pocket," she recalled, "the way a boy would do, so if Father wanted one, I'd have it handy. I tried to anticipate his wishes, like Mother. They were so close, those two. I knew they loved me as much as they loved each other, but I *felt* excluded. I guess I wanted to be first with both of them."

Rennie felt sorry for Heather. How could she have thought that Oliver and Daphne excluded her from their love? It was ridiculous. Heather knew that, too—now. Yet a shred of that childish dissatisfaction lingered. Did one carry it around all one's life?

"You think your parents are bad!" Rennie cried. "You should have mine!" Or is it just because they *are* my parents that I feel this way? she wondered suddenly. They smothered me with attention. Still, with three big brothers, I was lonely, too.

"I'm more patient with my children than Mother was with me," Heather continued. "She had so much temperament. She could get very upset. If she thought a person or an animal was being mistreated—or something beautiful—it aroused more emotion in her than in other people. I used to envy girls who had stolid mothers. I never quite got over her being so different."

"But weren't you proud?" Rennie asked. "I wish my mother did something interesting. It would take her mind off me."

"Indeed I was proud! At exhibitions, when people admired a picture, I wanted to cry out, '*My* mother painted that!' But at school the other girls wore lipstick and dated. I wasn't permitted to. And that plain language! If any of my classmates heard my parents speak to me, I was mortified."

"I think it's cool."

"That's because your parents didn't use it." For an instant her childhood annoyance blazed in Heather's eyes. Then she laughed. "I guess there are some things I'll never come to terms with," she said, getting up to leave.

Rennie detained her. "Heather, your father talks about taking Daphne to New York for the exhibition. Is she up to it?"

"I don't know. She seems more frail this summer than a year ago. But Father thinks seeing her pictures in the Museum of Contemporary Art will make Mother so happy, it's worth the risk. I hope Stephen and I can come for the opening."

She cares so much about her mother, Rennie thought, as Heather disappeared out the door. Why can't she lay those ghosts and let her love pour out the way Daphne does?

That afternoon it was like old times. Daphne and Rennie, just the two of them, sat on the back porch sipping iced tea.

Rennie was happy. "Won't you be excited," she exclaimed, "walking into the museum and seeing your pictures?"

Daphne smiled. It could be the lopsidedness, Rennie thought, but it looks like a pretend smile. She doesn't believe she'll go.

"Heather told me how proud she used to be at exhibitions. I'll feel the same way. I'll want to say, '*My* cousin painted those!'"

Was Daphne really more frail? After the initial shock, Rennie had become so interested in her personality and her art that she scarcely paid attention to her physical condition. Except when she longed to speak, she was always serene—none of the temperament Heather made so much of. If Daphne thought she was slipping . . . Rennie had an impulse to reach out and take the paralyzed hand, to ward off anything that might befall. Instead she said the thing she knew would please Daphne most: "I like Heather."

A few hours ago Rennie couldn't have said it. But now it was true. Behind the arm's-length reserve she'd seen a lovable though rather pathetic woman.

"Funny, isn't it, that Heather and I never met before? Second cousins—" All the summers Rennie's family might have spent here! "I wish Mother and Daddy'd drive up before I leave. If the

Meeting approves, we could have the wedding the very next week-end, couldn't we? Mother and Daddy'll understand that with our family and Peter's and all the Kendal Friends, there won't be room in the meetinghouse for outsiders. And after the ceremony we can just have punch and wedding cake out on the lawn."

All at once her happiness became panic. She turned and stared out across the yard. They'll come, won't they? They wouldn't re-fuse to come to my wedding, just because it's different?

Turning back, Rennie saw her doubts reflected in Daphne's eyes.

"I guess," Rennie said slowly, "I ought to try to tell them why I want to be married here. That was always my gripe—that Mother and Daddy never gave me sensible reasons for decisions they made. I owe them a decent explanation. As soon as the committee on clearness passes us—*if* they pass us—I'll phone home and ask Mother and Daddy to drive up right away. Will that be okay?"

Daphne nodded eagerly.

"It'll be my chance to show them Firbank. I'll row Daddy across the pond." And, meanwhile, what would Rennie's mother do back at the house? Would she just sit around and try to talk to Daphne? Of course not. She'd be in a fever, making plans for this imminent wedding—the gown, the veil, the bridesmaids. The whole routine would be set in motion again. Oh, no! Rennie cried to herself. I can't face it. She had a sudden inspiration. "Daphne, do I have to have bridesmaids?"

Daphne shook her head.

"Do I have to wear a veil?"

Daphne shook her head again.

Realizing that she had nerve, proposing this to a great artist, Rennie still couldn't resist asking, "Would you design my wedding dress? You know, the kind that's right for a Quaker marriage?"

It was one of those moments when speech would have been redundant. Daphne's face radiated pleasure.

"Wait," Rennie said, jumping up. She ran to the woodshed and returned with Daphne's watercolor pad, her colors and her brushes. Then she took the water jar and filled it afresh.

In the palest blue gray Daphne sketched a shadowy outline of

Rennie's figure, topping it with red fuzz. She proceeded to clothe the outline in a long, simply flowing gown, rounded at the neck. Cocking her head, Daphne held the paper up before her.

"I love it," Rennie declared.

But Daphne had another idea. She placed the paper on the table again and started a new sketch. Rennie, sitting beside her, watched a whole series emerge, each one a little different.

"I love them all," Rennie cried. "I don't know which to choose." There was something mysterious about them—more dreamlike than real, something only Daphne envisioned.

Then she made an even more fanciful sketch. This gown wouldn't stun the wedding guests like a designer's creation. Just the opposite. Breathtakingly beautiful though it seemed to Rennie, it was unobtrusive, a natural part of that self she'd give to Peter. In this sketch Rennie held a tiny, old-fashioned bunch of flowers.

"The bouquet!" Rennie cried, recalling the big, stiff arrangements her sisters-in-law had balanced on their forearms at their weddings. "I want that sweet little bouquet."

In a corner of the paper, Daphne drew the bouquet as it would appear to Rennie when she held it and looked down—a harmony of colors—cerulean merging with rose madder, pale yellow with aquamarine—transparent, flowing into one another. Then, down the margins of the paper, Daphne reproduced the individual flowers in a different style—life-size, detailed, like the botanical plates she'd done as an art student.

Daphne was still working on the flowers when Heather and Oliver returned. Heather went to the kitchen to start supper. Oliver, stooping to kiss Daphne, looked fascinated as he saw what she was doing.

"My wedding dress," Rennie explained, pointing to the last sketch Daphne had made. "Isn't it neat? And that's the bouquet. Would you tell me the names of the flowers so Mother can tell the florist?" Because Daphne had decided on them, it became terribly important to Rennie that she have just these, no others.

Taking the chair on Daphne's other side, Oliver produced a pencil from his pocket and began writing under each flower: blue flag, marsh marigold, robin's plantain. Halfway down the line he stopped, looking puzzled, and turned to Daphne. As they exchanged glances, the puzzled look disappeared and a little smile began to form around the corners of his mouth. They were sharing a secret. Rennie couldn't have felt more left out. Now I know what it was like for Heather, she thought.

Oliver had turned back to the sketch and was writing in the rest of the names: starflower, coral honeysuckle, bird's-foot violet. That's a wild flower, Rennie realized. Is that out in the fall?

When he'd finished, Oliver smiled at Rennie. "It'll be the most beautiful wedding," he exclaimed, "at the loveliest time of year!"

Daphne and Oliver were still looking at each other, sharing the secret, when the telephone rang. It was Clara Ludlow. She was sorry to be calling so late, she said, but she'd just found out that she and John and Neil and Alice would all be free this evening for the interview. Would Rennie and Peter have supper with them at the upper end of the beach?

As soon as Peter came from work, he rowed Rennie over. They walked along the shore until they found the Ludlows and the Hills, sunning themselves, with picnic things around them.

After they'd all been swimming, John started a fire. Rennie and Peter went with Neil in search of more driftwood.

"Neil," Rennie asked, "do violets grow around here in the fall?"

"No. End of May."

"What about marsh marigold and blue flag, do they come out in the fall?"

"Those are all spring flowers. Last of May, beginning of June, the Firbank woods are full of them."

How strange that Daphne shouldn't know!

Arms loaded with branches and old planks that had been washed ashore, they returned to the fire. Clara was heating a huge kettle of chowder. Alice had baked biscuits. Corn from Neil's garden was laid on the embers. A feast! But first they stood in a circle, silent, watching the crimson sun sliding into the sea. Neil and John reached for Rennie's hands.

These people weren't about to grade Peter and her, she thought.

Their function was to find them, catch up with them where they were—be their companions on this pilgrimage.

That's what it is. A pilgrimage! We're trying to realize our humanity the way Oliver and Daphne did. One could make a pilgrimage standing in a circle, digging one's toes into the sand while the sun went down.

They sat around the fire, eating all they could hold, joking. It was more like a family celebration than an interview, Rennie thought. When the chowder was all gone and the bowls had been rinsed in the ocean, everyone gathered around the fire again. No one spoke now. It gradually dawned on Rennie that this wasn't because the Friends couldn't think how to begin. They were trying to focus on what was important, collecting their forces.

Rennie looked over at Peter. He seemed frightened. On the point of whispering, Are you afraid they won't pass us? she held back. She had a suspicion his answer might be, No, I'm afraid they will. What had come over him? He was the one who was so crazy to write that letter.

John Ludlow was explaining that the original function of a committee on clearness had been only to determine that a man and woman who wished to marry were clear of all other engagements, but that nowadays it was to make sure the two people were clear in their minds about the sacredness of the step they were taking. He looked searchingly from Peter to Rennie. "Why do you want to get married?"

"We love each other," they said together. But, in the flat half-light, Rennie could see expectancy on all four of the faces that were turned to hers and Peter's. She thought, What they're asking is, How will it be different from the way things are now? In spite of their simplicity these people were with it. They didn't need to go into Rennie and Peter's sex life. Like Oliver, they could guess.

How *would* it be different?

"I think I know what you mean," Peter was saying. "And I guess the answer is, We don't know. But I'm sick of playing house, like a couple of little kids. It would have been better to wait till we graduate. We can't. It's too hard."

"You're young," Neil observed, "but you're speaking like a man. Still, need shouldn't be the whole reason for marrying."

Clara Ludlow asked, "How do your parents feel about your getting married?"

"Mine want me to," Rennie said. "Peter's don't really, but they're being nice about it." By the light of the fire Rennie discerned unease on the faces of the Friends.

"Maybe," Clara suggested, "you need to discuss this with them further. It takes time for a meeting of minds. We wouldn't feel very comfortable, you know, if your parents weren't in accord."

Now why did Rennie have to go into all that? Would they flunk them, just because of their parents?

Alice Hill started to speak, but stopped, weighing the words first. Finally she asked, "Are you familiar with our queries?"

"No," Peter said.

"We don't have a statement of belief, you know, only a set of questions relating to personal conduct. From time to time these are read in Meeting. The queries remind us of what we want our lives to be. So when we haven't been living up to our potential—and who does?—they make us dissatisfied, though we're only answerable to ourselves. The query on marriage sums up my ideal: 'Do you make your home a place of friendliness, refreshment and peace, where God becomes more real to those who dwell therein and to all who visit there?'"

Rennie thought, "Where God becomes more real!" How can I make it that? "Friendliness, refreshment and peace"—it had never occurred to her that their apartment would be more than a place to sleep and have snacks in. But to make that apartment another Firbank—to transform four walls into a place of highest significance! She was being led to envision an ideal beyond anything she had imagined.

When the sun went down, the sea breeze died but the air grew colder. So did the sand. Rennie thought suddenly, That's how I'd be if Peter left me. No! I have to generate my own power. When Peter had asked her to stay away for a whole week, she'd had no one to fall back on but the girls in the dorm, not herself. Now she was about to give that self to Peter. Did she really possess it? Maybe all along I didn't really love Peter. Is that possible? Wasn't I just hanging on to him for dear life? But now— Now!

"As far as I'm concerned," Clara was saying, turning to John and the Hills, "Rennie and Peter are clear for marriage."

"I approve of that," each of the other three said.

Rennie reached out to hug Peter. They had passed!

"As for the date," John said slowly, "perhaps you will give that a little more thought."

This was all. The interview was over. But they stayed sitting by the fire, gazing at the embers, in a silence like the one that preceded the close of Meeting. Then the Friends appealed to her and to Peter to perceive their own strongest feelings, their central wish. They urged them to wait for that which was near them, which could guide them. In different words they were saying what others had said the first time Rennie went to Meeting, when she'd resolved to listen to Peter.

I'm listening to him now! I hear what he's saying. He doesn't want to marry me yet, but he can't help himself. I asked for it. I begged to be dependent. I have to let go now, even if it should mean losing him.

John Ludlow reached out and took her hand. The others shook hands. It had been a Friends Meeting, here, by the fire.

The men stood up and stretched. They gravitated toward the water's edge while Rennie helped the women pack the dishes.

It was such a clear night. Rennie stopped working for a minute and looked up. She was sure she could see every one of the eighty-eight constellations and five thousand stars that Peter had once told her were visible to the naked eye. Suddenly she felt a surge within her, an irresistible impulse to wish on the whole sky full of stars. She didn't shut her eyes. They were trying to encompass the universe. This was her central wish—she had it at last! Nameless, infinite, beyond her grasp, yet as real as herself. Such a secret wish—how could she share it with Peter? It would take a whole new medium to express it, a lifetime to live out the glowing perfection that Rennie envisaged now.

If divine assistance—whatever that might be—could see Peter and her through their whole marriage, why wouldn't it see them through till they graduated? Why wouldn't it help them to wait till Peter had the independence his manhood craved?

Only I can give it to him, Rennie realized suddenly. Only I can give it to myself. Once they both had this independence, *then* they could depend wholly on each other, like Oliver and Daphne.

Daphne! That's what she was trying to tell me with those spring flowers! Oliver got the message right away. All along they'd had reservations about our getting married before we graduate.

Rennie jumped up. She didn't run to the water's edge; she flew. Seeing her coming, Peter opened his arms wide.

"We can wait," she whispered as he held her close. "It's only nine months till graduation. When we want our baby, we'll have to wait that long."

CHAPTER SEVEN

ON THE way home to Neville on the bus, Rennie got to thinking about her parents—about that day back in January when they'd suggested she and Peter get married. In all fairness she had to admit that her parents had been reaching out to her then. "You're still our little girl," her father had said. "Mother and I love you very much." And her mother kept repeating, "We just want you to be happy." It troubled them that they couldn't give Rennie the security she needed.

Suddenly, Rennie saw why her parents had wanted such a spectacular wedding. They had been worrying about her life-style. To try to reason with Rennie would have been useless. So they decided that the way to give her security was to get her married with a big splash, overlooking the fact that Rennie scarcely knew what marriage was all about.

I ought to have let my own parents come along on my pilgrimage, she thought miserably, but I pushed them away. I didn't think they'd understand.

Now she was returning to Neville firmly resolved to change all this. Her original plan had been to stay at Firbank until after Labor Day. Austin wanted Peter to work that long. But when she and Peter were writing their second letter to the Meeting, she had this sudden impulse. "It will make Mother and Daddy happy to have me there on my birthday," she told him. "Next year I'll celebrate it with *thee!*"

"And every year thereafter," Peter declared happily.

In their second letter they informed the Meeting that they didn't plan to be married till May 31. Would Friends postpone considering their marriage till January? They'd be able to come to Kendal during intersession.

Rennie hoped Oliver and Daphne wouldn't feel she was running out on them when Heather was about to leave for England. "It's just that I have this sudden impulse to explain to Mother and Daddy."

"What Woolman would have called a 'motion of love,'" Oliver observed, assuring her that he and Daphne would be all right.

But when she finally got to Neville, nothing was quite the way she'd pictured it. She offered to cook supper and was told to set the table. Her mother wasn't about to turn over her kitchen to anybody. "I'm getting on," she said, "but I can still run my house."

It was the same with the plans for the wedding. "What will there be for *me* to do?" her mother asked. "If you're not having any attendants and no proper reception, our friends will think—"

"They're not going to be there. The meetinghouse is too small."

"You said it seats over a hundred. Even with the two families there'll be room for the Dixwells, the Goffes—"

"No, Mother. Kendal Friends will fill every bench. There'll be Oliver and Daphne, the Ludlows, the Hills, all the Youngs, Mary Lancashire—she remembers Great-grandmother—the Ashaways and Billy Green. He's the kid who stole a car. Peter's been spending a lot of time with him."

"You mean," Rennie's father exclaimed, "Pete's keeping that kind of company?"

"All the younger men in the Meeting are doing things with Billy," Rennie explained. "Trying to act like his big brothers."

"Daddy and I don't know any of those people," Rennie's mother complained.

Then Rennie's father said something that surprised her. "Joan," he broke in, "let's not make this hard for Rennie. She's got new friends. Oliver's given her ideas." There was a touch of bitterness in those last words, but as he turned to her, she saw that his love superseded all else. "Maybe we did overdo it a bit when we planned that June wedding. We only have one daughter. We wanted to give her the best. But if you prefer to be married in Kendal, we'll go along with it. Won't we, Joan?"

"I don't think we're being given a choice."

"With one exception, Rennie. I insist on giving you away. Every father does that."

And Rennie, who wanted so much to sound like an adult, blurted out, "You don't own me, Daddy. How can you give me away? I'm giving myself to Peter. He's giving himself to me."

Rennie's father looked hurt, but he came over and put his arm around her. "Look, honey, a lot may change in nine months. The Meeting isn't going to finalize the arrangements till January, right? Very well. Let's forget the whole thing till next year."

Forget the whole thing! Rennie'd left Firbank, left Peter, so she could give her parents some insight into how she felt about this wedding. And now her father wanted to forget the whole thing! His tone suggested that by January the whole thing might be off. Rennie couldn't take it. She simply went upstairs.

Reviewed in the privacy of her room, her remark about her father not owning her seemed pretty stupid. Of couse he didn't. He never said he did. It was the significance of that walk down the aisle that he regarded—his responsibility for his daughter. He'd taken this responsibility all her life and only he could hand it over to Peter.

But this is going to be a *Quaker* marriage, Rennie argued, as if she were still downstairs.

Nothing was simple anymore; nothing was all good or all bad. Even Daphne and Oliver. How could such a perfect marriage as theirs have had negative side effects? Yet it was a fact that, much as they loved Heather, when she was young they had failed her.

Sighing, Rennie began to unpack. Her room didn't feel like home, even with Serenity's Woolman on the bedside table. Coming back had been a mistake.

The day after her twentieth birthday, Rennie went back to college for her senior year. When her bus rolled into Tilbury, Peter was waiting, his bright yellow head thrown back as he scanned the windows. It seemed forever before Rennie reached the door and jumped down. He put his arm around her shoulder, bending a little to smile lovingly at her.

"I thought I'd never get here," she said.

Too happy to talk, they crossed the campus. It was crawling with students. The upperclassmen acted as if they owned the place, but the freshmen looked lost. "Poor kids," Rennie finally murmured. "I'm glad I'm not young anymore."

Peter laughed. "How was your birthday?"

"Fine. Mother and Daddy gave me an electric skillet. Daphne and Oliver sent me a little watercolor of the house. It's in my bag. I'll show it to you later."

"I have something for you, too," Peter said.

"What *is* it?"

"Wait till we get somewhere that isn't so public."

When they reached the college garden, Peter drew Rennie to a bench and took a small package out of his pocket. She untied the white ribbon slowly, savoring her anticipation.

"It was my mother's," Peter said as Rennie looked down at an amethyst set in a narrow gold ring. "She wanted you to have it."

"Oh, Peter!" Rennie looked at the ring, then at Peter, then at the ring again.

He reached out for it and took her left hand. "This is only the first one I'm going to put on your finger," he declared as he bent to kiss her.

That afternoon, as soon as Rennie had unpacked, she sat down to write a thank-you letter to Mrs. Holland. Peter's mother answered by return mail, and after that Rennie got a letter from her every week, as Peter did. It was also signed "Mom."

Carrying extra courses—now that she had switched her major to art history—turned out to be harder than Rennie'd foreseen. She worked all the time. So did Peter. They saw little of each other during the day now that Rennie was staying out of his dorm. At the far end of the reading room in the library there was a row of tall windows, each with a cushioned seat beneath it. That was where they studied every evening.

Before they knew it, Christmas vacation arrived.

When Rennie got home, her mother was in tears. She had bursitis in her right shoulder. The doctor had immobilized her arm.

"What'll I do?" she wailed. "The whole family's coming Christmas Day. Larry and Victoria, Jonathan and Matty, Eddy and Jane, all the children. I was looking forward to it so. How can I cook with one hand?"

"No problem," Rennie declared, laughing. "After a summer at Firbank I'm equal to anything."

This time her mother was more than willing to let Rennie take over. Rennie spared no effort. She baked gingerbread men, candied sweet potatoes, creamed onions, hot rolls, while her mother sat at the kitchen table, watching in awe.

Rennie's father brought her old high chair down from the attic for Larry's baby, and placed telephone directories on the dining-room chairs for Edmund III, Vicky and Jocelyn. The other three children were big enough to sit at the table.

There were sixteen at Christmas dinner. Lawrence Ballantine Ross was in his high chair, picking up morsels with his chubby fingers and stuffing them in his mouth. Rennie smiled. Then, looking around the table at her parents, her brothers and their wives, she had a moment of anxiety. Would they understand the simplicity of her wedding? To them the pageantry was the best part.

She had no time to consider this further, because Vicky and Jocelyn left the table and started tearing through the kitchen. When I have kids, Rennie told herself, almost tripping over Vicky as she carried in the flaming plum pudding, when I have— But she stopped herself, recalling how obnoxious she'd been not too long ago. No wonder her mother was fit to be tied half the time!

Nobody finished the pudding, because the children suddenly made a dash for the presents under the tree and began opening them in an orgy of torn wrapping paper, cards and ribbons.

Rennie received enough kitchenware, silver spoons, towels and knickknacks to set up housekeeping on the spot. Peter had sent the reproductions of Daumier caricatures that he knew she wanted. Her brother Larry had given her a magnificent new edition of *Walden*, illustrated with colored photographs of the pond and surrounding woods in all seasons.

"Only that day dawns to which we are awake," Rennie thought, turning to a picture of the pond taken in early morning. Am I just now beginning to wake up?

Deeply moved, Rennie went over to Larry and thanked him.

It was a relief when everyone went home. And yet, after Rennie had disposed of the mutilated wrappings; after calm returned to the house and her parents had gone to bed, Rennie stayed downstairs. She turned out all the lights except the ones on the tree. There was something special about this Christmas that she wanted to hold on to, to savor.

With all the uproar the kids had made, it was still precious, Rennie's last Christmas at home. She missed Peter, but not the way she did before—when she thought she'd die without him, or worried about his falling for some other girl. There was no ache now. Inexplicably she had seemed to carry him with her all day.

In a week it would be January. Her father's implied prediction of last summer—that the wedding might be permanently called off by then—was proving unfounded. Peter was coming New Year's Eve! And on the second they'd leave for Firbank.

AUSTIN Young surprised Rennie and Peter by meeting their bus. "Thought I'd save Oliver coming in," he explained. He looked glad to see Peter again. "How're the books?" The question, merely good-natured banter on the surface, revealed the secret regret of a man who hadn't had a college education.

Peter pointed to his suitcase. "See that? It's full of them. We've got a lot of studying to do, next couple of weeks."

Firbank was glistening under a blanket of snow when they arrived. But indoors, all was warmth and hearty affection. When they walked into the living room, Daphne leaned forward and Rennie rushed to embrace her.

Then, standing in the middle of the room, looking around, Rennie suddenly felt lost. One thing she'd thought she could count on was that Firbank wouldn't ever change. But the walls looked completely different. The pictures were not the same ones.

Oliver sensed her uneasiness. "It's our preview of the exhibition," he explained. "Miss Chase, the director of the museum, came to see us before Christmas and selected these pictures out of the lot thee starred last summer. I thought Daphne'd get a better idea of how they harmonize if they were hung." Taking Rennie's arm, Oliver drew her to the fireplace. "Thee sees, this is where one walks into the gallery. The first thing one encounters is Grandmother's portrait." He commented on each picture as he steered Rennie around the room. Suddenly remembering his domestic duties, he let go. "Look in the dining room. I'll join thee in a minute, soon as I've basted the chicken."

On the threshold of the dining room, Rennie stopped short. She was face-to-face with her portrait. The light wasn't the same here as in Oliver's study. It came from the north rather than the east. Was that why the portrait made a fresh impact on her, as if she'd caught an unexpected glimpse of herself in a mirror?

Oliver came in from the kitchen.

"It looks more like me," Rennie blurted out.

"No," he said gently, "*thee* looks more like *it*. What a lovely work to end the exhibition with! Wait and see—I believe it will elicit the approval of the critics more than anything else there."

They returned to the living room. "The Museum of Contemporary Art," Oliver said, turning to Daphne and shaking his head incredulously. "What an honor!"

He must believe she'll make it to New York, Rennie thought, or he wouldn't go on about it like this.

Apart from the preview of the exhibition, nothing at Firbank seemed changed. Rennie would stay in the ell, and Peter was given

the room in the main wing that Heather used last summer. When they sat down to supper in the warm kitchen, with the familiar blue-and-white plates, the pewter teapot, the loving silence, it was as if they'd never been away.

After supper Rennie peeped into the woodshed, curious to see what Daphne was working on. As she opened the door, intense cold hit her. The potbellied stove was unlit and there was no sign of any painting in progress. Rennie shut the door quickly.

"It's awfully cold in the woodshed," she told Oliver when she went back. "I should think Daphne'd freeze."

"That stove heats it up good and fast," he replied. "Anytime she wants it. But she hasn't been inclined to paint lately. Thee's right—it's cold tonight. Going to be a hard freeze. I'm worried about my little plants down in the forest."

So he was still struggling with his antidefoliation project.

The next morning Rennie jumped out of bed and ran to the window. "Hi," she called to the ice-covered pond, "I'm back!" After breakfast she and Peter went sledding. They were tingling when they came back and stood around the fire in their ski socks. Oliver made cocoa. Daphne sat in the armchair, listening eagerly as they told her about the fun they'd had. She seemed to be reliving the days when she had enjoyed the winter woods.

It's almost, Rennie thought, as if we're standing in for her.

The days were full. Friends invited Rennie and Peter over to dinner. They never stayed late because they had to be up early to help Oliver before they began to study.

Although they'd brought that suitcase full of books, Peter and Rennie missed the college library. There were things they wanted to look up. So one morning Oliver telephoned Professor Anselm, the chairman of the forestry department at the university.

"Everything's arranged," Oliver announced when the conversation ended. "You're to go to his office at ten o'clock tomorrow morning. He's going to introduce you to the librarian. She'll supply you with the books you need."

Professor Anselm was a short, bald man who treated Peter and Rennie as if they were old friends.

"I remember when you came over to Firbank last summer," Rennie told him. Then, emboldened by his friendliness, she asked, "Professor Anselm, do you thnk it's ever going to be a success—Oliver's Vietnamese Forest?"

"That experiment of his for restoring contaminated soil? If you mean, has he found a formula that will do the trick, I don't know. Most likely not. But that is immaterial. Until Mr. Otis pricked our consciences by putting his own limited resources and strength into his work, few American scientists thought it was our duty to do something about the destruction in Vietnam. It's his intentions that have been significant, not his results. The rest of us will take it from there."

When they were crossing the campus to the library, Professor Anselm asked Peter, "Where are you going to graduate school?"

"I'm not applying yet. We're getting married the end of May. So going to grad school will have to wait."

"People have been known to do both," the professor observed.

Later, on the way home, Peter was silent for a long time. Then, suddenly, he turned to Rennie. "Someday you'll go to grad school, too, Rennie. Maybe even get a Ph.D."

"*Me?*"

"Of course! How do you think you can become an art historian if you don't?"

"We don't know where we'll be—whether it's near a university."

But contemplating the possibility Peter had just held out—that she might have not just a job, but a lifework—Rennie realized how close this came to being part of her central wish. I could write a doctoral dissertation about Daphne's paintings and drawings! she thought. Daphne can supervise it: the first scholarly evaluation of her work.

A doctoral dissertation! Could she do it? Convey the incredible beauty of Daphne's work, explain her technique to others, as Daphne had explained it to her?

Yes, Rennie thought, feeling a surge of confidence she'd never known before. With Daphne looking over my shoulder, inspiring me, maybe I can.

It was too cold for Rennie and Peter to ride to Monthly Meeting in the back of Oliver's truck, so they took Austin's, dashing ahead to get there before Sam and Jorim. They wanted to be the ones to carry Daphne into the meetinghouse tonight because tomorrow they were leaving for school. "It'll be our way of saying thank you for the beautiful vacation," Rennie told Peter.

They stood in the drive, by the syringa bush, waiting. Finally, Oliver's truck appeared and stopped beside them. Rennie watched Peter lift Daphne out and lower her into the wicker chair with awkward gentleness. Triumphantly they carried her in. When she was installed on the bench she always occupied, Rennie and Peter joined her. Oliver, coming in last, took the place beside Peter.

A table had been placed in front of the lowest facing bench. The presiding clerk, Edith Ellis, and the assistant clerk, a man Rennie didn't know, were sitting behind the table, going through a pile of papers. Suddenly Edith Ellis stood up. "At Kendal Monthly Meeting of Friends, convened for business on First Month twentieth," she announced. Then she sat down.

Rennie thought that if they had to work through all those papers, Friends had better get going fast, but instead they bowed their heads and settled into silence.

Rennie began thinking of what Oliver had told them—that they'd be asked tonight to choose the four Friends who would have oversight of their wedding. Of course they wanted Oliver and Daphne. As for the other two, Peter had suggested the Youngs and Rennie had agreed. She liked Austin and Judy, though she'd never quite forgiven Austin for saying that Firbank ought to be sold.

There was indeed a lot of business tonight—the reading of the minutes of the previous session, the report of the finance committee, news from Quaker relief workers overseas—the agenda went on and on.

They never voted. The clerk "took the sense of the Meeting," as if she might be taking its temperature without a thermometer. Then she framed a minute and read it aloud.

Rennie was surprised to find that Friends disagreed on almost every item, for not everyone perceived truth the same way. Oliver once remarked that the very steadfastness that made Quakers willing to endure persecution for their belief could become downright stubbornness in the face of lesser issues.

After what seemed an eternity to Rennie, Edith Ellis came to the last item on the agenda. "Now," she said, "may we have a report from the committee appointed to look into the clearness for marriage of Peter Holland and Serenity Ross?"

John stood up and said simply, "The committee met with them last summer. We found them clear for marriage."

"Thank thee, John Ludlow. Do Friends feel comfortable about taking responsibility for the accomplishment of this marriage?"

Suppose there was a difference of opinion on this matter, too! But no, there was immediate unity.

"Then we'll appoint a committee of oversight. Peter and Serenity, are there Friends you would like to have as overseers?"

Peter stood up and answered gravely, "Yes. Oliver and Daphne Otis, and Austin and Judy Young." When these four had agreed to serve, they were appointed and the session was over. Yet instead of going home, Friends bowed their heads and sank into a profound silence again.

Despite herself, Rennie wriggled. Another silence! She was impatient to telephone her parents and let them know that they were free at last to issue the invitations. Then she asked herself what fun her parents would have, working on the list, when there was no room for people like the Dixwells and the Goffes, her parents' lifelong friends, who meant as much to them as the Kendal people did to Peter and her. Looking around, Rennie wondered whether she could squeeze in an extra person on each bench. No, it would be too tight.

Rennie imagined herself walking down this aisle with Peter, heading for the facing bench in the gallery, which was used at weddings. On New Year's Day, Peter'd told her father that he felt the custom of the bride entering the meetinghouse with the groom put as much responsibility on the groom as when the father of the bride gave her away.

"I promise you, Mr. Ross," Peter had said, "that even if you don't

234

give Rennie to me in the meetinghouse, I'll take the best care I can of her as long as I live."

Listening to Peter make this solemn declaration, Rennie had remembered that childish outburst of hers last summer, when she told her father he couldn't give her away because he didn't own her. No argument of hers, however logical, no defense of her life-style, would convince them. She was really losing her parents.

Like if they died suddenly, she'd said to herself then. The possibility had shaken her. It had never crossed her mind that her parents might die before they were very old.

They'll die for me right now, she'd said to herself on New Year's Day, if I don't do something quick to hold them.

What she said then must have sounded strange, coming from her, but Rennie'd meant it. "I don't want you to give me away," she'd told her father. "I want to stay yours and Mother's, even after I'm married. How can I ever not be? I'll walk through life with Peter the way we'll walk into the meetinghouse, but I'll be yours, too." Then she'd gone over and kissed her father.

He looked flustered. Still, he didn't protest.

Acting on another impulse, Rennie had sat down on the couch next to her mother. "You used to sew a lot when I was young— those cute smocked dresses. Remember? Mother, would you— Wait!" Rennie ran up to her room and returned with Daphne's sketches. "Look, this is the wedding dress I want. Could you make it for me, maybe out of organza? I'd be so proud, getting married in a gown you made, instead of bought, for me."

That was the first time Rennie's mother showed any enthusiasm. Her face lighted up. But then, as Rennie had added, "I'm not wearing a veil, or stuff like that," she looked disappointed.

"Not even a cap?"

Rennie shook her head.

Now, sitting in the quiet meetinghouse, Rennie thought that when it came to the veil, she'd handled matters with her mother in the same old way. She sighed. For the first time she grasped how Daphne saw her in the portrait, almost like two people—the person she wanted to be projecting from the person she still was.

235

Just as if this were a Meeting on First Day, Neil Hill stood up and began to speak. "At our wedding Alice and I had the feeling that the Lord was joining us together. That feeling has pulled us through many troubles. What I want to say is, I hope Rennie and Peter will have the same feeling when they're married, and that it will be a good service to them on all occasions."

Neil sat down and Friends bowed their heads.

Caught up in the silence, Rennie became aware of a strange jerking beside her. Daphne was extending her good arm, trying to grab the back of the bench in front of her, struggling to get to her feet. Instinctively, Rennie put her hand under Daphne's elbow to steady her till she was standing upright.

Daphne felt moved to speak! She had a message for Rennie and Peter, too. Judging by her expression, it was a beautiful message. She looked as if she were envisioning the loveliest scene she ever painted. Not frustrated, as she usually was when she opened her mouth this way, but perfectly serene, Daphne stood there a minute in the awesomely quiet meetinghouse. Then she let go of the bench, and Rennie supported her till she was seated again.

I heard thee, Rennie told her just as silently, bowing her head, fighting back the tears. I understood every word. Thank thee!

CHAPTER EIGHT

The last day of March, when Rennie woke up in her college room, she told herself happily that in just two months she and Peter would both be bachelors (of art) and both married! This term was passing so quickly that it wasn't hard to wait. If only Peter had a job—anxiety about the future was getting to him again.

As she was lying there, thinking of Peter, the telephone rang. The moment she heard the anguish in Oliver's voice, she knew.

"Serenity." That was all he said.

No, Rennie thought. No! It's not that bad. She's had a stroke, but she'll recover, just like last time.

"Daphne's left us."

"Oh, Oliver!"

"Yesterday afternoon around four o'clock. Must have been almost instantaneous. She was still holding her brush. Thee knows, the past six months, she wasn't up to working. But yesterday she said she wanted to paint. So I lit a fire in the woodshed and took her there. Then I went to the kitchen to make tea. I looked back from the doorway to be sure she was comfortable, and she gave me the most radiant smile! Maybe she knew it was our farewell."

"Oh, Oliver." That was all Rennie was able to say.

"Heather's flying over as soon as she can arrange it—tomorrow or next day. We're having a Meeting of thanksgiving in Kendal Friday afternoon at two. Even if thee and Peter can't be there, I wanted you to know."

"I'll come. Peter can't. His senior project's due next week. But I'll come tonight."

"*Will* thee?" The tone of those two words told her how grateful he was, how much he needed her. "Oh, and Serenity, will thee notify thy father?"

She called him right away. He said of course he'd go.

"Won't Mother come, too?"

"I doubt it. She doesn't like funerals and it's a terribly long ride. But I'll pick you up in New York."

"No, Daddy. I don't want to wait till Friday. Oliver's there alone. I want to be with him."

As soon as her father hung up, Rennie pulled on her clothes and ran to Peter's room. This was the first time she'd been there all year. It looked familiar and strange.

"I have to go," she sobbed, after she'd told him about Daphne.

Peter took her in his arms. "Of course you do. We'll leave right after breakfast."

"Can you go? What about your project?"

Peter stroked Rennie's hair. "I'm not letting you go alone. I want to be with Oliver, too. I don't have that much left to do on my project. Anyway, what good is it, if there are no jobs?"

"The exhibition," Rennie said, suddenly realizing. "It's only three weeks away, but Daphne'll never see it. And the wedding! She won't be our overseer, Peter."

He wiped her eyes with the palm of his hand. "Go get your stuff together. I'll call Austin, see if he'll meet us."

It was raining in Tilbury, but when their plane came down in Rhode Island, the sun was out and spring was in the air. Austin said almost nothing till they reached Firbank. Then he asked Peter whether he'd help him fix up the meetinghouse Friday morning.

"We think there'll be more people than we have seats for. Folks from out of town—the art crowd and all their other friends. Probably reporters, too—can't tell you how many have been here, bothering Oliver, just when he has so much on his mind."

Reporters! Rennie thought. Was Daphne *that* well known?

"So if you'll go in with me Friday morning," Austin was saying to Peter, "we can bring up some extra benches from the basement. They'll give us about forty-eight more seats."

"Oh," Rennie cried. "I didn't know you could do that." Her parents' friends. There'd be room for them at the wedding!

When Rennie and Peter walked into the house, the dogs greeted them with such a clamor that Oliver came to the front hall. For the first time he looked like an old man. The vitality had gone out of his face. Nevertheless, Rennie and Peter saw at once how pleased he was by their coming.

Not that he was alone. Jorim was bringing firewood into the living room, and Judy came in with a platter of sandwiches. "You two must be starved," she said. "Sit down on the couch."

Oliver set a little table in front of them, and Judy poured the coffee. As soon as Peter had eaten, he went out to help Jorim.

The preview of the exhibition was still up. Rennie wondered whether Oliver hadn't really hung the pictures for Daphne because he knew all along that she'd never get to New York. Over the mantel, Serenity smiled down at the dog or child at her feet but, as usual, ignored her great-granddaughter. Below her, Lion and Duffy dragged themselves around Daphne's armchair, whimpering, unable to find peace. As she watched them, Rennie felt something inside her snap.

About to remove the little table he'd placed in front of her for lunch, Oliver saw it happen. He put the table down again and looked at her with deep tenderness. "After her stroke, Serenity," he said slowly, "Daphne kept asking why her life had been prolonged, what it was good for, the condition she was in. When thee came, she discovered there was something she was still called to do. Thy coming gave the remainder of her life meaning."

Suddenly overcome with emotion, Oliver left the room.

When Oliver and Peter and Rennie sat down at the round table and held hands before supper, it seemed unbearable. But out of the silence Oliver said something which comforted Rennie. "When Grandmother died," he recalled, "Daphne and I found solace in words someone quoted at Meeting: 'We think not a friend lost because he is gone into another room. . . .'" Letting go their hands, he murmured, "I've been reminded of that all day."

Early the next morning, while Rennie was washing the breakfast dishes, a strange car drove in. A man got out and came to the back door. Professor Anselm! As soon as he heard about Daphne, he'd rushed over!

But when he came in, happy to see Rennie again, jovially asking for Oliver, she realized that he couldn't have heard. Breaking the news was almost too much for her.

Professor Anselm looked terribly embarrassed. "I didn't know," he said. "Forgive me. I just happened to be over this way and I thought I'd say hello to Mr. Otis, see how those plants of his are doing, now that spring's here." He backed toward the door. "Do give him my sympathy."

"Wait. Don't go away. Peter's outside feeding the hens. He'd love to go down to the forest with you. I know Oliver'll be sorry he wasn't here."

As Professor Anselm started to leave, he shook his head. "Poor Mr. Otis. What's going to become of him here, alone?"

"I don't know," Rennie answered.

WHEN Heather arrived, Rennie'd expected her to take command of the house, the way she had the last time, but Heather was too upset to even try. She went right up to her room.

"It isn't just the shock," Rennie told Peter when he came in.

"It's those guilt feelings. She keeps wishing she'd appreciated her mother more. Why didn't she think of that sooner?" Looking at Peter, Rennie thought, He's different—more relaxed. "Has something happened?" she asked.

"Professor Anselm wants to see me."

"What about?"

"I don't know. He just asked would I come when I've finished my project. It's funny—he's more interested in what I'm going to do next year than anyone at Tilbury."

"Maybe it's a job!" Rennie said hopefully.

"I don't think so. I'm not in his field."

After supper Heather helped Rennie wash up. She talked incessantly, seeming to lean on Rennie for support. "You're so serene!" she exclaimed.

Rennie turned to her swiftly. "I *am?*"

"Yes. Last summer you seemed to be all agog."

"I was. Before I came here, I was mixed up, with everyone telling me the kind of person I had to be. But your mother gave me a new image of myself, something so much larger than I'd ever dreamed of. My own mother can't see how much I want her to understand this. She isn't even coming Friday."

"I thought your parents always came when someone died."

"Just Daddy. He'll arrive at two and leave right after the Meeting. There won't be time for him to see Firbank." Suddenly, Rennie had an idea. "Heather, do you think your father'd mind if my parents came Thursday night? It's a long ride for one day."

"I'm sure Father wouldn't mind. He's always regretted not being in touch. There's no one else of that generation left. Stephen and I want him to come back to London with me, but he says he belongs at Firbank. I wish we didn't live so far away."

Rennie hung up the dishcloth. "England! I'd love to go there sometime. It'll be years before Peter and I can see the museums your mother told me about."

That night when Rennie asked Oliver whether he'd mind having her parents come Thursday night—if she could persuade them—his face lighted up. "That would be first-rate!" he exclaimed.

Rennie rushed to the phone.

"No," her father said flatly. "Funerals depress your mother."

"It's not a funeral, Daddy. Daphne left her body to the Harvard Medical School so other stroke victims might be helped. This is just a Meeting of thanksgiving for her life, a memorial service. Oliver will be so pleased if you spend the night. Friday morning we'll row across the pond to the dunes and look at the ocean. Please come, Daddy, and bring Mother. Tell her I want her very much."

"Well, I'll speak to her."

By Thursday afternoon Rennie was becoming more and more apprehensive about her parents' visit. Would they come? And if they did, would it be a success? Rennie desperately wanted her father to find Firbank all that he'd remembered for over fifty years. She wondered suddenly whether that was why he never came back, except for those rare occasions when he felt it his duty to put in a quick appearance. Was he afraid that the reality wouldn't live up to his dream?

I must make his dream real, Rennie told herself, willing this with all her might. I must make him happy again at Firbank.

Around nine o'clock in the evening, when Rennie'd just about given up hope, her parents arrived. It was twenty years since her father'd been to Firbank, and the old farmhouse at the corner of the road that used to signal the turning into the Firbank lane was no longer there. So they'd wandered in the dark from one end of Salt Pond to the other.

Oliver welcomed them, his pleasure at seeing his cousin glowing in his face. But Rennie's father was stiff, out of his element. Her mother looked impressed by the genuine antiquity of the house she'd heard so much about, yet as she mumbled the phrases she believed were required of her on entering a house of mourning, she was pathetically ill at ease. Rennie noticed her startled expression when Oliver answered, "Thank thee."

Surprisingly it was Heather who eased the situation. While Rennie was taking her parents upstairs to the large front bedroom, Heather made tea and got out some cookies. By the time the Rosses came down again, Heather was sitting in the living room

241

behind the little table with the tea tray and Daphne's lovely Spode china, which delighted Rennie's mother.

And Peter—dear Peter! Unaffectedly he took the teacups from Heather and carried them to his future in-laws.

All at once Rennie's father jumped up, rattling the teacup in its saucer, almost dropping them both in his excitement.

Rushing to the fireplace, he exclaimed, "That's Grandmother!" He stood looking up above the mantel with the loveliest expression—the way he used to look at Rennie when she was small, before she began that painful struggle to become self-reliant.

"Hasn't thee ever seen this, Ed?" Oliver asked. "Daphne painted it shortly before Grandmother died. Well, thee only came here on those sad occasions, when thee wouldn't have gone into my study. It used to hang in there. Nice, isn't it?"

Rennie's father nodded, smiling. "She used to look down on me just this way. Joan, come here! See? That's what I've been trying to tell you about all these years—her warmth, her gaiety."

As Rennie's mother joined him, he turned to her with shining eyes. "See what I mean? She really had serenity."

Peter quietly took the threatened cup and saucer, putting them down on the tray. "Let me show you something else," he said. "It's even better." His eyes were shining, too, as he led the way into the dining room.

On FRIDAY morning Rennie's parents came down late, apologizing for oversleeping. It was ten thirty by the time they started for the pond. Only a few hours to recapture her father's childhood dream before driving to the service at Kendal.

In the rocky field, the oaks still had their brown last-year's leaves. The cedars and junipers were dull gray green. Another week or two and life would be returning, but Firbank looked bleak now, which depressed Rennie's parents.

Nothing turned out as she had hoped. Her father brightened when he saw the old boathouse. But he shook his head when Rennie, pulling in the painter, asked him to row. "Out of practice," he said.

Getting the two of them into the boat was *something*. When they reached the mud flat below the dunes and Rennie was trying to figure out how to put her parents ashore to see the ocean, they told her they'd rather not try. It wasn't worth the trouble.

"The ocean looks the same everywhere," her mother said, laughing. "We can see it anytime from the Goffes' porch."

Not *Daddy's* ocean, Rennie wanted to retort.

"By the way," she announced instead. "There'll be room for them at the wedding. And anyone else you'd like to invite. There are forty-eight more seats than I thought."

She expected this news to delight her parents, but it didn't have much effect. "Doubt if they'll come," her father muttered. "Way off here— Still, we'll give it a try."

Disembarking from the rowboat was even worse. Hanging on to the dock, Rennie watched anxiously as her father hoisted himself out. He puffed when he bent to give a hand to her mother, who was afraid to make the leap. By the time they got back to the house, Oliver and Heather had left for the Meeting.

Rennie put some food on the round table, thinking, as the three of them sat down, that probably this was the first time anyone ever ate here without pausing for grace. Suddenly tired, she longed for the comforting silence that would have eased her tension over the morning's failure.

While they were eating, her father mentioned the portrait for the first time. "Wonderful likeness!" he said. " "Why didn't you tell us you'd posed for it?"

"I did."

"Hm, I don't remember. But it's a gem. We've talked it over and we intend to have it. Do you think Oliver'd give it to us?"

"It's a beautiful thing," her mother said. "We ought to offer to pay for it, Ed."

Rennie didn't want her portrait hanging in Neville. "It has to stay here," she blurted out. "With your grandmother's. *The Two Serenitys*—they belong together."

"Shouldn't mind owning Grandmother's, either," her father murmured. "You should have told us a lot of things, Rennie. I never knew Daphne was a painter—an important one. Not till I read the write-up in the *Times*. She was about to have a show at the Museum of Contemporary Art. Did you know that?"

"Yes," Rennie answered wearily. "I should have told you."

WHEN they got to the meetinghouse, Rennie was recalling how she and Peter had triumphantly carried Daphne in the last time they were there. She didn't think she could stand looking at the wicker chair this afternoon. But she felt better the moment she caught sight of Peter, helping Sam and Jorim with the parking. So many cars! Rhode Island, Connecticut, Massachusetts, New York. For the first time Rennie realized that she had known only one small segment of Daphne's long life. The rest of it had touched hundreds of others, who had traveled great distances simply to give thanks for having known her.

The vestibule was jammed. Someone—was it Peter?—had removed the wicker chair.

Inside, the hushed room was already packed. The only three seats left together were on one of the extra benches.

"Isn't there any organ?" Rennie's mother whispered as they sat down. Rennie shook her head.

Sitting between her parents, wondering whether Peter would find a seat when he came in, Rennie couldn't seem to center down. She kept imagining how her mother was feeling in this homely place with no music to soothe her, so different from anything she had ever experienced. But what can I do? Rennie asked herself miserably. How can I make what's right for me right for her, too?

With relief she saw that Peter, Sam and Jorim had come in. They were standing at the back. Down front, near where Oliver and Heather were sitting, John Ludlow was getting up to speak.

"We're meeting to give thanks for the life of our friend Daphne Otis," he said in a steady voice, "as well as for the love by which her husband and daughter made her last years victorious. And they were victorious in every sense—professionally, but even more in the impact they had on other people's lives. No one could visit Daphne without feeling uplifted.

"At the beginning of their life together," John went on, "Daphne and Oliver resolved to turn all the treasures they possessed into the channel of universal love. And that was what they did. It was the business of their lives. Their home became this channel."

As John Ludlow sat down, Rennie bowed her head and thought of Daphne and Oliver deciding to throw over the jewelry job and live at Firbanks—speeding twenty-nine miles an hour to break the news to Serenity.

Rennie lifted her head and looked at Oliver. John's words had brought tears to his eyes. Rennie thought they were quite possibly tears of joy. This was something she'd noticed during the past few days, the joy that had gradually surmounted his grief. He and Daphne had created a perfect relationship. If there had been bad moments—no couple lived happily ever after—Oliver had forgotten. He had nothing to regret. He sat now simply rejoicing in the perfectness he'd shared with Daphne.

Her father bumped against Rennie's arm. He was fidgeting, as he used to do when he came here with his grandmother. Now he was getting old. Rennie's effort to re-create the delights of his childhood had fallen flat. He didn't even climb the dune to look at the ocean. But Serenity's portrait—that had stirred him. Serenity's love, Rennie thought. All these years—he's never forgotten.

His grandmother's serenity, which her father remembered wistfully and Rennie craved, wasn't, she realized now, a virtue in itself. It was only the state of mind that seemed to come naturally to those who looked for the divine spark in everyone to appeal to, knowing also that it didn't always get the upper hand.

Now Mary Young was getting to her feet, hoisting herself up by gripping the bench in front, just as Daphne did the last time Rennie was here. Mary was a homely old woman, the wife and mother of potato farmers, whose knobby hands and thin body proclaimed how hard she'd worked all her life.

She turned to pick up a book that lay on the seat beside her purse. "When my husband died," she said, "Daphne Otis brought me this book, *Some Fruits of Solitude*. Daphne said the reflections in it meant a great deal to her. I'd like to read a few of them now.

"They that love beyond the world cannot be separated by it.

"Death cannot kill what never dies.

"Nor can spirits ever be divided, that love and live in the same divine principle, the root and record, of their friendship.

"Death is but crossing the world, as friends do the seas; they live in one another still."

Mary shut the book and slowly let herself down onto the bench.

Did Daphne live in Rennie still? Wasn't that exactly what Rennie'd kept trying to have happen with Serenity? Because she was her descendant, her namesake, she'd believed she might become the kind of person Serenity was. But when she looked at the portrait, her great-grandmother refused to speak to her.

She spoke to Daddy, though. Right away!

He'd known her. Was that what made the difference?

The silence overtook her, that infinity that couldn't be contained in words. It reached beyond the world, loosening Rennie with the assurance that she could let go because she wouldn't drift away forever. She'd come back.

What Daphne'd given her she could pass on to others someday, when she had training and experience; when she could make art live for other young people the way Daphne had made it live for her, not as pigment on canvas, but as the projection of a spirit.

Someday. But right now it's Heather who needs Daphne—what Daphne gave me. Why can't I pass that on to her? When this Meeting's over, Rennie said to herself, I'll speak to her. I don't know what I'll say, maybe nothing. In its own time, way will open. But I'll bring her this thing of Daphne's that's in me—the root and record of our friendship.

Suddenly the silence evaporated. All around the room people were shaking hands and murmuring. Smiling at her father and her mother, Rennie reached out her hands to both.

Her mother heaved a sigh, as if she'd been holding her breath. "They made dying seem so beautiful," she murmured. She looked relieved, as if a fear she'd carried with her all her life was fading away. Then she said, looking around the room, "That dress she

246

designed will look perfect here. I'm going to hunt for the material tomorrow. It has to be just right—ethereal."

Rennie gave her mother's hand a squeeze.

The crowd they were caught in moved slowly toward the door. Peter was waiting there. He put his arm around Rennie's waist as they went down the steps, out into the sunshine.

Mary Lancashire was standing on the lawn, looking up at the Ross family. Happy expectancy shone in her wrinkled face. "Edmund!" she called before he reached the bottom step. "Edmund! I knew thee when thee was so high. Thee used to come to Meeting with Serenity Otis."

Rennie's father walked toward her, smiling. "Right. Couldn't sit still then. Can't now." He laughed. "To think you've remembered me all these years!" He was in no hurry to leave.

Nancy and Sandy were running across the lawn.

"Rennie! Peter! We're coming to your wedding!"

"Of course you are," Peter told them.

"You know the little table? Can we carry it?"

"What little table?"

"The one with the certificate—that long thing. After the boy and girl promise to love each other forever, two people carry the table over to their bench so they can sign their names. Haven't you ever been to a wedding?"

"Not one like that. And we didn't know about the little table, but you're the only two people we'd let carry it for us."

After Nancy and Sandy had taken off across the lawn again, Rennie glanced at her father anxiously, certain he'd be impatient with her for keeping him waiting. But he was still listening raptly to Mary Lancashire, turning to Rennie's mother from time to time to make sure she was taking in every word.

"Peter," Rennie said, "let's ask Mary Lancashire to be the other overseer. She knew Daphne for years. Is that okay with you?"

By way of answer, Peter drew Rennie nearer to the old woman, whose recollections still made her wrinkled face glow. How happy she looked when Rennie asked her! "Thee reminds me of thy great-grandmother," she said, as she always did.

Rennie's father beamed. He'd come home.

Oliver and Heather were standing near the syringa bush, surrounded by a host of friends. Rennie let go of Peter's hand. "Be right back," she said. "I'm just going over to see Heather."

Ten days later Professor Anselm returned to Firbank.

He was afraid Oliver might decide to leave and he wanted to impress on him how important it was to keep the Vietnamese Forest going. The National Academy of Sciences, he explained, had made a study showing that nature alone couldn't repair in a hundred years the ecological damage caused by defoliation chemicals. But, the professor believed, American scientists might succeed, if they only understood the need to tackle the job. Oliver must persuade them.

Rennie wouldn't have known all this if Professor Anselm hadn't told Peter when he went to see him at the university. The professor repeated what he'd said to Oliver: he absolutely must publish an account of his experiment. Professor Anselm realized that Oliver couldn't write and work outdoors at the same time. So if this was agreeable to Oliver, he was going to offer Peter a fellowship. Not in astronomy—that wasn't his to give. But if Peter wished to switch later, he'd have a master's degree in forestry to his credit. Since Firbank was within commuting distance of the university, Peter could help out with the experiment while Oliver wrote.

Oliver had thanked the professor. Nothing, he said, would make him so happy as having Peter and Serenity living with him. Firbank belonged to Serenity, too. And if anyone would nurse his seedlings faithfully, it was Peter.

"You mean," Rennie cried, when Peter got back to Tilbury and told her, "we're going to live at Firbank? Oh, Peter!"

"I never thought I'd go to grad school so soon! Only, Rennie, this isn't going to be much fun for you—just keeping house."

"At Firbank? I'd love it. But you want to be an astronomer."

"Going into another field may be a good thing. Some of the most original research is being done today by scholars who've cut across disciplines. I may want to do something I haven't thought of yet."

The following week, when Daphne's exhibition opened for a private showing, Rennie and Peter were in the middle of exams. Peter couldn't leave, but Rennie rushed down to New York for the afternoon.

At the door of the museum, Heather was waiting for her. She looked much more relaxed than she had after the Meeting of thanksgiving. In fact, Heather looked happy. "I couldn't wait for you inside any longer," she said, hugging Rennie. "I'm so impatient to tell you what's just happened."

Before the opening, the trustees of the museum and Miss Chase, the director, had given a luncheon in honor of her father and herself. "Of Mother really," Heather said sadly. But then the happiness returned. Over coffee, she said, the chairman of the board announced that they intended to publish a monograph— a biography and comprehensive study of Daphne Otis and her art! Miss Chase had assured Oliver that he was the only person who could do justice to the book. Would he undertake it? Naturally he'd have to engage someone to assist him. The museum was prepared to underwrite the expense.

"When Miss Chase mentioned an assistant," Heather told Rennie, "Father turned to me and exclaimed, 'Who but Serenity? She'll be living at Firbank! Next to thee, she's the only one who could really help.'"

Rennie thought she'd collapse from joy, right on the sidewalk. A monograph! It could be the basis for her doctoral dissertation.

"You're the only one I'd want to have interpreting Mother's lifework," Heather was saying. "You understood her. But first you and Peter have to have a holiday. You've worked much too hard and will again, come September. So Stephen and I would like you to visit us—fly to London right after the wedding."

"Heather!"

"I'm serious. Stephen and the children and I are coming to Firbank in July. Meanwhile you and Peter can stay in our flat. Or you can drive our car to Yorkshire, where Mother spent her childhood. Seeing the beauty and wildness of the moors will tell you a great deal about her."

A pilgrimage, Rennie said to herself. We'll be making a pilgrimage and ending up at Firbank, like Oliver and Daphne. But she shook her head. "We don't have the money. Even if we stayed with you, the trip . . . Maybe someday."

The museum was jammed. Oliver was standing in the lobby, talking to some men and women. When he saw Rennie, he broke away and came over to greet her. "It's marvelous! The way the pictures are hung, the lighting! I'll take thee up to the gallery." He handed her a book.

How happy he looks, Rennie thought. He's experiencing the pleasure for both of them. "They live in one another still."

Heather was already surrounded by people who wanted her to tell them about her mother. "First come and meet the trustees," Oliver was saying to Rennie. Taking her arm, he drew her toward the group he'd just left and introduced her.

It hadn't occurred to Rennie that anyone but Oliver and Heather would notice her here. So she wasn't prepared for the reception. These people had been looking forward to meeting her. They wanted to see how her real-life face compared with Daphne's drawing. Her cheeks got hot, but she managed a smile.

Then Oliver led Rennie up a long marble staircase. In the gallery, there was such a mob that it was impossible to see the pictures. Rennie's portrait was completely hidden.

"Thee and Peter will have to come after exams," Oliver said. "By then the crowds may have thinned out."

"Won't they be even worse, when it's open to the public?"

"Maybe." Oliver's face was shining. "Heather told thee about the monograph? I thought thee'd be pleased. We'll have a lovely time, working together!"

Before Rennie could answer, some people buttonholed Oliver. While he talked to them, Rennie stood in the middle of the gallery, awed by the grandeur of the place, the intensity of the crowd. Looking down, she noticed the book Oliver had given her. She'd been so overwhelmed that she hadn't realized it was the catalogue. *The Two Serenitys*, the title read. There was Rennie's great-grandmother on the front cover! And on the back, Rennie!

Peter, she cried inside herself. Peter, I need you! This is too much joy and sadness and beauty to bear alone.

Heather caught up with her then and led Rennie off to a quiet corner. She wanted to tell her how relieved she was that her father wouldn't be doing the heavy work anymore. "You and Peter are an absolute blessing," she said.

Then, to Rennie's amazement, Heather began referring to conversations she'd been having with Mrs. Ross.

"Wait a minute," Rennie broke in. "You and Mother have been talking? What about?"

"The wedding festivities. Father's looking forward so eagerly to having your family at Firbank. He wants this to be a memorable occasion. Before flying home on Wednesday, I'm going to get everything arranged. Your parents and the Hollands will stay at Firbank. The Ludlows and Hills and Youngs have offered to put up your brothers and their families. Father's planning a dinner the evening before the wedding, and your mother said she'd like to provide the food. It's going to be just lovely!"

"Oh, Heather, I wish you were going to be there."

"So do I. But now that you'll be living at Firbank, there'll be lots and lots of time for us to spend together."

CHAPTER NINE

OLIVER's prediction was accurate—Rennie's portrait stole the show. Neville couldn't have been more impressed if she had been chosen Miss Universe. Car pools formed to go and see the portrait, and one morning Oliver called to say the museum wished to acquire it. The Rosses were the most talked-of people in town.

Rennie hardly dared go home. But on their last free weekend before graduation she and Peter braved it.

When Rennie went to her room, she found the wedding dress hanging in the closet. Her hand trembled as she took it out and held it at arm's length on its hanger. Filled with apprehension, she decided to try it on now, while she was alone. The material was lovely—ethereal, as her mother had put it.

But I mustn't expect it to look like that sketch Daphne made, Rennie warned herself. How could Mother— No one could.

Stretching for the zipper, smoothing the skirt, Rennie finally faced herself in the long mirror. She was overwhelmed. Rennie had been certain that no material, however gossamer, could translate Daphne's sketch into an actual garment. Yet here she was, clothed in that mysterious dreamlike beauty Daphne had envisioned.

Running down the hall, she burst into her mother's room and threw her arms around her. "This is heavenly—more beautiful than I ever believed it could be! How did you manage it?"

Rennie's mother surveyed her, looking, Rennie thought, satisfied with her daughter's appearance for the first time in years. "I almost didn't. You'll never know how close I came to giving up."

"What happened?"

"I'm not sure. Daphne's sketch made me visualize how she saw you, but I wasn't able to transfer the idea to a pattern. Then maybe it was seeing you at Firbank or seeing the portrait—I don't know—but in the meetinghouse I seemed to be saying to myself, It's not how Rennie's going to look in that dress that's important. It's how she'll feel. That was a revelation. Suddenly I knew I could do it."

Rennie hugged her mother again. "I'm so happy with it."

After dinner that evening Rennie's father made a little speech. He was in a festive mood, but Rennie knew that he was having trouble controlling his emotions.

There was a time, he said, when the generation gap between them had seemed insurmountable. Luckily that was over. "I don't know," he observed with a touch of humor Rennie didn't think he had, "whether it's because you've grown older or Mother and I have grown younger. At any rate, we're very pleased with the way things have worked out and we want to say this, not just in words, but with a little gift for your graduation." He fished in his pocket and handed Peter an envelope. "It's for you both."

Rennie could see by the way Peter fumbled with the envelope that he was having trouble controlling his emotions, too. When Rennie took in what he was holding, she gasped. Round-trip tickets on the *Queen Elizabeth,* and a check with the memo: "For travel in England."

"Daddy! Mother! That's no *little* gift!"

Peter was baffled.

"Heather and Stephen invited us to spend the summer," Rennie explained. "I didn't tell you before, because I didn't think we could go. But Mother and Daddy must have found out from Heather." She turned to her parents. "Thank you so much!"

PASSPORTS, luggage, the marriage license, graduation—it was all beautiful, but enough to make one dizzy. Then, at last, the peace of Firbank! Now Rennie could begin to live.

All the windows were open, and Oliver, in his shirt sleeves, was polishing the antique brass handle on the front door, when she drove up with her parents. Inside, everything was shining, reflecting the enthusiasm with which Oliver and Heather had washed and polished in anticipation of this weekend.

A blue air letter, addressed to Rennie, lay on the table in the entrance hall. It was from Heather, saying how much she wished that she could have stayed for the wedding. But she wrote:

At the precise moment—eight o'clock in the evening here— Stephen and I will be centering down in the sitting room, joining Kendal Friends as they celebrate your marriage. A fortnight later we'll be driving to Southampton to meet your ship!

Peter arrived the next day, with his parents and his two shy sisters, Beth and Evey. Rennie's mother was bustling around the kitchen. Her father was helping Oliver extend the dining-room table. The way he welcomed the Hollands, one would have thought it was his house. After the greetings and introductions Peter took his family up to their rooms.

The Hollands had barely arrived when Jane and Eddy drove up with their brood, and right behind them were Larry and Victoria. The children exploded into the yard. Rennie's father had been looking forward to this moment. "All aboard!" he shouted. "We're going over to the dunes. You'd better come along, too, Larry and Eddy, just in case someone has to be fished out. And," he added firmly, "to row."

It was almost dinnertime when they returned, and by then Jonathan and his family were just driving in.

Rennie wandered through the house, talking to everybody. In the kitchen, four Ross women ran around hunting for serving dishes in the strange cupboards, bumping into each other. At the front door, the Ludlows and the Youngs, Mary Lancashire and the Hills were arriving.

At last dinner was ready. The grown-ups sat down at the huge dining-room table. The children had their own place at a picnic table under the window. Oliver, seated at the head of the table with Rennie's and Peter's parents on either side, looked around the room happily. He thanked everyone for coming. Then he asked his guests to join in giving silent thanks for the meal, for the beautiful occasion that brought them together, for the love that bound them one to another.

At the foot of the table, Rennie, sitting with Peter and his sisters, thought her heart would burst with happiness as hands were held all around. She couldn't eat much. Turning to Beth and Evey, she tried without success to make them talk.

"I suppose all these Rosses are a bit overwhelming," she finally said, laughing. "The Hollands are outnumbered."

Beth surprised her. "You'll be a Holland yourself, tomorrow," she said.

WALKING in from the vestibule with her hand in Peter's, entering the gathered silence their friends and relations had prepared, Rennie felt it was just like coming into the meetinghouse on First Day, expectant and quiet. This was no different, except that their parents and the overseers were on the facing benches, waiting for them. Rennie's mother and father sat next to her side of the narrow marriage bench. Peter's parents were on his side. Oliver, Mary Lancashire and the Youngs sat behind them.

Looking down at her bouquet, Rennie thought that if she and

Peter had been married last fall, Daphne would have been sitting up there. But Daphne wouldn't have been happy. She wanted them to wait.

Early this morning, the last day of May, Peter went out into the Firbank woods and picked every one of the wild flowers Daphne had sketched, all but the robin's plantain, which he couldn't find. So he brought Rennie a fistful of tiny bluets with bright yellow centers instead. "Quaker-ladies," Oliver'd called them.

Rennie was approaching her parents. They looked spellbound. Whether it was the dress—with the afternoon sun shining through the tall windows, it actually did have that mysterious shimmer Daphne had envisioned—or whether they were asking God's blessing, they seemed entranced.

As Rennie glanced up at Oliver, he gave her the affectionate nod she loved.

Turning and sitting down with Peter, Rennie faced all the rest of the company. Awed, she thought, I've become the girl on the third-floor landing—the one I used to talk to when I was small!

Her brothers, their wives and wriggling kids, the Hills and the Ludlows—was everyone here? Yes, row after row, clear back to the door, the benches were occupied. Not only had Kendal people come, but friends of Rennie's parents had traveled all the way from Neville. Not now, Rennie admonished herself. Later, out on the lawn, I'll see everyone.

Now she must turn inward, focus on the solemnity of the moment. All that came to her, though, was the rush of joy she had felt, standing at the kitchen door this morning, watching Peter go off to pick the wild flowers.

After he'd disappeared in the dark woods, Rennie stood there a little longer, feeling the smooth floorboards under her bare feet, smelling the spring freshness. The tulips were still tightly shut, asleep. So, apparently, was everyone in the house. Only she and Peter were awake, seeing the rosy dawn.

Now, when she turned, she saw that he was giving the signal. It was time. She rested the bouquet on the bench. They stood up and he reached for her right hand.

Looking at her with his whole self in his eyes, Peter said clearly, "In the presence of God and these friends, I take thee, Serenity Ross, to be my wife, promising, with divine assistance . . ." For a second he paused, searching her eyes, as if to make sure she believed it. Then he went on. "To be unto thee a loving and faithful husband as long as we both shall live."

Longing to communicate to him that her heart stood in perfect sincerity, Rennie looked at Peter and said softly, "In the presence of God and these friends, I take thee, Peter Holland, to be my husband, promising, with divine assistance, to be unto thee a loving and faithful wife as long as we both shall live."

Peter slid the ring on Rennie's finger. Then he bent over and kissed her.

They sat down again.

Bowing her head, Rennie stared at her hand. While she was still trying to take in the full significance of the wedding ring, Nancy and Sandy carried in the little table and placed it in front of Peter. The long certificate was rolled out on the table, with a weight laid over each edge to keep it from curling up. The weights were maroon cushions filled with sand, used only at weddings. They had been in the Otis family for generations.

As Peter took up the pen that lay beside the right weight and signed his name, Rennie noticed how beautifully the certificate was embossed in large italic letters. *Whereas Peter Hallburt Holland . . .* He put the pen down. Nancy and Sandy moved the table a few inches nearer to Rennie. She wrote carefully under Peter's name, *Serenity Ross Holland.* How strange it looked!

With great dignity Nancy pushed the weights aside and picked up the certificate. Mounting the steps to the gallery, she handed the long scroll to Oliver. He took it and then stood, holding the certificate up before him.

"*Whereas,*" he began reading, "*Peter Hallburt Holland, of Charlesbury, State of Ohio, son of Hallburt Holland and Ann, his wife, and Serenity Millburn Ross, of Neville, State of New York . . .*"

Rennie knew the words. But Oliver's voice invested them with more than their inherent meaning. When he came to the promises,

Rennie told herself that they would resound in her soul forever.

"*And Peter Hallburt Holland, taking Serenity Millburn Ross by the hand, did on this solemn occasion declare that he took her to be his wife, promising, with divine assistance . . .*"

Tears of joy sprang to Rennie's eyes. We're married!

"*And we,*" Oliver concluded, "*having been present at the solemnization of the said marriage, have, as witnesses thereto, set our hands.*" Rolling up the certificate, Oliver asked everyone present, including the children, to sign it at the rise of the Meeting. Every guest, he explained, was a witness.

Friends were bowing their heads, settling into silence.

We're married! Rennie exulted again. We don't have to stay apart anymore! Sinking into the quiet, she thought, Still, the last nine months were the best. We felt free. We were helping each other. We were staying apart *together*. It was hard, but for us it was the right thing.

Turning toward Peter, Rennie saw that his mother was standing up. Could *she* be about to speak?

Mrs. Holland looked out over the room in a shy but friendly way. Then in her musical voice she said, "My husband and I understand that anyone who feels led to speak is welcome to do so. There's something we want very much to say and we decided I should be the spokes*woman*." Her expression became downright mischievous. Mrs. Holland went on, turning serious.

"My husband and I are teachers. We're deeply concerned about young people—not just our own, but those entrusted to us at school. That has made us appreciate the care Kendal Friends gave our son and our new daughter, helping them to grow into an understanding of the commitment they've just made. May God bless them and all the folks who gave them a spiritual home."

She'd said this beautifully, Rennie thought. And now we're part of the ongoing creation, Peter and I. Tonight we'll be starting a home at Firbank, a place inside our encircling arms for our children to come to someday. Can I really make it a place of friendliness, refreshment and peace, where God becomes more real to those who dwell there and those who visit? It's my central wish.

Looking at the opposite benches, where her brothers sat with their wives and children, Rennie said to herself, I want them all to come. Summer vacations, Thanksgiving, Christmas, all through the year. I hope that from our encircling arms serenity will spill over onto everyone.

Oliver was touching Peter's shoulder, indicating that the Meeting was about to end. The two of them should walk out while their friends were still supporting them in silence.

Getting up, Rennie turned toward her parents. She'd see them again in a few minutes, outside at the reception on the lawn. But right now she wanted them to know how deeply she loved them. Her eyes sent them the message.

Hand in hand Rennie and Peter started for the door. Peter was drawing her forward so fast, they were almost running. Skimming over the gray carpet, they dashed through the vestibule, out into the sunshine. There wasn't a soul around.

Peter took Rennie in his arms.

"Wasn't it beautiful?" she gasped as he squeezed the breath out of her. "I thought I was going to be scared, but it felt just like any First Day. It is *our* first day."

Agreeing joyously, Peter let her go. "What were you thinking about during the silence?"

"Oh, Peter, to tell thee that is going to take as long as we both shall live!"

I Take Thee, Serenity is the third of Daisy Newman's novels which revolve around the warmth and spirit of Kendal, a small Quaker community in Rhode Island. Not surprisingly, it is a book which expresses the author's own religious feelings.

Born in England of American parents, Daisy Newman spent virtually all of her childhood in Europe, where her father's

business had taken the family. She attended schools in France and Switzerland and, later, Radcliffe College in Massachusetts. All that early traveling, she feels, is at least partly behind her development as a writer. "Writing was something I could do wherever I went," she explains.

However, the real force behind Mrs. Newman's work, she says, is "the joy of family life and, from that, the joy that overflows into other relationships." Her experiences with her children—she has a grown son and daughter and is a grandmother several times over—have led to a deep and abiding interest in young people.

Daisy Newman

Indeed, as *Serenity* was being written, a group of graduate students and young professionals were gathering regularly at Mrs. Newman's home in suburban Connecticut. "We talked about ourselves and our lives," she says. "They knew a little about *Serenity*, of course, and what they said confirmed what I had written. It made me feel that what I'd done had validity in their lives."

In addition to the Kendal books, Daisy Newman's works include another novel, *Now that April's There;* a history of Quakers in America entitled *A Procession of Friends;* and two children's stories.

The deeply moving story of Bill Wilson,
co-founder of Alcoholics Anonymous

Bill W.

A CONDENSATION OF THE BOOK BY
ROBERT THOMSEN

ILLUSTRATED BY GEORGE JONES

Who *was* Bill W., a man who helped change the lives of a million people throughout the world?

A small-town Vermont boy, brought up by an idealistic grandfather, married to a beautiful and spirited city girl, Bill W. was a tangle of contradictions. He was a leader, as he found out during World War I, a powerful persuader, proved by his glittering career on Wall Street, but he was not his own man.

As his dependence on alcohol increased he more and more lost control of his life's direction, of personal relationships—save for the continuing loyalty of his wife—until after one night of terror in Akron he found a fellow sufferer on the same path to self-destruction. Dr. Bob was a Yankee like Bill, a surgeon and a drunk. It took one to know one. It took one to save one. And so Alcoholics Anonymous was born.

How two desperate men, starting from the bottom, parlayed what they had learned from helping one another into a unique worldwide fellowship makes an almost incredible story. At last count, there were twenty-two thousand AA groups in ninety-two countries, plus four hundred or so "loners" who keep in touch by mail and telephone, either with the General Service Office in New York or their nearest local group. In the United States and Canada, so widespread is AA it would be hard to find a telephone book which hasn't an Alcoholics Anonymous number listed for people in need to call.

The story of Bill W. is a stirring spiritual odyssey through triumph, failure and rebirth, with vital meaning for men and women everywhere.

CHAPTER ONE

WHEN he stood beside his father, Bill Wilson never felt too tall and skinny or that his ears stuck out too far, and he was never afraid that he was going to do something awkward that would make people laugh and call him "Beanpole." He was realizing it had always been true that if his father was nearby, there was nothing to fear. But tonight everything was different, wild and dangerous, and whatever his father was doing inside that shed at the quarry's entrance, he wished he'd hurry, come out and join him.

It had to be midnight now, because it had been after eleven when they'd passed the church, and once again the thought of the old clock high above the silent town filled him with wonder. Never in his life had he been awake and out riding through the night when everyone else was sleeping. How many times had he been warned by his mother that God did not approve of nine-year-old boys being up past bedtime! But his mother and God had no connection with what was happening here.

It was one of those clear September nights when a three-quarter moon against a sky ablaze with stars makes the shadows doubly dark. Ink-black fir trees grew above the quarry, then sloped down to frame the clearing where he waited. The only spot of light on the mountainside was this open shelf, and here everything glistened. Slabs of Vermont marble, ten, twenty feet high, towered above him, and beneath his feet marble chips glittered like snow, their eerie whiteness adding to the hush that was settling over the world.

His eyes slid to the lighted window, and he listened for some indication that his father was still there. But there was no sound, and when finally all he could make out was the distant jangle of a harness as the mare shifted about, he turned and took several tentative steps toward the door with the sign G. WILSON, MANAGER hanging over it. As he did so, both his hands reached up and out—an almost automatic movement, with fingers spread wide, that his family said he'd been making ever since he was an infant— trying to feel and grab hold of moonlight. Tonight the light had no warmth and the fingers relaxed; his hands fell to his sides. A shiver of excitement—not quite fear—gripped his body. Something was going to happen and it had to do with him, with his father and with the fact that no one in the world knew they were here.

In the last few hours he had moved so far from the ordinary, so far into danger, there had been no time to review the steps that had brought him here. It had begun while he and his sister had waited at the supper table. Out in the kitchen they had heard voices; first his mother's, shrill and frightening, then his father's, not arguing, just quietly stating some fact. On and on it had gone, but he couldn't make out the words. Then there had been the shocking silence, and when he had been able to bear it no longer, he'd pushed back his chair and run into the kitchen. And there he had found them, confronting each other: his mother, head high, shoulders squared, one hand grasping the side of the table, and his father, not three feet away, looking deep into her eyes.

In an instant he knew what was happening. His father had told her something, but—he could read this in the tilt of her head, the rigid stance of her body—whatever it was she would not believe it. Then, when he looked back at his father, he saw what he had never seen before. His father nodded, accepting her terrible judgment, and without a word went out the door to the yard. And Billy watched him go, and he knew that his mother was watching too.

At supper and afterward, when they'd sat silently in the little front room until his mother said she felt one of her headaches coming on and asked if he would put his little sister to bed, his mind had shot off in all directions, searching for an explanation. There had been quarrels before, usually, Billy thought, because of something he had done or that he and his father had been involved in together; then his father had always spoken out. To-night he had stood there; he had not argued.

Billy was aware that his father had to be on guard, just as he had to be, or his father too could be placed on probation and would have to think up some method of winning his way back into her affection. And somehow, knowing this had made all sorts of things easier. But now his father must have committed a wrong Billy knew nothing about.

Up in his own room, he had flung himself across the bed. *Why* hadn't his father answered? As the alarm clock ticked off endless minutes, one thought demanded attention: If his father could walk away and not return for supper, might he not walk away and *never* come back? It was ten thirty when he heard the front door open. The wave of relief that poured through him seemed to take every particle of his strength.

Other boys had told him you could tell when a man was drunk by the heavy way he walked. The opposite was true of Gilman Wilson. Billy listened to the light footsteps coming carefully up the stairs. Outside his door they paused, but only for a second; then there his father stood, swaying slightly, looking down at him. Their eyes met and held, and still saying nothing, his father turned and started away with a slight jerk of the head, and Billy knew he was to follow.

Downstairs, he was sure they'd go out back, where they could talk without being overheard, but instead his father opened the front door and he could see, standing there, a horse and buggy from O'Reilly's livery stable. His father got in and patted the seat beside him. Billy crawled up, drawn like someone in a dream, and they started off through the silent town. A jug of whiskey was on the baseboard by their feet, and occasionally his father picked it up and took a swig, but their eyes were focused straight ahead and neither one said a word.

He never knew how long the trip had taken, he never cared, for as they trotted along he was seeing it all—the moon, the road ahead as bright as day, the fields enameled over with tiny white flowers—and he was seeing it with such awareness that he knew it was being recorded, that he would remember it all the days of his life. Even when they reached the quarry gate and the old mare strained on up the mountain, even when his father stopped and tied the reins to a tree, even then Billy had not worried.

But when his father disappeared into the shed and left him to wait, he could no longer tell what had happened and what was a dream. Superimposed over the picture of his father walking away was the memory of the two of them facing each other and his father nodding. Billy dug his hands into his pockets and squinted at the sky. How *could* his father give in and just walk away? He felt deserted, betrayed.

Once he was about to run and push the shed door open, but he stopped himself. He was supposed to wait. In time his father would come out, put his hand on his shoulder and explain. And everything would be made right again.

But when his father finally stepped from the shed, he moved off and leaned back against a tree, looking across the valley, and when he spoke it was not at all what Billy had expected.

"You'll take care of her, won't you, Billy?" he said. "You'll be good to your mother, and to little Dotty too." And he reached out a hand and mussed Billy's hair. "Sure you will," he said. "Sure. You're okay, Billy." And Billy knew that this was it.

In his right hand his father was carrying the jug, and Billy watched him lift it to his lips and take a long, slow drink. *This was it.* No explanation would be given. And Billy knew, instantly and with complete certainty, that this was as it had to be. His father was silent now as he had been before his mother, and Billy could see his silence was not weakness, it was strength. If he'd felt he must put it all into words, it would have stirred up the ugliness, made it live again. Women and little children put everything into words. They had to. Men didn't. This silence, this acceptance, in no way made his father less. And suddenly, looking at the plain bony face in the moonlight, Billy felt closer to his father than he'd ever felt to anyone; he felt a part of him.

When Gilman Wilson spoke again, it was as they always talked when they were outside at night: about stars and the moon and the mountains—the great Taconic range and the Green—and how they had been here even before there were men to call them mountains. But behind the words this time Billy felt another, deeper meaning that he couldn't quite grasp. He did know that it was serious. And listening to the voice he knew better than any other, it came to him that he didn't only *feel* a part of his father, he *was* a part of him—just as his father was part of Billy's grandfather and he in turn of *his* father. Suddenly he understood why, when they walked together through town and met someone and his father would say, "This is my son," he always had that same solemn feeling inside. He was aware of something *ancestral* in himself.

Billy listened to everything his father said now about the vast galaxies sailing through space. He knew how long it took a speck of light to come down and reach the two of them on their mountain and he was speaking of trillions of miles and billions of years, and he told Billy that they weren't just citizens of Vermont or even just the United States; they were citizens of this whole tremendous universe.

Such talk, he said, could sometimes make a man despair. Against the immensity of the cosmos his own insignificance could make him feel lost and no-account. But in this instant Billy Wilson was feeling the exact opposite. The thing he'd learned, the awareness of his descent, was still with him and he knew this was actual and perfect, while everything else—people laughing at him, or fights with his mother—was trivial and unimportant.

In time his father rose and, placing his great hand on Billy's shoulder, led him back to the buggy. By the time they reached the pike Billy's eyelids were heavy. He let his head fall against the prickly tweed of his father's sleeve, and slept. Years later Bill Wilson could still remember the feel of his father's coat.

When he awakened in the morning his sister, Dorothy, was waiting to tell him that their father had gone away.

This was Rutland, Vermont, in the autumn of 1905.

IN THE town of East Dorset word of the final separation of Gilman and Emily Griffith Wilson came as a shock, but not really a surprise. There had never been much that was surprising in the story of this handsome, healthy young couple who'd been born in the same year, 1870, in the same township, had attended the same schools, the same church. It was true they had been separated briefly when Gilly had gone off to Albany College in New York State and Emily to the normal school in Castleton, but they were together for the holidays and it was not long before they fell in love and married. There was no question that these young lovers from the oldest Vermont stock seemed meant for one another. Yet from the start—and everyone who knew them sensed this—these were two proud and strong individuals with marked differences of temperament.

The Griffiths had always been loners. When they arrived in Vermont they chose a rugged piece of farmland just below the timberline. Years later Bill was to describe his mother's family as people of extreme intelligence, with immense will, immense valor and fortitude, who became lawyers, teachers and judges, but were not dearly loved.

The Wilsons, on the other hand, seem to have felt some deep need for the warmth of others. Tall, rawboned, they were likable men who laughed easily and were superb storytellers. For generations they had been quarrymen, often moving rapidly up from worker to manager. On occasion they might stay too late in the taverns, and sometimes they may have arrived home slightly under the weather, but with the Wilsons such little failings were easily forgiven. At the close of the Civil War, William C. Wilson, Gilly's father, had wisely chosen for his bride Helen Barrows, one of whose ancestors had built the largest house in town. For years this had been run as an inn, the old Barrows House. Soon after the wedding William discovered that he quite enjoyed managing an inn, and changed the name to the Wilson House. After his death in 1885, Helen Wilson, with the aid of her young sons, George and Gilman, kept the place going. It was congenial work, she said, making strangers comfortable.

Griffiths and Wilsons. For all the doughty New England virtues they shared, it would be difficult to imagine two more disparate ways of living. But this appears not to have worried either Gilly Wilson or Emily Griffith when, in 1894, Gilly asked Fayette Griffith for his daughter's hand in marriage.

The newlyweds set up housekeeping in the rear of the Wilson House, and here—fittingly enough—in a small room behind the bar, William G. Wilson was born on November 26, 1895. Two years later came little Dorothy. By then Gilly was overseeing two quarries, and his advice was being sought about quarry sites by people in Boston and New York, which meant he'd often be away for several nights running. In 1902 he was offered the management of the entire Rutland-Florence operation. He found a house on Chestnut Street in Rutland and moved his family in, hoping perhaps that this promised a change in a marriage that had begun to bog down in domestic problems.

Emily's life at this juncture appears to have been devoted to an effort to analyze and dominate her circumstances. It was almost as though she had begun to see the behavior of others as part of a pattern which her superior knowledge and training should enable her to interpret. But Gilly approached life with no theories at all (or so it appeared to Emily). Keen as he was in assaying the quality of a quarry, he admitted there was always something mysterious to him about people. He approached life as a healthy, contented animal, sure that if he were ever to understand the motives of others, he'd still find them admirable, even lovable.

By the time the Wilsons had moved to Rutland these two outlooks had begun to create in Gilly a kind of disturbance he'd never known before and had no way of handling. And Emily could do nothing about it. She had loved Gilly, but she could not like him. She was perhaps constitutionally incapable of giving the unquestioning adulation he and all Wilson men needed.

By 1904 others had begun to notice something wrong with the marriage. Then in 1905 an incident occurred, probably while Gilly was off in New York. There was talk, which was more than the proud Emily could stand. Gilly left town.

Emily's behavior remained impeccable. She let it be known that her husband had gone west. In time she sent word to her father in East Dorset and asked him to drive up and collect her and her children. Calm, completely a Griffith, she had plotted the future. She was thirty-five years old, with a son and a daughter. She would, of course, consult with her father about financial matters, but there was no reason the children could not stay with her parents, no reason she could not move to Boston to study and launch herself on a brand-new career.

Arrangements for a divorce—shocking as that word might be to many old Vermonters—would be handled by a lawyer down in Bennington. It would all be done discreetly. If for any reason Billy or Dorothy should ever have to examine the divorce records, they would find only a slight reference, couched in the legal terminology of the day, to Gilman Wilson's utter irresponsibility.

IT WOULD be like going home, Billy's mother had said. He and Dorothy had been born in East Dorset and knew everyone in town. This was true, but there was a difference now, and sometimes he wondered if his mother just didn't care to talk about it.

In Rutland they'd had a home all their own. He'd been part of a family with a mother, a sister and a father. Now, no matter how kind and loving his grandparents might be, he was a guest. And it was as though his father were dead—worse, really, because people talked about the dead, but no one ever mentioned Gilly.

Then, the day before his mother was to leave for Boston, she told them they were to go on a picnic, just the three of them, because there was something they had to discuss, and with a terrible tightening in the stomach he knew what she was going to say. It was on that crisp, clear October afternoon at Dorset Pond—the summer folks had renamed this Emerald Lake—that he came to understand that there were different kinds of shock. There was the kind that could catch you totally off guard; there was also the kind that a part of you had been expecting, but for some reason you weren't prepared for—and he guessed he didn't know enough to tell which kind was worse.

As his mother started to talk, Billy sat on a long, flat rock that jutted out into the water, hugging his knees while his eyes studied the little patterns of ripples on the pond. Their father, she said, was out in British Columbia now, and she'd just learned that some of his old Rutland gang were going west to join him. He'd found work there, and he wouldn't be coming back—ever.

He heard the words, but his mind seemed to go numb. He literally could not accept what she said. Once, when she rose to hand him a sandwich, he turned and looked up at her, but he wasn't seeing her as she was—tall, handsome, with the afternoon sun shining on her hair; he was seeing her as she had been that evening when she'd taken him out behind the shed and thrashed him with her hairbrush, when she had made him drop his trousers so his bare bottom was exposed before her. He couldn't remember what he'd done to provoke that thrashing, but he remembered the wild anger in her eyes and his own impotent terror as he was forced to stretch out, naked and ashamed, across his mother's lap.

It was wrong, and he knew it, to be thinking about this. He should speak up. ("You'll take care of her, won't you, Billy? You'll be good to your mother, and to little Dotty too. . . .") Now in his role of son and big brother more was expected of him. Yet aside from such phrases as "Don't worry," or "Things will work out," which had no meaning, he could think of nothing to say. Not then. Not when they went for a walk around the lake. Not even driving back to East Dorset. After a time he stopped trying.

When Dot and his mother went into his grandfather's house and he had secured the old mare to the hitching post, he started to follow them inside, but halfway up the path he twisted around, darted up the hill toward an ancient oak tree, the oldest and tallest tree he knew, and started to climb—higher and higher until he reached the topmost branch that would hold him. Here he would not be seen, he would not have to search his mind for words; he was gasping, panting for breath, but he knew now he was going to be all right.

From that night on the feeling of being sheltered in the arms of the ancient oak was seldom completely absent from his mind. It became a sort of symbol: a place he knew he could run to, if necessary. In fact, he never climbed it again.

It was during that first year of staying with Grandpa Griffith that he made another discovery: he was living in what seemed to be two different worlds. Sometimes he thought there might even be three, but he couldn't quite pin down the third one. The first was the world of men and animals, of getting up and going to bed, of school, people, chores. Then there was the world in which he dreamed and imagined things. The third one had somehow to do with what had been here before he was born and would go on after he was dead. But the strange thing was that whichever world he happened to be in, a shadow from one of the others, like the shadow of a cloud crossing a field on a summer day, could at any moment fall over him. He was sure that when he was older he would understand about all this. Meanwhile, he was also sure it was best not to talk about it.

But even if he had wanted to talk about it, he didn't know exactly whom he'd tell. Certainly not the boys in school. They were not friends, they were rivals. With them it was always a question of who was stronger or taller, or could swim the farthest, fastest.

In place of a confidant he guessed he still used his father—a character he was making up half out of memory, half of imagining. Alone in his little attic room, he would carry on long conversations with this wondrous man who did perhaps drink a little too much, but who *had* to drink now because of the perilous nature of his work out in the wild Northwest. Some nights his father would confide in him, telling Billy he wanted him to leave Vermont, hitch a ride west because he needed him. But for some reason, instead of feeling better after these conversations, he often felt worse. He knew they were what his father in reality would call indulgence, something babies or little girls might do, and in time he grew self-conscious and gave them up.

Of course he knew he might talk to Rose or Bill Landon next door, or with old Frank Jacobs, Rose's father, who lived with them. Old Frank had been the town's shoemaker. He hadn't had much education, but he knew just about everything there was to know about nature. It was from him that Bill learned how to track down honeybees; and with him he would wait for hours on end for special birds that could be seen only on certain days of the year.

Bill Landon too could always find time for Billy and soon took it upon himself to train and make a crack shot out of the boy—even persuading the Griffiths to invest in a 25-20 Remington, a rifle Billy was to keep and love all his life.

The supreme moment of Bill Landon's life had occurred some forty years before, when he was a sergeant on the staff of General Philip H. Sheridan down in the Shenandoah Valley. Landon seemed repeatedly compelled to share every detail of it. The rebels had crushed the Union defenders until the meadows and lanes around Cedar Creek had become a chaos of wagons and fleeing men. Then suddenly a beautiful jet-black charger had appeared, bearing General Sheridan himself. Above the din they heard the general cry out, "Back. We will go back and retake our camps!" as, vaulting his horse over a wall, he galloped to the crest of the field. "We will go back. . . ." Bill Landon would repeat these words as if they were some holy incantation.

Ignominious defeat had been turned into victory through the action of one man, Philip H. Sheridan. As Billy listened, drinking it all in, he could see the gray columns of retreating, stampeding horsemen, see the foam that flecked Sheridan's black stallion, hear the roar of musketry and smell the gunpowder.

If Bill Landon was the first to feed Billy's world of dreams, Landon's wife, Rose, also contributed. "Barefoot Rose," as she was called, had been a great beauty, and had possessed so remarkable a voice that a man in Albany wanted to finance her, so that she might sing at the opera in New York. But instead she'd married Landon and had had a great number of children.

Billy got to know Rose through the errands she sent him on. "You, Willie," she'd call. "The well's most dry again." This meant he must make the run to the drugstore. There he'd be handed a small packet wrapped in tinfoil. Her surcease, Rose called it. Once he unfolded the tinfoil and found it to contain a chunk of something that looked like beeswax with a lot of white dust all around, and it smelled like a bunch of poppies. Rose always kept one of these in her apron, and as they talked she'd nibble at it. Sometimes, sitting in her porch rocking chair, she would lift her head in such a way that the blue of her eyes would completely disappear and he'd be looking only at the whites. Then, it was true, Billy would be frightened.

But he kept going back to Rose, because she was the only person who would tell him about his father. Not surprisingly, Rose tended to side with Gilly. But she was always careful not to speak unkindly of Billy's mother. Gilly's fault, she declared, if fault it was, was that he couldn't love just one special woman; Gilly Wilson loved all people, all men, all women. And she would say this as though she spoke of a rare and most admirable quality.

Then one summer afternoon, possibly without realizing she was doing it, Rose was able to offer Billy an escape every bit as exhilarating to him as her opium was to her.

A gentleman from Manchester, riding in a fine buckboard, had arrived in East Dorset looking for a place to open a library. Rose suggested her father's empty cobbler's shop. The following Saturday five hundred books were in the shop and Barefoot Rose Landon was the town's librarian.

Billy had been only a casual reader. He'd done homework and book reports, with occasional excursions into the Horatio Alger series. Now, suddenly, all manner of new excitements entered his world. Rose would lend him five or six books at a time, and alone in his room he would view the carnage of Troy with Ulysses, and with Sydney Carton look down at Paris.

One sensation he didn't understand was that many of the novels Rose lent him seemed not only written especially for him, but about him too. He felt so close to what the hero was going through, it was as though he were reading his own story. Then there were other books that left him with the most tremendous questions—about justice and truth, even about the wisdom of God Himself. He had no one to turn to with such problems. He thought of writing his mother—letters from her came regularly from Boston—but he wasn't sure she'd approve of his asking; one had to be on guard with her.

So, often, he turned to his father. The very thought of Gilly could change the climate of whatever world he was in. It seemed incredible to him that his father would want to be away, that he wouldn't even write a letter. Lying in bed, his sense of aloneness became most acute. Something he had done, he was sure, or something he lacked had made his father stay away. For this was a fact: Gilman Wilson, unlike any father he knew about, had walked away not only from his wife, but from his son.

If only his parents had loved him more, they wouldn't have separated. And this meant if he had been more lovable, it never would have happened. It always came around to that. It was, it *had* to be, his fault. He was the guilty one.

These late-night questionings invariably ended in the same way. Finding no answer, unable to absorb the feelings of rejection, the nameless guilts, he would get out of bed and study himself in the mirror. Then his bony jaw would set, his eyes would flash back into his own. So his father wanted no part of him. . . . Very well, he would show him. *He'd show them all.*

And as though he'd found his answer, he'd repeat, "I'll show them all," get back into bed and begin to read again. Though at first the words mightn't make sense, he'd read stubbornly on and on. He was training himself to focus all his thoughts on what he was doing. If he didn't, he knew he'd be completely lost.

THERE was nothing in any way eerie about Fayette Griffith. But at times the old man seemed able to read Bill's thoughts.

One evening in the late summer of 1907, Fayette looked at the boy and it was as though he sensed the immense determination that was forming and understood that such a passion must be given some direction. "It's an odd thing," he said casually. "I've been reading an article about Australia. No one seems to know why Australians are the only people in the world who can make a boomerang."

Bill looked up into his eyes. "The only people?"

The next day Bill borrowed two books from the library, both about Australia, and took to bed a volume of the *Encyclopaedia Britannica* to look up "boomerang."

That Saturday he went down the road to visit a French wood-cutter and spent the afternoon talking with him about the best grades of lumber for shaping a weapon three feet long, weighing no more than eight ounces. As summer shifted into fall, every scrap of paper in the house seemed to be covered with diagrams, and there were constant sounds from the shed of wood being sawed, carved, whittled. The cow was never milked on time, eggs were seldom collected. In November a note came from school. Bill was failing all subjects. His grandmother grew concerned. This was plain silliness, and a boomerang was a deadly weapon, as dangerous to the thrower as to the target. She spoke to Willie. And to his grandfather.

Fayette nodded and said he'd have words with the boy. But this wasn't quite the time. The time for worry would be when Willie gave up, when he would have to admit failure.

FAYETTE Griffith, a man of honor and quiet faith, was to become the most important person in Bill Wilson's young life. But at sixty-four, when he took on the responsibility of rearing two children, he was also a deeply troubled man, though he would not have admitted this. Great reader that he was, Fayette Griffith always found it difficult to express any of his feelings about himself, his family or his country.

He'd been only a young infantryman in 1862 when he heard Lincoln's message: "We shall nobly save, or meanly lose, the last best hope of earth." And that pretty well summed it up for Fayette. If the Union could be saved, then, he believed, other nations would follow our example and the world would be one great republic with free men everywhere. After the war this feeling, like a great wind down from the mountains, swept across the land and he was part of it, it was part of him. To some, democracy might seem a mystical concept, but to Fayette it was as plain as the kitchen table.

He always thought of those years after the war as his confident, glad years. Glad, not easy, for they had been years of endless work, hoeing stubborn rock soil on a sidehill farm, doing battle with every kind of pest. But he had married a strong woman—by some standards you could say his Ella was stronger than he—who bore him two daughters and his boy, Clarence. Ella made every stitch the children wore. And they were both mindful of the small amenities that make a family a family. No matter how late supper had been, there was always time for reading aloud, and time for Fayette to be alone with his books.

As things eased he bought timberland and moved to the house in East Dorset. But nothing of importance changed. Fayette thought, remembering, that his most satisfying moments might have been at night when his boy would move into the next room with his violin. Fayette would sit for hours listening to him practice, Clarence knowing that certain passages were difficult, knowing too that there was only one right way to play them. Hearing the comfortable sounds of the girls upstairs preparing for bed and in the next room the young man's vigorous striving, Fayette felt sure of his link with the future.

And this place where he had chosen to live was peculiarly right for him—a place of beauty among the vast mountains and, best of all, a place of good people where Fayette saw the Lincoln theories about democracy in practice every day. Belief in self and in the future gave warmth and meaning to his days and was part of the legacy he would hand on to his son.

Then in 1894 Clarence died. His lungs, Dr. Bemas said.

Fayette had gone on. One does, he wrote later, not because one wills to, but because one must. In time he prospered.

In time also his daughters, Emily and Millie, married. He went on, read his Bible, supported the church, but there was a verse from Matthew that would return to torment him: *If the salt have lost his savour* . . . And it seemed he could never clear his mind of one picture—of Ella putting the violin away in the attic—or of the sound of her locking the trunk.

Then Emily had brought her children to him. They were bright children, and kind. Fayette tried. He knew in theory what they needed. But there is a difference, and not simply a matter of age, between a grandfather and a father. There were many things he felt he should be saying, but even as he tried to form the words, they sounded hollow and he left them unspoken.

Sometimes he would stand by the door of the shed and watch Bill working, so concentrated on his three-foot slabs of wood he'd not even realize he was being watched, or he'd walk with him to an open field and listen to his description of the proper stance. "You must pivot on your spine, that's the trick, then make a half turn before you let go." And he would watch the boy, his long legs spread wide, the weapon in his right hand as he'd eye the field. Then, slowly stretching his arm into position, he'd whirl around on his left foot and let the missile spin out. It would go curving off sometimes fifty feet, Bill's eyes following it, his body hanging in the air. After a perfect half circle the missile would fall with an ugly crack. Bill's arm would drop, he'd shake his head, and back to the shed he'd go to start work on another kind of wood.

On many occasions Fayette had looked deep into the boy's eyes and he had always found the same thing there, intense determination and intense self-doubt. He had tried to do something about the self-doubt by suggesting little projects, and in part the boy had responded. But whatever he did easily he immediately lost interest in. Fayette knew Bill hated to do things that were difficult, but it was as if the boy sensed he would find no peace until he conquered them. Where could this lead? How would that extraordinary drive accept its failures? The boy seemed goaded by some dark desire that his grandfather could not understand. Finally, Fayette saw that the problem he was facing had nothing to do with Bill. It grew out of the bitterness in his own soul, because the boy he was rearing was not his Clarence.

Late on a cold February afternoon the change occurred.

That afternoon Bill led him not out to the open field, where every boomerang trial had so far ended in failure, but to the graveyard beside the church. They stopped by a headstone at the edge of the yard. Bill took his stance, legs spread, weapon in hand. Then, after a moment in which neither of them spoke, the boy stretched out his arm, spun his body around and the boomerang flew out, curving farther and farther over the graves, taking on momentum as it sped in a perfect circle until—there was no question about it—it was definitely coming back, right toward them, with the long, low, whistling sound of a giant beetle. Suddenly, Bill let out a yell, and they threw themselves flat on the ground as the boomerang cracked against the headstone.

For a full minute they lay side by side on the frozen earth, panting, hardly able to take it in. They might have been killed. Very slowly they sat up. "I did it," Bill whispered. "I did it." With a wild leap he was on his feet, and the banshee cry he let loose could have been heard in Manchester. "*I did it. . . .*"

That evening little else was talked about at supper, but the thing that struck Ella was not the triumph, nor even their close call; it was the miracle of change, the quickening of old Fayette Griffith. Her husband never stopped talking. "The very first American to do it. Our Willie. The number one man."

After the meal his voice was quieter as he spoke to her. He said he would like her please to give him the key to the trunk in the attic. He turned to Bill. It did seem a pity, he said, to have a violin locked away, not doing anyone any good.

CHAPTER TWO

So THE boomerang marked a turning point for both Bill and his grandfather. Fayette had found someone he wanted to talk to, someone for whom he could feel a wholehearted respect. And respect, of course, was what Bill needed most. When he'd heard himself called the number one man, all the lights in the room had seemed to come up brighter. He was filled with a kind of power.

He could feel it spreading through his body as if some potent drug had been released.

The yearning to be foremost was not new. In Rutland, when his father had taken him to the circus, he'd wanted to outride Buffalo Bill. He'd wanted to outbat Ty Cobb ever since he'd heard of him. To be number one and to keep the feeling he had at this minute would be worth any investment of energy or of time.

And at that same moment, still at the supper table, he made one other discovery. Six months before, he had known nothing about a boomerang, but he had worked, he'd asked, he'd listened; and each time he'd failed he'd carefully appraised what had gone amiss. *He was capable of learning.* From that day on, Bill was a learner, a listener, a watcher.

One evening after they had completed an errand down in Manchester, Bill watched his grandfather draw their buggy up beside the statue of a Continental soldier, on the green in front of the church. On its base were the names of all the local men who'd served in American wars.

From the expression on his grandfather's face Bill was sure he wanted to tell him something, but not until they were well up the Dorset road did the old man speak.

Now, just as old Landon had made him see the romantic side of battle, his grandfather made him understand why a group of Vermont boys, who'd known no more of the United States than their own county, had gone off to fight and be killed for an idea. The idea of democracy, he said—and Billy was not to forget it—was that all men are equal and that the things they have in common, that hold them together, are stronger than anything that tries to separate them. Everything depended on people knowing and remembering this. For the whole world was watching to see if this tremendous experiment could work.

Fayette kept it concise, but another time he made the point about the difference between law and justice. Laws could make mistakes, but justice never. Remember that the noblest thing a man could do was add his bit to the world's tiny store of knowledge, then join his weight to our unending battle for justice.

These were heady words that sent a thirteen-year-old to bed with his mind so giddy with new ideas there was no hope of sleep. Bill's fantasies kept changing. Now he saw himself as a lone attorney arguing his case for the people in the Supreme Court building in Washington, D.C., and some nights he could even make out an elderly gentleman, Mr. Fayette Griffith, sitting in the spectators' gallery, nodding respectfully.

Their neighbors soon grew accustomed to seeing the two of them walking together or just leaning back against a rail fence, sometimes talking, sometimes not. For Bill was learning not only from words, but from what was being left unsaid.

And this again was not new to him. That night on the mountaintop, when he had realized why his father had kept silent, he knew he'd been close to some vital understanding. Now, although he knew his grandfather and Gilly to be very different men, he could feel the same power in their silence. And as time raced by he had to find out about every kind of power a man might have.

The winter months were punctuated by the Christmas visit from his mother. Always he made long lists of the questions he planned to ask her. She would appear laden with gifts and the latest news about her classes, and since she was now enrolled in the Massachusetts College of Osteopathy and since very few women had ever attempted this, Billy wondered if she too understood the need to be number one. But before they knew it, New Year's would arrive, she'd be gone and none of his questions asked.

He was also learning from the whole incongruous mixture of individuals who make up a small New England town. Perhaps they sensed the determined reaching out in this tall boy who'd stop at their gate to wish them good evening, because now, as his young body began to take on its final shape, as his long arms found their comfortable hang, these people told him many things and their stories traced deep lines in his mind. Years later, when he tried to list their names, he had to give up; there were too many. There was, of course, dear old Frank Jacobs and Bill Landon and Barefoot Rose. . . .

And then there was Mark Whalon.

NEITHER OF THEM could remember a first meeting—they were neighbors, they just naturally knew each other—and although Mark was ten years older and they saw each other mainly when he was on vacation from the state university, he became Bill's first friend. Mark made him laugh and, as Bill put it, not take himself so damn serious.

Mark was a tall, thin, slow-moving fellow with a great crop of unruly brown hair. He was a jack-of-many-trades, for he had worked the quarries, been a lumberjack, and a lineman for the phone company. In the summer of 1908 he had a job in the general store, with access to a delivery wagon, which meant he and Bill could go driving off and visit neighboring towns. No day was lost for them if they were allowed a few free hours to draw up on a main street, sit back and watch the world move by.

It was true Mark did kid Bill unmercifully, but Bill was never offended. Mark had brought back from college a great store of green, fermenting information, and as they'd go rattling along in the wagon, he would recite long passages from Shakespeare and Burns and writers Bill had never heard about—Robert Ingersoll, Karl Marx. And he loved to argue. In contradiction to all Bill had been taught, Mark believed it had not taken six days to create the world, but that each of those days represented millions of years. He introduced Bill to the theory that man had ascended—he never said descended—from apes. And all his ideas were presented in such a buoyant manner that Bill was often puzzled as to whether he was serious or just getting off another of his good ones. For Mark, with a New Englander's distrust of all authority, enjoyed no role more than that of devil's advocate. Years later Bill recalled one time when he had played this part with more than his usual relish.

They were returning from a hunting expedition; their Remingtons and a half dozen squirrels lay on the wagon floor. Bill had been going on with his grandfather's line about how the whole world was watching the American experiment. Mark at last began to answer. The doctrine of democracy, he admitted, was a noble concept. But as to the proposition that men were equal, well, it seemed to him Bill should give that a little more thought.

The experiment, as he saw it, had to be based on the idea that all men had been endowed by their Creator with both the desire and the ability to improve themselves. And this, he said, was where the rub came in, because only a blind-drunk optimist could fail to notice that people might be good, but they were also greedy, timid and often bone lazy. What was more, these defects of character were more pronounced the farther down the social ladder you chose to look.

The expression "social ladder" was new to Bill. Sensing his confusion, Mark made a turn so they would pass the Manchester poor farm. He made no reference to this. The poor farm represented the ultimate disgrace, and you just naturally rode past it in silence. Mark didn't say anything either as they entered the outskirts of Manchester and trotted by unpainted houses with straggly fences.

It wasn't until they were riding past the stately row of old homes on the main street that Mark began his lecture on Manchester's social structure. Using the butt end of his rifle, he pointed out architectural graces Bill had never noticed—delicate fanlights above doorways, cornices, and white fences with carved pineapples on their posts. Then he indicated the sidewalks—broad slabs of marble, often out of line from having been pushed up by the roots of ancient elms. Not every American, Mark said, walked on marble sidewalks.

A few generations back, Manchester had begun to get a reputation as a summer resort and now each year it was visited by "fashionable folks" from Boston, New York and Brooklyn. Indeed, Bill had always thought of the town as divided into only two groups, summer people and Vermonters. He knew that some had much more money than others and had accepted this. But now Mark was trying to make him see that there were differences among the natives and among the visitors too, and it wasn't only a matter of the *amount* of money a person had. Old family money, Mark was saying, was one thing, but new money—the money a man earned, or maybe made at the track—that was another matter. Where the money came from was what decided which social rung a person belonged on.

Bill knew this was the most grown-up conversation he'd ever had and he tried to follow it, but Mark's vision of all of life as a ladder on which people tried to climb seemed awfully remote. Now he was going on about "the best people" and a certain "x quality" that set them apart. Perhaps since making a living wasn't so all-fired important to them, Mark said, they were freer to give themselves over to other interests. The whole feeling of the conversation embarrassed Bill, everything in him resisted it, resented it. What Mark was saying might be right in foreign countries with kings and noblemen, but didn't Mark know that here people had rights, that they could move ahead? That a man could pull himself up?

Of course, Mark conceded, there were exceptions. There were some right here on Main Street, and he pointed to a large, handsome white house. This, Bill knew, was the Burnham house; he'd often seen a family of golden-haired children playing in the garden. Dr. Clark Burnham, Mark explained, was a physician from Brooklyn and he had many wealthy patients. Bill was right—a doctor with his special skills could move up or down the ladder. So could a minister, perhaps, or sometimes a lawyer. . . .

Bill felt he'd scored a point—it was education that mattered.

Yes, Mark agreed. But that was only part of it, because here it was not how much you knew but where you learned it. All the men of the old families had been to Yale or Harvard, possibly Dartmouth, and before that they had gone to St. Paul's or Andover; the only boys and girls who got invited to their dances were the few who attended Burr and Burton Academy.

Burr and Burton was one of the oldest schools in Vermont, a gray stone edifice on a hill overlooking Manchester. Its students were mostly from out of town. You could always spot the boys by their tweed trousers, and jackets with belts in the back. In East Dorset they were considered snobbish, but now Bill wondered if there wasn't something about them he'd secretly envied, their special x quality?

Any man, Mark declared, who wanted to get ahead had better understand what he was up against and the rigidity of social patterns. Oh, he was wound up that afternoon.

Always before, when Bill left Mark, his spirits had been high, but not that night. If this talk had come from anyone else, he could have dismissed it, but he knew that Mark loved and respected people as much as his grandfather did. Did Mark, being younger, see the world more clearly than Fayette? If class distinctions meant so much, was this the real reason Bill had always felt a misfit, a guest? His mother was studying to be a doctor; did this mean that she understood what Mark was saying? Would her skills enable her to move up the ladder? But where and how would *he* acquire the power to climb? Soon he'd be a man. Who would this man be? Where would he belong?

The following Saturday, just as Bill was settling down to do his homework, he heard the delivery wagon drawing up. He had an examination Monday morning and he'd promised his grandfather he would study. What was more, he wanted to study, but at Mark's call, without thinking twice, he went out and joined him.

They drove over to Danby to make a delivery. On the way back there was a decided chill in the air, and as they passed an old tavern Bill had seen a hundred times, Mark said he thought he needed to wet his whistle.

Coming in from the sunshine, it took a minute to adjust to the dimness—and to the noise too. The room was full—there must have been twenty or thirty men—and everyone seemed to be talking or laughing at once. Something happened to Bill then. As they stepped through the door, they were greeted by the warm, friendly smell of wet sawdust, spilled beer and whiskey. But that wasn't it.

Mark had a drink, and somebody handed Bill a mug of cider. After a time he and Mark got separated, but it didn't matter. This was the friendliest gathering he'd ever been in. Some of the men had to be in their seventies, and over by the wall there were a couple of fellows not much older than he, but everybody was talking together. And soon he began talking himself, swapping stories with people, kidding, laughing. He knew he should feel guilty. He hadn't done the work he'd promised he would do. Yet here he was, talking right up with a bunch of strangers and feeling he belonged with them and that everything was all right. He glanced around, looking for Mark, and just at that moment Mark looked over at him and winked; then they both grinned.

It was already dark when they left, but Bill felt only a crazy happiness. He had laughed so hard that the muscles of his stomach ached, but his whole being was relaxed. Mark was a little drunk, he guessed. That didn't matter; the horse knew the way and the night was crisp and clear and this new lightness inside lasted all the way back to East Dorset.

Bill kept remembering that afternoon and his feeling of being at home. He wanted it again. But he sensed this *had* to be wrong. What could this have to do with being a lawyer in the Supreme Court building, with his lifelong plan to be number one? Still he couldn't *feel* it wrong. Those men in the bar were not only of different ages, they were from all rungs of Mark's ladder, yet the bond that existed among them proved everything his grandfather had been saying. So didn't they give the lie to Mark's theories about rigid class patterns? He wanted to go back, go hunting with those people, or just sit among them and listen to some old fellow playing his fiddle. And yet . . .

Yet if he did, how would he acquire the skills, the secret power his whole life told him he must have? As the weeks went by it was as though he were two people. One kept saying, "Go. Get Mark to take you back." And the other argued, "No. Stay here. Work." Then, just as he had long ago, he would look in the mirror and set his jaw. But now, instead of "I'll show them," his words were "I can. I can do it."

WHILE he had been wrestling with two sides of his nature, his grandparents had been watching and waiting. They approved of his new friendship. Like everyone in town, they enjoyed Mark Whalon. It wasn't that. What concerned them were changes in Bill himself. Each week the boy was coming to look more like Gilly Wilson, and this was no mere matter of coloring or cheekbones. It was an attitude, a stance of strong shoulders, an independent tilt of head. They said nothing about this, but each knew the other had noticed.

Then, and without any reason being given to Bill, a decision was reached. In the spring of 1909 his grandfather told him that after consulting with his mother, an application had been made for him to enter Burr and Burton Academy. He had been accepted.

THE years at Burr and Burton raced by, as if by the simple act of stepping out of East Dorset all of life moved faster. Afterward Bill remembered the times when he was happiest. But he also remembered days of the overwhelming loneliness that perhaps only boys of fourteen or fifteen ever know.

At his little schoolhouse he had been considered good at athletics, but here, up against boys who—as Mark would have pointed out—had had time to indulge in sports, he felt clumsy and out of place. And another obsession began. He'd show 'em, he'd be the best baseball player in the school. He so overdid his practice that he injured the socket of his right arm and developed a condition which to the end of his life prevented the arm from being fully extended. But he developed a deadly aim, speed and an ability to throw curves, spitballs, knuckleballs. In his second year he was pitcher, in his third year captain of the team.

Baseball was by no means his only obsession. A remark would be made, a casual remark not meant unkindly, but Bill would take it amiss and immediately determine to right the situation.

Once, returning from a baseball trip, the team was singing in the back of a wagon when someone next to Bill moaned and said to him, "For God's sake, take it easy." The following day Bill called on Mrs. Brooks, the headmaster's wife, who had been a professional singer, and asked if she would give him singing lessons. Poor Mrs. Brooks agreed, only to discover that Bill's voice had almost every fault that a young, unsure baritone can have. But the following spring Bill and a tenor sang a duet with the glee club.

The violin was another example. When his grandfather had taken the fiddle from the attic it was a battered instrument with one string. Bill repaired it and got a set of strings and an old jig book with a violin fingerboard chart. Then he beavered away at scales and arpeggios until he was playing in the school orchestra.

With each triumph a new dimension seemed added to his life. He began to feel more at ease. Most of his classmates were indeed from the upper rungs. The stories they brought back from holidays, lurid tales about girls and booze, were alien to Bill. But he joined in their late-night bull sessions and developed a reputation as a raconteur. By the spring of his junior year he knew he was accepted by his classmates. He intended also to be admired, envied.

Then, as always, something happened that Bill had not taken into account. He was a young, healthy, attractive male, and Burr and Burton was a coeducational school. Girls had so far played no part in his life, because until now he'd considered his face too homely to attract a girl. Besides, he had been otherwise occupied. Now he saw and was seen by Bertha Banford, the prettiest, brightest and surely the most charming girl in school. He fell in love—deeply, completely in love—and Bertha loved him.

There was a rare and special quality about Bill's loving, and there was a very special quality about Bertha herself. Hers was not the conventional prettiness of a sixteen-year-old, though she had her share of that—great dark eyes and a fine chin line softened by the gentle curve of her cheeks. But there was a glow about the girl, a promise. Everything, her young body, her manner, her eyes, spoke of the woman she was about to be.

Bill forgot he'd ever been shy. And he made a miraculous discovery: when someone thinks you handsome, you are handsome.

In chapel every morning their eyes would meet, then with an effort withdraw. When classes were over, Bertha was waiting. And in the evenings he called at the Banfords' Manchester home. It was Bertha who led Bill into the real world and gave him a sense of importance and freedom. Now there appeared to be hundreds of paths he might follow, nothing he couldn't do. He covered himself with honors. He was head of the YMCA, captain of a victorious ball team, and then was elected president of next year's senior class. And all this was done easily and with a tremendous, contagious joy. For Bertha was a girl who was delighted with life and shared her delight.

All that spring and summer there was a new aliveness everywhere, a resplendent haze over the world, and—this may have been part of their blessing—they both knew it. Another important element, and they both realized this too, was Bertha's family. Her parents were unlike anyone Bill had known. Her mother came from Louisville, Kentucky; her father, born in England, was rector of St. Luke's; and they both treated Bill as if he were a grown man whose ideas interested them. When he brought up, for example, some of Mark's social theories about the changes needed in the world, he found the rector agreeing and taking him a step further, hoping that Bill and Bertha would work and develop their minds, so that when the time came for them to strike out for change it could be with force and meaning.

One night after such talk Bill and Bertha sat side by side on the front-porch steps for a while, neither of them speaking. Bill knew that she was with him, going over in her head as he was in his what her father had said—about how from the beginning, even the very earliest forms of life had wanted to be something *more*, to break through into a new dimension. And from that wanting had come the doing—as he thought about this, Bill stretched out his hands—and from the doing came the means with which to do.

Bill turned and looked at Bertha. She was slowly moving her fingers, studying them one at a time. "Then . . ." she said—and if there'd been any doubt about her being with him, thinking the same thoughts, her words would have answered his doubt—"then what does it mean? It means we are not finished. It means man will always want to break through. We'll always want more. . . ."

And she said one other thing, her voice no more than a whisper. "It's almost as though we owe them something, all those who went before." She looked up into Bill's eyes. "If we aren't the most that we can be, then aren't we letting them down, going back on all that's happened, all their wanting?"

It was a question he knew there was no need to answer, as he also knew the time had come for him to leave her. He wanted to take her in his arms, press her body close against his, his mouth hard against hers. It was hell being a man and just holding a girl's hand and mumbling good night.

There were nights that summer when he ran all the way to East Dorset. And when at last he had made his way up to his room in his grandfather's house, he would lean out the window and stare down at the sleeping town. He knew who lived in every house and he loved them all now in a way he'd never imagined, realizing that they, like him, were filled with hungers and desire.

He was in love, he could not sleep, and it seemed sometimes that he could feel all the wanting in the world pouring in on him. He was in love, and his love reached out to encompass all people—all men, all women everywhere.

IT HAPPENED on a bright November morning.

Bertha had gone down to New York with her family for three days. She had promised to write, and Bill was late for chapel that morning because he'd stopped at the post office, but there was no letter. They were already singing a hymn when he sneaked into a place in the last row.

At the close of the hymn Mr. Brooks, the headmaster, stood up to address the school. Bill saw him reach into his pocket and bring out a yellow piece of paper. Looking down at it, Mr. Brooks cleared his throat and said he had just received a telegram from New York City and someone very dear to all of them, Bertha Banford, had died the night before following emergency surgery at the Fifth Avenue Hospital. That was all he said. Then he sat down. A little murmur, like a wave, moved across the chapel. A few heads turned toward Bill. Then there was silence until someone started playing another hymn and everyone got up and filed out.

Bill went to his first class; he went to his second and third. Girls came up to him and mumbled things, but they were all teary and he didn't hear them. Boys just looked at him and shook their heads, but it didn't matter because none of it was really happening.

At recess he had to get away. He walked up in the hills, walked all afternoon until it was dark. He could see Mr. Brooks, he could hear what he said; still it had no reality.

Three days later there was a memorial service at the church. He put on his blue suit and a dark tie and he sat way over at the side.

There would be no burial now, they said, because it was November and the ground was frozen. Bertha's body would be placed in the crypt at Factory Point Cemetery.

For a long time he looked hard at the Reverend and Mrs. Banford, thinking this would make him believe. He moved, he talked to people, he understood what they were saying and even answered them, but nothing touched him, nothing had any connection with him, with Bertha.

THE night after the service he walked out to the cemetery. It was a cold night, with a sharp wind down from the mountain. As he was pushing open the little squeaking gate at the entrance, he remembered that at the end of the play Romeo had gone to Juliet's crypt. Only—he moved on, closing the gate behind him—only Juliet hadn't been really dead; it was just a play.

Around the crypt there was a low granite shelf and for a time he sat on this, his long legs stretched out before him. Romeo, thinking Juliet was dead, had killed himself, but then Juliet awakened and . . . His mind went blank; he couldn't remember how it ended. Bertha remembered every plot. She would tell him.

He leaned his head back and peered up at the sky, searching for some familiar star, but the clouds hung too low. Bertha would not tell him. Not now. Not ever. Beneath him the earth felt hard, covered with a matting of dry, strawlike weeds. In time Bertha's body would become part of this. Her voice would never speak again. But the weeds would go on; they would bud in the spring, come to blossom, go to seed and bloom once more. He sat for what must have been hours. Weeds would go on, but he would never hear her whisper again.

When finally he rose, the clouds had moved on and a few stars were out. Over the town he could see Venus. Somewhere a dog barked and another answered. The worst, the very worst of it, was that the extinction of a young girl's life did not matter. It did not make the slightest difference or in any way affect the movement of the world.

He hesitated by the gate as this thought took shape in his mind;

then automatically his arms began to stretch up and out, his fingers spread as if trying to grasp some wisp of moonlight. But he knew now, and he let his arms drop to his sides. His need didn't matter a good goddamn. His hunger, his loving, meant nothing to the ongoing forces of creation.

He would never forget this truth which he saw that night.

HE CONTINUED to attend his classes. For a while he tried to go on with his other activities. At midyear he failed almost every exam. By spring it had become clear that he could not graduate; the class president couldn't graduate. His mother was sent for and a series of angry meetings followed, some of them in Mr. Brooks's office. Bill simply could not promise that he'd improve; he wanted to, but he just wasn't able to concentrate, and finally it was decided that he'd probably do better if he moved to Boston and lived with his mother.

His young years were over.

CHAPTER THREE

As BILL walked alone through the suburbs of Boston or made his way down bustling city streets, there was only one thing he knew: he too would die. Under what circumstances he did not know, but the fact of death was with him always. Time heals wounds, people said. He saw no reason to believe them. His time with Bertha had been the one point in his life with any meaning; he was not ready to be torn away.

The summer of 1913 his grandfather, perhaps in an effort to distract him, took him to Gettysburg, Pennsylvania. It was the fiftieth anniversary of the famous battle, and bent old men from every part of the country, rebels as well as Yanks, were gathering to sleep in tents, to talk and remember. Their camaraderie, their warmth, reminded Bill of the tavern he'd gone to with Mark. It was not the same, of course. For these men had been brought here by something important that had happened to them. Each had moved with and been moved by a tremendous event that had changed the course of a nation; and as Fayette had put it to him so often, what they had in common was stronger than anything that separated them. As he listened and felt this bond that existed among them, Bill was lifted beyond himself by something he only partially understood. For this brief period the whole American idea seemed alive and true and possible.

What he did not want to think about was the secret these men shared. Each of them had seen someone die, someone close. Yet they had accepted what he could not accept. He wondered if this had given them the faith he did not have.

As he and his grandfather boarded the train and headed north, his depression grew. Those great emotions belonged to the old men. What was happening to *him* had to do only with his own inadequacies. Among these men he was an outsider. He knew too that there had always been places where he didn't belong, where he was just passing through.

These dark moods, as his mother called them, these feelings of just passing through were like a disease growing inside him. Emily said they were little depressions and a natural part of growing up; one learned to override them. She kept harping on the point. Life had not treated Emily Wilson gently, but Emily had gone on, and she took pride in this. She was determined to pass her fortitude on to her son. One must have the proper mental attitude, she insisted, and whenever they were separated she wrote Bill long letters with the word succeed in every paragraph.

Above everything, he wanted to be engaged in some high purpose, but he was held in a paralysis he was powerless to shake off. Emily, who was then lecturing on nervous diseases, began to fear it was only a matter of time before his health would be affected.

He tried to exorcise all thoughts of Bertha and concentrate on the job at hand. In late summer he returned to Burr and Burton and passed the senior examinations. Then, Emily having decided that because of his boyhood interest in science he was cut out to be an engineer, he attended preparatory courses during the winter and took the entrance exam for the Massachusetts Institute of Technology. He failed almost every subject. After that a search began for a college which required only a high school diploma, and Norwich University, the state military academy, accepted him for the fall of 1914.

One thing that summer promised to relieve the discouragement. After a series of jobs, Bill at last made a trip west to visit Gilly in British Columbia.

His father was the same tall, gaunt figure he remembered, the same outgoing, contented man. He took Bill everywhere, introduced him to all his friends. "He must know a million stories," Bill wrote Dorothy. "The men all love Dad, and you know, I never heard him tell the same story twice." Yet somehow Gilly was not the same. He was a man in charge now, in charge of his men, his place in the world and in charge of himself. And possibly it was this that Bill had not expected.

At last, he had thought, they would be able to talk; his father would understand. But there was no way to broach a single problem. All Gilly wanted was for his son to be a generous, decent, untroubled young fellow. So—it was easier—he played that role. His father, it appeared, had another interest: Christine Bock, an attractive schoolteacher just his age, whom he planned to marry.

The trip home was one of the most forlorn times of his life. From the train window he watched the continent unfold, and tried to sort out his feelings. His father loved him, or loved what he saw him as, and his father was a good, a genuinely happy man, the sort everyone should want to be. So once more what had gone wrong had to be his own fault. He had expected answers from his father that would put his life in focus, but he had not dared to ask his questions. Still another door had closed. Did he belong nowhere? Deep inside him he was sure there was a man, struggling to be free. But free to go where, to do what?

Norwich now represented a challenge, a chance to get hold and find out who he was.

BILL entered Norwich just before his nineteenth birthday. This was a fine age to be, everyone said, when all life stretched ahead. And certainly it was a glorious time to be an American. In Europe

297

dark clouds had gathered. Germany had declared war on Russia and then on France, and England had retaliated in the same week and was now at war with Germany. But all this was four thousand miles away, and the prevailing view, especially among the students and young doctors who gathered in Emily's Boston apartment, was that Europe's troubles, though tragic, were none of our concern. America had too much to do. We were moving at last.

Bill had found no way to hitch in with this bright optimism. He'd been at Norwich only a matter of weeks when he began to sense that though the setting was new, he was the same, plagued by the same old fears. With Bertha he had believed himself a winner—and he *had* been one. Without her—he had to face it—he was second-rate. Not that his classmates were socially superior; they were simply better at everything they did.

He tried out for baseball but didn't make the team. It took all the concentration he could muster to maintain passing grades, and when fraternity rushing was on in late fall he didn't receive a single bid. He developed an overwhelming need for sleep. When reveille would sound at six a.m. it seemed more than he could do to get himself up. One morning when the ground was covered with ice and he was rushing to class, he fell and knocked his elbow out of joint. X rays showed a simple fracture, but since it was his right arm, the one already crooked from excessive pitching practice, he insisted upon going to his mother in Boston.

Dr. Emily had the fracture reduced, and after he'd had a suitable rest she sent him back to college. But the thought of the discipline, the drills, the reminder of being second-rate were too much. He was waiting at the Boston station when his heart began to pound and skip beats; his body was swept by a wave of panic, and alone on the platform, he was convinced he was about to die. On the train he developed a shortness of breath, his fingers went rigid and a paralytic spasm immobilized his legs. But far worse was the feeling that he could not get enough air. In a panic, he stumbled from the coach and threw himself down in the vestibule between cars, his nose close to a crack in the flooring, frantically fighting for air.

Back at Norwich there were more attacks. It was mental, the

college doctor said, nothing to worry about. One afternoon Bill overheard the word heart mentioned. Since no one had bothered to explain that although his palpitations were called a heart condition, it meant simply a functional disorder that would be cured by time and rest, he immediately dropped into a pit of hypochondriacal terror.

In February it was decided in another humiliating family conference that he should leave college and go to his grandparents. But at East Dorset he was no better. Later, Bill wrote that it required no profound knowledge of psychiatry to understand what had been going on: he had seen no reason to live—part of him wanted to die, but another part was terrified by death.

There were times, especially after a visit from his mother, when even this terror was trivial, compared with his feeling of inadequacy. Manhood and character, these were the things he must have. Everyone seemed to be waiting, expecting too much. Part of him, he was sure, wanted to be like others, to love and be loved, to live without excuses. Yet as the winter wore on he was convinced that the ability to do so had been taken from him.

EVEN in Vermont winter cannot last forever. The coming of spring is special everywhere, but in the valley between the Taconic and the Green it has a rare and heady quality. The first hint of change is in the winds coming off the mountains. The wind is no longer an enemy. It carries a sense of expectancy, of new beginnings. Old men feel this in their joints.

When this happens, old Frank Jacobs had once explained, a curious thing occurs: the spiritual life of the valley moves hand in hand with the physical. Men smile without knowing why. In this spring of 1915 the weather held, warm and dry and sunny, and Bill had these handsome days to do with as he chose, to wander with his gun past a clear mountain pool, or sit and study a cloud sliding over a greening hill. Sometimes he would hike it down to Manchester to watch the town stretching itself back to life in preparation for the summer people: houses deserted all winter being painted, gardens being tended. In the bustle, Bill gradually found himself wondering who would be back this year, found himself looking forward to seeing some of them again.

The Thacher house was always one of the first to open. Bill had known the Thacher sons at Burr and Burton, five beer-drinking fellows from Albany, all fine company. Dr. Burnham's house was rented, he'd heard. The family would stay out at their camp on Emerald Lake. Rogers Burnham, the elder son, was just Bill's age, and his passion in life was automobiles. Bill had the feeling Rogers expected his whole life to be one fast, sweet ride. It would be good to see him again. Then too, Rogers had sisters, in particular one older sister, Lois. Bill wondered when they were coming up.

Lois wasn't like any girl Bill knew. She was a good-looker, all right, but it wasn't that which made her different. There was a kind of force about Lois. It wasn't necessarily a force he wanted to tangle with now or believed he could ever handle, but his mind kept returning to her—maybe it had to do with spring—and he wasn't at all sure how he felt about seeing her again.

MARK Whalon had first pointed to Dr. Clark Burnham of Brooklyn Heights as one of the rare individuals who was able to move up or down in Manchester society. If Mark had traveled more, he'd have known that this man would be at ease anywhere. The doctor was small, at least eight inches shorter than Bill Wilson, but because of his chiseled good looks and his almost contagious good health, no one considered this. People instinctively responded to his confidence, his supreme fearlessness in what he knew to be this best of all possible worlds.

When Clark Burnham graduated from a Pennsylvania medical school, he started practicing in Brooklyn, where he lived in a boardinghouse and visited his patients on horseback. At the turn of the century the house calls were being made in a three-horse buckboard. By the time Bill came into their lives, the Burnhams were dividing their time between their homes in Vermont and Brooklyn, and the buckboard had given way to a series of touring cars—Peerlesses, Pierce-Arrows.

Clark Burnham had reason to be satisfied with himself and the fortunate background against which his story was unfolding. In those first years of the century the United States of America seemed God's own country, a land of plenty. In the West, fresh territories were opening up with grain and cattle. We had the know-how to build great cities. Enough for everyone. Just come and get it. And we were powerful too. Surely we were capable of whipping any force brash enough to challenge Uncle Sam.

The doctor's family also represented a central ingredient in his satisfaction. His two sons and three daughters were robust and very fair. Among the summer colony these were the golden children. Both Clark and his gentle wife, Matilda, took quiet pride in this. The young ones talked constantly and laughed a great deal, but their voices were soft, and they were never allowed any breach of manners. Just where their special style came from has always been a question—was it something the doctor acquired on his upward climb, or was it a natural part of Matilda's endowment? Whatever the source, a distinction in dress and manner was a mark of all the Burnhams. They were at home in their bodies and their bodies were at home in the world.

Lois, the eldest of the children, had the doctor's good looks, his slim, athletic body and his smile—a smile that appeared first in her eyes, which suddenly grew wider. But this was only for a second; her lips would part and her entire face would become involved. And the smile had a way of lingering on at the edges of her eyes.

She looked radiant and utterly alive, for she'd also inherited her father's passion for adventure. Yet her vivacity could not quite hide her seriousness, and it may have been this that gave her what Bill called "Lois's famous social sense," her belief that no matter what the situation, she could rise above it. And the situation she found herself facing now surely demanded something. For early in the summer of 1915 Lois Burnham, in her middle twenties, discovered that she was deeply smitten by Bill Wilson, who was nineteen.

WISE men since the beginning of time have warned that we had best be careful about what we want in our youth, because we may find in our later years that life has given us just that. But it must be added that had Lois known all the terrors the next twenty years would hold, there cannot be the slightest question that she would still have done exactly what she did.

Bill had first become aware of Lois the summer before. Foolhardily, he had challenged her to a race on Emerald Lake. She was sailing a tight little skiff; he had an old rowboat with tattered sails. But it was not the winning that mattered, Lois said, it was the fun of racing. She was full of such sayings, but with Lois they never sounded pompous or cliché. They were just what she honestly felt.

He had been a little shy about seeing her this summer, but he soon found he was completely at ease with her. She and Mark Whalon were the only people, he realized, who never seemed to treat him as someone other than he was. Here was a girl he could be friends with, without fear of misunderstanding.

Bill began turning up at the camp every few days without really thinking about it. Then he got into the habit of staying on later and later until Mrs. Burnham was obliged to invite him for supper. Meals at the Burnhams' were usually an uproar, because they were all talkers and their conversation was laced with family jokes which at first were unintelligible to an outsider, but in no time he was no longer an outsider.

Of course, if Lois had known all about Bill and had devised a a plan to attract—or to heal—him, nothing could have succeeded as well as this carefree time she gave him. For what was happening was very simple. When Lois stepped into Bill's life, she brought with her a built-in family, complete with a father, a mother, two sisters (Barbara, seventeen, and Kitty, fourteen), two brothers (Rogers, nineteen, and the baby, Lyman, eight). They moved over and made him another member of their circle, and Bill was too bedazzled, too hungry for affection, to question anything.

When he and Lois were alone there was a wonderful sense of freedom. They discovered they felt the same way about all manner of things, and sometimes these were the ones people didn't often mention: patriotism and honor, ideals and the meaning of loyalty. Lois would use such words with no embarrassment at all. Bill learned that the Burnhams were all Swedenborgians, and the mystical aspects of their faith fascinated him. He also learned that Lois had graduated from the Packer Collegiate Institute in Brooklyn, had had two years of art school and was now very involved in something called the Young People's League and the fine work they were doing. Although she kept filling him in with details about herself, she never pressed Bill about his plans. She admired his character, and it never occurred to her that someone she admired might not be totally worthy of admiration.

If as the summer went on Bill was aware that he and Lois were growing close, he didn't question it. He was returning to the world, so startled to feel alive, so flattered by the attention, he asked no more than to go on, one day at a time.

Then suddenly, early in September, everything changed.

Norman Schneider, a friend of Lois's from the Young People's League in Canada, had been visiting the Burnhams. When it was time for him to return, Bill and Lois walked with him to the station to see him off. When the train had pulled out, Bill said, quite naturally, "You'll miss him, won't you?"

Lois nodded, then she went on about the fine work Norman was doing and his wanting her to join him in it. Whether she meant to imply that Norman was asking her to marry him or just to work with him in Canada, Bill's reaction was instant and terrifying. Somehow he managed to ask if this meant she was in love with Norman.

Lois hesitated and—this can happen—time seemed to stop. Bill waited, his eyes riveted on her. Then she shook her head. She admired Norman, she always would, but . . .

The old weakness in Bill's arms and legs swept over him as he realized that the whole secure world he'd been a part of could evaporate in an instant and he would be alone again with his doubts and fears. Only gradually as they walked did he begin to focus on what she was saying. Then, if she didn't love Norman, he asked, did this mean she was in love with someone else?

It was impossible later for either of them to reconstruct what was said that night. But by ten o'clock he could not help it—he reached out and she was in his arms.

303

She had never been so beautiful. Or so happy. And she wanted him to know just how she felt. She believed in him so, and she knew everything was going to be perfection just as soon as he found out what he was going to do. For one fleeting moment the thought did shoot through Bill's mind that there were some things a man would have to find out on his own, but any such thoughts were pushed away by the look of her and by the knowledge of his miraculous rescue. By eleven they were engaged.

Lois left for Brooklyn the following morning. Bill promised he would write every day, and he did manage to get off three or four letters a week. Sometimes these would be brief, because halfway through an opening paragraph Lois's face would be back before him, so clear and so beautiful he could not see around it; then, when there was barely time to catch the last mail train, he'd scribble a request for her to write him "some more mush," promise to do the same himself and sign his name, always, "I.L.Y. I.L.Y.—Billy." As he did so, joy was mixed with incredulity that he could feel this way again.

He wrote about Mark Whalon, the only person in town he'd confided in. "She loves you because you are Bill Wilson," Mark had said. "So never try to be anything but just your plain ordinary self." He told her about Mark's drinking, which was heavy now, and his own concern at the signs of what alcohol was doing to that noble mind. He described his father, and poured out his ambivalent feelings toward him. Two themes ran through all his letters: Bill's desperate need to make enough money to get down and be with Lois, and his need to know that now they had found each other she would help him, teach him, guide him.

He was definitely going back to college in February. In his new ease of mind he was able to recover his old closeness to Fayette, talk with him. He began chopping wood for his grandfather at four dollars a cord. Also he got a job as fiddler with a small band, the Aeolians, who were developing something of a reputation around the state. They were busy with big engagements through the Christmas vacation. In January, Bill went to Brooklyn.

NOTHING HAD PREPARED Bill for Clinton Street. He had never stayed in such a handsome house. Always before, life with the Burnhams had been easy and natural; in the camp beside the lake a fellow could be himself, wear what he liked and think nothing of it. Brooklyn Heights was another matter.

That a house might be beautiful as well as functional had not occurred to him. At 182 Clinton he saw that the colors of the walls, the covers of the chairs and sofas had been chosen with care. The walls were lined with engravings and paintings the likes of which he had never beheld. Along with the constant family chatter there was a sense of excitement which he couldn't quite pin down, a suggestion of great events, of people arriving and departing, of young men driving up in expensive automobiles, calling for the Burnham girls. *Here Lois belonged.*

On the first night, when he found himself alone with Dr. Burnham before dinner, he was not comfortable. He couldn't escape being judged as a potential son-in-law. The doctor did not refer to this, but Bill knew it was no time to relax, and made an effort to keep the conversation rolling. It was the doctor's authority that put him off, as if he were always speaking from some great height which Bill doubted he himself could ever reach. It would have been different, he knew, if he had a job or if Lois didn't have one, or if he had money. . . . It wasn't the only time that weekend he remembered Mark's ladder.

At dinner there was another awkwardness. Beside his place there were several extra forks and spoons, and which one he was supposed to use presented an insoluble problem. But as they sat down he felt Lois nudge him. Whether this was accidental he wasn't sure—he was sure of nothing now—but then he saw Lois smile and pick up her outside spoon. Any girl who could do a thing like that without making a man feel a fool was no ordinary girl. From then on everything was right. The family behaved as if it were the most natural thing in the world for Bill Wilson to be here for a visit, and before long he was telling stories, everyone was laughing and he was as much at home as he would have been on the dock at Emerald Lake.

305

Lois's smile and her showing him which spoon to use marked the beginning of what was to be the perfect holiday. There was the Metropolitan Opera one night, the next a Broadway play with Elise and Frank Shaw, who were newlyweds. Elise was an old school friend of Lois's, and Frank had an important-sounding job with a Wall Street firm. They weren't at all what Bill had imagined sophisticated New Yorkers to be. He liked the Shaws. Then there was a party to meet more of the Burnhams' friends. But through everything Lois was beside him and Lois was taking care.

It was the start of what Bill called his social education. The point to remember is that he asked to be taught. And Lois Burnham was a born teacher. Not that Bill was in any sense the backwoods clown he sometimes enjoyed painting himself. But he was young, and his manner was more like the plain, sturdy wood of his grandfather's house than the urbane mahoganies of Clinton Street.

Saturday they set out for Manhattan to buy a ring. Lois led him to a modest jeweler in Maiden Lane, but Bill had set his heart on Tiffany's. He was adamant, and Lois saw she had no choice. To her amazement, if not to Bill's, there was a ring at precisely their price, a small amethyst for twenty-five dollars.

And Bill would remember the two of them late at night. After Barbara and Kitty were back from their parties and the family had gone to bed, the house was silent. They turned the lights low in the parlor, and when he pulled her to him and kissed her, she made herself small in his arms and tilted her face up to be kissed again. A new confidence filled him then and he knew that he was loved.

On his way back to Vermont Bill stopped off in Albany to visit the Thachers, those five brothers from Manchester summers and Burr and Burton days, and here too he was moving in a beautiful world where any problems that might arise would never be about money or finding the right job so you could marry a girl. Ebby and his brothers took him to his first nightclub. There was a lot of drinking and talk of joining some girls. Bill at this point was unashamedly afraid of drinking and interested only in one girl. Still he felt comfortable with the Thachers, and he returned to East Dorset elated. He was on his way now, he must keep moving.

Years later Bill said he had been slow in maturing; he wrote that when Lois came along "she picked me up with all the loving care a mother might have shown for a child."

But there was another factor in Bill's growth—one which a man may not fully recognize in his own story—and that was the important and mysterious matter of timing. Bill and Lois fell in love at the beginning of World War I, and the war was to affect every segment of his being—his view of society, society's view of him and, to a great degree, his view of himself.

WHEN he returned to Norwich in February 1916, Bill was still technically a freshman, enrolled to finish out his second semester. This was not an easy time for him. In the last few years he had developed no habits of study. Some subjects interested him and he did brilliantly; others bored him and he failed miserably. He made innumerable fresh starts, flunked and started again, and reported it all to Lois. Then came the Mexican incident.

All spring, newspapers were filled with accounts of revolutionary activities south of the border, and congressional pressure mounted for intervention. When Pancho Villa pushed into Texas, President Wilson ordered General Pershing to head a punitive expedition and pursue Villa back into Mexico. At the same time he called up various state militias to patrol the border.

For generations the Norwich cadets had been a proud part of the Vermont National Guard. Early in June they were sent off to Fort Ethan Allen, and Bill found himself a corporal in charge of drilling recruits. His letters to Lois became mere scraps: "Am first in line for promotion to sergeant. . . . Tried to get away to telephone you, but couldn't get permission. . . ." "It was wonderful of you to think of marrying me before I go. We'll talk. . . ."

On June 30 the First Squadron boarded a train. The rest of the camp, including Bill, gathered to see them off. There was a feeling of high adventure. These men were no longer playing at being soldiers, they were off to face the great unknown. Unfortunately, they got no farther than Brattleboro before they were told they were no longer needed, and were returned to Ethan Allen. Within a week the cadets were back at Norwich. For all practical purposes the Mexican adventure was over.

But for Bill it had been a beginning. He had worked hard and well, his work had been respected and he knew he'd done it on his own, needing no one's guidance. Indeed, the new recruits had turned to *him* for guidance. And this represented something of immense importance, as if some crucial element of his nature had been restored.

If those weeks had given him a sense of himself, they had also given him the feeling of being part of his country. The Mexican episode was a minor incident; still, a connection had been established and he felt a responsibility beyond his personal feelings. Along with this he had gained a new awareness, a widening of interest; if he was a part of the national scene, then he wanted to know about that scene.

In 1914 the mood of the country had been fiercely noninterventionist, but as the situation in Europe worsened and our relations with Germany grew more tense, many prominent citizens began lending their support to a preparedness movement. By mid-1916, at the time the Norwich cadets were discharged from Ethan Allen, the demand for action against Germany was growing daily. Congress finally passed a defense bill which called for an army of 175,000, and authorized an officers' training corps.

As the preparedness movement helped change the mood of the country, it also brought young Bill Wilson a curious local prestige. Everyone in East Dorset knew he'd done a stretch with the guard and that he was continuing to prepare himself in a military college. What he was doing mattered now. The next time he met with Dr. Burnham it was without his former diffidence, his subservient desire to please. They were two men who knew what they were about, and they immediately began swapping jokes about old Teddy Roosevelt's latest blast at "the cowardly crew in Washington."

Though Woodrow Wilson was reelected President in November on the slogan "He kept us out of war," there was a feeling of impending drama. Bill and his fellow cadets seemed imbued with a sense of purpose that gave a reason for accepting the tough strictures of military discipline. In January, when the President called for a negotiated settlement, "peace without victory," the cadets didn't know what to think. But the German government, by immediate resumption of submarine warfare—allowing only one American ship to sail each week into one British port—helped them make up their minds. The indignity of being *permitted* one ship and that one having to be marked like a barber pole was too much, and as a body they wanted to know what the hell the President was waiting for.

It was actually only a matter of days before Wilson formally broke relations with the German Empire. Bill and Lois were together when they heard newsboys shouting, "Extra!" They bought a paper and read the President's address:

> It is a fearful thing to lead this great peaceful people into . . . the most terrible and disastrous of all wars, civilization itself seeming to be in the balance. But the right [of mankind] is more precious than peace, and we shall fight for the things which we have always carried nearest our hearts. . . .

They looked up at each other and their eyes were misty. The thing they had dreaded and dreamed of was now a fact.

CHAPTER FOUR

THINKING back about his war years, Bill remembered them as having held a sense of exhilaration, of days racing by, filled with events that seemed to leave no more of a mark than a passing image leaves on a looking glass. Yet there were incidents that worked their way inward to become a part of him.

In April 1917 he had volunteered for enlistment in an ROTC unit and was shipped out with a contingent of his classmates for training at Plattsburgh, New York. The discipline of the Norwich cadets quickly set them apart, which was good for their egos, especially Bill's.

The first moment that so impressed itself upon Bill might have had no significance to another cadet. He was handed a piece of paper and told to sign his name beside the branch of service he wished to enter: aviation, which sounded daring—flying creaking crates in combat; infantry, which he knew meant danger; field artillery; coast artillery. He'd heard the coast artillery was training in the South, with large guns that were to become part of the mobile artillery, and they would surely be sent abroad. However, they said the training took a long time and the eight-inch howitzers usually operated some distance behind the lines.

That afternoon two sides of his nature met and waged their own brutal war. He wanted to live, to hold on to what he had finally built up. He could see Lois as clearly as if she had been beside him, her smile, the funny tilt of her head. He did not want to be wounded, maimed, not now before he had lived out his life with her, before he had lived with her at all. But just as he was about to sign his name, he remembered old Bill Landon's stories of Sheridan and the battered infantry rising as one man. "Back. We will go back and retake our camps!" The glory and the wonder of those words, that beautiful, gut courage, had been a part of him once. As much a part as Lois was now. And yet . . .

To go along with it he would have to sign up for infantry.

Slowly he let his eyes move up the list, and at the sight of the word infantry a half-forgotten terror swept through his body, he could feel the weakness rising from his legs. In panic, he tightened his shaking hand and signed for coast artillery.

That should have been the end of it—he had friends in the artillery who welcomed him aboard—but the night they departed for Fort Monroe in Virginia, a group of cadets came down to see them off, yelling and cheering. And just as the train pulled away, four or five of them began to jeer directly outside Bill's window. "The artillery. Yeah, yeah . . . playing it safe . . ."

All that night, as the train headed south, he kept hearing those jibes and seeing his grandfather, the old boys at Gettysburg, Bill Landon. And he remembered a skinny ten-year-old kid charging up a hill, his Remington at the ready, pretending. "Back. We will go back. . . ."

BUT THERE WAS no time to regret his decision. At Monroe he was surrounded by engineers and technical experts, and the student officers were worked sixteen hours a day. If Emily had believed Bill cut out for a career in engineering, that belief was being put to a grueling test. And if occasionally there was still the feeling of playing a role, he was sure others were feeling the same.

Whenever there was hope of a few free weekend hours, Lois would come down and check in at a nearby inn—and in this summer of 1917 the sight of a beautiful woman on the arm of a tall young soldier was about the most touching America could offer. Lois, more than anyone he knew, understood and responded to drama. She saw the wonderful qualities war can bring out in people, and most of the time she could find the right words for her feelings; at other times her laughing eyes would fill with tears just at the thought of what Bill was doing.

To this accelerated, hypnotic rhythm, believing the nation behind him, Second Lieutenant William Wilson marched off to war.

THE next incident just happened. There was no premonition to warn him. After Monroe, Bill was stationed at Fort Rodman, Massachusetts. One evening he was invited along with some other young officers to a party in New Bedford. Although he had stayed with the Burnhams and the Thachers, he had never imagined anything like the Grinnell mansion or the kind of lavish entertaining the Grinnell daughters extended every weekend to "our brave boys in uniform."

The party was under way when he arrived, filling the great main hall and two vast drawing rooms, overflowing onto a terrace. In one room a small orchestra was playing and a few couples were dancing. He edged his way around them to the terrace and saw the gardens below filled with little tables and Japanese lanterns.

He stood by the garden steps, trying to appear nonchalant. It was like the first evening at Clinton Street—he didn't know what to do with his hands—and there'd be no Lois to nudge him here. As far as he could see, people were herding into little groups—he was the only one adrift. On his way in he had noticed a long bar set up beneath the stairway, and although it was surrounded by confusion, it seemed to represent a haven where a man alone would not be conspicuous. Across from the bar he had spotted a side entrance and was considering it as a possible exit when someone spoke to him.

She was tall, not young, with a bony face and what East Dorset would call a socialite manner. Her hand rested on his arm and she immediately began asking questions—wasn't he enjoying himself; didn't he think the orchestra divine—and he could not think of a thing to answer.

He tried to smile, then a waiter with an immense tray paused before them and the girl took two glasses. This was something new, she said, as she handed one to Bill—a Bronx cocktail. She held up her glass in a silent toast. Thinking he had never felt more miserable, Bill held up his glass. Then they drank.

In a matter of minutes the waiter was back and Bill's new friend took his glass and handed him a fresh one. For a long, long moment he looked at the beautiful glow shimmering in the glass, then he emptied it in one swallow. It seemed to happen instantly—the relaxing, the warm glow seeping into all the corners of his being. Then, unaccountably, the room was tilting. But gradually everything evened off; he found he was talking—and apparently he was amusing. When she laughed this girl was far from homely.

There were people she wanted him to meet. . . . Locking her arm in his, she ushered him about. Soon groups were forming around him. How quickly the world can change! He couldn't stop laughing; he must have been witty because his remarks were being repeated—"Did you hear what old Bill said?"—and before long, strangers were asking if he could come to a party next weekend and what about the one after that. . . .

At one point—after his third or fourth drink—he hesitated, the glass halfway to his lips. Faces around him became hazy, his mind seemed to be slowing and he felt the old pounding in his chest. It lasted only a moment, then an older, wiser Bill seemed to take possession. He straightened up and, standing considerably taller than those around him, thanked a girl for an invitation to supper, and continued his conversation with a captain and a major. It was a miracle. Smiling, he looked around him. These were friends. They liked him and he liked them. Enchanted by the way he was handling himself, he signaled the waiter with authority, and when he had another full glass, bowed politely and excused himself.

With a thrill of pride at the magnificent clarity of his thoughts, he walked quietly across the hall and through that side door. It led onto a driveway. Standing there, he looked up at the star-spangled sky and smiled at the night and held his glass out before him—he was Gilly's son, and more than that, oh, much more, he was himself.

As he made his way down the drive, easily, gracefully, he felt as though all his life he had been living in chains. Now he was free.

It was always amazing to Bill that anything which in the end could drag a man so low could in the beginning lift him so high. For there was never any doubt that the Grinnell party ushered in the highest, happiest time of his life. A barrier which had always existed between him and others had been dissolved. With a few drinks under his belt, what a wonderful world it was.

There were minor problems. He seemed to lack any inner sensor to warn him when he'd had enough, and often he would be sick and have to dash to a men's room. The next morning he would be hazy about things everyone else remembered. But this was all part of it, he guessed. He'd just passed out, the older officers said. No reason to be concerned.

His work was not affected. He was up at reveille, the first on the drill field, and his performance there was watched with awe by his new buddies. The only explanation was that at twenty-two Bill Wilson had the constitution of a horse. And he had to admit a secret pride in his resilience.

His one concern had to do with Lois. Not that the Burnhams were teetotalers. He was sure Rogers would be a fine drinking companion, and he knew the doctor's cellar in Brooklyn was beautifully stocked with wine. But the first time Lois came to Rodman he noticed that she had a way of sipping a drink, then putting it

down. And he could see she was disturbed when he'd had too many, although she didn't say anything.

But he also saw how easily Lois could find her explanations. The tensions they were living with, the terrible uncertainties were, she knew, enough to make any man take too much. He could find no way to make her see that there might be something else involved, something important and personal.

There were tensions all right. The post was a hotbed of rumors about which units were to be shipped out and when. It was this that made Bill and Lois decide to move their wedding date ahead. They'd planned to be married the first of February, and invitations had been ordered; but by Christmas it seemed likely that Bill would be off to France at any moment, and the invitations were changed to announcements. They were married in a Swedenborgian ceremony in Brooklyn on January 24, 1918.

Rogers Burnham stood as Bill's best man, Lois's sister Kitty and four girls from Packer were bridesmaids, Barbara maid of honor, Elise Shaw matron of honor. Dr. Emily, due to a sudden attack of flu, was unable to come from Boston, and Dorothy stayed behind to nurse her mother. Also, perhaps because of the rush, Fayette and Ella were not there. But not even a lack of family on the groom's side could dim the quiet glow of the occasion—a young lanky soldier standing beside his bride—and no one who was at the church or the reception on Clinton Street was apt to forget it.

They took the night train for Boston, and next day, after paying their respects to Bill's mother and Dorothy, they hurried on to the little upstairs apartment in New Bedford, close enough to Rodman, that Bill had rented for thirty dollars a month.

Now that they were lovers in every meaning of the word, Bill felt he'd taken a giant step toward becoming the man he had waited all his life to be. Here in their own apartment, complete with piano and wood-burning fireplace, they were at that early stage of loving where they could not stay apart and had no need of any other person. At the same time, Bill's feeling for Lois seemed to be enlarging his feelings for family and old friends. These were golden days.

In April the Sixty-sixth Coast Artillery Corps was transferred to Newport, Rhode Island. Fort Adams was a last stop before embarkation, so Bill had to sleep on the post. Lois stayed in a boardinghouse, and they had only weekends. Still, a spring weekend in wartime Newport, when the most famous hostesses in America were opening their villas to servicemen, was an experience. Sometimes at a great gala, when Bill would wander off for a snort with the boys, he would glance back and see Lois sitting at the edge of a group, but she was never uncomfortable, never apologetic. She was still Lois, still confident.

To Lois, it was almost as though she had actually seen Bill growing. He seemed taller, stronger. He'd put on a little weight; he also was putting on a new authority. On afternoons when the public was allowed on the base to watch a parade or a maneuver, Lois always had a place at the front of the grandstand. When the band struck up, there'd be a tingling through her body, and when she saw Lieutenant Wilson lead his men across the field, tears would blur her vision. These afternoons made one thing crystal clear. Clark Burnham's daughter had married a leader.

THEIR last night together was in July. The Sixty-sixth CAC was to sail from Boston on the eighteenth, and on the night of the seventeenth they went out to the shore for a lobster supper, along with another young army couple. And there, high on a cliff overlooking the sea, one of those things happened that for many years made Bill think he was unlike other men.

Drinks at supper did little to lift the dark mood that had fallen over them. Afterward, Bill and Lois walked off alone. Without speaking, they sat on the cliff and looked down at the harbor, at two battleships anchored side by side, at pleasure boats moored closer in, at tiny white launches darting about. They sat, his arm across her shoulder, and as stars appeared and a breeze came up from the sea, their bodies relaxed and their nerves calmed. Occasionally he brushed his lips over her hair, his fingers barely touched her fingers; yet in all their nights of loving they had never been so close or read one another's thoughts so clearly. There was a possibility that Lois was pregnant and somehow this now seemed part of all they were feeling. In the morning he would sail, he would do what he must, then he would return—he was convinced of this— and she would have borne his child. The idea filled him with a joy and wonder he had never known; it seemed to draw him on toward some distant reality. Was this what old Fayette had meant when he spoke of his son, his link with the future? What Gilly had been saying when they stood under the stars? Was it part of an answer to his fear of dying, to all those agonizing questions he'd battled with when they had buried Bertha? Was a man's son a kind of immortality?

Still without speaking, he got to his feet, took a long breath and pulled Lois up beside him. Some deep intuition told him there was a path toward something larger, finer than anything he so far had known. And just knowing it was there filled him with a particular kind of pride.

They ran then like two children all the way down the cliff. And in the morning some part of the feeling was still with him, and when they stood by the train and finally had to part, it was nothing like what he had imagined. Their eyes met, their eyebrows lifted slightly, and in that look there was an awareness that separated them from everyone else on the platform. They knew they were together and indestructible.

Two other moments, or incidents—Bill never knew what to call them—occurred before he reached France.

When the old British liner *Lancashire* sailed from Boston, there was a tremendous sense of adventure about everything. Ten days out, however, when they were moving into the Irish Sea, which they knew was filled with subs, the mood changed dramatically. Blackout regulations were strictly enforced, and all junior officers were issued revolvers and put on watches, manning the stair landings to control any panic in case of a hit.

The last night out Bill drew his watch, midnight till four a.m. His only question was the old one of how he would perform in an emergency. He was aware of his fingers caressing the leather holster and he wondered if he would have the nerve to take the pistol out and actually use it. But as the hours slipped by, cut off from land, from his past and his future, he relaxed, and for a long moment time stood still. As he was examining this heady feeling, there was a tremendous crash. In another second every man was out of his bunk and racing for the stairs. Bill had dealt instantly with his wave of nausea. His pistol was drawn and he was barking orders. And there was no doubt in any mind that he meant to use it on anyone who dared take another step. They waited, all eyes staring up at him. But there was no second crash. Later, they found out that a destroyer at their side had spotted a sub and dropped an ash can, and the impact so close to the *Lancashire*'s hull had given every indication of a direct hit.

When finally Bill was relieved of his watch, a thin rim of gold had appeared on the horizon, and at its center he could see a shadowy outline of land ahead. They had made it. The speck of land looked hospitable. But more, much more than this, *he* had faced terror and come through. There'd been no panic on his deck, because he had been there.

And there—it was the damnedest thing—was once again that mysterious sense of being on the edge of some understanding.

THE other moment occurred in England. They were stationed outside Winchester, awaiting departure for France. Having wangled leave, Bill set off alone one August afternoon to visit the town and its ancient cathedral.

Possibly he was worried. News from the front was not reassuring. Americans had been thrown in everywhere to block the German advance toward Paris, and England buzzed with stories of a second battle of the Marne. But the moment he stepped into the cool hush of the cathedral all thought seemed to be taken from him. He moved slowly up the main aisle, then halfway to the altar he stood transfixed, gazing up at a shaft of light streaming down from the uppermost point of a stained-glass window. Hardly knowing he was doing it, he moved into a pew. Absorbing the total silence around him, he became aware for the first time in his life of a tremendous Presence. He was completely at peace. When he finally left, the great bells in the tower had begun to ring and he paused in the old graveyard, a little beyond the entrance, listening. Something had happened, something he was sure could happen again. And one day he might be able to grasp what it was.

He was not to know another such moment for years, yet at times it seemed more real than anything happening around him.

LIKE thousands of others, Bill and Lois had worked out a private code that was designed to get past the censors. If he signed his letter Billy with the *y* going straight down, she would understand that he was safe in some rear area; if, on the other hand, the *y* had a curve, it meant he was near the front. In all his time abroad he used a straight *y*. His letters showed high spirits. Even to the news that Lois was not pregnant he wrote that they had the rest of their lives to try again.

He believed deeply in what the war was about, and aside from missing Lois, he was where he wanted to be. He loved France and the French—the bright cafés at night, the old men arguing over their wine and everywhere the young lovers embracing in public—and he loved their feeling for Americans. He drank, as always, when there was a drink available, and in France there always was.

When the armistice was signed in November, the CAC did not immediately disband. It was not until March that Bill sailed for home. That winter and spring were extraordinary times to be alive. Four years of slaughter had ended with nine million dead. And yet as the SS *Powhatan* steamed into New York harbor, the course ahead—for the world, for the country and for Bill Wilson—seemed clear and straight and hopeful.

CHAPTER FIVE

WHEN Bill returned from France, there was a marked change not only in the amount he drank but in the reasons for his drinking, in what drinks did for him. He knew that certain situations seemed to bring out his sense of responsibility, while others played upon his insecurity. The period immediately following the war did both, because now he was living in a city, for the first time face-to-face with a highly competitive world.

His first weeks back were everything a returning hero could wish for. But more important than the adulation was what Bill felt about himself. He had been part of a great endeavor; he had done something worthwhile. Once, as a schoolboy, he had known such sureness and lost it. He was determined to hang on to this. Never again would he think of himself as Dr. Emily's little boy or the Burnhams' backwoods son-in-law. The time had come when he must brace himself for what was called the serious business of living. Everyone said he'd have no problem, he could write his own ticket. But a ticket to where?

Most of the veterans were eager to take up their interrupted lives. But before the war, before Lois, he had had no life. Each morning he pored over the help-wanted ads. There appeared to be limits as to what a former lieutenant with no college degree qualified for.

For several weeks he worked on the New York Central piers, driving spikes into planks that carpenters had sawed and laid. Then he decoded cablegrams for twenty dollars a week, but he soon grew bored and listless. He wanted a job with some purpose. Confused, angered and gnawed by self-pity, he got into the habit of stopping by a pub on his way home—why was it easier to think straight in a bar? By the time he headed for Brooklyn, he quite often had reached the conclusion that tomorrow—next week, any-how—he'd look for the right job. And always as he approached Clinton Street he'd say a little prayer that tonight Dr. Burnham would *not* ask how things had gone at the office.

Dr. Burnham, whom Bill now referred to as "Boss," was still a man of influence and he pulled strings for Bill, but it was the old story: no college degree, no job.

Bill became aware of a subtle change in the family. Oh, Lois's family loved him, he knew it, and he loved them, but the girls had grown into young women. Their talk was all about their work, and the young men who called were serious suitors now. Rogers was still overseas, and sometimes Bill wondered whether he would understand, either. It was not only the Burnhams who seemed assured of their world. Dr. Emily had no doubts about her course, and Dorothy was writing from Chicago, where she was studying, about her future with a young med student, Leonard Strong. Everyone was moving toward something new.

There were days when he believed this even of people he passed on the street. Everyone had a role; only he did not. Of course, the way to cope, as Bill realized, was to appear as confident as anyone else, and nothing helped with that like a drink.

Some of this he could talk over with Lois. Some he could not. And if she suspected how concerned he really was, she had her overwhelming faith. Everything would be all right. She would make it be.

At the end of his first summer back they decided to take a walking trip. They took a boat up to Portland, Maine. Then, carrying packs and pup tents, they started across to New Hampshire and Vermont. Almost the first day they were out of the city a change began to take place.

All Bill's life, part of him remained a country boy who responded to every aspect of nature—to wind and rain, the stars, the shifting autumn colors. It was as though nature helped him keep his soul his own. While hiking, he said, he saw himself in perspective. And Lois was a constant delight. He knew he could have looked the world over and never found another girl who so enjoyed the things he enjoyed or had such confidence in him. This was what amazed him. As they'd stride along he'd look down at her and wonder what it was that had given her this faith.

At sunset, or sometimes dawn, they would stand on a mountain-top, having skinny-dipped in a mountain stream, and look out over endless miles. Then they'd lean back against the wind, and all their worries seemed to be sucked up by the sun. They were in love and they knew in their very beings that all was right with them. They also knew that if only they could keep this, they could do anything. But *how* to keep this while penned up in an office? As they neared East Dorset the question plagued them.

AT FIRST EAST DORSET appeared exactly as Bill remembered it. All the old folks were there—his grandparents, old Bill Landon, Barefoot Rose—but he soon became aware of change. There wasn't one house where he didn't hear a story about some young person taking off for the city. Mark Whalon, as eager as ever to explain the world, said of course there was a change, not only in Vermont, but everywhere. Americans had fought a great war and now they wanted to return to what the Republicans were calling normalcy. It was too late for that. Americans always moved forward, not backward. And Mark whistled "How Ya Gonna Keep 'Em Down on the Farm (After They've Seen Paree)."

The electricity being installed all over town and the number of automobiles were symbols of the change. When everyone had his own tin lizzie, pretty soon they'd see a web of highways clear across the state. It was inevitable, he insisted, and there'd be alterations in everything, in how folks shopped, traveled, did business, in how the young ones courted. . . .

Although most people were less aware than Mark, Bill kept hearing the word progress. Only his grandfather seemed to question it. Fayette was much the same, with the same rough-hewn handsomeness, the same inner quiet and the old, unique ability to clear Bill's mind of cobwebs and leave him with a shining wondrous excitement about what lay ahead.

Fayette saw Bill's conflict about the line of work he wanted to pursue as a reflection of attitudes across the nation that to him were profoundly dangerous. The old ideals had been basically individualistic; now he could see us becoming a nation of giant corporations. Worse—he paused and Bill waited to hear the rest of the thought come rolling out in the clipped Yankee cadence—much worse, he could see our great cities being run by corrupt political machines. But if our experiment in government was to succeed at all, it must be brought about by the people themselves. "For," he said, exactly as he always had, "there's no other capital fund I know of to draw on."

As to what line of work Bill should follow, well, he said, he'd always been of the opinion that there were only a few careers worthy of an honest man's efforts. One of these he still believed was farming, but the greatest one . . .

Bill knew before he spoke the word. And he knew, too, why as a boy he'd always wanted to be a lawyer.

BACK in the city there were problems. Bill could not be a full-time student; he would have to find a way to carry his own weight financially. Lois was happy to accept an occupational-therapy job at Brooklyn Naval Hospital, and after a time, through a friend of sister Barbara's, Bill was taken on as a bookkeeper for the New York Central at $105 a month. With Lois's salary, this meant they could move into an apartment of their own and he could enroll for night courses at Brooklyn Law School.

These were full days. Bill's work load would have felled a less rugged constitution, for the job was a constant, tedious strain, and the study of law seemed to be more about torts and liens than the philosophy of justice.

He was, though, blessed in finding two professors who looked upon the law also as one of the humanities. In their classes Bill saw that the law not only defended the existing power structure, but also facilitated tremendous changes. Often it seemed that the young men gathered here to learn to use the law were actually being trained to run the world.

After class a group would move on to a speakeasy (Prohibition was now in effect). Over steins of beer, talk would grow heated, with opinions of famous jurists—Marshall, Holmes, even the new man, Brandeis—quoted back and forth. On such nights it was natural to think of oneself as a link in a glorious chain, part of a noble tradition. A man couldn't pull out and take such feelings down into a subway. At such a time he just had to order another round. Often Bill was the last to leave.

The next morning the alarm would go off and there'd be the long trip into Manhattan, the agonies of adding figures, and at five p.m. once more the rush-hour crowds to Brooklyn.

First-year students were urged to attend trials, and whenever he could wangle the time, Bill was in the courthouse on Chambers

Street. He liked the solemnity, the drama of a trial, the seriousness of jurors and witnesses. He studied judges and attorneys, and learned that their impact depended on one thing: their knowledge of the law. Finally, it was his terrible slowness in acquiring this that became so painful. For he knew he had within him the makings of a fine lawyer. But to succeed in such a profession required total concentration, and his days were being wasted. If only he had some other way of making a living. He went back to the want ads.

One morning a notice appeared asking young men of all-around abilities who considered themselves capable of close observation to write a letter to an address in New Jersey. He wrote, and in time was called to the Edison Laboratories in West Orange for a qualifying examination. There, on a Saturday in May, along with some fifty others, he was led into a long room with drains and sinks and laboratory equipment along the walls, rows of tables on which their examinations lay. In a far corner was a battered desk. Sitting at it, lost in thought, was Thomas Alva Edison. His clothes were stained with chemicals, and across his cheek was the faint scar that Bill knew had come from an experiment with nitric acid.

Edison had always been a hero of Bill's. He knew a thousand details of this man's life and could quote him endlessly. He knew that Edison had had no more than three months of schooling. He had trained himself, read, tinkered with machines, trusted hunches. Now here he was, the authentic American genius. It took Bill a while to focus on the papers before him. There were some three hundred questions—about the diameter of the moon, overtones on a stringed instrument, or the kind of wood used for oil barrel stays. Many were tests of observation.

As the others turned in their papers, Bill plowed on. He'd answered all the questions he could immediately and then gone back to the stickers. Finally, when he was the only applicant left in the room, he glanced up. The great man was standing beside him. He asked if Bill found the exam difficult, and Bill said yes, he did. They talked for a time, quietly and easily, and then Bill rose, thanked him and left.

Weeks passed. Hearing nothing from West Orange, he applied for a job with United States Fidelity & Guaranty Company. When a definite offer came he accepted it.

The work was investigative, mostly looking into defaults of brokerage firms on Wall Street. This was Bill's first exposure to the Street, and as he said later, it was a case of love at first sight. For here was much of the drama he'd sensed at a trial, plus the excitement of changing times. In the summer of 1921 America was more than ever aware of its incredible potential. Ambitious men everywhere were going into business for themselves, and Wall Street, not Washington, was becoming the real seat of power. That spring the Street was a place where anything could happen—and often did—at a wildly accelerated pace. A man couldn't help catching some of the contagion.

Then late one night the apartment doorbell rang and a reporter from *The New York Times* came upstairs. William G. Wilson was a winner in the Edison exams, the prize a chance to work in the laboratories. It was a moment of extravagant happiness for Bill and Lois. The reporter wanted to hear all about him.

But before he went to bed that night, he had made his decision. He would follow his hunch and stay on the Street. He already knew a few key men in brokerage houses. Barbara Burnham had worked for Baylis & Company, and had introduced Bill there. Frank Shaw, husband of Lois's friend Elise, was quite high up at J. K. Rice, Jr., & Company. And Bill was making new friends on his own. Men took an immediate liking to him. Possibly they sensed he represented no competition. There was always something a touch incongruous about the lanky figure, a battered brown hat on the back of his head, leaning back comfortably in an office or in one of the downtown speakeasies. It was that bit of the hayseed that never completely left him—in his speech, in the bright, friendly blue eyes. He was at ease, that was the thing. Men trusted him, talked freely with him and began giving him tips on the market.

Lois was making $150 a month at this point and Bill about the same. They moved to a larger apartment. While Lois busied herself in the evenings decorating the flat, Bill, who was fascinated by the new radios, worked at building himself one of the first super-heterodyne radios in Brooklyn. In time he built others, which he sold at a considerable profit.

Bill's dreams may have been growing, but he and Lois lived simply. They often went hiking on weekends, and it puzzled Lois that on these treks Bill never seemed to need a drink. It was as though the air and exercise furnished some essential ingredient that away from the country he could get only in booze. During the week it was another story. Then his days were spent in the dim chasms of the financial district, his evenings at Brooklyn Law, and both places gave him a good excuse for a couple of snorts. With Bill a couple always led to a couple more. Only occasionally, after his friends had left, did he remember that all the bright talk had been about another man's money, another man's plans. Then a signal to the bartender would bring the medicine he needed.

In late December, Bill received word that Grandmother Griffith was very ill. He hurried to Vermont alone, because Lois was suffering from the first of what was to be a series of miscarriages. On New Year's Day, Ella Brock Griffith was dead.

He was back in Brooklyn in time for the beginning of the winter semester, but he was spending more time reading market analyses than lawbooks. And now more and more he was drinking alone, fighting the old ugly awareness of not really being part of the scene. Everyone he knew was involved in building a family, a secure place for himself. His sister, Dorothy, had married her doctor. Living up in Tarrytown, she already had one child and another on the way. The Frank Shaws, whom he and Lois visited on Long Island, were prospering, with a whole batch of kids. Maybe, he would tell himself, it was all right to be different. Didn't evolution depend on variations from the norm? Wouldn't it follow, then, that all social and moral changes would begin with groups with differing values?

Then the next question would come up. Just what were his values? Finding no ready answer, he would have another drink.

But during this period there were wonderful, happy highs too, and some of these Bill shared with Lois. They would start out with a few short ones at home, and gradually, beautifully, the whole world would open out. They would move on to a restaurant, enjoy an insanely expensive meal with the best of wines, and Bill would seem the wittiest, handsomest man in town.

But, as Lois learned, it was only a question of time. After the sixth or seventh drink he'd be just as happy, but interested only in what *he* was saying. It didn't matter who was with him.

It's a lonely business being with a drunk, and when finally Lois had to take him home, she felt like a child deprived of something that had been, a few hours before, so real, so promising.

Sometimes next day they would talk and talk. What had caused the change? They'd walk all day discussing this, trying to understand, to find a cure. On other mornings his behavior became the one subject they both avoided. For Lois these mornings were often a time of self-reproach. In some way she was failing him. For Bill they were a time of silent remorse.

By December 1923, there had been so many bad nights followed by so many silent mornings that at Christmas, Bill wrote on the flyleaf of their family Bible:

> Thank you for your love and help this terrible year. For your Christmas I make you this present: No liquor will pass my lips for one year. I'll make the effort to keep my word and make you happy.

Two months later there was another such vow. As time passed, there would be others.

THE death of Ella had been like the loss of a mother, but Bill had no words to describe the impact of Fayette's death. Fayette had been his anchor and his polestar, his link with the past and, in a way, with the future too, because it had been old Fayette who'd made him see that through a son a man might live on beyond his years. Bill didn't want to think of that now. His link with the future would have to be worked out some other way. The spring before, Lois had had her third miscarriage. (His mother had written them most sympathetically and in the same letter had announced her intention of marrying again.)

Fayette, he remembered, had never had to sign a contract for the sale of his lumber. A handshake had sealed the deal, and when Bill had asked about this, he'd been told, A man's word is his bond. These words seemed to epitomize all the values that Fayette believed had made life vital and civilized.

As Bill walked back from the little hillside cemetery where his grandfather lay surrounded by his ancestors, a century seemed to separate him from Wall Street and the frantic pressures of Brooklyn Law. But that was the world he lived in now. Or almost lived in. Because as he said his good-bys to old friends and relatives, he couldn't escape the knowledge that he hadn't done much of a job of living in either world. He no longer belonged in East Dorset, and he had no real place in the city. That night on the train he understood one thing: he'd accomplished nothing. For six years he'd been drifting, waiting for the break that would not come, and now there'd be no Fayette to turn to.

ONE might suppose these would be sobering thoughts, but for Bill they had the opposite effect. Somehow he was able to hold down his job, but that was all he was doing. There was no hope of its leading him to higher ground. Law school had seemed to hold the answer, but he hadn't latched on, and there were young men in his class far brighter than he. At his final exams he was too drunk to see the questions.

As the hot summer nights settled over the city, he was determined to halt the terrible drift. Always—and he knew this might be part of the problem—he'd been trying to please others. Decisions had been made by others or by his desire to please them: Lois, his mother, his grandfather, Gilly. In some corner of his mind he had always been seeking Gilly's approval. But he would change all that. He had done it before. Once, and not too far back, *he* had been in command.

Buoyed up by this decision, he began what he thought of as a personal inventory. As he worked with his radios in the evening—

conscientiously cutting down on the drinking—he remembered the boy at Burr and Burton. A loner, surrounded by adversaries, he had determined to become the number one man. He smiled at the phrase, but admitted pride in that boy who would formulate a plan and pursue it. The pursuit had guided his every action. Now, as he remembered, another plan began to form in his mind.

Ever since he'd started working around Wall Street, one thing had been a puzzle to Bill. That was why everyone—not just the amateurs, but the big operators—would take such ridiculous chances and invest in companies they knew nothing about. In the past years Bill had developed certain investigative talents, and he knew something about the market. The few stocks he owned (mostly General Electric, purchased back in 1921 at $180 a share) were now, through splits, worth $4000 or $5000 a share. Why not go out, make a study of various companies, evaluate their potentials? Then sensible decisions could be reached, based on facts and a scientific prognosis.

He presented his plan to Lois in Vermont terms. Before his grandfather bought a cow, he would look at the cow, feel its legs, discover how much milk it produced, what its antecedents had been, etc. So why shouldn't they, he and Lois, go out on the road and apply this principle to the purchase of stock? Once the spark had been ignited, nothing could stop him. He borrowed three hundred dollars from Mrs. Burnham to buy a Harley-Davidson motorcycle, complete with sidecar; he bought Moody's manuals and every available book on market analysis. For weeks he studied the histories of industries that he believed warranted investigation.

Lois liked the idea; it would keep them together, away from bars. They were so much in agreement on this, so carried along with their own momentum, that when Bill presented the proposition to Frank Shaw at Rice, and to several other houses, and was met with a startling lack of interest, it in no way discouraged him.

In fact, the lack of support for his brainchild seemed to provide the exact stimulus he needed. They would be moving into uncharted seas. Of course, cautious brokers and bankers, whose businesses had hundreds of years of tradition, would be skeptical.

The more they said no, the surer he became. And the more they suggested that he was taking his wife across a desert with no compass to guide him, the more appealing it sounded. If there were no rules for such an enterprise, he would make his own.

They gave up the apartment, put their belongings in storage, mapped itineraries, packed the sidecar, then, counter to all advice, set off to investigate American industry. Bill was his own man now. The motorcycle was their covered wagon. They started out with pioneer innocence, ingenuity and hope.

CHAPTER SIX

THE motorcycle trip began in mid-1925. A psychiatrist might find it of interest that when they at last started off on the road to adventure, Bill headed first for East Dorset. They stayed at the Burnham camp, had late-night talks with Mark and hilarious evenings in Manchester drinking with Ebby Thacher. Then one July morning they were ready to move on.

The plan was to stop where night found them, cook supper, sleep in their explorer's tent and start out again at daybreak. The Harley-Davidson was a powerful machine, and Bill raced along, a roar across the countryside. Farmers put down their hoes to stare. Chickens, geese and children ran for cover, but the only sound the Wilsons heard was the wind in their ears, cheering them on.

Their first destination was the General Electric plant in Schenectady, New York, and as they leaped toward it, Bill was as happy as he had ever been, feeling in glorious control of his destiny.

On the outskirts of Schenectady they camped at the edge of a pleasant farm, and the next morning Bill called on General Electric. Here he learned his first lesson about dealing with management. He had put on his good suit and had presented himself as a small stockholder eager to find out about the company. He was received courteously, but perhaps his incisive questions baffled the men he spoke with—how much had he a right to know, how little could they tell him? When he left he'd learned not a thing.

There was a delay at this point because of their rule never to dip

331

into savings. Starting off with a hundred dollars, they had decided to stop when they ran low and work until they had earned enough to move on. East Dorset had made a dent in the wallet, so they looked in a Schenectady paper and found that a man on a nearby farm needed help. In the midst of a downpour they raced to Scotia. The place was run by a couple named Goldfoot and the man was no farmer. He'd been a coachman for Samuel Insull and a turnkey in a local jail. Crops and cattle overwhelmed him. Still, it took all afternoon to persuade him that Bill was the assistant he was looking for, and that Lois could really take care of the house and prepare three meals a day for a lot of farmhands. He hired them for seventy-five dollars a month. It was to be a strangely idyllic month, which gave no hint of the extraordinary events waiting just ahead.

Adjacent to the Goldfoot farm were several nondescript buildings on a large expanse of land owned by General Electric, where, they were told, GE conducted experiments. Lois was afraid at first that this might be a reminder to Bill of his missed opportunity, but as time passed and no reference was made to the subject, she relaxed. Toward the end of their month, Bill wandered into Scotia. There he fell into talk with several young men and, hearing that they worked for GE, bought them some beers. They learned of his great interest in electronics, and finally late at night drove him out to their research laboratory to show him what they were doing.

This was a night Bill would never forget. For stretched out before him was a wonderland like one of H. G. Wells's fantasies of the future. He saw experiments in sound motion pictures, work on magnets, on shortwave radio. He was given a complete preview of what General Electric was to become. By sheer chance he had stumbled upon top secret information it might have taken years to acquire. It was a confirmation of all he had gambled on.

The following day he sent a partial report to Frank Shaw. The rest he would hold to present in person.

THE next company Bill investigated was Giant Portland Cement, a small corporation whose stock was listed on the Philadelphia exchange. Here he began with a job in the plant. "Walking the rails," as he put it, was to become a key factor of Bill's method; by going in at the employees' entrance, he found out all he needed to know. At Giant Portland he discovered how much coal they were burning to make a barrel of cement; he read the meters on their power input; he saw the exact quantity they were shipping out. He noticed the new equipment—super synchronic motors and the like— that was being installed and, figuring out what this would mean to future production, estimated they would be able to make cement for less than a dollar a barrel. Yet for some reason their stock was dawdling on the market at only fifteen dollars a share.

Armed with a few shares of stock he'd bought, he marched into the front office and confronted them with the facts. It was an absurd situation. The management apparently had no faith in their own potential. Indeed, individual members of the firm were actually selling their stock as fast as they could. To Bill it was incredible, and feeling like a man who had fallen into a gold mine, he sent a signal to a Philadelphia broker to buy Giant Portland.

At this point there was one of those benign ill winds. A letter came from Bill's brother-in-law Leonard Strong, telling him Dorothy and the baby had been in a serious auto accident. There was no question, the Wilsons had to go to Tarrytown. While Lois nursed and tended, Bill was able to get into the city.

He went immediately to Rice and described the situation at GE and Giant Portland. It was a brilliant presentation and resulted in Rice's buying five thousand shares of Giant Portland and carrying Bill for a hundred shares. This was his first experience with a hundred-share lot of anything, and, of course, with this flurry of buying, the price per share jumped from fifteen to twenty-five dollars. Eventually, Giant Portland was to wind up at seventy-five dollars a share.

Rice's attitude toward Bill was totally reversed. Were there other companies they'd like him to look into? There were. The Aluminium Company of America, American Cyanamid, certain power companies that had been behaving oddly on the board. He might investigate Florida real estate.

A time to remember and a beginning.

THERE IS ONE INGREDIENT in all great adventures that the adventurer seldom acknowledges: that is the role played by chance. Like most men when life goes well, Bill could take the credit himself. And like all true adventurers, Bill believed he was born to be free.

With the family in Tarrytown on the way to recovery, and with winter coming on, Bill and Lois picked up the motorcycle and headed south. The next segment of Bill's story—indeed, the next four or five years—might be described in terms of one of those silent movies that were becoming so popular. Two wild riders, he and Lois raced through Virginia into the Carolinas, across Georgia, on to Florida. At Fort Myers they paused to visit Bill's mother and her husband, Dr. Charles Strobel, who were spending the winter on a houseboat. They took an afternoon off to wander around the island of Sanibel, and noticed a huge yacht anchored offshore and two figures dressed in dusters, collecting shells along the beach. There was no doubt whose yacht it was, or who the two figures were. They were Henry Ford and his wife.

Here the movie camera might move in for a close-up of Bill. For as Lois introduced herself to the Fords, Bill stayed back. What might be revealed in such a close-up, as he stood watching the great tycoon relaxing, talking with his wife? Bill never wanted to be an observer of great men; he wanted to be center stage. At this point he was on his way to becoming a Mr. Big in certain Wall Street circles, but wasn't he still obsessed with the notion that someday he too would be a number one man? Whatever his thoughts that afternoon, he watched and made no move to join the group.

From Florida they headed north and the film began to roll again. They examined phosphate mines; they camped on the shores of the Tennessee to study the wonders of Muscle Shoals; they were ferried across rivers on old stern-wheelers. Bill prepared voluminous reports on coal, iron and rail companies owned by U.S. Steel. Then on north to Holyoke, Massachusetts, to visit American Writing Paper, in which Bill and Frank Shaw were developing an interest, and later still—there was no sense of sequence—on to the wild lands of Canada and to the Aluminium Company.

THE SPRING OF 1926 found them back in Brooklyn for Kitty Burnham's wedding. There were also business conferences with Frank Shaw, who was doing so well he was considering branching out on his own. At these meetings there were frank discussions about Bill's drinking, but Shaw was a man with a keen eye for the long-haul situations Bill was unearthing, and their arrangement was proving so profitable he had no thought of changing it. Besides, when he was around the Street, Bill rarely drank until the exchange closed at three p.m. Then, realizing the magnitude of the deals he was involved in—he had a twenty-thousand-dollar credit with which to buy any stock he chose—he would head for the nearest speak and gradually make his way uptown. He'd be pretty much out of commission by Fourteenth Street, and completely lost by Fifty-ninth. By midnight he might have blown five hundred dollars. This Shaw knew, but he also knew Bill Wilson was not the only man on the Street who enjoyed tying one on.

Indeed, looking back at this latter part of the 1920s, it is easy to believe that the whole city, the whole country, was getting drunk along with Bill. In the course of a few years, established patterns had broken down everywhere. Men who before Prohibition never thought of drinking suddenly took it up with no concern about breaking the law; it was simply the thing to do. And with this the underworld moved in. Everyone wanted his share of the good things—bathtub gin, new cars, membership in the country club— and everyone wanted them now. If it can be said that any single force ever motivated a generation, surely in the 1920s that force was our will to succeed through selling ourselves or our product. Having fun and making your fortune became a mass movement. But what made Europe watch us in awe was our production, our promotion and our talent for creating great wealth. We went about this with all our cocksureness, our wit and resilience, laughing, as Carl Sandburg said of his Chicago, "as an ignorant fighter laughs who has never lost a battle."

Bank loans and installment buying paid for the show. Bill met businessmen who admitted they had borrowed ten times more money than they owned to speculate in the market. In those days everything fed the great miracle machines of American prosperity. Perhaps someone, especially someone in Washington, should have read the signals and given a warning, but as the governor of the Federal Reserve said, "How are you going to stop a million people from doing what they want to do?"

The carnival spirit didn't, of course, touch everyone. There was poverty and savage injustice. Bill and Lois had camped near the shack of one Robert Lee Brown for their first Christmas on the road. Brown was a sharecropper trying to raise tobacco. He invited the Wilsons to Christmas dinner with his family—sons, daughters-in-law and six younger children. Dinner consisted of turnip greens and sweet-potato custard, the only presents a package of jelly beans, and a knitted cap for the baby. At this point, when prosperity was nearing its peak, it was calculated that a family needed two thousand dollars to provide the basic necessities, yet sixty percent of U.S. families lived on less.

The signs were there. But the simple faith, the blind confidence were there too. Destiny was on the side of America all the way. Bill believed this in his heart. And didn't a rising tide lift all the boats? Later, when he was secure, there would be time—and he hoped he would use it—to do something about the Robert Lee Browns. Meanwhile the trick was to ride the waves.

IN MUCH the same way he rationalized his drinking.

He was not a drunk, he told himself, he was a man who drank badly at times. He must remember to eat when he drank; then, when things simmered down, he'd be all right. He was sorry his drinking upset Lois. He knew that on occasion it had been a real humiliation.

Bill was changing now. Some nights it was difficult to see any trace of the easygoing Vermonter everyone had loved. It was as though old snubs still riled him deep inside, and with a few drinks he felt a compulsion to even scores.

In 1928 they moved into a new apartment on Livingston Street, but even this wasn't grand enough, and when an adjoining apartment became vacant Bill rented it, paying for two years in ad-

337

vance and having the dividing wall knocked out to make one huge apartment. He needed the sense of spaciousness, he explained.

Curiously, during this period, when he was making such financial strides yet because of his drinking was sinking into a sump of hostility, there was one couple he never fought with: his sister, Dorothy, and her husband, Dr. Strong. Bill respected Leonard Strong, and Leonard was able to point out to him the progressive nature of his drinking. Leonard made an appointment with a colleague in New York for Bill to have a complete physical examination. Bill had a bad hangover the morning of the exam; but the young doctor found him to be in perfect health and saw no reason why with a little of "the old willpower" he shouldn't be able to drink in moderation. Bill thought the doctor an ass, but now the words willpower and moderation had been planted in his mind.

A definite pattern was beginning to develop. For weeks he would stay off the booze, then he would have a few, just a few in the evening, then there would be a party out on Long Island or up in Connecticut, and suddenly his drinks would hit him. Someone would make a remark and he would sense some implication behind it. The argument that followed would be grim and out of hand. For the one talent Bill seemed to have at such times was the ability to recognize an opponent's weak spot and move in on it. The next morning he would apologize, claim that when he'd had too much he wasn't himself.

Bill believed this, but only in a way. He knew that the words that came out of him during these drunken fights emerged from a deep part of him. The realization was profoundly shocking at first, but he made a serious effort to look at it.

Long ago, when people had first started talking about his drinking, he'd made what he called his list of nevers, things he'd never done. As long as he never did them, he knew he was not an alcoholic. He had never stolen, or begged for a drink. He'd never been violent with a woman or intentionally cruel. Old Fayette's rule that a man's word is his bond was of supreme importance. Of course, it was true he had gone back on pledges, but the point was they had been made to another, not to himself. Only in trivial things did he ever lie to himself—saying, for instance, that he would stop in a bar for just one drink, knowing he'd have three or four. That was just kidding oneself.

There were so many things about drinking that others didn't understand. There was no way to explain the constant tensions and the necessity to relax. There was *no* way of explaining that it was important to get away after the daily racket—to find out what he himself thought. With a few drinks he was a clearer, brighter man. And—why not admit it?—in a bar with men he liked, he was a gentler, more loving man.

But then—and he knew he had to look at this too—someone could say something and the world could change. That was occurring too often now. But he didn't want to think about it, just as he did not want to think about that other thing, the attacks. These attacks were new, and he'd found no way of coping with them. They had something to do with fear, but no fear he could label. One could hit him with no warning in the midst of a conference, a terrible floating anxiety he couldn't shake off. The only thing that would quiet it was a quick shot of whiskey.

But most important of all was what happened to him after his first few drinks. If he was ever to make peace with himself, he knew he would have to look at that first warm, loving interval. Look at it straight. And about this he was of two minds.

No matter what others said, he knew that what happened in those brief hours did *not* derive from anything evil. It was as though all the warring sides of his nature were in harmony then, functioning at their best and on a slightly higher plane than usual. The world in the evening with a few quiet drinks was the world as it ought to be, as he had always wanted it to be.

Wanted. Was that it? *Did* he want more than other men? Once a bartender had told him, "Trouble with you, Bill, is you want double everything—double whiskies, double laughs, double sex and double loving. Double everything." He'd laughed and felt he'd been paid a compliment; but he also felt the truth in it.

One winter night when he was alone—it may have been the time Lois took off to test him, leaving a note that when he'd gone six days without a drink he was to let her mother know and she would come back—he awoke in the night, reached out and found only the emptiness of the bed. He got up then, stumbled across to the window and stood looking out at the moon-white streets of Brooklyn. Then he held out his arms and said, "I want, I want . . ." Was this some curse inherited from his father? Or were there other men with their arms stretched out, wanting, wanting in the night?

His hands were spread up and out, his fingers open. There seemed something familiar in the gesture, but at first he could not place it. Something connected with moonlight? With Winchester Cathedral? He searched for a glimpse of the innocent years, but they were too distant, and all he could recall was the more recent past, restless, angry. Then he remembered—front-porch steps and a pair of hands reaching up beside his, Bertha Banford in a long white dress, Darwin and evolution. Always from the earliest times men had wanted life to break through into another dimension. And from this wanting had come the doing, from the doing the means with which to do. "Then," she had said, "it means man will always want to break through . . . always want more."

He and Bertha had believed that if they didn't want more, they would be letting down all those who had gone before. It was more than sex, this wanting in the night, though sex might be a part of it; more than a desire for peace or a surcease from compulsion. It was part of life in him, in all men. It had been here always, before there were men to give it a name.

For one moment he understood all the striving and desire everywhere. But as he tried to put it in words, it was gone. All that remained as he poured himself a drink was a sense of having been close to his answer. In the morning there was only a sense of having failed again. Well, the main thing was to keep rolling, and not indulge in childish fancies. He was doing all right. At any cost he must keep moving.

If there is a line, as Bill came to believe, that every alcoholic crosses, it may be that he crossed it at that point. He began to drink as never before, drinking his booze straight in order to dream, as he put it, dreams of greater glory. He began to envision himself as an independent operator, sitting on this or that board, graciously giving advice to Morgan and Company. In fact, at the start of 1929, Bill Wilson was living in what many would call an alcoholic's paradise.

AN ALCOHOLIC's paradise, as every drunk knows, can become in no time at all an alcoholic hell. The summer of 1929 Bill could no longer deny what Leonard Strong had told him about the progressive nature of his drinking. He had believed the attacks would disappear with financial security, but they only increased. It was undoubtedly an attempt to combat them that made him decide to spend some time in Vermont.

By now he had broken all connections with Baylis & Company, Shaw, and Rice. He saw himself as a big-time operator, the lone wolf of Wall Street—an image he enjoyed projecting on the Manchester scene. His portfolio was extensive. Late in the summer he worried because the market seemed a bit wobbly, and returned to the city. But specialists whose advice he respected told him everything was rosy, high and going higher. American Tel and Tel was over 310, General Electric 403. It was a time to enjoy. A time to get drunk.

Then it happened.

On October 23 there was a tremendous drop in the last hour of trading, and the following day, Black Thursday, thirteen million shares changed hands. The worst had to be over, everyone insisted, and Bill hung on, but on October 28 and 29 sixteen million shares were thrown on the market for whatever they might bring. Within a matter of weeks the paper value of common stocks had dropped thirty billion dollars. Bill was in a hotel, quite drunk, the night of the twenty-ninth. It was over. The end of the big bull market. The end of "normalcy." The merry-go-round had come to a stop, the structure broken down.

Leaders in Washington and on the Street said conditions were still fundamentally sound; it was a natural readjustment. But the leaders had lost all touch with the realities.

Bill's first reaction was typical and in a way it was even gallant.

On October 29 he was a man sixty thousand dollars in arrears, with a wife to support, a grand double apartment they could sublease only at a loss, and practically no ready cash. His response was one of almost boyish excitement; he saw it as a personal challenge. "Back," Philip H. Sheridan had said. "We will go back and retake our camps!" And why not? He'd show them.

His first move toward rallying his forces was to contact Greenshields and Company, a brokerage firm in Montreal with which he had done some lucrative business. Canada had not been quite so hard hit. By the middle of November he had received a wire from Dick Johnson at Greenshields to come on up, they would give him a job. He and Lois set off. He was on his way again.

But it was later than Bill Wilson realized.

THE Canadian venture began modestly, but by May he was making money and dreaming once more of omnipotence. They joined the country club and dined in only the finest restaurants. And Bill drank, starting with nips in the morning. By fall the partners of Greenshields were agitated about fights at the country club and in city bars, too often with potential customers. But Bill seemed unable to curb his life-style. Finally the partners agreed they had no choice: they had to let him go. It was unbelievable to Bill—ten months of big operations and nothing to show for it.

The word from Clinton Street at this moment was also grim. It was feared that Mrs. Burnham had cancer, and she was undergoing X-ray treatment. Feeling she had to be with her mother, Lois took off, leaving Bill to sublease the apartment if possible, store the furniture and sell their one real asset, a Packard touring car.

Being fired from Greenshields marked another ending and another beginning. With Lois gone he drank around the clock, and his memories of the next month, the next year were unrelated fragments. One—Christmas 1930—was to stand out. He'd somehow got back to Clinton Street, and Lois was looking into his eyes, telling him her mother was dead—that woman who was all love, who had a capacity for loving greater than that of any soul he'd ever known—and Lois was saying she was dead. Then the terrible knowledge that he'd got drunk, too drunk to pay Mrs. Burnham the tiny respect of attending her funeral or offering her daughter any kind of support.

The look in Lois's eyes remained in his memory, superimposed on a thousand details of that winter: breadlines, crowds going nowhere, just standing and waiting.

He and Lois were alone with the doctor on Clinton Street now, the family scattered. Even young Lyman had married and was practicing medicine out in Jersey. Bill again found himself a guest. This was no easy role for a man who prided himself on being the great provider. He knew the doctor had suffered heavy losses, and suspected that most of his patients were being carried on credit. One evening Lois asked if they didn't think it would be a good idea if she got a job, she was sure she could, and it would only be temporary, of course, until Bill got hold.

It was not the sort of question Bill knew how to answer, but when he was offered a humiliating job at Stanley Statistics at a hundred dollars a week, he knew he had no choice; he accepted.

Not too long after he had been hired, he got involved in a barroom brawl. He remembered a pair of sinister-looking thugs in the melee, and that he had mislaid his briefcase, but most of the details were blacked out. A few afternoons later he got a mysterious phone call at the office. The man wanted to know if Bill remembered everything that had been in his briefcase. Maybe they could work a deal, he said. He called the next day and the next, with insinuations about information he had picked up on Bill, and Bill's panic grew. He could do nothing all day except sit at his desk and stare at the phone, terrified—for the horror of it was that whatever the man was suggesting could be true. He had no idea what he had done that night. A policeman could walk in and accuse him of any crime at all; he would have no defense.

He could never remember if this threat of blackmail had been the cause of his dismissal from Stanley Statistics. All he remembered was cold terror that at any moment, sitting at his desk, he might lose complete control of himself. Then one Friday night he was told that he need not report for work on Monday morning.

Lois began working at R. H. Macy in May for nineteen dollars a week, demonstrating a new kind of collapsible card table. She enjoyed it, she said, as each evening at the supper table Dr. Burnham asked her, not Bill, "How were things on the job today?"

Bill would have found it difficult to describe what he did each day, and wholly impossible to share the thoughts and feelings that absorbed him as he made his way along the Street.

When he first got back from Canada he'd been shocked—and not only by the fear he sensed everywhere or the growing lines of unemployed. He understood the economic consequences of the crash—the decline in sales, decreased demand for goods forcing curtailment of production, wage cuts, firing. Unemployment had tripled in 1930, would double again in 1931 and would probably go on up to twelve or thirteen million. He knew all this. It was those who pretended *not* to know who disturbed him—chairmen and presidents of banks who stepped from their limousines and sailed into inner offices as though their right to wealth were ordained by the Almighty, as though nothing had changed.

Something had changed irrevocably. Bill would fall into talk with some man he'd find on a corner, take him into a delicatessen, buy him a beer and listen. After a while all their stories seemed the same—each a fragment of the saga unfolding all over the country. He felt a kind of guilt, almost as if he owed them a debt, for he was learning that the difference between a man with fifty thousand a year and a man whose wife worked and gave him beer money was negligible in comparison with a man who had nothing. He wanted to help, yet he felt isolated, as if his few advantages disqualified him. He felt a part of these hapless men, yet separate from them. For to Bill they were lost. They had no ability to adjust to circumstances. Out of work, they evidently saw themselves as victims. Bill did not yet see himself as a victim.

It would take a long time before he understood what was happening around him and to him. At least what he saw had shocked him out of total absorption in his self-centered world, and he was aware that there was an aching pain across the land that one day must be tended. But he was only dimly aware. Too much else filled his mind, primarily the necessity of proving to Clark Burnham and Lois that he was still capable of staying sober and making his living and doing something they would consider important. When the supper dishes had been put away he would wander out for a stroll, under the pretext of wanting some fresh air. He'd stop in a small speakeasy he'd discovered that sold whiskey for twenty-five cents a shot. Over what was to be just one little drink he would begin to organize a plan. He would start out tomorrow when Lois went to work, and perhaps see Frank Shaw, or Baylis, admit he'd been foolish, then remind them that he had done some important investigative work for them and wanted to start again; he was still an honorable man, no one would question that. He knew what suit he would wear, the way he would walk in, the way he would greet the secretary. Tomorrow morning. At ten o'clock.

Since everything was settled, why not have just one more drink? Tomorrow was a certainty.

So he would have one more. And one more . . .

Yet night after night, morning after lost morning, he never was without belief that for him there would be one more chance. And curiously, about this at least he was right.

CHAPTER SEVEN

It was through Lois's brother-in-law Gardner Swentzel that Bill first met Arthur Wheeler. Gardner liked Bill and respected his theories about the market. Artie too made up his mind that Bill had many ideas he could use. Artie, only son of the president of American Can, certainly had capital Bill could use. With Frank Winans, a banker from Chicago, they formed a long-term speculative syndicate based on the notion that if one had enough capital and enough patience, there was a vast fortune to be made out of the recovery that was bound to come.

Wheeler and Winans, however, were conservative and cautious. Before drawing up the contract, they investigated Bill's background and discovered his drinking history. They faced him with it frankly. Winans insisted on an addendum to the contract, which stated in the clearest terms that if ever during the life of the syndicate Bill took so much as one drink of alcohol, he would forfeit his entire interest in the enterprise.

On April 8 Bill signed. To this he would be true. He was Fayette Griffith's grandson. A man's word was his bond.

Spring came early that year, and it was an extraordinary, beautiful spring. It was also a beautiful time at 182 Clinton Street. Lois, privately reprimanding herself for having too little faith, took a day off and bought new dresses. She was younger than she had been in years, pretty and chic again.

But it wasn't only Lois. People everywhere were delighted. A man Bill hadn't seen in months called one day to ask if he'd care to investigate a new photographic process at the Pathé studios in New Jersey.

Driving out to Jersey with a group of engineers, Bill had never felt better. Five weeks without booze, a corner had been turned. At Bound Brook they checked into a hotel. After dinner a deck of cards was brought out; Bill had no interest in cards. He sat at the side and kibitzed. One of the men produced a jug of applejack. It was something special, they insisted, real applejack, Jersey Lightning. But Bill shook his head and was amazed at how easy it was to refuse. Sitting there, he thought back over just what he'd had in his thirty-six years. The Bronx cocktail in New Bedford at the beginning, brandies on the ship, wines in France. It became a kind of game, listing them, and he wondered if there was any kind of alcohol he hadn't tasted in the long road between 1918 in New Bedford and May 1932.

"Bill"—the jug had come around again—"you ought to try it."

There *was* one thing he'd never tasted. Jersey Lightning. "Why not?" One taste. He smiled and took a swig.

They were right. There was nothing like it. It was then, that night in New Jersey, that he learned there was not, and never would be, such a thing as just one drink.

The next thing he knew, it was morning and the engineers had gone off to Pathé without him. His room was flooded with blinding sunlight. His head was spinning and he was sure he was going to be ill. On the bureau he could see a jug with an inch of apple-jack at the bottom. He rose, staggered to the bureau, lifted the jug to his lips and, with great determination, swallowed what was left in one long gulp. But the shakes were still there. He rang for a bell-boy and ordered another crock of Lightning.

There must have been other calls to other bellboys. He knew nothing until what turned out to be three days later. As from a great distance he heard a bell ringing and gradually woke to the fact that it was a telephone. New York was calling. Mr. Wheeler. And Arthur Wheeler said what Bill knew he would say. The contract was canceled.

The contract was canceled. And there was something worse from which he had to run—something he had done to himself and could never undo. He didn't remember how he got back to Brooklyn, but he remembered Clinton Street and the dozens of eyes pinned on him as he stumbled along. Then someone's arm was behind his back, and as he let himself be guided, he clenched his jaw and tried to stop shaking, but he could no more stop the tremors racking his body than he could halt the terrible waves of sickness. At 182 everything went wrong. As he leaned forward to rest his head on the railing, he realized that if he didn't lower himself to the steps, he would fall, fall into a space that was opening out before him, huge and dark and growing darker.

THE worst of the Jersey Lightning experience was that it changed Bill's picture of himself. He could never again think of himself as a man of honor. His word was not his bond. Now he drank simply to escape. He was unemployed and unemployable, his life blown apart; and what he had done represented the antithesis of everything he'd been reared to believe in.

Yet at the same time he felt a kind of personal hurt, as though some outside force he could not label had betrayed him. He wondered if there indeed might be forces over which a man had no control. And to this thought there was a frightening corollary. By admitting that there could be forces more powerful than he, a door was opened to the idea that such forces might win out. And with this came the secret terror of insanity. He could already be on his way to complete loss of control.

But he was still Bill Wilson, still a man of pride. His pride, however, was of a special order. It was based not on accomplishments, but only on what he believed he could do—and for this reason, perhaps, he was always forced to find new challenges.

In the summer of 1932 the challenge was alcohol. He was going to prove he could control his drinking. He managed to stay sober for weeks, through fear and constant vigilance. Then he would try just a few, and having started, nothing could stop him. When he wound up passed out, he saw it now as due to some specific factor outside himself—he'd forgotten to eat, or his drinks had been spiked, or he'd gulped them too fast.

The following winter he thought a lot about powers greater than the individual. There was an air of foreboding all over America. One out of every four workers was unemployed. The faces on breadlines were no longer bewildered; they were angry, desperate. Now that people had radios, they were better informed than ever before about events in the world. But they could neither understand nor control these events. As he wandered the streets alone, Bill was filled with a sense of men waiting for a leader, and his picture of the sort of leader who might emerge troubled him profoundly. For Bill had been brought up by Fayette Griffith to carry steadily in his mind an image of independent democracy, and this was a legacy that, drunk or sober, he could not easily forget.

Fayette's words, though, seemed quaint these days. And Bill tried to accept the fact that he lived in a world where dreams die, just as with most of us love must die, or, in some rare cases like his Lois, refuses to.

But love was a thought he was becoming adept at putting from his mind. Whenever a picture of Lois threatened, an image of her going off to work and leaving a few dollars for him on the bureau, he knew the trick of immediately ordering another drink, or making a joke if there was someone near. By now their relationship had passed through every phase classic to the drunk and his devoted wife: fury, despair, resignation. There had been times when, remembering how alive and beautiful she had been, he literally could not accept what he had done. He knew she had probably, and often, turned to him with needs he could not satisfy, just as he had gone to her with hungers she could not even sense. There had been mornings—usually after a horrendous fight—when she seemed to understand nothing and control everything, and he felt the very essence of himself threatened. Home had become an armed camp— each one watching, waiting for the other's next move. Now, in the winter of 1933, they had arrived at a quiet period. There was solicitude and kindness. Lois treated him almost as if he were an invalid, gently encouraging him, and both of them always avoided any mention of what was really wrong.

Bill was living and doing his thinking in a strange twilight area between fantasy and fact, between shaking fear and outbursts of rage at what he believed was taking place around him. The murder of the dream. But nothing compared to his despair when, after weeks of sobriety, he'd find himself lost in a wild, drunken haze, stretched out in the vestibule, bloodied, with no memory of how it had happened. Lois would have to get him into the house and up the stairs to bed. Fortunately, Dr. Burnham had remarried early in 1933 and moved from 182, so there was no one except Lois to witness the pitiful bravado, the unbearable humiliation.

For one thing must be made clear: Bill was involved as never before with his struggle to master alcohol.

He saw that he had a tendency to relax after staying on the wagon for a time, to think he had it made. In a way, staying sober destroyed the challenge. His pride now needed to prove to him that he could handle a few drinks. Yet a pride that forced you to go on again and again with all the odds against you was a kind of insanity. Still he tried.

He allowed Leonard and Dorothy to put him in a hospital several times. He underwent the regulation detoxification, took vitamins and listened to the doctor's advice about willpower. He kept trying Vermont and outdoor living. He studied everything written on the subject of alcohol, all the self-help books. He even spent hours reading Mary Baker Eddy's *Science and Health*. He knew, however, that Christian Science could work only if he had faith, and faith, he had decided on the subway one night, was not something that could be reached by thinking.

The shocking thing about his behavior that night was that he was completely sober. The car was almost empty, but across from him sat a father and mother and three young boys. They sat quietly, huddled together, and there was about them a look not only of poverty and pride, but of unmistakable hunger. He knew they were in the subway not because they were going anywhere, but because it was dry and relatively warm.

Another passenger, an elderly priest, had been watching the family too. Now his eyes met Bill's. A beatific smile lit his face. "Do not worry," he said quietly. "God will provide."

Suddenly, Bill was on his feet. "When?" He towered above the priest. "What God?" he demanded. "And what will He provide?" He was like someone possessed, his words pouring out with fury. How, he wanted to know, could a God of love watch innocent children starving? He didn't believe in the priest's God, or in heaven and hell. They were not facts. He and his church were making people believe through fear and medieval superstition. And he gestured toward the poor, suffering family.

He had never felt such cold hatred as he felt at that moment, and when the train stopped and he got off, he was embarrassed. But he couldn't be sorry. He might be a poor sinner, he might not be a man of honor, but damn it, he refused ever to be solaced by anything his rational mind could not accept.

OF THOSE few who still tried to reason with Bill in this period, only one spoke to his condition, Dr. William Silkworth. Four times in 1933-34 Bill was a patient at Towns Hospital, a drying-out establishment on Central Park West, and it was probably during his second visit that he had his first talk with Silkworth. What was unique was that the doctor showed no condescension. He was speaking to a patient he knew to be very ill. He made no bones about this. And Bill recognized that this slight little man with compassionate blue eyes peering out from beneath a shock of pure white hair spoke from profound medical knowledge. Bill's drinking, the doctor said, was an obsession that condemned him to drink against his will. There was no question that Bill wanted to stop. There was an additional complication: he had become physically allergic to alcohol, his body could not tolerate it; hence his hangovers, his strange mental deviations. Their job, and he used the word *their*, was to break the obsession. He didn't preach; he presented Bill with this double-pronged bind.

Bill's reaction was indescribable relief. He had found someone who understood him. With such a man as Silkworth, who made a patient feel that his recovery mattered tremendously to them both, he was convinced they could handle it.

He stayed at Towns until he believed the poison was completely removed from body and mind. When he saw Lois again, he was filled with hope, and he was learning that hope was the first requisite of courage. The homecoming was an evening such as Clinton Street had not seen for years, the house filled with flowers, all Bill's favorite foods for dinner. They made plans for trips. They'd start hiking. Most important, he'd keep in touch with Silkworth, who'd told him he didn't know if deep psychological problems caused alcoholism, but he was convinced that alcohol caused psychological problems. Together they would go into those.

This was it. They were absolutely sure. In their wild high hopes they could be lovers again. He'd be a man again.

EVEN years later, no matter how hard he tried, Bill could not remember the circumstances of his next drunk, or even when it started. He knew only that it was impossible to stop.

Now there was almost nothing he would not do for a drink. He begged drinks, shamelessly, others said, but the truth was that some bit of him withered every time he did it. He stole, at first just a few bills from Lois's purse when he needed to buy a fifth of gin. Then he began taking small objects from the house to a pawnshop on Atlantic Avenue. He became cagey, conniving, and did not even cringe when he was called an out-and-out liar. Drunk, sober, sober, drunk, a man forever driven and forever blocked.

351

In July, Bill went back into Towns Hospital. Again there was a memorable session with Silkworth. But this time the interview was between Lois and the doctor.

To the doctor these interviews had become very much of a type, with the reaction of the wife often as baffling as the drunkenness of the patient upstairs: gallant women always believing he had some magic to put their lives back in one piece; women who went on hoping when there was no cause for hope. They were the strongest people God ever made. Yet he knew they might be part of the cause and, if not that, that they often went on feeding the flames of destruction—all in the name of love. They needed miracles to save them, and who could furnish miracles now?

As he fumbled with his papers, Dr. Silkworth felt painfully aware of his inadequacies. He never knew how to say the words that could signify the total failure of all a wife had worked and prayed for. But there was no escaping the intense blue eyes that looked up at him that evening, or the questions Lois forced herself to ask: "Why? What causes it?" Perhaps the American Medical Association was right: obsessive drinking was a moral defect and not a medical concern.

"What," she asked, "do we do?" He answered gently. He had hoped that Bill might succeed because of his desire to stop, because of his intelligence. But the obsession was too deep and the physical effects too severe. He already showed signs of brain damage, and if he went on, they would have to fear for his sanity.

"And"—Lois never took her eyes from him—"and what does that mean exactly?"

"It means you will have to confine him, lock him up somewhere, if he is to remain sane. He cannot go on for another year. . . ."

When he left Towns, Bill was told some of this prognosis, enough to frighten him into staying sober for more than a month. Silkworth's warning of brain damage put a foundation beneath the suspicion he'd been living with for years. The idea that incarceration could actually have been discussed caused such tension that soon he was forced to reach out for the only relief he knew.

Bill was alone now most of the time, because Lois had to leave at eight and didn't get home till after six. Most mornings he didn't mind seeing her go. There was a kind of relief in the empty house. Usually he'd get up and have coffee with her. But some mornings, from what he knew were the best of intentions, she would turn in the bedroom doorway and smile lovingly and say, "Why don't you just go back to sleep?" as if to imply, Bill, you don't have to get up for anything. How *could* she, how could *anyone,* say it? Those words would fill him with a wild rage: *You don't have to get up for anything.*

As soon as he knew it was safe, he would make a systematic check of his supplies. He had bottles stashed away in every part of the house—in the coal bin by the furnace, behind books on the shelves, under his shirts. Whether it was a day when he was drinking or one when he was coming off a drunk, he had to know a bottle was there, had to actually feel the cool glass against his fingers. For the fear of being without in case he had to have one was as obsessive as his terror of the "crazy house."

His world was gradually narrowing, and he was acutely aware of it, but he made few objections. In the evening he no longer had to excuse himself. He had only to keep peace with Lois.

His concept of self was narrowing, too, as he grew more conscious of the forces operating beyond his control.

One problem he never seemed to solve was when to get up, when to go outside. If he rose and left the house with Lois, the streets were filled with men and women hurrying along to work. He didn't belong with them. If he waited and went out at noon, he seemed to see nothing but idle old men or nursemaids airing babies. He belonged nowhere. That he was living in an inane vacuum he recognized as true. But he was careful to avoid anyone who might point it out. If he happened to run into an old acquaintance, he was ready with excuses for hurrying on. If, entering a bar, he sensed there might be someone who'd recognize him, he'd move on to another place. And all of this, he told himself, was because he was now in his natural state, a complete loner. In reality he was a man with an almost desperate need for any kind of friendship.

ON ARMISTICE DAY, 1934, there was no problem about when to get up. It was a handsome, crisp fall day and Bill felt fine. He decided to go to Staten Island and play a few rounds of golf.

After getting off the ferry at St. George, he boarded a bus and found himself sitting beside a man who was carrying a target rifle. They fell into easy conversation, and Bill talked about his old Remington. Halfway across the island their bus broke down, and to kill time they went into a nearby restaurant. Bill's new friend wanted a drink, but Bill said no and ordered a ginger ale. He explained that he was an alcoholic; he even described Silkworth's theory of an obsession combined with an allergy, and was quite pleased that he'd made his points so clearly.

It was past noon when a substitute bus carried them on to the golf course. By now they figured it was lunchtime, and, still together, they went into the club inn. A group of early drinkers were gathered around a piano, singing happily. While his friend ordered a Scotch, Bill again asked for ginger ale—but the bartender put two Scotches before them. "On the house," he announced in a cheery Irish brogue. "It's Armistice Day. Drink 'em up, lads." And Bill reached out for the Scotch.

He was aware of his friend staring at him. "After what you've told me," he said, "if you drink that, you have to be insane."

Bill returned his look. "I am," he said.

IN SOME way he reached 182, but there he stopped, unable to ring the bell. He dropped to his knees, stretched himself out and slept all night in the vestibule.

Lois found him there when she left for work in the morning.

CHAPTER EIGHT

A MAN with an active and naturally curious mind who suddenly finds himself a recluse can be distracted by any living thing. Even a dog stopping to sniff a tree can rivet his attention. Since Staten Island, Bill had been in total seclusion, venturing out only to replenish his supplies, then sitting for hours at a kitchen table, alone with a fifth of gin. When, late in November, his old friend Ebby Thacher phoned and said he'd like to stop by, Bill was wildly excited. Ebby Thacher had always been a rare one. Bill had sometimes envied him the glorious irresponsibility of the moneyed drunk. But no one could harbor ill feeling toward Ebby, with that straightforward smile and the kindness in his eyes.

Bill tidied the kitchen and brought out a fresh bottle of gin. It had been well over a year since he'd seen Ebby. It would be good to see such a character again. Bill hurried toward the stairs, deciding he'd shave for this reunion, he'd even get out of his pajamas. But at the foot of the stairs his eye fell on a folded-over mattress at the side of the hall. In an instant—it was as though a thundercloud had passed across the sun—all light disappeared from the hall. The night before last, Lois had helped him carry the mattress downstairs and he'd slept down here—or tried to—because she had been afraid he might try to throw himself out of the bedroom window.

He stared at the mattress, one hand gripping the stair rail, and suddenly his whole body was swept by a wave of panic and deep shame as he remembered every detail of the past two nights and the Staten Island night before them. Until Staten Island, when he had seen his face in the mirror across the bar and realized suddenly that he himself was the enemy of everything he believed in, that he himself was everything he had vowed he would never be—until then, booze had been his friend. No matter what happened, he'd always known that booze would bring a glorious oblivion. But since that night the opposite had been true. Now, instead of blocking out memories, alcohol opened doors and set all manner of demons free to sweep through his reeling brain.

Only it wasn't his brain now—that was the hell. As he had prayed for sleep, just a snatch of sleep, and no sleep came, he was tortured with terrors that rose from subconscious depths over which he seemed to have no control. These demons had no connection with conscious thinking. At Towns he'd heard other men, drunks, describe their d.t.'s—wild hallucinations that took over and became the only reality. They said there was nothing you could do. But there had to be something. . . . He had pulled himself out of bed

355

and stumbled to the window, searching for some answer, wondering if he ever would desire anything again, except to sleep, now and forever.

It had been as he stood at the window, trembling, covered with sweat, that Lois had awakened and, as if reading a thought before he actually reached that thought, asked him to help her carry this mattress downstairs.

Waiting for Ebby, he stared at it, then went back to the kitchen and swallowed a slug of gin. The only sensation it gave him was that there was a sense of movement now, a blind tumbling forward of everything. If once life had seemed a merry-go-round, now it was a high greased slide. His descent would be rapid, inexorable. He could not live if he went on drinking. He could not stop drinking. And he was terrified of death.

Possibly if he drank with Ebby, someone he knew and trusted, if he could laugh again, it might make the difference.

As soon as he opened the door he knew something was different, but it took several minutes to understand what. Ebby Thacher was cold sober. When Bill led him to the kitchen table, with the bottle and glasses on it, Ebby shook his head.

"No?" Bill studied him. This was an unheard-of situation.

"No."

"Why not?"

"I don't need it anymore."

It was a terrible letdown. Bill tried to cover it with a little joke. All the more for him, he said. They both laughed, but it was clearly not a subject a man could pass over. "What's it all about?"

"I've got religion," Ebby answered simply.

Bill wasn't sure he'd heard right, but in the silence, as he looked into Ebby's eyes, he knew he had. "Well . . ." He felt embarrassed and somehow betrayed. "What brand have you got?"

Ebby smiled and said he didn't think it had a brand name. He'd simply fallen in with some wonderful people, the Oxford Group.*

---

* In 1938 the movement became known as Moral Re-Armament. [Editor's note.]

Bill vaguely remembered having heard of them, rich folks mostly, all very chic and high-minded. Ebby said that when he'd been arrested on one of his sprees, three of them had come to his rescue and promised the judge to work with him. . . . And he went on about the group, which, it seemed, had started at Oxford University and moved on to South Africa. Many of their precepts, Ebby said, such as taking stock of oneself, confessing one's defects and being willing to make restitution, were truly international. Ebby Thacher should have been the last man on earth to be taken in by such easy salvation, Bill was thinking, and Ebby said he guessed Bill would gag, but they had asked him to pray to whatever God he believed there might be.

It wasn't that Bill gagged; he just stopped listening. Then he began picking up fragments of sentences. . . . As Ebby tried praying . . . keeping an open mind . . . drinking problem had been lifted . . .

It had nothing to do with being on the wagon, Ebby said; that had always been a struggle and he didn't have to tell Bill about the hell of failure. . . . As he said this their eyes met and held. And in that look there was no judgment. They were two drunks looking at each other with total understanding. The word hell moved them to a true communion.

After that, nothing Ebby could say would block out or even veil that contact, that thing that had existed between them for a moment. Bill did find much that Ebby said extremely hard to take. Still he listened.

It was simply a matter of admitting you were licked, Ebby insisted, of accepting the fact that booze was more powerful than you. Then Ebby began speaking, not of God, but of a "higher power," and Bill experienced a very definite and very curious physical reaction. He felt a chill run up his arm, and suddenly he was listening not so much to Ebby as *for* something, for some intimation beyond Ebby's words, and he was filled with a strange expectancy, as if he were hovering close to a new dimension of perception. He knew he had had this feeling before, this sense of approaching a truer reality, but he could not remember when.

Ebby stood up. In a moment he was gone, and Bill was alone.

357

PART OF BILL FELT hope for the first time in months, while another part kept dismissing almost everything that had been said. If it all depended on the God bit and giving oneself over to that; it had to be the same old malarkey. And yet . . .

And yet Ebby Thacher was sober.

Bill stayed in the kitchen and drank on into the night, and the inner debate seesawed back and forth between hope and resentment at being asked to accept what sounded like the sentimental garbage religious nuts handed out on the street. When Ebby phoned again and said he would like to stop by with a friend, Bill's resistance was at its peak.

The friend he chose to bring along was Shep Cornell. This was a mistake. Cornell was handsome, well built and well born, a cheery young fellow ready to confess to quite a drinking career of his own. But about this Bill had his doubts—probably too many sherries at a Junior League cotillion. But God knew he was sober now. And God knew they both seemed to be enjoying their sobriety. Ebby and Shep talked incessantly about the serenity of their new life, their newfound sense of purpose, a new kind of loving. Fortunately they did not stay too long.

When they were gone, Bill went straight for a bottle, and the drinks he poured himself were stiff ones. His reaction to Cornell didn't bother him; its origins went back to his resentment of Burr and Burton boys. But the change in his old drinking pal was another matter.

Ebby was not only inwardly reorganized; his very roots seemed to grasp new soil. He had suggested Bill pray to anything he'd ever had faith in. This might work for some people, but he was by training and inclination a materialist. They wanted him to give up the one attribute that set man above the animals—his inquiring, rational mind—for an illusion. What he had believed in was man, the spearhead of evolution, the rebel spirit who wanted to reach out into a new dimension.

As for love, he would not let himself think of love, of what he had done to Lois. His mind literally could not accept the picture of himself as a drunk lying in bed, hopeless and impotent.

His FIRST THOUGHT ON awakening the next morning was of Ebby, sober, with no hangover. What *had* happened to Ebby? Had he truly made a connection with a power he believed greater than himself? Did he honestly believe in God, or did he only long to believe?

Bill had been an investigator, a professional who had earned a reputation for being able to get at the facts of complex situations, so by midday it appeared logical that if he wanted to know about the source of Ebby's sobriety, he should go into New York and make an investigation of the Oxford Group. He started off for their headquarters in old Calvary Episcopal Church, which he knew to be on Gramercy Park, and to have a look at their mission, which he believed to be on Twenty-third Street.

At that time Twenty-third Street was abloom with bars, and he managed to hit most of them. It was late afternoon before he remembered why he was in the city. He was staggering when he finally made it to the mission, only to be greeted at the door by one Tex Francisco, a huge ex-drunk who ran the place and who immediately made it clear he was capable of running him out. But at that moment Ebby materialized from the shadows and suggested that they go upstairs for something to eat.

After a plate of beans and a great deal of coffee, Bill appeared a little more sober, and Ebby asked him to join a meeting in the main hall. The large room was lined with benches and filled now with men in every stage of decay, the bedraggled waste of a city. There were hymns and prayers. Tex spoke about Jesus and the possibility of a new life. A few people stood up and gave brief testimonials. Bill listened without judgment. There was no denying he was with his fellow drunks. Each stumbling account of each private hell was part of Bill's own story.

Tex called for penitents to come forward. Ten or twelve shuffled up, and suddenly, impelled by he knew not what, Bill found himself rising too. He stood at a railing surrounded by sick, sweating, stinking ghosts. Tex mumbled a few words, then they all headed back to their seats. But now Bill was filled with an uncontrollable impulse to talk. Later he had no idea what he had said, or why.

He thought afterward that he'd been operating in a mood made up partly of penitence, partly of showmanship. There had been an audience. He had to speak to them.

And he knew that when he walked back along Twenty-third Street to the subway, he never thought of stopping in a bar.

In the morning, instead of the bad hangover he'd expected, he had only a mild headache and a slight case of the shakes. But this was enough to make him take a quick drink as soon as Lois was out of the house. To taper off, he told himself.

Lois found him upstairs, passed out across the bed.

For three days he never left the house and seldom left the bedroom. No questions led to satisfactory answers now, nor did he any longer believe they would. He was doomed to intolerable alternatives: dependence on some spurious faith, death or incarceration. He drank now as he never had. He could eat nothing and he drank simply to stay alive.

Still he struggled. He knew Ebby was trying to lead him to some new ground of belief, but perhaps he was one of those who could never be led, who must always make his own discoveries. He understood that the ultimate reality must, of course, exist independently of his senses. Yet his senses were all that a man had to perceive with; therefore, whatever he saw could only be a reflection of his own sick, twisted psyche.

For now there was no question that he was ill. Silkworth's pronouncement about brain damage loomed as a monstrous truth. His once-lucid mind could not sustain a thought, much less develop one, and he knew this was not just the dimness of gin. Back of the fog something was no longer functioning.

Finally, on the morning of the fourth day after his visit to the mission, he knew he could no longer in any way trust himself. If he went on drinking throughout this day, he'd have no control of his actions, or of his thinking. And drink he surely would.

He roused himself to dress, scribbled a note for Lois and headed for Towns Hospital and Dr. Silkworth.

On the street he discovered he had only a nickel, the subway fare into the city, so, stopping by a grocery where Lois had some credit, he talked a clerk into giving him four bottles of beer. The last of these he drank as he arrived at the hospital door, holding the bottle by the neck.

Silkworth greeted him—Bill had to look away to avoid the hurt he knew would be in the good doctor's eyes—and then placed an arm across his shoulder and said quietly, "Well, now, boy, isn't it time you got upstairs and went to bed?"

He was home now. In a small room with a bed, one chair and a bureau, he was safe. He would be cared for and comforted. He was a man of thirty-nine. He felt and thought as a child.

His first night in the hospital he heard two nurses by his door. He picked up only one phrase, "incontinent in bowel and bladder," and although they were not talking about him (he had just been bathed and was in clean pajamas), his instant reaction was one of unspeakable shame: he knew that once, only a few weeks back, they could have been talking about him.

After a few days of sedatives, belladonna and a massive quantity of vitamins, his physical being seemed restored. His mind cleared, but as the boozy fog lifted, a great black depression, the worst one of his life, settled over him. When Ebby stopped by, therefore, and repeated his formula about admitting you were licked and being willing to turn your life over to the care of God, Bill nodded. And it was not just his head—it was as though his whole being nodded in response. He was so lost he was willing to believe anything. Anything could be the answer. He had no mind with which to argue, no energies to fight with. When Ebby left he made no move to see him out. He just sat there passively.

He never walked down the hall, never went to the window. The very thought of leaving this place covered him with a cold sweat. Out there were three choices. He could stop drinking. Or go insane. Or die. Alone, lost and terrified, he was an animal caught in a trap, crying out, thrashing about, flailing himself murderously.

He must leave the hospital. Silkworth would come in anytime now and tell him he must go. And what then? His pride had always been based on what he could do. Now he knew he could do nothing. Alcohol had already killed his mind, his will, his spirit. It was only a matter of time before it would kill his body. Yet with the last vestige of pride, the last trace of obstinacy crushed out of him, still he wanted to live.

His arms slowly reached out and up. "I want," he said aloud. "I want . . ." As far back as he could remember, he'd been saying just that. Now it had its ending. *He wanted to live.* He would do anything, anything, to be allowed to go on living. "O God," he cried. "If there is a God, show me. Give me some sign."

As he formed the words, in that very instant he was aware of a great white light that filled the room. He seemed caught up in an ecstasy he would never find words to describe. Everywhere now there was a wondrous feeling of Presence akin to but far beyond what he had sensed at Winchester. Nowhere had he ever felt so complete, so embraced.

This happened as suddenly and as definitely as a shock from an electrode. When it subsided—and whether it was in minutes or longer he never knew—the Presence was still there about him, within him. And with it there was a sense of rightness. No matter how wrong things seemed to be, they were as they were meant to be. There could be no doubt of ultimate order in the universe.

Now, in place of the ecstasy, he was filled with a peace such as he had never known. He had heard men say there was a bit of God in everyone, but this feeling that he was a part of God, himself a living part of the Higher Power, was a new and revolutionary feeling. And it was as feeling that he wanted to hang on to whatever had happened. Now, for a brief moment, he fell back on the bed and shut off thoughts and explanations.

Gradually—and again there was no awareness of time—he sat up and allowed himself to think. But along with rational thought, fear returned. Had it been hallucination, some phenomenon a doctor would spot as a symptom of a damaged brain?

As he recognized the signs of approaching panic, he walked into the hall and asked a nurse to find Silkworth.

He told the doctor everything, every detail he could remember.

Silkworth asked probing questions, and Bill replied as best he could. The doctor then sat back in his chair, his brow knitted.

Time seemed to stop. Finally, Bill could stand it no longer. "Tell me," he asked, "was it real? Am I still . . . sane?"

Then Silkworth answered, "Yes, my boy. Perfectly sane, in my opinion." Bill, he went on, had obviously undergone a tremendous psychic upheaval. Silkworth, a man of science, didn't begin to understand what some would call a conversion experience. But he knew it could happen, and something obviously had happened to Bill. "So," he said, and he looked deeply into Bill's eyes when he said it, "whatever it is you've got, hang on to it, boy."

IT WAS shortly after leaving Towns that Bill first heard the line of an old spiritual, *Young man, young man, your arm's too short to box with God.* In a way, this said it all for him. To Bill there seemed nothing supernatural or supernormal in his experience. It had happened. That was all he needed to know. Those who were close to him were interested to see what he would do, where he would go, now that he was sober. The question baffled him. Why go anyplace? He was here now.

CHAPTER NINE

"WHEN the pupil is ready the teacher appears."

This was another saying Bill latched on to. For him three remarkable teachers had now appeared: Silkworth; Sam Shoemaker, rector of Calvary Church; and a group of ex-drunks who met each week in Stewart's cafeteria. And there was no doubt about his being ready. He was standing straight, his step was resilient, and often, for what seemed no good reason, he found himself wanting to laugh aloud. All his tremendous energy was back. There were times that winter of 1934-35 when he felt so alive he could hardly believe he had ever lived before.

Talks with Silkworth often went on late into the night, and the doctor contributed so profoundly to Bill's understanding that it's hard to imagine what the next years would have been without him. "Silky" explained the mechanisms of the lock that hold the alcoholic in prison. More than that, he was Bill's safety valve; he kept bringing him down to earth.

In discussing the doctor's ideas about alcoholism, it should be remembered that he was a neurologist, not a psychiatrist. He had wanted a hospital of his own, but all of his dreams had crashed in the upheaval of 1929, and since then he had worked instead for Charles Towns. The conviction grew that one day there could be a cure for the insidious malady that was wrecking the lives of millions of men and women, and the hope of contributing his bit to the cure guided Silkworth's life. At Towns he had developed his theory of a mental obsession combined with a physical allergy. It has been estimated that he treated more than fifty thousand alcoholics. Bill wrote that Silky's compassionate attitude toward alcoholism would have been remarkable at any period in medical history, but in 1934 it seemed unique.

Silky's method of treatment—and from a psychiatric point of view this was the rankest sort of heresy—was to direct an alcoholic away from deep examination of the past. He went straight at the problems that were obvious and conscious, assuming the unconscious would take care of itself. By charging a great deal of behavior to the nature of the illness itself, he was able to take a patient off the hook of guilt, shame and morbidity. Then doctor and patient together would search out those defects of character that were blocking recovery. Silkworth was able to do this, Bill knew, because of his extraordinary talent for spotting the good in people and pointing out how these fine qualities had been run over by the obsession.

Of all the tools in Silkworth's kit two became a vital part of Bill's future work. First was the doctor's rare capacity to engage the confidence of a drunk. As if by some miracle, he seemed able to stay with a drunk and step into the special cave in which he lived. The second was his insistence that alcoholism is an illness, an often fatal one.

As to the changes in Bill himself, his ability to look at defects which might threaten his sobriety, they discussed these too; but

Bill was beginning to believe that much of his own inner revolution was now the province of Sam Shoemaker and the new friends he was making in the Oxford Group.

THE timing of his introduction to Shoemaker, the dynamic leader of the New York group, always struck Bill as more than coincidence. For if Silkworth described the mysteries of the lock that held the drunk in prison, Shoemaker—or so Bill believed—offered the keys to free him.

Sam Shoemaker was a tall, handsome man, heavier in build than Bill. Like Bill, he seemed to possess a special extra dose of life. Like Bill, he could bring himself down to any man's size; and unlike any other clergyman Bill had ever met, he appeared more willing to talk about his own shortcomings than anyone else's. People invariably turned to him, as if sensing that here was a man who could make things happen.

The spiritual principles he acted on—self-examination, acknowledgment of faults, restitution for wrongs done and, above all, constant work with others—were the principles upon which the Oxford Group was based, and they seemed to create an atmosphere in which Bill believed he might begin to grow.

Perhaps the most important contribution Sam Shoemaker made to Bill was his interpretation of prayer as primarily a method of discovering God's will, that it was more important for one to listen than to plead.

If to some it seemed strange that a man who had built up such a powerful resistance to the whole vocabulary of religion could now find himself so receptive, Bill had one simple answer: "A dying man can become remarkably open-minded." If some of the disciplines of the Oxford Group were beyond his grasp, if some of their tenets —absolute purity, absolute honesty, etc.—were to prove too strict a diet for a drunk, it didn't bother Bill. He was sober. That was the fact of his life.

Then too, he knew now exactly what he was going to do.

Within ten days of his release from Towns, he had run across a small group of ex-drunks who had developed the habit of going around to Stewart's cafeteria after Oxford Group meetings. He sensed at once the source of the special communion among the little group. They were never more than a small handful—Grace McC., Roland H., Ebby, of course, and perhaps one or two others. Bill knew immediately that these were his people. He could say anything to them and they to him. Over mugs of coffee and too many cigarettes they would talk until the place closed for the night, giving one another the most horrendous accounts of their drinking, laughing unashamedly. Or they could look at each other, as he and Ebby had at Clinton Street, and know they didn't have to describe what they'd been through. They had all at one time hit bottom, each beaten into defeat by the same thing—booze. Was that what brought them so beautifully together, or was it that they had found a common means of escape? He knew only that these people who had been drunks were now sober, and living proof that a good life for them was possible.

It was with them that Bill learned that his experience at Towns was not unique. He could never recollect who—Ebby or Roland— had given him a copy of William James's *The Varieties of Religious Experience*, but he remembered the impact of the book. It was James's theory that spiritual experiences could have a definite objective reality and might totally transform a man's life. Some, but by no means all, of these experiences, James believed, came through religious channels. All, however, appeared to have their source in pain and utter hopelessness. Complete deflation at depth was the one requirement to make someone ready for a transforming experience.

Deflation at depth. These words leaped at Bill. Hitting bottom— wasn't this the story of every ex-drunk he knew?

Roland H., for instance, the man who had come to Ebby's rescue, was the son of a prominent Connecticut family. He'd drunk his way through a fortune and in 1930 had wound up in Zurich, a patient of Dr. Carl G. Jung's. For over a year he worked with the great analyst, until he believed he had a full understanding of his obsession and could go on and live a sober life. But in a matter of weeks after leaving Zurich, Roland H. was drunk, unaccountably drunk. When he returned to Jung, the doctor was frank. There was nothing more that medicine or psychiatry could do for him. There was only one hope; occasionally alcoholics had shown signs of recovery through religious conversion. Jung had no advice about how Roland might find this, but he would first have to admit his personal powerlessness to go on living. Then, perhaps, if he sought, he might find.

What Roland had found was the Oxford Group. Roland had carried the message to Ebby, Ebby to Bill. Powerlessness. Deflation at depth. Then, only then, was an alcoholic ready.

As Bill read William James, as he reviewed Roland's story and his own, his mind raced ahead. He saw what had happened—one drunk taking the word to another—and he began to envision a vast chain reaction that someday would encircle the globe—a chain of alcoholics passing these principles along, one to the other. And it could begin here. Now. With this little group in Stewart's cafeteria. He knew he wanted to work with alcoholics more than he had ever wanted anything.

AND Bill Wilson worked with them. With the compulsive dedication of the twelve-year-old boy challenged to make a boomerang, he set off to sober up all drunks everywhere. There was no besotted derelict who staggered into the mission he didn't buttonhole, no fine executive wanting a quick drying out at Towns he didn't try to reach. He was all over New York, indefatigable and incorrigible, convinced that if *he* could do it, they ~~could. But~~ he was spectacularly unsuccessful.

Later he described his behavior at this time as twin jet propulsion: part genuine spirituality, part the old power drive to be number one. If he sensed a certain coolness and lack of support on the part of the bigwigs of the Oxford Group, he simply ignored it. If they weren't able to share his vision yet, he would just have to work harder and eventually show them. There was a kind of young madness in this new and magnificent obsession.

The reaction of the group shouldn't have been surprising. They had had bad luck with drunks. To them, drinking was a moral issue. No one seemed to understand Silkworth's idea of alcoholism as an illness. In an effort to show his gratitude to people who had done so much for him, Bill began to put less emphasis on the physical aspects of his story, more on the mystical awakening. But the effect on potential recruits was exactly the same.

Occasionally he would think he'd found a live one—Ed W., Walter P. He would take them back to Clinton Street and never leave their sides, but after a few days, or a week at the most, they'd slip away. During this period only Lois seemed to understand and approve. She would get home from her department store never knowing whether she was to cook supper for three or ten, go off to a meeting with Bill, or sit up half the night with some stranger who was trying to sweat it out. There was, however, one thing she knew: the work was keeping Bill sober.

In April he had a session with Silkworth. The doctor had gone out on a limb for Bill, risking his professional reputation by letting him talk with patients. When Bill asked him what he was doing wrong, he gave it to him straight.

"For God's sake, stop preaching. You're scaring the poor drunks half crazy. They want to get sober, but you're telling them they can only do it as you did, by some special hot flash. . . ." Religion, he said, usually filled a man with guilt or rebellion, two things guaranteed to send a real alcoholic running for a drink. He begged Bill to shift his emphasis from sin to sickness. "You've got the cart before the horse, boy. Hit them with the physical first and hit them hard. Tell about the physical sensitivity they are developing that will condemn them to go mad or die. Say it's lethal as cancer." Coming from Bill, another drunk, Silkworth believed this might crack their rugged little egos and crack them in depth. "A drunk," he said, "must be led, not pushed."

Money problems now began to fill Bill's mind. There was only Lois's salary coming in. True, they were able to stay on in Clinton Street by paying the bank only twenty dollars a month against the mortgage, but hints were arriving from every direction that the time had come for Bill to start earning.

He returned to the Street, and almost immediately found himself involved in a complicated proxy fight over control of a small machine-tool factory in Akron, Ohio. By joining forces with the secretary of the company and two other men, who had started buying and selling company stock, he got hold of a packet of proxies. It seemed a wise move for them all to go to Akron for the annual meeting. But the opposition had got there first, had spread stories of Bill's drinking history, his power drive and probable ambition to be president of the company—all of which were plausible—and they won control.

Bill's new friends hopped a train for New York, leaving him stranded in the Mayflower Hotel with exactly ten dollars.

There was no way he could think of to report his failure to Lois or to the Oxford Groupers, who'd seen him off with such high hopes. He began to pace the lobby, considering his next move. Directly across from his path of march was the entrance to the Mayflower bar, and with every step he took he was growing more aware of the cool, inviting darkness just beyond the entrance, the sweet, crackling sound of ice in a cocktail shaker. Why not? Who would know? And what harm could one drink do?

Instantly he panicked. For the first time fear overrode his rationalizing alcoholic mind. But even as he noticed his shaking hands, he felt a sense of relief. Maybe sanity could be restored.

There was one thing he knew he had to do—and do immediately. As he'd been pacing out his beat, he'd been vaguely aware of a glass-enclosed sign beside the telephones. A church directory. For a long moment he studied the names. Then, choosing a minister at random, the Reverend Walter Tunks, he stepped into the booth.

Mr. Tunks answered and Bill began his story: he was an alcoholic from New York and it was vital that he find another alcoholic to talk with. Later he wondered what must have been going through the minister's mind as he listened. Tunks had had some experience with drunks and had always worked on the theory that one at a time was enough, but he did give Bill a list of persons he might call.

Ten names. Bill decided to start at the top and, if necessary, go right down the list. A few were out, a few others were busy, a few said they would be happy to see him in church tomorrow. The last name on the list, a Mrs. Seiberling, was familiar. He'd heard of a Seiberling who'd been president of Goodyear Tire. He didn't see how he could tell this man's wife about his problem, so he stepped out of the booth and again began to pace.

The bar was still there. The laughter was louder as a happy Saturday afternoon crowd began to arrive. He watched a young couple wander in, arm in arm, then he went back to the phone booth and called that tenth name.

A soft Southern voice answered—not Mrs. Frank Seiberling, but her daughter-in-law, Henrietta—and after only a few sentences she interrupted to tell him that she understood perfectly, and proceeded to give him specific instructions for getting to the Seiberling estate, where she was living in the gatehouse with her two small sons.

Nothing had prepared Bill for the charm, the warmth or the understanding of Henrietta Seiberling. She was not an alcoholic, she explained, but she had had her troubles and found many answers in the Oxford Group. She knew just the man for Bill, a prominent surgeon, one of the finest in Akron, but his drinking had got so out of hand that few of his colleagues and practically none of his patients could trust him. Dr. Robert H. Smith.

Henrietta tried to phone the doctor, but his wife, Anne, said he was in no condition to see anyone. Undaunted, Henrietta made a date for five o'clock next day.

The following afternoon Bill met a man some fifteen years older than he, a man who had clearly cut an impressive figure and still tried to carry himself with dignity. But he was stooped now, his eyes were red and at times his hands shook uncontrollably. His first remark was one that any alcoholic in the world would have made. He said he could stay only a few minutes. So with no ado, Henrietta ushered the two men into her library and left them alone.

There were two completely new elements in Bill's approach to "Dr. Bob." One came from a decision on his part to follow Silkworth's advice for once and hit the physical first. The other welled up from a deep need of his own that he had not recognized until, alone in the Mayflower lobby, he had known with a desperate certainty that he had to talk with another alcoholic.

He started by admitting that he was there because he, Bill Wilson, needed help. Then he told his own story, describing as he had never done to anyone the horror of the suicidal obsession that had forced him to go on drinking, and the physical allergy his body had developed. He quoted Silkworth about the illness and its obvious prognosis: insanity or death.

From Dr. Bob's point of view, this was undoubtedly the only thing he would have listened to. He did not need, as Bill was to learn, any spiritual instruction. He was far more versed than Bill in such matters. And he thought he had heard everything there was to hear about alcoholism. Yet, ironically, as a doctor he had paid little attention to the physical aspects of his own case, and it was the obvious scientific soundness of Silkworth's statements—those twin ogres of madness and death—that finally delivered the telling blow. For Dr. Bob could not deny that here before him was something new: another alcoholic holding out hope in one hand and stark hopelessness in the other.

They talked on for hours. When they parted after eleven o'clock, something had radically changed in them both. Although they could not be specific about what it was, a spark that was to light future fires had been struck.

A few days later Bill moved in with Anne and Dr. Bob on Ardmore Avenue. He sent word to Lois, and to his associates in New York, that he'd be staying in Akron. To his surprise they wired him some cash and suggested that he investigate the possibility of fraud at the stockholders' meeting. Thus he was no longer penniless, but his primary interest was his work with Dr. Bob and the uncanny parallels they were discovering in their stories.

Both were Vermonters, Bob the son of a judge in St. Johnsbury. Both had taken up drinking at an early age, Bob at Dartmouth before medical school, and from the beginning they had both gone at booze heavily. Each, except for the hells created by drinking, had had a happy marriage; each admitted he must have been born with an iron constitution; both had wrecked brilliant careers.

The interior parallels were equally striking: the guilt, the defenses they'd constructed, the passionate desires and the futile efforts to be in control; and finally they had both wound up trying to give shape and meaning to their lives by adhering to the excruciatingly high standards of the Oxford Group. But now two pragmatic Yankees began working in tandem to make these lofty concepts part of the real world and to apply them in a practical way to their alcoholic natures.

As they talked on night after night, they were struck by the fact that they were speaking more openly than either had ever spoken to another person. They discussed Bill's failure in the five months he'd been storming around New York trying to reform drunks, and they decided it was his ego that had got in the way. He'd concerned himself too much with being successful and, consciously or not, with straining for the Oxford Group's approval. His fear of failure had made failure even more likely, whereas when he had met Bob at Henrietta's there had been no question of impressing anyone. He had needed Bob and told him so; therefore, they had been able to talk as equals, almost anonymous equals.

One thing they learned, one they felt they should have known, was: *You can never talk down to a drunk.*

As time passed, there seemed to be two issues they were mainly talking about. The first was how they could survive. The other they may not have stated in words, but they both sensed that they might have stumbled on something that could reach far beyond the two of them. Bill felt his dreams begin to take fire.

But again life wasn't to proceed as he expected.

One morning Dr. Bob mentioned the American Medical Association convention in Atlantic City the following week. He had always attended these gatherings and wondered what Bill thought about his going this year.

Bill tried to ignore the look of dismay that shot across Anne's face. Finally he and Bob concluded that since they wanted to live in the real world, and conventions, where people drank, would always be part of that world, they'd have to face it. Perhaps he should go to Atlantic City and test himself.

He went. For two days Bill and Anne tried not to give any sign of their apprehension when they heard nothing. Surely, Bill told himself on the third day, Bob would know what their natural concerns would be. But how many times had he, had any drunk, stopped to call home?

Pictures of what might be going on in Atlantic City tormented Bill; it was his fault. They had been safe together. He had encouraged Bob to go. He didn't know how to handle this, refused to admit how much of his own life seemed at stake in Bob Smith's safety. And he couldn't mention his feelings; Anne was as anxious as he. So they told stories and made feeble jokes, but each knew the other was thinking of only one thing.

Then on the morning of the fifth day there was a call from Bob's secretary-nurse. Bob had phoned from the station about four a.m., dead drunk, and she had picked him up. He was at her place. Would Anne come and get him?

As they put him to bed, Bill's heart sank, only to sink still lower when Anne reminded him that on Monday—three days away—Bob was scheduled to perform an operation. It was a complex, intricate operation, which they'd hoped would be his comeback.

As a team then, working around the clock, Bill and Anne Smith decided they'd sober him up. They used sedatives, masses of vitamins, even a special diet Bill had heard sometimes worked with hangovers; and they never left his side. Just before dawn on Monday morning, Bill, who was sleeping on a cot in the doctor's room, happened to look across at Bob and saw he was wide-awake and sitting up in bed.

"I'm going to do it," Bob said, though he was shaking miserably. "I'm going through with it." Thinking he meant the operation, Bill said of course he would, but Dr. Bob shook his head. He didn't mean that, he said. He meant the things they'd been talking about, the thing they'd been working on. Then he slept for another hour.

Bill drove him to the hospital about nine o'clock, and the sight of the surgeon sitting beside him and every now and then holding out his right hand, testing to see how steady it was, was a picture Bill would not forget.

In front of the hospital, Bill reached into his pocket, took out a bottle of beer and handed it to Dr. Bob. He watched him move slowly up the steps and into the building. Then he drove back to Ardmore Avenue. Again Bill and Anne waited hour after agonizing hour—far beyond the time the operation should have taken. Finally they could bear it no longer; they phoned the hospital. The operation had been completed and had apparently been successful, but Dr. Bob was not there.

This was early in the afternoon. There was nothing they could do, so they sat, trying not to think, and waited. It was five thirty when they heard his key in the door.

After leaving the hospital he'd had a few calls to make, he said, a few amends that needed tending to, doctors he'd wanted to apologize to, tradespeople he had owed some money.

This was June 10, 1935. After the beer Bill had handed him outside the hospital, Dr. Bob Smith never had another drink.

THE next morning Dr. Bob said he and Bill should get going on working with others. They could begin at Akron City Hospital. Dr. Bob explained to a receiving nurse that they wanted to talk with an alcoholic patient, and introduced Bill as a man from New York who had come across a cure for drunks. The nurse, knowing Dr. Bob, listened politely, then said she hoped he had used it on himself. He promised her he had, and she led them into the ward and pointed to a young fellow she described as "a *very* tough" repeater. He'd arrived the previous night with a bad case of d.t.'s, and had blackened the eye of the nurse who had put him to bed.

This was Bill D., and he was indeed in poor shape. As they sat beside his bed and told him their stories, he listened with apparent interest, but at the word God he shook his head. It was no use, he said. He believed in God, but God no longer believed in him. It wasn't an encouraging visit. But they asked if they could come again. Bill D. made no objection.

When they arrived the next afternoon, Bill D.'s wife was with

him. These, he said, were the men he'd been talking about. Then, before they could say anything, he told them how he hadn't slept all night and had decided that if they could do it, maybe he could; maybe they could do together what they couldn't do separately.

Bill D. was an attorney-at-law. A week after he checked out of the hospital he was back in court, sober and arguing a case.

Although it would be four more years before Alcoholics Anonymous would have a name, it had been founded by Bill W. and Dr. Bob in Akron, Ohio, and now it had a third member.

CHAPTER TEN

THE years immediately following Bill's visit to Akron were, despite disorder and uncertainty, a period of tremendous activity, of constant work with others and a continuous sense of growing.

He was on his way. The newness and the feeling of living completely in the here and now, which had been such a part of him after leaving Towns, had not worn off, nor had he lost his true gut-level gratitude for having been given a second chance. But he found that this awareness could become a now-and-then thing.

One experience could invariably bring it back: that sudden flash of recognition, the first faint spark of hope in a drunk's eyes; then the full wonder of what had happened would wash over him and he'd be totally alive.

He and Dr. Bob had talked about this awareness and how to make use of it. They'd come up with what they called their twenty-four-hour plan. They had stumbled on the phrase while working with new men. Neither of them would ask a drunk if he wanted to stop forever. A world stretching on ad infinitum with no booze was impossible to contemplate; they asked if he thought he could stop for one day. If this seemed too rough, they would bring it down to an hour.

In the last years of their own drinking they knew they had lived only in the past or in the future. Haunted by memories of what they had done the night before, terrified of what might happen tomorrow, they had had no present tense, and they discovered the same thing was true of every alcoholic they met. They came to see that their little trick could work for other problems too; for by thinking in terms of *now*, a man was able to concentrate on the job at hand instead of only on results.

Some men, such as Bill D. and a newer fellow, Ernie G., seemed able to latch on immediately and, with no trouble at all, take up their old lives. Most, though, could grope their way back to life only gradually. As soon as their minds cleared, some other obstacle would turn up. And when it became overwhelming, a man would look for answers where he had looked before: in booze. For them, Bill and Bob knew, there had to be some plan.

As THE summer of 1935 raced by, there were no further developments in Bill's proxy fight, so his time was his own. In July, Lois came to Akron and, seeing what Bill was learning, gave the project her full support. By the time she returned to Brooklyn, all four of them, Wilsons and Smiths, were agreed that a practical program of recovery had top priority.

It was not an easy project. Still, it was the only thing Bill wanted to do. He knew that few men forty years old find a vocation that can totally absorb their energies. And few vocations could have proved more fascinating—or more insanely frustrating—than trying to understand an alcoholic.

They thought at first they could use the Oxford Group's dynamic program as their model. They went daily to Akron City Hospital, talked to drunks and brought hopeful prospects back to Ardmore Avenue. They never stopped. There were heady moments when their wildest hopes seemed justified. There were great laughs, because some they brought home were born clowns. There were also moments of heartbreak. And one hot summer night the entire project almost ended when one Eddie R. threatened to kill Bill and Anne with a carving knife. But by the end of August, when Bill had to leave for New York, there were five, possibly six men staying sober and trying to help others. There had been mistakes, but Bill left Akron, as he wrote Bob, with more humility and understanding.

BACK ON CLINTON STREET, Bill aroused enough interest to hold meetings every Tuesday night. Usually there'd be two or three drunks staying in the house; once in a while there would be six or eight in various stages of recovery. One would locate a bottle; then most of them would proceed to get royally soused. On such nights Bill would remember his times with the Smiths as downright idyllic. At this point, however, support came from two brand-new men, Hank P. and Fitz M.

There could not have been two more contrasting personalities. Hank was a redhead, a football player, who went at life with the heartiness of a supersalesman. Fitz was thin and aristocratic, with the charm of the Southern gentry. Both saw the infinite possibilities of the fellowship Bill was trying to establish. Hank and Fitz not only shared his vision, they fed it.

If throughout his history there seemed to be characters who entered Bill Wilson's life at the moment of need, as though in answer to a call, this was never truer than with these two.

Fitz, Hank and Bill were extraordinarily healthy males who never let themselves forget what had happened to them and what they were now—men who had meant to live life passionately but whose ambitions had been derailed. To their new outlet they brought a wonderful young exuberance. They believed, these three, that they had heaven in their hands to give to others, and they traveled everywhere—to Towns Hospital, out to Jersey, up into Westchester—if they heard there was a drunk who might be interested. Hell-bent that others should have what they had, they attended innumerable Oxford Group meetings.

It was in connection with one of these that an incident occurred on Clinton Street which is memorable only because of a later development. Bill had on his hat and coat when he noticed that Lois wasn't ready. He told her to hurry up or they'd be late.

Suddenly, at that moment, Lois Wilson had had it. It had been a long day at the store, she'd cooked supper, washed the dishes. . . . In a towering rage she reached for the nearest object, which happened to be a shoe, and hurled it across the room. "You and your damned meetings," she cried.

In the doorway, Bill turned. Nothing more was said, but in the look that passed between them nothing was held back. Their two lives were spread out before them. For twenty years Lois had done everything possible to support and nurture Bill, always confident that through her love he would somehow get sober. And he had done what she had dreamed of and slaved for. But he had done it in a way she had nothing to do with and had no control over. She was no longer needed.

That is what happened that night. They stood looking at each other for a long moment. Then Bill turned and left the room, and Lois hurried to finish dressing. These are the facts, not what legend would build them into. They were different people and moved at different tempos. But there is one other fact. In that moment, in that exchange of looks, a seed had been dropped and it had fallen on receptive soil.

That evening, however, Lois simply picked up her shoe, put it on, grabbed her coat and went out through the door Bill had left open.

DURING the next six months Oxford Group meetings became progressively less important for the three alcoholics than their own Tuesdays. By mid-1936 a small but solid group had developed on Clinton Street. After a man had taken what they called the first step and had admitted he was powerless over alcohol, he began to see that staying away from a drink was more important than his wife, his job or his reputation, more important than anything, for in the end everything depended on this one thing. Each man who came was struck by all he had in common with the rest; not just in their stories of drink, but in the tremendous emotions that controlled their lives.

To Bill it was incredible that he had ever believed himself the only man whose life had been ruled by the need to succeed, the terror of failure, or by deep resentments. He began to sense a pattern. Nine times out of ten these men's troubles were of their own making. Although they wouldn't admit it at first, they all had been extremely self-centered. By definition, a drinking alcoholic was a

prime example of self-will run riot. Of course, he was always finding himself in head-on collision with someone else.

They were so many actors wanting to run the show. This meta-
phor struck a responsive chord every time Bill used it. The alcoholic was forever trying to arrange everything his own way—lights,
ballet, scenery, all the other players. And when it didn't work out,
he'd start blaming someone else. Convinced that he could wrest
happiness out of life if only he was allowed *his way*, he'd turn
angry, self-pitying.

As Bill saw it, they had to find some way to eradicate their self-
centeredness. They must stop trying to play God. Above all, they
must rid themselves of resentment.

Resentment was poison, deadly poison. Drunks nursed resentments, and by concentrating on the wrongdoings of others, they
gave others power over their lives. Finally they built up such
frustration that there was no way out but a drink. Even in the
earlier stages—Bill could think of many examples in his own case—
resentments blocked off any hope of spiritual growth.

These were the things they talked about, openly and frankly,
and Bill could feel a closeness and a tremendous lift that he'd never
experienced with other men. There was such an assertion of life in
the old Burnham parlor those Tuesdays that, watching it grow, he
couldn't help smiling from ear to ear.

As in Henrietta Seiberling's gatehouse he'd accepted his dependence on Bob Smith, so on Clinton Street he knew he needed
these men as much as, or more than, they needed him.

He loved people and they returned that love. Since that night at
Towns he had been nourished on spiritual reality. He had no more
argument with God. Absorbed in his work, he was no longer a
loner forced to compete and win. For all these reasons, meetings
may have been easier for him than for others, but that is not to
imply that this was an easy period. For one thing, there was mounting criticism from the Oxford Group of his concentrating on
drunks. One evening Bill discovered that alcoholics from the mission had been forbidden to come to Clinton Street. At large
Oxford Group gatherings it was bandied about that, after all, the

Wilsons were not "really maximum," a phrase foreign to Bill and Lois, but nonetheless upsetting. Finally "the divergent work of this secret group" became the subject of a Sunday morning sermon at Calvary Church. Yet in a curious way, instead of distressing Bill and his associates, this criticism stiffened their resolve.

Problems within the group were harder to handle. When a member they had known and loved for months would turn up drunk, a terrible apprehension would settle over the meeting. Who would be next? It was like a death in the family. But, as at times of death, there was also a new awareness of life, an unspeakable gratitude for being alive themselves.

For Bill too there was the old financial problem. Theoretically, men who stayed at the house contributed to their room and board, but they rarely did. Household expenses had to be met. And Bill was bringing in no money. He'd tried to connect with some Wall Street deals without success. What made the situation even more difficult was that each week he was with men who were back on the job, earning fine salaries, while he remained what he had been for years—a man whose wife was working.

Then with no warning his whole picture seemed to change.

ONE afternoon Charles Towns asked Bill to stop by his office. He wanted him to move his entire operation to the hospital. He would give him an office, a drawing account and a healthy slice of the profits. Bill would be a lay therapist, and if "Charlie" knew anything about it, in no time at all he'd be the most successful therapist in New York. The number one man.

Bill was stunned. He promised Charlie an answer in the morning. On the subway back to Brooklyn a hundred thoughts jammed his mind: what it would mean to Lois, to the creditors he still had on the Street and to the group. Then he realized this was a Tuesday and he wouldn't have to put off telling them. As he walked into the house and kissed Lois, he was more hopeful than he had been in years.

There was a good crowd that night, the parlor was full. He tried to keep a lid on his excitement and present the case exactly as

Charlie had. A row of impassive faces stared up at him. When he finished, an old-timer held up his hand. They had all been worried about Bill's finances, he said, and knew something would have to be done about them. But what Bill was suggesting didn't seem like the answer. Others spoke with real understanding of what the opportunity meant, but they all agreed about the problems they were sure they would encounter at Towns.

Finally one man stood up. He hadn't been with them long, but Bill knew his sobriety meant everything in the world to him. Fumbling for words at first, he said he wanted to appeal to Bill and to something he didn't know how to describe—the thing that bound them together. If such groups as theirs were to go on, this thing would have to prevail. And these feelings, as he now called them, his voice growing surer, could not be bought and paid for. This had nothing to do with patients and therapists. What they had here, what the whole thing was based on, was one poor drunk bastard coming eye to eye with another poor drunk bastard. There could be no substitute for that, he almost shouted.

Others made similar points, but Bill went on trying to hammer home his position. And then abruptly he stopped arguing.

There were to be no bosses. All decisions were to be made according to the group conscience. He and Bob had had this theory from the beginning. Now he, Bill Wilson, was being asked to put it into practice.

He phoned Charlie Towns that he couldn't accept the offer.

THAT call to Towns marked a decisive step in Bill's understanding that individual survival depended on group unity. From this point on it was clear that they must remain nonprofessional.

Almost immediately another decision had to be made. Bill would have liked to postpone a split with the Oxford Group, because in addition to his gratitude he felt a tremendous fondness for Sam Shoemaker. But it was apparent that alcoholics could not stand up against Oxford Group pressures. Silkworth was right: drunks had to be led, not pushed.

The Oxford Group was too authoritarian for alkies. Also, among

Bill's cohorts were atheists, agnostics, men of differing faiths. Bill might believe that certain steps were essential to spiritual growth, but this must not be made a condition of membership. Lastly, they were discovering that drunks needed anonymity. And the whole notion of anonymity went against the Oxford Group grain.

When in mid-1937 Bill saw that these differences were basic, he was able at last, and sadly, to make the break.

From then on his collection of nameless drunks operated as a fragile but completely independent group. The house on Clinton Street had become both a home and a laboratory, for there was always someone in some stage of sobriety waiting to talk with Bill. That summer the first female drunk checked in. Hank got a meeting started in his home in Upper Montclair, New Jersey. Fitz, who had returned to his family in Maryland, was trying the same thing in Baltimore. In Ohio, a second group was meeting each week in Cleveland.

In November, Bill had to make a trip to the Midwest in connection with a brokerage job he was trying to nail down. Although nothing came of the job, it gave him an opportunity to visit Dr. Bob. Bill had been sober almost three years, Bob two and a half. It was time, they figured, for them to take stock.

There had been failures galore. Some who had sobered up for a brief period had slipped away. So had some stalwarts. Ebby Thacher, Bill's sponsor, his rock, had gone off to Albany and come back drunk. And there had been one recent tragic suicide in Bill's own house: Bill, returning from a business trip, had found one of those he was caring for lying across the kitchen floor with his head in the oven.

Both men were very conscious of these failures as they settled down in Bob's living room. But as the afternoon wore on, they found themselves facing a staggering fact. They knew forty alcoholics who were staying sober, and at least twenty of them had been completely dry for more than a year. Every single one had been diagnosed a hopeless case. Forty men were alive tonight because of what had started in this very room. The chain reaction they had dreamed about—one alcoholic carrying the word to another—was a reality. They were filled with something akin to awe at this mysterious force they had helped set in motion.

But no sense of awe could stop these two Yankee pragmatists for long. The number of alcoholics in the world had to be reckoned in the millions. They must change their whole approach if they were even to begin to pass on their proven know-how to those sufferers. They must never again think of themselves as a small and secret society.

Since any decision about how to spread their knowledge would require the support of the entire fellowship, Bob got on the phone to arrange a meeting of the Akron group. In the interval before the meeting—it was only a few days—Bill had a thousand ideas. The stalled motor of his imagination was turning again, working once more in conjunction with the rational, investigative side of his mind. And the old power drive was coming back full force.

In order to reach out to drunks they might never meet personally, they would first of all need quantities of printed matter—books, pamphlets. Bill saw that these might serve a twofold purpose. They would tell the group's stories. At the same time they could clarify and keep straight its method of working. And they both knew this would be a great step forward, because as long as they remained dependent on word of mouth, there was a danger that everything they had developed might become garbled, distorted beyond recognition by some unstable member.

Also, since most hospitals refused even to recognize alcoholism as an illness, perhaps they ought to have their own establishments. Of course, such dreams would have to be subsidized, but Bill had not the slightest doubt that they'd be able to raise the money. Dr. Bob liked the idea of a book—to codify their beliefs in print. But as to running their own hospitals and raising millions of dollars, he had his doubts.

By the night of the meeting Bill was raring to go. He hoped for some opposition, because any argument would come like the smell of gunpowder to an old war-horse. He was going to show them all.

There were eighteen members present and the meeting began promptly at eight. They were still talking at midnight. Bill had launched his plan and they had started in on him at once. They went at him from every conceivable angle.

As Bill listened to them expressing their views, he was overwhelmed by the electricity that was being generated. These were his people: men who had wanted double everything and now were fighting for principles that had, they were convinced, saved their lives. The sheer animal energy of a recovered drunk was wildly stimulating. Bill knew that if only this force could be channeled, it could accomplish anything he had suggested and more.

Most were against going into the hospital business. It would be regarded as a commercial racket, and what, they demanded, would this do to the spirit of the group and their principle of carrying the message to other drunks, with no strings and no money attached?

Bill's point that word of mouth was too slow and too limited a way of carrying the message seemed to make sense. But some could see no reason for having a book or even a pamphlet. They pointed out that Christ's disciples had done all right without printed matter. And as for money raising, they were convinced it would spell the end of the fellowship.

But when the vote was taken, Bill was authorized, by a majority of two, to go ahead with his plan, return to New York and, if necessary, start raising money.

SOMETHING had been let loose in the world, a force that no one in the group at the time could fully understand. To some it was extremely frightening. All of them had questions. What would the changes mean to them as individuals? As they reached out along such grandiose lines, would they be able to stick together? Would they cling to the simple, sturdy raft that had brought them to safety? The one thing that could wreck all they had built up would be their own alcoholic power drives, those ballooning egos that had so recently been deflated. Would they soar up again and blow everything apart, or could they somehow be held in check?

Recently there had been few signs of Bill's old obsession to become number one, but these were canny alcoholics he was working with, and they knew that because an obsession has nodded off, it may not be permanently asleep. What if, as he started out to conquer new worlds, he found himself thwarted? What if Bill Wilson reached for a drink? Everything was being put in one man's hands, and this man was a drunk.

A few of the Akron group who saw Bill off for New York were admittedly deeply concerned. As the train came in, Dr. Bob put his hand on Bill's arm and said just one thing. "For God's sake, Billy, keep it simple."

WHEN Bill got back from Akron, the Clinton Street group, to his amazement, fell right in with his proposals. So did Fitz M., who was often in town that winter. And Hank P., the greatest high-pressure salesman Bill had ever known, always took fire from any idea Bill had. If a worldwide movement was going to take millions of dollars to launch, no problem; they'd raise millions.

The two of them immediately set to work approaching every rich man and every charitable foundation in Manhattan. But the wealthy can have remarkably deaf ears. They saw no real reason to help drunks, who after all had brought their problems on themselves. Perhaps if Bill or Hank could come up with a method of preventing alcoholism, they might be interested. There was a moment of hope when, through Bill's brother-in-law Dr. Leonard Strong, they took their case to John D. Rockefeller, Jr.

Rockefeller was impressed. He saw a parallel with early Christianity, and he spotted a combination of medicine and religion that appealed to all his charitable inclinations. However, he wanted to be careful to do nothing that could in any way harm an organization with such potential. And money, he was sure, might. He would place a check for five thousand dollars in the treasury of Riverside Church for their personal use, but he didn't want to be asked for any more. He was convinced that if ever a movement must be self-supporting, it was this one.

It was a shock. They had seemed so close. Yet curiously, Bill did not regard it as a setback. He felt the same sense of adventure he'd had on the motorcycle trip with Lois. Once again he was setting out on a quest with no precedents to guide him.

However, after further fruitless weeks of canvassing, Bill finally came to understand that if they were registered as a tax-free organization, people would look more kindly on them, and if they had a board made up of nonalcoholics as well as alcoholics, it might create more confidence. In April 1938 the Alcoholic Foundation was established. The board of trustees held meetings each month, though they had little to do except commiserate about their lack of funds. The book was the one project they could afford. So every morning, in an office Hank had in Newark, Bill began dictating to Hank's secretary, Ruth Hock.

There was remarkable timing in Bill's starting to write exactly when he did. It was as though it threw an inner switch that had been waiting to be thrown. He'd been sober for some time, but he was still close enough to the suffering, the raw emotions, the self-loathing, the terrors, to be able to call them up and present the ugly facts of the obsession that had ruled his life and finally placed him beyond human help. Also, he was in direct touch with the simple truths that had been guiding him since his first meeting with Dr. Bob.

The difficulties of stating these truths were immense. He didn't want to pretend to answer the riddles of alcoholism; he did want to cut through the vast bog of ignorance and misunderstanding surrounding alcoholism. He knew the message that would catch and hold a drunk had to have depth and weight. It had to be honest. He understood that the truth he was trying to pass on, the insight that might cause a psychic change in the alcoholic reader, had to be grounded in a Power far greater than himself.

A professional writer would have run from such an assignment, but Bill sat down at his desk in Newark each morning and talked simply, honestly, unashamedly. In no time he had the first two chapters finished, and Ruth Hock typed them up. There would be problems ahead, big ones, but these early chapters held the strength and the exuberance of a man who has discovered something on his own. Nothing is more readable.

It was so readable, even to nonalcoholics, that when one of the foundation board members showed it to Harper & Brothers they offered at once to publish it, with an advance royalty of fifteen hundred dollars. This was a beautiful day for Bill W.

The happy news spread quickly through the fellowship, and it is not known whether it was Hank or Bill himself who had the first doubts. Certainly a few days later they both were expressing misgivings. If this book was to be their basic text, and if the fellowship was to grow as they hoped, it didn't seem right that their main asset should be owned by outsiders. Besides, Harper's must believe it would sell, in which case thousands of inquiries might start pouring in and they'd have no money to cope with them.

Hank had contacted the Cornwall Press and had learned that such a book as they were planning could be printed for about thirty-five cents a copy and could sell for, say, $3.50. Even if they had to give bookstores a discount, their net had to be tremendous. Obviously they should form a corporation, sell shares and raise the money to publish their book themselves.

Bill was sure that the trustees would never go along with this. He was right. They said he must certainly accept the Harper offer. Not wanting to go against his friends on the board, but finding Hank's figures persuasive, Bill called Harper's religious editor, Gene Exman, to explain his dilemma. To his amazement, Exman agreed that an organization such as theirs should control its own literature; he understood perfectly and wished Bill the greatest success.

When Bill saw Hank next, the walls of the little office in Newark were covered with charts and diagrams, the desk drawer filled with blank stock certificates. Across the top of each certificate they wrote, "Works Publishing Inc. par value $25." Since they were sure this book was to be only the first of many publications, it seemed a fitting title. There was no way they could fail.

But it was tough going. Why, they were asked, should anyone invest in a book that hadn't even been written? It was a good question, Bill agreed. But his excitement was contagious. In the next few months he and Hank managed to sell over four thousand dollars' worth of shares, enough to keep the office going.

That fall and winter were among the most productive times in

Bill's life. He spent his days writing and his evenings at meetings, reading aloud what he'd written, defending it, sometimes rewriting it. The group at this point appeared evenly divided: conservatives, led by Fitz, who felt that since the movement was based on Christian doctrine, they should say so; and liberals, led by Hank and Jim B., another salesman who'd recently joined them, who wanted a strongly psychological emphasis. Bill's old friends the agnostics backed Hank and Jim. Bill listened to everyone, because even then he knew that the book had to speak for all of them.

And so it went, strong but warmhearted arguing, until Chapter Five. That was where Bill wanted to explain exactly how they worked, to pin their objectives down in specific steps, to plug the loopholes through which a rationalizing alcoholic could wriggle away. He set to work to break down the program into smaller pieces and, if possible, broaden and deepen its spiritual implications. When he finished he had outlined twelve steps in all. These steps opened Chapter Five.

Frankly pleased with them, he was in no way prepared for the violent reactions of the group. The fights raged on for weeks. At first Bill joined the battle, sensing all the old excitement of combat; then something made him decide to change his tack, to sit back and listen. It was the canniest decision he ever made. Without that shift, and without the way Lois had of turning up at opportune moments with fresh pots of coffee and a reminder that everything didn't have to be settled that minute, these evenings might have become totally destructive. Instead, something was created that blended the finest qualities of the opposing views. It was agreed that they should always label their steps a *Suggested* Program of Recovery, and The Twelve Steps were eventually accepted in Chapter Five. Before long they were to be looked upon as the foundation stone of the fellowship.

In mid-January the book was finished. But it had no title, and the question of what it should be threatened to become another battle of the steps. The New York group had been referring to themselves as a "nameless bunch of alcoholics," and from this had come the phrase "alcoholics anonymous." No one knows who first

THE TWELVE STEPS

1. We admitted we were powerless over alcohol—that our lives had become unmanageable.
2. Came to believe that a Power greater than ourselves could restore us to sanity.
3. Made a decision to turn our will and our lives over to the care of God as we understood Him.
4. Made a searching and fearless moral inventory of ourselves.
5. Admitted to God, to ourselves, and to another human being, the exact nature of our wrongs.
6. Were entirely ready to have God remove all these defects of character.
7. Humbly asked Him to remove our shortcomings.
8. Made a list of all persons we had harmed, and became willing to make amends to them all.
9. Made direct amends to such people wherever possible, except when to do so would injure them or others.
10. Continued to take personal inventory and when we were wrong promptly admitted it.
11. Sought through prayer and meditation to improve our conscious contact with God as we understood Him, praying only for knowledge of His will for us and the power to carry that out.
12. Having had a spiritual awakening as the result of these steps, we tried to carry this message to alcoholics, and to practice these principles in all our affairs.

used it. Bill thought it catchy, and an appropriate title for the book. So did the Akron group. The New Yorkers and others vehemently favored *The Way Out*. At one point Bill considered *The Bill W. Movement*—the ego had not yet been totally deflated—but he was quickly talked out of that. Bill sent a wire to Fitz in Maryland, asking him to go to the Library of Congress and find out how many books with the title *The Way Out* were registered. Fitz informed him that there were already twelve, but as far as he could discover, no *Alcoholics Anonymous*. That did it. No drunk was going to risk being the thirteenth anything. The book had its title, the fellowship had a name.

The first reactions to mimeographed copies they had distributed had begun coming in and they were heartening. Dr. Harry Emerson Fosdick, pastor of Riverside Church, was completely satisfied with the book. So were other ministers, medical men and psychiatrists, Protestant and Catholic alike. Hank, Ruth and Bill were so carried away by these responses that they placed an order with the Cornwall Press for a first printing of five thousand copies. This was optimistic, since they had no more than one hundred members as of January 1939. Edward Blackwell, the president of Cornwall, was a little aghast at their offer of only five hundred dollars as a down payment, but he finally agreed to play along and start the presses rolling.

But more buyers of Works Publishing Inc. stock were not forthcoming. And in April 1939 there seemed no money anywhere. Back in the fall, when hopes were high, Bill had talked Lois into giving up her job, so now, four and a half years sober, he wasn't even a man with a wife who worked. Then, to compound the situation, the week the book was published they learned that the bank which held the mortgage on 182 Clinton Street had found a buyer. They were told they had to be out by the first of May.

Without publicity, neither shares nor book would sell. If ever there was a moment for a miracle, this was it. And it was Hank P. who came up with it. He had been talking with a new man, Morgan R., and discovered that he was a friend of Gabriel Heatter's. Heatter, as everyone in America knew, was the MC of "We, the

People," a fantastically popular radio interview show, broadcast over a national hookup. Hank's plan was to get Morgan on "We, the People," have him describe his fall, his salvation through AA, and then put in a plug for the book. Heatter agreed, a date was set, and then someone came up with the question—they'd been stung too often—What if Morgan got drunk? After all, he'd been with them only a short time.

There was obviously one way to handle that. Hank found another new member, another solvent one, who happened to belong to the Downtown Athletic Club and was willing to foot the bill for two adjoining rooms. Morgan was checked into the club, and various older members worked shifts guarding him, never letting him out of their sight.

Morgan didn't care for the idea, but he stayed in his room, and on the night of the broadcast he was cold sober. And he was brilliant. In New York and out in Ohio, members sat glued to their sets. They knew their troubles were over. Out of their sufferings and struggles a best seller had been born.

The mail brought two orders for *Alcoholics Anonymous.*

CHAPTER ELEVEN

THERE are times in a man's life when all the waves of his history seem to be joining, building to some terrifying crest. In the spring of 1939 Bill could feel such a time approaching.

When he stood on Clinton Street and watched their possessions being carried out of the house and packed into a van, he didn't have the money even to pay the movers. All their furniture, including many of Dr. Burnham's finest pieces, was put in hock to a storage company.

And Bill was a man with a wife to support, no home, no job, no roots and no prospects of establishing any. He and Lois began a gypsy life in apartments people lent them. This was disturbing enough. Worse was what Bill felt happening to himself. When later anyone asked how he and Lois had got through the next two years, he'd say, "We were invited out to dinner a lot."

With Clinton Street gone, the New York group met for a while in Bert T.'s tailoring establishment on Fifth Avenue, then in a rented parlor in Steinway Hall. Meanwhile, the Jersey groups were beginning to branch out and there was always hopeful news coming in from Ohio, where a series in the Cleveland *Plain Dealer* had brought in a hundred new members in a month. AA was growing, but much more slowly than Bill had dreamed. Now whenever he'd see a copy of the book, it was a rebuke, one more example of Billy Wilson failing again.

Of course, there were signs of growth. When the Wilsons lived in Monsey, New York, for a time, they learned that Dr. Russell Blaisdell, the head of Rockland State Hospital, was sending busloads of alcoholic inmates to AA meetings in Manhattan and New Jersey. Almost every week, it seemed, Bill would meet a new man who would tell him that through AA he had become a brand-new person. But after each encouraging incident he would be obsessed by the thought of the hundreds of thousands of others they were not reaching, and the need to find a way plagued him.

When an article called "Alcoholics and God" appeared in *Liberty* magazine in September, they were at first dubious about it. *Liberty*, however, forwarded more than eight hundred pieces of mail to AA in Hank's Newark office, and books began moving from the warehouse. More pins appeared on the office map indicating possible recruits, and Bill's days were filled answering letters, explaining their work. This, along with his concern for every drunk he met, kept him from sinking wholly into depression. Still, he knew something was wrong—not in the program; in himself. But he could not pin it down. Throughout that fall and winter there was a growing contradiction between the easygoing, confident role he was playing and what he truly felt about himself.

At the end of 1939 there was another blow. Hank's business completely collapsed, and they were forced to move the AA office into one tiny room. Through it all Ruth Hock had stuck with them, often taking a few shares of Works Publishing stock in place of a salary. And then one morning Ruth found in the mail a clipping torn from an unidentified paper and sent in anonymously. It was

393

a three-line prayer. She read it and was instantly struck by how much AA thinking could be compressed into three short lines. On her own, Ruth had the prayer printed on cards; and without asking anyone, she began slipping a card into each piece of mail that went out from the Newark office.

> *God, grant me the serenity to accept the things I cannot change,*
> *Courage to change the things I can,*
> *And the wisdom to know the difference.*

And so the "Serenity Prayer" became part of the AA canon.

Every small, tightly knit group develops its own language—and its own humor. AA was no exception. To outsiders who attended meetings—they were referred to as civilians—the members' laughter was often shocking. But to the drunks it was curiously therapeutic. When a sick and shaking man, who has been living alone with his secret guilts, suddenly finds himself roaring with laughter at his own behavior, that man is beginning to grasp some perspective. And when this happens in a room full of other guilty drunks, he is no longer alone.

In a way, the same effect was achieved through sharing their special "in" language: a combination of barroom jargon and the purest spirituality, much of the latter from the wording of The Twelve Steps. (A visit to a potential member was a "twelfth step call" or "twelfth stepping.") But there was a sound reason for the reality of their talk. It was almost as though some men consciously used four-letter words in one sentence, knowing that in the next they could then use love, tenderness and humility. The frankness of their speech also helped them to focus on their real enemy—booze. Booze was too lethal a subject to dress up in fancy phrases. These men were talking about something that had to do with staying alive or with dying.

THERE had been no word from Mr. Rockefeller in three years. Then early in 1940 the board was informed that he had been keeping an eye on AA and had decided to give them a dinner.

It was to be quite a dinner, at the Union Club on Park Avenue.

Mr. Rockefeller had made up a tentative guest list, which appeared to include every prominent name in the New York financial world. Bill saw at a glance that their combined wealth would add up—literally—to billions of dollars. Bill was to arrange for the speakers and invite whatever members he wished. Dr. Fosdick agreed to speak for religion. Dr. Foster Kennedy, who had defended them in *The Journal of the American Medical Association,* would speak for medicine, Bob and Bill for AA.

Bill had seen to it that at least one AA member was at every table. Over the first course an elderly, bewhiskered banker sitting beside Morgan R. asked which institution he was connected with, and Morgan answered that at present he had no connection with any institution, but he added happily that he had recently been released from Rockland State Hospital.

Because of illness, Mr. Rockefeller was not able to attend, but his young son Nelson explained his father's great interest in AA and introduced the speakers graciously. Bill talked about the growth of the fellowship, about new meetings in Chicago, in Washington, Detroit and many other cities, and about their first "mail order group" in Arkansas. A loner there had straightened himself out after reading the book, and now, through correspondence with the office, he'd been off the juice for six months and had a small group going in Little Rock. Across the nation, they figured, there must be by now two thousand recovered drunks, and Bill tried to describe how the groups functioned.

When he'd finished—and he was an experienced enough speaker by then to be able to judge an audience's reaction—he knew that he had captured not only the interest of his listeners, but their deep concern. With the meeting open to questions, fielded extremely well by his colleagues, he sat back on the dais and gazed down at the sea of opulent faces. Why, he wondered, had they had to wait so long for this night? It didn't matter—he half smiled as he rose to answer a question—it had happened. Whatever God and John D. had had in mind, it was all right.

When the last question had been asked and answered, Nelson Rockefeller thanked the guests for coming to witness with him what his family believed was the birth of an important movement. Then he reiterated his father's faith in AA and his belief that its power lay in the fact that the message was always carried from one man to the next without any thought of financial income or reward. For this reason, he concluded, his father was convinced that AA must always be self-supporting. All they needed from men such as were gathered here was their confidence and their goodwill.

And with that the guests broke into loud applause. After hearty handshakes, friendly slaps on the back and many cheery good-bys, Bill watched as the whole billion dollars' worth walked out of the paneled dining room, out of his life.

It took a while for Bill to understand his own reactions. The dinner was to become a landmark in AA history, a turning point in their attitude toward outside contributions. It was to lead them to a policy of corporate poverty. But this was in the future. Now Bill saw he must begin to take things into his own hands.

The dinner was almost, but not quite, his last contact with the world of high finance. Mr. Rockefeller sent a letter to several hundred of his friends and acquaintances, once again proclaiming his faith and saying that he personally was contributing one thousand dollars to AA—undoubtedly a hint that they could do likewise. He also purchased and mailed out a few hundred copies of *Alcoholics Anonymous*. If his friends caught the hint, they probably balanced their incomes against Mr. Rockefeller's and decided to contribute accordingly. One international banker sent in a check for ten dollars.

The wire coverage of the Union Club dinner was extensive. Some of the accounts were on the wild side—the New York *Daily News* carried the headline ROCKEFELLER DINES EX-SOTS, NOW RUM FOES—but on the whole the AA story was presented with dignity. Mail inquiries increased, and to Bill, the clippings that came in from all over America made heady reading. Maybe news releases would be the way.

Hank P., their grand promoter, of course agreed with this idea instantly. They should get going at once with a barrage of arresting, shocking stories. But Hank's own shocking story became at this point Bill's first concern. Not only was his business gone, but he was being sued for divorce and was now being forced to accept what he called a degrading job out in western New Jersey. His plan was to take the book business and his secretary, Ruth Hock, with him. When Ruth refused to go and Bill pointed out that Works Publishing had to stay near their mailing address, Hank became totally irrational, flailing out at everyone, especially at Bill. It developed that Hank had asked Ruth to marry him, and when she had said no, he'd put all the blame on Bill. A few weeks later, at a stockholders' meeting, Hank was unable to give any kind of accounting. He'd apparently kept no financial record of the publishing moneys. When questioned, he began inventing tales about his office being robbed and his records disappearing. It was at this meeting that Dr. Silkworth saw signs of what he considered paranoia, and warned Bill that Hank might become dangerous.

Hank had begun to drink within a couple of months of the Union Club dinner. Every step of the ruthless progression of his emotional state was as clear as a graph on a fever chart. He was withdrawing, while they watched, into a private world of hostility, cynicism and resentment. Bill was powerless to stop the classic pattern, once started, from running its course. By the time Bill and Ruth had located an office on Vesey Street in Manhattan, Hank had become unapproachable to every member of the group. His state was a shock to all of them.

And to a few, Bill's reaction, indeed all of Bill's behavior for the next six months, was almost as alarming, because he too was launched on a course no one could check. Ever since the Rockefeller release he had been smitten by the excitements of big-time publicity. Now he went on the road. A group somewhere would ask him to speak, and he'd get the chairman to tip off a local reporter, who after the meeting would interview him. The next morning his picture would be splashed across page one, with a rousing account of the number of hopeless drunks Bill W. had saved. In the beginning many AA groups went along with this. But only in the beginning.

"Who does he think he is?" "What the hell is he pulling?" and "What about Dr. Bob?" The objections multiplied. But Bill could rationalize his every action. Secrecy might be all right for others, but the public had a right to know who AA's founders were.

With that one phrase, "all right for others," Bill began to think of himself as an exception. The resulting dissension excited him. *He* could command as much publicity as anyone. With his old zest the Burr and Burton boy was showing them. And no one could deny that the promotion was getting results. More drunks were turning up at meetings.

Then one night an old-timer told him that he might indeed be the co-founder, they might owe their lives to him, but he'd better watch himself because he was sure as hell acting like a man on a "dry drunk." It was a phrase Bill had never heard, and he saw the truth in it and it gave him pause. There were times when he felt himself driven exactly as he had been when he was drinking, only without the stimulus of booze to support and propel him. Then too, there were other times, usually at night when he was alone, when he would remember the yearnings, the constant reaching out that had been part of him before the drinking had taken over: in a starlit marble quarry, with Bertha, in Winchester Cathedral, alone in the Brooklyn house. Only now it seemed his hunger was for a state of being he had once had and let slip away.

Unable to place what it was he craved, finding no answers, but only a vague sense of loss, of having failed again, he knew it was better to keep moving, keep going with the tide.

Two remarkable people had entered his life the year before. Marty M. was one of the first females to sober up in AA. An intelligent young woman with tremendous charm, she possessed a drive which Bill immediately spotted as equal to his own. In time Marty was to become one of the great pioneers in the field of alcoholism education, but at this point she was primarily one of AA's spectacular recoveries.

A patient at Blythewood Sanitarium in Connecticut, she'd attended a Clinton Street meeting, had instantly caught the message and spread the good word among the other alcoholic inmates of her hospital. By 1940 she and Bill and Lois were fast friends. And she had introduced Bill to Dr. Harry Tiebout, the chief psychiatrist at Blythewood, who had been frankly astonished by the change he'd noticed in his alcoholic patients after a brief exposure to AA. Seeing the same attitude achieved by patient after patient, Harry Tiebout began in 1939 what was to become his lifelong absorption: a thorough scientific investigation into the techniques and principles of Alcoholics Anonymous.

He and Bill had liked each other at once, and Bill had decided soon after their first meeting that if ever his own problems grew insupportable, Tiebout was a doctor he could turn to. In his early days at Towns, Bill had often discussed with Silkworth the question of psychotherapy for alcoholics, and they had agreed it was usually wise for a man to have a prolonged stretch of sobriety before delving into his psychic disorders. Bill still believed this. In fact, he was so convinced that the answers lay in the program, it was to be another four years before he would seek Tiebout's help. He continued addressing meetings, constantly carrying the message to larger audiences, yet at the same time sensing that he personally was slipping farther and farther away from the true meaning of the program.

Apart from the knowledge that he had Tiebout to turn to, there was another important factor that kept Bill from going overboard during this dry-drunk period. The New York members, restive about having no permanent meeting spot, had rented an extraordinary little building on West Twenty-fourth Street which had been built as a stable up a narrow alley behind two brick houses.

In many respects it was an ideal AA clubhouse, with a meeting room on the ground floor and a general room and two tiny bedrooms upstairs. Bill and Lois eventually moved into one of these, but months before he actually lived there, Twenty-fourth Street had become the warm center of Bill W.'s life.

Lois too, at last, had an outlet of her own. While the regular meetings went on, she and other wives began to meet in the upstairs room and discuss their own problems, their methods of adjusting to their new way of life. Some believe that this was the actual start of AA's family groups. The clubhouse was a special place to both Lois and Bill at a moment when both needed it. For here Bill began to realize that his wildly active schedule was a release for pent-up fury at himself, at his failure to transform AA into the big-time operation he knew it must be.

Deeply depressed, he began to question his motives on these speaking binges. And he did not like what he saw. Did he go to meetings now to share with his fellow alcoholics? Did he still feel gratitude for what had happened to him? Did he honestly think he still needed the others? Hadn't he, in fact, become their teacher, their preacher, the one others depended on? Was he now seeing himself as some great moral leader? He again examined his famous drive, and he saw that it served to cover failure, impatience, eternal frustration at not being able to move things as he wanted to. And with the depression there was a sense of guilt that he could feel this way, he who had been given so much. This led to a new and hideous fear. What if he, Bill W., should crack up as he had seen other men crack . . . ?

He had no answer. Then one wintry night, when Lois was away and he was alone in the tiny bedroom at the club, an extraordinary thing happened. He was as low in spirits as he ever remembered being. A storm was beating on the tin roof overhead. He was wondering if the pain in his middle could be an ulcer, when he heard the doorbell ringing downstairs. Old Tom, the ex-fireman who occupied the other bedroom and served as janitor, announced that there was a bum from St. Louis asking to see him.

Before he could protest, a little man, dripping wet, limped into the room and sat down. He introduced himself as Father Ed of the Jesuit order, here on a pilgrimage to talk to Bill. Then he said, "*I thank my God upon every remembrance of you,*" and he smiled. "Philippians One: Three." And as he began talking about his work with alcoholics, Bill found himself looking into a most remarkable pair of blue eyes.

He'd become interested in AA, Father Ed said, through studying The Twelve Steps, in which he found parallels to the Exercises of Saint Ignatius, the spiritual discipline of the Jesuit order, and when

Bill confessed he'd not known this, he appeared utterly delighted. On and on he talked, and Bill could feel his body relaxing, his spirits rising. Gradually he realized that this curious little man was radiating a kind of grace, filling the room with that sense of Presence he'd felt at Towns. Father Ed wanted to talk about the paradox of AA, the strength arising out of total defeat, the loss of one's old life as a condition for achieving a new one. And Bill nodded and agreed, and soon found . . . But he never had words for what he found that night. There was no way to explain it. He didn't question Father Ed, any more than a man would have questioned the word of God.

As a matter of fact, they talked most of the night about the word of God. Bill told him that he no longer understood God, that he had lost what once he thought he had understood so clearly. And Father Ed said that our idea of God would always be lacking, "for to comprehend God is to be equal to God." But our concept could grow. He spoke of the responsibility referred to in the eleventh step, "to improve our conscious contact."

Bill told Father Ed about his anger, his mounting dissatisfactions. Father Ed quoted Matthew: *"Blessed are they which do hunger and thirst."* When Bill asked if there was never to be any satisfaction, the old man snapped back, "Never." There was only a kind of divine dissatisfaction that would keep him reaching out. Bill had made a decision, Father Ed reminded him, to turn his life over to the care of God, and having done this, he was not now to sit in judgment on how he or AA or the world was proceeding. He had only to keep the channels open—and accept. For, like it or not, things would proceed in God's good time, not Bill's.

And as he listened, Bill accepted and believed every word the old man said.

Eventually, Father Ed got up and hobbled to the door. As a parting shot he said that if ever Bill grew impatient or angry at God's way of doing things, if ever he forgot to be grateful for being alive right here and now, he, Father Ed Dowling, would make a trip all the way from St. Louis to wallop him over the head with his good Irish stick.

Bɪʟʟ's ʀᴇʟᴀᴛɪᴏɴꜱʜɪᴘ ᴡɪᴛʜ Father Ed was to prove unlike any other in his life. But he was soon given a chance to see that the outcome of their first meeting, the truths he had learned from his new Jesuit friend, were not unlike those which many members had been learning for themselves.

In the winter of 1940 a reporter from *The Saturday Evening Post*, Jack Alexander, was sent to see if there was a story in AA. In showing Alexander around, Bill had the opportunity to listen to older members in a great many groups discuss their experiences, and there seemed to be a common pattern. A man turned to AA quite simply because he knew he would die if he didn't. At the start he depended on the fellowship, the philosophy—the spiritual principles, if you like—to stop his drinking. Then, as things straightened out in his life, he tended once more to seek happiness through his own powers and desire for acclaim. From this point the stories all differed slightly. Through some incident, some sharp reversal, perhaps, their eyes were opened still wider, and they learned a new lesson; they returned, and as if entering another new level of feeling, they could truly accept AA's teaching.

For Bill too it seemed a new lesson, but there was also a returning to something he had let himself lose sight of. Now he was finding it true and valuable, as he had at first.

And as they said out in Akron, for Bill W. it was just in the nick of time.

Jᴀᴄᴋ Alexander was an experienced, cynical reporter who had his doubts about doing a story on a society of recovered drunks. But in interviewing and getting to know the members, he was won over completely. His article was a magnificent piece of journalism. It appeared in March 1941, and Bill at last had the publicity he had so desperately wanted when the book came out. It now became clear that they could not have coped with it then. "In God's good time," Father Ed had said.

For with the publication of the *Saturday Evening Post* story, the world of AA—and of Bill W.—was changed irreversibly. The floodgates opened. Pleas for help began pouring in by the thousands.

There seemed no possible way that the little group of nameless drunks could handle the demands being made on them.

For better or worse, in the year 1941 Alcoholics Anonymous was established as an American institution.

THEIR pioneer days were over, but Bill knew in many areas they would be flying blind. Fresh groups were springing up with such fantastic speed, there'd be no way of controlling them. They had proved that drunks could stay sober. But could such large numbers of erratic personalities work together, with no experienced person to guide them? Because of the very nature of the alcoholic character, problems of money and of individuals striving for power would cause tensions. Would they even stay sober? And mightn't their fights create schisms that could split the whole fellowship apart?

It would be years before Bill would have answers to these questions, but within days of the *Post* story's hitting the stands, he and Ruth Hock knew what they were in for. As they plowed through the avalanche of telegrams and letters, and tried at the same time to cope with the endless calls at the office—some of which were hilariously funny, others stark and tragic—they saw they could never handle the situation alone. Each plea for help had to be answered personally. Any sort of form letter would deny their whole premise and betray their basic belief.

Bill sent out a call for anyone who was sober and could type or had a wife who could. The Twenty-fourth Street clubhouse was transformed into emergency headquarters. Even this battery of volunteers working with Lois around the clock made only a tiny dent.* The prodigious chain reaction Bill had envisioned had become a fact.

It was self-multiplying. They'd answer a letter, send the book, and if there was another potential recruit in the same vicinity,

---

* In the year 1941 membership jumped from fifteen hundred to eight thousand, which meant that they probably dealt with another ten or fifteen thousand who looked in the door, turned around and went out. In time Bill was to learn that two-thirds of these would one day return.

they'd urge the two to get in touch. Any member whose business took him on the road would be sent a list of people to look up. Within weeks they'd hear of a new AA group. The new group had problems. And all problems were referred to New York, which meant that they became Bill Wilson's responsibility.

Obviously he needed full-time paid assistants. Reenter two AA bugaboos: money and the old question of professionalism.

It was an absurd situation and one that took on an alarming urgency as more and more members understood what was at stake. Some method had to be devised to unify AA. If it fell apart—which at times it showed every sign of doing—all would be lost.

It is not surprising, therefore, that many old-timers came to view the goings-on with alarm. They were no longer afraid Bill would get drunk—they'd followed him through too many catastrophes—but they were aware of Bill's peculiar pride. They watched him become the captivating center of all that was happening, a leader sending out his messages to an ever-widening domain—and they worried.

There was, however, one thing that no one fully appreciated, and that was the change in Bill W. The imprint of the past months made him not only ready for this role, but uniquely suited to it. Until now his energies had been involved with his own growth, and with the interplay of certain individuals upon his life and that of the organization he had dreamed up. He still cared passionately about individuals, but the focus of his life had shifted. Now his concern was for large groups of drunks, for finding the structure by which AA groups could function as a whole.

FORTUNATELY, at this time of frantic growth, living conditions for Bill and Lois took an unexpected turn for the better. A Mrs. Griffith had shown up at one of their meetings. She was a woman of some means who was wildly interested in houses, building new ones or fixing up old ones. She was appalled at the notion of Bill and Lois living on at Twenty-fourth Street. They would be suffocated in the crush, and she had the perfect house for them in Westchester. It was a preposterous idea—there was no money—but one afternoon, while visiting Bur S. in Chappaqua, they drove over to have a look at Mrs. Griffith's house.

Bill loved it on sight—the great living room with its huge stone fireplace, the kitchen and three bedrooms on the ground floor, the long hall and master bedroom upstairs. To Lois it seemed impossible. But Lois had underestimated Mrs. Griffith. Mrs. Griffith wanted the Wilsons in her house. She would let them have it for sixty-five hundred dollars—no money down and forty dollars a month.

So in the spring of 1941 they moved to Bedford Hills and, in the fashion of the day, gave their house a name—fittingly, Stepping Stones. It was not a settled time anyplace, but in 1941 Bill and Lois, after twenty-three years of marriage, got their first taste of that special security that comes from having a house of one's own.

The news from the rest of the world was grim. The Low Countries and France were occupied by Germany, and the papers Bill read on the commuter train were filled with accounts of the German invasion of Russia. There was still a strong spirit of isolationism, but Bill had an ominous sense that America too was moving into war.

At the office he tried, successfully most of the time, to put his forebodings aside. The problems of AA were absorbing as groups continued to mushroom everywhere. Also, the New York office corresponded with a number of AA loners—men who had been able to make it on their own. These represented a kind of miracle to Bill, for they seemed to deny his basic premise: that the message could be transmitted only through close person-to-person relationships. Here was a sailor writing during a long night watch, or a farmer on some remote ranch: "hopeless alcoholics" who'd read an article or been given a name—AA or Bill W.—to whom they wrote for advice and encouragement.

Nevertheless, as Bill never let himself forget, it wasn't the office mail that was spreading the word. It was the band of tireless recovered alkies who carried it day after day. It was thanks to their often unorthodox efforts that each week new pins appeared on the office map—a few now also in Canada. But with each new pin the need for a group directory, for proper office help and the money to pay for it, became more apparent.

Finally, Bill hit upon a scheme. He and Dr. Bob had agreed there could never be dues for AA membership, but there seemed no reason why groups could not voluntarily make contributions to headquarters—say one dollar per member per year. It was a simple plan that would impose no hardship on anyone, yet might ensure a more efficient operation. The trustees approved. They sent contingents of stalwarts out to promote the idea. Most groups endorsed it wholeheartedly. Of course, some objected, and as always the objectors grew vociferous. But by early 1942 enough group contributions had trickled in to pay two assistants. Unfortunately, just at this point a dangerous situation developed in Cleveland.

The phenomenal growth of groups in the Cleveland area was unique. They had solved many problems in ways that would in time become models for other groups. The idea of individual sponsorship for newly enrolled members, for instance, began there. But it had not always been peaceful. Groups broke apart in bitterness, and so the struggle for power and prestige among several of the early founders sometimes got out of hand. Then too, the rumors about "grand rackets" Bill was promoting, which Hank P. had ignited when he took off, all flared up again. New York headquarters began to hear reports of Cleveland groups that wanted to break off all connection with Bill W.'s brand of AA.

Bill had constantly to remind himself that these were not just schemes of a few power-hungry malcontents. There were serious men and women who were genuinely distressed by what they regarded as commercialization. What AA needed, they insisted, was not more money or a central organization, but more dedicated twelve-step work.

Finally the charges of commercialism grew so out of proportion that Dr. Bob and Bill decided to go to a gathering of recovered drunks in Cleveland. It was a melancholy occasion. After dinner they were ushered into a hotel parlor, where they were met by an interrogating committee, a lawyer and a certified public accountant, and the stories all came out. Someone who had talked to a trustee in New York "knew for a fact" that the previous year Bill and Bob had divided sixty-four thousand dollars. Someone else knew of Bill's close relationship with the Rockefellers; he was said to have been seen quite often coming out of John D. Junior's bank.

Bill and Bob heard them out, and then Bill spoke. He had brought with him a certified audit of all AA financial affairs from the beginning. It showed that although Dr. Bob was supposed to receive a royalty on the book, he had got none—everything had gone back into AA work. He still received a stipend of thirty dollars a week from the fund John D. Rockefeller, Jr., had started, but that was all. Bill had been getting the same thirty, plus, for the past year, twenty-five a week from the book company. His total income was fifty-five dollars a week. The committee's accountant studied the statement, then testified to its accuracy.

The committee apologized. Some were chagrined; they had only wanted to get the record straight, and they would do all they could to squelch the rumors—but this never really happened.

It was painful, and Bill did not pretend to hide the pain.

HENCEFORTH, Bill was determined, all AA financial dealings, whatever their nature, must be recorded in the simplest, clearest way. The books would always be available for any group's examination. And he was more convinced than ever that the fellowship must become totally self-supporting.

Meanwhile, mail continued to pour in, and the dilemmas of the groups seemed endless. Clearly they were facing problems of two kinds: those that might be called organizational, and those that sprang from the old alcoholic desire for power and glory. Certain patterns of trouble recurred so consistently that Bill began to wonder if there couldn't be some statement of principles, some form of what he referred to vaguely as a code of traditions. There seemed a genuine need for some great unifying set of truths that could apply to all group problems, much as The Twelve Steps provided guidelines for individuals. And whatever form such a code might take, it could be offered only as suggestion. No governing body in New York City was going to dictate to AAs. They might take advice, but orders, never. The only authority they would, or should, recognize was what they called their group conscience.

Bill could think of no other society, church group or political party that was not able to exert some form of discipline over its members through regulations. All nations, all societies had to be governed; and the authority to govern was the essence of organization. Yet Bill knew in his heart that AA was, and had to be, the exception to this.

As he wrestled with these questions, he saw the world around him being torn apart. Weighed against the horrors of the war, the problems of AA had to appear, as they would have said in East Dorset, of no real account. But that was the world into which AA was born and in which Bill W. worked to consolidate its traditions.

Within months of the Wilsons' move to Bedford Hills, in the year that the *Post* story appeared and AA's fantastic growth began, the Japanese air force attacked Pearl Harbor, and overnight a nation that had been divided was suddenly united. Bill immediately applied for a commission in military intelligence. One can only guess at his feelings when he learned that he, a patriot, a Vermonter, a veteran of World War I, wasn't even acceptable to his country as an old retread. But there can be no doubt about the result of this rejection. If earlier Bill's relationship to AA had been that of a father to a son, or an artist to his creation, in 1942 it became more that of a lover and his girl. During the 1940s there was not the smallest segment of AA that he did not know, study and love. And he drew from this new relationship a joy and a sense of security that he had never before experienced. The love affair was to last for fourteen years.

CHAPTER TWELVE

MEN who worked beside Bill in this period have said that in his private life Bill Wilson could make mistakes, horrendous ones, but as far as AA was concerned he was never wrong. This is not true. Bill made mistakes with AA, but each time he instinctively sensed his error and never made that one again. Nothing stood between him and his love, not even his devotion to Lois and their life in Bedford Hills.

A measure of his absorption was his reluctance to leave the office at night. One more drunk might wander in who had to talk with someone, and evening hours were the best for talk. This was a development, he learned later, that many AA couples faced. When a man has begun to live again and is filled with all the potentials of his rebirth, it is not always easy to share the excitement with a spouse who, no matter how devoted, has not changed in the same ways. The spouse's view has to be colored by what one was, not merely by what one is and will be. Some hopes of the recovered alcoholic are too intoxicating to share.

But however often Bill's head was still in the stars, his feet were planted in an office where day by day he was struggling to organize a group of unpredictable drunks.

Any two or three alcoholics—rampant, antisocial, critical, anti-religious or even anti–each other individuals—could collect a few kindred spirits and announce that they were an AA group—and they were, if *they* thought so. To many this seemed simple anarchy. There was a story going the rounds about a group that had posted a sign in its clubhouse: ANYTHING GOES HERE, EXCEPT YOU MUSTN'T SMOKE OPIUM IN THE ELEVATOR. It was a story that amused Bill W., though not the trustees.

Still, Bill persisted: they could only make suggestions. All letters to groups—and this practice has continued throughout AA's history —carried some such phrase as "Of course you are at liberty to handle this matter any way you choose, but the bulk of our experience does seem to suggest . . ." To Bill it was remarkable how often his advice was taken.

But the nonalcoholics remained skeptical. To the psychiatrically oriented all this liberty was an example of the alcoholic's refusal to grow up. To them it was only a matter of time before the adolescent egos would blow up and totally wreck what had been created. Yet as the years passed they had to admit that something was holding AA together.

For Bill this something had to do with the surprising willingness of the individual to place the welfare of his fellows above his own desires. AA was not a course of behavior. It was an attitude of mind and of heart, essentially spiritual, it seemed. The something appeared to fall into two parts.

He knew that within every recovered drunk there were two built-in authorities which the outside world could never understand. First, in the life of each member there still lurked a very real and ruthless tyrant. His name was booze. And every member had learned how deadly his weapons were.

To Bill there could be no more forceful restraint than this. Yet it took more than fear to bind these anarchists together—for this second authority Bill knew he'd not found the proper words. To himself he called it an inner voice; in talking with others he would say higher power, life-force, or any words the listener might be comfortable with. By whatever name they cared to use, it was this that brought about those moments of insight which drew members close, that brought forth the kind of loving Father Ed spoke of, which outsiders sensed but could not share.

Individual alcoholics would never need other directives than these, but the groups and their troubled relationships with members and other groups and the world around them were another matter. Finding guidelines for them was not to be easy. What would become of the fellowship if anything should happen to the handful of old-timers who were trying to mediate group problems? What about finances? What about breaks in anonymity?

Bill was absorbed through the 1940s in providing answers to these questions. The seeds of what were to grow into the Twelve Traditions were planted. As had been the case with the Twelve Steps and the book *Alcoholics Anonymous,* each tradition was arrived at the hard way, from lessons learned in groups and Bill's own involvement in their hassles. For example, whenever he discussed professionalism, he told of his temptation to work for Towns Hospital, and how the wisdom of a group conscience had finally made him turn down the offer. His arguments were disarming, because they were based on irrefutable personal experience.

Eight of the traditions focused on the internal workings of

411

groups, only four on their position with respect to the outside world. Good public relations, Bill knew, would always be essential to growth; over half the membership, he figured, had originally been drawn to AA by some favorable coverage in the media. But underlying all the traditions was the idea of anonymity.

In the beginning the whole notion had come from fear of public mistrust and contempt. The newcomer needed the protection of anonymity—no man wanted his boss, possibly not even his friends, to know he was joining a group of lowly alcoholics—and the groups needed it to protect themselves from members who might go shooting off on wild publicity binges of their own.

These binges still occurred, and Bill, who himself had been driven by a passion for personal acclaim, understood the temptation. Whenever he spoke about breaking anonymity, his talk was peppered with his own stories, especially from his conspicuous dry-drunk period. But he also knew that staying sober presented enough problems without adding to them the awesome responsibility—and the tensions that would invariably go with it—of realizing, if one should slip, what the ensuing publicity might do to the fellowship. That seemed an additional burden no recovering drunk should have to take on.

There were cases involving certain professional people which were not easy to resolve. But if the practical reasons for anonymity sometimes seemed not to apply, the spiritual reasons were, for Bill, conclusive.

About this there was no confusion in his mind. But as with the mysterious ingredient that he knew was holding AA together, he had not yet found a vocabulary to describe the spiritual side of anonymity.

For one thing, he didn't know if what he felt applied to others, or only to his own condition. He never questioned the importance of it in his life. When he was not Bill Wilson the co-founder, but just a drunk talking to and recognizing himself in another human being, then always he felt himself drawing closer to some indefinable force. Then he was truly living in the now, in some area of being that was outside the clash of opposites, outside past versus future. Conscious simply of the person he was with, he would become aware only of the immensity of the moment. Sometimes when this happened it was almost as if distant chords of music had begun to sound, but he could never say what struck them. He felt at times he was nearing a great truth which was in some way implicit in his concept of anonymity, and the inner excitement of being on the verge of grasping it, comprehending this mysterious power, constantly beckoned him on.

IN 1945 someone suggested that the draft of the traditions should be sent out to groups for their reactions. The office had by now moved to larger quarters uptown to accommodate new, special services, among them translators to handle inquiries from foreign countries, an enlarged mailing department and a monthly magazine, *The Grapevine*. After some discussion this had seemed a suitable forum in which to present the Twelve Traditions.

At about the same time there were two other major developments. One had to do solely with Bill's personal life. The second—his notion of forming a board of representatives from various sections of the country to take over the running of the fellowship—probably had more to do with ensuring AA's future than any idea he ever had.

Bill's private decision was to begin regular sessions of therapy with Dr. Harry Tiebout. To the members who learned of it, this was curiously disturbing. It seemed inconceivable that their Bill, who'd been released from his alcoholic obsession, had not been freed from every other. Seeing him at meetings or lolling around the office, relaxed yet always in control, radiantly alive, they could not, did not, want to believe that this man could on occasion be so crippled by depressions that he finally would have to turn to an outsider for help.

For Bill, going to Tiebout represented a tremendous venture in open-mindedness. In an essay he wrote later, he speaks of the Sixth Step, in which the alcoholic becomes ready to have his defects of character removed, as the point that separates the men from the boys. From the beginning he'd insisted that the AA way of life demanded rigorous honesty with oneself and had pointed to the perils of hanging on to old ideas. His own attempts at rigorous honesty had not been nil. But he recognized that if he was still being immobilized by spells of depression, if he was still burdened by ancient guilts, then he was still a man hanging on to old ideas, possibly even displaying the typical alcoholic's desire to nurse his guilts. But however Bill viewed it, for him at this point, just about to turn fifty and with all the prestige of a spiritual leader, to admit he needed professional help was more than open-mindedness; it was an act of courage.

In any case, the two men had a profound impact on each other. This is apparent in their writings. In the papers Tiebout presented after 1945 there are many signs of a new understanding both of conversion as a psychological phenomenon and of aspects of alcoholism. And Tiebout's influence is clear in Bill's pieces for *The Grapevine* and in his next two books. One example: in discussing the inner child who lives on in everyone but most obviously in the alky, Tiebout quoted a phrase of Freud's. And for Bill, remembering himself standing in a bar, king of all he surveyed, demanding that his will prevail, it seemed the perfect description of that kid inside who often took control, whom Freud had labeled "His Majesty the Baby."

Unlike most patients in therapy, Bill knew his goals. And his spiritual underpinnings were secure. Ever since their stormy night at the clubhouse, he'd remained in close contact with Father Ed Dowling. The two men corresponded, and they saw each other whenever the little Jesuit was in the East or when a trip took Bill near St. Louis. Soon after they met, Father Ed had presented Bill with a copy of the Prayer of Saint Francis. And it was never far from Bill's thoughts. Just saying it over, or repeating a particular phrase: "That where there is despair, I may bring hope . . . where there is sadness, I may bring joy . . . Grant that I may seek rather to comfort than to be comforted . . . for it is in self-forgetting that one finds . . ." Simply remembering these words would clear away his fears and misunderstandings, and he would be able to return once again to his real search.

IT WAS THE NEWS in 1947 from Akron that threw Bill's thinking into another dimension. Dr. Bob had been stricken with what was probably a terminal illness. And in what seemed no time at all Anne Smith died. Anne's death and Dr. Bob's illness were terrible reminders that life was narrowing down, closing in. Bill realized that he must start moving, and quickly, on his idea for a board of representatives—or, as he called it, his conference plan.

Until now, the only link between the members of what was becoming a fellowship with worldwide services and AA itself had been Dr. Bob, Bill W. and the secretaries who sent out the letters. Outside New York City no one even knew the names of the trustees; yet if something happened to Bill and Bob, the running of AA would be in the hands of these men, who—fine characters though they were—might be strangers to the drunks. It wasn't that the members lacked confidence in them; they did not know who they were. To have a board of trustees isolated like a tiny island in the midst of a fellowship that was spreading out across several continents struck Bill as completely untenable. He saw only one solution: a conference of men elected by the drunks themselves, in all sections of the country, who could represent the groups, meet once a year and inspect headquarters, and to whom the trustees would be accountable.

The trustees begged Bill to put the idea aside and relax. But in spite of Tiebout and Father Ed, relaxing when he met resistance was not something that came easily to Bill. He decided to go out to the grass roots and explain his plan to the groups. And from one of these trips—and there were a great many in 1948, 1949 and 1950—he returned to New York with a bonanza, a gift from God, a ten-strike. For what Bill had come across without even looking for it was the beginning of AA family groups.

In town after town he'd been hearing about the wives of members holding meetings on their own, not to discuss their husbands' problems, but to find ways whereby they themselves might better understand and use the program.

Perhaps he could have anticipated it, but he hadn't. Topsy-like, with no guidance, it had just grown. Wives and husbands of drunks were also victims of alcoholism, their lives twisted out of shape. And they could share their problems only with someone who'd been through the same thing.

When their spouses were drinking, they too had been filled with bitterness and self-pity. Marriages that had started out alive with young hopes had deteriorated, some into the relationship of a wayward boy and his protective, possessive mother. Then, when the drunk sobered up and the great honeymoon with AA began, to everyone's shock the problems were often worse. There was jealousy, often deep hurt, that strangers had done the job they hadn't been able to do. Sometimes the emotional scenes after AA were devastating, imposing cruel scars on any children involved.

But the important thing—to Bill, the glorious thing—was that all on their own they had the courage to look at these facts and see that changes must be made—*made in themselves*. It was this, and not their spouses' failings, they were meeting to discuss in little rooms, in kitchens and parking lots all across the country.

What they needed at this point was very much what AA had needed in 1935—confidence, some sense of organization and possibly, for contacting one another, a sort of central clearinghouse.

When Bill got back after discovering this new development, Lois was right there as always, waiting at the station.

There is some disagreement about Lois's first reaction. Bill remembered that she understood the whole situation at once and leaped at the idea of trying to help. Lois's memory is slightly different. She had a home in the country; she loved it, loved puttering in her gardens. She also had every reason to believe she had done her work. Only gradually, she recalls, did she decide she really had no choice. She would have to do what she could to unify these groups which had been born of such tremendous need.

Once the decision was reached she began to move, and all of Dr. Burnham's daughter's amazing vitality was put to work.

IN JULY 1950 some three thousand members gathered at an international convention in Cleveland. For several years the traditions had been discussed throughout AA and honed down accordingly.

THE TWELVE TRADITIONS

1. Our common welfare should come first; personal recovery depends upon AA unity.

2. For our group purpose there is but one ultimate authority— a loving God as He may express Himself in our group conscience. Our leaders are but trusted servants; they do not govern.

3. The only requirement for AA membership is a desire to stop drinking.

4. Each group should be autonomous except in matters affecting other groups or AA as a whole.

5. Each group has but one primary purpose—to carry its message to the alcoholic who still suffers.

6. An AA group ought never endorse, finance, or lend the AA name to any related facility or outside enterprise, lest problems of money, property and prestige divert us from our primary purpose.

7. Every AA group ought to be fully self-supporting, declining outside contributions.

8. Alcoholics Anonymous should remain forever nonprofessional, but our service centers may employ special workers.

9. AA, as such, ought never be organized; but we may create service boards or committees directly responsible to those they serve.

10. Alcoholics Anonymous has no opinion on outside issues; hence the AA name ought never be drawn into public controversy.

11. Our public relations policy is based on attraction rather than promotion; we need always maintain personal anonymity at the level of press, radio, and films.

12. Anonymity is the spiritual foundation of our traditions, ever reminding us to place principles before personalities.

Now, on a hot summer afternoon, in a roaring shout of approval, the Twelve Traditions were adopted—the means, they all believed, whereby AA could go on, function and hold together.

Several weeks later Dr. Bob was to undergo an operation. Bill paid him a visit, both men realizing that this might be their last time together. They talked of many things, but of one in particular. The future of AA, when the two of them were gone, depended on the conference plan. Bob knew about the dangers, the politicking that might go on when districts had to choose delegates, but he agreed that a governing body representing the drunks could guarantee the future. Perhaps they should call a conference, show them the offices and the books and let them decide how much responsibility they should take. Dr. Bob was as convinced as ever that decisions should be made not by Bill or himself or by trustees, but by the drunks themselves.

When Bill had to leave, Bob rose and saw him to the door. After Bill had moved down the steps, he turned and looked back. Dr. Bob was standing there, erect as always, but his face was white and his suit seemed much too big for him.

As Bill smiled, Bob lifted his arm in a wave. "Remember, Billy," he said. "Don't louse it up. Keep it simple."

Bill waved back, smiled again and hurried on. Dr. Bob Smith died November 16, 1950.

THERE are those who have wondered why Ohio's groups got off to a more solid start than New York's, and as the reason, some have suggested that Bob was a physician, trained to accept men as they were and to work with them as they were, whereas—and AA can thank its God for this too—Bill was always reaching for a new dimension. Even in his spiritual life with Father Ed, Bill found little comfort. His quest hounded him. Yet he sensed that that quest was what was keeping him sober.

And in that November of Bob Smith's dying, remembering the strange communion of their first meeting, he knew he was still seeking that source of inner power, still trying to find the real meaning behind his concept of anonymity. But whatever his final answer might be, he knew that Bob Smith in his quiet daily living was nearer the truth, closer to that secret power, and so perhaps closer to his Creator, than any man he had ever known. Perhaps AA needed them both, the quiet doctor who kept his inner life simple, and Bill W., to whom nothing was ever simple.

CHAPTER THIRTEEN

ON A hot July afternoon in 1955, Bill W. stood on the platform of the Kiel Municipal Auditorium in St. Louis and looked down at the rows of faces lined up before him. As he slowly straightened his back before speaking, his mind seemed to be apart, and for an instant he could see that all his years had been leading him toward this moment and what he knew he would have to say.

There were five thousand members with families and friends in the audience. For three days they had been celebrating the twentieth anniversary of Alcoholics Anonymous. Now, on their last day, a peculiar tension could be felt in their silence.

So far the speeches had followed the general pattern of those at open meetings. On the first night Bill had talked of what he called the first of their three legacies: Recovery.

His second talk had dealt with their second legacy: Unity.

Bill told of his struggles to establish a governing body, his conference plan, which now, after four years, had moved well beyond the experimental stage. The first conference of elected representatives had been held in New York five months after Dr. Bob died. The delegates met the trustees and headquarters staff, examined the financial books with a microscope and, in session after session of debate, resolved many knotty problems. One outcome of that conference was that the name of the board of trustees had eventually been changed from the Alcoholic Foundation to the General Service Board. The word foundation implied charity, even high finance, and the members wanted none of this.

Bill knew that something momentous had happened. He told his audience in St. Louis that it was clear that these first delegates had proved his point and Dr. Bob's: the group conscience should

419

be their sole authority. Bill went on to give an account of AA's growth, not only in the United States and Canada but all over the world, illustrating with stories of groups that he and Lois had visited; stories about the wondrous, rationalizing French, who'd kept insisting that wine wasn't liquor and so it shouldn't count; the secretive British, who had taken their anonymity so to heart that they were often impossible to find; the Oslo group, which to his delight had been founded by a Norwegian coffee-shop owner from Greenwich, Connecticut, a man who had lived as virtually a derelict until he'd found AA. For the first time, then, he wrote his family in Norway, telling them all that had happened in his twenty years in America. Word came back that his brother too was a hopeless alcoholic, about to lose his job on an Oslo newspaper and, they feared, his life. The coffee-shop owner packed up and headed for home. Three years later, when Bill and Lois arrived in Oslo, a large delegation of AAs was waiting at the airport.

To some, these stories were the high points of the St. Louis convention. For others, it was the Lasker Award, the bronze Winged Victory that had been presented to AA on the recommendation of twelve thousand physicians of the American Public Health Association, or the simple sincerity of the telegram from the White House; the contagious exuberance of Sam Shoemaker, perpetually enthusiastic about God and AA, or the sight of Bill's mother, Dr. Emily, now eighty-five, as proud and handsome as ever; or the radiance of Father Ed Dowling, oblivious to his painful lameness, who filled the auditorium with what Bill called his touch of the eternal. Everyone would remember Lois standing beside Bill, her hair graying, but her blue eyes dancing with delight as she told about Alanon, as the family groups were now known. There had been sixty when Bill discovered them. There were seven hundred now, plus groups in ten foreign countries.

But what no one who was in the auditorium that last afternoon would ever forget was the sense of expectancy when Bill stood before them to speak for the third time.

He seemed a little larger than life, a man who just naturally created memories; a tall, thin man, completely relaxed, yet with a tremendous inner energy; a personality that carried over big spaces. A warm light played over his face as he squared his shoulders and then leaned slightly forward across the lectern, like some old backwoods statesman who'd stopped by for a chat.

People thought they knew what he would say. He was to talk about the third legacy: Service. It was understood that then a resolution was to be presented concerning the organizational changes. No one was prepared for Bill to offer the resolution himself.

He was silent for only half a minute, perhaps, but as he looked into the faces below him, he had a quick flash of understanding. These were his people, assembled here to honor him for something that had not really been his doing. To many of them he had become a symbol, the custodian of their deepest beliefs and of that faith which somehow had created dignity and peace out of their unbelievable hells.

He had no objections; people needed symbols and some would always want leaders. And in this instant he knew—as he had known once long ago in the state militia—a sense of responsibility that went beyond any personal feelings or desires, and he understood that he must never allow private concerns to mar or obscure this trust. Then, as he cleared his throat to speak, he was struck by one further truth. These people were not children; their lives were no longer unmanageable. For twenty years he had tried to guide them and establish a structure within which they could grow. But now AA had come of age.

The resolution Bill proposed was put in the simplest terms. It declared that the time had come for the fellowship to take its affairs entirely into its own hands, and that the General Service Conference—the annual meeting—should now become the permanent successor to the two founders. The chairman, Bernard B. Smith—who had worked with Bill to see this plan brought to fruition—offered the resolution to the delegates for confirmation. They gave their consent by a show of hands.

There was nothing more to do, except for Bill and Lois to find some way to say good-by.

Lois spoke, thanking the convention, trying to express her feelings about what the afternoon had meant, and Bill saw that she too was a symbol, not only of the suffering the alcoholic's spouse must endure, but of the courage and hope of families in AA.

When she finished he moved back to the lectern. The well-meaning parent, he began, who tries to hang on to his authority and overstays his time, can do much damage. He never wanted to see this happen in AA. He'd be around, happy to help out in pinches, but that would be all. When it was time for the old guard to be relieved, he believed it right and fitting for them to march off briskly to the strains of a good quickstep. Still, he couldn't resist a few last admonitions.

But—for Bill—it was a short talk. When he finished, when he had grinned and waved at the crowd, who would not stop cheering, had helped his mother and Lois off the stage, he felt warm inside and good clean through. A little half smile kept playing across his lips. He knew that AA was safe at last—even from him.

BILL W.'s life did not end in St. Louis. When he finally dismounted the tiger he had been riding for twenty years, he was an extremely young fifty-nine, a man of tremendous virility, with an adequate income, good health and a stock of unanswered questions. He still possessed the curiosity of the schoolboy who'd wanted to learn everything there was to know about a boomerang. And a remarkable and quite sudden expansion of his interests took place.

Though he had announced—and believed—that he would no longer be the AA handyman around the office, he did maintain an office at headquarters* and kept fully informed about all activities. He had one pet and perennial concern: it had been for a long time of paramount importance to him that the majority of trustees, if only a majority of one, be alcoholics. It now became his own private war, and he was willing to risk anything, any relationships, to win a battle or even a small skirmish.

He admired the nonalcoholic members. They were some of the finest men in America, some of his closest friends, including his

---

*The General Service Office and AA World Service headquarters are now at 468 Park Avenue South, New York, N.Y. 10016.

own brother-in-law, Dr. Leonard Strong. All of them had devoted themselves to AA without stint. But on this one subject Bill W. was bullheaded. The thought of nondrunks having a majority stuck in his craw. Someday he'd *show* them.

The day was a long time coming. Not until 1966 was a system of rotation finally agreed upon to ensure that alcoholic trustees would always outnumber the nonalcoholics.

In other areas Bill did a better job of adhering to his autumnal plans. For example, he did a tremendous amount of writing: essays, books, pieces for *The Grapevine*, pieces in his kitchen-table style, so filled with humor and insight that members kept them and read them over and over.

These were also years of travel for the Wilsons, renewing old friendships and family ties, touring all of America and part of Europe. They would set off resolved to be just Mr. and Mrs. W. Wilson. But the word would get around: Bill W. was staying at the inn. A delegation would turn up, wanting to talk, wanting advice, or simply wanting to look at him. And Bill was honest about this: it was not displeasing. He might write about ego deflation, but His Majesty the Baby had never abdicated completely. Billy Wilson enjoyed being recognized.

Once, on a Caribbean island, they met Dr. and Mrs. J. Robert Oppenheimer. Bill and the great physicist took an instant liking to one another. After several long walks and many long talks, "Oppie" became convinced that Bill should join him at the Institute for Advanced Study at Princeton. He was eager to have Bill there to evaluate some work that was being done on the possible chemical composition underlying neuroses—especially depression.

Bill did not go to Princeton, but Oppenheimer had opened his eyes to new worlds. While he had been concentrating on arresting alcoholism through what he called spiritual means, many scientists had started looking into the interrrelated social, psychological and biochemical aspects of the illness. The social and psychological aspects were not news to Bill, but now for the first time he began to explore the biochemical. Soon after his talks with Oppenheimer, two men who were to have a great influence on this work entered his life: Dr. Abram Hoffer, of Saskatchewan, Canada, and Dr. Humphrey Osmond. In the course of research with schizophrenics these two physicians had tested hundreds of hospitalized alcoholics, who proved to be suffering from previously undiagnosed mild forms of schizophrenia. The possibilities inherent in these findings and the simple vitamin therapy—B_3, niacin—they were using, with what seemed remarkable results, fascinated him.

Until these three met, the Hoffer-Osmond research had been ignored by the medical profession despite two carefully controlled studies reported in several publications. The doctors explained philosophically that indifference, even hostility, was often the response to new findings. But Bill could not share this philosophical approach; it held too many echoes of early attitudes toward AA. Clearly what they needed was organization, a unifying force, some sort of clearinghouse for their information. In these areas Bill W. had had experience.

He immediately went to work for them, and for the next six years this became his primary concern. In true Bill W. fashion he was able to attract to the project eminent figures from a variety of medical fields and, in the course of the next several years, was responsible for disseminating great quantities of information about vitamin B_3. There are men who believe that in the long view Bill's work with this therapy may prove one of the major contributions of his life. But for the purposes of this narrative it is Bill's attitude toward the work and its relationship to AA that is significant. During his time with Hoffer and Osmond he never at any point forgot the traditions of anonymity and of not endorsing outside causes. His name was never associated with the undertaking. He insisted that all correspondence concerning it be addressed not to the office but to a post-office box in Bedford Hills.

Meanwhile, his relationship with AA groups was changing. Often after a day in the city or an early supper with Lois, he would feel like driving to a nearby town and dropping in on a meeting. He'd arrive a little late, find a place at the back of the room, stretch out his long legs and listen.

It was always wonderful. But eventually he would be recognized and the atmosphere would change in a subtle way. He would be called upon to talk—not as a member, but as co-founder.

He knew what was expected of him. If he spoke of his doubts and failings, they'd be disconcerted. They wanted him to proclaim a message of faith and to do it with a consistency unaffected by any of his own ups and downs. As he drove home he would sometimes realize he was getting almost as tired of the person he was supposed to be as of the person he really was.

What he wanted to be, what he needed to be, was a member of AA, and this he had never been. One night, as he was heading the car into the garage, he thought of himself as a sort of minor Moses. He had led his people across the wilderness, but for some reason God had not wanted him to enter the promised land. Such high-flown thoughts could stop him; but it did seem a paradox that he had been a channel through which others had found a truth that he still sought. He knew this had been a blessing for AA. The fact that he'd aligned himself with no church left the door open for people of any faith. But he had tried. He had studied religions, ancient and modern; and it sometimes seemed that what he was seeking was deeper and far simpler than anything they offered.

IT WAS one day in the early 1960s, when the AA headquarters were located on East Forty-fifth Street, that Bill was going through his files and suddenly found himself prompted to write a letter to the great psychotherapist Dr. Carl G. Jung in Zurich.

He began by introducing himself, and apologized for his long-overdue expression of gratitude for the critical role Jung had played in the founding of AA. He referred to Dr. Jung's conversations with Roland H. in 1930, and then in the simplest way he related what had happened to Roland after he'd left Zurich: Roland's spiritual awakening, his meeting Ebby and carrying the message to him, Ebby's carrying it to Bill. It was not a long letter, but he got everything in: the chain reaction and some details of his own experience at Towns. And he ended with the statement that Jung's place in the affection and history of AA was like no other.

Jung replied immediately. He remembered Roland H. with

warmth, explained that in those days he had to be exceedingly careful of what he said, because he had found he "was misunderstood in every possible way."

> But what I really thought about was the result of many experiences with men of [Roland H.'s] kind.
>
> His craving for alcohol was the equivalent, on a low level, of the spiritual thirst of our being for wholeness, expressed in medieval language: the union with God.°
>
> How could one formulate such an insight in a language that is not misunderstood in our days?
>
> The only . . . legitimate way to such an experience is that it happens to you in reality and it can only happen to you when you walk on a path which leads you to higher understanding. You might be led to that goal by an act of grace or through a personal and honest contact with friends, or through a higher education of the mind beyond the confines of mere rationalism. I see from your letter that Roland H. has chosen the second way. . . .
>
> I am strongly convinced that . . . an ordinary man, not protected by an action from above and isolated in society, cannot resist the power of evil, which is called very aptly the Devil. But the use of such words arouses so many mistakes that one can only keep aloof from them. . . .
>
> I am risking [this explanation] . . . because I conclude from your very . . . honest letter that you have acquired a point of view above the misleading platitudes one usually hears about alcoholism.
>
> You see, "alcohol" in Latin is "spiritus" and you use the same word for the highest religious experience as well as for the most depraving poison. The helpful formula therefore is: *spiritus contra spiritum.*

°"As the hart panteth after the water brooks, so panteth my soul after thee, O God." (Psalms 42:1)

There is no way to express what this letter meant to Bill. It was a confirmation of all that he had come to believe—and more. It came at a moment when he needed it, shortly after the death of Father Ed, who more than any other had understood the divine dissatisfaction that would keep him reaching out.

Ever since Bill had read Jung's *Modern Man in Search of a Soul*, he had looked on the great doctor as not wholly a theologian or a pure scientist, but as someone who seemed to stand, as Bill felt *he* did, in that strange no-man's-land that lay between. And now he had passed on the formula: *spiritus contra spiritum*.

Bill kept the Jung letter. In time it was copied, read at meetings, reprinted in *The Grapevine*, but the original stayed in his top desk drawer, and sometimes, even though he knew it by heart, he would open the drawer, look down at the signature and reread a phrase.

IN THE last years of his life Bill developed the habit of coming into the city on Tuesdays. Most of the time he stayed in his office, but occasionally he'd wander down the hall to study the pins on the world map that indicated fifteen thousand groups in the United States and eighty-eight other countries.

When the office would close for the evening, Bill would stay on at his desk, looking out the great window as light left the sky. He had no delusions about getting older. The doctors were after him to quit smoking, scaring him about emphysema. In the mirror he caught glimpses of a bony-faced old Vermonter, as though nature were returning him to his origins. He didn't mind getting older. It was like mountain climbing, an ancient Vermonter once told him: the higher you go, the more out of breath you get, and you're tireder too, but the view's a lot more extensive.

Still, he knew he would like to leave a message, some word to say to the future: I was here. But he knew his message would have to do with anonymity, because that was where the philosophy he could never formulate and the spiritual power he was always trying to understand seemed to join.

There were arguments now that the anonymity in AA had outlived its usefulness. Alcoholism was recognized as a disease, they said, so who need feel shame? Why not advertise your recovery? And help others by doing so?

Sensible, even praiseworthy. And yet at the very root of his being Bill knew that this aspect of the program was more than a symbol of what the ego gives up, and more than a shield for the

427

fellowship against the binges of relapsed drunks. Surely the first time he had called on Bob there had been more. Neither of them knowing or caring who the other was, they had been free to speak directly, openly, about their needs; and because of this they had discovered each other *not* from without, but from within. And this was not unique; it had happened to him too many times, and to too many other thousands. Somehow he knew he was always more at home with his own spirit when he was simply an anonymous drunk working with and sharing with another drunk.

It was a feeling that could not stand the strain of being woven into a creed; and maybe because he had always found it impossible to describe, he had felt that it brought him closer to the secret power he had always been seeking. "For if you can name it," Father Ed had once said, "it is not God."

In the end he knew he need not put it into a message.

As he sat looking out at the lights of the city, he realized that his feeling about himself and AA was very much the feeling of a boy who had stood on a mountain beside his father, gazing up at the stars, awed by the vast distances, not knowing if there was a meaning and overwhelmed by the mysteries, yet feeling safe, knowing his father was beside him. All his life since then, as a boy and as a grown man, he had been trying to force answers, to shape and improve people. Now he was beginning to think that from here on, all that might be asked of him was to relax, keep the channels open and to be a touch more loving.

HE COULD share fragments of these thoughts with visitors, but how much of them he was able to hang on to in the last months we cannot know. We can only hope they were nearby as the threatened emphysema developed and his life was taken over by oxygen masks and around-the-clock nurses. It was not an easy dying.

He and Lois had gone to Bermuda in the spring of 1970, to try to build up Bill's strength for the annual conference, but at the conference he was put to bed in his hotel room. In May and June they were with Dr. Ed Boyle of the Miami Heart Institute, trying to get Bill strong enough for a convention in Miami in July. He appeared there briefly in a wheelchair. He was in and out of hospitals in New York until early in January, when it was decided he should return to Dr. Ed. He died in Miami on January 24, 1971.

THE news of Bill W.'s death was carried on the front page of *The New York Times*. It spread as a big story around the world.

On Sunday afternoon, February 14, memorial services were held in New York at the Cathedral of St. John the Divine, in Washington at the National Cathedral, later at St. Martin's-in-the-Fields in London and in the chapel at Norwich University. In hundreds of churches, men of all faiths, of all nations, and in many languages tried to find the meaning in what Bill had done. Some old-timers could almost hear Dr. Bob saying, "For God's sake, Billy, keep it simple." But behind all the rolling cadences, the memory many people took with them was the sound in the voices of AA members when they read their Serenity Prayer, or a few little lines from Saint Francis, "Where there is despair, I may bring hope . . . where there is sadness, I may bring joy."

In New York it only seemed that every AA member was in or was trying to get into St. John the Divine. In Greenwich Village, one member, Joe B., who had been sober three years, unlocked the door of the tiny storefront they used for regular Sunday meetings.

It was two o'clock, just the time he had planned to take the subway uptown to the memorial service, and he wasn't at all clear about why at the last minute he'd decided to come here instead. The world would not end if for once they skipped a meeting.

Joe left the door open to air the place, and set to work, plugging in the coffeepot and unfolding the chairs that were stacked up against the wall. He didn't know exactly why he had wanted to go to the service. He was not a religious man. He was just curious, he guessed, to hear what they would say about Bill.

He'd met Bill only once. It was when they had all been talking about *Time* magazine's wanting to put Bill's picture on the cover, and he had said no. Such humility, such self-effacement, had impressed everyone at the gathering, but Joe remembered Bill shaking his head. For a quick moment their eyes had met, and there was a sparkle like a wink in his eye when he said that he guessed his turning *Time* down would be remembered a lot longer than having his face spread over a magazine for a week.

Joe had thought him a very shrewd Yankee trader. And he knew he owed him something. Still, that didn't explain why he was here this afternoon.

Over the little platform they had built for speakers there was a framed sign. It hung beneath the Twelve Steps.

> I AM RESPONSIBLE.
> WHENEVER ANYONE, ANYWHERE, REACHES OUT FOR HELP,
> I WANT THE HAND OF AA ALWAYS TO BE THERE.
> AND FOR THAT, I AM RESPONSIBLE.

It was a good saying, and Joe approved, but—he looked up at the clock—it was nearly two thirty now and no one had showed. No newcomer had needed his hand, so he walked slowly back to the coffeepot and began pouring himself a cup. He guessed he'd just lock up, go on, call his girl, maybe take in a movie.

He'd filled his cup and was looking around for a spoon when he heard the footstep. He turned, and there, standing in the doorway, was a man. He wasn't old, wasn't young; he wasn't poorly dressed or well dressed, but his hands, even though they were clasping the front of his coat, were trembling in an uncontrollable way that Joe recognized. And there was something about his eyes.

"Come in," Joe said. But the man did not move. "Yeah. . . ." Joe smiled. "This is the right place."

Then he held out his cup and the man took a slow, tentative step into the room.

"You look like you could use some coffee. . . ."

430

Robert Thomsen

As a young man, Robert Thomsen left his native Baltimore for an acting career in New York. He graduated from the American Academy of Dramatic Arts, and appeared on Broadway in *Stage Door*, with Margaret Sullavan, and *Mamba's Daughters*, with Ethel Waters, and was well on his way. At the same time he was writing plays, none of which got further than summer stock tryouts, he recalls.

Then came World War II and overseas duty as an ambulance driver with the American Field Service. Afterward, Thomsen turned permanently to writing. He did TV scripts for *Topper*, and published short stories and books, among them *Carriage Trade*, a historical novel.

He knew Bill Wilson for twelve years. The two had often discussed the book that might one day be written about AA's co-founder, and after Bill's death in 1971 Thomsen started work. With Mrs. Wilson, he traveled to Vermont to talk to Bill's family and childhood friends. He also visited Wilson's associates around the country and, he says, read everything Bill Wilson had ever written. In all his research, nothing touched him more than one yellowing scrap of paper. It was dated February 29, 1904, when Bill was eight, and was a letter he wrote on his typewriter to his little sister, Dot. The signature read: "Your unknown friend, Willie G. Wilson."

That phrase, your unknown friend, was to haunt Thomsen throughout his work on *Bill W.* and his attempts to pin down the elusive personality of a man whose vision had changed the lives of a million people.

Writing the story, he says, was an education in the invincible human spirit, for as he neared the end of the book he came to see that, in the words attributed to Voltaire, "after all it is no more surprising for a man to be born twice than it is to be born once."

It took the tragedy of war
and a woman's enduring love
to build

A TOWN

LIKE ALICE

A CONDENSATION OF THE NOVEL BY

NEVIL SHUTE

ILLUSTRATED BY CONNELL LEE

Jean Paget, at twenty-four, felt drained of life. England was so green and beautiful, she wanted to forget the war. She took a job as a secretary and tried to become an "ordinary person" again. But the bitter past kept crowding back—the killing march as a captive of the Japanese; the brief, poignant memory of Joe Harman, the Australian POW; the unspeakable scene under the tree by the British tennis courts. . . . So when Jean inherited a legacy, she knew she must return to Malaya, where something had been left undone.

In this timeless classic of a Scottish girl saved by her own courage and a man's self-sacrifice, master storyteller Nevil Shute reveals what the same courage, and determination, can do in a world at peace.

ONE

ONE afternoon in January 1948 I got a telegram from Ayr. It read:

REGRET MR DOUGLAS MACFADDEN PASSED AWAY LAST NIGHT PLEASE
INSTRUCT RE FUNERAL

DOYLE   BALMORAL   HOTEL   AYR

I had to search my memory to recollect who Mr. Douglas Macfadden was, and then I had to turn to the file to refresh my memory with the details of what had happened thirteen years before.

It was in 1935 that I met Douglas Macfadden. He was a client of
Owen, Dalhousie and Peters, the firm of London solicitors of which
I am now a senior partner. He wanted to redraft his will, and since
he was too unwell to travel down to London, I agreed to stop off at
his lodgings at Ayr on my way back from a fishing holiday in
Scotland. He was a quite affable gentleman, a semi-invalid, and
pleased that I had come to visit him myself. Though he was hardly
more than fifty years old at that time, ten years younger than I was
myself, he was as frail as an old lady of eighty.

He told me something about his life. He seemed to be an educated man, and he spoke with a marked Scots accent, although his
father, James Macfadden, had been born and had lived for many
years in Australia. He told me that he had no close relatives at all
except his sister, Jean Paget. She had married a Captain Arthur

Paget, who after World War I had been employed on a rubber plantation in Malaya, where their two children, Donald and Jean, had been born in 1918 and 1921 respectively. Arthur Paget had recently been killed in a motor accident in Malaya, and his wife had returned to England to make a home near Southampton for the two children.

Under the terms of Mr. Macfadden's will, his sister was his sole heir. "But you must understand that Arthur Paget was alive when I made that will," the old gentleman explained to me. "I expected that he would be there to guide her in matters of business."

He seemed to have a fixed idea that all women were incapable of looking after money. Accordingly, he wanted to create a trust to ensure that her son, Donald—at that time a schoolboy—should inherit the estate intact after his mother's death.

"Supposing," I said, "that Donald and his mother should die before you? The estate would then pass to the girl, Jean. I take it the trust would terminate when she reached her majority?"

"Ye mean," he asked, "when she became twenty-one?" He shook his head. "I think that would be most imprudent, Mr. Strachan. A lassie of that age is at the mercy of her sex. I would want the trust to continue till she was forty, at the very least."

I stated my own view that twenty-five would be a reasonable age, and very reluctantly he receded to thirty-five, a position from which I could not budge him.

I went back to London to draft the will, which I sent to him for signature. I never saw my client again.

It had been my custom to take a fortnight's fishing holiday each spring in Scotland with my wife, and I thought that the next year I would again call on Mr. Macfadden. But in the winter of 1935 Lucy died. We had been married for twenty-seven years and—well, I hadn't the heart to go back to Scotland.

One has to make a clean break at a time like that. I sold our house on Wimbledon Common and took a flat in Buckingham Gate, just across the park from my club in Pall Mall. Work all day, lunch at my desk, to the club for dinner and a rubber of bridge. There soon was another interest: the war. I became a civil defense warden, and I was on duty in my district of Westminster all through the London blitz and the long years of war that followed it. In those years I never took a holiday. I doubt if I slept more than five hours in any night. When finally peace came in 1945, my hair was white and my head shaky and I had definitely joined the ranks of the old men.

That, then, was the background to the telegram I got in 1948 informing me of Douglas Macfadden's death.

I sat at my desk, reread the telegram, and put in a call to Ayr. Mrs. Doyle, the landlady who had looked after my client's needs for many years, knew of no relations who might handle the funeral arrangements; I should have to go to Ayr myself. I had a talk with Lester Robinson, my partner, cleared my desk, and took the sleeper up to Glasgow after dinner that night. In the morning I went down in a slow train to Ayr.

At the Balmoral Hotel, I found the landlord and his wife in obvious distress; they had been fond of their lodger of many years. I made arrangements for the funeral. Then I settled down to look through the papers in Macfadden's desk. I found a letter from his sister written from Southampton seven years earlier, in 1941, which revealed significant news about the children. Both of them were in Malaya at that time. The boy, Donald, who must have been twenty-three years old then, was working on a rubber plantation near Kuala Selangor. His sister, Jean, had gone out to join him in the winter of 1939, and was working in an office in Kuala Lumpur.

At about five o'clock I put in a call to my partner in London. "Lester," I said, "I have arranged the funeral for day after tomorrow. The only relations I know of used to live in or near Southampton. In 1941 the deceased's sister, Mrs. Arthur Paget, was at 17 Saint Ronans Road, Bassett—that's just by Southampton somewhere. She had two children, Donald and Jean, but they were both in Malaya then. I wouldn't waste much time looking for them, but there were some Paget relations in the district, including the parents of Arthur Paget. Would you do what you can to find them and tell them about the funeral?"

Lester came on the telephone to me next morning. "I've nothing very definite, I'm afraid, Noel," he said. "I did discover one thing. Mrs. Paget died of pneumonia in 1942, so she's out of it. There are seven other Pagets in the telephone directory, and they've nothing to do with your family. But one of them thinks Arthur Paget's parents are the Edward Pagets, who moved to North Wales after the first Southampton blitz."

"Any idea whereabouts in North Wales?" I asked.

"Not a clue," he said.

"Go on looking," I replied. "I've just been to the bank, and there is quite a sizable estate. We're the trustees, you know."

In fact, we found the heir without much difficulty. Young Harris, a clerk in our office, got a line on it within a week of my return to London, and presently we got a letter from a Miss Agatha Paget, who was headmistress of a girls' school in Wales. She was a sister of Arthur Paget and confirmed that his wife, Jean, had died in Southampton in 1942. She added that the son, Donald, had died while a prisoner of war in Southeast Asia. Her niece, Jean, however, was alive and was employed by a concern called Pack and Levy Ltd., whose address was The Hyde, Perivale, London, N.W.

I reached for the telephone directory and looked up Pack and Levy to find out what they did. Presently I got up from my desk and stood looking out of the window. I like to think a bit before taking any action. Then I went into Robinson's office.

"I've got the Macfadden heir," I said. "The daughter. The son's dead."

He laughed. "Bad luck. That means we're trustees for the estate until she's thirty-five. How old is she now?"

I calculated for a minute. "Twenty-six or twenty-seven."

"Old enough to make a packet of trouble for us."

"I know."

"Where is she?"

"She's employed with a firm of handbag manufacturers in Perivale," I said. "I'm just about to concoct a letter to her."

I went back to my room and sat for some time thinking out that letter; it seemed important to set a formal tone when writing to this young woman for the first time. Finally I wrote:

Dear Madam,

It is with regret that we have to inform you of the death of Mr. Douglas Macfadden at Ayr on January 21. As executors to his will we have experienced some difficulty in tracing the beneficiaries. If you are the daughter of Jean (née Macfadden) and Arthur Paget formerly resident in Southampton and in Malaya, you may be entitled to a share in the estate.

May we ask you to telephone for an appointment to discuss the matter further? It will be necessary for you to produce evidence of identity, such as your birth certificate, National Registration Identity Card, and any other documents that may occur to you.

I am,

Yours truly, for Owen, Dalhousie and Peters,

N. H. Strachan

She rang me up the next day. "Mr. Strachan, this is Miss Jean Paget." She had the voice of a well-trained secretary. "I have your letter. I wonder—do you work on Saturday mornings? I'm in a job, so Saturday would be the best day for me."

I replied, "Oh yes, we work on Saturday mornings. What time would be convenient for you?"

"Should we say ten thirty?"

She was shown into my office punctually at ten thirty on Saturday. She was a girl of medium height, dark-haired, good-looking in a quiet way; she had the tranquillity, the grace about her that you see frequently in women of Scottish descent. I got up and shook hands with her, and gave her the chair in front of my desk.

"Well, Miss Paget," I said. "I take it that you are the daughter of Arthur and Jean Paget, who lived in Southampton and Malaya?"

She nodded. "That's right. I've got my birth certificate and my mother's birth certificate, as well as her marriage certificate."

She took them from her bag and put them on my desk, with her identity card.

After reading these documents, I had no doubt that she was the person I was looking for. "Tell me, Miss Paget," I said. "Did you ever meet your uncle, Douglas Macfadden?"

She hesitated. "I couldn't honestly swear, but I think it must have been him that Mother took me to see once in Scotland, when I was eleven. We all went together, Mother and I and Donald."

"Is your brother still alive, Miss Paget?" I asked.

She shook her head. "He died in 1943, while he was a prisoner. He was taken by the Japs in Singapore when we surrendered, and then he was sent to the railway."

I was puzzled. "The railway?"

She looked at me coolly, and in her glance I saw tolerance for those who had stayed in England. "The railway that the Japs built between Siam and Burma. It was two hundred miles long, and one man died for every tie that was laid. Donald was one of them."

There was a little pause. "I am so sorry," I said at last. "Was there a death certificate?"

She stared at me. "I shouldn't think so."

"Oh. . . ." I leaned back in my chair and took up the will. "This is the will of Mr. Douglas Macfadden," I said. "I have a copy for you, Miss Paget, but I think I'd better tell you its terms in ordinary, nonlegal language." I then explained that since her mother and her brother had died, she would enjoy the income from the trust, and inherit it outright when she reached the age of thirty-five, in 1956. "You will appreciate that it is necessary to obtain legal evidence of your brother's death," I pointed out.

She hesitated. "Mr. Strachan, I understand that you want some proof that Donald is dead. But after this is done, do you mean that I inherit everything that Uncle Douglas left?"

"Broadly speaking—yes," I replied.

"What is the amount?"

I picked up a slip of paper. "After paying death duties and legacies," I said carefully, "the residuary estate would be worth about fifty-three thousand pounds at present-day prices."

She stared at me. "Fifty-three thousand pounds?" I nodded. "How much a year would that yield?"

I glanced at the figures on the slip before me. "Invested in trustee stocks, as at present, minus income tax, you would have about nine hundred pounds a year to spend, Miss Paget."

"Oh. . . ." There was a long silence; she sat staring at the desk;

then she looked up at me and smiled. "It takes a bit of getting used to. This means I need never work again—unless I want to. But I don't know what I'd do if I didn't have to go to the office," she said. "I haven't any other life. . . ."

"Then I should keep on going to the office," I observed. "I'm an old man now, Miss Paget, and I've learned one thing—it's never very wise to do anything in a great hurry. If I may offer my advice, I should continue in your present employment for the time being and should refrain from talking about your legacy just yet. For one thing, it will be some weeks before you gain possession of the income from the estate. Tell me, where do you live, Miss Paget?"

She said, "I've got a bed-sitting-room at 43 Campion Road, just off Ealing Common. It's quite convenient . . . though I don't know very many people in London. I was a sort of prisoner of war in Malaya for three and a half years. Then when I came home two years ago, I got this job with Pack and Levy."

I made a note of her address upon my pad. "Well, Miss Paget, I will consult the War Office on Monday morning and obtain the evidence about your brother as quickly as I can. As soon as I get that, I shall submit the will for probate. Tell me his number and unit." She did so, and I wrote them down.

She looked up at me. "Tell me about this trust," she said. "I'm afraid I'm not very good at legal matters."

"Of course. The object of a trust is this. The trustees—in this case, myself and my partner—undertake to do their best to preserve the capital intact and hand it over to the legatee—to you—when the trust expires."

She thought for a minute, and then she said, "So you're going to look after the money for me till I'm thirty-five and give me the interest to spend in the meantime? Nine hundred a year . . . How do you get paid for doing all this, Mr. Strachan?"

I smiled. "That is a very prudent question, Miss Paget. You will find a clause in the will which entitles us to charge for our professional services against the income from the trust."

She said unexpectedly, "I couldn't ask for anybody better. I know I'm going to be in very good hands, Mr. Strachan."

"I hope so, Miss Paget. At times you may find this trust irksome.
I shall do my utmost to prevent it from becoming so. You will see
in the will that the trustees have the power to realize capital for
the benefit of the legatee in cases where they are satisfied that it
would be genuinely to her advantage."

"You mean, if I really needed a lot of money—for an operation
or something—you could let me have it, if you approved?"

"Yes, certainly." She was quick, that girl. "I think that is a very
good example." I went on. "Inevitably this legacy is going to make
an upset in your condition of life, and if I can do anything to help
you in the transition, I should be only too pleased." I handed her
the copy of the will. "Well, there is the will, and I suggest you take
it away and read it. I am sure there will be a great many questions
to which you will want answers."

She said, "I know there'll be all sorts of things, but I can't think
of them now. It's all so sudden."

I turned to my engagement diary. "Well, suppose we meet again
next week. What time do you leave your office, Miss Paget?"

"Five o'clock."

"Would six o'clock on Wednesday evening suit you, then?"

"Isn't it a bit late, Mr. Strachan? Don't you want to get home?"

I said absently, "I only go to the club. . . . Perhaps if you are
doing nothing after that you might like to come on to the club and
have dinner in the ladies' annex. I'm afraid it's rather subdued, but
the food is good."

She smiled and said warmly, "I'd love to do that, Mr. Strachan.
It's very kind of you to ask me."

I got to my feet. "Very well, then, Miss Paget—six o'clock on
Wednesday. And in the meantime, don't do anything in a great
hurry. It never pays to be impetuous."

She went away, and I cleared my desk and took a taxi to the
club for lunch. Afterward I walked aimlessly up St. James's Street
and wondered how that lovely young woman was spending her
weekend. Was she out with a young man? She would have plenty
of men now to choose from, because she was a very marriageable
girl. Indeed, considering her appearance and her evident good

nature, I was rather surprised that she was not married already.

On Monday I telephoned the War Office and the Home Office about the procedure for establishing the death of a prisoner of war. I found that where a doctor was available who had attended the deceased in the prison camp, he could provide a certification of death. In this instance I learned that there was a general practitioner called Ferris, located at Beckenham, who had been a doctor in Camp 206 in the Takunan district on the Burma-Siam railway.

I rang him up next morning and went to see him that evening.

I got to Ferris just as he was seeing the last of his patients. He was a cheerful, fresh-faced man not more than thirty-five years old.

"Lieutenant Paget," he said thoughtfully. "I remember Donald Paget quite well. Yes, I can write a death certificate, though I don't suppose it'll do him much good."

"It will help his sister," I remarked. "There is a question of an inheritance."

He reached for a pad of forms. "I wonder if she's got as much guts as her brother."

"Was he a good chap?"

He nodded. "He was delicate-looking, but a very good officer, the sort the men like. It was a great loss when he went."

"What did he die of?"

He held his pen poised over the paper. "Well, I don't really know. He'd recovered from enough to kill a dozen ordinary men. . . . He had a huge tropical ulcer on his left leg that we were treating—he got that because he was one of those chaps who won't report sick while they can walk. Well, while he was in hospital with the ulcer, he got cerebral malaria. We had nothing to treat that with except our own quinine solutions for intravenous injection; a frightful risk, but there was nothing else to do. Paget got over it quite well. Then cholera went through the camp. I never want to see a show like that again. We'd got *nothing*—no drugs and no equipment. But would you believe it, he got over his cholera, and about a week after that he just died in the night. Heart, I fancy. I'll put down for cause of death—cholera. There you are, sir. I'm sorry you had to come all this way."

I took the certificate, and on the ride back to London I sat thinking how easy by comparison my own war had been.

When Jean Paget came to see me on Wednesday evening, I went through one or two formal matters connected with the estate. Then I said, "I've got your brother's death certificate."

"What did Donald die of, Mr. Strachan?"

I hesitated. I did not want to tell so young a woman the unpleasant story I had heard. "The cause of death was cholera." I felt that I must say something else. "I had a long talk with the doctor who attended him. He died quite peacefully, in his sleep."

She stared at me. "That's not the way you die of cholera. Did he have anything else?"

Well, then, of course there was nothing for it but to tell her everything I knew. I was amazed at her knowledge of such things as tropical ulcers, until I recollected that she had been a prisoner of the Japanese in Malaya, too.

I turned the conversation back to legal matters, and presently we got a taxi and went over to the club to dine.

I had a reason for entertaining her, that first evening. I knew practically nothing of her education or her background. I wanted to give her a good dinner with a little wine and get her talking; it was going to make my job as trustee a great deal easier if I knew what her interests were and how her mind worked. I ordered her a sherry. "What did you do over the weekend?" I asked as we sat down. "Did you go out and celebrate?"

She shook her head. "I didn't do anything much. I'd arranged to meet a girl from the office for lunch on Saturday, so we did that."

"Did you tell her about your good fortune?"

"I haven't told anybody. It seems such an improbable story," she said, laughing. "I don't know that I really believe in it myself."

"You'll believe in it when we send you your first monthly check. It will be about seventy-five pounds. I take it that you will hardly wish to go on with your present employment?"

"No. . . ." She sat thinking for a minute. "I wouldn't mind a bit going on with Pack and Levy, if it was a job worth doing. But— well, it's not. We make ladies' shoes and handbags, and small attaché cases—the sort that sell for thirty guineas in Bond Street to women with more money than sense. It's all right if you've got to earn your living, and it's been interesting, learning all about that trade. But with all this money, one ought to do something more worthwhile . . . except I've got no profession. I never had any real education—taking a degree, or anything like that."

"May I ask a very personal question, Miss Paget?"

"Of course."

"Do you think it likely that you will marry in the near future?"

She smiled. "No, Mr. Strachan, I don't think it's very likely that I shall marry at all."

"Well, had you thought about taking a university course?"

Her eyes opened wide. "No, I'm not clever enough." She shook her head. "I couldn't go back to school. I'm much too old."

I smiled at her. "Not quite such an old woman as all that."

For some reason the little compliment fell flat. "When I compare myself with some of the girls in the office," she said quietly, and there was no laughter in her now, "I know I'm about seventy."

To ease the situation I suggested that we go in to dinner. When the ordering was done I said, "Miss Paget, tell me what happened to you in the war. You were out in Malaya, weren't you?"

She nodded. "I had a job in an office, with the Kuala Perak Plantation Company. That was the company my father worked for, you know. Donald was with them, too."

"Were you a prisoner?"

"A sort of prisoner," she said.

"In a camp?"

"No," she replied. "They left us pretty free." And then she changed the conversation very positively and said, "What happened to you, Mr. Strachan? Were you in London all the time?"

I could not press her to talk about her war experiences, so I told her about mine—such as they were. Then I found myself telling her about my two sons, Harry in his submarine on the China Station and Martin in his oil company in Basra, and their war records, and their families. "I'm a grandfather three times over," I said ruefully. "There's going to be a fourth soon, I believe."

445

Presently I got the conversation back onto her own affairs. I knew of several charitable appeals that would have found a first-class shorthand typist, unpaid, a perfect godsend, and I told her so. "Surely, if a thing is really worthwhile, it'll pay," she said. She evidently had quite a strong business instinct.

"Well, you can take your time," I said. "You don't have to do anything in a hurry."

She laughed at me. "I believe that's your guiding rule in life—never do anything in a hurry."

I smiled. "You might have a worse rule than that."

With the coffee after dinner I found out that she had little social life, which seemed a pity to me.

"Would you like to come to the opera one night?" I asked.

She seemed pleased. "Would I understand it?"

"Oh yes. I'll pick something light, and in English."

She said, "It's terribly nice of you to ask me, but I'm sure you'd be much happier playing bridge."

"Not a bit," I said. "I haven't been to the opera for years."

"Well, of course I'd love to come," she said.

We sat talking till half past nine, when she got up to go. I went with her, because she was leaving from St. James's Park Station, and I didn't care about the thought of her walking across the park alone at night. At the station, she put out her hand.

"Thank you so much, Mr. Strachan, for the dinner, and for everything you're doing for me," she said.

"It has been a very great pleasure to me, Miss Paget," I replied, and I meant it.

She hesitated, and then she said, smiling, "Mr. Strachan, we're going to have a good deal to do with each other. My name is Jean. I'll go crackers if you keep on calling me Miss Paget."

"You can't teach an old dog new tricks," I said awkwardly.

She laughed. "You can try."

"I'll bear it in mind," I said. "Can you manage all right now?"

"Of course. Good night, Mr. Strachan."

"Good night," I said, lifting my hat.

In the following weeks during probate of the will I took her to a good many things. We went to the opera, to the Royal Albert Hall, and to art exhibitions. In the course of these excursions she came several times to my flat in Buckingham Gate, and made tea when we came in from some outing. I had never entertained a lady in that flat before except my daughters-in-law.

The will was probated by March, and I was able to send her her first check. She did not give up her job at once. She wanted to build up a small reserve of capital; moreover, she had not yet made up her mind what she wanted to do.

That was the position one Sunday in April. I had arranged a jaunt to Hampton Court for her that day. And then it rained.

She came to the flat just before lunch. We stood watching the rain beat against the palace stables opposite, wondering what we should do that afternoon. She seemed to be thinking about other matters. Over coffee before the fire it came out. "I've made up my mind what I want to do first of all, Mr. Strachan," she said. "I know you're going to think this very odd. You may think it very foolish of me, but—it's what I want to do. I want to go back to Malaya, Mr. Strachan. To dig a well."

I WAS completely taken aback. Jean must have felt reproof in my silence, because she said, "I know it's a funny thing to want to do. May I tell you about it?" She paused. "It all seems so remote, as though it happened to another person, years ago."

"Isn't it better to leave it so?" I asked.

She shook her head. "Not now, that I've got this money. You've been so very kind to me. I do want you to understand."

HER life, she said, had fallen into three parts. First, she had been a schoolgirl living with her mother in Southampton. Of the period before that, in Malaya, she had only confused memories, because they had left when she was eleven. Jean and her brother, Donald, lived the life of English children—school, holidays, and the great annual excitement of three weeks on the Isle of Wight in August. They all spoke Malay, first as a joke and as a secret family language, but later for a definite reason. After Arthur Paget's death, the directors of the Kuala Perak Plantation Company wrote to the widow offering to keep a position for Donald as soon as he became nineteen. That shrewd Scotswoman, their mother, saw to it that the children did not forget Malay.

What Jean remembered best of all about her childhood in Southampton was the ice-skating rink. It was connected in her mind inevitably with Waldteufel's "The Skaters" waltz. "It was a lovely place," she said, staring into the fire. "I suppose it wasn't much, really—a converted wooden building—but the music, the clean, swift movement, all the boys and girls, the colored lights . . ."

She turned to me. "You know, out in Malaya, when we were dying of malaria and dysentery, shivering with fever in the rain, and nowhere to go because no one wanted us, I used to think about the rink at Southampton more than anything. It was a sort of symbol of the life that used to be—I promised myself that one day I would go back and skate at the rink again." She paused. "Directly I returned to England I went to Southampton, and the rink had been blitzed. It was just a blackened, burned-out shell. I stood there on the pavement with the taxi waiting behind me and my skates in my hand, and I couldn't keep from crying with disappointment. I don't know what the taxi driver thought of me."

Her brother had gone to Malaya in 1937, when Jean was sixteen, and she entered a commercial school in Southampton, where she earned a shorthand typist's diploma. She then worked for about a year in a solicitor's office. During that year a future for her in Malaya was taking shape. The chairman of Kuala Perak was very satisfied with Donald's progress on the plantation, and at Mrs. Paget's suggestion, Jean was given a job in the head office at Kuala Lumpur, two hundred miles northwest of Singapore. The war broke out while all this was in progress, and to begin with, in England, it was a phony war. There seemed no reason to upset Jean's career, so she left for Malaya in the winter of 1939.

For nearly two years she had a marvelous time. Her office was near the secretariat, a huge building erected in more spacious days to demonstrate the power of the British rule. It faced a club across the cricket ground, with a typical English church to one side. Here everybody lived a very English life, with tropical amenities: plenty of leisure, plenty of games, and plenty of servants. Jean got a room in a private hotel for unmarried girls.

"It was just too good to be true," she said. "There was a dance or a party every single night. One had to beg off doing something in order to find time to write a letter home."

When war came in the Pacific, although her brother was called up to serve in Malaya, it hardly registered as any immediate danger with her or with any of her set. December 7, 1941, which brought Japan and America into the war, meant no interruption in the round of parties, but young men began to appear in uniform. Even when the Japanese landed in the north of Malaya there was little thought of danger in Kuala Lumpur; three hundred miles of mountain and jungle was itself a barrier against invasion from the north, and it didn't mean a thing to a girl who had just rejected her first proposal.

As the Japanese advanced down the peninsula through jungle no troops had ever penetrated, the situation became serious. Jean's chief called her in one morning and told her that the office was closing. She was to pack a suitcase and take the first train down to Singapore. Five other girls in the office got the same orders.

The Japanese at that time were reported to be near Ipoh, about a hundred miles to the north. Jean went to the bank and drew out all her money, about six hundred Straits dollars. She did not go to the railway station; by that time the line was completely blocked with military traffic coming up to the front. Instead she took a bus to Batu Tasik, about twenty miles northwest of Kuala Lumpur, to see some friends, the Hollands.

Mr. Holland was a man of forty, the manager of a tin mine. He lived in a pleasant bungalow near the mine with his wife, Eileen, and their children—Freddie, aged seven, Jane, four, and Robin, ten months old. Eileen Holland was a motherly woman between thirty

449

and thirty-five years old. The Hollands never went to parties or to dances; they stayed quietly at home and let the world go by. They had invited Jean to stay with them soon after she arrived. She had found their company restful and had visited them several times. In Kuala Lumpur, the day before, she had heard that Mr. Holland had brought his family into the station but had been unable to get them on the train. Jean felt she could not leave without offering to help them; Eileen Holland, though a good mother and a first-rate housewife, was singularly unfitted to travel with three children in the turmoil of evacuation.

In Batu Tasik, Jean found Mrs. Holland alone with the children. All trucks and cars belonging to the mine had been taken by the army, and the Hollands were left with their old Austin Twelve with one tire worn down to the canvas and one with a large blister on the wall. This was the only vehicle they had for their evacuation to Singapore. Mr. Holland had gone into Kuala Lumpur at dawn to get new tires, and he had not come back.

In the bungalow, everything was in confusion. The amah had left, and the house was full of half-packed suitcases. Freddie had been in the pond and was all muddy, Jane was sitting on her pot among the suitcases, crying, and Mrs. Holland was nursing the baby and cooking lunch and attending to Jane and worrying about her husband all at the same time. Jean turned her attention to Freddie and Jane, and presently they all had lunch.

Bill Holland did not return till nearly sunset. He had had to walk the last five miles for lack of transport, and he was soaked to the skin and utterly exhausted. In addition he came empty-handed. All tire stocks in Kuala Lumpur had been commandeered. However, a native bus was leaving the city for Singapore at eight in the morning, and he had reserved seats on that.

Jean stayed with them that night, wakeful and uneasy. By morning the Japanese advance patrols had infiltrated behind the British forces as far as Slim River, less than fifty miles away.

The Hollands packed the Austin in the first gray light; with three adults, three children, and all the luggage, the car was well loaded down. Before they had gone two miles the tire that was showing canvas burst. The spare, the one with the blister, took them another half mile before going flat. In desperation Mr. Holland drove on; the wire wheel collapsed after another two miles, and the Austin had run to its end. They were about fifteen miles from Kuala Lumpur, and it was seven thirty.

There was no assistance to be had, and it seemed best to get back to their bungalow. They set out to walk the five miles, leaving the luggage in the car. They reached home exhausted.

An hour later a truck stopped at the bungalow and a young officer came hurrying in. "You've got to leave this place," he said. "I'll take you in the truck. How many of you are there?"

"Six, counting the children," Holland said. "Can you take us to Kuala Lumpur? Our car broke down."

"No, I can't," the officer replied. "The Japs were at Kerling when I last heard. They may be farther south by now." Kerling was only twenty miles away. "I'm taking you to Panong. You'll get a boat from there down to Singapore." He did not have time to return with the truck for their luggage.

Kuala means the mouth of a river, and Kuala Panong is a small town at the entrance to the Panong River. By the time the truck reached there, it was loaded with about forty men, women, and children picked up for evacuation from the surrounding estates.

The truck halted at the district commissioner's office and the DC came out. "God," he said quietly as he looked at the women and children, and the few men among them. "Well, drive them to the accounts office over there; they must sit on the veranda for an hour or two and I'll try to get something fixed up for them. Tell them not to wander about too much." He turned back into the office. "I can send them down in fishing boats, I think," he said. "That's the best I can do. I haven't got a launch."

The party were unloaded at the accounts office. Jean and Bill Holland left Eileen sitting on the shady veranda with the children about her, and walked into the village to buy what they could to replace the luggage they had lost. They were able to get a feeding bottle for the baby, a little quinine, some salts for dysentery, two tins of biscuits and three of meat. Jean got herself needles and thread and, seeing a large canvas haversack, she bought that, too. She carried that haversack for the next three years.

They went back to the veranda. Toward sunset the lighthouse keepers at the river mouth telephoned the DC to say that the customs launch—a large diesel-powered vessel—was coming into the river. The DC's face lit up; here was the solution to his problems. The launch could take all his evacuees down the coast out of harm's way. He walked down to the quay to meet the vessel. As she came around the bend in the river, he saw with a sick heart that she was loaded with troops, small stocky men in gray-green uniforms, with rifles and bayonets taller than themselves.

The Japanese rushed ashore and occupied the place without a shot. The evacuees sat numbly on the veranda. Facing leveled rifles and bayonets, they were ordered to give up all fountain pens, wristwatches, and rings. They did so silently, and suffered no other molestation.

When night had fallen, an officer came and inspected them in the light of a hurricane lamp, a couple of soldiers hard on his heels with rifles at the ready. Most of the children started crying. The inspection finished, he made a little speech in broken English. "Now you are prisoners," he said. "You stay here tonight, tomorrow you go to prisoner camp perhaps. You do good things, obedience to orders, you will receive good from Japanese soldiers. You do bad things, you will be shot directly. So, do good things always. When officer come, you stand up and bow, always. That is good thing. Now you sleep."

Kuala Panong lies amid mangrove swamps, where the mosquitoes are intense. All night the children moaned fretfully, preventing what sleep might have been possible for the adults. Jean dozed a little and woke at dawn stiff and aching and with swollen face and arms. The prisoners were in a very unhappy state.

No food was provided that morning. The prisoners were taken to the DC's office, where a Japanese captain, whom Jean was to know later as Captain Yoniata, sat with a lieutenant, who was making notes. At the end of the interrogation the captain said, "Men go to prisoner camp today, womans and childs stays here. Thank you."

They had feared this, but had not expected it to come so soon. Holland asked, "Where will the women and children be sent?"

The officer said, "The Imperial Japanese Army do not make war on womans and childs. Perhaps not go to camp at all, if they do good things, perhaps live in homes."

It is usual in war for men to be interned in separate camps from women and children, but it was hard to bear. Jean felt her presence was unwanted with the Hollands, and sat alone on the veranda. One thing was certain: if they were to spend another night there, she must get some mosquito repellent. She remembered a chemist's shop in the village from yesterday's visit.

She attracted the sentry's attention and pointed to her mosquito bites; then she pointed to the village, and stepped down from the veranda to the ground. Immediately his bayonet advanced toward her; she got back onto the veranda in a hurry.

There was another way: the latrine behind the building, where there was no sentry because a wall prevented any exit. Jean moved out of the back door, sheltered from view. Some native children were playing in the yard.

She called softly in Malay. "Girl. You, you girl. Come here."

The child came toward her; she was about twelve years old. Jean asked, "Do you know the shop where a Chinese sells medicine?"

The child nodded. "Chan Kok Fuan."

"Go to Chan Kok Fuan, and I will give you ten cents. Say that the *mem* has *nyamok* bites"—she showed her bites—"and he should bring ointments here, and he will sell many to the *mems*."

The child nodded and went off. Jean went back to the veranda and waited; presently the Chinese man appeared carrying a tray loaded with little tubes and pots. He gestured to the sentry, indicating his wish to sell his wares. After some hesitation the sentry agreed. Jean got six tubes of repellent, and the rest was swiftly taken by the other women.

Presently a Japanese orderly brought two buckets of a thin fish soup and another half full of boiled rice, dirty and unappetizing. There were no bowls or utensils. There was nothing to be done but to eat as best they could.

That afternoon the men were separated from their families. Bill Holland turned from his wife, his eyes moist. "Good-by Jean, good luck." And then, "Stick with them if you can, won't you?"

She nodded. "I will. We'll all be in the same camp together."

The seven men were marched off under guard.

The remaining party consisted of eleven married women and two others—Jean and an anemic young woman called Ellen Forbes. There were nineteen children, varying in age from a girl of fourteen to babies in arms; thirty-two persons in all. Most of the women could speak no language but their own; a few, including Eileen Holland, could speak enough Malay to control their servants, but no more. They stayed on the veranda for forty-one days.

The second night was similar to the first, except that the doors of the accounts office were opened and they were allowed to use the rooms. There was a second meal of fish soup in the evening, but no beds, no blankets, no mosquito nets were provided. Some of the group had blankets, but there were far too few to go around. Mrs. Horsefall, a stern-faced woman, asked to see Captain Yoniata and protested the harsh conditions, and asked for beds and nets.

"No nets, no beds," he said. "Very sorry for you. All Japanese sleep on mat on floor. You put away proud thoughts, very bad."

"But we're English," Mrs. Horsefall said indignantly. "We don't sleep on the floor like animals!"

His eyes hardened; the sentries gripped her arms, and he hit her four stinging blows on the face with the flat of his hand. "Very bad thoughts," he said, and turned on his heel and left.

Undaunted, Mrs. Horsefall asked for a water supply the next morning. She pointed out that washing was necessary for the babies and desirable for everyone. A barrel was brought into the smallest office that afternoon and was kept filled by coolies; they turned this room into a bathroom and washhouse. In those early days most of the women had money, and following the example of Chan Kok Fuan, the shopkeepers of the village came to sell to the prisoners.

Gradually they grew accustomed to their hardships. The children quickly learned to sleep on the floor without complaint; the younger women took a good deal longer, but the women over thirty seldom slept for more than half an hour without waking in pain.

The food issued to them was the bare minimum to support life—fish soup and rice, twice a day. Later, Captain Yoniata added to the diet a bucket of tea in the afternoon, as a concession to English manners. They received no medical attention. At the end of a week dysentery attacked them, and the nights were made hideous by screaming children stumbling with their mothers to the latrine. Malaria was always in the background, held in check by the quinine they could still buy from Chan Kok Fuan.

Jean shared with Mrs. Holland the care of the three Holland children. She suffered from a feeling of lassitude, but she slept soundly most nights until wakened. Eileen Holland, who was older, could not sleep so readily upon the floor. She lost weight rapidly.

On the thirty-fifth day Esmé Harrison, a child of eight, died. She had grown weak and thin from dysentery; she slept little and cried a great deal. Then for two days she ran a high malarial temperature. Mrs. Horsefall told Captain Yoniata that the child must see a doctor and go to a hospital. He said he was very sorry, but there was no hospital and the doctors were all fighting with the victorious Imperial Japanese Army. That evening Esmé had convulsions, and at dawn she died.

She was buried that morning in the Moslem cemetery behind the village. Her mother and one other woman were allowed to attend the burial. They read a little of the service out of a prayer book before the uncomprehending soldiers and Malays, and then it was over. Life went on as before in the accounts office, but the children now had nightmares of death to follow them to sleep.

At the end of six weeks, as Captain Yoniata faced them after the morning inspection, the women stood worn and draggled, holding the children by the hand. Many adults and most of the children were thin and ill. He said, "Ladies, Imperial Japanese Army has entered Singapore. All Malaya is free. Now prisoner camps are at Singapore and you go there. I am very sad your life here has been uncomfortable, but now will be better. Tomorrow you start to Kuala Lumpur. From there you go by train to Singapore. In Singapore you will be very happy. Thank you."

From Panong to Kuala Lumpur is forty-seven miles; it took a minute for his meaning to sink in. Then Mrs. Horsefall said, "How are we to travel to Kuala Lumpur? Will there be a truck?"

He said, "Very sorry, no truck. You walk, easy journeys, not more than you can go each day. Japanese soldier help you."

"We can't walk, with these children. We *must* have a truck."

His eyes hardened. "You walk," he said.

"But what are we to do with all the luggage?" she asked.

"You carry what you can. Presently the luggage is sent after you." He turned and went away.

The women, in desperation, sorted helplessly through their possessions, trying to make packs of the essentials. Mrs. Horsefall, a former schoolmistress, moved among them, helping and advising. She had one child herself, a boy of ten, John. It was possible for a woman to carry the necessities for one child, but the position of those with several children was bad indeed.

Having lost their luggage, Jean and Mrs. Holland had less of a problem. What extra clothing they had could go into Jean's haversack. They had acquired two blankets and some food bowls and cutlery, which they made into a bundle; one would carry the haversack and one the bundle. The biggest problem was their shoes, which were quite unsuitable for marching.

That evening, when they were alone, Mrs. Holland said quietly, "My dear, I shan't give up, but I don't think I can walk very far. I've been so poorly lately."

"It'll be all right," Jean assured her, although deep in her mind she knew that it was not going to be all right at all.

Soon after dawn Captain Yoniata appeared with a sergeant and three privates—who were to be their guard on the journey. "Today you walk to Ayer Penchis," he said. "Fine day, easy journey. Good dinner when you get there. You will be very happy."

Jean asked Mrs. Horsefall, "How far is Ayer Penchis?"

"Twelve or fifteen miles. Some of us will never get that far."

The little group walked down the tarmac road in the hot sun, seeking the shade of trees. Jean walked with Mrs. Holland, carrying the bundle of blankets slung across her shoulders as the hotter and heavier load, and leading the four-year-old, Jane, by the hand. Seven-year-old Freddie walked beside his mother, who carried the baby, Robin, and the haversack. Ahead of them strolled the Japanese sergeant; behind came the three privates.

They went very slowly, seldom covering more than a mile and a half an hour, with the frequent halts as a mother and child retired into the bushes. The journey became one of endless waits by the roadside in the hot sun, for the sergeant refused to move on while any of the party remained behind. Within the limits of their duty the Japanese soldiers were humane and helpful; before many hours had passed, each was carrying a child.

The sergeant had made it very clear that there would be no food or shelter till they got to Ayer Penchis. As that first day wore on they began to suffer from their feet, the older women especially; many of them were limping painfully. Jean watched some of the children go barefoot, then took her own shoes off. She got along better, but Eileen Holland refused to try it.

Shortly before dark they stumbled into Ayer Penchis, a Malay village which housed the labor for a number of rubber plantations. The women were herded into a palm-thatch barn, where they sank down in a stupor of fatigue. Presently the soldiers brought a bucket of tea and a bucket of rice and dried fish. They drank cup after cup of the tea, but few had any appetite.

With the last of the light Jean strolled outside and looked around. The guards were busy cooking over a small fire; she asked the sergeant if she might go into the village. He nodded; away from Captain Yoniata discipline was lax.

In the village she bought a dozen mangoes. At Kuala Panong there had been little fruit. She went back to the barn and distributed her mangoes to the others. They were such a success that she went back and got four dozen more. When the soldiers came in with a bucket of tea, they got a mango each for their pains. Thus refreshed, the women were able to eat most of the rice. They slept, exhausted and ill, though the barn was full of rats. In the morning it was found that several of the children had been bitten.

It did not seem possible they could march again, but the sergeant forced them on to a place called Asahan, ten miles away. It was a shorter trip than the one the day before, but it took as long. The delay was chiefly due to Mrs. Collard. She was a heavy woman of about forty-five with two children, Harry and Ben, aged ten and seven. She suffered from malaria and dysentery, and was very weak; she had to stop and rest every ten minutes. The younger women took turns walking beside her to help her along.

By afternoon her ruddy face had gone a mottled blue, and she was complaining of pains in her chest. When they finally reached Asahan she was practically incapable of walking. Their accommodation was another barn. They half carried Mrs. Collard inside and sat her up against the wall. One of the women fetched water and bathed her face, and then took the children outside to wash them. When she came back, Mrs. Collard had fallen over on her side and was unconscious. Half an hour later she died.

That evening Jean got more fruit for them, mangoes and bananas, and some sweets for the children. The Malay woman who supplied the sweets refused money. "No, *mem*," she said. "It is bad that Nippon soldiers treat you so. This is our gift." Jean went back and told the others what had happened, and it helped.

In the flickering light of the cooking fire outside the barn, Jean and Mrs. Horsefall held a conference with the sergeant, who spoke only a few words of English. They illustrated their meaning with pantomime. "Not walk tomorrow," they said. "Walk tomorrow, more women die. Rest tomorrow. Walk one day, rest one day."

"Tomorrow," he said, "woman, in earth."

They seized upon this as an excuse. "Tomorrow bury woman in earth, stay here tomorrow."

Later he came to Jean, his face alight with intelligence. "Walk one day, sleep one day," he said. "Womans not die." She called Mrs. Horsefall, and they all nodded vigorously together, beaming with good nature; they gave him a banana as a token of esteem.

The effects of the march began to show that night in different forms. The women under thirty, and the children, were in most cases healthier than when they had left Panong; they were cheered by the easier discipline, and stimulated by the exercise and by the improvement in the diet brought by fruit. For the older women exhaustion outweighed any benefits; they lay listlessly in the darkness, too tired to eat and even, in many cases, to sleep.

In the morning the Malay headman showed them where they could bury Mrs. Collard—near a rubbish heap. The sergeant got two coolies to dig a shallow grave, and they lowered Mrs. Collard into it, covered by a blanket. Mrs. Horsefall read from the prayer book. Afterward they took away the blanket, because they could not spare it, and the earth was filled in. Jean found a carpenter who made a little wooden cross, and on it they wrote "Julia Collard" and the date of death with an indelible pencil.

Captain Yoniata turned up at midday, driving the district commissioner's car. He got out and abused the sergeant for some minutes in Japanese, then turned to the women. "Why you not walk? Very bad thing. You not walk, no food."

Mrs. Horsefall faced him. "Mrs. Collard died last night. We buried her this morning, over there. If you make us walk every day like this, we shall all die. You know that."

He walked into the barn and stood looking at two or three women sitting there wearily. At the door he turned to Mrs. Horsefall. "Very sad woman die. Perhaps I get a truck in Kuala Lumpur. I will ask." He got into the car and drove away.

His words cheered the women quickly; they would finish the journey to Kuala Lumpur by truck; there would be no more marching. They would be sent by rail to Singapore, and there be put into a proper camp, where they could settle down and look after the children. A prison camp would have a doctor, too, and some kind of hospital for those who were really ill. Their appearance was a great concern to them that afternoon. Kuala Lumpur was their shopping town, where people knew them; they must get tidy before the truck came.

Captain Yoniata appeared again before sunset. He said, "You not go to Kuala Lumpur. English destroy bridges, so railway no good. You go to Port Swettenham, then ship to Singapore."

There was a stunned silence. Then Mrs. Horsefall asked, "Is there going to be a truck to take us to Port Swettenham?"

"Very sorry no truck. You walk slow, easy stages."

From Asahan to Port Swettenham is about thirty miles. She said, "Captain Yoniata, please be reasonable. Many of us are quite unfit to walk any farther. Can't you get some transport for the children, anyway?"

He said, "Englishwomans have proud thoughts, always. Too good to walk like Japanese womans. Tomorrow you walk to Bakri." He got into his car and went away; that was the last they saw of him.

The next morning they started on the road again. Only one private remained to guard them, with the sergeant. This was of no consequence to their security, because they had no desire to attempt to escape, but it reduced by half the help the guards had given them with the younger children.

Mrs. Holland was walking so badly that Jean now carried the baby, Robin. She went barefoot as before, and found that the easiest way to carry him was to perch him on her hip, as the Malay women did. Surprisingly, Robin was thriving the best of the three children; Freddie and Jane had become thin and gaunt.

They slept that night in a bungalow that had belonged to the manager of the Bakri tin mine, an Englishman. It had been occupied by troops of both sides and looted by the Malays; now little remained of it but the bare walls. Marvelously, however, the bath was still in order, and there was wood for the stove that heated water. The sergeant allowed them a day of rest, and they made the most of the hot water for doing laundry and for bathing. With the small improvement in conditions their spirits revived.

They marched next to a place called Dilit, following cart tracks through rubber plantations. The tracks were mostly in the shade of trees, and even the older women found the day bearable.

In the afternoon, while barefoot, Ben, the younger son of Mrs. Collard, trod on something that bit him with poisonous fangs and got away. Mrs. Horsefall sucked the wound to draw out the poison, but the foot swelled up quickly and the inflammation traveled to the knee. Mrs. Horsefall carried him for an hour, and the sergeant took him for the rest of the way. By the time they got to Dilit the ankle was enormous and the knee was stiff.

Dilit was a typical Malay village, the houses of wood and palm thatch raised about four feet from the ground on posts, leaving a space beneath where dogs slept and fowl nested. The thirty prisoners waited wearily while the sergeant negotiated with the Malay headman. The village could prepare a meal for the party, but the headman wanted payment, and he said flatly that there was no accommodation; finally he agreed to provide a house for them.

Jean secured a corner for their party, and Eileen Holland settled in with the children. A few feet away, Mrs. Horsefall was working on Ben Collard. With an old razor blade she cut the wound open a little, in spite of the child's screams; then she put in permanganate crystals, bound it up, and applied hot fomentations.

Jean wandered outside. Nearby, the headman was at the top of the steps leading to his house, squatting on his heels and smoking a long pipe; he was a gray-haired old man wearing a sarong and what once had been a khaki drill jacket. Jean crossed to him and said rather shyly in Malay, "I am sorry we have been forced to come here, and have made trouble for you."

He stood up and bowed. "It is no trouble. We are sorry to see *mems* in such a state." He invited her into the house, and she sat with him on the floor at the doorless entrance. Presently his wife came in bearing two cups of coffee without sugar or milk; Jean thanked her in Malay, and she smiled shyly and withdrew.

The headman said, "The Short One"—he meant the Japanese sergeant—"says you must stay here tomorrow."

Jean said, "We are too weak to march each day. It will help us a great deal. The sergeant says he can get money for the food."

"The Short Ones never pay for food. Nevertheless, you shall stay."

She said, "I can do nothing but thank you."

He raised his gray head. "It is written in the fourth sura of the Koran, 'Men's souls are naturally inclined to covetousness; but if ye be kind toward women and fear to wrong them, God is well acquainted with what ye do.'"

They rested all next day and then marched to Klang, three or four miles before Port Swettenham. Ben Collard was neither better nor worse: the leg was very much swollen. He had not eaten since the injury, for nothing would stay down; none of the children by that time had any reserves of strength. The headman of Dilit had directed the villagers to make a litter for Ben, and the prisoners took turns carrying it.

At Klang, they were installed in an empty schoolhouse and the sergeant went off to report to a Japanese encampment nearby.

Presently an officer arrived, at the head of a guard of six soldiers. This officer, whom they came to know as Major Nemu, spoke good English. He said, "Who are you people? What do you want here?"

They stared at him. Mrs. Horsefall said, "We are prisoners, from Panong. Captain Yoniata sent us to be put on a ship to Singapore."

"There are no ships here," he said. "You should have stayed in Panong."

"We were sent here," she repeated dully.

"They had no right to send you. There is no prison camp here."

The women stared at the major in blank despair. Mrs. Horsefall summoned up her flagging energy. "May we see a doctor? Some of us are very ill—one child especially."

"I will send a doctor. You will stay here for tonight, but cannot stay for long. I do not have sufficient rations for my own command, let alone for prisoners." He turned and walked back to the camp.

A new guard was placed on the schoolhouse; they never saw the friendly sergeant or the private again. A young Japanese doctor came and examined them one by one for infectious disease. They made him look at Ben Collard's leg and asked if he could be taken to the hospital. He shrugged his shoulders. "I inquire."

They stayed on in the schoolhouse. By the third day Ben was worse. Reluctantly the doctor ordered his removal to the hospital in a truck. On the sixth day they heard that he had died.

Jean Paget sat beside the fire in my sitting room; outside, the wind brought the London rain beating against the window.

"People who spent the war in prison camps have written a lot of books about what a bad time they had," she said quietly. "They don't know what it was like, *not* being in a camp."

THREE

THEY stayed in Klang eleven days. On the twelfth day Major Nemu assembled them at half an hour's notice, allocated one corporal to look after them, and told them to walk to Port Dickson; a ship might be there to take them to Singapore.

That was the middle of March, 1942. It took them till the end of the month to travel the more than fifty miles to Port Dickson. Mrs. Horsefall went down with malaria, and although she was walking again within a week, she never recovered her vigor. The leadership fell more and more upon Jean's shoulders.

By the time they reached Port Dickson their clothes were in a deplorable condition, and Jean took another step toward the costume of the Malay woman. Already she was barefoot; now she sold a little brooch to an Indian jeweler for thirteen dollars, and with two of the precious dollars she bought a sarong.

A sarong is a skirt made of a long strip of cloth; you wrap it around your waist, pleating in the surplus material. When you sleep you loosen it and use it as a covering. It is the coolest of all garments for the tropics. For a top, Jean cut down her cotton dress into a sort of blouse. At first the other women disapproved of this descent to native dress; later most of them followed her example as their clothes became worn.

There was no ship for them at Port Dickson. They were allowed to stay for about ten days; then the Japanese commander put them on the road to Seremban. He reasoned, apparently, that they were not his prisoners and so not his responsibility.

At Siliau, on the way to Seremban, tragedy touched the Holland family. Little Jane developed fever during the day's march. They gave her what quinine was left, but it was too late. Jean and Eileen Holland stayed with her, fighting for her life in a smelly shed where rats scurried around. On the second evening Jane died.

Mrs. Holland stood it better than Jean had expected. "It's God's will, my dear," she said. "He'll give her daddy strength to bear it when he hears, just as He's giving us all strength now." She stood dry-eyed beside the grave, and helped to make the little wooden cross. Jean woke later that night and heard her weeping.

They got to Seremban, which lies on the railway, about the middle of April, but there was no train to Singapore. Before they were forced upon the road again, they lost another member of the party. Ellen Forbes was the other young woman—the anemic one. She had come out to get married and hadn't, a circumstance that Jean could well understand by now. Ellen was vacuous, undisciplined, good-humored, and much too free with the Japanese troops. At Seremban they were accommodated in a schoolhouse which was full of soldiers. In the morning Ellen simply wasn't there, and they never saw her again. Jean's inquiries went unanswered.

Two days later they were marched to Tampin, where there was so little food they nearly starved. After urgent entreaties the commandant sent them under guard to the port of Malacca. But there was no ship and they plodded back to Tampin in despair. Then Judy Thomson died. To stay at Tampin meant more deaths, inevitably, so they asked to continue to Singapore on foot. A corporal was detailed to take them to Gemas.

On the way, Mrs. Horsefall developed dysentery and died in two days. It was in the middle of May. Mrs. Frith, a faded little woman past fifty who always seemed on the point of death, took over the care of Johnnie Horsefall, and it did her a world of good.

They got to Gemas three days later, and as usual they were put into the schoolhouse. The Japanese commandant, a Captain Nisui, came to inspect them. Jean explained that they were prisoners being marched to camp in Singapore.

He said, "Prisoner not go Singapore. Strict order. Where you come from?"

She told him, with the calmness born of many disappointments. "We've been traveling for over two months. Seven of us have died already—there were thirty-two when we were taken prisoner. Now there are twenty-five. We *must* get into a camp."

He said, "No more prisoner to Singapore. Very sorry for you, but too many prisoner there."

464

"Well, can we make ourselves a camp here and have a doctor?"

His eyes narrowed. "No prisoner stay here. I tell you where you go tomorrow."

The news meant very little to the women; they had fallen into the habit of living from day to day, and Singapore was very far away. "Looks as if they don't want us anywhere," Mrs. Price said heavily. "Bobbie, if I see you teasing Amy again I'll wallop you just like your father. Straight, I will."

Mrs. Frith said, "If they'd just let us alone, we could find a little village and live till it's all over." Jean stared at her. It was the germ of an idea, and she put it in the back of her mind.

Captain Nisui came the next day. "You go to Kuantan. Woman camp in Kuantan, very good," he said. "Kuantan on coast."

Behind Jean someone said, "It's hundreds of miles away, the east coast. Can we go there by railway?"

"Sorry, no railway. You walk, ten, fifteen miles each day. You will be very happy."

Jean said, "Seven of us are dead already, Captain. If you make us march to this place, more of us will die. Can we have a truck?"

"Sorry, no truck," he said. "You get there very soon."

From Gemas to Kuantan is about a hundred and seventy miles; there is no direct road. Jean reckoned it would take them six weeks, by far their longest journey.

They left next morning with a sergeant and a private as guard. The east coast railway wasn't in use and they walked along the railway line, which meant being in the sun most of each day.

They went on for a week, marching about ten miles every other day; then a fever and rash broke out among the children. At Bahau, four of them died: Harry Collard, Susan Fletcher, Doris Simmonds, who was only three, and Freddie Holland. By that time grief and mourning had ceased to trouble the group; death was a reality to be avoided and fought, but when it came—well, it was just one of those things.

Jean's concern now was for Mrs. Holland. With both the older children dead, she gave the baby, Robin, to his mother, not because she wanted to be rid of him but because she felt Eileen Holland

465

needed an interest. The experiment was not a great success; Eileen was so weak she could not carry Robin on the march or summon the energy to play with him. Moreover, the baby obviously preferred the younger woman to his mother, having been carried by her for so long.

"Seems as if he doesn't really belong to me," Mrs. Holland said. "You take him, dear. He likes being with you." From that time on they shared the baby; he got his rice and soup from Eileen, but he got his fun from Jean.

They left four tiny graves behind the railway station at Bahau, and went on down the line carrying two litters on bamboo poles for the weakest children. The Japanese guards, uncouth in their habits, were yet humane and reasonable, and devoted to the children. For hours the sergeant would plod along, carrying one child piggyback and at the same time carrying one end of the stretcher, his rifle laid beside the resting child.

Mrs. Frith, who had taken on a new lease of life since adopting Johnnie Horsefall, now marched as strongly as any of them. She had lived in Malaya for many years, and she was quite happy that they were going to Kuantan. "Much healthier over there than in the west," she said, "and nicer people. We'll be all right once we get there." As time went on, Jean turned to Mrs. Frith more and more for comfort and advice.

At Ayer Kring, Mrs. Holland came to the end of her strength. She stumbled into the village on her own feet, but she was changing color as Mrs. Collard had, a bad sign. They got the village headman to turn the people out of one house for them. They laid Mrs. Holland down and made a pillow for her head and bathed her face. She took a little soup that evening but refused all solid food.

"I'm so sorry, my dear," she whispered late in the night. "Sorry to make so much trouble for you. If you see Bill, tell him not to mind about marrying again. It's not as if he was an old man." Then later, "I do think it's lovely the way baby's taken to you, isn't it?"

In the morning she was unconscious, and at about midday she died. They buried her in the village cemetery.

They were now entering the most unhealthy district they had

passed through yet. The central mountain range was to the west as they marched north through marshy country full of snakes and crocodiles, infested with mosquitoes. By day it was steamy and hot; at night a chilling mist came up.

After two days several of the party were suffering from fever, and there was little to treat it. The Japanese sergeant advised them to get out of this bad country as soon as possible. Jean was running a fever herself; everything was moving about her in a blur.

"What he says is right, dearie," Mrs. Frith declared. "We won't get any better staying in this swampy place."

They marched each day after that, stumbling along in fever, weak and ill, and it took them eleven long days to get through the swamps up to the higher ground past Temerloh. They left Mrs. Simmonds and Mrs. Fletcher behind in graves, and little Gillian Thomson. Jean was very weak, but her fever was gone.

Four days later, in the evening, they came to Maran. A tarmac road runs through the village, which has perhaps fifty houses, a school, and a few shops. It overjoyed them to see evidence of civilization. And there, in front of them, were two trucks and two white men working on them while Japanese guards stood by.

One of the trucks was jacked up and both white men were underneath it working on the back axle. They wore shorts and army boots without socks; their bodies were brown with sunburn and smeared with grease. They were lean but muscular—the first white men the women had seen for five months.

They crowded around the trucks, and their guards began talking with the truck guards. One of the white men, shifting on his back, wrench in hand, said slowly, "Tell the bloody Nip to get those bloody women away so we can get some light."

Mrs. Frith laughed. "Don't you go using that language to me, young man."

The men rolled out from under the truck and sat staring at the women and children, at the brown skins, the sarongs, the bare feet. "Who said that?" asked the man with the wrench. "Which of you speaks English?"

Jean said, laughing, "We're all English."

He stared at her, noting the dark hair plaited in a pigtail, the brown arms and feet, the sarong, the brown baby on her hip. There was a line of white skin showing on her chest at the V of her tattered blouse. "Straits born?" he hazarded.

"No, real English—all of us. We're prisoners. Are you?"

He got to his feet, a fair-haired powerfully built man about twenty-seven years old. He smiled. "Are we prisoners? Oh my word."

"Are you English?" she asked.

"No," he said in his deliberate way. "We're Aussies. We come from Kuantan. We drive trucks fetching stuff down to the coast."

She said, "We're going to Kuantan, to the women's camp there."

He stared at her. "That's crook for a start," he said. "There isn't any women's camp at Kuantan, just a little temporary camp for us. Who told you that there was a women's camp at Kuantan?"

"The Japanese."

"The bloody Nips say anything. I thought you were all boongs. You say you're English, dinky-di? All the way from England?"

Jean nodded. "That's right. Some of us have been out here for ten or fifteen years, but we're all English."

"I never thought the first time I spoke to an English lady she'd be looking like you."

"You aren't exactly an oil painting yourself," Jean said.

The Australian smiled. "Where did you come from now?"

"Panong," Jean said. "We're being marched to Kuantan."

"Not all the way from Panong? Oh my word," he said. "That sounds a crook deal to me. How do you go on for tucker?"

She did not understand him. "Tucker?"

"What do you get to eat?"

"We stay each night in a village. We eat what we can get."

"For God's sake," he said. "Wait while I tell my cobber." He swung around to his buddy, the other Australian. "You heard about the crook deal that they got? Been walking all the time since they got taken, never been inside a prison camp." He turned back to Jean. "What happens if any of you get sick?"

"We get well or we die. We've got practically no medicines left,

469

so we mostly die. There were thirty-two of us when we were taken. Now we're seventeen."

The Australian said softly, "Oh my word."

"Will you be staying here tonight?" Jean asked.

He said, "Will you?"

"Yes—and tomorrow, too, unless they'll let us ride down on your trucks. We can't march the children every day. We walk one day and rest the next."

"If you're staying, Mrs. Boong, we're staying, too. We can fix this bloody axle so it will never roll again, if needs be." He paused in thought. "You got no medicines?" he said. "What do you need?"

She did not correct his reference to her as Mrs. Boong. Instead she asked quickly, "Have you any Glauber's salt? We need quinine, and something for all these skin diseases the children have."

He said slowly, "Have you got any money?"

Mrs. Frith snorted. "After six months with the Japs? They took everything we had. Even our wedding rings."

Jean said, "We've got a few bits of jewelry left, if we could sell some of those."

He said, "I'll have a go first, and see what I can do. You get fixed up with somewhere to sleep, and I'll see you later."

Jean went back to their sergeant. Together they found the headman and negotiated for the loan of the school building and for a supply of rice.

At the trucks, the Aussies got back to work. "I never heard such a crook deal," the fair-haired man said to his cobber. "What can we do to fix this bastard so as we stay here tonight?"

The other said, "Take the whole hub off for a look, 'n' pull out the shaft from the differential. That makes a good show of dirty bits. Means sleeping in the trucks."

"I said I'd try and get some medicines."

"How you going to do that?"

"Petrol, I suppose. That's easiest."

It was already growing dark when they extracted four feet of heavy metal shafting from the back axle and showed it to the Japanese in charge as evidence of their industry. "*Yasume* here tonight," they said. The guard was suspicious, but agreed; indeed, he could do nothing else. He went off to arrange for rice for them.

The fair-haired man left the trucks and slipped quickly behind a row of houses. He came out into the street toward the end of the village, where a Chinese man kept a decrepit bus; the Australian had noted this place on his various journeys.

In his deliberate manner he said, "Johnnie, you buy petrol? How much you give?" It is extraordinary how little barrier an unknown language makes between a willing buyer and a willing seller. At one point in negotiations the Australian wrote "Glauber's salt" and "quinine" and "skin disease ointment" in block letters on a scrap of wrapping paper.

In the darkness, at about ten o'clock, he came to the schoolhouse where the women were quartered. The Australian saw the guards squatting near the trucks, and crept silently to the school.

At the open door, he paused and said quietly, "Which of you ladies was I talking to this afternoon? The one with the baby."

Jean was asleep. They woke her, and she fastened her sarong, slipped her top on, and came to the door. He had several little packages for her. "That's quinine," he said. "I can get more if you want it. I couldn't get Glauber's, but this is what the Chinese take for dysentery. If it's any good, keep the label and maybe you could get some more in a Chinese drug shop. I got this Zam-Buk for the skin, and there's more of that if you want it."

She took the packages gratefully. "That's marvelous. How much did it all cost?"

"That's all right. The Nips paid, but they don't know it."

She thanked him again and asked, "When are you leaving?"

"We should be back in Kuantan tonight," he said, "but Ben Leggat—he's my cobber—got the truck in bits, so we had to postpone it. We might stretch it another day, though it'd be risky."

There were six of them driving trucks for the Japanese, he explained, between Kuantan and a place on the railway called Jerantut, a distance of about a hundred and thirty miles. They would drive up one day, load the truck with ties and railway track taken up from the line, and drive back to Kuantan the next day, where the materials were unloaded to be sent by ship to some unknown destination. "Building another railway somewhere, I suppose," he said. When they failed to reach Kuantan before dark, they spent the night in a village. He had been driving trucks for about two months. "Better than being in a camp," he told her.

She sat down on the steps, and he sat on one heel on the ground, somewhat the way natives did but with his other leg extended.

"Are you a truck driver in Australia?" she asked.

"No bloody fear. I'm a ringer."

"What's a ringer?"

"A stockrider," he said. "I was born in Queensland. My dad, he came from London. He used to drive a cab and so he knew about horses, and he came out to Queensland to work for Cobb and Company, and met Ma. I've been working in the Territory, over to the west, on a station called Wollara. That's about a hundred and ten miles southwest of the Springs."

She smiled. "The Springs?"

"Alice," he said. "Alice Springs. Right in the middle of Australia, halfway between Darwin and Adelaide."

She said, "I thought the middle of Australia was all desert."

"Oh my word," he said. "Alice is a bonza place. Plenty of water in Alice; people there leave the sprinkler on all night, watering the lawn. Course, the Territory's dry in some parts, but there's usually good feed along the creeks. You take a creek that only runs in the wet, say a couple of months in the year. You get a sandy billabong, and you'll get water there by digging not a foot below the surface, like as not, even in the middle of the dry." His even tones were strangely comforting. "There's water all over in the outback, but you've got to know where to find it."

"What do you do at this place Wollara?" she asked. "Do you look after sheep?"

He shook his head. "It'd be too hot for sheep. Wollara is a cattle station."

"How many cattle have you got?"

"About eighteen thousand when I come away. It goes up and down, according to the wet, you know."

"Eighteen thousand? But how big is it?"

"Wollara? About two thousand seven hundred."

"Two thousand seven hundred acres. That's a big place."

He stared at her. "Not acres. Square miles. Wollara's two thousand seven hundred square miles."

"But however many of you does it take to run it?"

His mind ran lovingly around the well-remembered scene. "There's Mr. Duveen, Tommy Duveen—he's the manager; and then me—I'm the head stockman, or I was. Tommy said he'd keep a place for me. I'd like to get back to Wollara again, one day. . . ." He mused a little. "We had three other ringers—whites. Then there was Happy, and Moonlight, and Nugget, and Snowy, and Tarmac. . . ." He thought for a minute. "Nine Abos we had."

"Nine what?"

"Black stockriders. Aborigines."

"But can fourteen men look after all those cattle?"

"Oh yes," he said thoughtfully. "Wollara is an easy station, because it hasn't got any fences. It's fences make the work. Of course, these bloody Abos are always going walkabout."

"What's that?" she asked.

"Walkabout? Why, an Abo ringer, he'll say one day, 'Boss, I go walkabout now.' And he'll go wandering off just in a pair of trousers and an old hat, with a gun if he's got one. Then when he's had enough wandering, he'll come back and join up for work again."

They sat quietly in the tropic night, exiles far from their homes. Over their heads, the flying foxes swept in the moonlight with a rustling of leathery wings.

She asked, "How big is Wollara—how long and how wide?"

"Oh, about ninety miles from east to west, and maybe forty-five to fifty, north to south, at the widest part. But the homestead is near the middle, so it's not so far in any one direction. Over to the Kernot Range is the farthest; that's about sixty miles."

"How long does it take you to get to the farthest point, then—to the Kernot Range?"

"To go over to the range and come back? Might take about a week. That's with horses; in a utility you might do it in a day and a half. But horses are best, although they're a bit slow. You never take a packhorse faster 'n a walk, not if you can help it. It isn't like you see it in the movies, people galloping their horses everywhere. That way you'd soon wear out a horse in the Territory."

They talked for over an hour, then the ringer got up. "I mustn't stay any longer, case those Nips come back and start creating. My cobber, too—he'll be wondering what happened to me."

Jean got to her feet. "It's been terribly kind of you to get us these things. Tell me, what's your name?"

"Joe Harman—Sergeant Harman—Ringer Harman, some of them call me." He hesitated awkwardly. "Sorry I called you Mrs. Boong today. It was a silly kind of joke."

"My name's Jean Paget."

"That sounds like a Scotch name."

"It is," she said. "My parents came from Perth."

"My mother's family was Scotch," he said. "From Inverness."

She put out her hand. "Good night, Sergeant. It's been lovely talking to you."

There was great comfort in his masculine handshake. "Look, Mrs. Paget," he said. "I'll try and get the Nips to let your party ride down with us. If they won't allow it, I'll make darn sure there's something crook with the truck. What else do you need?"

"Could you possibly get us soap? I've got a gold locket from one of the women who died. I was going to see if I could sell it."

"Keep it. I'll see you get soap." He hesitated and then said, "Sorry I talked so much, boring you with the outback and all that. There's times when you get down a bit—can't make yourself believe you'll ever see it again."

"I wasn't bored," she said softly. "Good night, Sergeant."

In the morning the Australians had a smart argument with their guards, who refused point-blank to let the prisoners ride. The weight of seventeen women and children might well have brought about the final breakdown of the overloaded trucks. Harman and Leggat went to work to put the back axle together again. When they were finished, Joe Harman said, indicating the Japanese guard, "Keep him busy for a minute while I loose off the coupling." Presently the trucks started, Harman's in the lead, dribbling petrol from a loosened pipe joint, unnoticed by the guard. It was just as well to have an alibi when they ran out of fuel, having parted with six gallons to the Chinese man.

Next morning the women began the march down the tarmac road. Jean looked for Joe Harman's truck all day; she was not to know that it had been stranded overnight at Pohoi, short of petrol.

They stayed next day at Buan in a shed, and the women took turns watching for the truck. They never saw it pass through, but a Malay girl came to them in the evening with a brown paper parcel of six cakes of Lifebuoy soap. It was addressed to Mrs. Paget, with a note which read:

Dear Lady,

I send some soap which is all we can find at present but I will get more later on. The Nip won't let us stop so I have given this to the Chinaman at Maran and he says he will get it to you. Look out for us on the way back, and I will try to stop then.

Joe Harman

The women were delighted. "Lifebuoy," said Mrs. Warner, sniffing it ecstatically. "My dear, wherever do you think they got it?"

"I'd have two guesses," Jean replied. "Either they stole it, or they stole something to buy it with."

The next day the women marched to Berkapor, through much better country. The road wound around hillsides and was shaded by trees. At Berkapor, just before dusk, the two trucks drew up, driven by Ben Leggat and Joe Harman. They were headed for the coast.

Jean and several of the others walked across the road to greet them. "Ben's got a pig," Joe whispered.

"A pig?" They crowded around Ben's truck. Lying on top was a black pig, already covered with flies. Ben had seen it on the road and chased it for a quarter of a mile before the Japanese guard beside him shot it. Harman told Jean, "We'll have to let the Nips eat all they can. Leave it to me; I'll see there's some for you."

That night the women got about thirty-five pounds of boiled pig meat, conveyed surreptitiously in several installments, and made a stew with their rice ration. They sat about after they had finished, and presently the Australians came across to talk to them.

Jean said to Joe, "We've been eating and eating, and there's still lots left. I don't know when we last had such a meal."

"There's not a lot of spare flesh on any of you, if I may say so." He squatted down on one heel in that peculiar way he had.

"The pig was a godsend," she said. "That, and the fruit—we got some green coconuts today. We've been very lucky so far that we've had no beriberi or that sort of thing."

"What were you all doing in Malaya?" he asked her.

"Most of us were married. Our husbands worked here."

"All the husbands got interned separately, I suppose?"

"That's right," said Mrs. Frith. "I think they're in Singapore."

"It seems to me," said Harman, "the way they're kicking you around, it might not be too difficult to just stay in one place, and live there till the war's over."

Jean said, "I know. I've thought of this ever since Mrs. Frith suggested it. The trouble is we'd have to earn our keep somehow, and I don't see how we could do it."

Harman said, "It was just an idea," and then presently, "I believe I know where I could get a chicken or two. If I can, I'll drop them off when we come up-country, day after tomorrow. You ladies need feeding up."

Jean said, "We haven't paid you for the soap yet."

"Forget about it. I didn't pay cash for it. I swapped a pair of rubber boots for it that I took from a sleeping Nip."

Jean said, "Don't take any risks."

"You attend to your own business, Mrs. Boong," he said, and smiled. "And just take what you get."

She smiled back at him and said, "All right." The fact that he had called her Mrs. Boong pleased her; it was a little tenuous bond between herself and this strange man that he should pull her leg about her sunburn, her native dress, and the baby that she carried on her hip like a Malay woman. "Tell me," she said. "Is it very hot in Australia, the part you come from? Hotter than this?"

"It can be hot when it tries," he said. "At Wollara it can go to a hundred and eighteen. But it's not like here. It's a dry heat, the sort that does you good and makes you thirsty for cold beer."

"What does the country look like?" she inquired. It pleased this man to talk about his own place, and she wanted to please him.

"It's red," he said. "Red around Alice and where I come from, red earth and then, the mountains are all red. . . ." He paused. "I suppose everybody likes his own place. The country round about the Springs is my place. Some say Alice is a lousy town. To me, it's beautiful. Where do you come from?"

Jean said, "Southampton."

"Where the liners go to? What's it like there?"

She shifted the baby on her hip. "Quiet, and cool, and happy," she said thoughtfully. "There is an ice rink there. I used to dance on the ice. One day I'll get back there and dance again."

"I've never seen an ice rink," said the man from Alice. "I've seen pictures of them in the movies."

Presently he got up to go; she walked across the road with him toward the trucks, the baby on her hip, as always. "We start at dawn tomorrow," he said, "but I'll be coming back up the road the day after. I'll see if I can get you those chickens."

She turned and faced him, standing beside her in the moonlit road. "Look, Joe," she said. "We don't want meat if it's going to mean trouble. It was grand of you to get that soap for us, but I know you took a fearful risk, pinching that chap's boots."

"You can run rings round these Nips when you learn how," he said. "Don't worry about me. I won't go sticking out my neck."

"You'll promise that?"

"Don't worry," he said. "You've got enough troubles on your own plate. But we'll come out all right, so long as we just keep alive. That's all we got to do till the war's over."

"I'd never forgive myself if you got caught in anything, and bought it," Jean told him.

"I won't," he said. He put out his hand as if to take her own, then dropped it again. "Good night, Mrs. Boong."

She laughed. "I'll crack you with a coconut next time you say Mrs. Boong. Good night, Joe."

They did not see him in the morning, though they heard the trucks go off. They marched on to Pohoi the next day.

That evening a little Malay boy came with a green canvas sack to the house in Pohoi where they were staying; he said that he had been sent by a Chinese man in Gambang. In the sack were five black cockerels, alive, with their feet tied.

Jean regarded the kind gift uneasily. It told her something of the temper of a man like Joe Harman. No risk would deter him from getting what he considered to be helpful for the women.

And how would they cook the cockerels without drawing the attention of the guards? Jean wished she knew where the birds had come from; it would be easier to frame a lie, then. She consulted with the other women, and it was decided regretfully to make a gift of one of the cockerels to the sergeant. It would flatter him and involve him in the affair besides. Accordingly, she took a chicken in the sack and sought him out, with much bowing.

"*Gunso,*" she said. "Good *mishi* tonight. We buy chickens." She opened the sack and smiled innocently. "For you."

It was a great surprise to him. "You buy? Where get money?"

For one fleeting moment Jean hesitated, feeling that it would be better not to mention the Australians. But she had already agreed with the others on the best story to tell. "Man prisoner give us money for chickens," she said. "They say we too thin. Now we have good *mishi* tonight, Japanese and prisoners also."

The sergeant smiled at her and walked off with the sack under his arm.

That day there was a row in progress at Kuantan. The commanding officer was a Captain Sugamo, whose duty in Kuantan was to oversee the evacuation of railway construction material from eastern Malaya and its shipment to Siam for use in the construction of the Burma-Siam railway. He lived in the house of the former district commissioner, who had kept a fine flock of Black Leghorn fowls imported from England. When Captain Sugamo woke up that morning, five of his twenty Black Leghorns were missing, with a green sack that had once held the district commissioner's mail and now was used for grain for the fowls.

Captain Sugamo was a very angry man. He set the military police to work; their suspicion fell at once upon the Australian truck drivers, who had a record for petty larceny unsurpassed in that district. Their camp was searched for any sign of telltale feathers, or the sack, but nothing was discovered.

Captain Sugamo became more angry than ever. A question of saving face was involved, because this theft from the commanding officer was a clear insult to his position, and thus to the Imperial Japanese Army. He ordered a search of the entire town of Kuantan, and on the following day troops under the direction of the military police entered every house, but there was no sign of the black feathers or the green sack. Next the soldiers' barracks were searched, with no success from that either.

There remained one further avenue. Three of the trucks driven by Australians were up-country on the way to or from Jerantut. Next day Sugamo dispatched an army jeep up the road, manned by four military police, to search for the trucks and to interrogate the drivers and the guards. Between Pohoi and Blat the police came upon a crowd of women and children walking along loaded with bundles; ahead of them marched a Japanese sergeant with his rifle slung over one shoulder and a green sack over the other. The jeep stopped with a squeal of brakes.

For the next two hours Jean kept repeating her account of how the Australian had given her money and she had arranged at Berkapor for the fowls to be sent to them at Pohoi from a village called Limau, two or three miles off the road. When they felt her attention wandering they slapped her face, kicked her shins, or stamped on her bare feet with army boots. She stuck desperately to her story, knowing that it was unconvincing but not knowing what else she could say. A convoy of three trucks came down the road; the driver of the second one, Joe Harman, was recognized by the sergeant of the military police and brought before Jean at the point of a bayonet. "Is this man?" the sergeant demanded.

Jean said desperately, "I've been telling them about the four dollars you gave me to buy the chickens with, Joe, but they won't believe me."

The military policeman shouted, "You steal chickens from the *shoko*. Here is bag."

The ringer looked at the girl's bleeding face and feet. "Leave her alone, you dirty bastards," he said angrily. "I stole those chickens and I gave them to her. So what?"

DARKNESS was closing down in my London sitting room. The girl sat staring into the fire, immersed in her sad memories. "They crucified him," she said quietly. "They took us all down to Kuantan, and they nailed his hands to a tree and beat him to death. They kept us there, and made us look on while they did it."

FOUR

"MY DEAR," I said. "I am so very sorry."

She raised her head. "You don't have to be sorry," she replied. "It was one of those things that seem to happen in a war. It's a long time ago—nearly six years. And Captain Sugamo was hanged—not for that, but for what he did upon the railway. It's all over and done with now, and nearly forgotten."

THE execution had taken place at midday at a tree overlooking the tennis courts; as soon as the maimed, bleeding body hanging by its hands had ceased to twitch, Captain Sugamo stood the women and children in parade before him. "You very bad people," he said. "No place here for you. I send you to Kota Bharu. You walk now."

They stumbled off without a word, desperate to get clear of that place of horror. The sergeant, who had shared the chickens, was ordered to continue with them as a punishment. All prisoners are dishonorable creatures in the eyes of the Japanese, and to guard them is a job fit only for the lowest type of man.

So they took up their journey again, living from day to day. It was the middle of July. Jean anticipated it would take them two months to walk the two hundred miles to Kota Bharu.

480

On the first day they got to Beserah, a fishing village on the sea. They slept little that night, because the children were awake and crying with memories of the horror they had seen. They could not bear to stay so close to Kuantan, and traveled on the next day.

Gradually they realized they had entered a new land, the northeast coast of Malaya, with rocky headlands and sandy beaches fringed with palm trees, and swept by fresh winds from the sea. Moreover, there is an abundance of fresh fish in all the villages. For the first time since they had left Panong the women had sufficient protein with their rice, and their health began to improve. Most of them bathed in the warm sea every day, and the salt water began to heal the skin diseases they suffered from.

They all improved except the sergeant. He seldom carried a child now or helped them in any way. He seemed to feel the reproofs that he had been given very much, and he now had no companion of his own country to talk to. Upon this route they met very few Japanese. He moped a great deal, sitting sullenly aloof from them in the evenings; once or twice Jean caught herself consciously trying to cheer him up, a queer reversal of the role of prisoner and guard.

As they traveled up the coast, the condition of the women and the children altered greatly for the better. They were now very different from the helpless party of six months before. Death had eliminated the weakest members and reduced them to about half the original number, which made problems of billeting and feeding far easier. Having learned to use the native remedies for malaria and dysentery, and to dress and live in the native manner, they had far more leisure. The march of ten miles every other day was no longer a great burden. Presently Mrs. Warner, who had been mistress of an elementary school, started a class for the children on their day of rest.

Jean began to teach her baby, Robin Holland, to walk. He was getting quite heavy to carry, for he was now sixteen months old. He crawled about naked in the sun, like any Malay baby.

Slowly they moved up the coast, through the fishing villages. They rarely spoke of the horror at Kuantan.

It was Mrs. Frith who sought for the hand of God in the awful event. A devout little woman, she said her prayers morning and evening faithfully and always knew when Sunday was—she would read the Bible aloud for an hour to those who cared to listen. Brooding over the text of the Crucifixion, she was struck by certain similarities in the Australian's death. Beyond all doubt, the party had been blessed since then. God had sent down His Son to earth in Palestine. What if He had done it again in Malaya?

Men and women who are in prolonged distress often long deeply for the help of God. As the weeks went on, accurate memory of the Australian began to fade, replaced by a roseate portrait. If what Mrs. Frith believed could possibly be true, it meant indeed that they were in the hand of God. Nothing could touch them; they would win through, live through all troubles. They marched on with renewed strength.

Jean, the youngest of the women and the only unmarried one, had formed a very different idea of Joe Harman. For her he had been a very normal, human man who had made her feel prettier in his presence. He had called her Mrs. Boong, and she had never corrected his impression of her as a married woman with a baby on her hip. It had been a defensive measure; if he had known she was unmarried, anything might have happened between them in the hot tropic nights. Her grief for him was far deeper than that of the other women, and more real.

Toward the end of August they came to Kuala Telang, on the south bank of the Telang River, a pretty place of palm and casuarina trees, and long white beaches on which the rollers of the South China Sea broke in surf. There was a sort of village square with native shops grouped about it; behind this stood a rice godown, empty at the time, and it was in that warehouse the party was accommodated.

The Japanese sergeant had fallen ill with fever here, probably malaria. He had been sullen and depressed, and seemed to feel the lack of companionship very much. As the women had grown stronger, so he had grown weaker. At first they had been pleased that this ugly, uncouth little man was in eclipse, but as he grew more unhappy they suffered a strange reversal of feeling. He had been with them a long time and had done what was possible to alleviate their lot; he had carried their children willingly and had wept when children died. So they took turns carrying his rifle and tunic and pack. They arrived in the village, a queer procession, Mrs. Warner leading the little yellow man clad only in his trousers, stumbling along in a daze; behind came the other women, carrying all his equipment as well as their own burdens.

The village headman was called Mat Amin bin Taib. He was about fifty and had close-cropped hair and a small clipped mustache. He was naked to the waist and wearing a sarong.

Jean explained the situation to him. "We are prisoners, marching from Kuantan to Kota Bharu, and this Japanese is our guard. He is ill with fever, and we must find a shady house for him to lie in. We must also have a place to sleep ourselves, and food."

The headman said to Jean, "I have no place where *mems* would like to sleep."

Jean said, "We are not *mems* any longer; we are prisoners, accustomed to living as your women live. All we need is shelter and a floor to sleep on, some rice, a little fish or meat, and vegetables."

"You can have what we have ourselves," he said, "but it is strange to see *mems* living so."

The headman's wife cared for the sergeant all night. He was still in a high fever by morning and much weaker. He was giving up. The women took turns all day sitting with him and bathing his face; they tried to talk to him, without success.

In the evening Jean sat with him; he lay inert and unanswering.

In his clothes she found a photograph of a Japanese woman and four children standing by the entrance to a house. She said, "Your children, *gunso?*" He looked at it without speaking, then motioned to her to put it back again. Later she saw tears oozing from his eyes. Very gently she wiped them away.

Two days later he died. They buried him in the village cemetery, and most of them wept for him as an old and valued friend.

They were now prisoners without a guard, and they discussed their unusual position at length that evening. "I don't see why we shouldn't stay here," said Mrs. Frith. "This is as nice as anyplace we've come to. That's what *he* said, we ought to find a place where we'd be out of the way, and just live there."

Jean said, "If the Japs find out we're living here, the headman will get into trouble. They'd probably kill him." She paused. "And we can't expect this village to go on feeding seventeen of us."

"We could grow our own food," Mrs. Frith said. "Half of the paddy fields we walked by haven't been planted this year."

Jean stared at her. "That's right—they haven't. I wonder why?"

"All the men must have gone to war," said Mrs. Warner.

Jean said slowly, "Suppose I tell Mat Amin that we'll work in the rice fields if he'll let us stay? How would that seem?"

"I wouldn't mind working in the paddy fields if we could live comfortable and settled," said Mrs. Warner.

Mrs. Frith said, "If we were growing rice, maybe the Japs would let us stay here. After all, we'd be doing something useful, instead of walking all over the country like a lot of whipped dogs with no home."

Next morning Jean went to the headman. She put her hands together in the praying gesture of greeting, smiled at him, and said in Malay, "Mat Amin, why do we see many of the paddy fields not sown this year?"

He said, "Most of the men, except the fishermen, are working for the army." He meant the Japanese army.

"Are they coming back to plant paddy?"

"It is in the hand of God, but I do not think they will come back for many months."

"Who, then, will plant the paddy, and reap it?"

"The women will do what they can."

Jean said, "Mat Amin, if there were a man among us he would talk for us, but there is no man. You will not be offended if I ask you to talk business with a woman, on behalf of women?" She now knew something of the right approach to a Mohammedan.

He bowed to her and led her to his house. They sat facing each other on the floor of the rickety veranda, and he called sharply to his wife to bring out coffee.

"We are in a difficulty," Jean began. "Our guard is dead, and what will become of us is in our own hands—and in yours. We were taken prisoner at Panong, and since then have walked hundreds of miles to this place. No Japanese commander will receive us, because each commander thinks it is the duty of the other; so they march us from town to town. One by one we shall all die. That is what lies ahead of us, if we report to the Japanese."

Mat Amin replied, "It is written that the angels said, 'Every soul shall taste of death, and we will prove you with evil and with good for a trial of you, and unto us shall ye return.' "

She thought quickly; the words of another headman came to her. She said, "It is also written, 'If ye be kind toward women and fear to wrong them, God is well acquainted with what ye do.' "

He eyed her steadily. "Where is that written?"

She said, "In the fourth sura."

"Are you of the faith?" he asked incredulously.

She shook her head. "I do not want to deceive you. I am a Christian; we are all Christians. The headman of a village on our road was kind to us, and when I thanked him he said that to me. I do not know the Koran."

"You are a clever woman," he said. "Tell me what you want."

"I want our party to stay in this village," she said, "and work in the paddy fields, as your women do." He stared at her, astonished. "This will be dangerous for you," she said. "If Japanese officers find us before you have reported that we are here, they will be very angry. And so I want you to let us go to work at once with one or two of your women to show us what to do. We will work all day for our food and a place to sleep. When we have worked so for two weeks, I will go to an officer and tell him what we are doing. And you shall come with me and tell the officer that more rice will be grown for the Japanese if we are allowed to work."

"I have never heard of white *mems* working in the paddy fields," he said.

Jean asked, "Have you ever heard of white *mems* marching and dying as we have marched and died? We are in your hands."

The headman was silent.

"If you allow us to stay," Jean continued, "you will get great honor when the English *tuans* return after their victory."

He said, "I shall be glad to see that day." They sat sipping the glasses of coffee. "This is a matter that concerns the whole village," the headman said. "I will talk it over with my brothers."

Jean went away, and that evening she saw a gathering of men squatting with the headman in front of his house; they were all old men, because there were very few young ones in Kuala Telang at that time. Later, Mat Amin came to the godown and asked for Mem Paget; Jean came out to him, carrying the baby.

"We have discussed this matter that we talked about," he said. "It is a strange thing, that white *mems* should work in our rice fields, and some of my brothers are afraid that the white *tuans* will not understand and will be angry when they come back, saying we have made you work against your will."

Jean said, "We will give you a letter now, that you can show them if they should say that."

He shook his head. "It is sufficient if you tell the *tuans* this thing was done because you wished it so."

She said, "That we will do."

The seven women and ten children, including the baby, Robin, went out to the fields next day with two Malay girls, Fatimah and Raihana. The headman gave them seven small fields covered with weeds, an area they could easily manage. There was a roofed platform in the shade, where they left the youngest children.

Rice is grown in little fields surrounded by a low wall of earth, so that water from a stream can be let into the field at will to turn it into a shallow pool. When the water is let out, the earth bottom is soft mud, and weeds can be pulled by hand and the ground hoed and prepared for the seedlings, which are then planted in rows. The field is flooded again, and the seedlings stand with their heads above the water in the hot sun. After a few days the water is let out again to permit the sun to get to the roots. With alternating flood and dry the plants grow quickly to about the height of wheat, with feathery ears of rice on top of the stalks. The rice is harvested by cutting off the ears with a little knife, and is taken in sacks to the village to be winnowed. Water buffalo are then turned in, to eat the straw and fertilize the ground, and soon it is ready for sowing again. Two crops a year are normal.

Working in rice fields is not too unpleasant. There are worse things in a very hot country than to put on a large palm-leaf hat and take off most of your clothes and play about, damming and diverting little streams of water. By the end of two weeks the women had settled down to the work—the children loved it from the first. No Japanese had come near the village.

On the sixteenth day Jean started out with Mat Amin for the twenty-seven-mile walk to Kuala Rakit, where a Japanese detachment was stationed; they carried the sergeant's rifle and equipment, his uniform, and his paybook.

On the evening of the second day they came to Kuala Rakit, a very large village. Here Mat Amin took her to see an official of the Malay administration, Tungku Bentara Raja, a thin little Malay who spoke excellent English. He was genuinely concerned at the story that he heard from Mat Amin and from Jean.

"You must stay with us tonight," he said. "Tomorrow I will have a talk with the Japanese civil administrator."

In the morning Jean went with Tungku Bentara and Mat Amin to see the civil administrator. He was sympathetic, but declared that prisoners were the concern of the army. He took them to a Colonel Matisaka, the military commanding officer.

It was quite clear that Colonel Matisaka considered women prisoners a nuisance, and he told the civil administrator to make what arrangements he thought best. The civil administrator told Tungku Bentara that the women could stay where they were for the time being, and Jean started back for Kuala Telang with Mat Amin.

They lived there for three years.

"It was three years wasted, just chopped out of one's life," she said. She looked at me hesitantly. "At least—I suppose it was."

"You don't know if it was wasted until you come to the end of your life," I said. "Perhaps not then."

"I suppose that's right. They were so very kind to us. They

488

couldn't have been nicer. Fatimah, the girl who showed us what to do in the rice fields—she was a perfect dear. I got to know her very well indeed."

"Is that where you want to go back to?" I asked.

She nodded. "I would like to do something for them, now that I have this money. We'd all have died before the war was ended if they hadn't taken us in and let us stay with them. And now I've got so much, and they so very, very little. . . ."

"Traveling to Malaya is a very expensive journey," I said.

She smiled. "I know. What I want to do for them won't cost much—not more than fifty pounds. We had to carry water in that village—that's the women's work—and it's a fearful job. You see, the river is tidal at the village, so the water's brackish; you can use it for washing, but drinking water has to be fetched from the spring, nearly a mile away. We used to go for it with gourds, two in each hand with a stick between them, morning and evening—a mile there and a mile back—four miles a day."

"That's why you want to dig a well?"

She nodded. "It would make life easier for them, as they made life easier for us. A well right in the middle of the village, within a couple of hundred yards of every house. I thought if I went back there and offered to engage a gang of well diggers to do this for them, it'd sort of wind things up. And after that I could enjoy this money with a clear conscience." She looked up at me again. "You don't think that's silly, do you?"

"No," I said. "The only thing is, traveling there and back will make a very big hole in a year's income."

"If I run out of money, I'll take a job in Singapore or somewhere for a few months and save up a bit," she said.

"Why didn't you stay out there and get a job?" I asked.

"In 1945 we were all dying to get home. We were flown down to Singapore, and there I met Bill Holland and had to tell him about Eileen, and Freddie and Jane." Her voice dropped. "All the family, except Robin; he was four years old then, and quite a sturdy little chap. They let me travel home with Bill, to look after Robin. He thought of me as his mother, of course."

She smiled a little. "Bill wanted to make it permanent. I couldn't do that. I couldn't have been the sort of wife he wanted."

I said nothing.

"When we landed, England was so green and beautiful," she said. "I wanted to forget about the war and be an ordinary person again. I got this job with Pack and Levy, and I've been there two years—ladies' handbags and attaché cases, nothing to do with wars or sickness or death. I've been happy there, on the whole."

She was very much alone when she got home. Her mother and her brother, Donald, were dead. She stayed a few weeks with her aunt Agatha at Colwyn Bay, in Wales, then went down to London to look for a job.

I asked her why she hadn't gotten in touch with her uncle, the old man at Ayr.

"I only saw Uncle Douglas that once when I was about ten years old," she said, "and it never entered my head that he would still be alive. If it had, I wouldn't have known where he lived. . . ."

JEAN Paget went on with her work at Perivale, and I with mine in Chancery Lane, but I was unable to get her out of my mind.

There is a man called Wright, a member of my club, who was in the Malay police and was a prisoner of the Japanese during their occupation of Malaya. I sat next to him at dinner one night, and I could not resist saying, "One of my clients told me an extraordinary story about Malaya the other day. She was one of a party of women that the Japanese refused to put into a camp."

He laid his knife down. "Not the party who were taken at Panong and marched across Malaya?"

"That was it," I said. "You know about them, do you?"

"Oh yes," he said. "It was most extraordinary. Finally they were allowed to settle in a village on the east coast somewhere, for the rest of the war. A very fine girl was their leader; she spoke Malay fluently. She wasn't anybody notable; she'd been a shorthand typist in an office in Kuala Lumpur. A very fine type."

I nodded. "She's my client."

"Is she! I always thought that girl ought to have got a decoration of some sort. If she hadn't been with them, all those women and children would have died. There was no one else in the party of that caliber at all."

JEAN Paget found a line of intermediate-class cargo ships that took about a dozen passengers for a modest fare to Singapore, and she booked a passage to sail from London on June 2. I saw her from time to time in the weeks before she left. She gave notice to her firm to leave at the end of May. She had told Mr. Pack about her legacy, and he had accepted the inevitable.

I made arrangements for her income through September to be available to her in Singapore. As the time for her departure drew closer, I became worried that she would get into difficulty over expenses. Nine hundred a year does not go very far for a person traveling about the East.

"Don't forget that you're a fairly wealthy woman now," I said about a week before she left. "You're quite right to live within your income, but don't forget that I have rather wide discretionary powers under your uncle's will. If you really need money, cable me at once. If, for example, you should get ill."

She smiled. "That's very sweet of you. But honestly, I think I'll be all right. I'm counting upon taking a job if I find I'm running short. I haven't got to be back in England by a given date."

I said, "Don't stay away too long."

She smiled. "I shan't, Mr. Strachan."

She was giving up her room in Ealing, of course, and she asked if she might leave a trunk and a suitcase in the boxroom of my flat till she came back to England. She was taking only one suitcase.

"But what about your tropical kit?" I asked. "Have you had that sent on?"

"I've got it with me in the suitcase. Fifty antimalaria tablets and a hundred sulfa pills, some mosquito repellent, and my old sarong."

I drove her down to the docks in a taxi. The ship was new and clean, and when the steward opened the door of her cabin she stood back amazed. "Just look at all the flowers! Wherever did they come from? Not from the company?"

"Make a nice show, don't they, miss?" the steward said.

She swung around on me. "I believe you sent them." And then she said, "Oh, how perfectly sweet of you!"

"English flowers," I said. "Just to remind you to come back to England soon." I must have felt a premonition, even then.

Before I could realize it, she had kissed me on the lips. "That's for the flowers, Noel," she said softly, "and for everything." And all I could say was, "I'll have another of those when you come back."

I didn't wait to see her off. I went back in the taxi to my flat alone, and I stood for a long time looking out of my sitting-room window, thinking of her. She was just such a girl as one would have liked for a daughter.

She traveled across half the world in her tramp steamer and wrote to me from most of the ports—from Marseilles and Naples, Alexandria, Aden, from Colombo, Rangoon, and Penang. She stayed only one night in Singapore, and took the morning plane to Kota Bharu. I'd arranged for the British adviser there, a Mr. Wilson-Hays, to meet the airplane. Jean was surprised to find an official and his wife waiting to greet her.

I met Wilson-Hays at the United University Club a year later, when he was on leave, and he said that she had been embarrassed; she did not seem to realize that she was a well-known person in that part of Malaya. Wilson-Hays had arranged to lend her his jeep and driver for the hundred-mile trip to Kuala Telang. He said that British prestige was higher there after the war, due solely to this girl; she'd earned the use of a jeep for a few days.

When she left next morning she wore sandals, carried a Chinese umbrella, and had done up her hair native-style on top of her head. In a palm-leaf basket she took a toothbrush, a towel, a cake of antiseptic soap, and a few drugs. She took one change of clothes—a new sarong and top to match—and some Woolworth brooches and rings for her friends. That was all.

It took fourteen hours over very poor roads to reach Kuala Telang. When they arrived after dark, a buzz of excitement swept through the village and people came from their houses. The jeep stopped in front of the headman's house and Jean got out wearily,

put her hands up in the praying gesture, and said in Malay, "I have come back, Mat Amin, lest you should think the white *mems* have forgotten all about you when their need is past."

People thronged about her. Fatimah approached with a baby in her arms and a toddler hanging on to her sarong. Jean pushed through the crowd and took her by the hand. "It is too long since we met." Fatimah presented her young husband, and Jean bowed before him and wished that she had brought a shawl to pull over her face, as would have been polite when being introduced to a strange man. She put her hand up to her face and said, "Excuse me that I have no veil."

He bowed to her. "It is no matter."

She went with Fatimah to her husband's house, and they made her a supper of rice and *bĕlachan*, the highly spiced paste of ripe prawns and fish that the Malays favor. And presently, tired out, she lay down on a mat as she had done a thousand times before, loosened the sarong around her waist, and slept.

Next morning she had a talk with Fatimah and other women, squatting around the cooking pots behind the house. "Every day I have thought of you all living and working in this place," she said, "as I did. I was working in England in an office, at books, in the way that poor women must do in my country." The women listened and Jean went on. "But recently my uncle died; he had no other relatives, and I inherited his money. Now I need not work unless I want to."

Other women drifted up to enlarge the circle as she continued. "Having money for the first time in my life, it came to me that I should give a thank offering to this place. A present from a woman to the women of Kuala Telang, nothing to do with the men."

There was a pleased, excited murmur, and then she told them about the well. "So that you could walk out of your homes and there would be a well of fresh, cool water to draw from whenever you had need of it." She described the well for them; it would have smooth stones around its base for the women to sit on, and nearby there would be a thatch-covered house for washing clothes, the sinks arranged so that the women could face each other and talk while they worked, with a wall high enough so that the men could not look in. "I will engage well diggers and carpenters and masons," Jean said to an excited buzz.

A long clamor of discussion followed. Once they were used to the idea, the women savored it, examining it in every detail and discussing where the well should be and where the washhouse, the concrete pools, and the drain. Jean was satisfied that it would fill a real need.

That evening she sipped coffee with Mat Amin on his small veranda. "I have come to talk with you," she said, "because I want to give a thank offering to this place, that people may remember when the white women came, and you were kind to them."

He said, "The women have been talking of nothing else all day. They say you want to make a well."

Jean said, "That is true."

He paused. "The spring was good enough for their mothers and grandmothers. They will get ideas above their station in life."

She said patiently, "They will have more energy to serve you faithfully and kindly if they have this well. Do you remember Raihana, who lost her baby when she was three months pregnant, carrying water from the spring? It would not have happened if she had had this well."

"God disposes of the lives of women as well as those of men," Mat Amin said.

She smiled gently. "Do I have to remind you, Mat Amin, that it is written, 'Men's souls are naturally inclined to covetousness; but if ye be kind toward women and fear to wrong them, God is well acquainted with what ye do'?"

He laughed and slapped his thigh. "When you lived here you said that, whenever you wanted anything, but I have not heard it since." Then he said, still laughing, "I must consult my brothers."

The men of the village sent for Jean next morning, and she squatted a little to one side as is fitting for a woman, and they asked her where the well was to be put and many other questions. She said that everything was in their hands, but it would be convenient for the women if it was in front of Chai San's shop. They went to see the ground and discussed it from all angles, and the women of the village stood and watched their lords making this important decision, and "Djeen" talking with them almost as an equal. She did not hurry them. It took them two days to make up their minds that the wrath of God would not descend on them if the well was constructed.

There was only one family on the coast, about five miles from Kuantan, who could be entrusted with the skilled work. Mat Amin dictated a letter to be sent to them, and Jean ordered five sacks of cement from Kota Bharu. Then she settled down to wait.

She went out with the fishermen on their boats. She bathed and swam a good deal, playing on the beach with the children, and she worked for a week in the rice fields at harvest-time. She had lived so long with these people that she had learned to be patient; moreover, she wanted to consider what to do next with her life. She did not find the three weeks of idleness tedious.

The well diggers and the cement arrived about the same time. The diggers were an old gray-bearded father, Suleiman, and his two sons, Yacob and Hussein. They worked quickly and well, from dawn till dusk, one at the bottom of the shaft and the other two disposing of the soil on top; they bricked the shaft downward from the top as they worked, supporting the brickwork upon stakes driven into the earth sides.

Old Suleiman was a mine of information, for he traveled up and down the coast in his work. The men and women of Kuala Telang would gossip with the old man, getting news of their acquaintances and relatives in other villages. One afternoon Jean said to him, "You are from Kuantan?"

"From Batu Sawah, two hours' walk from Kuantan."

"Do you remember the Japanese officer in charge at Kuantan in the first year of the war—Captain Sugamo?"

"A very bad man," Suleiman replied.

"Captain Sugamo is dead now," she told him. "He was sent to the Burma-Siam railway, where he caused many atrocities, many murders. The Allies executed him after the war was over."

The old man nodded and called down the well with the news.

Jean said, "He did many evil things in Kuantan. When we were starving and ill, a prisoner helped us. The Japanese crucified him with nails through his hands and beat him to death."

"I remember," Suleiman said. "He was in hospital at Kuantan."

Jean stared at him. "Old man, no, he died."

"Perhaps there were two." He called down the well to Yacob. "The English soldier who was crucified at Kuantan, tell us, did that man die?"

Hussein broke in. "The one who was crucified was an Australian, not English. It was for stealing the black chickens."

"But did he live or die?" the old man said.

Yacob called up from the bottom of the well. "Captain Sugamo had him taken down that night; they pulled the nails out of his hands. He lived."

FIVE

IN KUANTAN, in the evening of that day in July, 1942, a sergeant had come to Captain Sugamo and reported that the Australian was still alive. Captain Sugamo found this curious and interesting, and he strolled down to the recreation ground to have a look.

Covered by a great mass of flies, the body still hung by its hands, facing the tree. Blood had drained from the blackened mess that was its back and had run down the legs to form a pool on the ground. But when Captain Sugamo approached, the eyes in the face opened and looked at him with recognition.

It is doubtful if the West can ever fully understand the working of a Japanese mind. Captain Sugamo bowed reverently and said, "Is there anything I can get for you before you die?"

The ringer said distinctly, "You bloody bastard. I'll have one of your black chickens and a bottle of beer."

Captain Sugamo's face was completely expressionless. He turned upon his heel and, back at his house, commanded his orderly to fetch a bottle of beer and a glass, but not to open the bottle.

The man protested that there was no beer. Captain Sugamo sent him to the town to see if he could find a bottle of beer. In an hour the man came back and with considerable apprehension informed his officer that there was no beer in all Kuantan.

Death to Captain Sugamo was a ritual. Having offered to implement the last wishes of his victim, he was personally dedicated to see that those last wishes were fulfilled. By doing so he would have set an example of chivalry and Bushido to his troops. Unfortunately, it was impossible to provide the bottle of beer, and since the soldier's dying wish could not be met in full, he could not carry out his own part in the ritual. Therefore, the Australian could not be allowed to die, or he himself would be disgraced.

He ordered his sergeant to take a party with a stretcher to the recreation ground. They were to take the man down from the tree, and put him face downward on the stretcher, and take him to the hospital.

To Jean, the news that the Australian was still alive came like the opening of a door. She slipped away to the beach to consider this incredible fact. She felt as if she had suddenly come out of a dark tunnel that she had walked down for six years. She started to pray, "Lighten our darkness, O Lord, and of Thy great mercy . . ." and repeated it over and over to herself.

That evening she spoke to Suleiman again, but neither he nor his sons could tell her how long the Australian had been in the hospital; they knew only that when he was sent by ship to a prison camp in Singapore he had been walking with two sticks.

So she had to leave it, and she stayed in Kuala Telang till the work was completed. On the day that water was reached at the bottom of the well, the carpenters erected posts for the thatched washhouse, and both the well and the house were finished about the same time. They had an opening ceremony: Jean washed her own sarong and the women crowded into the washhouse, laughing, and the men stood at a distance, wondering if they had been wise to allow anything that made the women laugh so much.

The next day she dispatched word to Wilson-Hays asking him to send the jeep for her. Two days later Jean left in a flurry of shy good wishes, with her eyes moist. She stayed in Kota Bharu with the Wilson-Hayses that night, putting off her native clothes for the last time. What she thought about, lying in the cool, spacious room under the mosquito net, was Ringer Harman and the red country around Alice Springs.

In the morning, she walked with Wilson-Hays in the residency garden and told him of the well and washhouse in Kuala Telang. He was enormously interested and said, "Where did you get the plan of it—the arrangement of the sinks and all that sort of thing?"

"We worked it out ourselves," Jean said. "They knew what they wanted." They strolled along the muddy river and she told him about Joe Harman. "Do you think I could find out anything about him in Singapore?" she asked.

The Englishman thought about it for a minute. "You say he was an Australian? I think you'd have to write to Canberra. They ought to have a record of all prisoners there. Happen to know his unit?"

"I'm afraid I don't."

"Might make it difficult—there may be several Joe Harmans."

Jean stared across the river at the rubber trees. "He worked before the war on a cattle station called Wollara, near Alice Springs." Wilson-Hays suggested that she write to that address, and she answered slowly, "I might do that. I would like to see him again. You see, it was because of us that it all happened."

That evening she told Wilson-Hays of her intention to wait in Singapore for passage to England. "Would there be a hotel at Kuantan, if I stopped there for a day?" she asked.

He looked at her kindly. "Do you want to go back there?"

"I think I do," she said. "I'd like to see the people at the hospital and find out what I can."

He nodded. "You'd better stay with David and Joyce Bowen— he's the district commissioner and would be glad to put you up."

"I don't want to be a nuisance to people," Jean said.

"Why, Bowen would be very disappointed if you didn't stay with him," Wilson-Hays told her. "Let me arrange it for you."

The Bowens were on the airstrip at Kuantan next day to meet her. They sat over tea in the DC's house, where Captain Sugamo had sat so often, and Jean told them about Joe Harman. After tea they drove to the hospital. Sister Frost, the matron in charge, an Englishwoman of about forty, received them in her office.

"There's nobody here now who was on the staff then," she said. "Nurses in a place like this—they're always leaving to get married. We never seem to keep them longer than two years."

Bowen said, "What about Phyllis Williams—wasn't she here?"

"Only for the first part of the war," the sister said, "until she married. But she might know something about it."

As they drove away to find Phyllis Williams, Mrs. Bowen enlightened Jean about her. "She's a Eurasian, very dark, married to a Chinese, Bun Tai Lin, who runs the cinema. What you'd call a mixed marriage, but they seem to get along all right."

The Bun Tai Lins's rickety wooden house was up on a hill overlooking the harbor; they had to leave the car in the road and climb a short lane littered with rubbish. Phyllis Williams, a merryfaced brown woman with four children, took them into a shabby room, the chief decoration of which was a large lithograph of the king and queen in coronation robes.

She spoke very good English. "Oh, yes, I remember that poor Joe Harman," she said. "I nursed him for three or four months. None of us thought he'd live when he came in, but he must have led a very healthy life—his flesh healed wonderfully." She turned to Jean. "Are you the lady that was leading the party of women and children from Panong? You know, he was always wanting to know where you'd gone. . . . Excuse me, but I forget your name."

"Paget. Jean Paget."

Mrs. Bun Tai Lin looked puzzled. "That wasn't it. I wonder now, was he talking about someone different? I can't remember what he called her, but it wasn't that."

There wasn't much more she could tell them about Joe Harman that Jean didn't already know. Though his recovery had been good, it would be years before the muscles of his back were strong again—if, indeed, they ever were.

It was only after they left and were picking their way down the lane that the Eurasian woman called from the veranda. "I just remembered who he was always talking about. Mrs. Boong. Was that one of your party?"

Jean laughed and called back. "That's what he used to call me!"

On the way to the DC's house they passed the recreation ground. The tree where the tortured man had hung still overlooked the tennis courts, and underneath it some Malay women sat and gossiped. It all seemed very peaceful in the evening light.

Jean wrote to me from Singapore, where she flew next day. It was a long letter, the ink smudged a little with the sweat from her hand. She told me about Kuala Telang and the well diggers, and that Joe Harman was alive. And then she announced:

> I hope it won't be too much of a shock, Noel, but I'm going on to Australia from here. I still have about a hundred and seven pounds, not counting next month's money. The fare to Darwin is sixty pounds by Constellation, and I can get a bus to Alice Springs for very little. I thought I'd get to Wollara, and someone in that district is bound to know where he is now.
>
> Some very nice young merchant officers at the hotel here tell me I can get a ship back to England probably from Townsville, on the east coast of Australia, or certainly one from Brisbane. I've arranged with the bank in Singapore to transfer my next month's money to the Bank of New South Wales in Alice Springs. Write to me there, because I know I'm going to feel a long way from home. . . .

She ended by expressing the hope that she would be in England by Christmas at the latest. I sat in my office reading and rereading the smudged pages, bitterly disappointed. I suppose I had been making plans for when she came back. Old men who lead a somewhat empty life get rather stupid over things like that.

IT MUST have been a week later that Derek Harris, the clerk, came into my office. He said, "Could you spare a few minutes for a stranger, sir?"

"What sort of stranger?"

"A man called Harman," he said. "He came about an hour ago and spoke with me, since you were engaged. But it's you he really wants to see. Something to do with Miss Paget, I understand."

It was quite incredible. I asked, "What sort of man is he?"

He grinned broadly. "A colonial, I should think. Probably Australian. He's an outdoor type, anyway."

It was all beginning to fit in, and yet it was unbelievable that an Australian stockrider should have found his way into my office in Chancery Lane. "Is his name Joseph, by any chance?" I asked.

"You know him, sir?"

I nodded. "I'll see him now."

Harris went to fetch him, and I stood by my window, wondering what this visit meant and how much I should tell this man. Harris showed him in, and I turned from the window.

He was fair-haired, about five feet ten in height, thickset, between thirty and thirty-five years old. He was deeply tanned and had bright blue eyes. His face was too square for handsomeness, but it was good-natured. He walked with a curious stiff gait.

I shook hands with him. "Mr. Harman?" I said. I was unable to resist looking down at the huge scar on the back of his hand.

He sat down in the client's chair and said, "I don't want to keep you long." He was ill at ease and obviously embarrassed. "I was wondering if you could tell me about Miss Jean Paget," he said. "Where she lives, or anything like that."

I smiled. "Miss Paget is a client of mine, Mr. Harman. Are you a friend of hers?"

"Sort of. We met in the war, in Malaya that was. I'll have to tell you who I am, of course. I'm a Queenslander. I run a station in the Gulf country, about twenty miles from Willstown." He spoke very slowly and deliberately. "Midhurst, that's my station."

I made a note on my pad, and smiled at him again. "You're a long way from home, Mr. Harman."

"I don't know nobody in England. I came here for a holiday, you might say, and I thought perhaps Miss Paget might be glad to know that I'm here, but I don't know her address."

"Rather a long way to come for a holiday?" I asked.

He smiled sheepishly. "I struck it lucky. I won the Casket."

"The Casket?"

"The Golden Casket. Don't you have that here?" I shook my head. "Oh my word. We couldn't get along without the Casket in Queensland," he said. "It's the state lottery that gets the money to build hospitals. I won a thousand pounds. I always take a ticket, because even if you don't get a prize you get a hospital. You ought to see the hospital the Casket built at Willstown. Three wards it's got, with two beds in each, and rooms for the sisters, and a separate house for the doctor, only we can't get a doctor yet, because Willstown's a bit isolated."

"Tell me, Mr. Harman," I said, "how did you get to know that I was Miss Paget's solicitor?"

"She told me that she lived in Southampton," he said. "So I went to a hotel there. I never saw a city that had been bombed before—oh my word. Well, I couldn't find out nothing except she had an aunt in Wales at a place called Colwyn Bay. So I went to Colwyn Bay. I think her aunt thought I was up to some crook game—she wouldn't tell me anything. She said that you were her trustee, whatever that means. So I came here."

"Did you fly from Australia?" I asked.

"Five days ago, by Qantas. You see, I got a good stockman looking after Midhurst for me, but I can't afford to be away more'n three months."

Flying to England, I thought, must have made a considerable hole in his thousand pounds. I looked him directly in the eyes, and smiled. "You must want to see Miss Paget very much."

He met my gaze. "I do."

I leaned back in my chair. "I'm sorry to disappoint you, Mr. Harman, but Miss Paget is abroad. She's traveling in the East."

He stared down at his hat for a moment. "I see."

I couldn't help liking and respecting this man. It was perfectly obvious that he had come twelve thousand miles to find Jean Paget, and now he wasn't going to find her.

"While I can't give you my client's address, Mr. Harman," I said, "I suggest that you write her a letter and bring it to me tomorrow morning. I will send it on with a covering note. Then if she wants to see you, she will get in touch with you herself."

"You don't think she'll want to see me?" he said.

I smiled. "Mr. Harman, I'm quite sure that when she hears you've been in England looking for her she will write to you. However, I'm not in a position to give her address to anyone who comes into this office." I paused. "There's one thing that you'd better know," I said. "Miss Paget is a fairly wealthy woman. I'm not saying that you're after her money, but I *am* saying that you must write to her and let her decide if she wants to meet you."

He stared at me. "I never knew that she had money. She told me she was just a typist in an office."

"That's quite true," I said. "She inherited some money recently."

He was silent. I glanced at my engagement diary. "Suppose you come back tomorrow morning at, say, twelve o'clock. Write her a letter saying whatever it is you want to say, and bring the letter and I will forward it to her. Where are you staying, Mr. Harman?"

"At the Kingsway Palace Hotel."

We got up together. "All right, Mr. Harman," I said. "Tomorrow at twelve."

I spent most of that evening wondering if it had been right to refuse Mr. Harman the address. But one thing puzzled me: why had he suddenly wanted to meet Jean Paget again, after six years? A question or two on that point seemed in order, and I prepared a small interrogation for him on his next visit.

Twelve o'clock next morning came, and he didn't turn up for his appointment. I waited till one, then went to lunch. By three o'clock I was concerned. If he should vanish, Jean Paget would be very cross with me, and rightly so. I put in a telephone call to the Kingsway Palace Hotel. I was told that Mr. Harman had gone out after breakfast, and had left no messages. I left one for him, asking that he ring me as soon as he came in.

By ten that night I had not heard and I rang the hotel again. He was not in.

At eight o'clock next morning I rang again. They told me that his luggage was still in his room, but that he had not slept there.

As soon as I got to the office I sent for Derek Harris. I told him briefly what had happened and asked him to ring the various police courts. "I have given him some unwelcome news. It's quite possible he's been out on a binge," I said.

Harris came back in a quarter of an hour. "You must have second sight, sir. He's coming up at Bow Street this morning, drunk and disorderly. They had him in the cooler for the night."

I instructed Harris to get down there right away and pay the fine, if necessary. He was then to take Mr. Harman to my flat. There was nothing urgent on my desk that day, so I was able to get to the flat in time to catch the charwoman at work and to have her order food and make up the spare-room bed.

Harris arrived with the Australian half an hour later. Harman was cheerful and sober after his night in jail, but disheveled. "I've been on the grog," he said.

"I thought perhaps you'd rather clean up here than at the hotel. If you want a bath and shave . . ." I showed him the geography of the house.

Then I went back to the living room, where Harris was waiting. "Thanks, Derek," I said. "There was a fine, I suppose?"

"Forty shillings," he said. "I paid it."

I gave him the money. "He was cleaned out?"

"He's got four and fourpence halfpenny," he replied. "He thinks he had about seven pounds, but it doesn't seem to worry him."

I sent Harris back to the office and settled down to write a few letters. Presently Harman finished with his bath and came into the living room. "I dunno what to say," he apologized. "Those jokers got all my money last night, but I can pay you back. The bank in Brisbane gave me a letter of credit."

"You didn't bring me the letter for Miss Paget," I observed.

"I changed my mind." He went to the window. "I won't be writing any letter." He turned to me. "I had a good long think about it. That's why I didn't come back."

I suggested that perhaps he'd like to talk about it after the charwoman served him some breakfast. He came back to me a quarter of an hour later.

"I'd better be getting along now," he said awkwardly.

I got up and offered him a cigarette. "Tell me a bit more about yourself before you go. I'll be writing to Miss Paget in a day or two, and she's sure to want to know all about you."

He stared at me. "You're going to tell her I've been here?"

"Of course."

He stood silent for a moment, and then said in his slow Queensland way, "It would be better to forget about it, Mr. Strachan. Just don't say nothing at all."

"Is this because I told you about her inheritance?"

He grinned. "I wouldn't mind about her having money, same as any man. No, it's Willstown."

"Look, Joe," I said. "It won't hurt you to sit down for a few minutes and tell me one or two things." I called him Joe because I thought it might make him loosen up. "You met Miss Paget first in the war? In Malaya, when you were both prisoners?"

"That's right. In 1942."

"And you've never met her since, nor written to her?"

"That's right."

"Well, I don't understand. It's six years since you met her. Why the sudden urge to get in touch with her now?"

He looked up at me, grinning broadly. "I thought she was a married woman. I only found out this May that she wasn't. I met the pilot who had flown her out from Malaya."

He had driven fourteen hundred cattle three hundred miles from Midhurst station to Julia Creek with his stockman, Jim Lennon, and two Abo stockriders. They got to Julia Creek in May, and the job of loading the cattle onto trains took several days. One night in a bar Joe talked to a Trans-Australia Airlines pilot, and they discovered they had both served in Malaya.

"The funniest thing I ever struck," said the pilot, "was a party of women and children that never got into a prison camp at all. Spent most of the war in a Malay village working in the paddy fields."

Joe said quickly, "Where in Malaya?"

"Somewhere between Kuantan and Kota Bharu," the pilot said. "I flew them to Singapore. English, they were, but they looked just like Malays—all brown and in native clothes."

Joe said, "Was there a Mrs. Paget with them?"

"A *Miss* Paget. Hell of a fine girl; she was their leader."

Joe said, "Mrs. She was a dark-haired girl, with a baby."

"That's right—a dark-haired girl with a little boy she was look-ing after. He belonged to one of the women who died."

Joe stared at him. "I thought she was a married woman."

"I know she wasn't," the pilot said, "because the Japs had taken all their wedding rings and we had to sort them out. It was easy—they were all Mrs. So-and-So with the exception of this one girl and she was Miss Jean Paget."

"That's right," Joe said. "Jean was her name. . . ." He left the bar and stood leaning on a stockyard gate for a long time in the night, thinking things over.

That morning in my London flat, Joe told me something of what he had been thinking.

"She was a bonza girl," he said simply. "If ever I got married, it would have to be with somebody like her. And so—I came here."

"What about the Golden Casket?" I inquired.

"I didn't tell you right about that," he said a little awkwardly. "I *did* win the Casket—in 1946, the year after I got back to Queens-land. A thousand pounds, like I said. I—I was saving it, in case someday I got to have a station of my own, or something."

"How much do you think you've got left now?"

He said, "There's five hundred pounds on the letter of credit, and I suppose that's all. There's my pay as manager, of course."

I couldn't help being sorry for this man. Since he had met Jean Paget six years previously he had held her image in his mind, wishing for somebody a little like her. When he had heard that she was not a married woman, he had drawn the whole of his small savings and hurried half across the world to England, hoping to find her still unmarried. Clearly he thought little of his money if it could buy him a chance of marrying Jean Paget.

It was ironical that she was at that moment busy looking for him in his own country, but I did not feel that I could tell him.

"I still don't quite understand why you've given up the idea of writing to Miss Paget," I said at last.

After a pause he said, "I thought a lot about things after I left you, Mr. Strachan. I got none of them highfalutin ideas about not marrying a girl with money. But there's more to it than that." He paused again. "I come from the outback. Running a cattle station is the only work I know, and it's what I like. I couldn't make out in the big cities. I can run a station better'n most ringers, and I'll run my own someday—but I'll be staying in the outback. And, Mr. Strachan, that's a crook place for a woman."

"In what way?" I asked quietly.

He smiled wryly. "Take Willstown, as an example. There's no shop to buy fresh fruit or vegetables. There's no dress or ice-cream shop, nowhere a woman can buy a magazine or book, no swimming pool, although it can be hot. There's no telephone or doctor or other young women. Soon as they're old enough, they're out of it to the city." He paused. "It's a grand country for a man, Mr. Strachan, but crook for a woman."

I said, "Are all the outback towns like that?"

"Most of them," he said. "There's only one good one for a woman, Alice Springs. A girl's got everything in Alice—two picture houses, shops for everything, Eddie Maclean's swimming pool, plenty of young women, nice houses. Alice is a bonza town."

"What makes Alice different from the others?" I asked.

He scratched his head. "I dunno," he said. "It's just that it's got bigger, I suppose."

"What you mean is that Miss Paget wouldn't have a very happy life in Willstown."

He nodded. "That's right," he said, and there was pain in his eyes. "It all seemed different when I met her in Malaya. You see, she hadn't got nothing, and I hadn't, either, so there was a pair of us. But then I come to England and I see the way people live here, and when you told me she'd come into money I got thinking. . . . I never know it to work, for a girl to come straight from England to the outback. And for a girl with money it'd be worse still." He grinned at me. "So I went on the grog."

It seemed to me that he had taken a very reasonable line of action. "Look, Joe," I said. "Miss Paget thought you were dead."

He stared at me. "You knew about me, then?"

"Not very much," I said. "I know that you stole chickens for her, and the Japs nailed you up and beat you. It's been a very deep grief for her. You see, she thinks it was her fault."

"It wasn't," he said. "She told me not to stick my neck out, and I went and bought it. It wasn't her fault at all."

"I think you ought to write to her," I said. "Take a bit of time to think it over. When do you have to return to Australia?"

"I wouldn't be doing right by Mrs. Spears—that's who I work for—unless I get back by the end of October," he said.

"That gives you two and a half months," I said. "And you've got five hundred pounds left on your letter of credit."

"That's right."

I knew that the air fare to Australia was expensive and suggested that he might want to return by sea. "A tramp steamer would only cost about eighty pounds, but you'd have to leave pretty soon—within a fortnight, say."

"If there wouldn't be no chance she'll be coming to England that soon," he said a little wearily, "I'd better go back by sea, and save what's left of the money."

"I think that's wise," I said, getting up. Then I offered him the use of the spare room, assuring him that he wouldn't in the least be in the way, and he finally agreed.

When I went to my office I had, apart from my clients, plenty to think about. There was no denying this man's solid virtues; he had flown halfway across the world to look for the girl he loved; quite certainly he was kind and would make a good husband.

For the rest of his stay in England, I did my best to see that he enjoyed himself. He wanted to visit 19 Acacia Road, Hammersmith, where his father had been born. He wanted to attend a live broadcast of a radio show that he listened to on shortwave from Brisbane. He wanted to see all he could of thoroughbred horses and cattle, and was interested in saddlery.

The time passed agreeably, and not only did he attend his radio show; he was interviewed on a program called "In Town Tonight" as well. The announcer shepherded him skillfully, and he spoke for six or seven minutes about the Midhurst cattle station and the surrounding area below the Gulf of Carpentaria that he called the Gulf country. He visited my friend Sir Dennis Frampton, who has a herd of pedigreed Herefords at his place down by Taunton.

He had only three days there because I had gotten him a cheap berth on a ship of the Shaw Savill & Albion Line leaving that week for Australia. When he returned from Taunton I had a word with him about Jean Paget. "Joe," I said, "I shall write to Miss Paget and give her your address. I should think you'll find a letter from her at Midhurst. In fact, I know you will, because I shall write airmail, and she's certain to write airmail to you."

He brightened considerably at the thought. "I'll wait and write when I hear from her," he said. "I'm glad I didn't meet her over here, in a way. It's probably turning out for the best."

It was on the tip of my tongue to tell him then that she was in Australia, but I refrained. There was no reason to lay all her cards before him at this stage.

I saw him off at the docks two days later, as I had seen Jean Paget off a few months before. As I turned to go, he said gruffly, "Thank you for doing so much for me, Mr. Strachan. I'll be writing from Midhurst." And he shook my hand with a grip that made me wince, for all the injury his hand had suffered.

"That's all right, Joe. You'll find a letter from Miss Paget when you get back home. You might even find more than that."

I had reason for that last remark, because I had a letter from her in my pocket that had come by that day's mail, and it was postmarked Willstown.

WHEN Jean Paget arrived at Darwin Airport she was wildly and unreasonably happy. I think that till that time she had never really recovered from the war. Deep in the background of her mind remained the tragedy of Kuantan, killing her youth; she had very little zest for life.

She landed at Darwin at night, and as she finished with customs, a young man came up to her and said, "Miss Paget? The stewardess tells me that you're getting off here and you're staying at the Darwin Hotel. May I give you a lift into town? My name is Stuart Hopkinson; I represent the Sydney *Monitor* up here."

She said, "That's terribly kind of you, Mr. Hopkinson. I don't want to take you out of your way, though."

He said, "I'm staying there myself." And presently, as they drove along, he asked, "You're English, aren't you? Would you like to tell me why you're visiting Australia?"

She laughed. "It's only something personal—it wouldn't make a story. Is this where I get out and walk?"

"You don't have to do that. It's just that I haven't filed a story for a week," he said. "Come out to get married?"

"I don't think so."

He sighed. "I'm afraid you're not much good to me."

"Tell me, Mr. Hopkinson," she said. "I want to go to Alice Springs, and I haven't much money, so I thought I'd go by bus. Is that possible?"

"Sure, one went this morning. You'll have to wait till Monday now; they don't run over the weekend. It takes two days. Not too bad a journey, but hot."

At the hotel, she showered and went to sleep with a bare minimum of covering. Next morning she lay for some time in the cool of the dawn, considering her position. It was imperative that she find Joe Harman and talk to him; the meeting with Mr. Hopkinson had warned her of possible difficulties. However pleasant this young man might be, she had no desire to figure in the headlines: GIRL FLIES FROM BRITAIN TO SEEK SOLDIER CRUCIFIED FOR HER.

She invented a story for herself: she was going out to Adelaide to stay with her sister who was married to a man called Holmes who worked in the post office; that seemed fairly safe. She was traveling by way of Darwin and Alice Springs because a cousin called Joe Harman was supposed to be working there but hadn't written home for nine years, and her uncle in England wanted news of him. From Alice she would take the train down to Adelaide.

It seemed a pretty waterproof tale, and she got her chance to try it out on Stuart Hopkinson that morning as he showed her the way to the bus ticket office. The representative of the Sydney *Monitor* swallowed it without question. He took her into a milk bar and stood her a Coca-Cola. "Joe Harman . . ." he said. "What was he doing at Alice nine years ago?"

She sucked her straw and said innocently, "He was a cowboy on a cattle station." She hoped she wasn't overdoing it.

"A stockman? Do you remember the name of the station?"

"Wollara," she said. "That's the name. It's near Alice Springs, isn't it? Is it difficult to reach?"

"I don't know," he said. "I'll try and find out."

He came to her after lunch with Hal Porter of the Adelaide *Herald*, who informed Jean that Wollara was a good hundred and twenty miles from Alice Springs. "You mean Tommy Duveen's place, and there's no way of getting there except in a lorry or a utility," Porter advised. "By plane would be much the easiest. Maclean Airways run around most of those stations weekly."

On Sunday the two reporters took her around Darwin in a car. As they drove, the reporters told her about the city, and the picture they painted was a gloomy one. "Everything that happens here goes crook," Hal Porter said. "The meat works closed because of labor troubles. The railway was intended to go south to Alice and join up with the one from Alice down to Adelaide, but it stopped at Birdum. There used to be an ice factory, but that's closed down." He paused. "Everywhere you go round here you'll see ruins of things that have been tried and have failed."

"Why is that?" Jean asked. "It's not a bad place, this."

Stuart Hopkinson said cynically, "It's got outbackitis. You'll see a lot of this in Australia, specially in the north."

She asked, "Is Alice Springs like this?" It was so very different from Joe Harman's glowing recollections six years before.

"Oh, well," said Hopkinson, "Alice is different; it's a go-ahead place. Alice is all right."

That night she said good-by to her two friends, and at dawn she started for Alice Springs. The bus was streamlined and comfortable enough, although not air-conditioned, and it cruised down the wide, empty tarmac road at fifty miles an hour.

The country was wooded with stunted eucalyptuses—gum trees—which were interspersed with open meadows of wild land. Gradually the land became more arid, the trees more scattered, till by evening they were in country that was almost desert.

They stopped for the night at Daly Waters, which consisted of a hotel, a post office, and an airdrome. In front of the hotel, Jean saw three young men squatting on their heels with a leg extended in the attitude that Joe Harman had used; they wore jodhpur trousers and elastic-sided thin-soled boots, and they were intently playing cards on the ground. She realized that she was looking at her first ringers, and resisted an absurd temptation to go up and ask them if they knew anything about Joe Harman.

The next day the bus went on southward down the tarmac road; the vegetation grew sparser, the sun hotter, till by the time they stopped at Tennant Creek for a meal and a rest, the country had become pure sand. Toward evening they found themselves approaching the Macdonnell Ranges, lines of bare red hills against the pale blue sky, and at dusk they reached Alice Springs and drew up at the Talbot Arms Hotel.

Jean's room opened onto a porch, the hotel being a one-story bungalow-type building, like practically every other building in Alice Springs. Tea was served immediately—she had already learned that in Australian country hotels unless you are punctual for meals you will get nothing—and afterward she strolled slowly down the broad streets, examining the town.

She found it as Joe Harman had described it, a pleasant place. Despite the tropical surroundings and bungalows, there was a faint suggestion of an English suburb which made her feel at home. Each house stood in a small garden fenced around or bordered by a hedge for privacy; the streets were laid out like English streets with shade trees along the curbs. Alice was a bonza place, and she knew that she could build a happy life living in one of these houses, with two or three children, perhaps.

She strolled up the main street. The town had a hairdressing salon, dress shops, two picture houses . . . She went into the milk bar and bought an ice-cream soda. If this was the outback, she thought, there were many worse places.

After breakfast next morning she told the hotel manager the fiction about being on her way to Adelaide to stay with her sister. "I promised my uncle I'd stop in Alice Springs and try to find out something about a cousin of mine. He hasn't written home for nine years," she explained.

Mrs. Driver, the manager, was interested. "What's his name?"

"Joe Harman."

"Worked out at Wollara?" The woman shook her head. "He used to come in here just after the war. . . . Maybe one of the boys would know where he is now."

Old Art Foster, the general handyman, said, "Joe Harman? He got a job as station manager up in the Gulf country. Tommy Duveen, out at Wollara, would know where."

Jean asked innocently, "I suppose Joe took his family with him?"

The old man stared at her. "I never heard Joe Harman had a family. No, he's not married."

"My uncle back in England thought he was married." Jean deliberated for a minute, then asked Mrs. Driver, "Is there a telephone at Wollara? If Mr. Duveen knows Joe's address, I'd like to ring him up for it."

But there was no telephone line to Wollara, only a radio network that was operated by the flying-doctor service. Each morning and evening an operator at the hospital called up the forty or fifty stations on the radiotelephone, and messages were transmitted back and forth. "Mrs. Duveen is sure to be on the air tonight," Mrs. Driver said. "Her sister's in the hospital here for a baby, and she'll want to know if it's arrived yet. Write a message, and Mr. Taylor at the hospital will pass it on to them tonight."

Jean did so, and Mr. Taylor told her to come back late that evening. "They may know the address right off," he said.

That freed Jean for the remainder of the day. She went back to the milk bar for another ice-cream soda and made a friend there, a girl named Rose Sawyer, who was about eighteen and had an

Aberdeen terrier on a lead. She was very interested to hear that Jean came from England, and they talked about England for a time. "How do you like Alice?" she asked, with a touch of scorn.

"I like it," Jean said candidly. "I should think you could have a pretty good time here."

The girl said, "Well, before we came here all my friends said these outback places were just terrible, but it's not so bad."

Jean learned a little of the town's history from Rose Sawyer. In 1928, the year the railway reached it from Oodnadatta, it was about three houses and a pub. In 1930 the flying-doctor service was started, with small hospitals located in the surrounding districts. The hospital nurses had married furiously, and by 1939 the population was about three hundred; after the war it rose to about seven hundred and fifty, and when Jean was there it was about twelve hundred.

"People seem to be coming in here all the time now," Rose Sawyer said. "Of course, for myself, I'm a bit unsettled at present." She explained that she worked afternoons in a dress shop, but wanted a job for which she was better suited. She asked Jean if she might like to come swimming with her in the late afternoon. "I'll ring up Mrs. Maclean," she offered. "She's got a lovely swimming pool, out by the airdrome."

She drove Jean out there at five o'clock and they joined the party at the pool. Sitting and basking in the evening sun, Jean became absorbed into the social life of Alice Springs. Most of the women were under thirty—kindly, hospitable people, avid for news of England. None of them had ever been there, yet each cherished the ambition to go "home" for a trip one day. These pleasant people, who knew so much about her country, humbled Jean, who knew so very little about theirs.

That evening at the hospital, there was no address for Joe Harman, but Mrs. Duveen had promised to consult her husband and send a message on the morning schedule. Jean thought a good deal that night about Joe Harman. She was amazed that he had recovered enough from his injuries to carry on his work in the outback, but the man was tough. It would be impossible to leave Australia without seeing him again. She did not fear embarrassment at their meeting, but would tell him the truth frankly: she had heard of his survival and had come to satisfy herself that he was quite all right. If anything should happen after that . . .

She drifted into sleep, smiling a little.

At the hospital next morning, she learned that Joe Harman was the manager of Midhurst station, near Willstown. She had never heard of the place, so Mr. Taylor obligingly got out a radio-network map of Australia and showed her Willstown.

"It's a fair cow up there." He laughed. "It's got an airstrip but not much else. Oh my word. It's likely to be rough living."

"I've got to go there and see Joe Harman," Jean said. "Would there be a hotel?"

"Oh, there'll be a hotel. They've got to have their grog."

She left the hospital and went thoughtfully to the milk bar. As she ordered her ice-cream soda, it occurred to her that it might be a long time before she had another. Rose Sawyer found her there, studying bus and airline timetables.

"It'll be much easier to fly; everyone does these days, and you save on hotels and meals," Rose said. "I should take the Maclean service to Cloncurry, next Monday. If you want, you could stay with my family till then. Oh, please do! It's so seldom we talk with anyone from England, and the hotel's not very nice, is it? I've never been in there, of course."

Jean was already aware of the strict Australian code that makes it impossible for a woman to go into a bar. What a friendly gesture Rose's invitation was! "If you're sure it wouldn't be any trouble," she said gratefully, and presently went back to the hotel to pack her suitcase. Before going on to the Sawyers', she stopped off at the post office and spent a quarter of an hour sucking the end of a pencil. This was the telegram she finally composed to Joe Harman:

HEARD OF YOUR RECOVERY FROM KUANTAN ATROCITY QUITE RECENTLY PERFECTLY DELIGHTED STOP I AM IN AUSTRALIA AND COMING UP TO WILLSTOWN TO SEE YOU NEXT WEEK

JEAN PAGET

The Sawyers were kind people, and after the third day she could not bear to go on lying to them; she told Rose and her mother what had happened in Malaya and why she was looking for Joe Harman. She begged them not to spread the story, for fear that it would get into the papers. They asked her only to tell Mr. Sawyer about it when he came home from the office.

Mr. Sawyer had a lot to say that interested Jean that evening. "The Gulf country's not much at present," he said, "but Joe Harman's a young man and things can happen very quickly in Australia. This town was nothing twenty years ago and look at it now!" He went on. "The Gulf's got rain in its favor—thirty inches a year compared to our six or seven. That's bound to tell in the long run, you know." He sucked his pipe. "Mind you, it's not much good to them, that rainfall, because it all comes in two months and runs off into the sea. Water conservation, that's what the stations need."

Jean left Alice Springs on Monday morning and flew all that day in a Dragonfly. It zigzagged to and fro across the wastes of central Australia, depositing bags of mail at cattle stations, picking up stockriders and policemen to drop them off after a hundred miles or so. At each stop there would be tea and gossip with the station manager or owner, then back into the plane and away. Jean got to know exactly what a cattle-station homestead looked like and to have a good idea of what went on there.

At dusk they got to Cloncurry, a fairly extensive town on a railway that ran eastward to Townsville, on the sea. Here she was in Queensland, and she heard the slow, deliberate speech of the Queenslander that reminded her of Joe Harman at once. Cloncurry, she found, had none of the clean glamour of Alice Springs; it was redolent of cattle, with wide streets through which to drive the herds down to the stockyards, many hotels, and a few shops.

She spent the night there, and after breakfast, while the air was still cool, she walked up and down the main street. She looked in at a shop that sold toys and newspapers, but they were out of all reading matter except a few dressmaking journals. Back at the hotel, she lay on her bed and sweated out the heat of the day. Most of the citizens of Cloncurry were probably doing the same.

She was at the airdrome next morning with the first light. The aircraft again wandered around the cattle stations. At midday, after four or five landings, they came to the seashore, a desolate, marshy coast.

They got to Willstown in midafternoon. The countryside was well wooded and fairly green. The Gilbert River ran into the sea about three miles below the town; there was deep water in it as far up as Willstown. As they circled for a landing, Jean saw a wooden jetty, and the river running inland out of sight. All the other watercourses seemed to be dry.

The town consisted of about thirty low buildings spread along two intersecting unpaved streets. Only the hotel had two stories. From the town, dirt tracks ran out into the country in various directions, and nearby was a magnificent airdrome built there during the war for defense purposes. They landed on one of its huge runways and taxied toward a waiting petrol truck. The pilot said, "You're getting off here, Miss Paget? Is anyone meeting you?"

She shook her head. "I want to see a man who's living in this district, Joe Harman. He's manager of the Midhurst station."

"Al Burns, the Shell agent on the truck, knows everybody here."

They got out of the airplane together. "Morning, Al," the pilot said to the man on the truck. "She'll take about forty gallons. I'll have a look at the oil in a minute. Is Joe Harman in town?"

"Joe Harman?" said the man. "He's in England. On holiday."

Jean tried to collect her thoughts. She wanted to laugh. "I sent him a telegram to say that I was coming," she said foolishly. "I suppose he didn't get that."

"When did you send it?"

"About four or five days ago, from Alice Springs."

"Oh no, he wouldn't have got that," Al Burns said. "Jim Lennon might have it, out at Midhurst station. Joe went to England a month ago. He's expected back about the end of October."

The pilot turned to Jean. "What will you do, Miss Paget? Do you want to stay here? It's not much of a place, you know."

Jean bit her lip in thought. "When will you be taking off?" she asked the pilot. "You're going back to Cloncurry?"

"That's right. We'll be getting back to the Curry tomorrow morning. Take off in about half an hour."

Cloncurry was the last place she wanted to go back to. "I'll have to think about this," she said. "I'll have to stay in Australia till I've seen Joe Harman." She paused. "Could you suggest a nice place to stay?"

"Well, Cairns is a bonza town," the pilot said. "If you've got to wait six or eight weeks, you don't want to wait here, Miss Paget."

They discussed various ways of getting to Cairns. As usual, to travel by train would involve long delays. Jean was getting sensitive to the cost of flying these vast distances, but the alternative was almost unbearable. "It'd be much cheaper to stay here and go by the Dakota next week, wouldn't it?" she asked the pilot.

"Oh, much—about twenty pounds less."

"I suppose the hotel here is quite cheap?"

He turned to the Shell agent, busy with the fuel. "Al, how much does Mrs. Connor charge?"

"Ten and six."

Jean did a rapid mental calculation: by waiting here for the Dakota she would save sixteen pounds. "I think I'll stay here and see Jim Lennon and wait for the Dakota next week."

"It's a bit rough, Miss Paget. The whatnot's in the backyard."

She laughed. "Will I have to take a revolver to bed with me?"

The pilot was a little shocked. "Oh, you'll find it quite respectable. But, well, you may find it a little primitive, you know."

"I expect I'll survive."

By then another truck had appeared. The pilot took her suitcase and put it in back; the driver helped Jean up into the cab beside him. It was a relief to get away from the blazing sun. As they drove off, the driver asked, "Staying in Willstown?"

"Till next week, if Mrs. Connor can have me; then I'm going on to Cairns. I wanted to see Joe Harman, but he's away."

"Joe's gone to England. You're English, aren't you? My mother and dad both came from there—Sam Small's my name."

The truck left the runway and began bumping and swaying over the dusty track leading to town. Dust rose into the cab, the engine roared, and blue fumes enveloped them. "Why did Joe Harman go to England?" Jean shouted over the creaking and rattling.

"Just took a fancy, I think," Mr. Small replied. "He won the Casket a couple years back." This was Greek to her. "Nothing much to do on the stations this time of year."

The truck jolted over the landscape. A wooden shack appeared, then fifty yards away another; another short distance and they were in the main street. They drew up in front of a two-story building with a large faded sign over the first-floor veranda: AUSTRALIAN HOTEL. "This is it," Small said. "Come on in, and I'll find Mrs. Connor."

The hotel was a wood-frame building with iron siding. About ten small bedrooms opened onto the second-floor veranda. Mr. Small appeared with the landlady, a tall, gray-haired, determined woman who evidently had just awakened. Jean asked for a room, and Mrs. Connor looked her up and down.

"Traveling alone? You just missed the Cairns airplane."

"I know. They say I'll have to wait a week for the next one."

The woman looked around. "Well, I don't know. The men sleep on the top veranda. That wouldn't be very nice for you."

Sam Small said, "What about the two back rooms, Ma?"

"Aye, she could go there. It's on the back veranda, looks out over the yard." She showed Jean the room. It was clean and had a good mosquito net. "Nobody don't come along this veranda," she explained, "except Annie, the maid. She sleeps in the other room." She glanced down at Jean's hand. "You ain't married?"

"No."

"Well, there'll be every ringer in this district coming into town to have a look at you. You'd better be prepared for that."

Jean laughed. "I will."

Sam Small brought up her suitcase; she thanked him and he turned away, somewhat embarrassed. She had a shower and was ready for tea at half past six when the bell rang.

She found her way down to the dining room. Four men already seated there looked at her. A well-developed girl of sixteen, whom she came to know as Annie, indicated a small table laid for one.

"Roast beef, roast lamb, roast turkey," she said. "Tea or coffee?"

It was sweltering hot still. Flies were everywhere in the dining room; they lighted on Jean's face, her lips, her hands. "Turkey," she said; time enough to try for a light meal tomorrow. "Tea."

The plate was heaped high with meat and vegetables, hot and greasy. Tea came, with milk out of a can. The potatoes seemed fresh, but the carrots and turnips were evidently canned. The flies might cause dysentery, but she had plenty of sulfa pills. She ate about a quarter of the food and then escaped into the open air. On the downstairs veranda there were two or three deck chairs, a little distance from the entrance to the bar. She already knew enough about Australian conventions not to go near the bar, but since there was nowhere else in the hotel where she could sit, she hoped that she would not offend local manners.

She sat there looking at the scene. It was evening, but the dusty street was still flooded with golden sunlight. The only shop was a rambling building a hundred yards away on the opposite side, bearing the sign: WM. DUNCAN, GENERAL MERCHANTS. Outside Mr. Duncan's establishment were three Abo stockriders; one held the bridle of a horse. They were big, well-set-up young men, and they seemed to have plenty to laugh about.

Farther along the other side of the great street a six-inch pipe rose vertically from the ground to a height of about eight feet. From it gushed a fountain of water, which seemed to be boiling hot. A cloud of steam surrounded the fountain, and the stream running away into the background steamed along its length.

From time to time a man passed her and went into the bar, but she saw no women in the place. Presently a young man smiled at her from the road and said, "Good evening. I saw you come in with Sam Small this afternoon." He walked with the ringer's swaying gait, and wore jodhpurs and boots.

She smiled at him. "That's right," she said. "I came up from Cloncurry. Tell me, is that water natural?"

He looked where she was pointing. "That's a bore. Never seen one before? It's mineral—you couldn't drink that water. There's gas comes up with it as well." He went on to explain that the bore would make a flame five or six feet high. "Wait till it gets a bit darker and I'll light it for you."

She said that was terribly kind, and as they talked he told her his name was Pete Fletcher. Presently Al Burns, the Shell agent, came by and joined them. Before long there was a little gathering of men about Jean's chair. "Tell me," she said. "Why aren't the houses closer together? This town is so spread out."

A man she later learned to know as Tim Whelan, a carpenter, said, "There was houses all along here once, Miss Paget."

Al Burns said, "Oh my word. This was one of the gold towns, with thirty thousand people living here."

Jean asked, "How many are there now?"

"Oh, I dunno. How many would you say, Tim?" To Jean, aside, Al said, "He builds the coffins so he ought to know."

"A hundred and fifty," said Mr. Whelan.

"There's not a hundred and fifty in Willstown now. A hundred and twenty," shouted another man.

Sam Small joined them and a slow wrangle developed, so they set to work to count them. Jean sat amused while a census was taken. The result was a hundred and forty-six, and by then she had heard the names and occupations of most of the townspeople. "What happened? Did the gold come to an end?" she asked.

There was talk of the gold days and of how the cost of the mining machinery had ultimately not paid.

"But what happened to the houses?" Jean asked.

"They fell down, or were pulled down to patch up others," Al told her. "The people couldn't stay when the gold was done."

"Ghost towns," one of the men said. "That's what they call the Gulf towns. They became ghosts of what they were once."

While the men talked, Jean tried to visualize this derelict place as a town of thirty thousand inhabitants. Now all that remained was a network of tracks and odd buildings.

As the light faded, Pete and Al went out and lit the bore for Jean. They struck half a dozen matches before a flame shot upward; it lighted the whole town, flickering amid the water and the steam till finally it was extinguished by a gush of water. It was clearly the one entertainment that the town provided, and they were doing their best to give her a good time. "It's wonderful," she said. "I've never seen anything like that in England."

They were duly modest. "Most towns around here have a bore like that, that you can light," they said.

She was tired with her day of flying and at nine o'clock excused herself. She drew Al Burns to one side before she left. "I'd like to see Jim Lennon before I go on Wednesday. Will he be coming into town?"

"I'd say that he'd be coming in here Saturday for his grog," Al said. "If he doesn't, I'll run you out to Midhurst on Sunday."

"That's awfully kind of you."

"No trouble. Makes a bit of a change."

Breakfast next morning was at half past seven, and Jean found that the standard Willstown breakfast was half a pound of steak with two fried eggs on top. She surprised Annie by asking for one fried egg and no steak. "Breakfast is steak and eggs," Annie patiently informed this queer Englishwoman.

"Could I have just one fried egg, and no steak?"

"Just one fried egg on a plate by itself?" She came back from the kitchen with a steak topped by two fried eggs. "We've only got the one breakfast," she said, and Jean gave up the struggle.

After breakfast she sought out Mrs. Connor and asked if she could wash and iron a few things.

"Annie'll do them," Mrs. Connor said. "Just give them to her."

Jean had no intention of trusting her clothes to Annie. "She's got a lot of work to do, and I've got nothing," she said. "If I can just borrow the tub . . ."

"Good-oh."

Jean spent the morning washing and ironing on the back ground-floor veranda just outside the kitchen; in that dry, torrid place clothes hung out on a line were dry in ten minutes. Annie came presently and stood nearby, furtively examining Jean's washing. She picked up a carton of soap flakes. "How much of this do you use?"

Jean said, "I think it tells you on the packet."

The girl turned the packet over in her hands, scrutinizing it.

525

From the door Mrs. Connor said, "Annie don't read very well."

The girl said, "I can read."

"Oh, can you? Well, then, read us out what's written there."

The girl put the carton down. "I ain't had much practice lately. I could read all right when I was at school." After Mrs. Connor left, she asked Jean, "Are you a nurse?"

Jean shook her head. "I'm a typist."

"If you'd been a nurse," the girl said, "I'd have asked you for some medicine. I've been feeling ever so ill in the morning lately. I think I'll go up to the hospital tomorrow and ask Sister Douglas."

"I should do that," said Jean cautiously.

In the course of the morning she met most of the notable citizens of Willstown, including Mr. Bill Duncan in his store and Miss Kenroy, the schoolteacher.

She slept most of the afternoon, and when the day cooled off she went down to the front veranda, as she had the previous evening, and before long the ringers came one by one, unsure of themselves and yet unable to keep away.

She got them to talk about themselves; it seemed the best way to put them at ease. One of the men was leaving Willstown to work with his brother on the railway down at Rockhampton, and the talk centered on that.

Jean asked, "Is it better pay down there?"

"Well, no. The pay's all right here," Pete Fletcher said. "Trouble is this place. Nothing to do here. There's a chap supposed to come show films every fortnight—he hasn't been for a month."

"What about dances?" Jean asked.

There was a cynical laugh, then Pete explained. "There's about fifty of us stockriders, Miss Paget, and two unmarried girls to dance with. The girls all go to the cities. I'm going to Brisbane."

Jean said, "Don't you like it on a cattle station, then?" She was thinking of Joe Harman and his love for the outback.

Pete hesitated, uncertain how to put what he felt to this English-woman without using a rude word. "I mean," he said, "a fellow's got a right to have a girl and marry, like anybody else."

She stared at him. "It's really like that, is it?"

"It's a fair cow," said somebody. "No kidding, lady, a fellow hasn't got a chance of marrying up here."

Somebody else explained. "You see, Miss Paget, if a girl's normal and got her head screwed on right—say, like it might be you—you wouldn't stay here. Soon as you were old enough to go away from home, you'd be off to some place where you could make your own living. The only girls that stay in Willstown are the ones who are a bit stupid and couldn't get on well in any other place."

She was in her bedroom that night, still thinking about Pete's statement, when she noticed a figure standing on the veranda that overlooked the backyard. Only two bedrooms opened onto the veranda, her own and Annie's. She called good night to the girl, and Annie came in to her.

"I feel awful bad, Miss Paget. Mind if I ask you something?"

"Of course not, Annie. What's the matter?"

"Do you know how to get rid of a baby, Miss Paget?"

The morning's conversation had prepared Jean for this, and she felt a deep pity welling up for the child. She took her hand. "I'm sorry, but I don't think it's a good thing to do, you know."

"I thought you might have had to do it, and you'd know," Annie said. "Pa'll beat the daylights out of me when he hears."

"Why don't you ask the man to marry you, and have the baby?" Jean suggested.

"I don't know which one it was. They'd all say it was one of the others, wouldn't they?"

It was a problem that Jean had never had to face. She did her best to comfort her, but there was no way to help the girl.

On Saturday, Jim Lennon came into town, as predicted. He was a lean, bronzed, taciturn man, and he drove an International utility that Jean learned was the property of Joe Harman.

"I got an airmail letter yesterday," he said with the deliberation of the Queenslander. "Joe's starting back from England in a ship. Be here about the middle of October, he thought."

"I see," said Jean. "I want to see him before I go back to England. I've arranged to fly to Cairns on Wednesday and wait there for him. Mr. Lennon, what's Joe been doing in England?"

The stockrider laughed. "I don't know why he went. In yesterday's letter he said he'd seen a bonza herd of Herefords belonging to Sir Dennis Frampton. Maybe he went over to have bulls shipped out to raise the quality of the stock."

She gave him her address in Cairns, the Strand Hotel, and he promised to let her know the date of Joe's arrival.

That evening, as she was sitting on the veranda, Al Burns brought a bashful, bearded old man to her. He was carrying a sack. "Miss Paget, want you to meet Jeff Pocock," Al said. "He's the best crocodile hunter in all Queensland, aren't you, Jeff?"

The old man nodded. "Been hunting crocs since I was a boy."

"Show Miss Paget the skin, Jeff. Bet she's never seen one like it."

From the sack, Jeff Pocock took out a small rolled-up crocodile skin and spread it out on the veranda. "Cleaned and trimmed and tanned this one myself," he said, "though mostly we just salt 'em and sell 'em to the tannery. Pretty markings, ain't they?"

The sight of it brought back to Jean nostalgic memories of Pack and Levy Ltd. and the rows of girls at workbenches. She laughed. "I used to work in a factory that made these skins into shoes and handbags." She picked up the skin and handled it. "Ours were harder than this. You've done the curing very well, Jeff."

Other men drifted up, and her story was repeated until they had all heard about Pack and Levy. No one was certain what was done with the skins after they left the Gulf country. "I know as they make shoes of them," said Jeff. "I never see a pair."

A vague idea was forming in Jean's mind. She asked Jeff how many skins he obtained in a year. Eighty-two last year, he told her.

"Will you sell me this one?" she said.

"What do you want it for?"

She laughed. "I want to make myself a pair of shoes. That's if Tim Whelan can do up a pair of lasts for me. Here, how much do I owe you?"

But Jeff refused payment, and finally she accepted gracefully and said, "We'll want calfskin for the soles and some thicker stuff for the heels." She fondled the skin in her hands. "It's beautifully soft. I'll show you what to do with it."

SEVEN

THE business of the shoes assumed such importance in the life of Willstown that Jean put off her trip to Cairns for two weeks.

She made that pair of shoes, working on her bedroom dressing table—to be more exact, she made three pairs before she got one that she could wear. Tim Whelan made lasts for her of mulga wood, and Pete Fletcher produced some tanned cowhide of the right thickness for soles, and a piece of bull's skin for building up the heels. The only material for the lining seemed to be wallaby skin; Pete went out and shot and skinned a wallaby, and the tanning was done by a committee of Pete, Al Burns, and Don Duncan, working in the back of Bill Duncan's store.

The lining wasn't ready in time, so Jean used white satin for the first pair of shoes. She knew every process of shoemaking from the point of view of an onlooker, but she had never done it herself before, and the first pair were terrible. They pinched her toes, hurt her insteps, and the satin lining was messy with perspiration from her fingers. Still, they were shoes. She set to work on a second pair, which were better, but the whole job was finger-marked with sweat. Undaunted, she began a third pair. The final result was quite creditable. She showed the three pairs of shoes to the men on the veranda and they were awestruck, calling to each other to come and have a look.

"You made them yourself, Miss Paget?" one of the men said. "Oh my word, it's as good as you'd buy in a shop."

"Not really," Jean said, pointing out the defects. "I just wanted to show you what they do with all the skins Jeff brings in."

Jeff was out of town, so she could not show him the shoes that day. She left them with the men to take into the bar and talk over, and she went to have a bath. She had discovered how to have a bath in Willstown by that time.

Where the water from the bore ran off in a hot stream, a small

528

wooden hut had been built to span the stream, at such a distance from the bore that the temperature was just right for a bath. A rough concrete pool had been constructed, and you took your soap and towel, went to the hut, locked yourself in, and bathed in the warm saline water flowing through the pool.

The sunlight came in through chinks in the wooden walls and played on the water as Jean lay soaking. Since she had seen Jeff Pocock's crocodile skin, the idea of making shoes had been in her mind. From the time that she had learned of her inheritance she had been puzzled, and at times distressed, by the problem of what she was going to do with her life. She was a business girl, accustomed to industry. She had given up her work with Pack and Levy, but she had found nothing yet to fill the gap left in her life. Subconsciously she had been searching for the past six months to find something she could work at. The only work she really knew about was making and selling fancy leather goods.

She lay in the water, thinking. Suppose she could have a little workshop with about five girls, and a small tannery. Handpresses and a rotary polisher meant electricity—a small generator, or she could buy current from the hotel. An air conditioner to keep the shop cool and keep the girls' hands dry as they worked.

Could such a setup pay? Jeff Pocock got seventy shillings for an uncured crocodile skin. Pack and Levy paid about a hundred and eighty shillings for cured skins. Costs and labor would be cheaper in Australia, but there would be the cost of shipping the shoes to England, and an agent's fees. She wondered if Pack and Levy would sell for her. The major problem was not the business end of it, she thought. But could she train the sort of girl that she could get in Willstown to turn out first-class quality work, capable of being sold in Bond Street? That was the real problem.

That evening Sam Small came to her on the veranda. "About that pair of shoes you made, Miss Paget . . ." he said.

"Yes, Sam?"

"I been wondering if you could teach our Judy. You see, she's getting near sixteen, an age when she's got to do some work, and there ain't nothing here for her," Sam explained. "And I thought

this shoemaking, well, maybe it would do for her. We've got everything you need for it right in Willstown."

Jean thought for a minute. "It wouldn't work like that, Sam.
That pair of shoes you admire—they're rotten. I'm not saying we
can't turn out a decent shoe in Willstown, but we'd need proper
machinery and materials."

He looked at her keenly. "Was you thinking of a factory or
something, here in Willstown?"

They discussed the possibility of it. Sam estimated that Jean
could hire six or seven girls without much difficulty, girls of sixteen
or seventeen, just finishing with school. "How much would it cost
to put up a workshop?" Jean asked, and Sam calculated that it
would cost two hundred pounds. "I'd want it to have a double roof
and a veranda. It's got to be cool," Jean specified, and he raised
the estimate to four hundred pounds.

"Tell me, Sam, would people here like something of that sort?"

"You mean, if it kept the girls here in town, earning money,
instead of going off thousands of miles to the cities?" Sam paused
thoughtfully. "Oh my word, yes."

The next Wednesday she left Willstown for Cairns, a prosperous
town of about twenty thousand, situated on an inlet of the sea.
There were several streets of shops, and wide avenues with flower
beds down the middle. She liked Cairns from the start.

At the Strand Hotel she found a letter from me that had been
there for some days, and she replied by airmail:

My dear Noel,

I got your letter of the 24th when I arrived here yesterday, and I
wish I had a typewriter, because this is going to be a long letter.

First of all, thank you so very much for telling me what you did
about Joe Harman. You've evidently been very nice to him and, as
you know, that's being nice to me. I can't get over what you say
about him rushing off to England and spending all that money, just
to see me again. But people out here are like that. The ones that
I've met in the outback have all been like Joe Harman, very simple, very genuine, and very true.

And now, about Willstown. I don't know if Joe Harman will still be so keen on marrying me when he sees me; six years is a long time, and people change. I don't know if I'll be keen on marrying him. But if we were to want to marry, what he told you about Willstown is absolutely right.

It's just terrible, Noel. It's absolutely the bottom. There's nothing for a woman there except the washtub. I know that one ought to be able to get along without such things as radio and lipstick and ice cream and pretty clothes—I did in Malaya. But when it comes to no fresh milk or vegetables or fruit, it's a bit thick. I think that what Joe told you was right—no girl could come straight out from England and live happily in Willstown. I don't think I could.

And yet, Noel, I wouldn't want to see Joe try and change his way of life. He's a first-class station manager, and I wouldn't want to see him try and make his life anywhere else, just because he'd married a rich wife who wouldn't live where his work is.

Of course, you'll probably say that he could get another station near a better town; perhaps near Alice. I've thought a lot about that one. Midhurst gets more rainfall than in England; it seems to me that the Gulf country is a far better prospect than anything round Alice. I wouldn't like to think that he'd left good land for bad land, just because of me.

Noel, do you think I could have £5000 of my capital? I'm going to take the advice you always shove at me, and not do anything in a hurry. If when I meet Joe Harman he still wants to marry me, and if I want to marry him, I'm going to wait a bit, if I can get him to agree.

I'd like to work in Willstown for a year before committing myself to live there. I want to start a tiny workshop, making shoes and handbags out of crocodile skins. It's work I know about, and the materials are there to hand. I've written a long letter this morning to Mr. Pack to ask him if he would sell for me in England, and I've asked him to make me out a list of the things I'd want for a workshop employing up to ten girls, and what they cost; things like a press and a polisher, and a Knighton No. 6 sewing machine.

I should think the lot, including £400 for a building, would cost

531

about £1000. But I'm afraid that's not the whole story. If I'm going to start a workshop for girls, I want to open a shop to sell them things that women want. I want it to be a sort of ice-cream parlor with a few chromium-plated chairs and glass-topped tables. I want to sell fruit there and fresh vegetables flown in from Cairns. I want to sell fresh milk, too; Joe will have to keep a few cows. I want to sell sweets, and just a few little things like lipstick and powder and face cream and magazines.

The big expense here is the refrigerators. I think we'd have to allow £500 for those, and then there's the building and the furniture—say £1200 the lot. That makes, say, £2500 for capital expenditure. If I have £5000 of my capital, I should be able to stock the shop and the workshop and employ five or six girls for a year without selling anything at all, and by that time there should be some income. If there isn't, well that's too bad and I shall have lost my money.

I want to do this, Noel. Apart from Joe Harman and me, they're decent people in Willstown, and they've got so very little. I'd like to work there for a year as a sort of self-discipline and to keep from running to seed now that I've got all this money. I think I'd want to do this even if there wasn't any Joe Harman in the background at all, but I shan't make up my mind until I've had a talk with him.

May I have the £5000 to go ahead with this?

Jean

I got her letter five days later, and marked the passages about the money for Lester to read. He said, "I think we might let her have the money. She seems a responsible person."

"I'd like to think it over for a day or so," I said.

Accordingly, I arranged an appointment with Mr. Pack of Pack and Levy Ltd. He was coming to London on business the following Friday and agreed to call at my office.

He was a small, fat, cheerful man, and he brought with him a brown paper parcel. "Afore we start," he said, "these came in this morning." He unwrapped the parcel. It was a pair of crocodile-skin shoes. "They're what she made herself at this Willstown," he said. "With her own hands in her hotel bedroom, so she said."

I examined the shoes with interest. "Are they any good?"

"For selling in the trade they're bloody awful." He pointed out various crudities. "But if you take them as shoes made by a typist who never made a shoe before, well, they're bloody marvelous."

"She's told you what she wants to do?" I asked.

"Aye, that she did. I've had a letter from her."

"What do you think of her proposition, Mr. Pack?"

"I don't think she can do it," he said flatly. "I don't think she knows enough about the shoe business to make a go of it."

I must say I was disappointed, but it was as well to have the facts. "I see," I said quietly.

"She hasn't got the experience," he explained. "She's a good girl, Mr. Strachan, and she's got a good business head. But she's got no experience of making shoes to sell, and she's had no experience in keeping girls in order 'n' making them work for their money."

His suggestion was that Jean hire an experienced forewoman from England and pay her passage to Queensland. "I got a girl in my shop—well, a woman she is, thirty-five, and not living with her husband—who might be willing to try it. Aggie Topp the name is. You wouldn't get girls playing up with Aggie Topp in charge."

"Does Miss Paget know her?"

"Oh, aye, Jean knows her. Matter of fact, Aggie's getting restless, hands in her notice every two or three months. I asked her yesterday if she would like to go to Australia for a year to work with Miss Paget. She said she'd go anywhere to get away from standing in a queue for the bloody rations. She'd go out for a year if Jean wants her. They all liked Jean."

The woman's passage and pay while traveling would tot up to three hundred pounds, which seemed cheap to me if it would help the venture get started. Mr. Pack was willing to do the selling for Jean and would airmail her samples of style changes from time to time. "Mind, I don't know if she can make a go of it at the prices we can sell at, but I'd like to give it a spin."

I thanked him very sincerely, and he went away. I wrote all this out to Jean Paget, and I believe Mr. Pack wrote to her as well. There was an interval of several days before a letter arrived from

Jean. She remembered the gaunt, stern Aggie very well and
thought that it would be really something if Aggie would come to
Queensland. I think that she was beginning to feel very much alone
and among strangers while she waited for Joe Harman.

She told me later that the three weeks in Cairns was the worst
time of her life. Each morning she woke up convinced that she
could never settle down in this outlandish country, and that it
would be much better not to meet Harman again at all. The wise
course was to take the next plane back to England, where she
belonged. But by evening she knew that if she left she would be
running away from things that she might never find again her
whole life through. So she would go to bed resolved to be patient,
and in the morning the whole cycle would start off once more.

She found out when Harman's ship was expected to dock at
Brisbane. She also knew, because of the airline schedules, that he
must pass through Cairns before going on to Willstown. She wrote
to him care of the shipping line at Brisbane:

Dear Joe,
I got a letter from Mr. Strachan telling me that you had been to
see him while you were in England, and that you were sorry to have
missed me. Funnily enough, I have been in Australia for some
weeks, and I will wait at Cairns here so that we can have a talk
before you go on to Willstown.

Will you let me know when you will be coming up to Cairns? I
do want to meet you again.

Yours sincerely,
Jean Paget

She got a telegram on a Tuesday saying he would be flying up to
Cairns on Thursday. She went to meet him at the airdrome, feeling
absurdly like a girl of seventeen keeping her first date.

I think Joe Harman was in a position of some difficulty, too. For
six years he had carried the image of this girl in his heart, but, in
sober fact, he didn't in the least know what she looked like. The
girl he remembered had a pigtail down her back, was very brown,
wore a tattered, faded sarong and walked on bare feet. He must

have been distressed by the thought that he probably wouldn't be able to recognize Jean again.

She waited for him by the rails bordering the scorching tarmac as the plane taxied in. She recognized him as he came out of the machine, fair-haired, blue-eyed, broad-shouldered. He was looking anxiously about; his gaze rested on her a minute and passed on. She wondered if she looked very old, and saw him start to walk toward the airline office with a curious stiff gait. A little shaft of pain struck her; Kuantan had left its mark on him.

She walked quickly across the tarmac. "Joe!" He stopped and stared at her incredulously. It was unbelievable that this pretty girl in a light summer dress was the ragged figure he had last seen on the road in Malaya, with blood upon her face where the Japanese soldiers had hit her. Then he saw a characteristic turn of her head and memories came flooding back to him; it was Mrs. Boong again, the Mrs. Boong he had remembered all those years.

It was not in him to be able to express what he was feeling. He grinned a little sheepishly and said, "Hello, Miss Paget."

She took his hand impulsively. "Oh, Joe!"

He pressed her hand and looked down into her eyes, and then he said, "Where are you staying?"

She said, "I'm at the Strand Hotel."

"Why, that's where I'm staying. I always go there."

In the taxi as they drove into town she asked him about me.

"Mr. Strachan was fine," he said. "I stayed with him quite a long time, in his flat."

"Did you!" She had not known that part of it.

She did not ask why he had gone to England; he forestalled her by inquiring, "What have you been doing in Australia?"

She temporized. "Didn't you know I was here?"

He shook his head. "All I knew was what Mr. Strachan said, that you were traveling in the East. You could have knocked me down with a feather when I got your letter at Brisbane. Oh my word, you could. Tell me, what are you doing in Cairns?"

A little smile played around her mouth, "What were you doing in England?"

He did not know what to say to that. "We've got a good bit of explaining to do, Joe," she said. "Let's leave it till we get to the hotel and find somewhere to talk."

Jean's hotel room opened onto a balcony overlooking the sea to the green hills behind Cape Grafton. Joe met her there, and she asked, "What about a beer or two?"

He grinned. "Good-oh."

She ordered three beers for him and one for herself. When the waitress had gone and they were alone, she said quietly, "Let me have a good look at you, Joe."

He stood before her, examining her beauty; he had not dreamed that she was a girl like this. "You've not changed," she said. "Does the back trouble you?"

"Doesn't hinder me riding, but I can't lift heavy weights."

He stood beside her while she took one of his hands and turned it over, looking at the great scars on the palm and back. "What about these, Joe?"

"They're all right," he said. "I can grip anything—start up a truck, or anything."

They sat down in some deck chairs with the beer. He took a glass and sank half of it. "Tell me what happened—after Kuantan," he asked. "I do want to know."

She sipped her beer and told him about Kuala Telang. "They let us stay there," she said. "We just lived in the village, working in the paddy fields till the war was over."

"You mean paddling about in the water, planting the rice, like the Malays? Oh my word," he breathed.

She said, "It wasn't a bad life. I'd rather have been there than in a camp—we were all fairly healthy when the war ended. We started a school and managed to teach the children something."

"I did hear a bit about that," he said thoughtfully. "From a pilot down at Julia Creek. He flew you out to Singapore in 1945."

"I remember," Jean said slowly. "A thin, fair-haired boy. What did he tell you about me?" Joe said nothing. She coaxed, "Come on, Joe. Have another beer, and let's get this straight."

He took another glass, but did not drink. "He said you were a

536

single woman, Mrs. Boong. I thought the lot of you was married."

"Is that why you went rushing off to England?"

He met her eyes. "That's right."

"Oh, Joe! What a waste of money, when we're here in Cairns."

Then it was her turn to bring him up to date. She told him about inheriting the money, which he already knew about, and of getting the idea to do something for the people of Kuala Telang. Sitting there with the glass of beer in her hand, she described the journey back to Malaya, her friends in the village, and the building of the washhouse and the well. She came now to the difficult part: the discovery that he had survived. "I thought that you were dead, Joe. We all did. Then the well diggers told me you weren't. I went to the hospital in Kuantan, hoping to find out more about you. They told me you'd asked about us." She smiled. "Mrs. Boong."

"But did you come on to Australia from there?"

She nodded. "Yes."

"What for?"

"Well," she said awkwardly, "I wanted to see if you were all right. I thought perhaps you might be in hospital or something."

"You came on to Australia because of me?"

"In a way," she said. "Don't let it put ideas in your head."

"Well, you're a fine one to talk about me wasting money," he said. "We'd have met all right if you'd stayed in England."

She said indignantly, "How was I to know that you'd be turning up in England, and fit as a flea?"

They sat drinking their beer for a time. "How did you get here?" he asked. "Where did you come to first?"

She said, "I knew you used to work at Wollara and I thought they'd know about you there. So I flew from Singapore to Darwin, and went down to Alice on the bus."

"Oh my word. You went to Alice Springs?"

"I stayed about a week. I got your address at Midhurst from Mr. Duveen, over the radio. So then I flew up to Willstown. But they told me there, of course, that you were in England."

He stared at her. "You've been to Willstown?"

"I was there three weeks with Mrs. Connor, in the hotel."

"But why three weeks? Three hours would have been enough for most people."

"I had to stay somewhere," she said. "If you go running off to England, people who want to see you have to hang around."

"What did you do all the time?"

"Sat around and talked to Al Burns and Pete Fletcher and Sam Small, and all the rest."

"You must have created a riot." He paused, considering this. At last he said, "What did you think of Willstown, Miss Paget?"

She laughed. "Look, Joe, you can call me Mrs. Boong or Jean, but if you go on with Miss Paget, I'll go home tomorrow." The bell rang downstairs. "And we'll be late for tea, Joe," she said, "if we start on Willstown."

"Tell me," he said.

She looked up at him. "I thought it was an awful place," she said quietly. "I can't see how anyone can bear to live there." She laid her hand on his arm. "I want to talk to you about it, but we must have tea now."

"Too right," he said. "It's a crook kind of a place for a woman."

They went down to tea and sat at a small table, Joe deep in gloom. When they had ordered, Jean said, "When have you got to be back at Midhurst?"

"When I'm ready." He paused. "What about you?"

"I suppose I'll start looking for a boat home next week."

Their food came and he asked presently, "Been out to the reef?"

"No," she answered.

His face lit up. "Oh my word. You can't go home without seeing the Great Barrier Reef." He paused a moment. "Would you like to go out to Green Island for the weekend?"

She cocked an eye at him. "What's Green Island?"

It was a little coral island on the reef, he explained, with a restaurant and bedroom huts for guests. Jean felt that the bedroom huts wanted checking on, but the suggestion had its points. A weekend there with Joe Harman and they would certainly come back knowing more about each other.

"I'd like to do that, Joe," she said, and was glad for him as he beamed with pleasure. "But, look, it's to be Dutch treat. We'll both pay our own bills," she said. He objected strenuously until she warned that she wouldn't go otherwise. "I'll think you're plotting to do me a bit of no good."

He grinned. "Too right." And then he said, "All right, Mrs. Boong, we'll each pay our own whack."

After tea he went out to arrange boat transportation to the island, and when he came back they sat together in the quick dusk and darkness, talking of everything but Willstown. He described his scheme for preserving rainfall at Midhurst by constructing dams at the head of the creeks. "Trouble is, of course, to get the labor." He sighed. "You can't get chaps to work in the outback."

Jean had a very good idea of why this was so, but there was time enough later to pursue the subject. He told her about his horses and dogs. "You couldn't get along in the outback without a dog to sit by you in the evenings," he said. And she could picture the long, lonely nights that were his normal life.

At ten o'clock they said good night, to prepare for an early start in the morning. They stood together in the darkness outside her room for a moment. "Have I changed much, Joe?" she asked.

"I wouldn't have known you again."

"I didn't think you would. Six years is a long time."

"You haven't changed at all, really," he said. "You're the same person underneath."

"After the war I felt like an old woman," she said slowly. "After Kuantan, I didn't think I'd ever enjoy anything again—like a weekend at Green Island." She smiled.

They left next morning in a motor launch, chugging out over the smooth sea. Green Island appeared after an hour, the tops of coconut palms visible above the horizon, then the little circular island itself, fringed around with a white coral beach. There was a long pier built out over the shallow water of the reef; they landed and walked down this together, pausing to look at the scarlet and blue fish playing around the coral below.

There were no other visitors, and they were given two little bedroom huts in among the trees. The huts had open sides to let the breeze through, with curtains for privacy. They changed clothes at once and met on the beach. Jean's new white two-piece bathing costume got a flattering reception. "It's as pretty as a picture," Joe said. "Oh my word."

"I'll have to look out I don't get burned."

He stood looking at her, reluctant to take his eyes off her beauty. "You've been out in the sun up top, though."

"That's from wearing the sarong in Kuala Telang," she said. "While they were digging the well." Her shoulders and arms were tanned, and there was a hard line above her breasts, brown above and white below.

As they turned to go into the water, she saw his back for the first time, lined and puckered with enormous scars. Deep sorrow welled up in her. This man had been hurt enough for her already, she thought; she must not hurt him any more.

They rolled over in the blue translucent water; the sun made silvery ripples on the white coral sand around them. They had to keep close to shore because of the sharks. "In Kuala Telang, there were crocodiles in the river," Jean said. "All in all, I guess there's nothing to beat a good swimming pool in a hot country."

"I've never bathed in a swimming pool," Joe said.

"Mrs. Maclean's got a pool at Alice Springs."

"I know—built it a year or two ago. I've never seen it."

She rolled over on her back and watched a sea gull soaring in the thermals from the island. "You could have a pool at Willstown," she said. "You've got all the water in the world, from the bore, running to waste. You could make a lovely swimming pool right opposite the hotel."

"That water isn't running to waste. The cattle drink it."

"Wouldn't hurt the cattle if we borrowed it first and used it for a swimming pool," she said. "It'd taste all the sweeter."

"Might taste sweeter if you swam in it," he concurred. "I don't know about me."

After the swim they sat in the shade of the trees up from the beach for a time, then went back to their huts for lunch. Joe had arranged for a light lunch of cold meat and fruit, and while she struggled to eat a mango decently, she asked, "Why don't places like Willstown have more fresh fruit? Won't it grow there?"

"It will all right," he said, "but there aren't enough people in the country to grow it. We can't even get ringers on the stations. They won't come to the outback."

She said thoughtfully, "There were plenty of fresh vegetables at Alice Springs."

"Ah, Alice is different. Alice is a bonza little town."

They slept in the heat of the day and bathed again before tea; in the cool of the evening they fished from the end of a jetty.

Then they just sat and watched the sunset. "It's funny," Jean said. "You go to a new country and expect everything to be different. There's such a lot that stays the same. That sunset might be in England on a fine summer evening. Cairns is a lot like Ealing, where I used to live."

"When you go home," Joe asked, "will you live there again?"

"I don't know," she said. "I don't know what I'll do, Joe."

In the evening light, sitting together and watching the sunset over the water, she had expected some overture from him. She had expected to spend the whole weekend on the defensive, but he had not tried even to kiss her, and it was beginning to distress her.

At bedtime they said good night in the most orderly way, not even shaking hands, and retired to their huts with perfect decorum. Jean lay awake for a long time, restless and troubled. Nor were things any better the next day.

They bathed in the cool of the morning in that marvelous translucent sea. They walked out on the reef at low tide, paddled in a glass-bottomed boat to see the colored fish, and he made no gesture of intimacy. By teatime, conversation was an effort and restraint was heavy on both of them.

In the evening they decided to walk around the island on the beach. Jean went into her hut and called out, "Give me a couple of minutes, Joe. I don't want to go in this frock."

He turned in the half-light as she came out of the hut, and he was back in the Malaya of six years ago. Jean was wearing the same old faded cotton sarong. Her brown shoulders and arms were bare; she was barefoot, and her hair hung down in a plait. She was Mrs. Boong again. She came to him shyly and put both hands on his shoulders. "Is this better, Joe?"

She could never remember very clearly what happened in the next five minutes. She stood locked in his arms as he kissed her face and neck and shoulders hungrily; in the tumult of feelings that swept over her she knew that this man wanted her as nobody ever had before. She stood unresisting in his arms; it never entered her head to struggle or to try to get away. She never knew how they got into her bedroom hut, and now a new confusion came to her. The sarong was loosening. Standing in his arms, she thought, It had to happen sometime, and I'm glad it's Joe. And then she thought, I must sit down or I'll be stark naked, and at that she escaped from his arms and sat on the bed.

He followed her, laughing, and her eyes laughed back at him as she tried to hold her sarong up to hide her bosom. Then she was in his arms again. He said quite simply, "Do you mind?"

She reached an arm around his shoulder. "Dear Joe. Not if you've got to. If you *can* wait till we're married, I'd much rather, but whatever you do now, I'll love you just the same."

He looked into her eyes. "Say that again."

She drew his head down and kissed him. "Dear Joe. Of course I'm in love with you. What do you think I came to Australia for?"

"Will you marry me?"

"Of course I'll marry you." She looked up at him with fondness. "Anyone looking at us now would say we were married already."

He was holding her more gently now. "I don't know what you must think of me."

"Shall I tell you?" She took one of his wounded hands and fondled the great scars. "I think you're the man I want to marry and have children by." It did not seem to matter now that the sarong had fallen to her waist. "Marriage is a big thing, Joe, and there are things that ought to be done first. But if you say we can't wait, then I'll marry you tomorrow, or tonight."

He drew her closer and kissed her fingertips. "I've waited six years. I can wait a bit longer."

She said softly, "Poor Joe. I'll try and make it easy, and not tantalize you." She freed herself from his arms and pulled up the sarong and rolled it around. "Just get outside a minute and I'll put on some more clothes."

Presently they stood upon the beach in the bright moonlight, holding each other tight. "I never knew a man could be so happy," he said once.

SHE woke with the first light of dawn. At last, she felt, things would go right between them. She peered cautiously over at Joe's hut. There was no sign of movement anywhere, and she went down to the sea and had a bathe. Then she went back to her hut and dressed, and went over to the restaurant. It stood open, but there was nobody about. She made tea and carried a cup to Joe's hut.

He was lying on the bed in a pair of shorts, sleeping as easily as a little boy; the scars upon his back stood out with an appalling ferocity. She stood for a while watching him, knowing that she would see him so most of the mornings of her life to come.

As she put down the cup, he opened his eyes and looked at her. He raised himself up on one arm. "Tell me," he said. "Did what I think happened last night really happen?"

"I think so, Joe," she said.

He stretched out a hand. "Come and let me give you a kiss."

"Not on your life." She laughed. "Not until you're up and bathed and have some clothes on."

After breakfast they sat over a last cup of coffee. They had no difficulty in finding things to talk of now, and even their silences were intimate. Joe said, "I've been thinking. I'm going to give up Midhurst, as soon as Mrs. Spears can find another manager. We'll get a grazing farm near Adelaide or some other city, so that we could get into town anytime."

Jean didn't reply at once; this needed careful handling. "But what's wrong with Midhurst, Joe?"

"Adelaide's a bonza city," he said. "Oh my word. It's got streets of shops and cinemas and dance halls—"

"But Joe, is that the sort of work you want to do? Just buying cattle and fattening them? It sounds awfully dull to me. Are you fed up with the outback?"

"There's places that suit single men and places that suit married people," he said. "You've got to make a change or two when you get married."

The breakfast table was between them, separating them. "Let's go outside," she said, and they found a patch of sandy grass at the head of the beach in the shade and sat there together. "I don't think you ought to leave the outback just because we're getting married," Jean said.

He smiled at her. "The Gulf country's no place for a woman, especially one from England. The life's too different."

Jean went carefully. "You're afraid our marriage will go wrong at Midhurst, aren't you?" She took his hand in hers.

"Too right."

There was a long silence. "I'm afraid, too," she said at last.

He could not bear that she should be afraid of anything in their new life. "Of what?" he asked gently.

She said, "I'm afraid of changing your job." She paused. "You've been used to a property of two thousand square miles, Joe. What would a man like you do on a thousand acres?"

"Get accustomed to it pretty soon, I should think."

"I know you'd do it," she said quietly, "but sometimes you'd think of your old life in the Gulf country and how you had to give it up because of me. That would be between us all the time. That's what I'm afraid of, Joe. I think we ought to stay up in the Gulf country, where your work is."

"You just said you couldn't stand Willstown," he objected.

"I know I'm not being very reasonable," she said thoughtfully. "First I say it's an awful place, and then I say that you oughtn't to think of living anywhere else."

Now he clasped her hand, puzzled and distressed. "We've got to try and work it out some way to find what suits us both."

"There's only one way to do that," she said.

"What's that?"

She smiled. "We'll have to do something about Willstown, Joe."

THEY SPENT THE remainder of the weekend in a curious mixture of loving affection and serious economic discussion.

"You can't tell me that a country with three times the rainfall of the Northern Territory can't support a town as good as Alice," Jean said at one point. They had bathed and were sitting together in the shade of a coconut tree.

Joe held forth on the subject of rain conservation. "I'd start with little dams to hold back the water in the creeks, so's you'd get a little pool every two or three miles," he said. "You could add a lot of feed to Midhurst if you did that. It'd double the cattle stock."

"Then it would be worth spending a bit of capital on dams, wouldn't it?" Jean said.

"Mrs. Spears has already agreed to the cost," he said, "but you'd need a permanent gang of men for the job. It could be years before I get the men. You see, there's only three of us at Midhurst—me and Jim Lennon and Dave Hope—plus a few Abo stockriders."

"How many would you like to have?" she asked.

"With eighteen thousand head of cattle, I could use twenty men. There'd be fences and stockyards and all sorts of things to make."

They sat thoughtfully for a moment. "If all the stations developed like you say," she theorized, "that would mean three or four hundred ringers in the district, all with wives and families—we'd have room for a town of two or three thousand people."

He smiled. "You'll be making it as big as Brisbane next."

She looked at him. "Joe, listen, would you think it very stupid if I wanted to start a business in Willstown?"

"A business? What sort of business could you do in Willstown?"

"There's such a lot that you don't know about me." And he listened in amazement to her account of Pack and Levy, and the crocodile shoes, and Aggie Topp. "That's what I want to do, Joe," she concluded. "Do you think it's crazy?"

"I don't know," he said.

"I'd just make shoes to start with. A little workshop with six or seven girls—it wouldn't cost any more than I can afford to lose."

"You wouldn't keep six or seven girls six weeks. They'd all get married."

She laughed. "Then I'd have to find six or seven more."

They bathed again and lay in the clean silvery water, and presently she said, "You won't drown if I throw another shock at you? I want to start an ice-cream parlor in Willstown."

"Oh my word."

"I'm going to pay these girls a lot of money, Joe," she said seriously. "I've got to get some of it back."

"An ice-cream parlor in Willstown?" he said. "It'll never pay."

"Wait till you see what I charge for an ice cream—and fruit and vegetables, quick-frozen stuff, and magazines, and cosmetics," Jean remonstrated. "All the little things that women want. I even know a very pretty girl who might come and run it for me, Rose Sawyer from Alice Springs. She's been wanting a new job."

He said slowly, "If you get a girl like that, the women won't be able to get into the shop. It'll be full of ringers."

"That's all right, as long as they buy ice cream. Joe, can you imagine? On Sundays, with the bar in the hotel shut, all the men would take their wives and kids to the ice-cream parlor, just as they do in Alice Springs. Wouldn't it be wonderful?"

They got out of the sea presently; he would not let her stay in long for fear of sunburn. They sat in the shade under the trees, discussing the cost of these undertakings in relation to the money Jean had inherited. "I've got enough for it," she told him.

He turned to her. "Mr. Strachan told me you were a wealthy woman. Don't tell me if you'd rather not say, but if I knew about how much you've got, I'd be able to help you more."

"I've got about fifty-three thousand pounds. It's all in trust till I'm thirty-five."

"Oh my word."

"I admit I don't know anything about real business. I just think—well, we'd be using the money the way it ought to be used, in places like Willstown."

She kissed him. "You say men are leaving the outback," she went on. "Well, of course they will if they can't get a girl. For every girl I make a job for, I believe you'll get a man to work at Midhurst. I do want to try to start this business before we get married, Joe.

You know, I don't believe you'll waste much time starting a family. When is the cattle mustering?"

"After the wet—normally, the middle of February. Then there's the branding of calves and driving the stock down to Julia Creek."

"Could we get married after the mustering, say, early in April? I'd have nearly a year from now to start the business, then I could leave it for a month or two while we start our family."

"I'd call that good-oh." He grinned.

The weekend on Green Island ended, and the motor launch carried them back to Cairns. They visited a tannery and discussed crocodile skins and other shoe materials. The manager, Mr. Gordon, approved using wallaby for linings, and Joe arranged to send him half a dozen skins for sample bleaching and glazing by the next lorry.

They got back to the hotel at dusk. They had booked passage to Willstown on the morning plane. "Before we leave," Jean said, "I must write to Noel Strachan and tell him what's happened."

She sat on the veranda and wrote me a letter. Joe Harman sat quietly beside her as she wrote, at peace.

It was a long letter from a very happy girl, telling me about her love. I was delighted at the news, of course. I sat reading it with my breakfast, then I read it through again, and then a third time.

It was cold and raw out in the street, when I walked to the office in a dream, thinking about wallabies and laughing stock-riders, about blue water running over white coral sands, about Jean Paget and her sarong. . . . I had a client or two that morning, and I suppose I gave them some advice, but my mind was twelve thousand miles away.

By the end of the day I knew that long letter by heart. I took it with me to the club, and after dinner and a couple of rubbers of bridge I ran into Wright, who had been in the Malay police. I dropped down into a chair beside him and remarked, "You remember that girl Jean Paget I spoke to you about? She's got herself engaged to be married. Manager of a cattle station, in northern Queensland."

"Indeed?" he said. "What's he like?"

547

"I've met him," I replied. "He's a very good chap. I think they're going to be very happy."

"Is she coming back to England before getting married?"

"No," I said. "I think she'll make her life in Queensland now. She's got no ties in this country."

And then he said a very foolish thing, however well he meant it. I got up and left and avoided him for some time after that. I was seventy-three years old that autumn, old enough to be her grandfather. I couldn't possibly have been in love with her myself.

EIGHT

IN THE months of November and December that year Jean Paget worked harder than she had ever worked before.

Rose Sawyer was eager to give the ice-cream parlor a try, and joined her in Willstown within a fortnight. Aggie Topp sailed for Australia early in November. She came to see me before she left. A gaunt, rather prim woman, I could see at once that if anyone could make girls work she could. I gave her her ticket and a typed sheet of instructions for getting by air from Sydney to Willstown.

Jean was anxious to get the air-conditioning unit. She had not been able to find one in Australia, but I'd got hold of one. Mrs. Topp took it out with her, along with three cases of tools and lasts and formers and all sorts of things from Pack and Levy.

The day that Joe Harman and Jean arrived in Willstown, they met with Tim Whelan and his two sons in the carpenter's shop. They had already ordered lumber from Cairns and were planning the layout of the buildings. The workshop, with a three-bedroom annex for Jean and Rose and Aggie, was to be built first, and after that the ice-cream parlor next door, leaving space for the expansion of either building. Mr. Carter, the shire clerk, approved the plans and granted them a lease of the site on the main street. The rent for building on the land, he said, would be about a shilling a year for each hundred feet of frontage.

Jean went to Brisbane a week later. She stayed there for three days, ordered an electric generator, a large refrigerator, two deep freezers, a stainless-steel counter, eight glass-topped tables, thirty-two chairs, two sink units, glasses, plates, cutlery, and furnishings, as well as electrical fittings and cable. She made arrangements for all of this to be crated and trucked to Willstown.

When she came back to Willstown after making tentative arrangements for supplies of stock for her ice-cream parlor, she found the framework of the workshop already erected. It was a nine-day wonder in Willstown; old men used to stand around marveling at this midsummer madness of an English girl who proposed to make shoes there and send them all the way to England to be sold.

She visited Midhurst one Sunday when no work was in progress on her building. Joe Harman fetched her in his utility at dawn. Hitherto she had not been beyond the town. The land was parched and dry with the summer heat, covered with scorched grass and spindly gum trees so widely spaced that it was possible for a car or a truck to find a way between them.

Once in the twenty miles she saw half a dozen cattle, which stampeded wildly at the noise of the utility as it rocketed over the uneven ground. Farther on she exclaimed at three brown furry forms bounding away among the trees. "Oh, Joe—kangaroos!"

He corrected her. "Wallabies. They're smaller than 'roos. We don't get any 'roos up in these parts. I've got a tame wallaby to show you at the homestead."

At the entrance to Midhurst a fence of two wire strands tacked to trees crossed their path. Jean got out and opened an iron gate, and Joe drove through. "This is the home paddock," he said. "I've got about three square miles fenced off around the house."

The road swung around and she saw Midhurst homestead, situated on a low hill above the bend of a creek. A fairly large wooden building, with the familiar corrugated-iron roof, it stood on posts, so that you climbed eight feet up a flight of steps to reach it. The three bedrooms and one sitting room were surrounded on all four sides by a veranda twelve feet deep; masses of ferns and greenery in pots killed most of the direct rays of the sun. Suspended from the rafters was a large canvas water bag cooling in the draft, with an enameled mug hung from it by a string. There was a kitchen at one end and a bathroom annex at the other; the toilet was a little hut over a pit in the paddock, some distance from the house.

As the utility halted, five or six dogs greeted them noisily. Joe pointed out a large blue-and-yellow bitch like no dog Jean had ever seen. "That's Lily," he said fondly. "She had a bonza litter."

He took her up into the coolness of the veranda; puppies were surging about them, odd-shaped yellow-and-blue puppies. Joe dropped them one by one into a wire-netting enclosure in one corner. "I left them out this morning," he said. "They'll be big enough to go down in the yard pretty soon."

"Oh, Joe, this is nice! Who fixed up these plants?"

"Mrs. Spears, when she lived here. The women water them, morning and evening." He told her that three Abo women, wives of stockriders, shared the domestic duties and cooked for him.

They found the wallaby lolloping about on the veranda; it stood like a little kangaroo about eighteen inches high, and had no fear of them. Jean stooped beside it and it nibbled at her fingers.

The table was laid for breakfast, and presently a black woman appeared, with the usual egg-topped steak and a pot of strong tea. Joe told Jean this was Palmolive, wife of Moonshine, an Abo ringer. The steak was tougher than most. As Jean struggled with it she made a mental note to look into the cooking at Midhurst.

Joe took her out before the heat of the day to see the establishment. Although the property covered more than a thousand square miles, there were no more buildings than she had seen on a four-hundred-acre farm in England. There were four cottages for married stockriders and two small bunkhouses for unmarried ones. A shed housed the utility and machinery. There was a stable for six horses, and a saddle room, a butcher's room; a diesel engine drove a generator that pumped water from the creek. That was about all.

He said, "Can you ride a horse?"

She shook her head. "I'm afraid not, Joe. Could I learn?"

"Too right," he answered. He put his fingers in his mouth like a schoolboy and blew a shrill whistle; a seamed black face poked out of a cottage window. "Bourneville," he called, "Saddle up Auntie and Robin. I'll be down to help you in a minute."

He surveyed her cotton dress, then took her up into the homestead and produced a man's shirt, a faded pair of jodhpurs, and a belt for her. She went into a spare room and put them on, with a pair of elastic-sided boots that were much too big for her. It gave her a queer feeling of possession to be dressed in his clothes.

Once astride the patient fourteen-year-old Auntie she felt very safe. The saddle was like no saddle she had ever seen. It had a great horn and it rose up high behind her, so that she was seated as in a hammock and held securely in place. "I don't believe that anyone could fall off a saddle like this," she said.

He showed her how to hold the reins and use her heels, and took her up the creek and through the bush. He told her that the scurrying black forms she saw among the trees were wild boar, and once, when they passed a wide stretch of water, there was a violent swirl as a crocodile dived away from them.

They lunched on the veranda on more steak, and bread and jam. "Palmolive hasn't got much imagination in the matter of tucker," he said apologetically.

"She's looking very tired," Jean said. "Give her the afternoon off, Joe. I'll make tea for you."

He offered her a room to sleep in after lunch, but their time together seemed too precious to waste. "Let's sit out here," she said, pulling some long cane chairs to the corner of the veranda where there might be a breeze. "If I should go to sleep, Joe, it'll be just one of those things."

"It's not always as hot as this," he said. "Just these two months are bad ones. By January it will begin to cool off."

And she did fall asleep, just after he talked about poddy dodging. Poddies are unbranded calves, born before the last muster. "Cleanskins, we call 'em," he explained.

"But what is poddy dodging?"

As far as she could make out, it was a more or less friendly thievery among ringers, involving raids on each other's poddies; apparently it was common practice. "I see . . ." Jean said drowsily.

When she woke up the sun was lower, and Joe had left. She sponged her face in the bathroom, and saw him outside working on the engine of the truck. She went to investigate the kitchen.

There was an oilstove and a small kerosene refrigerator. Cooked meat was stored in a screened meat safe, with nearly as many flies inside it as outside. It was a nightmare of a kitchen.

She put on a kettle to boil for tea and looked around for something to cook other than meat. Eggs were plentiful at Midhurst, and she found some stale cheese; she made Joe a cheese omelet with eight eggs. He cleaned his hands and came and watched her. "Oh my word," he said. "Where did you learn cooking?"

"In Ealing," she said, and it all seemed very far away; the gray skies, the big red buses, and the clamor of the Underground. "I used to cook myself an evening meal on an electric stove."

"Afraid you won't find many electric stoves in the outback."

She touched his hand. "I know that, Joe. But there are things that can be done to make life easier. The kitchen needs altering. The rest is lovely."

"I'll get a toilet fixed up in the house before you come," he promised her. "It's all right for me going out there, but it's not nice for you."

They ate on the veranda, talking quietly, as the sun went down. "Will you be in town next week, Joe?" she asked.

He nodded. "Friday at the latest. I'm going up to the top end of the station tomorrow for a couple of days. I've got a feeling that Don Curtis, on Windermere station, has been at my poddies."

He drove her into Willstown at about nine o'clock that night; they halted outside the town to say good night in proper style. She leaned against his shoulder with his arm around her, listening to the croaking of frogs, the sound of crickets, the crying of a night bird. "It's a lovely place you live in, Joe," she said. "It just wants a new kitchen, that's all. Don't ever worry about me not liking it."

He kissed her. "It'll be all ready for you when you come."

"April," she said. "Early in April, Joe."

She opened the shoe workshop the first week of December, after Aggie Topp had arrived. There were five girls: Judy, the daughter of Sam Small; Judy's friend Lois Strang; and Annie, whose figure was beginning to deteriorate and who had been sacked from the hotel, plus two fifteen-year-olds who had recently left school. For cleanliness and to mark the fact that they were working in a regular job, she put them in green coverall smocks and hung a mirror on the wall so that they could see what they looked like.

From the first she found that the fifteen-year-olds were the best employees. They were used to the discipline of regular school hours; the monotony was irksome to the older girls, and she tried to relieve it by ordering a phonograph from Cairns, with a supply of records. The big attraction of the workshop, however, was the air conditioner. In the torrid summer heat, which sometimes reached a hundred and ten degrees, she managed to keep the temperature down to about seventy. The workshop was popular from the first, and Jean never had any difficulty in getting as many recruits as she could handle.

She spent a hectic fortnight getting the ice-cream parlor furnished and stocked, and opened it on December 20. On that first afternoon she stood outside with Joe in the blazing sunlight, looking at what she had done. The workshop windows were closed to keep the cool air in, but they could hear the girls singing Christmas carols as they worked—"Holy Night" and "Good King Wenceslas."

"Well, there it all is," Jean said. "Now we've got to see if we can make it pay."

"Come on and I'll buy you a soda," Joe said. They went in and were served by Rose Sawyer behind the counter. "I don't know about the shoes, but this part of it'll pay," he said. "George Connor is getting very worried about his bar, with you starting up."

As they sat at the little table, Peter Fletcher came in, sidled up to the counter, ordered an ice cream, and began chatting with Rose. Joe said, "I bet you don't keep Rose six months."

Now that the businesses were started, Jean felt slack and listless. As soon as work stopped that day, she said good-by to Joe and went to her room. It was refreshingly cool in the workshop building, and she lay on her bed, exhausted, and slept for twelve hours.

The next morning, as they had arranged, Joe met her at the hotel soon after dawn to take her out to Midhurst for the day. When they got there he made her sit in a long chair on the veranda with a glass of cold lemon squash. He brought her a breakfast tray. She sat there, relaxed, with the fatigue soaking out of her, content to have him fussing over her. Later he suggested she take a nap in one of the spare bedrooms.

When she woke it was nearly four o'clock and she was cool and rested and at ease. She came to Joe out on the veranda, full of fondness for him in his generosity. She kissed him and said, "Thanks for everything, Joe. I had a lovely sleep."

On the first Sunday she worked steadily in the ice-cream parlor with Rose from nine in the morning till ten at night. Dead tired, Jean counted the money in the cash register. "Seventeen pounds thirteen shillings," she said to Rose in wonder. "That doesn't seem bad for a town with a hundred and forty-six people."

Jean opened the ice-cream parlor after lunch on Christmas Day and took in twenty pounds. She had the phonograph from the workshop playing that evening, so that the little building poured out music and light into the dark street. Old, withered men and women whom she had never seen before came in that night, drawn by the lights and the music.

The workshop operated steadily under Aggie Topp, and just after Christmas two packing cases of shoes were dispatched to England. Jean had already sent a few early samples of their work to Pack and Levy by airmail.

On Boxing Day, clouds massed in great peaks that covered the sky till it grew dark. Then down came the rain, a steady, vertical torrent that went on and on.

Jean went with Joe to Midhurst soon after the New Year. All along she had been careful not to stay overnight at the station; if she was to make a success of what she had set out to do for women in the town, her own behavior would have to be above reproach.

She scuttled through the hot, streaming rain to the utility. As she got into the cab, she said, "What are the creeks like, Joe?"

"Coming up," he said. "Nothing to worry over yet." He had, however, been stocking the homestead with foodstuffs.

The two creeks between Willstown and Midhurst, wide bottoms of sand and boulders that she knew as hot, arid places, were now rather terrifying wide streams of yellow muddy water.

"It's all right," Joe said at the first one. "It's only a foot deep. See that tree there with the overhanging branch? When that branch gets covered, at the fork, it's a bit deep."

They drove through the water and emerged on the other side, forded the second creek, and got to Midhurst in time for breakfast. It was still streaming rain, too wet for outdoor activity, so they set to work to plan the new kitchen and the toilet.

They were measuring the kitchen when a man on horseback rode up about noon. It was Pete Fletcher; he handed his horse over to Moonshine and came up to the veranda, soaked to the skin, his boots squishing.

"The radio says there's some kind of trouble at Windermere," he said. "Don Curtis went up with an Abo ringer to the top end of Windermere three days ago. Now the horse is back without him."

"Tracked the horse back?" Joe asked at once.

"Didn't work. Tracks all washed out." The young man sat down on the edge of the veranda and took off his boots to tip the water out of them. "Jackie Bacon, the girl on the Cairns radio, got the news on the morning schedule. She called the Willstown mounted police station and got Sergeant Haines. He sent Phil Duncan to Windermere. I said I'd come round this way and tell you. Eddie Page is headed there from Carlisle—the station just to the north," he added for Jean's benefit.

Joe asked, "Do they know where Don was going on the station?"

"Up by Disappointment Creek."

Joe's mouth tightened. "For God's sake, he's been at my poddies again. The mugger's got a poddy corral up there. I'll tell you where it is," and the two men discussed the terrain of the adjoining Windermere station. "You know where Disappointment Creek runs into the Fish River?" Joe asked. "Well, up the creek about five miles you'll see a lot of thick bush with a bare hill behind. It's only about fifty feet high—the poddy corral's to the south. If you're going on a search party, I'd start off with that."

Pete put his boots back on. "Coming with me, Joe?"

Joe began putting on boots and rainwear. "Think I'll get up to the top end of my own station—maybe Don was after some more poddies and had his accident up there. If I can't find any trace of him, I'll go on to his corral and meet you there. I'll leave with Bourneville, as soon as I've run Miss Paget back to town."

The forty-mile trip to Willstown and back in these conditions would take Joe three hours, Jean realized. "Don't bother about me," she said. "I'll stay here till you come back. You must get away at once."

He smiled at her. "Might be a long wait. I'll tell Moonshine he's to take you into town anytime you want to go."

The rain had practically stopped, but the clouds were heavy and black overhead as Pete Fletcher rode away. Jean hurried to the kitchen to help Palmolive prepare food for Joe and Bourneville, while they loaded a packhorse with a tent and camping gear. Joe kissed Jean good-by on the veranda. "I'll see you in Willstown next week," he said; then he was trotting out of the gate with the Abo at his side and the packhorse behind on a lead.

The rain, which had begun again, made a steady drumming on the iron roof. It occurred to her that Don Curtis might have turned up and Joe's journey could be so much wasted effort. It was absurd that Midhurst had no radio transmitter. She made up her mind to have one installed after they were married.

She had never been alone at Midhurst before. She wandered through the house deep in thought, and the wallaby lolloped after her; from time to time she dropped her hand to caress it, and it nibbled her fingers. She spent a long time in Joe's room, touching his rough gear and clothes. It was here that he had dreamed and planned the fantastic journey to England in search of her.

At about three o'clock Dave Hope, one of Joe's stockriders, rode up. He had been in Willstown and had learned from the radio there that Don Curtis' Abo ringer, who had also been missing, had returned to Windermere. He and Curtis had separated, for some reason, and were going to meet back at camp. Curtis hadn't returned, and with the heavy flooding, the Abo couldn't track him.

Jean frowned with worry. Somewhere on the station a man was lying injured; he might be anywhere within a radius of fifteen miles, very probably unconscious by now.

"You'd better go and help," Jean said to Dave Hope. "I'm perfectly all right here."

Only about two hours of daylight were left when Dave rode off. He knew Windermere station well and didn't mind finishing his journey in the dark. Jean went on with the plans for the new kitchen, and presently Palmolive came in and cooked her some eggs for tea. When the maid went to her quarters, Jean was alone, with only the puppies and the wallaby for company. That evening she learned how much a lonely person turns to animals, and a little of the fortitude that a wife on a cattle station must develop.

She slept lightly and woke many times. The rain stopped. Before dawn she heard the sound of a horse's hoofs. She dressed and went out on the veranda, calling, "Who's that?"

"It's me, missy. Bourneville." The gray-haired Abo came up on the veranda, talking rapidly. "Missa Harman, him up on top end. Him find Missa Curtis, him leg broken. Him send me back fetch Missa Hope, drive utility up top end."

"Mr. Hope's not here. He's gone to Windermere," she said, biting her lip in thought. "Bourneville, can you drive the utility?"

"No, missy."

"Can any of the other Abos?"

"No, missy."

She thought deeply for a moment. She could drive the utility, with Bourneville as guide, though her experience did not exceed five hours in an ordinary car. To send Bourneville into Willstown for help would mean at least six hours' delay.

She asked, "What's the track like? Are there any creeks to cross?"

He held up three fingers. "Tree, but they not too deep, missy."

"All right, Bourneville," she said, "I'll drive the utility. You come with me on your horse."

He went off to get a fresh mount, and she changed into riding shirt and breeches.

557

She took along a waterproof tin trunk of bandages and medicines which she had discovered in Joe's room, together with blankets and food, in case she had to spend the night in the utility. Saying a prayer, she switched on the motor and pressed the starter. It both pleased and alarmed her when the engine turned over.

Then she drove off, with Bourneville riding ahead. She never got into top gear, and never exceeded ten miles an hour. She drove through the three creeks, and once the water rose above the floor-boards. But the utility came through, bounding from rock to rock with water pouring out of every hole and cranny.

NINE

JOE Harman sat by a fire in front of his tent, in a clearing near the corral. The logs that formed the gate of the corral had been pulled down and the enclosure was empty. Inside the tent, a man lay on a bed of brushwood covered with a waterproof sheet, with a blanket over him. Joe turned and asked, "What happened, Don? Did the poddies rush you when you had the gate down?"

"They knocked me down and about six of 'em ran over me."

Joe said, "Bloody well teach you to go muggering about on other people's land." There was a pause. "How many of mine did you get last year, Don?"

" 'Bout three hundred."

Joe laughed. "I got three hundred and fifty of yours." And from the tent Don Curtis said a very rude word.

Then there was silence and the darkness and a long stretch of waiting. Suddenly the silence was broken by the sound of a motor vehicle approaching. Joe jumped up from the fire and peered into the darkness. Bourneville appeared on horseback, followed by the chugging utility. Jean stopped it with a sigh of relief, and Joe came to her as she sat there. "What happened to Dave?" he asked.

She told him what had happened. "I've only driven a car three times. I don't think I've done it any good," she apologized.

He kissed her soundly, then asked, "What were the creeks like?"

"Came over the floor of the cab. Is Mr. Curtis here, Joe?"

"In the tent there. Got his leg bust—compound fracture, the bone's sticking out," Joe told her. "I made a sort of splint, but we've got to get him to the hospital as quickly as we can."

They set to work to strike camp. When they removed the tent from over the injured man, Curtis said, "Hello, Miss Paget. You don't remember me. I saw you in Willstown the day you arrived."

She smiled at him. "You'll be back there soon—in the hospital."

Joe rolled up the tent, and they worked a blanket under the brushwood. With infinite care they lifted Don Curtis into the utility. He was white and sweating, and blood showed on his bitten lips, but they could do nothing to ease his pain.

They started off at about nine o'clock, Joe driving, Jean riding in the back with Curtis, and Bourneville behind, leading the two other horses. The creeks were higher than when Jean had navigated them. They were able to cross the first, though water came into the cab and almost reached the floor of the truck body on which the sick man lay. At the second creek the utility ground forward through the swirling yellow water. Then it came down heavily on a boulder with a crunch of metal, and stopped dead.

Joe pressed the starter, but the engine was unresponsive. Oil appeared on the eddying water and slid downstream in black-and-yellow tails. "I've cracked the bloody sump," he said shortly.

He got down into the water—it was almost waist-deep—and called to Jean to pass him a coil of rope from the truck. Then, with Bourneville, he harnessed the three horses to the back axle, groping and spluttering underneath the water to do so. In ten minutes the vehicle was on dry land, a performance that awed Jean.

She got out and went to Joe, who was lying on his back under the front axle. He breathed a sigh of relief. "Crankshaft's all right. It's only the sump." He got to his feet. "I could patch it good enough to get home, but we haven't any oil. Only thing now is to have Don flown out."

"Where could an airplane land?" Jean asked.

"I know one place. It'd give 'em five hundred yards," Joe said.

He took his horse and rode off, while they unpacked the tent and arranged it over Don Curtis to protect him.

Joe came back in a quarter of an hour. "Think we can make an airstrip of it," he said. "It's only about a mile away." He hopped from the saddle, and they made a team of the horses again and harnessed them to the front axle of the truck. With Jean at the wheel, they set off, maneuvering through the bush.

They came to a grassy sward more than five hundred yards long. Studying it, Joe saw that the bushes and trees that blocked either end of the approach would have to be cut down. He produced an axe and a spade from the utility, but there weren't enough hands to finish the job. He said, "We'll have to get the boys up from Midhurst, and get a message down to Willstown about the airplane."

Jean said, "I'll ride down with Bourneville. He can bring the boys back and I'll go on to Willstown."

He stared at her. "You can't ride that far; it's forty miles. I won't have you trying to cross them creeks alone, on a horse."

She touched his arm. "All right, I'll take someone with me. From Willstown, we could get the Windermere crew to help."

Joe gave her the location of the clearing so that the airplane could find it. "We're about six miles west-southwest of the new bore." He made her memorize it and repeat it.

She asked, "What are you going to do?"

"Start felling these trees."

"You can't do that, with your back, Joe," she said. "Promise, or I'll take back what I said about not riding alone. I mean it."

He smiled at her. "All right." He led her over to mount Robin, his horse. It was a much bigger animal than she had ridden before, but Joe's saddle was sturdy and accommodating, and when the stirrups were adjusted she found herself fairly comfortable.

She started off with Bourneville at a slow trot through the trees, and so began a feat of endurance which she was to look back upon with awe for years to come. On her visits to Midhurst she had never been on a horse more than an hour and a half at a time. They waded through one creek, and at the second, Bourneville made her take her feet out of the stirrups and hold on to the horse's mane, prepared to swim. The rain began again and soaked her to the skin; very soon the wetness began to chafe her legs and thighs, and she could feel the soreness growing. There was nothing to be done about it.

It took nearly four bruising, wearying hours to reach Midhurst. By then she had a raging thirst and was half sick with fatigue. Moonshine and some of the other boys came running out to take her bridle and help her down from Robin; she could not manage the stretch from the stirrup to the ground. "Bourneville, tell Moonshine to saddle up and come with me to Willstown," she said. "Take all the other boys back to Mr. Harman. I'm going to have a cup of tea and some tucker, and then we'll start."

The brief rest stiffened her, and she needed all her courage to face the twenty miles that lay ahead. She did not dare to examine her sores; once started on that sort of thing, she knew she would never get going again. Every muscle in her body ached, and were it not for the sturdy saddle, her legs could not have held her on the horse. She and Moonshine crossed the creeks, now too deep for a car, and followed the car track. The last ten miles passed in a daze; Moonshine had to ride close to her side to catch her if she fell. She had been in the saddle eight hours when they reached Willstown. They rode past the ice-cream parlor with its lights streaming out, and came to a halt outside Sergeant Haines's combined police station and home. With a last effort she dismounted while Moonshine held Robin's head. But she could not stand at first without holding on to Robin's saddle.

"Why, Miss Paget," Haines said in the slow Queensland way, "where have you come from?"

"From the top end of Midhurst. Don Curtis is up there with a broken leg. Joe Harman found Don, and the Midhurst stockriders went up to build an airstrip to fly Don out in the morning."

While Moonshine went to bed down the horses in the police corral, Haines took Jean inside and Mrs. Haines brought her tea.

When Jean had finished her tea she got up. "I'm going home to bed. If I stay here any longer, I won't be able to walk at all." She staggered and almost fell, and Sergeant Haines rushed to assist her.

"I'm taking you to the hospital; I don't care if you want to go or not," he said. "Sister Douglas has everything you'll want."

Half an hour later she was bathed and in a hospital bed, with penicillin ointment on various parts of her anatomy. Back in his office, Sergeant Haines sat down at the transmitter.

"Eight Queen Charlie, Eight Queen Charlie," he said. "This is Eight Love Mike calling Eight Queen Charlie. Please come in."

And so the machinery was set in motion to fly Don Curtis to safety. The rescue was not accomplished without difficulty. The next morning, when the twin-engined Dragon took off from the airstrip at Cairns, it was misty and raining. Willstown was four hundred miles distant, with the first seventy miles over mountains, and the pilot had to fly low for visibility. Throughout the flight he was never more than two hundred feet above the treetops.

At the Willstown airfield he picked up a hospital orderly, then set out to find the meadow at Midhurst station where the injured man waited. The runway the ringers had prepared was pitifully short. He came in as slowly as he dared, missing the trees by a few feet. Throttling back, he brought the plane down toward the grass. He could . . . no, he could never stop in time. With wheels no more than two feet from the ground he jammed the throttles forward, held her level for a moment, and climbed away.

He turned to the orderly. "Got a pencil and paper? Write this. 'Sorry I can't make it. Strip must be a hundred and fifty yards longer. I will come back at four o'clock this afternoon.'" They put this in a message bag with colored streamers, flew over, and dropped it on the middle of the strip.

At four he was back over the meadow; the rain had stopped, the men had lengthened the strip, and he touched down at the near end, the plane bouncing on the uneven ground. He stopped the engines and got out; they took a stretcher from the cabin, and the orderly began the business of getting Don Curtis into the plane.

Joe asked, "Did you hear anything about Miss Paget, down in Willstown?"

The pilot said, "She's in the hospital. Nothing much wrong, they say; just tired and sore. She must be quite a girl."

563

Joe said, "Too right. If you see anyone from the hospital, leave a message for her that I'll be in town tomorrow."

"I'll do that," said the pilot.

The loading was completed now. The pilot got into his seat; the orderly swung the propellers, and they taxied back to the far end of the track. He opened out and took off down the runway, clearing the trees with fifteen feet to spare. Half an hour later he was on the ground at Willstown, helping to transfer the stretcher to the truck that was to take Don Curtis to the hospital.

In the hospital that afternoon, Jean showed Rose Sawyer the more accessible of her wounds. "Honorable scars," Rose said. The two girls chatted for a while, and then Rose said, "Tell me, Jean. Do you think there'd be work for a contractor up here? You know, making roads and buildings and things like that."

Jean stared at her. "A contractor?"

There was a young man in Alice, it seemed, with whom Rose had been corresponding, and he was considering a change in work, just as she had. "He's coming for a visit as soon as the wet's over," Rose confided. "His name's Billy Wakeling."

"He won't get any building contracts yet. But Joe Harman needs some dams on Midhurst. Is that in his line?"

"I suppose he could move anything with a bulldozer."

"Can he get hold of a bulldozer?" Jean asked.

"I should think so. His father's a contractor down at Newcastle and owns about forty of them."

Jean asked, "Could you scoop out a hole for a swimming pool with a bulldozer?"

"I'm sure you could. Do you want a swimming pool?"

Jean stared thoughtfully at the white hospital wall. "A nice big pool right by the bore, with a tower to cool off the water, and a lawn where people could sunbathe. Ask Billy to get hold of plans, and tell us what it would cost when he comes up."

"I'll ask him," said Rose. "Anything else?"

"A nice beauty parlor with a French brunette who could make one look like Rita Hayworth. That's what I want, sometimes."

Jean left the hospital the next day and walked awkwardly to the workshop. There was an airmail letter from Mr. Pack. He pointed out a number of defects in the shoes she had sent him, but finished by saying that he would try and market them. Jean and Aggie Topp interpreted this as high praise.

Aggie said, "Everybody's talking about the brave horseback ride you made to get help for that injured man."

"How on earth did they hear?" Jean asked.

"It's these little radio sets they have on the cattle stations," Aggie said. "You can't keep anything secret in this country."

Joe rode into the town that afternoon with Pete Fletcher. The creeks were up, and though he'd started from Midhurst spick-and-span, as befits a man going to see his girl, he had had to swim one of the creeks. He combed his hair and emptied out his boots and went to find Jean.

She was in her bedroom, writing a letter to me. She came out to him. "We'll never hear the last of it if you come in," she said. "Let's go to the ice-cream parlor." It was borne in on her that this was literally the only place in Willstown where young men and women could meet reputably. They picked a table by the wall; she looked around. "This won't do," she said. "I'll have to install some sort of booths where people can talk privately."

Joe went to the counter and came back with two banana splits. She ate a little of hers in silence. Then she said, "Joe, about those dams. Have you anyone to build them for you yet?"

He shook his head. "No good thinking about those until the dry."

"Could a bulldozer build them?"

"Oh my word. If anybody had a bulldozer, he'd build the lot inside a month," he said. "But there's no bulldozer around here."

"There might be one," Jean said, and told him about Rose Sawyer's young man, who was coming to visit. "Take him out to Midhurst and have a talk with him," she suggested.

"My word. If we had a joker with a bulldozer in Willstown, it'd make a lot of difference." He dipped eagerly into his banana split.

"Joe," she said after a while. "If we had a swimming pool by the bore, with cabins to change in and lawns to sunbathe on, and

565

diving boards, and a man to mow the grass and keep it clean—would people use it? If we charged, say, a bob to bathe?"

He smiled at her in curious wonder. "What comes after the swimming pool?"

She stared out at the miry expanse of street. "They'll get their hair wet in the swimming pool, so we'll have to have a beauty parlor. And after that, an open-air cinema, a laundry, and a decent dress shop. Don't laugh, Joe," she reproached him. "I started an ice-cream parlor and put Rose in it, and now her young man's coming with a bulldozer, so you'll get your dams built."

"You're ahead of the game," he said. "They aren't built yet."

"They will be soon."

He glanced around the ice-cream parlor. "If everything you want to do works out like this," he said slowly, "you'll have a town as good as Alice Springs in no time."

"That's what I want to have," she said. "A town like Alice."

TEN

ALL that happened nearly three years ago. I think that after the affair of Mr. Curtis she became more closely integrated into the life of the Gulf country. Even before her marriage there was a subtle change in her letters. She ceased to write as an English-woman living in a foreign land; she gradually began to write about the people as if she had become one of them, about the place as if it had become her place.

She married Joe Harman in April after the mustering. There was no church in Willstown, though one is to be built next year; the wedding was in the shire hall, and all the countryside came. They had their honeymoon on Green Island, and I suppose she took her sarong, though she did not tell me.

In the first two years of her married life she made considerable inroads into her capital. She always started one thing and got it trading smoothly before starting another, and she sent me accounts of her ventures, prepared by a young man who worked in the bank. But all the same, by the time her second son was born, the one she called Noel after me, she had had over eighteen thousand pounds for her various businesses. Although they all seemed to be making profits, Lester and I were growing concerned about the chances of a slump which would extinguish the thirty percent of her inheritance that we had let her have.

The climax came in February, when she wrote me a long letter from the hospital at Willstown, soon after she had given birth to Noel. She asked me if I would be one of his godfathers, and that pleased me very much, although there was little prospect that I should live long enough to discharge my duties to him. Rose Sawyer's husband, the young man with the bulldozer, was to be the second godfather, and since he seemed to be settled in the district I felt that Jean would not injure her child by giving him an elderly godfather who lived on the other side of the world. I decided to make a corresponding alteration in my will immediately.

She went on in the same letter to discuss Midhurst. Joe was doing very well as manager, she said—the cattle had increased from eight thousand to twelve or thirteen thousand, and because of the dams they kept building each year in the dry, the increase was likely to continue. Mrs. Spears, the owner of Midhurst, presently lived in Brisbane, and they had gone down to talk with her the previous October. "I didn't tell you about it then," Jean wrote, "because we had to find out if we could get a loan."

The upshot was that Mrs. Spears had offered to sell them a half share in the station, with an option to buy the rest on her death.

"It means getting hold of about thirty thousand pounds," Jean wrote. "The land is rented from the state, and there's seventeen years to go upon the present lease, which would have to be altered to include Joe's name. The bank is willing to advance us two-thirds of the amount. That leaves us with ten thousand pounds to find in cash, and that's what I wanted to ask you about, Noel. If we can't take over the station, Mrs. Spears will probably sell it, and we'd be miserable leaving Willstown now. It's turning into such a happy little town to live in."

Another ten thousand pounds would mean that we had allowed Jean to invest half of her inheritance in highly speculative businesses, which was by no means the intention of her uncle when he made his will. I spent a day or two thinking about it, but in the end it came to this: our duty was to do what Mr. Macfadden himself would have done in similar circumstances. Jean was no longer a young unmarried girl likely to be imposed upon. She was a woman of thirty with two children, married to a steady sort of man. Would Mr. Macfadden, in these circumstances, still have insisted on the trust being maintained in its original form?

He was a kindly man, I felt sure, and he would have wanted her to have her Midhurst station, since her home and her interests were there. But as a careful Scot he would have wanted to ensure that she got good value for this ten thousand pounds.

I talked it over with my partner, and Lester agreed that the chief question concerned the lease that had only seventeen more years to run. With the dams and other improvements Joe was making, he could not possibly go on with capital investments in the station until a much longer lease had been negotiated.

Lester said, "I think we ought to use the trust as a lever to get the lease put right for Mrs. Harman. Tell all and sundry that we won't release her money until the leasehold is adjusted to our satisfaction. Then she can have all the money she wants."

I smiled. "I wouldn't tell *her* that."

I sat down and drafted a letter to Jean. "The lease would have to be adjusted," I stated, "or the money could not be advanced."

I came to the main point of my letter next. "No doubt you have a solicitor that you can trust, but if it would assist you, I would very gladly come and visit you in Queensland for a few weeks and see this matter of the lease put into satisfactory order before you invest this money in Midhurst. It is many years since I have been away from England, and I would like to take a long holiday before I get too feeble. If I could help you in this matter, I should be only too glad to come and do so."

The answer came in a cablegram. She urged me to come out by air the end of April, since their winter was approaching then and the weather would be just like an English autumn. She said that she was sending me a list of clothes and things I might need for the journey. I was touched by that.

I LEFT London one Monday morning and arrived in Sydney on Wednesday night. It was fatiguing, sleeping two nights in a reclining chair, but I must say the plane was comfortable and the stewardess most kind and attentive. I rested in Sydney for two nights and then took the plane to Cairns, and here I had a great surprise, because Joe Harman met me. There was a twice-weekly air service to the Gulf country, partly on account of the growth of Willstown, he told me, and we would be able to go out on Monday.

The hotel in Cairns was a rambling building, and we sat together in the huge bar. Joe asked if I would drink tea or beer or plonk.

"Plonk?"

"Red wine," he said. I ordered some, and I must say I found it quite palatable.

"Jean was sorry she couldn't come and meet you, but she's feeding Noel so that ties her," he said. "She'll meet the plane on Monday in Willstown."

"How is she?" I asked.

"She's fine," he said. "Having babies seems to suit her. She's looking prettier than ever."

We settled down after tea on the veranda outside my bedroom and discussed Midhurst. He had brought copies of the accounts. Although he gave much of the credit for his success to Jean, I found him well able to appreciate the intricate points about the lease and his capital improvements. We talked for a couple of hours about the businesses that Jean had started in the town.

"She's got twenty-two girls in the workshop," he said. "It isn't doing quite so well. But all the others—oh my word." He showed me the figures for the ice-cream parlor, the beauty parlor, the swimming pool, the cinema, the laundry, and the dress shop. "They're doing fine. The fruit and vegetable shop, too." We totted up the figures and found that the seven of them together had made a clear profit of £2673 in the previous year.

"It'd pay her to run the workshop at a loss," he said. "She gets it back out of what the girls spend to make themselves look pretty for the ringers, and what the ringers spend in taking out the girls."

I was a little troubled about the workshop. "Can she lower the overhead by doing a bigger business?" I asked.

He was doubtful about that. "She's using just about all the crocodile skins Jeff Pocock and others can bring in," he said. "I don't think she can do much more in the workshop. She's got a hunch that in a few years the town will be so big we won't need it."

"I see," I said thoughtfully. "How big is the town now?"

"There's about four hundred and fifty people living in Willstown. The population's trebled in the last three years."

"Is that just because of the workshop?"

He said slowly, "Everything comes back to that, when you look at it. She's got three girls employed in the ice-cream parlor, two in the beauty parlor, three in the dress shop, two in the fruit shop, three in the cinema. She's never employed more than thirty-five girls at any one time, but since she started there's been forty-two girls married out of her businesses. They mostly marry ringers. Well, that's forty-two families starting, forty-two women wanting cinema and beauty parlor and fresh vegetables, besides the thirty-five girls she's still got employed. It kind of snowballs." He paused. "Take the bank. There's two girl clerks that never were there before, because of the bigger business. The contractor's got a girl in his office." He turned to me. "It's a fact, there's a hundred girls and married women under twenty-five in Willstown now. When Jean came, there was two.

"And the babies!" he went on. "There's more babies than you could shake a stick at. They've had to send a special maternity nurse to the hospital. That's another girl. She got engaged to Phil Duncan, the copper, last month, so there'll be another one."

I smiled. "Are there enough men to go around?"

"Oh my word," he said. "There's no difficulty in getting men to work in Willstown. I've had ringers from all over Queensland, and the Northern Territory, too. One chap came from Western Australia, two thousand miles or so."

We had a conference next morning with Mr. Hope, the solicitor, in his office, and wrote a letter to the Queensland land administration board suggesting a meeting to discuss the lease of Midhurst. On Monday morning we flew to Willstown. As we circled for the landing I was able to study the place. The sunlight glinted on the wide streets that were filling up with new houses everywhere. A line of shrubs had been planted in a formal garden down the middle of the main street, transforming the wide cattle track into two lanes, and tarmac pavements had been laid in this part of the town. Opposite the hotel I could see the swimming pool, just as Jean had described it in her letters. Then we were landing.

She was there to meet us in her Ford utility, which she had bought for running in and out of town to see to her businesses. More mature now, she had grown into a very lovely woman. "Oh, Noel," she said. "It *is* nice to see you. Are you very tired?"

"I'm not tired," I said. "Three or four years older, perhaps. You're looking very well."

"I am well," she said. "Disgustingly well. Noel, it was good of you to offer to come out like this. I wanted to invite you, and then it seemed so much to ask. It's such a very long way."

They drove me out immediately to Midhurst. There was no road in the accepted sense; Jean picked her way across country, following the general line of the tracks but avoiding the deep holes. When we came to the first creek, there was a sort of concrete causeway across the riverbed, marked by two massive wooden posts on either bank. "We haven't got as far as bridges yet," she said. "But this thing is a godsend in the wet, to know that you won't hit a boulder underwater."

There was a garden now in front of the homestead, bright with flowers, and great ranges of cattle pens. "We've got three zebu bulls now, and you need more stockyards when you start breeding," Joe said. He was keeping a small herd of dairy cows, too, and that meant more enclosures still.

"How many hands have you got now?" I asked him.

"Eleven white stockriders and ten Abos."

They put me in a long chair on the veranda with a cool drink. I was fascinated to see the life of the station: the stockriders, the cattle, the horses, and puppies playing with a half-grown wallaby. I could have sat there indefinitely, watching it all, watching the grace of Jean attending to her children and her Abo women. I did sit there for three days.

She took me into town one morning and showed me everything she had done. The girls at the workshop looked very smart in their green smocks, working at the leather goods, and the air conditioner was still a great lure.

She had arranged her other enterprises all in a row as a little street of shops. She had built a wooden veranda over the pavement to protect shoppers from sun and rain. Here she had the beauty parlor, with four private booths, and a glass counter and display case full of women's things; all very clean and nice. Next was the laundry, then the greengrocer's, which sold seeds and garden implements as well as fruit and vegetables; and after that the dress shop, with dummies clothed in summer dresses. I was interested to see a small, secluded part, served by a middle-aged woman, where the elderly could buy the clothes they were accustomed to, black skirts and flannel petticoats and coarse kitchen aprons.

She took me across the street to the swimming pool and the cinema. It was quite a hot day and I had had about enough, so we went to the ice-cream parlor and had a cool drink. I watched the people as they passed by. There were far more women than men, and at least half the women seemed to be in the family way.

"What comes next?" I asked. "Is there any end to this?"

She laughed and touched my hand. "No end," she said. "I keep on badgering you for more money, don't I? As a matter of fact, I think I can start the next one out of the profits."

"What's it to be?"

"A self-service grocer's shop," she replied. "The demand's shifting, Noel. When we started, it was entertainment we needed, because almost everyone was young and unmarried—the ice-cream parlor and the swimming pool, the beauty parlor, and the cinema. What the town needs now are things for the young family. A grocer's shop selling really good, varied food as cheap as possible.

And then, as soon as I can start it, we must have a household store."

I asked her, "How do your goods get here?"

"They come by train from Cairns to Forsayth, and by truck from there. It makes it very expensive, because there's no proper road, and a truck is worn out in two years' time. The roads commission is considering a tarmac road from here to Mareeba and Cairns. We might get it in two years, the town's growing so fast. Fancy being able to drive to Cairns in a day!"

The land administration board had answered our letter, and the next week I flew down to Brisbane with Joe Harman, after picking up his solicitor in Cairns, and settled the question of the lease. I stayed on in Brisbane after Joe left, while the draft of the final agreement was passed back and forth from me to the board. I was also in communication with Mrs. Spears's solicitors over the option for the final purchase of Midhurst. After a fortnight I was able to bring the papers to Cairns. Joe signed them, and my business in Queensland was done.

I went back to Willstown with Joe and stayed another week, largely because of an old man's sentiment. I asked Jean if she would be coming back to England for a holiday.

She said gently, "Not for a bit, Noel. Joe and I want to take a holiday next year, but we've been planning to go to America. We thought we'd get an old car and drive down the west coast to Arizona and Texas. Their problems must be just the same as ours, and they've been at it longer. I'm sure we'd learn an awful lot."

She touched me very much one evening when she said, "You're practically retired now, Noel. Why not give up London and stay here with us? You know we'd love to have you."

It was impossible, of course; the old have their place and the young have theirs. "That's very kind of you," I said. "I wish I could. But I've got sons and grandchildren. I must go back."

They drove me to the airplane. I cannot remember now what Jean said. I can only remember a great thankfulness that the plane on that flight didn't carry a stewardess, so that nobody could see my face as we circled Willstown after takeoff, and I saw the bright new buildings of that Gulf town for the last time.

IT IS WINTER NOW, nearly three months since I have been able to get out to the office or the club. My daughter-in-law Eve, Martin's wife, has been organizing me; it was she who insisted that I should engage a nurse to sleep in the flat. They wanted me to go into some sort of nursing home, but I won't do that.

I have spent the winter writing down this story, I suppose because an old man loves to dwell upon the past. And having finished it, it seems to me that I have been mixed up in things far greater than I realized at the time. It is no small matter to assist in the birth of a new city, and as I sit here looking out into the London mists, I sometimes wonder just what it is that Jean has done; if any of us realize, even yet, the importance of her achievement.

I wrote to her the other day and told her a queer thought that came into my head. We had discovered at the office that her money had come originally from the goldfields of Hall's Creek in Western Australia, where her grandfather, James Macfadden, had made it in the last years of the last century. When I thought of that, it seemed to me that I had done the right thing with her money and that James Macfadden would have approved, although I had run contrary to the strict intentions of his son's will. After all, it was James who made the money and took it away to England from a place like Willstown. I think he would have liked it when his granddaughter took it back again.

I suppose it is because I have lived rather a restricted life myself that I have sat here day after day this winter, dreaming of the blazing sunshine, of poddy dodging and black stockriders, of Cairns and of Green Island. Of a girl that I met forty years too late, and of her life in that small town that I shall never see again, that holds so much of my affection.

Since its publication in 1950, *A Town Like Alice* has been hailed around the world as a masterpiece. Sometimes described as two brilliant novels in one, it would certainly seem to have had two sources of inspiration.

Nevil Shute wrote of one in a postscript to the original edition. The march of the women prisoners in Malaya was  based on an event that actually happened in neighboring Sumatra when Japanese forces invaded that country. A local Japanese commander, reluctant to assume responsibility for some eighty Dutch women and children, sent them on a trek that lasted twelve hundred miles and two and a half years. Fewer than thirty survived. In 1949, Shute was a guest in Sumatra of a member of that party, Mrs. Geysel-Vonck. "Unable to resist the appeal of this true story," he wrote, "I want to pay tribute to the most gallant lady I have ever met."

Nevil Shute

The other source of inspiration was Australia itself. Shute was a successful aeronautical engineer as well as an author. In 1948, with a friend, he flew his own light aircraft from Britain to eastern Australia. He was fascinated by the vastness of the country, where "all kinds of things were going on." The story of how Alice Springs grew, from a backward settlement of fewer than fifteen hundred inhabitants to a booming town of more than six thousand and a mecca for tourists, fired his imagination. Through this novel he was able to communicate some of his vision about Australia's development.

Indeed, the year that the book was published, he and his family emigrated from Britain to Australia and settled on a large farm in the state of Victoria. He continued to write, publishing his autobiography and more than twenty novels.

He died in 1960, of a heart attack, at sixty-one. Shute had a large following in the United States as well as in Australia, where many readers were surprised to learn he was an Englishman, as they had come to claim this superb teller of tales as one of their own.

ACKNOWLEDGMENTS

Page 3: fabric illustration by Carol Inouye.

Page 336, lines 32-33: from "Chicago" by Carl Sandburg, *Complete Poems* by Carl Sandburg, published by Harcourt Brace Jovanovich, Inc.

Pages 390, 417: "The Twelve Steps" and "The Twelve Traditions," © 1952, 1953 by The A. A. Grapevine, Inc., and Alcoholics Anonymous World Services, Inc.

Page 426, lines 5-30: excerpt from a letter to William Wilson from C. G. Jung, January 30, 1961. Copyright © 1963 by Princeton University Press. Reprinted by permission.